Also by C Adrian Balson

Onward Christian Salesman
copyright © Clifford Adrian Balson 2013

The First of July
an Epiphanal Startling

By
C Adrian Balson

10th Samaritan Ministry
16602 North 25th Street
Unit 123
Phoenix, Arizona 85032

copyright © Clifford Adrian Balson 2014
All rights reserved

Library of Congress Catalog Card Number 2014906503

ISBN-13: 978-0615967868
ISBN-10: 0615967868

Book Cover Design by:
Quantum Design Lab
PO Box 483
Seaside Park, NJ 08752
http://quantumdesignlab.com

Photography
Angela Vargas
http://www.facebook.com/AngelaVargasPhotography

In memory of
John Adrian Balson and Christopher Gene Cahill,
two good men, gone, never forgotten.

"But seek first the Kingdom of God and His righteousness, and all these things shall be added to you. Therefore do not worry about tomorrow, for tomorrow will worry about its own things. Sufficient for the day is its own trouble."

Matthew 6:33, 34

Contents

Acknowledgements

The creation of a fictional piece is a daunting challenge that represents the opportunity to fashion, using imagination and creativity a unique means of portraying life and life experiences. For someone attempting to author such a work it can mean a great deal of soul searching. We that endeavor to do this find inspiration in many locales. It could come as a reaction to another literary work or from a chance encounter with someone that writes indelibly on our hearts.

The creation of this book took more than one year and during that time there were many such inspirations that helped me overcome the barriers that stand between an author and the page. These friends have and continue to provide me a great deal of support.

Since the book explores theories regarding the American Civil War, and specifically the battle of Gettysburg, I have called upon my recollections of the facts and the people that participated in the great battle. This battle has been the subject of much discussion and there are numerous books written on the subject. Having read several of them I give credit to two of them as having an impact on my opinions of the nature of the battle.

The first would be Michael Shaara's 'The Killer Angels'[1] (copyright© 1974 by Michael Shaara). This book while considered to be historic fiction by many brings the battle's combatants to life. It was studiously researched and competently written, winning its author the coveted Pulitzer Prize. The book has inspired a movie and has offered insight to many that viewed historic events with a detached and clinical eye. Each of the men that donned their country's colors were indeed very human and as such were much like you or I.

The second book was 'The Gettysburg Campaign – A Study in Command'[2] written by Edwin B. Coddington (copyright © 1968 Caroline Q. Coddington, Executor of Estate of Edwin B. Coddington). This book is a treasure trove of historic fact about the actions that lead to the defeat of the Army of Northern Virginia. With an extreme attention to detail the reader finds themselves immersed in the challenges that confronted the commanding generals as well as the political fabric of the time. The book because of its purpose is meant to enlighten and inform. The author accomplishes his purpose with alacrity offering a reader a panoply of perspectives.

Other influences that formed opinions come from a multitude of sources including the writing of C. S. Lewis, Frank Herbert and J. R. R. Tolkien. Their contribution, while they did not inspire content, was their ability to immerse the reader in a world that is familiar but is yet strange and alien. I am quite certain that these authors have had a profound impact on many other readers as well.

I received much encouragement throughout the process and would like to thank two people specifically. The first is my good friend Christopher Anderson whose work on the cover of this book provides the proper finish for a book that deals with the quest to manipulate time. His work is innovative and his service is first rate. The second person I would like to thank is Angela Vargas who took the photograph of me that was used on the back cover of the book. She is a talented photographer and she took a difficult subject and made it look good, at least I think so.

Finally I would like to take a few more moments of your precocious time to speak to you about a young man that I knew. His name is Christopher Cahill and he was born on January 30, 1987 and he left us on the January 30, 2014. Chris was a remarkable young man that I was blessed to know. He was my nephew and a friend. He had a loving heart and was fiercely loyal to those he loved and cared about. My father had a special attachment to Chris and Chris knew that his 'Pop' was always there for him should he need him.

Chris' offered me a great deal of comfort and his words touched me in such a way that it reflect God's love for us all. This was a man that intuitively 'got it'. As many of you know I made some very poor decisions and they cost me a great deal. While many others were trying to determine whether I should be given a second chance, Chris stated simply that 'I was his uncle and that he loved me'. What more can anyone hope for than that?

Cliff

Forward

I am going to ask you the reader to suspend your life as you know it and enter into the world of the twenty second century. As you look around your new surroundings you will find that things are not too different than they are today. There some very neat gadgets that can amuse you but you will find out quickly that life in this time has an uneasy feel to it. There is clearly something that is not quite right.

This is not a future of which most of us dream. It is not a future that many fear. Perhaps it is best described as a future that we will scratch our head in puzzlement and wonder simply- why?

As you will begin your journey you will meet a man on his way to work. He may be someone that you can relate to easily but then again he may not be. Philip Lee is a college professor about to start his routine day confident that it will all be the same, that his routine is secure. He is certain that nothing will change. Little does he know that around him everyone that he knows and loves is attempting to do what he is confident cannot be done, change everything.

Are you, the reader, a person that is seeking to change things, to change your life? Or are you someone that is counting on things remaining the same? Is your life so complete that you need nothing else? These are the questions that I hope you will have lingering in your mind as you read the next few pages. It will enable you to open yourself up to discovering the epiphany that may await you.

This book was written to illustrate one point of that can lead to such a change, there are others. It will hopefully become clear that while we are all seeking things that we want some of us are fortunate to find exactly what we need. The curious thing is that the journey that we must take to discover this can start with an event that might at first seem harsh and difficult to endure. It could also be something that is so familiar and so comfortable that we do not see the change until it overruns and surprises us. Our reaction then is that 'we did not see it coming'. It could begin today or it could already have begun. You could be sitting on a train, commuting to your job with a favorite book balanced on your knee as you ponder your life and observe the events that surround you. Don't look now but your destination may have changed and when you arrive, you may end up startled at what you find.

Chapter One

Philip Lee sat in the same seat he did every day as he rode the Pittsburgh Pennsylvania Harrisburg Intrastate Commuter Train from his home to the Harrisburg Interconnect where he transferred to the Lancaster Short Shuttle. He barely had time to get any work done on the first leg of the trip with the train traversing the distance in roughly thirty minutes.

A tattered copy of 'The Killer Angels'[1] rested on his knee as he took a few moments to glance at the screen-scape which displayed a sunny day that was always present on the way to work. The scenes were always the same, projected images designed to show movement because the Maglev trains did not give any sensation of motion except when accelerating or decelerating. They were created because once the speed exceeded three hundred miles per hour there were too many episodes of motion sickness occurred as the passengers looked out the windows at the country side speeding by. It became necessary not to show the true speed to the passengers at which the train was traveling. Soon Philip would begin to feel the gradual deceleration of the train. The windows would then go black and the cabin lights brighten as they would come to a stop at the Interconnect's main transit hub.

Across the aisle came a voice, "You know that on the trans-continental line they have trains that hit speeds better than four hundred and twenty miles per hour!" said the young boy standing on the seat across from Philip.

Philip looked at him and smiled and then asked, "Where did you hear that?"

The boy's mother shot Philip a look of disdain and pulled her son down into his seat and scolded him in a low voice, one that Philip could not make out what was being said. It was a shame that many people we so frightened to interact with others, he thought.

Philip picked up the book as it was beginning to slide off his leg and he could feel that the train was breaking harder now, they had almost reached Harrisburg. A pleasant female voice announced their imminent arrival and then the train's next destination.

Philip said, "Acorn, say time." and he heard his personal communications unit recite the time through his temple implant, "seven thirty two AM". He had eleven minutes until the Lancaster Short Shuttle departed. The train was exactly on time, to the minute. Even though the Short Shuttle was not as fast, the twelve minutes it took to reach its destination was barely enough time to get comfortable in one's seat.

The female voice indicated that the seven twelve from Pittsburgh was arriving at gate Seven 'A' and the small lurch indicated that the train was indeed stopped. Philip grabbed his brief case from under the seat in front of him and looked around the train to see if there was an advantage in exiting one way or another and as usual there was not. The long train had few empty seats and most of the thousand or so people were just as anxious to depart and move on to their next destination as Philip was.

Philip thought, if only the University of Pittsburgh had an opening in the American Studies Department he could get campus housing and walk to work every day, but his job at Franklin and Marshall had a great deal of appeal. The school remained small and well-funded. He had a great deal of freedom to pursue whatever curriculum that he thought appropriate. He only needed to publish once per year as opposed to once per semester that most universities required of their faculty. The only drawback was that there was no campus housing and houses in Lancaster and the surrounding area were impossible to find. So the commute wasn't all that bad he thought after all things were considered.

Philip's thoughts were disturbed by the voice of a man.

"Hey, are you going to sit there all day?"

Philip snapped back to reality and stood up and said, "Thanks" to the small rather plump man that let him get out of seat so that he could begin the brief walk to the Lancaster Short Shuttle. 'I'd better check the status of the train and see if it's on time.' he thought. He did this every day even though he had no reason to do so since in the past five years it hadn't been late once.

"Acorn, say status Lancaster Short Shuttle." he queried and the voice replied, "Departure time delayed seven minutes arrival at the scheduled time".

'How can that be?' he thought. The train is only capable of two hundred fifty miles per hour and that made it impossible for it to arrive at the scheduled time.

"There must be a lag in posting the delay in arrival time. I should call the school and let them know that I may be a few minutes late. Acorn call office." he said. The call was instantly placed and the electronic receptionist answered just as quickly.

"Good morning, Franklin and Marshall. How may I help you?" the pleasant voice answered.

"Philip Lee's office, please." he replied.

"Thank you, I will transfer you now." the receptionist responded. While he waited Philip walked behind what appeared to be an endless stream of commuters working their way down the long platform to the escalators ahead.

A pleasant female voice answered the phone, "Dr. Lee's office may I help you?"

Philip said, "Leave message".

He was then transferred to an automated attendant that said, "Thank you Dr. Lee, I am ready when you are."

He never got over the fact that the system recognized his voice even when used to disguise it to see if he could fool it. "Marsha, its Philip, I am probably going to be a couple minutes late, something up with the shuttle, tell Morgan to start the class on day one and I'll take it from there when I arrive. Thanks- Acorn disconnect." he said.

As he emerged from the platform area into the main concourse and as he did he glanced up at the transparent ceiling and saw that it was raining. 'Great, I hope it is not raining in Lancaster the walk to campus is more than twenty minutes just about as long as it took to reach Harrisburg from Pittsburgh and he had no rain gear. Why hadn't he checked the weather?' he thought.

"Acorn, say weather in Lancaster PA" he said.

He smelled the tempting aroma of coffee and decided to stop at the concession since he had an extra seven minutes until his train departed.

The PCU related the weather saying, "The current weather conditions in Lancaster Pennsylvania are partly cloudy skies with a temperature of eighty four degrees Fahrenheit and winds from the northwest at twelve miles per hour."

"I'll have a regular with light cream please" he said as he directed his attention to the automated coffee attendant while the coffee was brewed and poured into the cup.

"Thank you Philip Lee your account has been charged eleven IMC. Have a good day." he attendant stated cheerfully.

Great, he had forgotten how expensive the concession in the train station were. A good cup of coffee was only about five or five point five IMC elsewhere. He then determined that he should check his account balance. 'I might have to transfer funds to cover the rental this afternoon.' he thought and directed, "Acorn, say operating account balance."

The PCU replied, "Your operating account balance is one thousand three hundred twenty two point five IMC". Wow, he thought, this coffee was hot as it splashed against his upper lip as he walked toward the shuttle's platform. He was still arriving very early and at the least that would assure him of a good seat.

Philip kept his eyes cast downward as he walked, he liked looking at the mosaic tile that was used in the concourse. Its random patterns and vivid colors created optical illusions that his mind had difficulty bringing into focus.

"You have an incoming call from Morgan Lewis do you wish to accept the call?" the PCU announced.

"Acorn, Yes. Hello Morgan how are you?" he replied and greeted his graduate assistant.

"Phil I wanted to let you know that I got your message and we will begin with day one. How late do you think you will be?" Morgan said sounding worried, but then again he always did.

Philip wondered if he sounded that way when he was a graduate assistant. "You will do fine, I won't be but five or ten minutes late I think, it depends upon the train and..." Philip stopped in mid-sentence. In front of him on the overhead platform, where the Lancaster Short Shuttle was supposed to be, was a surprise.

"Morgan there is a Baldwin 200 sitting on the tracks where the shuttle should be. I might not be late after all!" he exclaimed.

The Baldwin 200 was the latest in rail technology. It was the basis for the trans-continental tube system design. It was purported to reach speeds approaching five hundred miles per hour in test runs that were done early the previous summer. The only apparent difference in appearance between the 200 series and the 100 series was the color and the fact that the 100 series had a slightly more rounded nose.

It seemed almost less aerodynamic then the previous generation trains but because the tube trains ran in a ninety five percent vacuum environment there was little friction to provide drag to slow them down, as a result aerodynamics were a secondary concern. The reason these trains were able to reach such speed was due to the new power sources that had recently developed cold fusion tera-watt generators that were so compact that they were roughly the size of four bales of hay.

The technology also depended upon the use of subterranean tubes which were created by extremely large movable particle beam units. The units constructed the tube using molten earth blended with silicon. These hulking monsters crept along at two miles per hour and could create 20 miles of tube in a single day. The conductive floor that produced the magnetic wave that propels the train through the tube was extruded from the back of the tube maker.

Philip continued walking toward the escalator that would take him to the elevated platform. The color of the beast was not what he would have chosen, he thought.

"Phil are you there?" Morgan queried.

"Oh yes Morgan, this train is something to see – it's... it's this emerald green kind of color. I really like the pearl white 100 series better. I'd better go. I'll see you soon, bye. Acorn disconnect."

Philip never waited for a reply, he was just amazed to see the train. He wondered when they had the time to make the tube. Even though it would only take a little less than three days to make the tube there were so many obstacles in the way, people's homes, businesses and even highways, though highway traffic was diminishing each year, he thought as he marveled at the machine.

The last he had heard was there were less than a million cars left in the national rental fleet. If you add that to the three or four hundred thousand private vehicles that remained in service it did not come close to the numbers of private vehicle that numbered in the tens of millions just sixty years earlier. It was no wonder that the train lines were being created as rapidly as they were.

Philip reached the escalator and he could hear the rain hitting the transparent ceiling, the sky had been darkening with the approach of the heaviest part of the storm. The people in the concourse were unaffected and because the lighting within the train station remained at a constant level of illumination adjusting to the changes in the light levels on the outside.

As he rose to the platform seventy feet above the concourse level the train came into full view. It had windows, he could actually see the seats through those heavily tinted windows but then as though by magic the windows suddenly disappeared.

"Now that is some fascinating technology." Philip said out loud.

"Yes it is." replied a man standing on the platform responded. He was a balding man that appeared to be in his early fifties.

Philip looked at him not really recognizing that he had spoken aloud. Then he said "I can't believe that it's here and it's - well that I am going to be actually riding on it." he then said to the man.

Jeremy replied, "Yeah, I know it is pretty cool."

Pretty cool? He must be older than I thought or just some weird older man that likes to use out dated expressions." Philip thought and the replied, "Yes, it's amazing."

"The name's Giles, Jeremy Giles." Jeremy said as he extended his hand.

'Wasn't he afraid of catching some disease like everyone else?' Philip thought while cautiously extending his hand saying, "I'm..."

"I know Dr. Lee, Philip isn't it?" Jeremy said with a knowing smile.

"Uh, yes it is, you have me at a loss." Philip replied slightly confused.

Jeremy then explained saying, "I met you four years ago, I work with your father- I'm on the tera-watt generator project, applied cold fusion. Your father's a great man but his theories are way too sophisticated for me. That's why I transferred to the Applied Engineering Division instead staying on at the Theory Division."

Philip tried to recall the memory of their meeting but he could not. "I'm sorry but I don't remember..." he then said.

"That's quite alright you were pretty upset about your brother's incarceration. By the way how is he? Austin is his name isn't it?" Jeremy asked. Philip nodded. There was something wrong here. This was too coincidental, the very day that Austin was getting out of prison. "Well how is he?" Jeremy pressed.

"He is okay I suppose, I haven't seen him in several months." Philip said keeping his guard up and thought that perhaps he worked for the government.

Jeremy turned and looked at the train again and smiled. "This is going to be one great ride." he added. "Philip, ya want to see the engine on this baby? I'm here to validate the energy generation protocol and have free access to the cab- I can even run the thing if I want. Pretty cool, huh?" Jeremy asked invitingly.

The lure of seeing the latest technology was too great to turn down. "That would be wonderful. If it's not too much trouble?" Philip agreed.

Jeremy then replied "No problem, let's go." and he was off. Philip looked at the seamless shell of the green train and it appeared to be a tube with a flat bottom skirt attached to it. The skirt must contain the magnetic propulsion that enables the train to levitate and move at the high speeds that it travels. The interior of the train was heavily shielded from the magnetic energy and there was virtually no magnetic energy detected in the cabins as indicated by the monitors that were placed throughout each car.

The train utilized a ribbed construction the enabled it to bend and flex almost snakelike in a very fluid motion. There was therefore little jerking or a sensation of motion even when the train was changing directions. This was a truly remarkable technology that had changed the way man traveled.

"Jeremy, when did they construct the tube?" Philip queried as he finally caught up with the short stocky man that moved quickly down the platform toward the front of the train.

"Last week, it took four days from start to finish. These Norwind Tube Manufacturing Platforms are truly awesome to behold. Have you seen one? I think that the one that did this tube is still outside of Lancaster. It is going to do the Baltimore run soon. That will take a little longer they have to go deeper than normal, I think. This tube is about on hundred fifty feet below the surface but to make the Baltimore tube they will have go down to almost three hundred feet. Here, in here." Jeremy said as he stopped about thirty feet from the front of the train, right below the Baldwin logo and looked quizzically at the train. He held up a cross shaped item with his right hand and seemed to press it with his fingers. There was a low hum as a doorway opened, appearing seemingly out of nowhere. Jeremy gestured for Philip to enter and followed him through the entrance.

They entered the train in the first passenger compartment just behind the control center cab. There were three women working between the seats arranging pillows and armrests. The seats looked to be very comfortable and they were mint green in color which contrasted the forest green carpeting which ran from floor to midway up the sides of the train. Philip felt the urge to sit in one but fought it off as he turned to the right to see Jeremy moving off in the direction of the control center.

The door opened with a whoosh and they stepped into a rectangular shaped room that was completely white in color. The dimpled metal floors were coated with a latex type substance that gave them a springy feel as Philip walked upon it. In the center of the room was a rectangular shaped column that was about three feet wide and four feet deep and its height was the full eight feet of the compartment. There was a low hum present that was barely audible.

Jeremy walked to the left of the column and entered a code into a numeric pad that was located just out of Philip's sight. The windows that were apparently present became transparent and Philip could see views of both sides of the train plus out of the porthole in the rounded nose of the train. Two chairs arose from the floor and a triangular shaped display descended from the ceiling and opened into the shape of an inverted pyramid. Jeremy detached the keyboard that was concealed and motioned for Philip to sit.

"I just have to run a quick diagnostic check before I... that's not right- oh yes there it is." Jeremy's fingers moved rapidly over the keys. "Okay, this is it Philip. Pretty cool, huh?" he stopped to say to Philip.

"What is the purpose of column in the middle?" Philip inquired.

"Oh that's the thirteen tera-watt cold fusion generator." Jeremy replied.

"Thirteen tera-watt? That's impossible." Philip replied in amazement.

"Nope, your dad's really proud of this baby- he says he will have a production model of a Three T-Watt generator that will fit in a briefcase in less than a year- now that it is way cool. You want to ride up here- the trip should take about nine minutes and I'll leave the porthole window on so you can see how the vacuum locks function. The engineers that designed the tubes did some really cool things with illuminated panels and lasers- quite a light show." Jeremy said and then turned back to his work not really paying attention to whether Philip was interested in riding in the control center or not.

Philip decided to get up and walk forward to see out of the nose porthole. The porthole was about three feet in diameter and offered a great view of the magnetic bed the lie ahead. The bed continued at the current elevation then gradually sloped out of view. The sound of the magnetic relays cycling brought Philip back from his half dream like state that he was in as he gazed down the bed. "What was that Jeremy?" he asked. Jeremy ignored him and continued to manipulate the keyboard.

The door opened and a man dressed in a blue shirt and pants came in accompanied by a woman. He looked at Philip and then at Jeremy, then he inquired, "Who is this Giles?" Jeremy ignored him.

Philip stepped up and extended his hand, "I am Philip Lee".

The man looked at him sternly, "Are you involved with this project Mr. Lee?" he replied without extending his hand. "Lee, wait. Are you related to Dr. Gregory Lee?"

"Yes, he is my father." Philip said.

"Okay, have a seat please we are about to depart. Jenkins switch on the stabilizers and raise two more chairs." he instructed.

The woman silently went about raising two more chairs on the far side of the cabin and proceeded to sit down. She too wore the same blue shirt and pants. Her appearance was unremarkable as case with most women in the work place. Her dark brown hair was cut short and her eyes were hidden behind glasses that indicated she used the older technology PCU display and not the temple hologram display that Philip used. It was nice not having to wear glasses, Philip thought. He watched as Jenkins lowered another pyramid shaped display from the ceiling and began to enter information and manipulate the keyboard.

"Alright, Giles are we ready?" the man in blue asked Jeremy. This time Jeremy paused long enough to give thumbs up.

"What does that mean Giles? Can't you even answer a simple question?" the engineer asked in an irritated tone.

"Ready." Jeremy mumbled and returned to monitoring his terminal.

"Mr. Lee, please have a seat - if you would like you can move your chair to the front. I am certain you will find the view interesting." engineer said without enthusiasm.

Jenkins looked up and said, "She's ready Mr. Engineer."

"Check doors." the engineer instructed and at that command the windows changed to views of each of the ten doors, all showing clear.

"Close doors." and with his command all doors closed immediately. It was at that point that Philip realized that the engineer's voice commands were being executed by the train's system and not Jenkins.

"Show cabin." he then said and the window displays changed show each of the ten compartments with views of each one's forty seats. In Cabin Four there were two people that were standing and talking in the aisle. The engineer looked at them and shook his head.

"I should start this thing and let them fall." he said under his breath and then he added, "Jenkins help Mr. Lee move his chair." Jenkins stood and showed him how to release the chair and move it. Not surprisingly it was suspended using magnetic force.

"Well they don't seem to want to sit down- display motion warning message and sound chime." he told the train. The chime was rung and the message displayed in a three dimensional hologram in each of the compartments. The two people finally took their seats.

"Finally - initiate starting protocol." he then ordered. The train silently rose approximately 7 inches from the bed.

"Engage forward protocol" and instantly the train began to slowly move forward.

"Accelerate to level one." and the train began to pick up speed.

"Display velocity on forward porthole" and with that command a display showing the velocity of the train appeared on the lower right portion of the round porthole. They were traveling at seventy miles per hour as the train began its decent into the tube.

Philip watched the train's path as they descended into the darkness of the tube. He caught sight of motion to his left as Giles slid his chair into position next to his. "Watch this Philip" and suddenly there was a path of blue light that illuminated the bed in front of them.

The speed registered '175 mph' on the porthole display and the odd thing was that there was no sensation of motion. The engineer called out to Jenkins, "First lock in thirty seconds- stand by". In front of them were crisscrossed laser lights in green and yellow dancing in front of what appeared to be a wall that they were headed directly for at a speed that now registered '215 mph'.   Then the wall was gone and the train continued to gain speed. "Initiate cruise protocol." the engineer called out and the train's speed increased rapidly to '300 mph', then three hundred fifty, and four hundred and finally when it reached '417 mph' it held steady.

The train passed through vacuum locks approximately every minute as it raced toward Lancaster.

"Initiate docking protocol" and the train began to slow to first '350 mph', then three hundred, two hundred and then it burst out of the tube into the daylight just two miles north of Lancaster. The trip was amazingly fast.

"Jenkins prepare for arrival" the engineer directed as the train slowed to '70 mph' and then to fifty and thirty and finally to five as it eased in the space next to the arrival platform. The side windows became transparent and a chime rung as the three dimensional hologram displayed the message 'Welcome to Lancaster'.

Jeremy stood up and said "Wow that was way cool!" Philip had been impressed, the technology was like that illustrated in science fiction novels that he read as child.

"Thank you Jeremy, that was a very interesting experience, I enjoyed it. Oh, will you, by chance, be seeing my father later today?" he then asked.

"Perhaps at the end of the day, why?" Jeremy replied.

"Can you tell him to remember that I will see him tonight around dinner time, you know he never answers his phone and doesn't believe in these things', he said as he motioned to the temple communication device that was inside of his head." Philip explained.

"Yeah- do you have the tooth mike also? I can't seem to get used to having that in my mouth." Jeremy answered.

"I don't even know that it is there most of the time, though the first one I owned used to feedback when I was in an area where there were heavy microwave transmissions. It would cause the tooth to vibrate and then heat up- I must say it was an unpleasant feeling but thank goodness that problem was corrected." Philip said.

"Wow that sounds totally messed up. Yeah, I will let your dad know- nice meeting you." said Jeremy as he extended his pudgy hand. He had short fingers and Philip felt as though he was almost shaking a child's hand and his grip was spongy and uncomfortable.   Philip withdrew his hand awkwardly and said, "Nice to meet you as well and thanks for the tour, this is one amazing train."

Philip turned to exit the cabin. Jenkins was standing in his way. He looked at her and smiled. Her facial expression did not change and she did not move. "Nice to meet you Miss Jenkins." Philip said as he extended his hand. Jenkins looked at him and then took his hand. Her grasp was warm and firm. For some reason Philip found it difficult to release her hand, he did not want to let it go.

"It was nice to meet you Mr. Lee and thank you for your patronage." she replied.

Now that was odd, Philip thought but brushed it off as her just being professional and courteous.

"Mr. Lee your book and your case." Philip turned to see that the engineer had his copy of 'The Killer Angels' in his hand.

"Thank you. I would have been lost in class today. We are starting to study the battle of Gettysburg today and I find this book helps bring a lot of the day's activities to life vividly." he said.

Yes he had done it again, gone off on a tangent that no one else could have any interest, except that Jenkins interjected, "The first of July, 1863, the turning point- I don't think there are too many more important days in the history of the world- modern history I mean."

"Really!" Philip said with a little too much enthusiasm. "I think you are probably right. Two or three different decisions and some luck and the outcome of the Civil War would have different". Jenkins removed her glasses revealing that she had what Philip thought were beautiful brown eyes that danced with life. Philip said "Unfortunately I am late for class, perhaps we could discuss this further at a more convenient time?" Jenkins nodded. "May I call you?"

Jenkins put her glasses back on and asked, "Ready?" Philip nodded and she depressed the send button on her glasses right ear piece.

"Acorn, store under Jenkins." said Philip. "Thanks Jessica. Would you like mine?" he asked.

"That's not necessary, I will wait to hear from you." she replied. As Jeremy brushed past him and he nudged him with his elbow.

"I will call you later- bye for now. Thank you Mr. Engineer." Philip said over his shoulder as he exited the train.

Philip looked down the platform to find the best exit to the street. It was a twenty minute walk to campus from the train station and the way things were going he would be on time for this first class after all. That was a good thing since he was going to be leaving early to go to Bethlehem, he reflected. Since the Allentown line was not completed the only way for him to get there was by automobile. The five hundred IMC charge for the rental was quite an extravagance but it was not every day that his brother was being released from prison, it was an expense that had to be paid.

On exiting the station Philip was hit by a blast of hot air. The early morning temperature was already eighty four degrees though the forecast called for rain which would offer a bit of relief. The crowds of people walking to their jobs had reached the apex and soon everyone would be off the streets in their climate controlled offices, classrooms or homes. Most work until eight or nine so that they could avoid the late afternoon heat. Everyone looked forward to winter when temperatures were in the sixty and seventy degree range most days. Thank goodness I don't live in the Midwest Philip thought.

"Acorn, say temperature in Kansas City Missouri."

"The temperature at six thirty AM was ninety seven degrees with a projected high of one hundred twenty two degrees today."

Philip walked past the downtown stores and turned the corner and saw the familiar row of dormitory apartments just across the street from the football field. The campus hadn't changed much in the past thirty years. The big additions at that time were the enclosed walkways between buildings. It took three years to install the movable sidewalks that made it extremely easy and fast to move between the buildings. Philip was fortunate, though, his office was just one floor from his classroom. He taught an average of four classes a day and had between twelve and sixteen students in each class. He was also lucky to have at least one graduate assistant working with him each semester.

This semester it was just Morgan but he was extremely motivated and really wanted to please. Philip picked up the pace and crossed the street without looking to see if there was any traffic. The odds were in his favor, though there were students whose parents would not have thought twice about spending the two hundred thousand IMC to purchase an automobile for their child. F & M was not inexpensive, but considering that many of the small independent schools were closing down this prestigious little school in Lancaster PA flourished with five hundred applicants for each of the four hundred positions available each September.

Philip entered the American Studies Building at five minutes passed eight and his class was just about to begin. He thought about letting Morgan have some fun and try his hand at starting the class solo but his ego just wouldn't allow him to do so. He enjoyed the subject of this class it was his favorite study in the Nineteenth Century American History class; the Civil War and its impact on the world. This period in time represented the last bastion of slavery and the fight for states' rights verses the centralized federal government, a battle that continued in the hearts and minds of many Americans well past the day the last shots were fired.

The impact of the Civil War was swimming in his head as he entered the classroom. Morgan sat at Philip's desk looking at the six students that were already in place. Philip said, "Thanks Morgan it turns out the new 200 series Baldwin train is now on the Harrisburg to Lancaster line now. I had the opportunity to ride in the control cabin, the technology is quite impressive." Morgan looked a little disappointed but smiled just the same. He pushed himself back from the desk and stood up. The remainder of the twelve students filed in as the eight ten class chime sounded.

Philip stood at the front of the room and said "Acorn, block all calls" and then turned to the class and said "Good morning". There was a less than enthusiastic response from the class.

"How many of you have had the opportunity to visit the battlefield at Gettysburg?" he asked. Three hands went up. "What were your impressions... uh Mr. Stenson?"

Jordan Stenson a smallish blonde haired be speckled sophomore with a true passion for history seemed taken aback by the question. "Uh, Dr. Lee I found it to be a very somber place, as though I was visiting a shrine."

"Really, well there are a lot of souls that met their end there and it was the bloodiest battle fought in American history in terms of American losses since all that died on both sides were Americans. Today's battles tend to be lethal only to those with whom we are fighting." There was a murmur and some slight giggling.

"Can you imagine twenty eight hundred men dying in less than forty five minutes? Charging across open terrain into a horseshoe shaped killing field... but I am jumping ahead- Does everyone have their text books and a copy of Shaara's 'Killer Angels?'" All heads nodded. "Let's turn to chapter two in the text and set the stage for the battle."

The fifty minute class passed too quickly for Philip. He really enjoyed picturing the gallant young men in futile combat that would shape the face of modern warfare, not so much at Gettysburg but those in the Wilderness Campaign where Grant's strategies had been reapplied and were utilized during that Second World War.

The chime for the end of class struck and in an instant his classroom was empty leaving only Morgan who stood in the back of the room staring out the window.

"Phil, have you ever seen anything like that before?" Philip turned his attention to where Morgan was gazing. The sky was dark was the thunderstorms approached from the northwest but then Philip saw it. The Norwind Tube Manufacturing Platform appeared to be just about one thousand meters from the northern edge of the campus. It was a massive unit that housed a remarkable collection of technology. The platform sat on tracks which enabled it to creep over just about any type of terrain. It was apparently in the process of beginning the next tube construction project, Lancaster to Baltimore. The ninety five mile tube would take twelve to fourteen days to complete and once done the commute time to Baltimore would be less than twenty minutes.

They could see the platform had extended the particle beam bore from under its base and it was targeting the initial excavation point for the tube. The particle beam bore would create the tube form fusing the earth and melting a hole that extended for a distance of ten to one thousand meters in a single burst. The typical burst calibration was five hundred meters and the bore would then be repositioned in the tube. Following after it would be the tube finishing system which would create the silicon based finish for the tube and it also extrude the metal floor which would be how sympathetic magnetic field was generated which enabled trains to run.

Since the particle beam cuts the tubes at depths of one hundred to three hundred meters below the surface there was some concern for damage or impediment to creation of tubes by ground water tables and occasional unstable geological plate activity in certain specific areas in the country. The fact that the tubes were typically run through rock meant that the likelihood of damage was remote and with the accuracy of tectonic monitoring, train activity was to be suspended during times of geological instability. Any damage could repaired within days with most of that time delay being caused by the need to wait for the Norwind equipment to arrive at the site.

Philip stared at the huge cube shaped platform with is four crawlers. It had the appearance of a huge odd shaped beast resting on its haunches. The crawlers were tracks like those you see on earth moving equipment and on each pod there were three sets of these crawlers. Above them were what one might call legs which were extended when the unit was in the move position. At that time the cube portion of the platform was elevated so that the unit could crawl along to it next position.

Once the particle beam bore had been put in place the platform was to begin its crawl to the next firing point. The subterranean operations ran on reserve power until they have finished the tube lining and magnetic floor. The timing of the arrival of the platform and the tube equipment was roughly the same. The platform was then lowered and a second particle beam bore was used to create a shaft so that an umbilical power cable could be lowered to provide the energy for the next firing. This process was repeated as many as twenty or more time in one day.

After the tube had cured for 24 hours the next team arrived to install the vacuum locks, the power couplings and the magnetic control systems. They worked around the clock to complete the tube so that twenty four hours after the platform arrived at the destination the tube was made operational.

Morgan turned to look at Philip and said, "I guess the new train line will mean that Lancaster will become even more crowded. I've heard that Baltimore has a housing crisis and with the banks not willing to build more without a pledge from the government that will guaranty their profits, relief is a long way off."

Philip shrugged and said, "I suppose so, my brother would be outraged though. He hated the Banking Consortium..." and then he stopped for fear of saying too much.

Austin Lee was finishing his five year prison sentence today. He had been convicted for conspiring to crash the World Banking Consortium's computer network. He had hoped that that would have led to the collapse of the economy. He had received the lightest sentence of the twelve that were convicted. There was only one that had remained at large, he was never captured and was presumed to be dead. My brother the criminal Philip thought. What was he thinking? I know he blames the banks for the wars and for Uncle Bob's death during the last war in the middle east, but how can one man's death in a meaningless skirmish in the deserts of Syria have any bearing on bringing about a total collapse of the world's monetary system, he thought.

"It just doesn't make sense." Philip stated aloud.

"Sure it does there is still some housing here in Lancaster and the surrounding communities people can commute the twenty minutes or so into Baltimore with little or no problem. Especially, if you put fifteen hundred seat trains on the line." Morgan responded.

"You are right." Philip agreed with Morgan. Very few people knew Austin Lee was his brother and if they did they most likely did not remember what he had done. Philip suddenly remembered that his phone was off line. He knew that he should check messages in case there were changes that he had to make regarding his trip to Bethlehem. "Acorn, activate and play messages."

"One message taken at eight twelve AM. Philip it's your mother don't forget to pick me upon your way to get your brother- I'll be ready at four o'clock sharp. See you then darling - love you. End of messages."

After hearing the message he said, "Acorn, erase message."

"Why Acorn?" Morgan asked. "I have always wondered. My access word is Thurgood, after Thurgood Marshall, the Supreme Court justice. I always liked the name."

"It is the nickname my grandfather used to call me. He said that I would grow up to be tall and strong. He got half of it right I am fairly tall at six foot four inches but I am far from strong." Philip answered.

Morgan replied, "Perhaps he meant in character." Philip pondered that statement as though the thought had never crossed his mind before.

"Yes perhaps." he responded as he pictured his grandfather speaking to him, the times that they had spent together when he was a young child. In many ways Philip had patterned his life after the man.

Joseph Harrington Lee, Philip's grandfather, was considered bright and seemed to be a caring father and husband but there also appeared to be a dark side to him that no one really knew. He was known as Harry to his friends and was an only child. There developed a rift between Harry and his father which Philip did not understand but it was clear that Harry harbored some very strong anger and resentment that may have been directed towards his father.

Harry became estranged from him when he left to go to college. He graduated from Temple University with a Bachelors of Arts Degree majoring in Art History. From there he went to New York University where he received his Masters and finally on to Cambridge where he received his Doctorate. He taught at Franklin and Marshall for quite a few years and finished his career at Temple as the head of the Art History Department.

While Philip had felt close to his grandfather when he was very young, his own son, Philip's father, apparently did not. For that matter his father a brilliant scientist/physicist seemed to be distant from everyone. He was always buried deep inside some project and as a result of the banks taking most of the real estate in the late 2040's, he became consumed with the idea of creating the perfect energy source as a means making life better for everyone. All his effort and energy seemed to go into it.

He met and married MacKenzie Alenni and when he was finishing his Doctorate at MIT. MacKenzie was a lively dark haired girl with big blue eyes and a winning smile. She had just finished her tour of duty in the army having served in the war in Argentina in 2069. She had distinguished herself when she rescued four of her fellow soldiers from capture and was given a bronze star. She was going to the University of Massachusetts as a sophomore when she met Greg at the Boston Common one spring day in 2073. They fell instantly in love and the affair became something much more when she became pregnant with Austin in July of that year.

They were married in a civil ceremony and in attendance was one lone family member, Greg's younger brother Bob, Robert H. Lee. Bob worshiped the ground Greg walked on but Greg never seemed to reciprocate though he always seemed to include Bob in every event that had meaning in his life; his marriage, the births of his children, Austin, Philip, Roger and Pam.

Uncle Bob was always around up until 2088 when he was called by his country to go to war for the first time.   When Bob returned he was different, more distant but he soon found happiness when he met Andrea. She had the same joy for living and she was deeply spiritual.   She convinced Bob to reevaluate his life and priorities shifting his thoughts to his life's purpose.   They married in January 2092. Bob's best man was Austin.   The nine year old idolized this man with the easy smile and you for living.

Philip remembered the wedding clearly, he was jealous of his brother standing next to Uncle Bob.   Austin had shown his little brother the wedding band that his uncle had entrusted him and he even saw the writing that was inscribed inside the yellow band, "I love you so much you see..."   He wasn't sure what it meant but he was certain that it was some kind of code from when Uncle Bob was in the war.

Morgan snapped Philip back to the here and now by calling his attention to the platform rising up on its legs and then jerking forward as it began its crawl to the rendezvous with the beam bore.   "I'll bet they have to repair the streets after that thing get through with them." Morgan interjected. Philip nodded his head.

"Incoming call from Roger Lee. Will you accept?"

Philip replied, "Acorn accept. Hello Roger how are you this fine rainy day?"

"Phil, I have a dreadful cold- it came on all of the sudden." his brother answered.

"So you won't be joining us tonight then?" Philip asked.

"No I'll be there, I can't miss seeing Austin- though I feel guilty about never going to see him even once. Do you think he will forgive me?" Roger asked.

"I am sure he has already Roger, he was never one to hold on to things, to...- Well accept when it came to Uncle Bob. Roger I'll see you at Mom and Dad's tonight then. I have another class coming in any minute." Philip said.

"Okay. Phil I will see you tonight - good bye." Roger replied, and Philip, instructed Acorn to disconnect.

The next class slowly filled their seats.   The class on Twentieth Century United States Politics was currently dealing with the race riots of the 1960s and they would end the week studying Martin Luther King's effect on the move toward racial equality one step closer to being reality, a reality that would take seventy more years to truly attain.   It was not attained by elevating the African American's status but by lowering the status of everyone else. This was excluding that chosen one percent of the population that controlled all the wealth and power. That was what had made Austin so angry, that was why Uncle Bob died, that was why life seemed to be so much drudgery for so many. Economic slavery had become reality of the mid to late Twenty First century.

Philip watched the final two students take their seats. The young blonde girl, a junior named Becky was always the last one to enter the classroom and was in serious danger of failing the class. She was clearly wasting her parents' money but it was their money, Philip thought. Becky smiled sheepishly as she sat down. The chime for the class to begin had rung several minutes before and normally Philip would have begun but he had been day dreaming about Austin, the train ride and the impressive platform that was now almost out of site.

Philip decided to call the classes' attention to the platform. "Class if you haven't seen the Norwind Tube Platform in action before please take a look at the one that is leaving our fair city." The class turned in unison save one, Becky, who was engaged with something that was on her personal communication device. She hadn't heard anything that Philip had said.

Philip shook his head and then said "Okay, now let's turn to page one hundred and six in our text and we will finish our discussion on the 1960 presidential election. Miss Forrest, perhaps you would like to give and opinion on why the winner was victorious?" Becky's expression went blank. Philip guessed that she didn't even know what class she was in at this point.

"Anyone want to venture into this?" he then asked. Three hands shot up and then one was slowly extended in the back of the room. Robert Unhu, the exchange student from Mozambique, tentatively had put forth his long thin arm with his large thin hand, his bony fingers slightly curled as it was waving back and forth. "Mr. Unhu, your thoughts please".

"Mr. Nixon lost for two reasons- one he looked physically terrible in the televised debate, sweating like a pig and two because dead people voted in Mr. Daily's Chicago."

Some of the class chuckled but most looked to Philip for his reaction before they would respond. Philip thought the answer was entertaining but not quite what he was hoping for, but then there were some good discussion points that could come from the statement and that was always a great opportunity to engage the students.

"Very interesting Mr. Unhu, please elaborate and of course I would like to hear from the rest of you - including Miss Forrest." Becky looked up from whatever she was doing and smiled weakly. Philip thought to himself, what a waste of a good seat.

The class time went by rather quickly and soon Philip found himself alone with some time to grade assignments and to catch on correspondence. "Acorn, say mail"

"You have twelve mail messages. Four are marked urgent, three are from students."

"Acorn, display list." The holographic projector that was located in the temple units created the pale green image of the mail list. Philip saw the urgent messages highlighted in bold letters. Two of the messages were from his mother and everything was urgent as far as she was concerned. Another was from Morgan and the fourth was from Marsha Meade his administrative assistant.

Philip said, "Acorn display number four." Philip scanned the message. It referred to one message that he had received earlier in the week. The Dean and College President was encouraging him to publish by the end of the semester and he was looking for an update and that update was required immediately. Great, thought Philip, he had not settled on the topic yet. It seems like this was a much higher priority than normal and he decided he must select a topic soon. "Acorn, reply to number four." Philip then dictated a quick note and as he spoke the words were written before his eyes. When he finished he instructed Acorn to send and then display the third message.

Morgan's message was just his usual panic when he wasn't certain his performance was up to Philip's standards. Philip composed a quick, nerve soothing response and moved on to the balance of the messages. His mother's messages did not warrant responses, they were reminders about the journey to retrieve Austin from prison.

Philip looked at the copy of 'The Killer Angels' resting on his desk and thought about Jenkins and the train ride. Philip always had difficulties establishing relationships, in fact he had trouble finding the courage to start a new acquaintance regardless of the gender. Philip pictured the train racing through the tube, the laser lights and guidance displays creating a spectacular effect. But then there was Jenkins curious remark about Gettysburg. He really was curious why she felt the battle was a pivotal moment in time.

"Acorn, call Jessica Jenkins." and as soon as he said those words he regretted the action as he stood up and walked to the window. The storm that had been anticipated and looked so ominous had apparently dissipated. There was a glimpse of the sunlight breaking through the clouds that were rapidly clearing from the late morning sky. The PCU pulsed a tone that acknowledged that the call had been placed and that acceptance had not occurred. The call was then transferred to a message handler.

"Jessica Jenkins is not able to accept your call at this time- if you would like to leave a message please do so, otherwise your name and number were recorded for later use."

"Jessica this is Phil Lee, we met earlier today on the Lancaster Short Shuttle. I have been thinking about your comment regarding the battle of Gettysburg and would like to discuss it more. Perhaps we could do that over coffee or dinner. Please call me when you have the opportunity. Good bye." Philip said and Acorn auto disconnected when it recognized him saying the words 'good bye'.

Philip stared out the window once again. This time he thought about Jenkins and whether he had done the right thing in calling. Time would tell, he thought and then he realized that he was getting hungry.

The food on campus was expensive, even under Lancaster standards. A cup of soup and small garden salad cost Philip twenty five IMC, more than most people earned for two hours of work. The walk to the main campus bistro was through the transparent enclosed walkways that crisscrossed the campus. Philip had taken his seat in the corner hoping to spend a few more quiet moments before his next class when Dr. Heidi Grunthal saw him and strode briskly to his table.

"Dr. Lee." she said as she approached his table.

"Dr. Grunthal would you like to join me?" he replied as he rose from his chair and gestured toward the seat across from his. Philip noticed that she did not have anything to eat in her possession, and that she must be on a mission, he thought. "May I get you something to eat or drink?" he asked.

"No thank you Dr. Lee, what you can get me is your topic for publication. The Dean has been calling me all morning. One of the trustees has been pestering him about you. He needs to have everything in order so that your actions cannot be questioned." she said firmly. Heidi had the utmost respect for Philip and appreciated his efforts and his expertise. She was letting Philip know that she was there to help him. At this point Philip was not sure what was amiss.

"I just sent to him a memo stating that I would have an outline to him by Friday, two days from now. What is the problem? I am ahead on publishing. What could be questioned?" he asked.

Heidi replied, "You haven't published this calendar year and while you did publish last semester, a truly fantastic study on the effect of the 1960s civil protests on the collapse of the United States Monetary system, the new requirement is to publish during the spring semester."

Philip hadn't heard of such a ridiculous requirement before this conversation. This meant he would not only have to have a topic but he must able to finish the paper and submit it for publication in less than five weeks.

"What!" Philip exclaimed. "What are they thinking?"

Heidi squirmed in her chair. For a woman that was nearly sixty she was extremely fit. Her arms were clearly defined only her face betrayed her age being weather-worn from too much exposure to sun in her youth. Her gray hair was pulled back and gather loosely in a clump on the back of her head.

Philip looked into her green eyes that intently stared at him and asked, "Heidi, what's going on here?"

She replied with question, "Do you know Norville Forrest?"

Philip thought for a moment and then replied, "Yes, he was just appointed trustee last fall after Nikki Takaka died."

Then Heidi asked, "Well, do you know Beckinvee Forrest?"

Then Philip's response was, "Oh." Becky Forrest's father must not be too happy that his daughter was not doing well in his class. Then he continued, "Yes I know her, she is failing my class."

"The Interim reports show that she has a four point zero in all her other classes." Heidi explained.

"I find that very hard to believe." Philip said and continued, "She has no interest in being here."

Heidi shrugged and leaned forward touching Philip's hand as he fidgeted with the small salad bowl in front of him. "Phil, give me your topic and I will get them off your back. You will publish a small piece and no will have any room to complain."

Philip looked at Heidi and then down at the table. "Okay, Heidi- Gettysburg- turning point in global history." Now he knew he had to find out what Jenkins meant by her comment.

Heidi sat back and said, "Now that sounds like a great piece and no one I know will do a better job with it than you will." A broad smile crept onto her face. "Thanks Phil, I knew you had something ready and were just keeping it secret until you felt it was the right time to disclose it." she said.

"Heidi, I just thought it up today." he replied.

"That's even better..." she interrupted. "I have to be in a meeting. I will speak to you later. Please enjoy your lunch. Good bye Dr. Lee." she said in a louder voice.

"Good bye Dr. Grunthal". Philip's eyes went down to his salad, he didn't know why he had chosen that topic except for the mysterious Ms. Jenkins seemed to be on his mind when he wasn't focused intently and deliberately on work. What if he never hear from her, how will he know what she meant? What was he thinking? He was considered to be one of this region's best resources on the battle of Gettysburg and its impact on United States History.

He had always considered it to an important battle but as Morrison argued so was Antietam. There were others that would site the Wilderness Campaign because it was the foundation for modern warfare tactics and that could also be cited as a turning point in global history. I can write a small paper probably in my sleep, he thought.

Those thoughts were disturbed by his PCU stating, "An incoming call Jessica Jenkins, will you accept?"

My goodness I didn't think that should return the call, he thought. "Acorn, yes. Hello, Phil Lee here."

"Hello Philip this is Jessica Jenkins, you called me." she said plainly.

"Yes, thank you for getting back to me- I called to invite you for coffee or perhaps dinner. Are you free tomorrow evening?" he asked.

There was a pause and then Jessica continued, "I would like to discuss Gettysburg with you. Perhaps we could have coffee, but tomorrow is inconvenient for me. I must travel to Chicago on company business I will be away for two or three weeks depending upon how the training goes. I am being considered for promotion to engineer. It is quite an honor. I could meet you tonight if you would like?"

Philip's heart sank, he had to pick up his brother. No, it wasn't that he had to, it was that he wanted to get his brother out of that place. "I am scheduled to leave on a short trip this evening myself and I did so look forward to talking with you."

"Oh." Jessica responded and her tone betrayed disappointment. "Where are you now? Do you have a little time?" she asked.

Without hesitating Philip said yes.

"Great, meet me at the train station in thirty minutes. I'll be in the main concourse at the Famous Coffee Shoppe. See you soon." she said.

Philip called Morgan and told him to take his first class of the afternoon and summarized what he was to cover. He told him he would be late, but to keep going and that it was his class to conduct and that he would be graded on his performance. The last part Philip threw into keep him on edge. It wasn't the kindest way to handle the situation but Philip could sometimes be a little less than kind.

Philip left campus and the comfort of the climate controlled sanctuary. The early afternoon heat was oppressive and greeted him as if he had opened an oven door. The humidity must be very high today he thought as he purposefully walked to the street. After crossing it he sought the entrance to the shops that made up the strip mall under the elevated dormitories of the school. Philip reached the entrance and quickly stepped inside.

My, that's a relief, he thought as he started down the corridor for the far entrance to the mall. The shops were sparsely occupied by people on their lunch break seeking to escape the heat or to make a quick purchase. The cavernous corridor echoed with a low pitch murmur of the people taking thoughtlessly on their PCUs.

Philip walked briskly to the far end of the building and exited once again into the heat of the day. It was three city blocks to the train station and he slowly proceeded down the sidewalk to his destination. The heavily tinted windows of the building showed his reflection as he moved through the oppressive atmosphere. It was almost like swimming in water. Beads of sweat started to form on his brow and at his collar. It had been quite some time since he had been out at this time of day and by the fact that he was the only one on the street most people had more sense than he apparently did.

"Acorn call National Enterprise Car Rental." he instructed.

The automated attendant answered, "National Enterprise how may we help you?"

"My name is Philip Lee and I have a rental reservation for this afternoon. I am calling to confirm delivery time and location." he inquired.

"One minute please Dr. Lee the Voltrun 90 will be delivered to your location at Franklin and Marshall College, Lancaster Pennsylvania at three fifteen this afternoon." they responded.

"Thank you." Philip replied.

"Is there anything else Dr. Lee?" they asked.

"Yes, will it be possible to have the car picked up in Harrisburg, PA this evening at ten o'clock." Philip said.

"Of course Dr. Lee, do you have an address you wish to give us now or would you like to call back with the information later?" the attendant asked.

"Please pick up at 1520 Juniper Avenue, Harrisburg PA." Philip instructed.

"I have 1520 Juniper Avenue Harrisburg PA scheduled as the pick-up location at ten o'clock this evening. Is that everything Dr. Lee?" they asked.

"Yes." Philip answered.

"Thank you for your patronage."

"Good bye" he said and Acorn terminated the call. Philip was breathing heavily but his spirits were lifted as he saw the door to the station a mere ten feet in front of him.

The rush of cool air caused a slight chill on his damp skin as Philip stepped into the station's entrance foyer. The station seemed to always have a good number of people milling about and today was no exception. There was a faint sound of some unrecognizable music playing over the noise generated by the people that were going about their business. Philip attempted to get his bearings but still wasn't sure where the meeting point was located.

"Acorn, display best route to Famous Coffee Shoppe." he instructed. The holographic display showed him his way. As he walked the display changed using an arrow to direct him. Before he knew it he was at the coffee shop and said, "Acorn, turn display off."

There was an elderly woman standing in the doorway of the shop who upon hearing his voice turned and said to him, "I beg your pardon?"

Philip realized immediately that she did not ascribe to the technology of the day, many of her generation reacted the same way his father had, and rejected it as being too intrusive. Philip couldn't seem to understand why they were so reluctant to embrace these fantastic inventions.

"I am sorry, I was speaking to my communication device." he said to her as he pointed to his temple.

"Oh." the woman replied and turn to some unseen person and continued speaking to them. Philip peered past the woman to see that the shop was virtually empty. Philip pondered whether the woman was just being rude or there was some other reason for her standing in the doorway. Halfway across the room, under a faux Tiffany lamp seated at a small octagonal table with her back to the door was Jenkins. It was the blue transit uniform that made him certain that it was her. Philip took a moment to study her appearance and other than her bronze coloring that was almost aglow in the dim light there was nothing remarkable. What caused him to be drawn to her, he wondered?

Philip elected to ask the woman blocking the passage to move, "I beg your pardon, may I pass through here please?"

The woman turned to him and she declared indignantly, "I suppose this time you were speaking to me." She did step aside never the less and Philip thanked her.

"Acorn hold calls." Philip whispered as he approached Jessica at the table.

Philip walked to the table and then around it so that he faced Jessica. "Hello Jessica." he said as he extended his hand. He could not help smiling. Jenkins looked up and directly into his eyes.

She returned his smile and extended her hand taking his firmly. The clasp, for it did not involve shaking, lingered and Jessica then became self-conscience and withdrew her hand saying, "Hello Philip."

Philip took the seat without asking and then pulled himself half out of it while awkwardly asking, "May I join you?" Jenkins nodded and smiled and then her gaze returned to her coffee.

Philip thought before he saw her sitting across the room that his main purpose for meeting her was to have her explain what she meant about the Battle of Gettysburg, but now he wasn't sure why he was there. He had impulsively left a class in the hands of a novice, something he had never done before. Then again there was the paper he had to publish, the 'publish or perish' mantra never had such a vivid meaning before now.

He thought he should get directly to the point by asking, "What makes you convinced that those four days in July were the most pivotal in modern history?"

Jessica looked at him and studied his face trying to see if this was a ploy. Was he sincere in his question or was this just some means to attempt to seduce her? He seemed sincere she thought but rather than blurt out the answer she elected to ask a question of her own.

"Do you think of the United States in terms of one of the great empires of civilization?" She paused and continued to watch his facial expressions change. He wrinkled his brow and did what she thought was a cute scrunch with his nose and as she waited for his response she found herself drawn to his eyes, a pale blue contrasted with the whitest whites she had ever seen. He's honorable she concluded but still waited for his response.

Philip thought or several seconds before answering the question. He fought with the term great. Greatness to him implied more than military might or financial domination. There were cultural contributions, spiritual aspects as well as humanistic issues that all folded into the definition of what a great civilization was or is.

"Powerful, influential and dominating, all of those things but not necessarily great - why do you ask?"

"Imagine a world without the United States as you know it. Replace it with two smaller factions that never resolved their differences and never develop the infrastructures necessary to be an impact on the balance of power during the First World War. Let us say that the war continued to languish and the struggle becomes a mortal stalemate that has the conflict persisted into the mid-1930s. At that point, let's assume that a certain corporal named Adolf Hitler is shot for cowardice. What is the world's condition in 1940?"

"You are making some very huge assumptions. Why do believe that the North would capitulate?" he asked in reply. Philip thought this argument was very familiar. Where had he heard it before?

He puzzled over it as Jessica responded with another question, "How many mistakes were made during the Gettysburg campaign by Lee and his generals, Dr. Lee?" she continued to respond by asking questions.

"I believe that Lee made one very large tactic error and one significant strategic one. His generals failed to execute several orders in either a timely fashion or they did not follow them according to specific directions." Philip answered.

"The one order, tactical error you said. Are you referring to Pickett's Charge?" she asked.

"Yes, even if Longstreet had...." he stopped in mid-sentence when he suddenly realized that what he was hearing were arguments made by Dr. Leopold Jenkins, Dean of American Studies at Berkley- this was his daughter. "You are Leopold Jenkins' daughter aren't you?" he asked in amazement.

"Philip I am surprised it took you as long as it did to discover that." she answered coyly.

"He has never published that theory to my knowledge, but I did meet him..." Philip said.

And Jessica interrupted, "Yes, I know three years ago in New York at his lecture on the Revolutionary War."

"How did you know, did your father mention me, I could not have said anything that brilliant or noteworthy." Philip replied though he was confused.

"No, you didn't but you did impress someone who was standing at his side." Jessica said while lowering her eyes and blushing. Philip tried to bring the conversation back to the forefront of his memory to see if he could recall seeing her or noticing her, which apparently he did not.

"I am sorry Jessica I have tried to recall the day and only remember your father's theory on the significance of the battle." he said. Philip felt as though he should remember her, after all she now seemed to be so very memorable.

"Don't be, I was off to the side speaking to one of my father's many admirers and didn't have the opportunity to introduce myself. The two of you were engaged in a very intense conversation, but then again all of my father's conversations seemed to be intense." she said with a laugh.

"How is your father?" Philip inquired.

"He died more than a year ago." Jessica said quietly. Philip felt a sense of immediate loss and also guilty about his intent to publish a theory that another had developed.

"I am so sorry." he replied and took the opportunity to touch her hand softly.

"Dad had always loved white water rafting and had been in Maine with two friends. They apparently ran into difficulties and two of them died. The other man, Sun Ya Yen, you may know of him, is now paralyzed though he has been in regenerative treatment for almost five months and I have heard that he will eventually recover most of his abilities."

"Sun Ya Yen, Senator Sun Ya Yen? I remember hearing about the accident when it happened. Why don't I remember your father's name being mentioned?" Philip asked with incredulity.

"That is because it was withheld for reasons I am not sure will ever be known." she replied.

"Jessica I feel terrible. I came here to meet you and to get to know you because I felt somehow drawn to you. I used the Gettysburg discussion as an excuse but also, and this is the part I am sorry about, I was hoping to use the idea for a paper I have to publish to keep my job.

Philip waited for a reaction but Jessica took his hand and then looked up into his eyes and said, "I was hoping you would want to publish his theory. I have only two requests, which are I have to be involved and you have to credit my father appropriately. This was his passion, his life."

Philip thought this is too perfect. There has to be something that will happen to ruin what was turning into one of most lucky days of his life. "I am stunned." he replied. "Thank you, of course you can be involved and your father will get all the credit for the subject and appropriate research. I see the chance of spending time with you as a very special bonus." He could not believe that those words had sprung from his lips. From where had all of this boldness come, he wondered.

"So we have a deal?" she queried as she placed her hand in his and held it.

"We most certainly do." Philip returned not knowing what to say next, his mind had gone completely blank.

"Good, I have a few pages of my father's notes that might be helpful. You can pick them up when I get back from my trip if you would like."

Philip thought that could be weeks before she returned and perhaps he could meet her later. No, he said to himself, he hadn't seen his brother in almost a year and this was the night of his release.

"Oh, I wish that I was free this evening or that you were not traveling tomorrow. Will you have any free time this weekend?" Philip asked.

"Yes, but I won't have enough time to travel back and forth." she explained.

"I could come there, if you take the notes with you." Philip said and again he found his mouth saying things that he never would have dared to think normally.

Jessica smiled. "That could work out I will call you and give you my schedule. Perhaps we could have dinner together, if you would like." Jessica said while she continued to hold his hand firmly as they talked about the battle and her father's theory. Philip had thought originally that it was not a plausible theory but that was before the words had come from Jessica's lips. He hung on every word, his head bobbing in agreement even when things rang a somewhat dis-harmonic chord.

Before he realized it he had been with her for an hour and knew he had to get back for the start of last class of the day. He had to teach this class before he went to meet his mother. He finally said, "Jessica unfortunately I have to be leaving." She squeezed his hand and smiled sadly.

"I should have left twenty minutes ago." she replied.

"I will call you later tonight if you would like. What time do you usually go to sleep?"

"I am usually in bed by ten o'clock but you can call me a little later than that if that will be more convenient for you." she said.

"No, I will call you around ten or perhaps a little before and then of course I will call you tomorrow to work out our dinner arrangements for this weekend. If that is alright with you?" he asked hoping to hear additional affirmation of her positive feelings toward him.

"That will be fine." she said. Philip stood up and Jessica did as well since neither wanted to let the others' hand go.

"Until tonight then." Philip said awkwardly as he released her hand and stood looking at her. He motioned to the door and as they walked he placed his arm around her waist and she moved closer to him. When they reached the doorway Philip ushered her in front of him and they emerged into the concourse which was bring and noisy in comparison to where they had been.

"Okay, I really must be going." Jessica said. "I am certain that I have been missed by now." Philip looked down and then did something again that was out of character he bent his head down and forward. Jessica saw his action and offered her cheek. Philip kissed her cheek softly hesitating briefly and then to his surprise Jessica turned her head and their lips met briefly as Jessica pulled back and said, "Good bye Philip."

"Jessica, good bye I will call you tonight at ten." he said as he watched her turn and walk away.

"Acorn, activate phone and check messages." There were no messages. Philip watched Jessica vanish in to the crowd and then turned and walked toward the exit. He had to venture into the heat of the day. Though it was clearly hotter than when he had been out earlier Philip did not seem to feel as oppressed by its effects. Before he knew it he was back inside the enclosed strip mall which was almost completely empty of customers. His foot falls echoed slightly as he walked deliberately to the exit. Then he was back on campus and climbing the stairway to reach his classroom. The chime indicating his class was to start rang out as he opened the door.

All eyes were on him in disbelief that Dr. Philip Lee could be late for any class. The perspiration dripped from his brow as he struggled to gain his composure and begin the class.

"Good afternoon ladies and gentlemen. I am sorry for being late today, it was unavoidable." he began.

At that moment interrupted by, "You have a phone call from our mother. Do you wish to accept?"

He replied, "Acorn, no and deactivate phone. My apologies again let us take out our text and begin in chapter six. Can anyone tell me who Jane Fonda was and why her actions during the Vietnam War were so divisive?" he asked the class.

The class time passed slowly. This was not a talkative group to start with and engaging them in a discussion on Twentieth Century American Wars was a difficult assignment for anyone. Even though it was incumbent upon the student to put forth effort to learn Philip also felt a strong obligation to make the material worthy of an attempt to learn it. Perhaps his enthusiasm for the topic was not as great as it was with other topics, he thought.

"Mr. Gupta, please explain why you feel that the United States was wrong in abandoning the people of South Vietnam in 1975?" he asked.

Felix Gupta began a long winded explanation of how the people were betrayed by a military that had lead them to believe that they would protect them as a reward for betraying their own people and their culture. Philip hardly listened as he droned on making the same point repeatedly. Philip had challenged him for this very reason knowing that he would usurp the remaining class time listening to his favorite voice, his own.

The chime sounded the notification of relief and the students jumped to their feet as Gupta continued his monologue.

Philip interrupted him by saying, "Mr. Gupta, I am sorry to interrupt you but class has ended. We can continue this next time. Thank you for your participation." Gupta smiled, stood, picked up his books and left. Philip had only a few minutes to get to the entrance and meet the car rental representative. As he gathered his things together he said, "Acorn, activate phone and play messages."

You have one message received at two fourteen PM today." "Philip, I haven't heard from you. Are you going to be on time or am I to consider you as having developed the same characteristics of your younger brother. Call me and let me know what I should expect. Remember your brother has been in that horrible place for five years and I want to get him out of there as soon as we can. I love you. Bye"

He then instructed the PCU to the erase message. Philip decided to call his mother while he was in transit. He walked out of the classroom as Morgan was attempting to enter.

"Ah Morgan, walk with me please. How did it go?" Morgan made a face as the both walked down the hall.

"I think it went alright. The class did not participate very much. I finally had to call on Neuman to get things going. You know how much she loves controversy and she did not disappoint." he told Philip.

"Sounds like you had a little fun." Philip replied.

"Yes, the end of the class was a war..." he began to elaborate.

Philip interrupted saying, "I am sorry but I have to pick up the car. I will be in tomorrow early. Let's get together and review the video of the class. I'm sure that you did wonderfully. If not, I guess I'll have to replace you." Philip teased with a smile and then reassured Morgan that everything was fine. "Meet me at seven fifteen tomorrow morning in my office - I will see you then." he said.

"Have a safe trip Phil. See you in the morning." Morgan said as Philip walked away.

When Philip reached the reception area he saw the representative from the rental company was standing close to the door. The uniform he wore was quite striking. It was a maroon suit with a collarless white shirt. The company's logo was in gold and stitched on his left breast pocket. Philip waved to get the young man's attention.

"Good afternoon, I am sorry that I am late." he said.

"Quite alright Dr. Lee. If you will permit me I will give you some brief instruction on the operation of the Voltrun 90." the young man said.

"Thank you that would be helpful." he replied.

Once again Philip found himself outside in the heat. They walked the short distance to where the vehicle was parked.

"Dr. Lee I am going to ask you to read aloud these instruction at a normal pace, not too slow, not too fast." the young man instructed. Philip read four sentences from a small laminated card. "That's great now please tell the car to open."

Philip said, "Open." and the door in the front of them opened.

"Now Dr. Lee please tell the car to start and set temperature to seventy degrees." Philip did so and the car started and a burst of cool air came from the cabin.

"Please come around to the other side and say 'open' and then get in." Philip complied with the directions. Once seated inside the young man gave him information on manual and automated driving. He recommended manual driving only be done in an urban settings but automated driving could be done one hundred percent of the time. High speed driving required reactions to be very acute and if he was not used to the controls he could easily override the safety features that are integrated into the vehicle he was told.

"That's about it Dr. Lee, are there any questions?" he said in conclusion.

"No, I think I will let the car do all of the driving." Philip responded.

"A very intelligent decision. You can even take a nap if you wish should you choose to allow the vehicle to function as it is designed." the young man said.

Philip took note of the young man and he did not appear to be affected by the heat. "You seem to be able to withstand the heat much better than I do." he commented.

"Yes, the uniform is equipped with a cooling system. It keeps me very comfortable." the young man said.

"Oh, thank you for your instructions." Philip said.

"You are welcome Dr. Lee and thank you for your patronage. Good bye and have a safe trip." the young man said as he turned and left.

"Good bye - close doors." Philip said. The Voltrun closed both its doors silently.

Philip sat in the seat behind the steering controls which were on an arm that extend from the dashboard with a joystick attached. The message 'What mode?' was displayed on the screen located below the windshield. Below that display was the environmental/proximity display that should the cars position relative to the surroundings. He saw the image of a car move up from the left rear and then he glanced at the heads up display located at the top of the windshield to see the vehicle approach. It was another Voltrun 90, its silver color betrayed the 90 designation since all Voltrun 90s were silver. The rounded shape, almost like an egg sliced in half and mounted on four wheel, was unmistakable as well.

"Automatic mode. Destination one twenty four East Market Street, Reading, Pennsylvania. Confirmed." he instructed.

"One twenty four East Market Street, Reading Pennsylvania. Commence journey?" the vehicle replied through his PCU.

"Yes." Philip confirmed. The Voltrun's wheels rotated ninety degrees and the car pulled away from the curb without hesitation. The guidance arm used for manual driving retracted into the dashboard as Philips seat rotated fifteen degrees toward the center of the vehicle giving him more leg room to relax.

The Voltrun rotated its wheels as it continued to move and began to accelerate. The ride was silent.

"Acorn, call mother." Philip said as he watched the Voltrun approached an intersection and it came to a stop and waited for vehicles with a higher priority status to proceed through the intersection. Once they had passed it once again began to move. Soon it was on State Route 222 heading for Reading at a cruising speed of seventy miles per hour.

"Hello mother, it's Philip I am in transit and should arrive slightly early. I will see you soon. Good bye."

The message was just the kind that would irritate her but since she had been bothering him all day about being certain that he would not forget his brother's release he felt justified in leaving the message. He had thought about this day every day for the past five years. He missed Austin, he admired him and most of all he loved him. This day was almost as unbelievable as the day that they arrested Austin for his role in the incredible plot. It had to be concocted he had thought, Austin was so much like their father, too was difficult to imagine that he would have broken the law.

The Voltrun slowed as it prepared to negotiate some road construction that was ahead of them. The roadways had received very little attention in the past fifty five years because of the collapse of the automobile industry which was brought about by the cost of fuel and its availability. When gasoline went to fifteen dollars per liter and ethanol was twenty two dollars per liter very few could afford to put fuel into their cars. Electric cars like the Voltrun were great alternatives but they cost too much for most to purchase. The regional rail systems became the solution. That also reduced the need for much of the air travel which cut overall fuel consumption and had reduced greenhouse gas emissions dramatically. It was going to take years but the consensuses of opinion was that the climate would eventually moderate.

Philip gazed out the window at the dairy farm that seemed to go on forever. The cows stood inside an environmentally controlled building that had a flat roof and its dimensions were approximately one thousand by one thousand feet, a million square feet under a single roof. The silhouettes could be seen milling about through the tinted windows as the cows were apparently anxious for the afternoon milking.

The dairy farm transitioned into a corn field that was under a canopy with a perpetual mist being sprayed into the air to provide a cool relief from the extreme temperatures. Philip took a moment to relax and closed his eyes as the Voltrun continued its mission to arrive at the destination in Reading. The scenery passed and Philip's mind wandered from planning lessons, to picturing Austin's face, to Jessica and finally to his train ride that took place in the morning. It was then that he decide to see what was going on in the world. He instructed the car to turn on the video display and play the latest news program available.

From out of the dashboard a collapsible screen display slid. The hand held screen was a square foot in size and about one sixteenth of an inch in thickness. It was flexible and very light weight, perhaps weighing two or three ounces. Philip detached it from the holder and held it resting on his knee. The news began to play and Philip watched the program half interested. The national unemployment rate was announced and it had fallen to less than thirty percent for the first time in almost thirty years. The retraining of the American workforce would be completed within the next five years and full employment was projected to occur within ten.

The prison population increased from eighty six million to almost one hundred twenty two million or twenty two percent of the population. The average sentence had still remained consistent at five years. The statistics were always disturbing. 'Twenty two percent. That meant that more than one in five people were in prison. Crime is certainly out of hand.' he thought.

The video program continued, "On a positive note the nations prison systems have generated enough revenue to finance most of the war effort. As a result of their contribution taxes will not have to be raised in the coming fiscal period." the newscaster continued.

"This is so depressing." Philip said out loud.

The message center displayed the alert that they would arrive at the destination in approximately ten minutes and Philip noticed the display that showed the current time as three forty two PM. That meant he would arrive at least five minutes ahead of schedule and his mother should have less to complain about.

Philip looked ahead and saw his mother standing on the sidewalk in front of his aunt's home with whom she had been spending the day. The houses were vintage and in poor repair. They appeared to be from the mid Twentieth Century circa 1940 to 1950 and they contrasted the new construction that was visible just three blocks further down the street. The car eased into the spot directly in front of the house but about ten feet from where his mother was standing.

"Car move forward ten feet and open passenger door." he said, and the car moved forward, stopped and opened the door.

MacKenzie Lee, a stout energetic middle aged woman, quickly entered and said, "My it certainly is hot out there." she said as leaned toward Philip so that they could exchange kisses and their respective cheeks.

MacKenzie continued, "How are you dear? I am impressed, this is a very nice car and you are on time too. Wait until I see your brother

Roger. We have to make him more timely." Philip sat back as MacKenzie continued to talk about her visit with her aunt and Philip interrupt her only to close the door, program the destination and commence the journey.

Philip studied his mother as she spoke. It had been only a couple of weeks since he had last seen her but she seemed to have aged. Her dark brown hair had slightly more gray and the wrinkles around her eyes seemed deeper and more pronounced. Philip knew that unless he asked a question there would be no reason to speak, MacKenzie would do the talking for both of them.

The Voltrun pulled on to the Pennsylvania turnpike and accelerated to the ninety five miles per hour speed limit without effort. Philip look at the power reserve indicator and it showed that power reserve was at eighty five percent. The driving range of these cars was almost one thousand miles on single charge but it was always good to make certain just the same, he thought.

There was a lull in the conversation so Philip decided to speak. "I saw on the news that the unemployment rate is finally going down." he said. That jump started MacKenzie again and she went on about how four or five percent unemployment seemed to be tolerable in the past but since the 'New Direction' there have been so many without jobs.

The car reached the northeast extension of the turnpike and made the turn north toward Bethlehem. The release time for Austin was slated for five o'clock and based upon their current position and the speed that they were traveling they would arrive around fifteen minutes early.

The roadway stretched on in front of them barren of any other vehicles. A small indicator displayed the image of a vehicle approaching from the rear and then another one as well. The cars must be manually operated since they were both exceeding the speed limit, Philip thought.

Philip glanced at the heads up display and saw a red dot approaching from behind. As it got closer he saw that the car was powered by an internal combustion engine. The vehicle was very small and apparently very fast. The car came upon them quickly and then shot by them as though they were standing still. The car in pursuit was a police interceptor, a Voltrun 200 capable of speeds up to one hundred and fifty miles per hour. The car slowed to allow the interceptor to pass and then resumed the maximum speed.

"My goodness!" MacKenzie exclaimed and then continued, "What would possess anyone to drive that fast- don't they know they could end up in jail?"

That's right Philip thought, depending upon the judge a person could be sentenced to a term of one to five years for such an offense. "Mother, people don't always make the right decisions." he told her.

"Philip if that a negative inference directed at your brother, I hope you stop that kind of thinking. Your brother needs our love and support, not our judgment." MacKenzie said sternly.

"I understand mother." he replied. Austin still had his mother's heart Philip thought, but then again he had nothing but positive feelings toward his brother. He really had missed him.

The Voltrun exited the turnpike at the Allentown/Bethlehem exit and continued to meander its way toward the prison. The message display indicated that it was approximately ten minutes until they reach their destination, but they could already see the prison in the distance, and why not, it housed one point two million inmates from traffic violators to murders. It also held state and federal prisoners and was considered to be a model on which all other prisons were to be built.

Philip found the visit there a year ago so troubling that he could not bring himself to return. The security was oppressive and visitors were made to feel as though they were suspected of crimes themselves. This was true even though there was little interaction with the guards. The guard population was less than six thousand or about a ratio of two hundred to one. The inmates ran the facility under the control of the guards and the automated systems.

The Voltrun slowed and turned onto the road that ended at the prison. Philip looked at his mother, he could see the stress written on her face. He felt his pulse pounding and reached to grasp his mother's hand. She instantly took his.

She sensed his apprehension as well and in the typical MacKenzie way said, "Remember, we are bringing Austin home. He's getting out of this place. That's why we are here."

Philip rejoined, "Yes, that's why we are here."

Chapter Two

"Hey Austin, you up fer a card game? me en Wills er gonna get ya back fer yesterday's whippin'." Junior called out to Austin.

"Not now Junior, I have to finish writing this letter, maybe when they let us out at two. Okay?" Junior shrugged his massive shoulders. The large muscular black man looked forward to playing cards with Austin every day, it helped to pass time, and it was his lone passion.

"Awright, see ya in about three hours then." Junior said and turned and exited the cell. Austin turned his attention back to his letter. He thought about how the mail service must only be for the prison system since couldn't remember the last time he received or sent a letter when he was on the 'outside'. He then paused to think again. When was the last time he had received one while he was in prison and who sent it? That's right, he thought, it was his mother about two months ago. Life on the outside moved far too quickly for people to sit down and invest any time in something as time consuming as letter writing. On the other hand Austin had written many unanswered letters not knowing what happened to them. Each one was a compilation of his thoughts, dreams and desires. Each letter offering a small amount of cathartic release that helped to purge the guilt he felt, the remorse and the need to repent for the harm that he had caused.

This letter was being written to Melinda. He couldn't help thinking about her, even though she was instrumental in his incarceration. He pictured the day that he first saw her. He was in Manhattan attending a shareholders meeting, one of those quarterly conferences that were meant to reassure investors that the company was performing at the level that they hoped that it would, when like most companies outside of the Banking Consortium they were clearly not. He was invited to an upscale restaurant for lunch by a young woman that was interested in more than investment tips. Austin had found her very attractive, though now he could not even remember her name or bring in a clear picture of her in his mind. He remember big blue eyes, a pretty smile and blonde hair but that was about all. There was a fashion show going on during the lunch hours and Melinda Royce was the designer whose clothes were being shown. She was a slightly built Asian woman with long jet black hair that reached the small of her back. Her dark eyes made contact with Austin when they met by accident as Austin and his date were leaving. Melinda's smile completely disarmed him. Days later he found himself consumed with trying to find a way to meet her, contact her, find her, he was smitten.

This letter had the same theme as the others he had written to her. The only significant difference was that it referenced the fact that he was being released from prison tomorrow at five in the afternoon. He shared a little of the unusual events that transpired since his last letter and then decided to close the letter with an invitation to come to see him at his parent's home soon. No one would approve of the offer, but he didn't care, he loved her and want to have her back if she were to consent to it.

Austin stretched his lanky frame out on the bunk. He could feel the metal shelf under the thin mattress. A rolled up towel covered by his top sheet was his improvised pillow since none were allowed. While it offered some support it was very hard and may as well have been a cinder-block when it came to comfort. The blue dyed woolen blanket was half draped on him to provide some additional warmth. The cells were kept cold and he slept fully clothed to stay as warm as possible. He adjusted his position trying to find a comfortable section. The top bunk had been his since his last cell mate had come in about six or seven months earlier. Austin gave up his bottom bunk status and he moved up top because 'Spud', as he was called, was a very short man and getting up and down represented a real challenge for him.

Austin had decided that he did not need to show up for work at the assembly line that day, he was being released. He had had enough of assembling personal communicators and then packaging them for shipment.

Prison labor had become the United States' great equalizer. What could be cheaper than laborers that were being paid one IMC per day? Ones that were paying you twenty IMC per day, since the inmates were required to pay the cost of their incarceration. Prison had become big business and with the collapse of many other US based businesses they provided a way to keep those at the top supplied with a low cost and profitable resource. Prisons were ranked tenth in their contribution to the Gross National Product. If things kept going the way that they had been trending the prisons would surpass the construction industry within a year and move into the ninth position.

The low murmur of talking drifted in from the day room outside his cell. It was getting close to ten thirty in the morning, Austin thought. Soon the cell doors would automatically close and if he was not in place he could be disciplined. The first and only time Austin let it happen he spent forty eight hours in the hole. After that experience he decided that being late was not a good thing, in fact unless he was eating, playing cards or working he tended to stay in his cell reading or writing.

Austin looked up to see Spud and his friend Kareem power walk past the cell. Spud always flirted with the lock in by waiting until the very last minute and laughing gleefully when he pushed his body past the slowly closing cell door. At that moment the ten thirty horn blew and the clang of the locking mechanisms rang out. The doors would begin to close in two minutes and then take fifteen seconds to close completely, Austin thought about this as he watched Spud walk by again. This time he smiled and waved. Austin shook his head and waved back half chuckling. He had seen this behavior too many times to let it phase him.

The doors began to close and still no Spud and then as though he was shot from a cannon Spud squeezed through the door and burst out laughing. "Man oh man that sure was a close one." Spud threw himself on his bunk and continued to laugh for several minutes and then Austin heard him snoring. His medication had caught up with him.

Austin closed his eyes and thought about Melinda but then he found his thoughts returning to that Wednesday morning in November when he was sitting at breakfast with his faithful dog Marti, the loveable, goofy boxer with whom he spent so much time. There came that knock on the door and when he answered it the police told him that his car had been vandalized and that he needed to come and see. When he stepped outside they hand cuffed him in front of his neighbors and in front of Marti who just cocked her head and looked at him confused. The police then called his brother Roger to come and take the dog. After that he was then whisked off for a day full of humiliation.

Austin then spent the next six months working on his case but was unable to have his bail reduced from the six million IMC it had originally been set at because of the nature of his offense. Finally his attorney came to him with a deal that he was told was too good to pass up. He would plead guilty to theft by computer and receive a sentence of three to seven years with five years of probation. He accepted the deal because all the other members of the conspiracy had received sentences from ten to twenty years in prison. At that point he felt that he had gotten a favorable sentence.

Austin still believe that the plot to topple the world currency market was the right cause, even though he had said many times that he was truly remorseful and regretted his actions. How can you regret trying to put an end to a society that imprisons and enslaves its people? Not like pre-Civil War slavery or as in the Hebrew people during their captivity in Egypt, but it just as real. Economic slavery that relegated all but a very select few to a treadmill existence where the faster you ran, the faster you got absolutely nowhere.

Austin remembered his Uncle Bob telling him one night before he left for his second tour of duty of mandatory service that every American had to fulfill, how President Ansterman had given a speech that was considered truly visionary. He had stated that because fuel prices had risen to the point where a person could no longer afford to own a vehicle and that he was calling for the rapid development of the transcontinental and regional rail systems utilizing new technology that would revolutionize train travel and limit air travel.

The President went on to say that the housing crisis would be averted by the government backed program. Work would be created by mandating that the economy would be expanded to seven days per week and twenty four hour a day operation. Each job would therefore require up to eight workers. The wages would be reduced slightly but peoples expenses would drop as well. In addition to these changes all debt would be eliminated and credit would be abolished.

He could remember Uncle Bob's facial expression, the intensity in his eyes, and the set of his jaw. He felt that Bob believed the President and he believed in his idea. Austin remembered the turmoil, how many people felt that the new system would be unfair and that they all would lose their freedoms. Bob had respond with, "What freedoms were we losing, we are all slaves to the banks." He used terms like slavery, indentured servitude, company store, most of which Austin did not fully understand at the time. Uncle Bob took him to rallies that supported the President's new agenda. There were many people at these rallies both for and against. Some rallies were extremely noisy and frightening as though they were being held back from mayhem by some invisible thread of conscience. Others were boring long winded affairs filled with monotone speeches that filled the air with little or no passion.

Uncle Bob was always the same at each of these events, he cheered the loudest in support and when it was time to show negative reactions he was yelling or booing while waving his arms or shaking his fist. He was called upon to speak at one of the rallies and Austin remember how proud he was of his uncle. Austin remembered cheering loudly when the crowd did not respond in the way he thought that they should. Austin yelled at them in the same fashion he had seen his uncle do many times. A tear formed in the corner of his right eye. Austin hadn't cried in years and he wasn't going to let himself fall into those feelings. He was getting out tomorrow at five o'clock, life in prison was almost over and life as an ex-con was about to begin.

Spud let out a loud snort and Austin changed his position on the bunk so that he could see out the small horizontal slit that represented a window to the outdoors, even though it was a false image since there were no actual windows in the prison it gave him the illusion that he could see the world outside. The view was of two barbed wire fences. There were motion detectors that monitored the area between the building and the fences. Between the two fences there were dogs. These dogs were just as much prisoners as the inmates. The only difference was that they were treated worse. Dogs, being social animals needed routine contact, much more that the ten or fifteen minutes a day that their handlers gave them, Austin thought.

Austin felt a kinship with them and had even named them Cops and Robbers. It had been one of his grandfather's favorite television shows. His grandfather had been teased by his Uncle Bob about his love of that show and the even though Austin did not quite understand what was being said he did enjoy that Uncle Bob and his Grandfather always laughed and the laughter was so contagious that soon everyone was laughing. Cops was slightly larger and apparently younger than Robbers who spent much of the day sleeping.

Austin wondered why it was necessary to have them out there at all. This was a maximum security prison. A person trying to escape would need significant amounts of explosives just to get outside. Then they would have to contend with the motion detectors and the two fences. After that there was the pit, an oily liquid filled trench that once someone fell in it they could only hope that someone would come and get them out before they drowned.

If someone made it past these deterrents they still had the electrified fence and more motion detectors and the final twelve foot cement wall with which to contend. There was no reason to even think of escape, and as far as Austin knew only one person ever tried and they didn't even reach the first fence before they had been shot.

The horn sounded indicating that it was time for lunch, it was eleven forty. The doors slowly started to open and before they were completely opened Spud had already grabbed his cup and plastic spork and shot through the opening. Austin threw his legs over the side of the bunk and let them swing freely for a moment. The door clanged into the open position and Austin could see the inmates scurrying toward the food dispenser. It was time to get down from his perch and eat one of his last four meals that he would eat there. At that moment he forgot what was on the menu for lunch.

Austin walked out of his cell into the day room. The room was trapezoid in shape with two doors. One exited into a small exercise area that was completely enclosed by cement walls and a wire cage ceiling and the other exited into the interior of the prison. There were many other blocks, each one identical to this one. Each one was four stories in height, or tiers, with fourteen cells per tier.

On the same wall as the exit door was the food dispenser. This station worked on a long conveyor system where resin trays were dispensed according to the inmate's wrist band. The band was held up to a scanner and the tray was dispensed through a slot below it. The inmate had thirty seconds to remove the tray or it was returned. Most trays were the same but there were accommodations made for special diet when it was determined to be necessary. A robot arm worked on a jukebox type of device in which the trays had been loaded. Inmates prepared the food and stock the dispensers. They also removed the returned trays which were reloaded into the dispenser when the wrist band was scanned for the second time. Everyone was therefore supposedly guaranteed to get food. Unfortunately some of the weaker or less intelligent inmates were exploited by others, after all it was prison.

Austin numbly, and that was it he was numb, queued up to receive his tray. "Hey Lee. You wanna sell your tray?" Austin turned to see a thirty-ish Hispanic male named Carlos, or Snake to his friends.

"No thanks Carlos." he replied. If Austin hadn't been respected by Snake, Snake would have pushed the issue but Snake moved on to find an easier mark.

There was always wheeling and dealing going on between the inmates. People trading trays for things that had been bought at 'the Store'. The Store was a weekly event where inmates could buy snacks and personal supplies at exorbitant prices, roughly twice as much as they cost normally on the outside. The prison had to make a profit on everything. Prisoners earned five IMC per week if they worked and everyone worked except those with medical conditions or those convicted of capital crimes.

The prison manufactured and assembled goods for sale. They also grew food to supply the prison and the surplus was sold to the surrounding community. The prison also ran the waste treatment and water purification facilities for the region. There was recently talk about the prison taking additional enterprises but with the area unemployment being so high it had been tabled. The Commonwealth of Pennsylvania received two hundred IMC per inmate, per month from the company that ran the prison. They in turn after all expenses had a net profit in the past year of two hundred million IMC. They also returned one hundred fifty IMC per inmate per month to the Federal Government or one and one half Billion IMC per year. That meant that for the entire prison system nationally, the payoff was ninety billion IMC or what would have been four hundred ninety five billion US dollars. 'The prisons are big business.' Austin thought as the line moved forward.

Austin hoped that the lunch would be one of the better ones though since he came to prison he had lost weight, dropping from one hundred ninety pounds on his six foot two inch frame to one hundred seventy two pounds the last time he had been weighed.

"Okay Lee, move it." a voice boomed from behind him. It was Austin's turn to scan his wrist band and get his tray. The conveyor moved and out came the brown resin tray. It was beef stew, though you would be hard pressed to find the beef in the stew. There was a lot of gravy and it was served over rice with two golf ball sized potatoes. There was a piece of corn bread along with a hunk of un-iced cake, a few pieces of lettuce without dressing and some black eyed peas.

Austin took his tray and went to one of the tables that were anchored throughout the day room. Jake sat at the table Austin settled at. Austin sat with Jake at lunch time almost every day. Jake was constantly attempting to get someone to trade his tray for one of the standard diet trays. Jake's tray had a slice of turkey with rice and no gravy, a half of an orange and a slice of whole wheat bread. No cake, Jake always complained that he had to have cake.

"This place is crazy man. Look at dose idiots over there. Can't they sit down- dogs eat standin up like that - not people. What did their mother do to raise such morons?" Jake complained.

Austin picked up his spork and thought, 'Wouldn't it be nice to be able to use a knife and fork again.' He now looked at Jake and said, "How are you doing Jake?"

"Not bad- you should be doing pretty good- tomorrow's the big day- I'll be right behind you though, only twelve more weeks for me." Jake said beaming.

"That's right Jake you'll be right behind me - ten years has been a long time, five years is…." and Austin trailed off think of all that he had missed during the time he had been in prison.

"Ain't nothing but ride up and a walk back." Jake replied with a chuckle. Jake was always adding little homilies and that was one of the reasons Austin enjoyed his company. They were quite an odd pair.

Austin whiter than white and Jake blacker than black. Austin tall and very thin, Jake short and portly.

"Gotsta have that cake." Jake would say. Jake was genuine there was nothing fake about him. He was straightforward, blunt to a fault. He was loyal to Austin as a friend and Austin reciprocated. Did they both have other friends? Yes. Were they even possibly closer in other ways? Yes, but there was something unique about this friendship, a purity where there were no expectations, no obligations other than being yourself.

"Austin what you goin to do when you first get out?" Jake asked with a mouth full of food.

"I'm having dinner with my family." he replied.

"What are they having for you?"

"I am not sure, but anything is better than this- uh, wait I shouldn't speak too fast my mother isn't a great cook." Austin said with a laugh. He had just done something he did not do often and that was he almost let his guard down. It had to do with the fact that he could feel that he had reached the end. He was less than thirty hours away from being released.

"me, I'm havin a big thick streak and a big think mamma to go wid it!"

Jake roared with laughter and Austin laughed again.

"You are too much Jake." he said shaking his head.

"What I ain't had a woman in ten years, you think I'm gonna let one night pass before I has one, maybe two. Hell, maybe three." He roared with laughter again.

Jake was on a roll and he kept laughing and joking and his laughter was so infectious that the other inmates at the other tables started smiling and laughing even if they didn't know why. Simple Steve saw this his chance to walk over and see if he could take advantage of the good spirits.

"Yo, Austin, can spare some food? I'm really hungry." he asked.

"What are you looking for Steve?" Austin asked in response.

"A soup, a Choco Roll. Hell anything. I'll take your tray off your hands. - I'm starving."

"I haven't been to the Store but you can have the cornbread." said Austin all the while knowing that he was being scammed.

"Thanks." Steve said as he scooped up the cornbread and then was gone, off to the next table to tell the same story in his attempt to scrounge for food.

"Why's you do that? Steve's an idiot. He has more stuff than anybody here- yet he's always beggin and scammin. You are an idiot for letting him do it to you." Jake chastised Austin.

"Jake it is only cornbread." Austin said returning his attention to his food.

"If you didn't want it then you should have given it to me." Jake complained.

"Oh now I get it. Hey aren't you supposed to be losing weight?" Austin replied playfully.

"No man, I needs my cornbread." he said and was laughing again. You just couldn't keep Jake from enjoying himself, though he often did it at other people's expense. Anything to make himself laugh. Things that were crude or mean spirited were also fair game. Even though Jake was in his fifties he was fearless and wasn't afraid to mix it up with anybody.

Austin ate the rest of the food on his tray, except for the cake. When he had finished he pushed the tray forward and motioned to Jake to take it. Jake looked at him and smiled and muttered under his breath.

"Gotsta have my cake."

Austin had decide to use his last soup later that night and that with the few remaining crackers should help him sleep through the night without being too hungry.

The horn sounded the five minute alert which signaled that all trays should be returned and the cell doors would once again be closed. The lock in would be for a little more than two hours and during this time Austin usually wrote in his journal. He had many interesting and disturbing memories captured on those pages. They illustrated the depths that he had reached in despair, his recovery from depression and fear that he had felt in this cold and inhumane fortress.

Austin queued up again in order to surrender his tray. He looked at the white walls, the gray floors and the doors. There was no color, no life to the drab antiseptic environment. He scanned his wrist band and surrendered the tray to the conveyor. The noise in the day room increased as the inmates all said their last words prior to being locked up.

Spud was walking the perimeter once again. He was very animated and Austin felt that things did not seem to be right for some reason. He was about to try to speak with him when Johnny grabbed his arm and asked if he was okay.

"Yeah sure, how about you?" Austin asked in replied.

"Jake said that you looked like something was bothering you. You'll be okay out there. I know you are not coming back." Johnny said.

"Thanks John, I appreciate the good thought. Life is certainly going to change tomorrow at five." Austin said.

"Yes, and for the better. Trust me it will be for the better." Johnny said with that Austin looked and saw Spud was flailing his arms and laughing as he power walked around the day room.

The second horn sounded and Austin told Johnny, "Talk to you at two." And then walked quickly to his cell. He crossed the threshold as the release clanged and the door began to move. Spud continued to walk alone around the day room. The door was at the half way point and Spud seemed oblivious to the need to get to the cell before the doors closed. The door was at the three quarter point of being closed when Spud seemed to realize that the doors were indeed closing. He sprinted to the door but it was too late to squeeze through. The door shut and the loud clang of the locks sliding into place rang out as all the doors were made secure.

Spud beat his fist on the door of the cell and then turned to wait and see how the guards were going to proceed. There were two courses of action that could be taken. The first and most typical action was the block guard could simply open the door and let the offender into their cell. When that was done the inmates in the cell would be locked in their cell for the remainder of the shift. They would lose their recreation time and their meals would be given to them to eat in their cell through the slots located below the reinforced windows in the cell doors. The second action would involve sending a detachment of guards to the block. This was done in the case where inmates did not willingly go back into their cells or to set an example which illustrated the consequences for non-compliance and wrongful behavior.

Austin resigned himself to being locked in and waited for the door to open. He had been locked in like this before when Spud had done similar antics. This time the door did not open. Spud started to pace back and forth, his actions more animated and erratic. He started making gestures at the guard that was watching from the control center window. The guard just stared at him. Suddenly the door directly below the control center opened and three special unit guards entered. These guards were dressed for trouble. Their black uniforms and hobnailed boots were normally intimidating on their own, but with riot helmets, vests, shields, and batons it was obvious that they were not there to play.

Spud saw them and became enraged. He started yelling obscenities at them. All Austin heard were muffled sounds through the bulletproof glass of the cell door. Austin knew that Spud's only chance to escape harm was to drop to the floor face down with his arms at his sides. Do it Spud, get down, he thought. Austin banged on the cell door and yelled to Spud to get down on the floor. Spud did not react. He continued to yell and pace back and forth. They approached him and closed off any route that he could use to escape them.

Suddenly Spud raced at the guard in the center kneeing him in the groin and grabbing his baton. Spud raised the baton and brought it down on the guard's helmeted head. One of the guards took his shield and drove it into Spud's calf. Spud swung the baton again hitting that guard on the arm in which he held his shield.

The remaining guard fired his stun gun. The darts hit Spud in the back and the buttocks. Spud turned as the guard depressed the trigger sending the voltage into Spud. He immediately flopped to the ground in convulsions. He lost control of his bowels and bladder and began to vomit. The guard gave the trigger another pull and Spud went limp. He was unconscious.

The guard that Spud had attacked got to his feet slowly. He walked over to Spud and promptly kicked him in the head. Spud had done some damage. He had broken the arm of one guard and had injured the other one as well. At that moment a blue uniformed team of medics arrived with a gurney to cart poor Spud away. They could have killed him, in fact they may have done so with the kick to his head. Austin sat on the metal disc stool that protruded from the wall. He stared at the floor and thought about what had happened. Why hadn't he gone to work today, he lamented. At the very least he would have not had to witness this. Why had they done that?

Austin climbed into his bunk and lay down. He tried to push the images out of his head just as he had many times before when something bad, something bizarre, or something sad had happened. This event was all three. Images of the past five years flowed through his brain. Inmates abusing inmates, guards abusing inmates, man's inhumanity toward man, each act brutal and unfeeling.

The intercom buzzed and a voice spoke, "Lee, the door will open in two minutes you are to get the mop and clean the mess on the floor that Lewis made. Do you understand? You will have five minutes to clean it and return to your cell."

Austin responded, "Yes" and awaited opening of the door. As foretold the door opened and Austin was met with the smell of urine and feces. The mop and bucket were at the doorway below the control center window. The guard motioned for Austin to hurry. Austin decided that he needed to work quickly and went to work on the small spot where Spud had been prone. He noticed a small pool of blood that may have been as a result of the kick to Spud's head. The smell of vomit and feces was overwhelming and Austin fought back the urge to vomit with a series of gags.

Austin completed the cleaning, wrung the mop out and returned the mop and bucket to where he had initially retrieved them. He returned to his cell but the door did not close immediately, it remained open. The odor from the day room began to fill the cell and Austin began to wish the door would close soon.

The best thing Austin thought to do was to get into his bunk and pull his blanket over his head and wait for the smell to dissipate. He climbed up and as he did he heard the door begin to close. Once on top of the bunk Austin decided that he did not need to hide under the covers. He looked at his black pants and the food stains that were present on them. He should have sent them to the laundry, he had thought that it would not matter since he was going to be leaving. Still he needed to remember that he was going back to civilization and people expected more than they did inside.

Black uniforms indicated that he was federal prisoner. He was one of three on the block. Jake was another one. He had robbed a series of banks and never would have been caught if he hadn't been in the habit of leaving snack food wrappers behind. They lifted his finger prints and DNA from the wrappers and the rest was history. The other colors; red, yellow, brown, gray, blue, pink and green all indicated various things regarding the nature of the offense. Red uniforms were murders and they were housed in the ultra-maximum security wing. The only way another inmate saw one of those people was if they working the laundry and delivered their clothes to the block, they were in maintenance and needed to repair a toilet or electrical problem, or they happened to be in the medical ward when one was being brought in or out. These people were always escorted and always wore shackles (handcuffs bound at the waist and leg irons). When Austin was arrested he was restrained like that and when he went to court he was as well. It was an extremely unpleasant experience, but then again being in prison was not fun at all, he thought.

Austin lay back in his bunk again trying to put this recent trauma out of his consciousness. He soon found himself drifting into a dream state. Prison did this to him, enabled him to fall asleep at any time to escape the here and now, fleeing to the arms of Morpheus to soothe the pain and suffering of the lucid mind.

Austin jumped awake, he was crying. He hadn't cried in his sleep for many months. His dream had been so real. He saw Uncle Bob's death, it was that video clip he had seen and then replayed far too many times. Each time it was if the incident had occurred yesterday and he had lost his favorite person, his hero all over again.

"One Charlie Twenty this is Zulu Echo Two come in." said the command center operator.

"This is One Charlie Twenty go ahead Zulu Echo Two." the pilot said as the Norwind Assault Chopper banked into attack position and then continued, "Zulu Echo Two is in position. Should we light 'em up?"

"Zulu Echo Two you are go to start the party." the command center operator said relaying the orders from the Division Commander. Without hesitation the rockets were fired. The pilot watch the missiles track in when he suddenly noticed a US soldier running from the building followed by two civilians. In the soldiers arms was a small child.

"Damn – Look..." he said as the rockets hit. The video camera caught Special Forces Sergeant First Class Robert H. Lee as he was instantly decapitated by shrapnel from the explosion. His head cleanly removed with a single slice and it bounced twice before coming to rest. The two civilians were incinerated by the fireball. The young child, a girl, was saved. Bob's body had acted as a shield as they fell to the ground.

It wasn't anyone's fault they said, but Austin knew where the blame lay. We were in another useless war to maintain the domination of the rich and powerful, it was to maintain the control of a select few in the world. The US was just the muscle, the brains were scattered through the world.

Austin had just gone from a very unpleasant event to the saddest memory of his life. He now thought about why he was here in that place. It was because he believed Justin Welsh, that they could topple those that had killed his uncle by collapsing the newly created IMC. He had been convinced that everything that those in power owned was bet on the successful conversion of all the world's diverse currencies to the new currency standard. The plan should have worked. He still marveled at the unanswered question of how did Justin escaped and why he hadn't been caught. What were the reasons - these question plagued Austin routinely, almost every day. Justin was a high profile personality, larger than life in the world of banking and high finance. He was wealthy, flamboyant and apparently a magician and able to disappear into thin air.

Austin thought about how he had met Justin. It was at a tremendously stuffy cocktail party he been compelled to attend as the junior member of the high profile investment banking team at Star Funding. He had Melinda on his arm to impress the old men that he knew would be there with their old wives. He was under orders to impress and make new contacts. He did, he came back with four and the highest profile, most dynamic and biggest fish in the pond had been Justin. They met at the bar, Justin was drinking a Bombay Sapphire martini with two olives. Austin ordered the same though he had never had a martini before that night. He fought his way through it and fought to stay sober enough to maintain control and stay on his mission.

The conversation centered on Justin's position at The World Bank. He was being encouraged to accept the vice-chairman position and he complained that he did not support the adaptation of a single world currency. It was for this reason he could not accept the position. He had a very powerful presence. Though he was clearly older than he first appeared because of his passion and enthusiasm he appeared to have the vitality of a man in his forties. Justin, Austin knew, was in his early sixties. He had done his homework.

Justin never became a useful contact for Star, but what did happen was that Justin saw in Austin a person that could help him fulfill his mission to stop the IMC from becoming the currency standard, a move that Austin later would find out would cost Justin much of his vast fortune. Welsh had bet everything he had amassed that the US would not succumb to the world currency movement. The US he had thought was the leader in the world, why should it compromise. Welsh had used his connections to wage numerous wars against the banks which struggled to have dominion over everything. He managed to show Austin how the Syrian campaign of the Middle East War was exclusively about having Syria capitulate and remove its objection to the IMC and to allow World Banco One Internationale to become the states only banking institution.

Currency control and all banking activities including oversight were privatized and the consortium of banks was and was led by WBOI. The behemoth was not a public company but a private one that had but a couple of thousand stockholders. They printed the IMC, they controlled its value and as such dominated the world's commerce and possessed the vast majority of the real estate holdings in the world. Everyone was captive to them through economic slavery which they controlled and oppressed all that struggled to survive.

Austin had heard a lot of this from his Uncle Bob who had told him how evil that the system was becoming. Bob Lee had tried to inspire his nephew to be socially aware and to recognize the value of people, all types of people. The catalyst for action was Uncle Bob's death, though Austin chose to think that he would have been a follower of what he saw as his uncle's ideals even if he had not been martyred in front of his eyes.

Austin closed his eyes again and drifted back to sleep. He was awaken by the horn that sounded the two o'clock recreation period and he heard the door sliding open. Time was passing, he was getting closer to his release, but rather than experiencing an overwhelming feeling of joy there was significant apprehension. Life had changed, people had changed. He was a convicted felon and his chances of landing a good job were not spectacular, especially with the unemployment rate being what it was. What will he do? Where will he live? He knew that he could live at his Mom and Dad's house, but Dad hadn't spoken to him since the day of his arrest. That was five years and seven months and twelve days ago. He remembered his father looking at him as he stood before the judge.

His Mom was in tears, and his Dad was just in shock. Austin pondered all of these things, they were a reoccurring theme pattern that repeated in endless succession, like the noise of leaky faucet dripping continually tormenting the insomniac who tosses and turns endlessly awake seeking some relief.

There was one person that always seemed to be in his corner was his brother Philip. Philip seemed to always write to him and he came to visit him more frequently than anyone else. He was also quick to send money so that Austin could have the few meager indulgences he had allowed himself to have. Philip unlike his brother Roger seemed to understand why he had done it even when there were times he, himself, couldn't understand why he had done it.

Austin exited the cell and looked about. Several inmates had exited their cells ahead of him and were gathered at the tables playing chess or various card games. He heard the hiss of the shower and directly ahead of him was an inmate that was trying to power up the video screen in order to watch what was being broadcast. He was jumping up and down trying to reach the power button. Austin decided to help.

"Allow me." he said. Little Georgie stepped out of the way and Austin stretched and turned on the video unit. The program showing was depicting a violent murder with all the blood and gore. It was just the type programming you would want to show to criminals, he thought.

The day room began to get noisier as more of the inmates came sleepily out of their cells. If one didn't work all that could typically be done was sleep, eat and seek diversion. Diversions were card playing, reading, sports, body building, or watching videos. After five years of doing the same thing. Austin was not certain that he could do anything else.

What could he do with his MBA from Wharton? "Maybe I'll be an accountant for some criminal enterprise." he thought and chuckled out loud.

Jake waddled up to him and told him, "Junior and Wills waz lookin for us cuz they wanna nuther wippin." Austin nodded and he thought an hour or two of card playing would help keep his mind off the many scrambled memories that he was dealing with today. If ever he could use one of Justin's martinis, today was the day.

Austin followed Jake to the table where Junior was already seated. Wills, on the other hand was pacing back and forth nervously. It was difficult for him to sit down for any length of time. Martin Wills was a criminal extraordinaire he had committed four hundred and twelve burglaries before he was caught and though they could see the similarities in the crimes the prosecution could only tie him to two. They were extremely disappointed but go some satisfaction when Wills received seven and one half to ten years, the absolute maximum for the two crimes. He was a real survivor and even though at thirty he should have been prey to some of the more violent or deviant types that abound in the prison, Wills somehow kept safe. To look at him you would have felt compassion. He looked much younger than his age because of his slender build and boyish face that had a lock of blonde hair always obscuring one eye down almost to his chin.

Junior was the opposite of Wills he was as black as Wills was white. He was a massive man that seemed perfectly content to stay at rest. To say that he was slow to anger would be an understatement, people just couldn't upset Junior. Jake used to say that Junior was like a Brontosaurus, you could kick him in the toe and it would take a month for the pain to reach his brain. Junior was not stupid and he had great reflexes. He was a great driver and in fact he was the getaway driver for a number of bank robberies. His luck ran out when his gas tank punctured and he ran out of gas during a high speed chase. Junior was finishing up a ten year sentence for that crime. Austin was certain that Junior would end up back in prison since all he did was talk about how he wanted to get behind the wheel again and this time he wouldn't get caught.

The card game started quickly enough with each player studying their hand intently trying to determine how much they would bid. Austin's hand was not very good so he passed. Jake shot him a look of disgust. Jake hated to lose at anything. This could be a long afternoon if the cards continued to be unfriendly, Austin thought. Being Jake's partner was something very few could handle on a regular basis. If he was winning everything was great but if he was losing look out.

Jake and Wills got into a bidding war and Jake finally backed down and he groaned and complained about Austin not having anything to help him. The hands went poorly for Jake and Austin at first but they rallied and were within striking distance of winning. The final hand of the game came down to a bidding war between Jake and Austin and this time it was his partner who was on the other side. Neither really wanted to give into the other. Austin knew that unless he backed down Jake would be impossible to deal with the next game and possibly the next several hours. Austin dropped out of the bidding. Jake confidently played the hand but they fell short and they ended up losing the game. Blame was assigned and naturally it was Austin's fault.

The hour and a half that was recreation time passed quickly and the horn sounded that indicated that lock in time was five minutes away. Junior threw his hand down in frustration and said, "Now that's the bess hand I got all day- figures." Jake gathered up the cards and the group disbursed without as much as a word to one another.

When the horn sounded again to signal lock in everyone was in their cell. There would be no repeat of the lunch time incident. Austin wondered about Spud's condition and whether he was alive. Now as the doors closed Austin had more time to think about all those crazy images of the past five years. The next time he would be allowed out of his cell would be to eat dinner in about two hours.

Why didn't he go to work today? He could have passed the day making those personal communication units, he thought. He was responsible for assembling and testing the new temple mounted models that were so popular. The components came to the prison and the units were assembled and packaged. It took Austin twenty minutes to assemble the unit, test it and then package it for shipment. That meant that during his shift he would produce twenty five sets and considering that Austin was one of two hundred inmates that worked on each shift and there were three shifts, that meant that the prison was producing five thousand units per day, seven days per week, fifty two weeks each and every year. The prison bought the components and then sold the units to distributors. The project had been so successful and the demand for the product so high that the prison planned to start a second production line that would boost total output to twelve thousand units per day.

The tooth microphone components were the most time consuming to assemble, Austin thought. They were also misappropriated on a regular basis. Even Austin had considered taking one as a souvenir but he was so concerned that if they caught him he would have the opportunity to spend some more glorious time in prison.

The Bethlehem Multiplex Correctional Facility, the fourth largest city in Pennsylvania had its own transit system and was a completely enclosed environment that provided revenue for the government and safety for the public. All of the criminals that society could identify could be absorbed into the huge networks of prisons that sprang up all over the country. All under one corporation, one very profitable corporation, that was owned by a few individuals and the Banking Consortium.

Austin tried to think of a business that wasn't controlled or owned at least partially by the BC. They were in the process of purchasing from the government the judicial system and the postal service (which naturally included what used to be called the internet but was now referred to as simple the Information Exchange). All citizens had to belong to the IE and the annual fees enabled you to receive communications both voice and data as well as to do research through the vast libraries of data that were housed in computer scattered throughout the world. The new PCUs also provided geographic positioning so your location was always known when the units were active, and they were active when they were attached to a person. That is how they derived their power, they actually siphoned off electrical impulses from wearer's brain.

The advertisement for these devices espoused how safe they were and they even encouraged you to wear them while you were sleeping. There was little or no risk of harm from the extraction of the energy form the brain, though there were reports of people having seizures from wearing them. Those reports were discredited and sales of the units remained very strong. The glasses units that they replaced were rapidly going out of style as being too intrusive and bulky as well as missing the valuable feature of geographic positioning and because of that the wearer couldn't receive directions by simply requesting them from you PCU.

Austin felt it was odd that you had to name your PCU, but his brother Roger, the computer scientist, explained that by picking a word or name that a person would rarely use the wearer could instruct the unit to respond once it recognized the code word. Many of his friends had chosen very creative names, while other had used obscenities. The use of obscenities had proved to be not a good choice since there would be times when you needed to address the PCU when you were in a situation where the use of profanity was inappropriate.

He had never liked glasses and wasn't sure how he felt about the temple PCU. He knew that he didn't like the tooth cap microphone (TCM). The TCM attached to one of your molars and while it was not designed to be a replacement for a tooth it could withstand significant pressure and function as a tooth. When Austin tested them he always felt as though he had something stuck between his teeth, it was not an enjoyable sensation.

Austin laid back in his bunk again. Dinner would be in a little more than an hour. By the time that he was back in his cell he would less than twenty four hours to go before he was to be released. Freedom, he wonder what it would be like? He could almost remember what the sky looked like, Austin thought. He tried to think about how it would be like to feel rain on his face, the wind blowing on him pushing him down the street as he walked in its path. Life's little things seemed to mean so much. He remember what it would be like to be able to eat what he want and when he wanted to do it. He thought about a pillow for his head, a knife and fork, the ability to shower where people weren't always watching, all of these were just the few things that immediately came to his mind. He then thought about seeing his family again and that was so much more important than all of those simple things.

Austin stood up and looked in the polished metal mirror that was directly above the stainless steel sink/toilet combination. His face was different. There were pronounced lines. He looked older than his years. His hair had not been cut in five years and he wore it gathered and pulled back in a ponytail. He also wore a mustache and a small circular patch of facial hair on his right cheek. That patch signified that he was under the protection of the Monks. He planned to shave it off tomorrow just before he left.

That patch had probably saved his life at least twice. The Monks were one of two gangs that dominated the prison's social fabric. The name's origin came about because of the austere lifestyle that the original members practiced. They would do anything to protect a fellow member. They had murdered many inmates before they established their reputation that guaranteed them respect and instilled fear.

Austin had earned their protection because of a favor he had performed for the Monk that was number two in the organization within the prison. He was facing an assault charge on an inmate and he had a weapon that had been fashioned from a toothbrush and a disposable razor. The inmate had been cut but the wound was not life threatening. Austin had taken the weapon from him prior to the guards' arrival on the block and had gone into his cell, broke it up and flushed it away. Without the weapon Gonzales was not able to be charged and Austin had made an important friend. Looking back on the event he still could not understand why he had accepted the shank and why he had taken the chance of being caught on video surveillance. It just come down to the simple conclusion that he had been too afraid to say no, he surmised.

If his father, the ever pious Gregory Lee, knew his son was a gang member he would probably drop dead from a heart attack, Austin imagined. Gonzales never spoke to Austin about the incident but a few days later when Austin was walking to work, two inmates grabbed him and hustled him into a closet, a closet that should have been locked. They didn't speak to him but one them pinned his arms to his side while the other took a razor and shaved him dry removing the beard that he had been growing. They left his mustache and a small round patch on his right cheek. It was just like the one that the two of them had on their right cheeks.

When he finished Ramirez stepped back and smile with his big grin showing his missing two front teeth. "Okay Bolillo, you're made, don't 'F' it up". From that moment on Austin was protected. This action had ensured that he would have no problems so long as remained in Monk territory and there was little reason to stray outside of the Monk's territory and it was something that he only did once. Fortunately nothing happened though, as he found out later he could been killed. Austin made sure that his patch was maintained and the he did nothing to show his fellow Monks that he was not proud to be one of them. Financial consultant turned gang member, he mused. Tomorrow afternoon the patch has got to go, he thought and then felt a small sense of loss.

Austin climbed back into his bunk again. He closed his eyes and as usual fell asleep again. There was nothing to remember from the dreams that he may or may not have had. Austin jerked awake wondering what time it was. That was another thing that he wanted, a way to tell time. The only way he could learn the time was by finding someone that had a wristwatch. No one outside the prison wore a watch, your PCU displayed the time and it could do anything. Just knowing you could find out the time, that you could have some idea when things happened or how long it was until they were supposed to happen seemed so important to him.

Dinner must be soon Austin thought, but then again he could be way off on his estimate or he actually could have slept through dinner. He couldn't tell. He tried to see if the shift had changed and there was another guard in the control center but there was no one visible. He decided that he would get back into his bunk and wait and just as before he feel asleep.

This time he was awaken to, "Austin, hey Austin, you eatin? If not kin I git yer tray?" called Jake.

He opened his eyes and said "Yeah, I'm eating. I'll be out in just a minute." Austin got down from his bunk hitting the floor hard with his stocking feet. He slipped his feet into his skippers, a slip on canvas shoe that were manufactured at the prison for both their own use and for sale. Austin could not imagine anyone ever wanting to buy them.

Austin shuffled out of his cell and directly to the tray dispenser, there was no line and he went through the process of picking up one of his last meals. There was nothing appealing about the meal but he would eat quickly in order to dull the hunger pangs that he constantly felt. Hot dogs and cornbread. There were no buns. This was the last dinner that Austin would have there. Only two more meals and less than 24 hours to go.

Suddenly there erupted a commotion behind him. He turned around and watched Junior stand and look menacingly at Squeak, a little effeminate boy of nineteen that constantly tried to steal food from other people's trays. Squeak ran away and Junior sat down again. It was not much of a problem. Austin had seen people fight over a carton of milk or a wrong look. Most people didn't want to fight because when they did happen everyone was punished. That meant that the whole block would be locked in for twenty three hours and would be given just one hour of exercise per day. This would go on for as long a time as the guards determined to extend it. Sometimes they were fair and kept the number of days to a reasonable number but other times they were not.

Austin took a seat at his usual table and began to eat. The food was bad but he wasn't certain that could remember how good food would taste. Since he was always hungry he ate with a ravenous edge and some might have thought he was actually enjoying it. He often thought they kept the portions small so that the inmates would eat quickly out of hunger. Then again how do explain Jake and Junior, they both seemed to have no trouble gaining weight. Of course they did buy a lot of junk food from the prison store and the over priced goods were predominately sweet and high in calories, and of course generally unhealthy. Many of these food items of questionable dietary value were manufactured at the prison and sold to the outside world as well. The prison had become the regional manufacturer and distribution point of some of the largest food corporations in the country.

Austin mechanically ate his food without speaking and perchance waking himself from a dream only to find himself years away from his release instead of twenty three hours or so that were left until the door swung open and he was free. Only two more meals in this place he thought again and again.

"Hey Austin, what chew goin' to eat first man?" Jake asked. He'd been asked that question at least six times in the past twenty four hours and had answered it differently each time.

"I plan on hot dogs and cornbread." he shot back to Jake.

"Dat's crazy man." and Jake burst out laughing.

Austin picked up his tray and returned it to the dispenser and then walked back to his cell. The horn had not sounded giving the inmates the five minute warning but Austin did not hesitate going in and climbing onto his bunk. He thought about his father and whether he would welcome him into the house or would retreat into his study claiming he had work that must be completed all the while hoping that he would not have to see the son that had caused him so much shame.

Sometimes when Austin sat still and allowed himself to become lost in thought when he opened his eyes he actually wondered where he was. Once he remember where it was that he sat he would ask himself several questions. Why was he here? Why was he involved? Why did he get caught?

Was he here because he wanted to pay them back for Uncle Bob's death? The war was fought over money, it was always because of money. Uncle Bob died so that a few rich men could become even richer. He was caught because he was stupid, he had made mistakes. The whole group had made mistakes though everyone blamed Melinda. They said she had told the government what was going to happen. Austin sat shaking his head thinking, how could that be, Melinda loved him and he loved her. She didn't know enough to bring down the entire operation, the best she could have done was implicate Austin. Someone else must have betrayed them, maybe it was Justin that had done it. Here he was more than five years later and there were still no real answers. The only thing that he knew for certain is that he wouldn't go back to prison ever again, not even for Uncle Bob's memory.

The horn indicating that the doors would close in five minutes sounded and startled him out of his thoughts.

"I really wish I had a watch." he muttered under his breath. He would sit there and watch the time drain by. Maybe an hourglass would be even better he could count the grains of sand as they slipped into the next second and in turn to the next minute yielding to hours and then the quick rush of free air, he would be outdoors and will have escaped from the bonds that have held him stuck in time for the past one thousand eight hundred twenty five days of his existence.

His mother and brothers would be arriving to get him and he knew that there would be tears. His sister and father would be at home waiting. He imagined opening the door and then walking through it. Walking through that door to his parents' home would be a difficult step to take, one that he had thought about too many times. Sometimes there was a joyous reUnion but more often it was a non-event. His father would look at him, disapproving of his appearance or condemning the circumstances. How could he not have felt the same way Austin felt about the death of his brother.

Austin felt that his father was always cold and impersonal. He never seemed to feel anything. How did his mother put up with him? What made her want to be with Gregory Lee? Maybe he was different when they first had met. All these questions seemed to surface when he thought of his father, the enigma. Trying to solve the mystery of Gregory Lee was like trying to solve the riddle of the Sphinx. He continued to puzzle over his father. If he stayed with these thoughts long enough he would begin to think of childhood remembrances. The little snippets that illustrated the detached relationship he had with this father. Most of the memories were of his father being too busy in his study or being away at work.

Austin had a very clear impression of who his father was. He was certain that there had to be more to him than what he saw but there was nothing to validate that assumption. He had a two dimensional view of his father and he had at times tried to emulate an image that was incomplete. Sometimes he blamed himself for not asking his father why he was the way he appeared to be. Perhaps that would have enabled him to understand or perhaps it would compelled his father to share, to open up the curtains and let him have a glimpse at what the brilliant physicist, husband to MacKenzie, father of four, brother to Uncle Bob and son of the illustrious Harry Lee was concealing from everyone. He felt that the reUnion tomorrow was going to unenlightening and frustrating and Austin resigned himself to that fact. All encounters with his father were that way. Of all the boys only Roger had seemed to have some way of getting through the facade and perhaps he had made even more of a breakthrough in the past five years. After all he had not seen either of them during that time period.

Roger Lee was a lot like his father, thought Austin or at least like what he thought his father was like. Roger resembled his father physically and he was roughly the same height, not as tall as Austin and certainly not as tall as Philip. He was solidly built weighing more than both of his brothers, though he did not appear to be overweight. His work ethic was a lot like his father's as well. He spent most of his time working on complex problems that most people didn't even know existed. He had created computer programs that had been the foundation for all the military's encryption programs as well as many other classified projects.

The horn sounded and the door began to close. Austin decided to close his eyes and get more sleep. The sleep would allow the twenty hours to pass more rapidly without having to think about all the potential trauma associated with his transition from confinement to freedom. He pictured the sun shining in a brilliant blue sky and tried to imagine a breeze blowing softly across a field and the aromatic scent of honeysuckle flirting elusively with his senses. What was it like to be outside? The video said that the climate had gotten even hotter. Maybe he could still enjoy the early spring and late fall days, he thought.

Two hours later the horn sounded the alert for everyone that evening recreation was now in progress. The doors opened and Austin did not move, his eyes still closed not wanting to get up and spend the next three hours playing cards and participating in the same conversation. It was emotionally draining to go through the motions, to fain interest, to laugh at the same jokes.

Austin finally moved, rocked himself up into a sitting position and then let his legs dangle over the edge of his bunk. Sitting that way was truly uncomfortable because the metal frame dug into the underside of his thighs and he felt the hard surface beneath his buttocks. This was still more comfortable than the metal disc shaped stools but just marginally.

He became aware that his frustration and sensitivity was probably heightened by the anticipation of his departure tomorrow. If he could just maintain his calm and serenity for just a few more hours, he thought, he could then force himself to sleep away another large chunk of time that he had remaining.

The card game that was not finished from before was waiting for him when he came out. The players all anxious to continue, all of them aware of Austin's upcoming departure but no one mentioning it. Only a few knew he was leaving since there were inmates that would have tried to either assault him out of their frustration or attempt to get him in trouble. They did these things because they resented when anyone was leaving because it wasn't them. Most people kept that information to themselves out of fear of some stupid reprisal spawned by these types of resentment.

"How you feelin man?" Jake asked.

Austin looked at him and said, "Anxious, just want the time to pass quickly."

"Yeah, don't we all." Wills interjected.

Jake chuckled and shook his head. "We're gonna miss you, who am I gonna get to be ma partner? None of these jokers can play wortha damn." Jake said and laughed again but the way he looked at Austin told him that he really was going to miss him and not just because he was a good card player.

The game continued and lead changed hands several times and it wasn't clear until the last hand that Jake and Austin would prevail. Jake celebrated by berating the completion. Austin just sat there and watched the spectacle.

Suddenly there were two sharp horn blasts and door opened below the control center opened. A short, thin Hispanic inmate wearing a green jump suit took one step inside and yelled, "Lee, medical."

Austin looked around and then stood up and walked to the door. Austin recognized the inmate as Juan Lopez. He was Gonzales' courier and assistant. He was also a convicted murderer.

"Hey Bolillo." Juan said quietly. Austin nodded. Austin's thoughts went in several directions simultaneously. What if they had found out he was leaving and wanted to make it difficult or something worse. Austin exited the cell block into the security lock. The door closed behind him and he stood silently with Lopez, both staring straight ahead, waiting for the door to connecting corridor to open.

There was a temptation to ask Lopez what was going on but he knew that Lopez wouldn't talk especially while they were on camera and being recorded. The door opened and they both walked out into the long white corridor that was brilliantly lit. At the end of the corridor Austin could see an inmate dressed in red mopping the floor. As they approached he apparently noticed Lopez and stopped. He moved back against the wall making certain that Lopez was given the respect that he obviously felt he deserved. The man eyed Austin but when he saw his patch he immediately put his head down. That was the kind of reaction that the Monks brand had on most people inside the prison, including the guards.

At the end of the corridor they made a right turn down the intersecting hallway. This corridor was also white but there were bluish gray doors that were unevenly spaced on each side of the corridor. The medical unit was on the left about one hundred fifty feet down the down the hall. There was no one in the hall but every twenty or thirty feet there was a ceiling mounted camera along with what appeared to be a fire extinguisher/sprinkler system. There were also boxes that protruded from the wall about six inches or so and there were doors, or more accurately stated, barred gates that could be closed to create small compartments should the need arise. Within each compartment there was one these boxes and it contained a system that released metal flakes that adhered to someone's clothes or skin. The box would pulse an electric charge sending anyone wearing as few as four flakes into convulsions. The only time Austin had seen a person with flakes on him, he was covered from head to toe with them and he was unconscious.

They arrived at the medical unit and Lopez pushed a button and the door opened after a short delay. He motioned for Austin to go in and said, "Later Bolillo." He extended his fist and Austin responded in kind.

"Thanks." Austin replied but Lopez had already turned and began to walk down the hallway. Austin then turned entered the medical unit, once inside he heard the door close behind him.

The room he found himself in was the same brilliant white that the hallway had been. There was no one in the room and there were two doors, the one that he had entered through and one directly opposite that he was now facing. There were no furnishing and a single camera in the ceiling represented the only contour in the room at all.

Austin stood motionless waiting. Nothing happened. He continued to remain still his hands clasped behind his back waiting for someone to tell him what to do. Finally the door opened and a woman dressed in white instructed him to enter. As he did he looked around and saw that there were only two others present, a guard and someone who appeared to be a doctor. The woman told Austin to follow the doctor and that he would be conducting the interview. At that point Austin thought, 'What interview?'

Even though he questioned the proceedings he followed because that was what you did in prison you followed or else! He had been conditioned to do what he was instructed to do. There was no outward hesitation he dutifully complied and trailed behind the doctor. The doctor led Austin down another corridor. Austin tried to recall when he had last been to the medical unit but he could not remember.

The doctor stopped in front of a door and said, "Open exam room number two" and the door opened. He then motioned with his head for Austin to go in and said, "Close exam room number two." Austin heard the door close behind him as he entered, it was at that moment he noticed that the doctor did not follow him into the room.

The room was dimly lit and there was a desk with a high backed chair behind it facing away from him. There was a familiar metal disc stool mounted in front of the desk on which the inmates were to sit. The chair swiveled around to reveal Gonzales slumped down in the seat.

"Mr. Lee it has been some time since I last saw you. I am glad to see that you are in good health." he said. There was no Latino slang or inflection in his speech. Gonzales' greeting completely surprised him.

"Mr. Gonzales, it has been quite some time." Austin replied.

"Please call me Hector." he rejoined.

"Only if you will call me Austin." asked replied.

"Agreed. Please sit." Hector said motioning with his hand. They looked at one another for several moments and then Hector smiled and said, "You are wondering why you are here. There are two reasons; one I need a favor from you and in exchange for doing that favor I am offering you a future favor and the other reason is to wish you well on your release tomorrow."

Austin wasn't sure in what he was about to become involved and he began to feel anxious. Gonzales connections reached far outside of the prison and Austin had to wonder what the price of noncompliance with the request would be.

"Thank you for your good wishes. What favor do you want me to do for you?" he asked calmly.

Gonzales chuckled, "Austin I know you must be thinking all sorts of strange and sinister thoughts regarding my request. Believe me if I needed something nefarious I have ample resources at my disposal."

"Okay." Austin rejoined, "What can I do for you then?"

Hector pulled a small pouch out of his shirt pocket. "Give this to my sister for me." Hector placed it on the desk and slid it toward Austin. "Go ahead look inside."

Austin opened the pouch and looked in. What he saw was a silver pendant on a fine silver chain. Austin looked quizzically at Hector and asked, "Couldn't you have sent this to her?"

Hector took a breath and said, "That pendant has been in our family for almost two hundred and fifty years. It is passed from generation to generation on the wedding day of the first male in our family. My nephew is to marry in two weeks. There is a good chance that this would be taken by the postal inspectors and never reach the destination. You must wear it out otherwise they could take it from you too." Austin looked at the pendant and studied it. It was clearly very old. Austin wasn't even sure that you find anything like it today. The replacement cost would be great.

"Okay." he said and then asked, "Where is your sister located?"

Hector replied, "She lives in Washington DC but she will meet you in Philadelphia on Saturday at ten forty five in the morning at City Hall. She will approach you and tell you her name, Lucy, and then she will say 'I believe that you have something for me from Hector'. Shake her hand while you are holding it in your hand, talk about anything for a few moments and then leave. That's it."

"Why the secrecy for the exchange?" Austin asked.

"Because I don't want anyone taking it or thinking it was something illegal, suppose you are followed." Hector said.

"Okay, I'll will do it." Austin agreed.

"Austin, thank you again. I owe you once again. If you ever need anything, send word to me in here I will help you." Hector said sincerely. Austin put on the pendant and stood up extending his hand. Hector stood and shook it.

"Good luck Austin, don't come back. Oh just one more thing make sure you are there Saturday on time." he said with a smile.

"Absolutely." Austin replied.

Hector leaned over and pushed a button on the underside of the desk. The door opened and Austin saw that the doctor had been waiting outside in the hall. The doctor looked at Hector briefly and then put his head down. Austin waited and no one came to escort him back to the cell block so he decided to retrace his steps until he reached the entrance to his cell block. The door opened and he entered the lock and as soon as the door behind him had closed the door to unit opened. All eyes turned to him briefly and then they went back to what they were doing. There was still well over and hour until lock in for the night.

His place at the card game had been taken by a young kid that Jake loved to abuse verbally. Austin decided to go to his cell. There was still no sign of Spud, He realized at that moment he could have inquired about him while he was in medical but that opportunity was gone and besides all that would have accomplished would be to give him information that he would have felt obligated to share with the others on the block.

Austin started to organize the things that he was going to take with him. He had planned to wait until tomorrow but there was nothing for him to do. He thought that he should read but he had too much nervous energy to concentrate on the words on the pages. He pulled all the envelops and folders out from underneath his mattress and started to go through the papers to see if there were any that he felt should be thrown away. He knew that he had done this exercise before but he continued to review the pages on the off chance he had missed something.

He had saved all the letters that he had received, though there were not many considering that he had been incarcerated for five years. Each letter had been read many times but there was one that had been read more than all the others. The ink on its tattered pages had blurred from being handled so often. That letter was the only time he had heard from Melinda and every time he read it had given him hope that he would see her again and that they could continue their relationship. Many times he felt he was living a fantasy when he considered that he had not heard from her in more than four years. He was not certain how he would react each time he picked the letter up to read it. Sometimes he had hope and other times he felt despair. He was drawn to reading it as a moth was drawn to a flame and every time he encountered the worn pages he could not stop himself from reading it. This time reading it was no different the all the previous times and when he reached the end a tear was rolled down his cheek only to hit the fragile paper, further blurring the already obscured writing. Perhaps it was time to let this go, he thought.

By the time Austin had reviewed all his papers it was nearly time for lock in. There were only two pieces of paper that were sitting in the pile of things to possibly throw out. One was an advertisement that he thought he had discarded earlier and the other was that letter. He tore the advertisement into small pieces and tossed into the toilet. He stood there with the letter in his hand and he grasped it as if to tear it. He hesitated but finally decided to proceed. At the end he tossed it slowly in and flushed the paper away. I was a new start, he thought.

The horn sounded for breakfast and Austin decided to stay in bed. He wouldn't starve, he was tired, and sleep had eluded him most of the night. The primary cause was most likely because he had slept so much of the previous day but it also was due to the anticipation of the day with only twelve hours more of the absurdity, he thought as he drifted back to sleep.

The horn indicating that it was eight thirty and time for the morning recreation period sounded and Austin still lay in bed in a state of semi-consciousness. His mind was all set to get out of bed but for some reason his body did not want to move. He thought that if he got up at that very moment he might be the first one to make it to the shower and he would not have to wait to take his last shower in prison. Another last time he thought. One in a series of lasts. Soon it would be his last lunch, his last meal would be upon him and then the last two o'clock recreational period and finally the last time the doors would lock him in.

Again he seemed to feel that there was no point in getting up, he could take a shower later. He closed his eyes again and drifted back to sleep. At some time later his eyes popped open and he then struggled to finally get up. He did have things to do and he had to start his day. It was almost ten when he finally made the walk to the showers.

He was in luck, there was no line. He walked in carefully put his change of underwear in his shoes and puling the towel through the mesh of the cage that surrounded the entrance to the shower. He quickly took off his clothes and carried his soap, shampoo and washcloth back to the showers. He selected the next to the last one and pushed the button. The water jetted out from the nozzle in a high pressure stream. The temperature was warm but quickly became hot. Austin lathered himself quickly and then proceeded to remove the cord that held his hair back. He washed his hair carefully and wondered whether he would keep his hair long. He knew his father's reaction would be against it. Perhaps he should consider cooperating instead of fighting with his father about something that really had no real importance. There would be lots of issues that they could disagree about that were more important, he thought.

He finished showering and was drying off when he noticed Squeak peeking in looking at him. Austin turned and finished drying and dressed quickly. There was no reason to make an issue about Squeak everyone knew he was homosexual and that he did things like that all the time, but making an issue could start a fight and delay his release and it was possible that was what Squeak was trying to do.

The horn sounded for the late morning lock in and Austin was working his prison issued comb through his long hair. The hair would probably not dry if he pulled it back but if he left it down it would in the way. He opted for wet hair.

The lunch horn sounded and the door slid open. Austin had just finished getting dressed and all that remained was for him to remove the Monk's patch. That was something he wouldn't do until they were locked in at three thirty.

Lunch was spaghetti and chicken. This was not one of Austin's favorites and he had never had anything like it before he come to prison and didn't plan on eating anything like it ever again. He sat with Jake. Jake as always was complaining about the food and that he needed to have his cake. Austin was trying not focus on the time or worry about what his life would be like tomorrow. The hours had been weighing on him and he looked worried.

"Here." he said to Jake offering him his cake.

Jake grabbed it. "I appreciate it." he said and laughed. "Gotsta have my cake. You gonna take that off?" he continued as motioned to his cheek.

"Yeah, when we lock in at three thirty." Austin replied.

"Good idea, you don't need that stuff following you. Where'd you git the chain?" Jake asked.

Leave it to Jake to notice Austin thought, but he already had thought up an answer. "My mother had it sent in but I never wore it, I figured since she was picking me up I had better wear it. That's a good idea don't you think?" he asked.

"Yeah that's real nice thing she did. You have to let your momma know that you appreciate her." Jake said sincerely with a smile.

Lunch was over and Austin was back in his cell. He stripped his bunk. He folded everything and put in a neat stack. When the cell door opened he was going to be ready to go. He paced back and forth in the cell thinking to himself that in two hours he would be out again and that he would spend his last hour and a half playing cards with Jake, Junior and Wills. He then thought about how Jake had befriended him and how Junior was always ready to step in and defend him. Both were good loyal friends the type of people he did not know on the outside. Something he thought that he should remedy.

The urge to use the toilet hit him as he paced. Lunch had not agreed with him and he was going to pay for it. Austin took one of his towel and tucked it into the space where the door met the top of the doorway. This covered the window in the door and gave him some privacy. He didn't look forward to sitting on the cold steel or feeling the rush of cold water that surged under the seat when the toilet was flushed, but it had to be done.

Soon two o'clock horn blared and Austin knew he was less than three hours away from the end of his ordeal. He instantly thought about that first day when he stood clutching his bedding, afraid and not knowing if he would survive, but he had. Sometimes he wasn't sure if he was completely changed or if he was completely the same. He had only one thing he could be certain about and that was that he had survived and was determined not to come back again.

The card game was just about over. Jake was happy he was winning. The five minutes warning horn sounded and they speedily played the last hand. "In your face fat man!" Jake said to Junior slapping the final card on the table confident of the win.

Austin stood up and offered his hand to Junior. Instead he smiled broadly and stood up and gave Austin a huge hug.

"I'm gonna miss ya man - don't come back."

Wills extended his hand, "Austin make sure you have that first drink for me."

Jake just looked at him and Austin could see tears forming in his eyes. Jake took his hand and pulled him close "You're awright for a white guy, take care man." He turned and walked quickly to his cell.

"See you around Jake." Austin called after him.

The horn sounded and Austin ran to his cell. He just made it in before the door closed. A couple of inmates yelled out there best wishes though Austin could only hear the sounds and could not make out what words were said. Less than one and half hours to go.

Austin stood at the door staring out, watching the two sanitation inmates cleaning the tables and sweeping the floor. The time was really going to drag on and on he thought. He sat down on one of the discs stools that were attached to the wall and looked at the lower bunk where Spud had slept. It was exactly as Spud had left it when he had gone yesterday.

Austin leaned over and opened the drawer that he had used to keep all of his possessions for the past five years. There were a couple food items, a sweatshirt, and some shampoo that he was leaving behind. If Spud came back they would be his as he had promised but if someone was put in here before that he had no control over what would happen to them. He decided to take them out and put them in Spud's drawer. The worst case Spud would never be back to claim them. That exercise took around ten minutes and Austin then wondered, 'Now what?'

Austin paced again and began thinking of things that ranged from his conversation with Gonzales, to the first time he saw guards brutalize an inmate. Then he remember the patch. He went to the mirror and looked at it. There were times when he actually felt pride in having it, a connection to something bigger than he was. It was safety, it was a statement of acceptance and belonging. He, Austin Lee, investment banker and gang member. He took the razor and began to shave. He shaved his face still leaving it in place and then he slowly removed it and he wondered why he had so much difficulty adjusting to change. Was he superstitious or was he afraid? He sighed and started to slowly remove the patch. He was now just Austin Lee, Federal inmate number 100930101, soon to be Austin Lee free man.

The time he thought would never arrive finally did. The speaker in his cell emitted a tone and a voice said, "Lee, prepare for discharge." The cell door opened. Austin quickly gathered all his belongings and his bedding in his arms and emerged into the empty day room. It was four thirty nine on Thursday and he was on his way. The door to the lock opened. The inmates began to bang on their cells in a salute (a custom that he had observed). Austin was now the one with tears in his eyes. He was leaving and going home.

Chapter Three

The Voltrun approached the front gate to the prison and came to a stop. A long boom extended from the outside wall to the left of the solid gate that represented the entrance to the prison. As he looked at the facility Philip thought that nothing short of a bomb blast could dent the formidable structure. The car window automatically rolled down. It was apparent that the car was being controlled by the prison at that point.

"State your name and business." the stern masculine voice demanded.

"Philip Lee, I am here to pick up Austin Lee, he is being released today." he replied.

"One moment please." the voice said. Philip looked at his mother who once again grabbed his hand and squeezed it.

The car window rolled back up and the temperature of the car began to recover to the seventy degrees that it was set to maintain after having been disturbed by the influx of oppressive late afternoon heat. The arm retracted to its original position and the gate began to raise so that the car could enter.

"I guess we are expected." Philip said nervously.

"Remember, we are bringing Austin home, that's why we are here." MacKenzie repeated. Philip began to realize that she was mostly saying that to keep herself focused on the positive reward at the end of the stressful and arduous task.

The car moved forward and entered the main court yard. From there it made a series of turns until it arrived at its designated birth, a parking space near the public entrance to the prison. As the car came to rest and Philip turned and looked at his mother. She was staring at the doorway that lead into the prison and her brow was creased with stress and worry.

"Mom are you ready to bring Austin home?" he asked.

"Philip I have been ready to bring him home for five years. Let's go get him." she said as she forced a smile.

"Open doors." he instructed the Voltrun and the car promptly opened both doors and rotated the seats to facilitate the exit by its occupants. Philip got out into the hot humid air and walked around to help his mother from the car. MacKenzie sat waiting for Philip to come and help her out of the car and as he approached she held her hand out for support and assistance.

"I tend to stiffen up when I sit like this for a while. I just need to get moving, then I am fine." she said.

Philip smiled and helped his mother out of the car and then put his arm around her shoulder. "We are going to get through this, all of us." he said. MacKenzie grasped his arm after he released her shoulder and they both began to walk to toward the door. "Close door and lock." he said over his should and the car complied. After one or two minutes it would shut off the environmental controls to conserve energy.

Philip and MacKenzie reached the door and they opened it. Inside they were met with a refreshing blast of cool air but the air had a strong antiseptic smell that was not quite pleasant. The large circular room had a single desk located in the middle with a rotating inverted pyramid computer display, similar to the ones that Philip had seen on the train. The floors were a glossy white and blue checked pattern and the walls were pale blue almost like the color of ice. This made the room appear to be colder than it felt.   There were no traces of any people or any noise as they walked toward the terminal, a female voice directed them, "State your names please."

"Philip Lee." he said and MacKenzie followed by stating her name.

"You are here to pick up Austin Lee. Correct?" voice asked.

"Yes." they said in unison.

"Please proceed to the security station for inspection and then follow the instructions you are given." the voice directed. The female voice was pleasant but it was rare to have a computer generated voice that wasn't pleasant. A door opened to their left and the light above it flashed indicating that they should enter. They walked deliberately to the door and crossed into the security section.

****

Austin left the block and walked down that long white corridor. There were three inmates at the end of the corridor being supervised by a guard. The guard seeing Austin instructed them to stand facing the wall so as to avoid any potential issues.

"Lee- you getting out today?" Cooper asked.

"Yes Mr. Cooper" Austin replied.

Cooper said, "Best of luck and don't come back."

"Thanks I don't plan on it." Austin said as he made a left hand turn down the same hallway he had been walking down yesterday only in the opposite direction. He reach his hand to feel the chain and pendant confirming that they were still there. Austin reached the end of the hall where the entrance to the prison transit system was located. He would have to take the train to the out-take facility. This was the most trying part of the trip. The train stops were the places where most of the assaults took place. He was no longer under protection and would be considered fair game.

"State your name and number." the station monitor instructed him.

"Austin Lee – 100930101." he replied.

"Proceed." it said and the door opened on to the train platform and Austin stepped inside. The door quickly closed behind him. The dimly lit platform was empty and the tunnel was dark in both directions. Austin was perplexed because he wasn't sure which train he was to take. Trains went in both directions and while he could get on any train and eventually get to his destination it was far better to get on the right one. He heard the train approach as he could hear the squeal of its brakes before its single light was visible in the tunnel. It approached at a fairly high rate of speed and continued on without stopping. The next train approached from the opposite direction and it too continued without stopping.

Austin began to pace nervously on the platform. The door that he had entered through opened and a guard ushered an inmate attired in red onto the platform. The noise of his shackles and leg irons chilled Austin as he remembered having to walk in those things and how they dug into his ankles and how he always felt as though he was going to trip. The guard nodded to Austin and the inmate glared at him.

"Lousy Fed prisoner." he grumbled. Austin just looked away.

The guard chuckled and said, "He's going home today Lester and you are going to be here the rest of your miserable life."

The inmate strained at the shackles causing them to rattle. "Lee, where's your patch?" the guard asked referencing his Monk's brand.

"Made me shave it off." he lied. Lester's facial expression changed and he put his head down.

"Anything you would like me to say to Hector or Julio?" the guard sadistically inquired. He knew that he was now torturing Lester.

"No, I said my good byes yesterday."

Another train approached slowing to stop at the platform. It stopped and the doors opened. "Inmate Lee, get in." a voice boomed. Austin clutching his stuff quickly got into the train. There were several inmates in the train and there was only one seat available. Austin elected to stand. All but two were clutching their possessions and were obviously going to out-take for processing and freedom. Everyone was quiet but they all appeared anxious.

The train stopped and a voice told the two inmates that were empty handed to exit and await escort, which they did. When the train continued on its way, the others began to talk.

A young man near Austin said loudly, "I'm getting out today, I can't believe it."

Everyone including Austin said, "Yes or Yeah me neither." almost in unison. The train continued on and Austin looked around. He noticed that one of the men was actually wearing a watch.

"Excuse me, what time is it?" he asked.

"Four fifty five." man replied.

"Thanks." There was no reply or acknowledgment, Austin realized that he probably answered that question thousands of times while he wore the watch in prison.

****

"Acorn, say time." Philip inquired and the PCU, responded with, "Four fifty six PM." Philip and his mother walked to the security screen and stood motionless while the scanners moved about them. The system indicated that they had no contraband or weapons and they were then instructed to follow the illuminated path to the train that would take them out-take processing. A single bar in the center of the floor illuminated progressively as they walked down the corridor and then made a series of turns before ending up at the platform where they would await the train.

They had walked quietly and now stood quietly not knowing what to say. Philip could see that his mother was getting upset and he reached over and put his hand on her shoulder. She mustered a weak smile and grabbed his had that was on her shoulder and then patted it. A train approached and slowed to a stop.

The door opened and a voice said, "Welcome, please enter this train to transport you the out-take processing facility."

Philip and his mother did as they were instructed to do. The train was empty and they took the first seats that they saw. The door closed and the train accelerated into the dark tunnel.

****

The train stopped and the doors opened but no one moved. They all were waiting for instructions. A loud voice announced, "Inmates Anders, Bukka, Chambers and Flante exit and follow the blue line to out-take processing. Inmates Guereny, Lee, Oshu, and Wilson exit and follow the green line to out-take processing." Austin exited the train first and began to walk following the green line. The walk took him to stairs and as he climbed them he counted them. When he reached the top he had counted twenty four. That was the most exercise that he had had in quite some time and didn't realize that he was in such bad physical condition.

****

When the train stopped MacKenzie sprang to her feet. Philip could see her impatience growing. Patience had never been a strong attribute of his mother. The doors did not open immediately instead a voice told them to follow the green line to out-take processing and as soon as the doors opened that's exactly what they did. Philip was half a step behind his mother as she walked briskly following the line. When she approached the escalator she climbed the stairs rather than let the stairs do the climbing for her.

****

The door to the out-take processing facility was directly ahead and Austin stopped within a foot of it. Austin could hear the others behind him and when it was apparent that they were all in close proximity to the door, it finally opened. The room, floor and furnishing were all green. It was in fact startling when Austin first saw it. There were a number of chairs in the middle of the room all facing three desks, two of which were occupied by a man and a woman. "Take a seat and wait until your name is called." a voice said.

Austin sat in one of the chairs facing the desks. The woman at the desk to the left looked up and Austin caught her eye. She frowned and shook her head then looked back at the pyramid shaped terminal in front of her. "Guereny, 122350122, Miguel." Guereny stood up and took a seat in front of the woman's desk.

"Lee, 100930101, Austin." the man said. Austin got up and walked to the desk and waited to be told to sit. The man working at the desk looked up and motioned for him to sit.

****

Philip was walking uncomfortably fast to keep up with his mother. Even at her age when she was motivated she walked at very fast pace. She could no longer maintain the pace for as long as she could in her youth but today she was extremely motivated and was showing great endurance as well. Philip had just finished climbing the escalator and his mother had already covered half the distance of the large room. At the other side were blue, red and green archways. The green one was illuminated to show them the correct way to proceed.

"Mom, please slow down, we are only going to have to wait once we get there." Philip called after her but she continued walking briskly. Philip elected to jog to catch up and did so just as they reached the archway entrance.

They arrived in a comfortably appointed room though there was a preponderance of green which Philip found disquieting. There were clusters of small sofas with large over-stuffed chairs arranged in semi enclosed rectangles. This was done to give visitors a feeling that appeared to be an almost intimate setting. At the far end was a reception area and behind the high desk stood a young woman dressed in a green jump suit. The slightly built Asian woman immediately reminded Philip of Melinda. He became instantly suspicious of her.

MacKenzie strode up to the reception area and told her that they were here to take Austin home.

"Welcome Mrs. Lee. Your son has just begun the first phase of the release process. If all goes well you can expect to leave in about thirty minutes. Would you care for some refreshments?" she asked.

MacKenzie replied, "No thank you." and turned on her heals and walked to the closest cluster with Philip in tow. They sat on the sofas facing one another, neither one knowing what to say.

"Didn't she remind of you of someone?" Philip asked. The room was virtually dead acoustically because of the thick green carpet and MacKenzie could barely hear what he had said.

"Who?" she replied.

"Melinda." Philip said. MacKenzie turned to look at her and stared, studying her appearance.

"Why because she's small and she's Asian? Aside from that I don't think so." she explained.

"I suppose you are right." Philip acquiesced for he didn't feel that it would be appropriate to engage in an argument with his mother at that time. "What do you have planned for dinner this evening?" Philip asked changing the subject.

"I have a real Italian meal being sent in, ravioli both spinach and cheese along with sweet and hot sausage, fresh garlic bread and an antipasto- oh yes and some amazing minestrone soup. Austin loves ravioli." she said.

"Yes he always did. It sounds like a wonderful meal." Philip replied.

"Yes, it is being sent from South Philadelphia by train and couriered from the station. They guaranty it will still be hot enough to burn the roof of your mouth." she said with a laugh.

"That's something I always look forward to, burning my mouth." Philip quipped.

****

Austin answered all the questions about his residence and then listened to the details concerning his parole and probation.   He nodded even though he was certain that he would forget the details but was confident that he would receive written instructions that he could read and follow.   The man continued to review the instructions and then reached into a drawer in the desk and pulled out a green flex screen. Austin was handed a stylus and told to sign it at the location indicating he had reviewed the information and had received the flex screen which contained the written instructions.   Once he signed the man rolled the screen up and inserted it into a tube that was about half an inch in diameter.

"Follow the green arrow to inventory control, good luck." man said disingenuously and then called out, "Oshu." Austin got up and walked in the direction of the arrow which pointed to a doorway that he had not noticed earlier.

****

"Mrs. Lee, your son has completed the first step and is on his way to inventory control after that he has a security screening and then he is done." the woman said.

"Thank you." Philip replied for her though he wasn't sure that she had heard or even cared that he had responded. An old Asian couple walked nervously into the room and up to the receptionist. Philip watch them humbly wait for the receptionist to look at them. They announced that the Oshua's were here to pick up their nephew. They were told his status and then found seats in one of the clusters choosing not to face the direction of the Lees.

****

Austin put his prison bedding plus he second uniform on the counter at inventory control. The inmate that was behind the counter punched up Austin's name and it showed the location of the civilian clothing that he had been wearing when he was arrested. The young man left and then returned with a garment bag and handed it to Austin. He pushed the bedding and clothes into a bin located on the opposite of the counter and motioned for Austin to follow the green arrow again.

Following the arrow took Austin around the corner where he encountered a guard. The guard pointed to a small room where he was told to remove all his clothing, squat and cough. This was the same routine he had to go through each time someone had come to visit him, once when he went to see the person and again when he left to return to the cell block.

"Okay, get dressed- wait what's that around your neck?" the guard asked.

"A pendant, a gift from my mother." Austin replied.

"Give it here, you don't need that." the guard demanded. Austin froze, standing naked in front of the guard that had his hand out.

"Come on quickly or it's back to the block with you." the guard said louder. Austin looked at him and thought of Hector. If he went back to the cell block he would be alive, if he gave up the pendant he would probably end up dead.

"Okay, back to the block." Austin said with very little conviction but he started to put his prison uniform on again.

"What are you doing? It's only a stupid chain." the guard told him.

"To you maybe, but to me it's a gift from my mother, I'll die before I give it up." Austin replied with more conviction.

The guard looked at him and said, "Don't be a fool, I can bang you for an assault charge and you'll be here for another ten years, and I'll beat your ass and take it anyway. Hand it over." he said.

Just then Miguel Guereny rounded the corner with his garment bag in hand. The guard had a witness with which he now had to contend, he had waited too long.

"Get dressed." he muttered and he turned to Miguel to check him. "Follow the green arrow and drop your clothes in the bin." the guard said. Austin quickly dressed in his civilian clothes. His shirt, a pale blue color, hung large on him. His pants were baggy and too big in the waist and though they would not have actually fallen down they could easily have been pulled down without opening them. He had no belt and his shoes had no laces. He had to wear his white socks that he had worn in prison since he had no socks when he was arrested. The memory of that day once again rushed back to him. He grabbed his possessions and the prison uniform and followed the green arrow.

He deposited the uniform in the bin as instructed and continued to walk down the corridor to another and yet another. He began to feel as though the journey would never end.

****

"Mrs. Lee your son is just about done he will be coming through that door any minute now." the woman said.

"Thank you." said MacKenzie as she popped up and walked quickly toward the door. Philip followed but hung back. This first moment was going to be reserved for his mother, she had wait so long for this day.

****

Austin's walk ended at a turnstile. A voice instructed him to insert his left hand up to the wrist in the slot above the turnstile. He did so slowly not sure what was going to happen. He felt a tug on his wrist band and then it was gone. He felt a sting as a tracking chip was embedded in his wrist that would enable the authorities to find him if they needed to locate him. It was a short range broadcasting chip and was effective for only ten or twenty miles depending upon terrain but it could be activated by any law enforcement agency. "Proceed." the voice said and the door opened and there was his mother standing at the entrance. He stepped forward into freedom and his mother's arms.

Austin kept his composure and smiled and shook his brother's hand and then hugged him. "Where's Roger?" he asked.

"He's not feeling well but he will see you at home, he wouldn't miss seeing you." Philip said.

Austin looked around and said, "I would like to get out of here, if you don't mind."

Before they realized it they were at the car and Philip was instructing the car to start and open the doors so that they could escape the heat. Philip gave the destination to the Voltrun and the front seats were rotated to face the rear seats and once this was accomplished they were off.

No one spoke while the car negotiated the internal drive and finally came to rest at the exit gate. The car remained motionless while a series of robotic scanners searched the car. The final check was to determine the occupants were not escaping inmates. Austin's chip indicated who he was and the scanners compared the images of Philip and MacKenzie with the occupants of the vehicle. All was in order and the gate opened. The car crept out of the prison and then came to life quickly accelerating to the legal limit.

MacKenzie smiled and leaned over to touch Austin. Austin burst into tears. Years of self-control, strength under duress, melted away in one emotional moment. He was free. Philip stared at his brother and a tear formed and slowly rolled down his face. What had they done to his brother, they had broken his spirit. They had hurt him badly. He watched as his brother's shoulders shake as he wept into his hands.

MacKenzie worked her way into the back seat and put her arm around her wounded baby, Austin responded and they hugged and she stroked his head and tried to comfort him. It was several minutes before Austin managed to regain control.

"I'm, I'm so sorry, you just don't know how long I've been holding that back." he said while he tried to smile but it would not quite form on his lips.

Philip continued to look at him and finally said, "You'll never guess what mom has planned for dinner?"

Austin replied, "Anything will be fine as long as it's not hot dogs and cornbread!"

With that he laughed and then the smile stuck and he began to grasp the significance of his last several hours. He was finally free.

The car pulled on to the northeast extension of the Pennsylvania Turnpike and accelerated to the legal limit. The conversation was lively but mostly superficial and light-hearted. Everyone want to just feel the joy of the moment. Later there would be time for reflection and for the planning for the future and the execution of that plan. At that moment it was time to revel in the joy of reUnion.

Austin glanced out the window during a brief lull in the conversation. He saw a red sports car approach them. It came up quickly and then slowed matching their speed. The driver looked familiar somehow. He had rather longish gray hair and he wore dark glasses. The driver of the red car removed his glasses and smiled giving a thumbs up. Austin knew him. It was Justin- it was him.

The car accelerated and Philip then commented, "Mom, isn't that the same car that passed us on our way to the prison, I guess the police didn't catch him."

"I don't know dear I really wasn't paying attention." she replied. Austin started to say something and then thought better of it. He was already questioning his memory and it couldn't be Justin, not here, not now. He thought that the next thing he would expect to see would be Melinda and with that he smiled and rejoined the conversation.

When they reached the east/west connection for the turnpike Philip received a phone call, it was from Roger. He accepted the call and said, "Hello Roger. How are you feeling?" Philip asked

"I'm okay. How is Austin?" Roger replied.

"He's fine, very thin and he has very long hair but I would also say that he is very happy to out of that place." Philip said.

"Great, tell Mom that I am on my way and to their house and I will have the table set and food ready when you arrive." Roger replied.

"Okay, we will see you in about forty five minutes to an hour. Bye."

"That was Roger he will take care of setting up dinner and will be waiting for us when we arrive." Philip said informing them of his conversation with the youngest brother.

"How is Dad doing?" Austin asked when he was finally able to bring himself to ask about his father.

"He is okay. He is looking forward to seeing you." Philip answered.

"Why do you say that?" Austin asked skeptically.

"Because he is, he told me so. Didn't he Mom?" Philip replied while looking for some support from MacKenzie.

"Yes, he talked about you all of the time, he did miss you." she answered. After that statement the trio became quiet. Everyone knew that Gregory was not known for demonstrating his feelings. Austin now was focused on the challenge he had thought about regularly over the past weeks as he awaited his release. How would his father receive him? What would they say to one another? The answer was less than an hour away.

The Voltrun turned down Juniper Avenue and slowed to the residential speed limit. Austin tried to keep his nerves in check as the car came to rest in front of 1520. It was a little past six thirty and the sun was glowing brightly on the horizon and heat was still oppressive. The evaporation from the Susquehanna River made Harrisburg very humid. The river had shrunk in the past decade and now was so shallow that it could easily be walked across in most locations.

Their house had been built in the last half of the nineteenth century and had been renovated and modernized several times in the two hundred plus years since it was first constructed. Each of the houses on the quiet street were unique unto themselves. The newest had been built in 1905 and been squeezed between two of the larger homes that had been the residences of members of the Pennsylvania Legislature but now all the houses on the street were occupied by scientists and low level banking executives. The scarce few remaining elements of the once majority that was the middle class.

Philip gave the car its last instructions and the doors opened and the passengers disembarked. "Close doors and lock." said Philip. Austin stared at the house and hesitated. He watched Philip help his mother up the four cement steps and up the walk before he forced himself to move. He began to climb the steps as he watched the progress his mother and brother were making. Soon they would climb the wooden steps to the porch and then be at the door. He picked up the pace and joined them on the porch as they were about to reach the door, but before they could open the door it swung open and there stood Roger beaming.

MacKenzie stood aside and Roger stepped out and hugged his brother forcefully. "Austin, by goodness, it is so great to see you!" When he stepped back it was obvious that he too had shed a tear. Austin just stood there his smile tentative, he was anxious about his next encounter. The aroma of genuine Italian cuisine hit him with a pleasant punch to the senses.

Roger ushered him in and called out, "Dad, he's here." he said loudly.

"Yes I know I..." as his father rounded the corner from the pallor. He stopped in mid-sentence and mid-step. Gregory was stunned by his son's appearance and he was overwhelmed with joy just to see him. He was so happy that when Austin extended his hand that he brushed it aside and pulled him into a hug. "Welcome home Austin, son I've missed you so." he said.

Austin was completely confused by the show of emotion. What had happened to his father? How had he changed so much since the last time he had seen him?

"Dad I'm, I'm so sorry I let you down."

Gregory responded, "No, son I let you down. Your uncle would have been very proud of you, doing what you believed in." MacKenzie watched the changing dynamic between her eldest son and the man she had always known was inside of Gregory Lee. She hustled her other boys into the dining room where the food was simmering in heated serving dishes.

"Where is our little princess? Sleeping I'll bet. Roger could you tell your sister that her brother is home and that it's time to eat. Thank you dear." she said. Roger left and went to find his sister.

Philip and MacKenzie busied themselves with making the food easily available. The food was on the buffet that stood on one wall and rather than transfer it to the table they decided to allow everyone to serves themselves and then be seated. Roger returned with Pamela who was still rubbing the sleep from her eyes as she trailed into the room.

"Hi Mom, where is he?" she said.

"He is with your father." MacKenzie replied.

"Oh." Pamela said with an ominous tone.

"No, your father welcomed him home and even hugged him." MacKenzie said reassuringly and Pamela looked at Philip who nodded.

"You're kidding, Dad hugged Austin. Is it snowing?" Pamela asked in disbelief. Everyone chuckled but the attention shifted to Austin and his father as they walked into the room.

"Look at you." Pamela exclaimed, "All that hair." She walked up to him and lifted up on her toes and kissed his cheek. "Welcome home, big brother."

Austin offered to hug her but she withdrew nervously.

"You look great Pam." he said. Then the room went awkwardly silent.

"Let's eat." said Roger with a plate in his hand.

Austin ate as though he hadn't seen food in a month. Everyone watched him. They all had some sense of pain and lingering anger at both the circumstances and at Austin for having put them all through the horrible experience. They all loved him but were truly embarrassed and disappointed. Now they were apprehensive about what Austin future would be like. Had he changed? Was he now transformed into a criminal having been made so by his association with all of those people?

MacKenzie studied her son as he continued to eat. "Well at least you got rid of that silly patch on your face." she said. Austin looked up and smiled with his mouth full of food and then nodded. "Why did you did you do that anyway? I thought it was very odd." she asked.

All eyes turned to Austin. He wasn't sure what he would say. Of all the things he had rehearsed in his head this is one that he had not prepared an answer. "Uh, it's a long story, perhaps another time."

His mother seemed to respect his answer but Pamela did not, she was inquisitive, she had to know something if someone else knew it.

"What did it look like Mom?" she asked. MacKenzie did her best to describe it as she had seen when she last visited and then she added that she had seen two others with similar patches on their faces and assumed it was a fashion statement. Roger then blurted out that it sounded like it was a brand and when he got quizzical looks from everyone, except Austin, he went on to explain that it was an identifying mark worn by members of the same gang.

"You weren't in a gang were you?" Pamela asked with wide eyed enthusiasm.

"I told you it was a long story." he replied hoping that she would leave the subject alone.

"Tell us the story son." Gregory implored, "You will not be judged, we are your family, we all love you."

Austin related the entire story about Hector, and how Austin had saved him from prosecution. He went on to say how it had made his time easier and safer. He ended the story with the favor that Hector had asked him to do regarding the delivery of the pendant. At the conclusion he pulled the chain out of his shirt and displayed it.

Philip lowered his head to take a closer look and said, "That is a remarkable piece of jewelry." he said.

"You are taking a risk having it son. Don't you think the authorities should be contacted?" asked his father.

"Dad I am in a difficult situation to which there is no comfortable and correct solution. I can surrender it to the authorities and have the Monks after me or I can give it Hector's sister and believe that that is the end of my involvement." Austin said.

"I see. I'll go with you on Saturday, and take you there myself and at least... Well at least it sounds plausible. Roger do you think there could be anything more to this than it just being a piece of jewelry?" Gregory inquired.

"Do you mean aside from the symbolic significance? Of course I could have it scanned to see if there is anything encrypted or embedded in it, I suppose." Roger responded.

Austin thought and then added, "No, it is better not to know, we should accept the face value of the story. Finding something more would change everything."

Philip thought about volunteering to go as well and then thought of Jessica. He finally decided that there would be time to do both. He could take the express from Philadelphia to Chicago and still be there in plenty of time to have dinner with Jessica.

"I'm going along too." he said. It was settled that the three would take the train to Philadelphia. Austin would meet Hector's sister and Gregory and Philip would watch from a distance.

The conversation became lighter as the Lee's brought Austin up to date with all of the latest news. There were also reminiscences of past family reUnions and embarrassing moments in each of the sibling's lives. Pamela was especially enthusiastic when it came to recounting the others' missteps but became indignant when her own were brought to light. There was some harmless teasing and a lot of laughter. Austin felt welcome and loved, something he had been afraid would not happen.

Philips PCU flashed a holograph message that it was approaching ten and that he had a phone call scheduled. He had the opportunity to execute the call or to wait. Philip excused himself from the group and decided to walk outside to place the call.

"Acorn, place call." he stated as he opened the door. The temperature was still in the mid eighties but there was no sun and a slight breeze that helped make being outdoors somewhat bearable. Philip noticed that the Voltrun was in the process of leaving. He wondered whether there was someone inside but that thought quickly passed as he found a chair on the porch to sit on as he waited for his call to go through.

"Hello Philip, you called earlier than I thought you were going to call." Jessica said answering the call.

"Hello Jessica. Is this a good time?" he inquired.

"It's fine, I suspect that you forgot that there is a one hour time difference that's all." she replied.

"Oh, you're right. How was your trip out and how has the session been so far?" he asked.

"The trip was uneventful I actually worked in the operations center on the way out. I don't start my classes until tomorrow. I am here a little early but that is alright." she said.

"Are you going to be available to have dinner on Saturday evening?" he asked.

"Of course what time can you be here? I am free after three. The rest of the weekend is my own, though I am certain there will be work to do." she said.

"I am planning on being there around that time. Where do you suggest that we meet?" he asked.

"How about at the hotel where I am staying. It's the Royale Ambassador on Wacker." she responded.

"I know the hotel. I will see around three and we will make plans then." he said.

"Great I'll look forward to it and yes I did remember to bring my father's notes in case you forgot the reason that you were coming." she said with a laugh.

"All business huh?" Philip teased back.

"Absolutely." she responded with a laugh.

"Okay then I'll see you Saturday. Have a good night." he said.

"You have to go?" she asked disappointingly.

"Yes I have people waiting for me I just stole a few minutes away to call you." he replied.

"Oh well then I won't keep you. Good night Philip." she said.

"Sweet dreams Jessica, Good bye." Philip said and stood up and went back to the door and opened it.

He was anxious to return to see Austin again, and while he was pleased to hear Jessica's voice, he was too consumed with the feelings of happiness that he had regarding Austin's freedom to dwell on Saturday. After all he had to work tomorrow and then there was this business about the pendant. Life, which had been dull and monotonous, had suddenly become mysterious and exciting.

As his hand grasped the door he hesitated then impulsively said, "Acorn re-dial last call."

"Philip is everything okay?" Jessica said answering his call.

"Yes I just wanted to tell you I am looking forward to seeing on Saturday and to ask you if I could call you tomorrow evening?" he asked sheepishly.

"Of course I will be available about this time tomorrow." she said.

"Great I'll talk to your tomorrow." he said.

"Philip you are an interesting man. I think you... well I better go my bath is about to run over. Good night." she said.

"Oh yes. Good night and good bye." said Philip who then turned the knob and was back immersed in Austin's stories before he had time to think about Jessica again.

They sat in the living room talking about everything and anything. Austin told some stories about prison life. He kept the violence limited since he knew it would deeply upset his mother. MacKenzie was not accustom to being up past nine and here it was almost midnight. She was fighting sleep so that she could be close to Austin. It was as though she was trying to make up for the five years of absence in one night. Pamela had already slipped into dreamland with her head resting on her father's shoulder and seemed content to stay there as long as she was allowed to remain.

Gregory interrupted Roger's story about his battle with encryption algorithms to tell MacKenzie that she should take Pamela and the go up to bed and that they would follow shortly. MacKenzie knew that it could be hours until her husband came to bed but she also knew that she was very tired. The relief of having Austin home was a burden that had been lifted. She could now relax and sleep a sleep of peace and contentment. "Alright young lady, let's go upstairs to bed." she said to Pamela.

Pamela opened her eyes and sat up bleary eyed. "Okay Mommy." she replied and though she was half asleep she stood up walked to Austin and said, "Nice to have you home Austin." as she touched his shoulder.

MacKenzie stood up and kissed everyone good night. "Don't stay up too late. Oh Austin, your room is made up and ready to go. Good night everyone." she said. They responded with good night wishes as MacKenzie and Pamela made their way upstairs.

"Well I suppose the encryption story might be a little too dry." Everyone laughed at Roger's realization that the world did not actually share the same passion for computer science that he did. "Austin it must have been terribly frightening at times." he said

"Yes, but most of the time it was mind numbingly boring. A constant repetition of the same things. Even work making those things that you are wearing was too much sameness, but there was an edge and violence that was very real." Austin said then told the story of Spud in as little graphic detail as possible. Everyone stared stunned by the inhumanity.

"That's was truly horrible, I had no idea that people could be allowed to do something like that and not suffer any consequences." Roger said.

"Dad, that's one of the reasons I was grateful to wear the Monk's patch, it saved me from inmates as well as the guards." Austin said.

"I think I understand." Gregory replied solemnly.

Gregory and his three sons continued to talk and everyone except for Austin poured themselves a cognac as they laughed and shared their good and bad experiences. As they relaxed the conversation became more frank. Finally Gregory decide to tell their sons about their great, great grandfather. "You know Austin you aren't the only family member that ever got into trouble."

Then Roger exclaimed, "You are not going to tell us that you had a checkered past!" Gregory laughed and said no but that their great, great grandfather's father in law did though. His actions caused quite a stir. Your great, great grandfather was completely humiliated by it. So much so that he never would share the information about it with the family. He even went as far as to change his name."

"What was the name before he decide to change it?" asked Philip.

"Leesop." Gregory replied. Philip took a moment to think where he had heard that name before.

"Christopher Leesop? Are we related to him?" Philip asked in amazement.

Gregory took a deep breath and said, "Yes, he was my cousin and he and he and your Uncle Bob were very close, very close. Austin, you actually met him once."

"Who is Christopher Leesop but more importantly what did that person do that made our great, great grandfather change his name?" Roger asked.

"Your grandfather is the only one that knows and he won't say. I have tried to find out through research but the on-line records were lost during the technology meltdown of 2050. So much was lost and we took a giant step backward as a species because of it. Some the paper records probably still exist but there is little chance that you can find them. Your grandfather is now the only source of that information."

"Christopher Leesop was the last man executed for treason in the US." Philip said.

"He wasn't a traitor, he was a spiritual man that was greatly misunderstood." Gregory added. This statement stunned all three boys. Their father had always seemed to be a supporter of the government and its plans to systematically place all the wealth and control in a very few individuals hands.

"Dad he advocated the overthrowing of the government." Philip stated.

"No, he wanted nothing to do with government he only expected it to protect and to serve all its people not serve only an elite class." Gregory replied.

Austin stared at his father and wondered why he had not said anything before about this to him. Had Uncle Bob followed Christopher Leesop? There were many followers, many that were underground and off the grid, because if they were in the open they would most likely be in jail. Austin had actually met one of his followers in prison. His passion for the teaching of Leesop was borderline maniacal, though there was no violence or mean-spirited behavior, just a fervor that could not be suppressed.

The room fell silent for a moment as they thought about the latest revelation. Austin finally asked, "What made you decide to tell us this today?"

Gregory twisted in his chair and said, "Perhaps I felt it was just time for you know so that if you wanted to know more you could talk to your grandfather about it. He had Christopher's journals and he might give you the information about his grandfather that he would never share with me."

"But why today?" Philip pressed.

"Because I believe that Austin did what I should have done and I wanted him to know that despite my failure at the time that I was weak then but now I've learned to be strong. But if you understand Christopher's teachings you will learn that change of this type cannot be made 'en mass' but must be done on an individual basis. Each of us must understand our purpose and seek to fulfill it with all our heart and soul." Gregory explained.

Roger had not spoken since his father had begun to tell them about their true heritage. He felt betrayed, that his life had been a lie. He was hurt because secrets had been kept from him. He wasn't Roger Lee he was someone he didn't know. At that moment he felt anger toward his father and grandfather. How could they let this happen?

"I'm going home." he announced.

Gregory sensed his son's feelings. "Roger, please stay, it's important for you to understand why I kept this from you." Gregory said.

And Roger replied, "Perhaps another day, I need to leave."

Philip stood up and followed his brother out of the room. "Roger I am just as shocked and confused as you are..." he said.

Roger interrupted him by saying, "I'm not shocked. I'm angry. We were lied to for our entire lives. We thought that things were one way and now we find out that things are completely different."

"Roger I'm going to see Old Harry soon I think that will clear some of this up. Please come with me. Austin can't leave the state and I need to confront the source. We need to do that." Philip said.

Roger looked at him, he loved his father and wanted to find a way to forgive him and put the blame elsewhere and Old Harry was the logical choice for a dumping ground.

"I'll let you know tomorrow. Good night." Roger said and walked out and into the moderating temperature. He had a half mile walk to the train and then a twenty minute ride to his home in Philadelphia. He was about to leave the porch when he remembered his brother Austin. He turned and there was Austin at the door. He opened the door.

They looked at each other shrugged and smiled and hugged. "Great to have you home Austin. I've missed you." he said.

"I've missed you too Roger. Perhaps we can catch up some more on Saturday when I go to Philly?" Austin asked.

"Yes, that would be great. Good night. I have an early day tomorrow." he said.

Austin watched his brother until he rounded the corner and was gone from sight. He then opened the door and walked into see his brother and father standing in the hallway waiting. "Is he okay?" Gregory asked.

"He is stunned and angry but I think once he has had the chance to think about it he will be okay." Austin said.

"Philip wants to go visit your grandfather and get more information." Gregory added.

"Austin I am glad you are home. After I get home from school tomorrow we can go out and do some exploring if you would like." Philip said.

"It sounds like a good thing to do." Austin said.

"Work still comes early and even though the trains get me to Lancaster fast the commute is a fairly long one. I am going to say good night as well." Philip said.

"Good night I will see you tomorrow." Austin said.

"Good night son." Gregory added.

Philip's departure left Austin and Gregory alone once again. "Austin it has been lonely without you son." he said as he held out his hand and shook his son's hand and then continued, "I have not always been easy to approach but I hope we can change the way we both behaved and share our lives together going forward."

"I think that would be something that I would like Dad." Austin replied.

"Let's go to bed I have to get up early also." he father said.

"Okay I'll be right up." Austin said. Gregory walked to the stairs while Austin went to the kitchen. He searched the refrigerator looking for left over sausage. He found it and a roll and put them into the microwave and within a minute he had something he hadn't had in more than five years, a midnight snack!

****

Austin heard a light tapping sound. It called to him from his unconscious state, then the flash, he had slept through breakfast and had not heard the horn. He sat up and looked around the room. For a moment he could not bring into focus where he was, then he knew. He heard his mother's voice calling from outside his door.

"Austin are you awake?" she asked.

"Yes Mom." he said sleepily.

"It's almost noon and I have to go out. Would you like some breakfast before I leave." she said.

"No, I'll find something in a little while. Thank you anyway." he replied.

"I'll be back in a couple of hours. See you soon." she said.

Austin looked around again. His room was the same as it was when he was in high school. It had been almost ten years since he had slept in this bed. He looked at the pictures on the wall and at his plaques, his high school and college diplomas. All of them, those things had some value in the past now simply collected dust and had little or no meaning. What was he going to do now? Where was he going to go? His career was gone. His love was gone, Austin broke down in uncontrollable weeping again. When he finally was able to collect himself, a minute later, and he swore that that would be the last time he would let that happen, no more self-pity.

Freedom turned out to be just as boring as jail when there was no one around. Austin thought it was great to be able to walk outside and see the sun shining though the heat was too oppressive for him to stay outside for more than a couple of minutes. Austin found a telephone and contacted the Federal Parole Office. They instructed him to report on Monday afternoon at four o'clock. The office was in Philadelphia so it appeared that he would be going there more than once in the next couple of days and that was then he frequently than he would normally have gone there in a year.

MacKenzie returned home at a little past three and found Austin asleep on the sofa in the living room. She looked at him as he slept. Her son had been through so much, the family had also suffered, everyone one of us, she thought and said, "Austin, Austin - Hello dear."

Austin stretched and yawned saying, "Hello Mom."

"Have you been sleeping all day?" she asked.

"I developed a terrible habit of sleeping the time away. Though for some reason this sleep is much more restorative. I actually feel rested when I wake up. The bed and the sofa are far more comfortable then the bunks in prison." he said.

"What would you like for dinner?" MacKenzie then asked.

"Anything will be fine." he replied.

"Let's order Chinese then." she said.

"It sounds great." he said enthusiastically.

"A little bit of lots of different things." she replied.

****

Saturday morning came and Austin lay in bed watching his clock and thinking about what was about to take place. It was five o'clock. He, his father, and Philip would catch the eight fifty train to Philadelphia, a train trip that was less than twenty five minutes. They would arrive with plenty of time to spare. The exchange would probably take only a couple of minutes and then he could spend the rest of the day fooling around with Roger. There was a baseball game at the new stadium perhaps they could watch that. He wasn't a fan and in fact he had never been to a game and perhaps that was the reason it sounded so appealing.

Austin decided to get up and get dressed. He thought he could go downstairs and get something to eat before everyone woke up. When he entered the kitchen he found is mother busily making pancakes. Bacon was frying, coffee was brewed and the kitchen table was set. "Good morning, Mom." Austin said and then kissed her on the cheek.

"You are up very early, I thought that I wouldn't see anyone for at least another half hour." she replied.

"I was just a little nervous about today. I want to put all of this behind me or at least start to do that." he said.

"I understand dear, I'll have breakfast on the table in just a couple of minutes. Are you afraid that something bad will happen?" she turned and asked.

"No, I don't think that anything will happen. I am fairly certain that Hector was being sincere." Austin replied optimistically.

MacKenzie returned to cooking and Austin stood up and poured coffee for himself and offered some to his mother. He knew that coffee was one of her passions. He studied her as she worked with speed and efficiency. Many had been critical of her cooking but Austin had always loved it. In fact he loved his mother very much and never doubted her love for him.

"Good morning." a deep voice said with the sound of someone who had just awaken. Philip struggled into a chair and rubbed his face trying to clear his head. He had been talking with Jessica until two in the morning before he had realized the late hour and the time when he had to get up. Today was going to be hectic for him. In fact the whole weekend was going to be that way.

"Good morning Phil." said Austin.

"Philip you don't look like you slept at all." his mother commented. Austin retrieved a cup of coffee and gave it to him. Soon they were joined by Gregory and the conversation gradually became livelier as they began to all wake up and come to life.

It was not long before the three were walking to the train station to take the intrastate service to Philadelphia, a train that originated in Pittsburgh and ran with two stops Harrisburg and Philadelphia. The morning air was heavy with humidity and the temperature was in the low eighties with a projected high of one hundred and ten degrees for the day. The sun was up just above the eastern horizon and hung as though suspended like some huge yellow balloon. They were going to arrive well before the time that needed to catch the train, and they might even be early enough to catch an earlier train. MacKenzie had encouraged them to leave in plenty of time she was always wanted to arrive early regardless of where she had to be.

The walk was a brief half mile and took them about fifteen minutes to complete. Philip had given Austin his old PCU glasses, similar to the ones that Jessica wore. It had taken a couple minutes to program them to Austin's voice and to load a couple of phone numbers into memory. Gregory did not carry a phone or use a PCU. Philip had always wondered why but it never bothered him enough to pursue asking him for his reasons.

They arrived at the station's main concourse at seven twenty, more than an hour early. The station had many shops and dining spots, most of which were closed at the early hour on a Saturday, but there were still a few that had followed the government's call to have the economy function twenty four hours a day, seven days a week.

A rotating news kiosk caught Austin's attention, he hadn't seen this technology before and was amazed by the clarity of the holographic images of the news stories. The kiosk featured lots of war highlights, the Middle East conflict was always center stage. After all it had been alternating from country to country for more than sixty years.

The war in the Netherlands surprised Austin he did not know that it was taking place. "When did that start?" he asked, pointing at the displayed images of a building being blown up by a missile fired from a US helicopter.

"Last month." Philip responded, "They rejected the IMC conversion again and the banks decided they had had enough."

"Another war over currency conversion." Austin commented.

"It's much more than that, it's about ownership and wealth control." Philip answered and then continued saying, "The Russians registered a complaint with the world court but it was rejected. It will be over in less than thirty days and the military will be off to fulfill the next mission."

Gregory left his sons and went to take care of Austin's rail pass. He was giving Austin a card that he could use to pay for his fare. Gregory used one since he did not use a PCU like Philip did. Philip and Austin watched the remainder of the news briefing and when it was clear that they had seen all of the current stories they started to walk in the direction that Gregory had headed. Austin stopped several times to look through the windows of the various shops. He was searching for things that had changed and to see the cost of the items. One thing he did notice was that there seemed to be fewer items that had more than one manufacturer. He remembered a time when you could see five or more different electric shavers on display in a store not he saw only two.

"Philip is there something going on regarding the variety of manufacturers of the products that are for sale?" he asked.

"If you are you wondering whether there are fewer manufacturers and brand choices, then the answer is yes, absolutely it's a way that we can preserve resources, rather than make too many items that could mean the depletion of a resource, the government is now licensing products and restricting the manufacturing to those that can prove their product is the best use of resources while at the same time being offered to the people at a fair price and a superior quality. Licensing is only for one year at a time and you must compete each year to maintain your license." Philip explained.

"Free market conditions or economic natural selection don't apply anymore?" Austin asked.

"No, it's considered wasteful. The companies are free to develop and refine products in test environments but must submit them to the licensing board prior to bringing them to the market." he answered.

"What incentive do they have to even try? It seems pointless." Austin commented.

"Licensing for the runners up can be awarded to other markets, so there are significant fortunes that can be made." Philip replied.

"How long has this been going on?" Austin inquired.

"About four years now but it has really starting to show in the marketplace now that most of the inventories have been finally depleted." Philip responded.

"There he is." said Austin, pointing at his father as he walked toward them.

"I've loaded five hundred IMC on this card." Gregory told Austin as he handed him the card. "That should last you for a while and it will work everywhere and you don't need one of those things." said Gregory as he pointed at Philip's PCU.

"Yes, I know all about them I sent more than three years putting them together and testing them." Austin said painfully.

"Let me know when you run low and I'll load some more on the card. All you have to do is peel off the adhesive strip and place your thumb on it and it will only be able to be used by you." Gregory told him.

After personalizing his card Austin placed in his shirt pocket. Philip motioned to the video board that showed the departure gates and the status of the various trains by destination. The next train to Philadelphia was departing in half and hour on track Seventeen C. They elected to head to the track platform and wait there since it would take them several minutes to make their way to the platform and this would assure them a good seating position.

When they arrived at the platform there were about fifty people already queued up in the various stalls. Each stall corresponded to a series of seats on a train and the seats that were available on the inbound train were indicated by an illuminated panel on the floor of the stall. A stall with three illuminated panels would be ideal for the trio. Philip spotted one about one hundred feet down the platform and they walked purposefully toward it.

They stood inside the stall and then relaxed as they waited for the train. Close by a holographic display showed a map of Pennsylvania and the relative location of the train. Below the image was a count-down which was rotating and showing the arrival time as eighteen minutes and twelve seconds. Each time the counter rotated the display changed. Austin stared at the greenish images and was amazed at how captivating and entertaining they were. He would have loved this when he was a child, he thought.

The train burst into the station and slowed rapidly stopping exactly with the doors aligning perfectly corresponding stalls. Each door with a vacancy opened and the three entered. They barely had time to take their seats when the train's doors closed and they were underway. The stop at the station was less than two minutes.

Austin looked at the displays of the simulated windows. The image did not correspond to the time of day but the view was pleasant enough. The train's movement was not apparent to Austin. He thought that the absence of the feeling of motion was remarkable. "This train is fantastic." he finally said out loud.

Philip smiled and then added, "Wait until you ride the new 200 series they are even more unbelievable..."

"Yes, I understand you had quite a ride the other day and that you were quite smitten but not by the train." Gregory interjected.

Philip smiled and then decided that he needed to talk about Jessica. "Yes, I did meet a fascinating woman." he said.

"Oh?" Austin said smiling, "Do tell."

"She is the daughter of a very famous historian Dr. Leopold Jenkins, unfortunately he passed away some time ago but she is following up on some of his work regarding the significance of the battle of Gettysburg." Philip stated.

"Oh." Austin added slightly disappointed.

"Yes she believes that if the South had prevailed that the entire world would be different today." Philip explained.

Austin thought for a moment and then asked, "Dad, what do you think of this?"

"I think Philip's found a soul mate." he replied and they both laughed. Philip was about to protest but elected to just smile. Further protestation would have gotten his brother to tease him about Jessica and that would betray the fact that his interest was more than a research collaboration.

The train began to brake as they approached Philadelphia. The station was actually located on the outskirts of the city and there were numerous shuttles that could speed people to every point within the city limits. When the train came to a halt the doors opened and everyone got out, exploding on to the platform busily heading to their connections since this hub was rarely anyone's specific destination.

The three men worked their way down the moving sidewalk to the city hall shuttle. These were two car trains that departed every ten minutes and made the ten minute trip entirely below ground. They descended using the moving sidewalks to the shuttle platform. The air was stale and slightly damp. This shuttle line used some of the same tunnels that were used by the elevated trains or El that dated back to the early part of the Twentieth Century. Moments after they arrived on the platform a train pulled up ready for boarding. There were no indications of where to stand like there were on the intrastate train, but there were only a few people on the platform and the arriving train was less than half full so they were able to find a seat without difficulty.

The short trip was noisy and the train bumped and bounced its way down the tracks. When they arrived at the city hall stop, they exited.

"Acorn, say time." Philip said and the PCU responded with, time telling him it was nine thirty seven AM. "We have about an hour and a half until it's time for you to meet... what was her name?" he asked Austin.

"Lucy." Austin replied.

"Do you know what she looks like?" Philip asked.

"No, but she knows what I look like." Austin answered.

"Okay what should we do?" Philip asked the two men.

"I think we should find a place where Philip and I can sit and watch you from a distance. Then you can wait by yourself. We can contact the police if there is trouble." Gregory responded.

"No police unless they try to kill me or kidnap me." Austin insisted.

"Why?" Philip asked.

"I will be signing my death warrant if I involve the police. Please understand that I appreciate your moral support but don't over react." Austin implored.

"Okay - agreed. Let's find a place to get some coffee where we can sit and wait." Philip said.

They exited the platform on to the moving sidewalk that eventually deposited them on Market Street, just across from City Hall. There was a Famous Coffee Shoppe on the corner and it appeared to Austin that it could be the best place for his father and brother to sit and wait. They could remain there while he stood and waited across the street.

They walked leisurely to the corner and entered the shop. They were greeted by the enticing aroma of freshly brewed coffee mingled with a swirl of freshly baked pastry. Philip noticed that there were several of overstuffed arm chairs very close to the window that would give them a good view of the rendezvous.

"You have an incoming call from your mother do you wish to accept?" his PCU alerted him.

He responded, "Acorn, yes. Hello mother, we are just getting ready to sit down and have a cup of coffee. Yes, everyone's fine and I will call you when this is all over. Yes. Yes. Okay. I will them and yes I love you too." Philip said responding to MacKenzie's comments.

"Your mother does like to worry." Gregory added.

"Well if you weren't somewhat worried you wouldn't have asked to come along. Isn't that true?" Austin said to his father.

"I suppose so but let's just call it more time to catch up on things." Gregory replied and directed his comment to Philip by saying, "Jeremy said you seemed impressed with the news train." It was far from a perfect segue but while Gregory had made significant progress in revealing his feelings, he did not want to spend too much time calling attention to them.

Philip took the opportunity to speak about the train and began by saying, "The train is very impressive and the new tunnel technology is something to behold. I sat in the control center and watched the train exceed four hundred miles per hour and we moved effortlessly between vacuum locks. They use lasers in the guidance system to trigger lock activation so there is quite the light show traveling in pitch black with multi-colored lasers lights crisscrossing in front of you. Austin, I think you would enjoy the ride perhaps Dad could arrange one for you."

"Why do you have connections in the transportation department?" Austin asked his father.

"No, I helped design the power generation system. My design and implementation teams have access to the three prototype trains whenever we need to review data or validate our current hypothesis." Gregory answered.

"The next time you have one of those evaluations please let me tag along." Austin said.

"I'll check with the team and see when they are going out next and maybe I'll tag along too." Gregory replied.

The server came to their table and took their order. Philip instructed his PCU to give him an alert when it became ten thirty. They had agreed that Austin should be waiting outside about fifteen minutes before the agreed to meeting time. They continued to talk about trains and the new power generation systems that Gregory had devoted all his time and energy to perfect. Every time the conversation stalled Philip was able to spark more conversation with another question about the trillion watt generators that were being created and how compact they were becoming.

"Yes, but they are still very expensive. I am hoping that one day they can be produced so that each community can afford one and we can do away with the centralized power monopolies." Gregory added. That thought process was considered by the government as being almost as evil as the action that Austin had taken in his attempt to bring down the IMC and the Banking Consortium.

"It is ten thirty AM." Acorn announced.

"It's time Austin." Philip stated as soon as his father finished his sentence and before he could continue. Austin reached into his shirt neck and pulled the chain and pendant over his head. He looked at it for a moment in the palm of his hand. Then carefully gathered the chain up in his palm and closed his right hand around it.

He stood up and looked at his brother and father and said, "I'll see you in about a half an hour."

"Good luck." Philip said and Gregory added, "Take Care." He turned and walked to the door and pushed it open. The air temperature had warmed considerably, it had to be close to ninety five degrees already, he thought.

He walked slowly to the curb and crossed the wide street at the designated crosswalk according to the signal. While there were a few cars and taxis on the street the threat of personal injury came from PTUs (Personal Transport Units). These single and two person three wheeled enclosed scooter like units were everywhere. And there had to be at least one hundred of them stopped waiting for the sea of pedestrians to cross.

Electrically powered and rented at kiosks located throughout the downtown area, they afforded the user a lot of mobility at a low cost and convenient means of getting from one remote location in Philadelphia to another. They were also air conditioned which made them much more desirable than walking.

Austin's glasses went to maximum tint and he activated the time display so that he could focus on how much longer the ordeal would be. The time was ten thirty nine when he took his position. He managed to move under the archway that led to the central courtyard of City Hall which protected him from the sun. The old building had a good bit of charm and was one that most Philadelphians were proud of because of its history and signature statue of William Penn.

The minutes slipped by and Austin struggled to remain calm as the heat and the anxiousness of the situation bore down on him. He began to feel self-conscience when people passed and looked his way. Did they recognize him as criminal? Was anyone monitoring him? It was then that he remembered the chip that was embedded in his wrist. What type of telemetry did it broadcast? His name? His crime? The sweat began to roll down his back. Why hadn't he gotten a haircut? The weather was far too warm for long hair, he thought.

Ten fifty eight was displayed and he felt as though he had been in a sauna for too long. He heard the sound of an internal combustion engine. It was the high pitch scream of a finely tuned engine not the low whine of the electric PTUs or cars that had been passing. He looked to the right and saw a red Ferrari coming down the multi-lane street. It stopped at the curb in front of Austin. The passenger door opened and a young looking Hispanic woman emerged. She was wearing a red pant suit that was apparently a size too small to fit her properly.

Austin watched as she approached. When she got closer it became apparent that she was clearly not as youthful as he had first thought. She was perhaps in her fifties or maybe even older. She held out her hand and said, "Hello Austin it's nice to see you."

"Hello Lucy." Austin replied and he extended his hand and passed the pendant and chain to her.

She talked to him for about two minutes and then said, "Thank you for coming." She approached him and leaned toward as though she was going to kiss his cheek and instead whispered to him. When she finished she pulled back and looked at him and laughed. She turned and went to the car. The driver lowered the window as she reached the car and opened the door. It was Justin. He smiled and stared. Austin couldn't believe what he was seeing. He decided to approach the car, but as he did Justin pulled away, tires squealing and then they were gone.

Austin had had enough of being outside in the heat. He crossed the street and rejoined his father and brother.

"How did it go?"

"Fine I suppose. I gave it to her." he said as he pondered whether he should share the fact that Justin was the driver of the car and that Lucy had given him further instructions. Both Philip and his father studied Austin intently.

"What else?" Philip asked.

"That's about it. She talked about the weather and...it was nothing I guess. I am just trying to get used to the idea that that part of my life is over." Austin said. They appeared to accept his statement as an adequate explanation because they began to relax and started to plan their exit and departure from Philadelphia.

Philip told them he was going to Chicago and from there he and Gregory could take the same train, the twelve forty five which stopped in Harrisburg was well as Dayton Ohio. It would be the one of the trains he would take on Sunday when he went to see Old Harry. Roger was to meet him in Lexington Kentucky where Harry lived.

"My, aren't we going to be busy." his father interjected.

"Yes, I have not been this busy on weekend since graduate school." Philip answered.

"And I think there was a girl at the center of that whirlwind of activity too if I'm not mistaken." Austin teased.

"I think you are right." Gregory agreed.

Philip blushed and tried to recover and asked, "You are going to meet Roger this afternoon?"

"Yes, in about an hour and a half." Austin replied.

Gregory pushed back from the small table and said, "I've had too much coffee I think and eating those pastries ruined any thoughts of eating lunch anytime soon. Let's get out of here and stretch our legs."

They exited the coffee shop and headed south to Chestnut Street. The street had been enclosed by an Invisasteel canopy that had been extended to meet the buildings on either side. The twenty block walkway had moving sidewalks and was completely climate controlled. There were many plants and areas of grass with fountains that gurgled and splashed water on polished stones. In the trees there were birds that sat and watched the procession of humanity stream by. This was one of the showcases that enabled Philadelphia capture an increasing number of tourist along with a growing population of young professionals. The comeback of what was once the premier city in the country that had fallen in stature since the end of the Civil War was truly remarkable. The last census had the city moving from the tenth position all the way to number six and if the trend continued it would soon be in the top five cities in the country.

The trio went east on the moving sidewalk walking along at a slow pace but moving continuously. The sidewalk had a protocol which common courtesy dictated. Fast walkers used a speed sidewalk located on the interior (left side), strollers used the middle and people that preferred to let the sidewalk do all the work used the outside walk which moved slowly. Changing tracks could be a little tricky at times, depending upon the number of people that were present.

When traffic was encountered at any of the several intersections the sidewalks were stopped when the traffic signal indicated that the traffic could pass. There were only a very few streets where traffic was still permitted and at those intersection there were garage like openings that allowed the traffic to flow through the tunnel. Sensors detected whether traffic could proceed and gates were closed to prohibit the pedestrians from straying out into the path of an oncoming vehicle. Between those safeguards and the level of sophistication of the new automobiles the chance of a person being harmed was very remote.

Unsure of where they were headed they continued to move at a constant pace talking about the area and the transformation it had gone through. Comments were made about the wide variety of shops and the number of people that were present. The people were there even though the economic conditions were not good and the number of manufacturers were shrinking. It was unlikely that there were that many that could afford to goods that were being sold and they speculated that many were simply 'window shopping'.

Gregory stopped talking in mid-sentence and looked ahead. They were approaching Independence Hall and he had been struck by the sight of the shrine that once was home to the Continental Congress and in whose halls the Declaration of Independence had been signed under penalty of death to the conspirators.

"Let's get off here." Gregory said inviting the boys to exit the moving walkway and explore history, something Philip had enjoyed doing at every chance he got. "Blast, we forgot to call your mother and to let her know that everything was alright. Philip?"

"Acorn, call mother." Philip said as lagged behind and he spoke briefly with his mother

Meanwhile Austin and his father joined the line of people waiting to visit Independence Hall. Austin was still thinking about his encounter at City Hall. He looked at this father and thought about telling him but decided, once again, to remain mute. He knew what his father would say or at least he thought he did, his father had changed significantly since the last time he had spoken with him, he actually felt for the first time that his father cared about him and had missed him. He felt guilt in that he had not missed him. All he had felt was dread when he had thought of his father during those five years in jail. This was certainly a confusing situation, a jumble of mixed emotions that did not seem to have a starting point to which he could untangle them.

"Austin, this room has always had a special place in my heart, I always felt that all that was good and right about this country was conceived and born here." Gregory was speaking though not to anyone in particular. It was if he were speaking to the room itself.

"Yes I know. I remember the times you brought us here as children, it is no wonder Philip became what he did. It's a surprise that Roger and I didn't as well." Austin replied.

"Except Pam, she could never bring herself to like anything that was old." Gregory commented and they both mused over Pamela's strength of character and conviction.

Philip caught up with them as they worked their way through the old building following the continuous flow of people, listening to a recorded voice explain the occurrences and significance of that which had taken place within those walls. Austin glanced at the time. It was eleven fifty eight. Soon his father and brother would be leaving. He must call Roger soon to change their plans, he thought.

They emerged from the building and made their way to the crossing where they would be able to gain access to the moving sidewalks that headed back toward City Hall. The walk back was a quiet one. There was little discussion and they did not walk but chose to stand and observe. When they reached Broad Street they exited the walkway and proceeded to the shuttle station. At the junction where the entrance to the east/west tram and the north/south tram converged they parted company. Austin shook hands with the two men and they said their good byes.

"See you at home later son." his father said.

"Have a safe trip Philip." Austin told his brother and he stood and watched them until they disappeared down the corridor.

"Melinda, call Roger." Austin waited for the call to be answered.

"Hello Austin, how did it go?" Roger asked.

"Without too much trouble. Though, it is very hot out." Austin replied.

"Yes, far too hot to stand outside for very long. What was she like? Was she attractive?" Roger queried.

"She was attractive for a woman in her mid-fifties though from a distance she did seem younger." Austin replied.

"Oh." Roger said disappointingly.

"She also likes to wear her clothes tight- it must be uncomfortable." Austin added.

"Really! That must have been entertaining." Roger said.

Austin knew where his brother was going to steer the conversation and did not want to play along. "Roger I am going to be about a half hour late, I need to run a quick errand. Can we meet at the Italian Market at one or one fifteen?" he asked.

"Sure I enjoy walking around down there. How about we meet at the tea shop at the corner of Catherine Street?" Roger replied.

"Sounds good I will see you then." Austin agreed.

Austin walked to the tram platform. He was headed south to the Italian Market as Lucy had instructed him. He was to go to Mario's Butcher Shop and there he would receive further instructions. Before he was able to get himself too consumed by fear or anger he found himself standing on the street getting his bearing. He moved east until he reached Ninth Street. He entered the climate controlled atrium that was the Italian Market. This was the home of legendary crime bosses, the food distribution center, and a great place to find items that weren't available anywhere else. While Austin had been at Wharton he had made a habit of getting to know Philadelphia and this was an area he had always enjoyed. There were foods available that had been signature pieces, culinary offerings, not 'haute' cuisine but common simple fair that lost favor because of health concerns yet continued to be offered in some obscure establishments in and around 'South Philly'.

There it was Mario's Butcher Shop. Austin walked across the street which had not been used as a thoroughfare for automobiles for well over one hundred fifty years. There were tables lining each side with fresh vegetables and fruits in abundance. Older men with large round stomachs called out special pricing and tried to tempt the passer by to stop and look and then hopefully buy. Austin felt a tug on his elbow as he passed a table in front Mario's.

"Look at these grapefruit. Fresh flown in today only one IMC a piece - it's a steal." the vendor said.

"No thanks?" Austin answered and the man without hesitation turn to the next person and repeated the same pitch.

Mario's window was filled with hanging sausages, what looked like goats that had been roasted and a suckling pig. Austin inhaled, grasped the door handle and pushed the door open. Austin was hit with the over powering fragrance of garlic. The shop was small with dark hardwood floors that were heavily scarred from and age and wear. They creaked when he walked in and as the door closed it struck an arm that caused a bell to ring. An Asian man wearing a bloody apron popped up from behind the display case. It contained many different cuts of meat, mostly pork products, but there was also some beef and a fair amount of poultry.

"Ah, you are expected." he said.

"You are Mario?" Austin asked.

"Oh no." the Asian man chuckled, "Mario died forty years ago I bought the shop from his daughter almost fourteen years ago. The name is well known, so I didn't change it. Please go through that door and down the stairs. You are expected." he said and pointed to a door that was partially obscured by a beaded curtain. Austin pushed through the beads and opened the door.

There was a light at the bottom of the narrow staircase and Austin could hear the muffled strains of music. The ceiling was low and even though Austin was able to descend the stairs standing fully erect he felt the need to bow his head slightly. Upon reaching the landing he soon saw another closed door with light shining through the spaces where the door did not fit its frame properly. Austin pushed the door open and saw Justin sitting in a chair to the right and three men standing along the opposite wall. They all turned and looked at him as he entered.

"Good to see you my boy." Justin said as he extended his hand but did not rise. Austin looked at him and then at the others. They all bore a striking circular patch of hair on their right cheek. They were obviously Monks.

"Justin I thought you would have left the country or I don't know what I thought." Austin stammered, "What happen? Why?"

Justin motioned for Austin to sit. There was a small stool that appeared to be off balance but seemed strong enough to handle his weight so Austin gingerly tested it and it held him.

"I suppose you are wondering many things but first I want to tell you thank you from Hector and Lucy they truly appreciate you bringing the pendant out. It means a great deal to them." Justin said.

"What does that have to do with you?" Austin asked.

"Hector is a good man, a friend. He has helped me in the past, as I have helped him. He made certain that you were kept safe while you were in prison." Justin explained.

"You are telling me that you had something to do with that? I don't believe it." Austin said incredulously.

"You remember Charlie here don't you?" Justin asked pointing to one of the men that were standing against the wall. Austin turned to look at the man Justin called Charlie. He appeared to look familiar.

"Show him your stomach Charlie or should I call you Iron, short for Iron Man." Justin directed. Charlie Shart pulled his black shirt up and exposed his stomach. There was a long scar that ran across his abdomen where Hector had cut him.

"That was you?" Austin asked in amazement as suddenly realized that his recruitment had been contrived. They had to have an excuse to make him a member and to keep him safe.

"You see Austin while I couldn't affect the outcome of your trial more than the sentencing and the date of your parole, I did all that I could to make it as easy on you as I could." he said with a smile.

Over the next half hour Justin explained what had gone wrong and how he had tried to help all of the members of the group as best he could. He also told him while he suspected Melinda of having a role in the failure of the plan, he could not find enough evidence to act on his suspicions.

"Act on it. You mean…" Austin said.

"No, just make certain that we kept her apart from future activities." Justin interrupted.

"What future activities? Count me out, I am not going to jail again." Austin said firmly.

"There is nothing planned at this point and there maybe never any plans, but I thought that if you and she were together it would…" Justin said.

Austin interrupted by saying, "No, no, I am not participating forget it."

"That's very understandable. Please do me one favor take this card it has a number that you can reach me at if you just want to talk or you should you need something. I will help you if you I can." Justin said.

Austin looked at the card that was extended toward him and assessed his options quickly. There was no harm in having it and perhaps he could use it later. He reached and took it. Justin smiled and said, "Melinda's new number is on it as well. I thought you might want that too."

Again Justin extended his hand "Good luck Austin, perhaps someday we will be able to see a better day for us all. He who serves the poor is rich beyond his wildest imaginations." he stated.

"That's a quote from..." Austin said not knowing where he had heard it.

Justin completed his statement saying, "Christopher Leesop, yes and inspiration to us all." Austin took his hand and shook it. He wanted to believe Justin. He had trusted him before perhaps he could trust him again.

Soon Austin was on the street again this time on his way to meet his brother at the tea shop. He thought that he should at least have something in his hand when he met him. He stopped at a stand and purchased some vegetables; corn, beans and tomatoes. He also picked out some fantastic looking strawberries remembering how much his mother enjoyed them. He then purchased six soft pretzels and realized that he was very hungry. He covered one with brown spicy mustard and ate while he continued to his destination.

People passed him as meandered from stand to stand. The meeting and all it represented faded from consciousness and he began to once again appreciate his freedom. For the first time he felt relaxed and his face showed a smile that could be suppressed.

As he approached the shop he saw that he was early, but he noticed his brother walking toward him, the timing was good, he thought.

"Austin you look like you are enjoying yourself, though the mustard on your face isn't the most attractive look I've seen." Roger said teasing him. Austin laughed and with his free hand attempted to wipe the mustard off and with some coaching he finally accomplished the task. "Let's go in I need to pick up some green and black teas." Roger said.

The two men foraged about in the small shop. Austin selected some tea, though he normally didn't drink it. Perhaps it was time for another new behavior, he thought. Roger made his selections quickly and they were soon back on the street.

"I am a little hungry. I missed lunch, worked straight through again. Are you interested in something to eat?" he asked Austin.

Austin thought for a second and said, "Absolutely, what do you suggest?" he asked his brother.

"Healthy or not?" Roger countered with a question.

"Not." Austin said resolutely.

"Follow me." Roger instructed him. They walked south on ninth street until they reached the end of the atrium coverage.

"Now we have to brave the elements for two blocks." Roger explained. They exited the temperature controlled enclosure through a rotating revolving door. The heat was overpowering as the sun blared down on them. Austin's glasses tinted immediately to their darkest level.

"Austin it is great to have you back. I am truly sorry about not coming to see you. It was too difficult to think of you in there and painful. I well I..." Roger said trying to explain why he did not visit him while he was in prison. Austin decided to let his brother stumble rather than rescue him with a reassuring, 'it's okay'.

"I was very angry at you and at the government and the banks and well everyone. Then I was just plain sad." he concluded.

"Roger I did a really stupid thing. I hurt a lot of people in the process. The unfortunate fact is that it was apparently done for nothing." Austin said.

"You can't bring Uncle Bob back." Roger stated.

"I really just want to make those I thought caused his death pay for it." Austin rejoined. The sweat was beginning to run down his back and his legs.

"It is really hot. Wang, display temperature." Roger instructed his PCU and its display showed one hundred and twelve degrees. "Yes, it's a warm one today- one hundred twelve degrees and it not yet reached its peak. Here we are." he told Austin.

They entered a small shop with darkened windows and no visible identification of what type of establishment it was. The smell of fried food dominated by onions was intense.

"Ah cheesesteaks! It's been almost twelve years since I last had one of these. I didn't think that you could still find a place that made them." Austin said enthusiastically.

"You have to be in the know, my boss told me of this place and two others. This one traces its origins back more than one hundred and fifty years to a place named Tony something or others." Roger said.

They ordered and sat down to wait for the food to be prepared.

"You know that these are definitely outside of the dietary code and that if the state had their way they will make selling these sandwiches illegal. No, really. The health risks put a strain on the medical services, it's the same argument they used to make cigarettes illegal twenty years ago. They have not been able to alcohol declared illegal though they just tried again last year." Roger continued to talk about the government even though in his field his primary employment came from government contracts.

"Another opportunity to add to the prison population." Austin said shaking his head.

"There you go, enjoy guys." the counterman said as he deposited two large sandwiches in front of them and at that moment all conversation stopped as they eagerly devoured their food.

Roger wiped the grease off his fingers using several paper napkins as he watch his older brother cram the last of his sandwich into his mouth.

"Now that was outstanding. Thank goodness I don't eat these often I would be even heavier than I am now, though you could stand to put on a few pounds, quite a few." Roger said.

"My goodness that was great. I've had nothing like that since I can't remember when." Austin replied.

"Where to now? Wait I've got it. There is a new holo-theatre that just opened. The technology is amazing. What do you think?" Roger asked.

Austin agreed by saying, "That sounds good to me."

The entrance to the holo-theatre was in front of them but Austin could not see how they were supposed to get inside. The sign said enter here, but there was no doorway, just a brick wall with a poster that hung on it with its bottom two corners flapping in a breeze that Austin could not detect.

"Let's go in." Roger said stepping forward and walking into and through the wall.

"That's a holographic image?" exclaimed Austin as he had not seen anything like it before, such realism, he thought.

Inside they found themselves in a lobby that advertised the five different programs that were showing.

Roger said, "They have a good sampling of different effects in all of them. I've seen them all, though the best is a remake of the movie 'The Double Helix'. It's a classic and the plot is a little too symbolic for me but the effects are truly the best." Roger explained and then asked, "What would you like to see?"

"Anyone but that one." Austin said and pointed to the title 'Cell Block 21', a prison movie.

"Okay, let's try 'The Double Helix'. I think the effects will impress you." Roger replied.

"Hey, the hologram at the entrance impressed me." Austin exclaimed.

Roger ordered the movie and they were lead to one of the two hundred theaters that were located in the building. Inside there were several chairs in the center of a black room. A lone spot light shown down on them. The attendant, a young man, removed the excess chairs so that there were only two remaining. He then positioned the remaining chairs in the center of the room.

"You must stay in your seat during the showing. Should you need to get up for any reason, please push the red button on the arm of the chair. To swivel the chair use the foot petals. I suggest you try them out before the feature begins so that you can maneuver them properly and get the most from the holographic experience. Any questions? Thank you for your patronage and enjoy the experience." The young man said and turn and left.

No sooner had the attendant left that Austin saw the shadows of various mechanical arms and projection equipment descend from the ceiling and rise from the floor. A slight mist was also introduced from vents in the floor. Music began to play softly then increased in volume. A young woman appeared to Austin's left and walked to a point where she was directly in front of the two men. She welcomed them and then began to explain the technology. She spoke of the effects and as she did fish swam by in midair through a blue ocean that melted into a landscape and then a train thundered down tracks that were directly in front of them. Austin watch as the train appeared again just behind them then trailed off into the horizon.

Instantly they were on a roller coaster and they looped and spun around. There chairs moved in concert with the motions of the coaster. Next they witnessed a gun fight between cowboys on the streets of Tombstone Arizona. The bullets tore into the loser and blood appeared to fly in the air toward them. Austin covered his face to protect it but of course there was no blood just spectacular three dimensional holographic effects.

The final image was a helicopter that appeared over a sand dune directly ahead. It hovered for a moment then fire a missile straight at them. The missile detonated. Sand and debris flew everywhere in front of them and then it was gone. The woman appeared again and continued to talk about other features and options that someone could choose. Austin heard little, he was thinking about Uncle Bob again. The helicopter, the missile, the carnage had triggered that memory once again. The movie began and he continued to dwell on his uncle's death even while the opening credits were being displayed. Then the first visual effect punched through his reflections and soon he became completely absorbed in the show.

On the train ride back to Harrisburg, Roger and Austin talked about the amazing special effects, but Austin's real passion awoke when Roger mentioned their lunch. Austin was still very full and had no interest in food though he was sure their mother would expect them to eat and of course they would comply. Roger brought up his trip to Lexington on Sunday and how he wished that Austin could come along with them. They would soon arrive in Harrisburg and take the walk through the late afternoon heat to their parent's home.

****

While Austin and Roger had been experiencing the Double Helix first hand, Philip was arriving in Chicago. The new train concourse was actually located in proximity to the O'Hare airport. The airport was still in use for international flights and for a very select few private charters, but much of it was now being modified to become the most modern train hub in the US. It represented the main interconnect for travel into Canada as well as being the point of origin of the Pan American line that would, within three years, connect Chicago and Buenos Aires, making it the longest train line in the world. For now it was still a work in progress and Philip negotiated the construction and walked for what he felt an extraordinary distance just to reach the local service that fed into the Chicago transit loop.

While Philip liked Chicago, he felt it was like being in one the largest little towns in the world, he was often confused by its transit system. He did not want to repeat his last visit when he had spent an hour riding on the wrong train. Philip searched throughout the concourse until he located an information kiosk. He inquired as the proper train and then instructed the directions to be loaded on his PCU. Acorn gave him verbal instructions which put him on the inner city shuttle. The wait was a short one but there were many people that were traveling into the center of the nation's fourth largest city. With every stop more and more people crammed themselves onto the train until Philip felt slightly claustrophobic.

Acorn instructed him to get off at the next stop and he pushed his way out through the crowded car and onto the platform, which itself was full of people. Holographic advertisements danced overhead. The air was an unpleasant mixture of different perfumes and the smell of electric motor's discharges. Philip finally emerged from the platform to the enclosed street above. The whole of downtown Chicago was environmentally controlled either under atrium or opaque covering. It was Impressive. Small three wheeled open taxis scurried about in special traffic lanes along with hundreds of PTUs like the ones he had seen in Philadelphia earlier.

The Royal Ambassador was only a four block walk and he jumped on a moving walkway and stood and looked at the stores, the people and floating holographic news displays, billboards and advertisements. Chicago was intensely alive with people moving at a fast pace going about their work or pleasure. What a contrast to Lancaster, he thought.

The city had changed a great deal in the past two years since Philip had last been there. It seemed to have come alive with activity that had been missing. It was curious that it would be that way, the country was still struggling. Unemployment was still at very high level. The new reforms had not yet manifested themselves and many efforts were bogged down with bureaucratic red tape from both parties in congress. The only people doing well were the ones that perpetually did well, the wealthy and powerful. What was happening here, Philip wondered as he approached the door to the hotel.

"Acorn say time." he instructed his PCU which recited dutifully, two forty three PM local time. At that point he decided that he was still a little early so he elected to go to the lobby and wait until three when he would call her.

Philip reached the door and it sprung open. "Good afternoon Mr. Lee, welcome to the Royal Ambassador." disembodied voice said. Philip did not particularly like this part of the technology, for the PCU betrayed his identity to anyone that wanted it.

The hotel was imposing. The large lobby had a cathedral ceiling that must have been one hundred feet from the floor to the intriguing mosaic design that covered it. There were four massive columns that stood equally placed that may well have been used for support as well as being ornamental. There were numerous little islands of chairs and sofas arranged throughout. Philip spotted one that was vacant and headed toward it.

"Philip." He heard his name called and turned. Jessica had seen him enter and waited for him to notice her. He had walked almost directly past her without registering that she was there. Philip could not restrain the smile. He walked to her but froze wondering if he should hug her, kiss her, offer her his hand or wait to see what she would do. He did not have to spend too much time thinking. Jessica came to him and hugged him and offered him her cheek to kiss. The greeting was warm and friendly. Philip was relieved that she appeared to be glad to see him.

"Jessica you look great. Have you been waiting long?" he asked.

"No only about five minutes or so, the session broke up a little early. How was the ride here?" she replied.

Philip told her about his day, leaving out the reason Austin had to go to Philadelphia. They talked and looked in to each other's eyes while standing in the center of one of the main paths to the registration desk. Finally after they noticed that people had been giving them disapproving looks, Jessica suggested that they sit down.

"I have my father's notes and journal in my room. I thought we could go over them a little later, unless you are pressed for time?" she asked.

Philip explained that he had planned on spending the rest of the day with her and that he had to catch the last train to Dayton which was at twelve fifty. He also added that he hoped that he was not being too presumptuous. Jessica smiled and said she was glad that they would have some time to get to know each other better.

They spent the next several hours talking about a wide variety of topics. Jessica was very interested in history thanks to her father's influence. She told Philip that she and her father were never very close because he was difficult to engage him in intimate conversation. His huge intellect was crippled by an inability to relate to people on a personal level. He was either unable or unwilling to drill down to the core and find that spark of commonality. Jessica spent most of her time speaking giving insight and clarity into what made Ms. Jenkins the transparent being to which Philip was drawn.

He on the other hand provided anecdotal and humorous stories that painted a comedic view of a quirky family. There was no depth, no real substance and tremendous omissions of feelings and truth that were furnished and gave little for Jessica to draw an accurate image. The family, but most specifically Austin, were portraits that were incompletely painted.

Dinner was finally suggested and they elected to wander the downtown area in search of a true Chicago dining experience. The search ended at a trendy seafood restaurant which Jessica ordered crab cakes and Philip ordered fresh oysters and Scallops Flambé. Both enjoyed the meal and while Philip was taken aback by Jessica reaching over and tasting his food, she could do nothing wrong in his eyes. It seemed the more time he spent with her, the more he wanted to spend time with her. He felt himself caught in a whirlpool of emotions in which he felt he had diminishing control.

After dinner they went to her room where they spent time reviewing her father's notes. Jessica had explained that Philip was free to take the material with him since they were copies but she felt it important to explain her father's index, referencing and his extremely cryptic shorthand. As they rode the elevator Philip gently grasped her hand and she responded with a soft squeeze. They stood there quietly waiting to the door to open.

When the door opened two young children, a boy and his younger sister quickly entered. They were carrying an ice bucket and were excitedly talking about their adventure to retrieve the ice for their parents. The elevator door closed and they ascended one floor and the two adventurers ran quickly out of sight. Four floors later the doors opened again and this time Philip and Jessica exited.

When Jessica opened the door the lights automatically illuminated several sections of the room. The room was a typical hotel room with the bathroom located to the right as you entered the room. Across from it was a dressing area which included a chest of drawers, a clothing rack and large mirror with a counter top where one could put cosmetics or other personal items. There was a short hallway that lead to a good sized room which had a table and chairs located in front of a full length window and on the opposite wall there was a bed.

The decor was tasteful and carpet thick and plush. The room was not too special but it was very comfortable. Jessica walked to the table and held up a folder. Philip joined her and they sat facing one another.

"See this section here? That was my father's idea of an index. You will need to understand his abbreviation scheme before you can find where the information you are seeking is located." Philip studied the pages, she was right this was very difficult to follow, he thought. Jessica then produced several pages of abbreviations and their meanings. The key was an integral part of the understanding anything that was written. The referencing of various supporting text was also somewhat difficult to follow and again Jessica produced another key which enabled the reader to decipher the references and apply the references in the appropriate places.

Philip wondered why the mystery, why had Jenkins gone to so much trouble to confound the reader of an obscure theory about a war on which volumes upon volumes had been already been written?

"Jessica did you father always make it so difficult to understand his research?" he asked.

"No, I keep thinking that there is more here than I have been able to uncover." Jessica replied.

Philip went through the first few pages, flipping between the two keys to so that he could discern what was being set forth. The premise was clear, Gettysburg, in the author's opinion, represented a pivotal point in time for the world. The paper stated that the theory would illustrate that there had been only ten or fewer such type of events in modern times. The paper than began the process of defining what constituted such a significant event. Jenkins call this type of event an 'Epiphanal Startling'. Jenkins stated that such an event would have to have global implications and would have to have significant probability of resulting in what he called a 'reversal', if the outcome of the event had been different. "What did he mean by reversal?" Philip pondered out loud.

Philip looked up from the pages asked Jessica, "Did you finishing reading all of this?" he asked. There had to be at least five hundred pages that represented the main body of text.

"No I only made it through page thirty five. I felt at that point I had a good idea of what he was thinking." she replied.

"He was a brilliant historian but I'm perplexed by this, there had to be something more than the face value indicates. This will take some time to comprehend." he added.

"I suspected it would." Jessica said and reached over and touched Philip's hand. Philip sat back in his chair and smiled at her.

"I think it would be best if I saved this for a time when I can concentrate more fully on it. But there is one point that I think needs some further attention now." he said returning his attention to the paper.

"Your father's definition of his invented term "Epiphanal Startling". It doesn't seem to add up to what the word epiphany represents in either a denotative or connotative framework." he said as puzzled over the two paragraphs under which Jenkins had set forth is hypothesis.

"My father had a flare for the dramatic at times and I took this use of terminology as just one of those occasions. He was using hyperbole, equating a man contrived event and giving it deistic implications." Jessica replied.

"I think there is more than that, I think there is something that is missing and is meant to be discovered. He claimed that the sheer discovery of the event was the epiphany and the startling was the dramatic results of the change of direction and how it would affect all that were involved, and that meant all of mankind. Wait a minute. He was stating that he believes that this could be done. That there are means to be able to affect this startling and such change life and that we would move from one time thread to another. It is interesting how he chose the word 'thread' as opposed to the once popular word 'stream'..." Philip said his voice trailing off while he maintained his concentration on the words in front of him.

Jessica smiled back and then looked down at the floor. She was concerned that Philip would attempt to move their relationship into an area she knew it should not go. Philip was here to help her validate her father's work and to solve the mysterious code that she had uncovered. He was one of a very few people that had the depth of understanding necessary to accomplish this. She had to keep him interested but not distracted by her romantically.

Philip emerged from deep thought and found himself beginning to play a fantasy in his head. He pictured himself standing up and pulling her from her chair toward him and Jessica falling into his arms and they embraced while their lips found each other. Philip's pulse quickened as he envisioned their passions exploding. Then he remember his vow to remain chaste until he married. He took that recollection as a sign for him to re-immerse himself in the project at hand, he needed to do this since his livelihood depended upon publishing.

Jessica continued to think about Philip and what he could do for her. He was an attractive man and he had a very charming personality. He was also very intelligent and that was the truly dangerous part. If she let herself start to see him that way she might find herself wanting what she felt and knew he wanted. What do I do if I get more involved? Will I be able to keep to my mission, she wondered to herself.

Philip did his best to pull himself back to the here and now and looking at Jessica again said, "I have to tell you, I am attracted to you."

"Yes I know." she said with a coy smile. They spent the next several hours talking and hold hands. During that time Philip would occasionally thought about kissing her but since she had not responded quite as he had anticipated to what he had hope he did not act on this thoughts. Philip wondered how she felt about him. She was warm and kind in her response but there was no demonstration of how she felt, not like she had been when she candidly shared about her family life and other feelings and thoughts she had revealed.

The time passed very quickly and it was soon time for him to leave. Philip gathered the papers together and put them in a large envelope. He wished at that point he had brought his briefcase. Jessica was sleepily watching him collect himself to leave. She wondered to herself why he hadn't he married or wasn't engaged. He was quite a good looking man, intelligent and he had a very respectable position. Then she instructed herself thinking 'Don't do this, you've been keeping things straight so far. Don't get confused'.

Philip had noticed that one of Jessica's shoes laces were undone. He bent down and got on one knee to tie her shoe. She watch him as he did, a lock of his dark brown hair dangling down covering one of his eyes while he intently tied her shoe. Then she sighed, if he keeps this up, I'm going to be in real trouble, she thought and when Philip stood up she stood as well. She smiled again, then raised up on her toes and quickly kissed him on the lips.

"You should leave. Call me tomorrow. Okay?" she said.

Philip came back to reality as he stepped onto the train headed for O'Hare. She does like me, a theme that kept playing repeatedly in his head. It took him until he was seated on the train to Dayton to begin thinking about the research in his possession. As the train doors closed he took out a few pages along with the keys and began to read. Blast she was beautiful, he thought.

Chapter Four

John Devers spun around in his chair and looked out of the full length windows of his one hundred and first floor office at World Banco One Internationale headquarters building in New York City. The haze clouded much of what would be a breath taking view yet one still had the feeling that one was suspended in midair, high above all those other insignificant beings and that made Devers smile. Devers was probably the sixth most powerful man at WBOI (White Boy as he privately called it) which placed him somewhere in the top twenty of the most powerful men in the world.

"You have an incoming call from Robert Nagatu do you wish to accept?" his PCU alerted him. Nagatu was in the Surveillance Division and had been assigned to follow Austin Lee.

"Rasputin, Yes. Well?" he asked Nagatu.

"Sir nothing has come of our surveillance as of yet. He has not made contact with Welsh, at least as far as we have been able to tell." Nagatu reported.

"Look Nagatu, we let Lee out of prison to lead us to Welsh. Welsh is a very dangerous man and has to be stopped at all costs. Do you understand?" Devers barked.

"Yes sir." he replied.

"Get it done quickly and there's a promotion in it for you. Otherwise it's back to the Congo for you - clear?" Devers threatened.

"Yes sir." Nagatu replied.

Devers instructed his PCU to end the call by saying, "Rasputin end call." Another incompetent idiot, he thought.

"Lewis!" he yelled. Samantha Lewis a short woman in her mid-thirties opened the door just enough to poke her head through. "Get in here." he ordered. Sam reluctantly opened the door and entered the office silently closing the door behind her. "I need the entire Philadelphia security team mobilized. Get me the director on conference along with Millings in DC. This has to happen now!" he said.

"Sir, it is Sunday and there are not many working today." Sam replied.

"Find them all- call them at home. Just do it!" he instructed.

"Yes Sir." she said.

Devers watched her leave. If she would just lose a pound or ten she could be worth pursuing, he thought.

"Rasputin call Fortesque." he had his PCU place the call to the vice chairman.

"Devers nice to hear from you old man." Fortesque said.

"Lionel, I think we may have acted rashly when we let Lee out of prison before we had the complete surveillance team in place." Devers said.

"We count on you to execute your assignment and trust you will handle these matters. Aren't your people up to the task?" Fortesque asked.

"We have traditionally worked in a defensive posture. Defend the bank at all costs and by whatever means, but this is a proactive operations and we are a little outside of my people's training and mind set." Devers explained.

"What do you suggest?" Fortesque inquired.

"We can subcontract the mission while we build up the capability. I think that is a capability that we will find useful in the future." Devers said.

"Who do you have in mind?" Fortesque asked.

"Either the FBI or the CIA, though I like the CIA's methods better and the FBI has had the problem before and fumbled it." Devers replied.

"Do it. Just let me know how much it will cost and when we can expect your team to be up to the level of competence to complete such a mission." Fortesque instructed.

"Nine months, tops." Devers informed him.

"I do hope this problem is ancient history by then or we may both be looking for other things to do with ourselves." Fortesque stated directly.

"It is top priority. We will have them both in custody or..." Devers said in an attempt to reassure the Vice Chairman.

"I don't need to know any more." Fortesque interrupted.

"Whatever the methods you utilized are your responsibility and at your discretion. Don't involve me. I am not requesting any more from you than for you to solve the problem. Understood John? I am so glad we had this chat I will let the others know your plans and will expect a report weekly and to updated immediately should things change in either direction." Fortesque said not expecting anything reply accept Devers agreement who responded automatically with a 'yes'.

"Good bye old boy." Fortesque said.

"Good bye Lionel." Devers replied.

Devers stood and stretched. "Lewis!" he bellowed once again. Samantha again opened the door. "Come in and sit down. I have a lot of things I need to get done. First, have you been able to set up the conference call yet?" he asked.

"Millings is on stand-by and we are tracking down the Philly director, Morrison and should know something in about fifteen minutes." she responded.

"Good. You must get me the name of the best, and I mean the best, contact we have at the CIA, their full dossier and then set up a meeting here for some time today. The sooner the better. Finally, do we have a contact in HA?" he then asked.

"I'm not sure sir. I am not even sure where I could find out that information." she answered.

Devers looked at her sternly with that 'what good are you?' kind of expression on his face. "Come on think." he implored.

Samantha squirmed in her seat and she crossed and uncrossed her leg while trying to think of who would know someone that was a gang member, especially that gang, Hell's Assassins.

"Okay try Yu. Wake him up, it's almost four out there any way. He has to be good for something. Get moving!" he said and turned his back.

"You have an incoming call from Charles Smith do wish to accept the call?" his PCU announce.

He replied, "Rasputin, Yes. What?"

"Mr. Devers sir. There is an attempt to hack into the Geneva Central System, we have traced the attempt to a four block area in Denver Colorado." Smith said.

"And?" Devers asked.

"We need your authorization to pursue or wait until we can pin down the location more specifically." Smith stated.

"Go get them now. Rasputin disconnect." Devers said. What a fool, Devers thought. That was a routine hack. They must have twenty of them each and every day. "Lewis!" he yelled again and again Sam peered into the office. "Who does that moron Smith work for?" he asked.

"Alphonso Leopold." she answered.

"Get him in here ASAP." he snapped.

"Anything else Sir?" she asked.

"No." Devers said abruptly.

"Sir, the conference call is available when you are." she said and replied.

"Connect me."

Devers heard the stuttered tone indicating that the conference was in progress. "Okay gentlemen what did Mr. Lee do during the past fifty hours of his freedom?" he asked without announcing his presences on the call. Millings told him of the satellite tracking and that nothing was observed that was of a suspicious nature. Greg Morrison told him of the detailed surveillance and when he spoke of the woman he met at City Hall and at that point Devers interrupted saying, "What woman? Did you follow her?"

"No, we were unable to do so. She arrived in a red sports car and walked up to him. They had a two minute conversation and she kissed his cheek and left." Morrison reported.

"Then she just drove off?" Devers asked the irritation being reflected in his abrupt tone.

"No, she wasn't driving." Morrison replied.

"Who was then?" he asked as the anger began to show dramatically in his voice.

"We couldn't tell from our vantage point." Morrison said.

"Great, what spectacular incompetence! Then what happened?" Devers asked impatiently.

Morrison talked about the rest of the visit and the phone call to his brother delaying the meeting. He then mentioned Mario's Butcher Shop.

"How long did you say he was in there?" Devers asked.

"About thirty five minutes." Morrison answered.

"What did he buy?" Devers asked.

"Nothing." Morrison answered sheepishly.

"Morrison didn't your people think that was odd? Did anyone think to go inside?" Devers asked.

"We thought it would compromise our surveillance." Morrison answered defensively.

"How about after he left, did you go inside and talk to anyone?" Devers asked.

"Uh, no sir."

"Morrison, you are done. Clean out your desk tomorrow and report to human resources for reassignment. That is of course if anyone will have you." Devers said.

"But sir." Morrison said trying to appeal his termination.

"Get off this call now." Devers said and then Morrison was gone and so was his career of twenty two years.

"Millings do you have anyone that you could recommend for the Philadelphia team position?" Devers asked.

"Foster, she's bright and energetic and is not afraid to take the initiative." he replied.

"Get her to Philadelphia today and get this surveillance up to the level at which it needs to be functioning. Start at the butcher shop and also see if there is any video that may enable us to get an ID on the car and driver. Got it?" Devers asked.

"Yes sir." Millings answered.

"I expect a full report tomorrow before six PM from both of you. Go." Devers ordered.

"Yes..." Millings replied as Devers ended the conference call abruptly.

"Lewis." he called.

Samantha came to the door, pushed it open and this time she walked in carrying a tray of food and a bottle of cold water saying, "Mr. Devers your lunch arrived. Also, CIA contact Juanita Fuentes will be in your office in about three hours and I found a contact for you that used to be a member of HA. He will be calling you soon."

"Finally some good news." said Devers as he watched Lewis unload the tray of food.

"Lewis, enjoy the rest of the day. Thanks for the quick results." he continued.

"Are you certain sir?" she asked as she looked up only to catch him looking her over. That made her skin crawl as it did every other time she had caught him doing it.

"Yes, go before I change my mind. See you tomorrow." he replied.

"Yes sir." she and quickly exited the room, grabbed her things and was at the elevator before Devers had time to taste his food.

"You have a call from an unknown caller do you wish to report the call to the authorities?" his PCU alerted him, and he replied, "Rasputin, Yes, no wait, accept call... Yes?"

"You Devers?" man asked.

"Yes." he replied.

"You wanted to talk to one of the brothers?" the man inquired.

"Yes." Devers answered.

"Bout what Devers?" the man questioned.

"A little freelance work that might involves religious fanatics." Devers replied.

"I see and you think we'd be interested in this kind of work?" the man said.

"Yes one of the individuals is a good friend of Hector G's." Devers said.

"Oh that could be interesting but also very dangerous. What's he to you?" the man answered.

"He is someone that is a potential problem when it comes to my life's work." Devers said giving him as little information as possible.

"So what do you have in mind?" the man asked directly.

"A permanent vacation when the time is right." Devers stated plainly.

"I see, let me check with my friends and see how they feel about this. Work like this is very expensive." the man said.

"Yes I know it will be, if you are interested let me know how much you want I will see what I can do accommodate you." Devers said.

"Be back to you soon Devers." the man concluded and the line disconnected. That went well Devers thought, now all we have to do is get Lee to lure Welsh out into the open and they will both be gone forever.

CIA operative Fuentes exited the elevator and found her way to the reception area which was manned by a large black man with what had to be a thirty inch neck. When he stood to take her to Devers she realized that, while she was almost six foot tall herself, this man was more than a foot taller than she. She followed behind the giant until they reached Devers' office door. The man gently tapped on the door.

"Yes." Devers' voice came bellowing from inside.

"Mr. Devers, Ms. Fuentes is here to see you." man said quietly.

"Come in." Devers said and with that the door opened and the man motioned for her to enter, then he closed the door behind her.

"Ms. Fuentes thank you for coming on such short notice." Devers said cordially.

"Ms. Lewis indicated that it was an urgent matter and since you are the head of international security Mr. Devers I thought it would be important to accommodate your request." Juanita replied.

Devers looked at her. He was trying to study her quickly to determine whether he would be able to trust her and then if he could dominate her or worst case manipulate her. He could not read anything, her expression was one of relaxed confidence. She was probably in her late thirties or early forties he thought. A rather plain appearance but she was not to be underestimated, her eyes told him so.

"As you may know we have been attempting to bring to justice a known terrorist, Justin Welsh for the past six years. And he has proved to be extremely elusive." he said then Devers paused and waited for some reaction or acknowledgment, but none was forthcoming. "Recently we allowed one of his accomplices to be paroled from prison so that we could revitalize the pursuit and bring him to justice."

"Has he left the country?" Juanita asked.

"No, not that we are aware of. In fact we think he is living somewhere in the mid-Atlantic region." he replied.

"This sounds as though the FBI would be your best ally in this operation." she said knowing where Devers was headed and wanting him to get to the point.

"They have had the case for six years and have not made any progress. For example Welsh was spotted in Philadelphia yesterday." Devers told her stretching the truth. He continued, "We have reasons to believe that he has developed an affiliation of some kind with a gang that I am certain is on your watch list, the Monks." Devers saw the first sign of a reaction.

"I can see how this can possibly have international implications." she admitted.

"Yes, quite. The Monks are said to be in Chile right now in an effort to take over the banking system in that country. A move that could thwart Chile's adaptation of the IMC. This appears to all be related." Devers explained.

"That rumor had no real foundation or evidence to support it." she countered.

"What kind of evidence would be compelling?" Devers asked as he believed that he had found his opening. Devers knew that the agency was not really interested in working within the US borders but there were many times in the past fifty years when they had. The pursuit of terrorist was the catalyst that had always initiated that action. Devers knew it, he wanted her to state it therefore agreeing to possible involvement. He had an ace he wasn't showing.

She knew that she must be careful, this was a very powerful and dangerous man. "If the Monks were involved in Chile and there was evidence linking Mr. Welsh not only to the Monks but to that action, then I think that the matter would warrant our attention." she said carefully choosing her word.

"Does there have to be direct linkage or can it be indirect?" Devers asked.

"Show me what you have and we'll see if it reaches to a level where we can justify our involvement." she said skeptically.

Devers studied her face. There was no indication whether he could trust her or whether she could be intimidated, though it did not tell him that he couldn't.

"I have evidence linking Welsh to the Monks, Welsh has a history of working against the Bank's efforts to install the IMC globally. These photos will show the Monks involvement in Chile. Do you see the man on the left?" Devers asked as he pushed the photo screen toward Fuentes.

"That is Julian Martinez, the number three man in the Monks New York Chapter. In the next image you will see him with Simone Chevez the vice chairman of the Chilean Ruling Cabinet and the next one he is seen with Mr. Welsh."

Fuentes looked at the photos carefully, she had seen them all before. Each one of them a carefully constructed fake and up until now she had not known the source or at least who she now believed to be the source. The next move she made could be a very dangerous one. She had to weigh her options carefully and be prepared for the consequences. She had one that would give her the best chance and that was to take the matter under advisement, bump it upstairs so to speak, she thought and then said, "Mr. Devers this could be in line with what we have been speaking about. May I have these to show my superiors?"

Devers sensed her suspicions but he couldn't back down at this point. "I thought that you had the authority to help me, if not put me in contact with the one that does." he demanded as he snatched back the screen and rolled it up quickly and then shoved it into its tube. The play did not work. Fuentes was the decision maker, they both knew it but she couldn't be bullied and she was apparently too intelligent to be trapped into acting.

"As you wish Mr. Devers. We will be in touch if we have further interest." she said and was on her feet quickly, extending her hand. Devers looked at her, stood slowly and shook her hand briefly.

"I assume that if I come across any other information you would be interested in seeing it?" he asked.

"Yes, but of course Mr. Devers. We are anxious to thwart any and all real terrorist threats to our country and its citizens." she replied.

"Of course." he said in response.

"Have a pleasant day, good bye." she said with a smile.

Devers watched Fuentes leave and no sooner had the door closed when he slammed his hand down on the desk. That women was going to be a problem. Not only won't she help but he now believed that she would start to investigate WBOI internationally and could unearth some very unpleasant details that wouldn't do the bank any good, he thought and then said, "Rasputin, call Girard – Girard."

Girard answered gruffly, "What dya want?"

"Devers here Girard, I need to see you as soon as possible." Devers exclaimed.

"Why?" Girard responded disinterestedly.

"A business matter. Someone needs to be removed from our equation." Devers elaborated.

"I see. When?" Girard asked.

"Soon- very soon." Devers implored. "I'll meet you tonight at the usual place." Girard agreed.

"Ten?" Devers asked.

"That's fine." Girard said and the call disconnected. Well that could be a mistake, Devers thought but he also knew he had time to sort it out. Worst case he could just not meet Girard or change the direction of the meeting to something other than killing people. Matt Girard also did some very good altered photos and forged documents, he was multi-talented.

****

Drew Morris was eating lunch with his youngest granddaughter. It was their first time out, just the two of them. Lillian Wantanabe was a precocious three year doing her best to act very grown up and she appeared to be older than her young age. She studied the menu intently and even though she could read some of the words, she relied heavily on the pictures to help her make her selection.

"I'll have that Gramps." she said as she pointed to the grilled cheese sandwich and soup.

"I think that looks great. If you don't mind I think I'll copy your choice. Okay?" he asked.

"Oh Gramps you can have whatever you want." she replied with a giggle.

Drew thought if she only knew how true that statement was. As president of WBOI only the Chairman and Vice Chairman were higher paid and more powerful. He owned roughly three percent of the company that was worth more than two trillion IMC. Still, he valued time with his family though it seemed that lately it was becoming more and more scarce. Things were supposed to be easier for the very rich he thought.

The server appeared and inquired as to whether they were ready to order.

"Go ahead Lillian, you order for both of us." he said with a smile.

"Okay Gramps. We will have this." she said and pointed to the picture of the sandwich and soup.

"What kind of soup do you want?" the server asked.

"That kind." she responded pointing again to the picture.

"Tomato?" they asked again.

"That kind." she said adamantly. Drew began to become irritated with the young woman.

"Bring us that kind!" he said emphatically.

"Uh, alright." the server agreed.

Drew responded with a terse, "Thank you."

"You have an urgent call from Devers do you wish to accept?"

"Tumbleweed, yes. What Devers?" he said quietly.

"Sir, we have a problem with the regional director of the CIA, she is not on board with the program." Devers informed him.

"And?" he replied.

"I have a meeting with Girard tonight on the Welsh matter and thought we could use a more suitable replacement." Devers explained and then went on to add, "We are seeking religious persecution."

"Extreme persecution?" Drew asked seeking confirmation of Devers intentions.

"Of course." Devers responded. Drew watched Lillian as she began to act her age by bouncing in her chair and fiddling with the silverware.

"I'll call you in an hour- no make it two. I have to think about the fallout. Tumbleweed disconnect." Drew smiled at Lillian, she was a pretty as her mother, he thought.

Soon the sandwiches and soup arrived. Vegetable soup and Lillian inspected it, nodded her head and ate with careless abandon. Drew Morris was an enigma. As kind and caring as he could be to those that he loved he could be completely and utterly ruthless to those who earned his wrath. His ire was quickly raised, his temper an instant boil as though his demeanor was at a constant simmer awaiting the slightest introduction of heat to have it roar to life.

Upon their departure he commented to the restaurant manager using a few well selected words regarding the prospects for long term employment of the server. Her position was severely in question from that point forward, though he never raised his voice he implied that the bank would not be inclined to continue to provide working capital to companies that did not meet the highest standards of customer service.

The Voltrun 190SC glided up to the curb and the doors opened as the car welcomed Drew by name. The spacious vehicle, valued at more than one million IMC, was just one more perk for a man that had anything he wanted, whenever he wanted it. "Home." he stated as he helped Lillian into her seat. The car sensed her weight and size immediately configuring the seat to accommodate the diminutive person

As the car pulled away from the curb all traffic stopped, because of its priority protocol. As the car moved through the congested thoroughfare everything in its path yielded to it. As a result the trip from Third Avenue to their home on the fringe of Central Park that would take a normal traveler fifteen to twenty minutes was accomplished in less than five.

Upon arrival the car stopped and before it opened its doors the seats rotated for easy exit. Morris was talking to Devers about the Welsh matter and gave him the authority to do whatever was necessary to effectively handle the situation. He watched his granddaughter bounce up and down trying to be patient but she wanted to go. She wanted to see her Mommy and play with her toys. Morris finally emerged from the car and instructed it park and after they both had exited it promptly took off for the garage that was located on the next block.

Lillian grabbed Gramps' hand and said, "Come on let's go Graaaaamps!"

"Okay little one." he replied.

As they walked hand in hand to the door of the building a series of transparent panels arose from the sidewalk forming a triangular passage that became filled with cool air. If you happened to be a pedestrian walking on the sidewalk at that moment you would be momentarily captured in the prism like structure, another perk for those wealthy enough to afford anything.

The Bush Tower had every conceivable amenity and its one hundred and forty one stories towered over all other building that overlooked Central Park. The security scanner read his image and the door opened and the 'Welcome Mr. Morris' message was played by the automated attendant. The express elevator at the far end of the hall opened and they walked to it. Upon entering the elevator doors closed and they automatically rose to the penthouse entrance, one hundred and forty stories above the street.

The doors opened and Lillian ran into the expanse of the penthouse. The one hundred and fortieth floor was one open room the size of the entire floor of the building. Its exterior walls were glass, a seamless wonder that made one think that the ceiling was levitating above you. In the center of the room was a spiral escalator that looked like the double helix of the DNA structure. Three small tubes extended upward through the floor and acting like a new age dumbwaiter system that allowed food that had been prepared in the kitchen one floor below to appear is if by magic.

The bathrooms were concealed in the floor and the six of them were scattered along the perimeter of the room. If one needed to use one you could simply stand on a specific spot indicated by a crescent moon insignia embedded in the floor. The panel hiding the entrance rose and you descended via escalator into a fairly large rectangular room. Once inside the panel closed and the occupant was able to privately fulfill your biological needs. No one could enter without using an override code that was unknown to everyone except the house steward Niles Bordon and the Morris family.

The large room had several areas where people could congregate. These were small islands where furniture was grouped together. The room could rapidly be transformed into a ballroom, a meeting room, large dining room or activity room. It could even become a tennis court should it be desired. Today the Morris's were entertaining their family though as he exited the elevator Drew noticed that there were two men dressed in business attire standing with their backs to him looking out the windows at the view. He recognized one of the men immediately, Sherwood DeMasters, Chairman of WBOI but the other man he was uncertain of his identity.

"Sherwood to what do I owe this pleasant surprise?" Drew greeted them with an extended hand and smile, all the while wondering why on a Sunday the Chairman would come to his home.

"Drew, good to see you. The view is spectacular. It makes me almost want to move back here." Sherwood said.

"It's the only reason I still live in New York. Has Gwen offered you something to drink? Perhaps a bit of lunch?" Drew said hospitably.

"No, we are fine. Drew, I don't think you have met Wa Li Chu. Chu here is in charge of real estate holdings, but I'm sure you already knew that." Sherwood said as he placed his hand Wa's shoulder.

"A pleasure." Morris said bowing first and then extending his hand.

Wa bowed but did not respond as far the hand shake was concerned, and said, "Mr. Morris, I am in New York for one reason."

"Come now Chu." DeMasters interrupted, "there are many reasons to come to New York." He then forced a laugh.

Wa did not share the moment of humor instead he continued by saying, "Our objective to control real estate holdings in South America is not being met, we are not where it was anticipated we would be at this time. Columbia, Chile, and Argentina are most problematic. Security, which is pivotal to our success has failed us."

"I see." Drew said looking at DeMasters who shrugged and smiled. "Let us sit down over here." Drew then said and gestured to a grouping of overstuffed chairs away from his family that was watching him from across the room. The trio moved to the seats and sat down. Wa, the shortest of the men, had an oval shaped face and with thin black hair that was combed straight back. His teeth were crooked but were brilliantly white and he kept his lips parted as he breathed. His eyes were obscured by tinted glasses (his PCU).

Drew summoned Bordon by saying, "Niles, please bring some water in a pitcher with glasses." Though Bordon was not within earshot he heard the call through his PCU which was set to monitor. Moments later Bordon appeared carrying a tray with the pitcher of water and three long stemmed glasses. "Mr. Wa the South American problems are only short term setbacks and most of them relate to Military Operations not security." Drew said.

"Chile?" Wa asked.

"What about Chile?" Drew responded as though he was not aware of any other issues regarding the currency conversion in Chile.

"We've heard that Justin Welsh is involved with a global gang of thugs, the Monks, and that they are intimidating the government officials and preventing our plans from being finalized. That falls under corporate security and is your Mr. Devers' role is it not?" Wa said angrily.

"Mr. Wa, I appreciate your passion, but there is no evidence to support that claim. I wish there were. We could then wipe the Monks off the planet without fear of repercussions." Drew responded.

"What repercussions?" Wa asked.

At that point DeMasters interrupted, his grandfatherly look gone from his face, and his brown eyes intently focused on Morris and said, "Drew are you up to this or do we have the wrong man living here?" He gestured with a wave of his right arm.

"We just can't act with impunity. I too want them gone. I want the same things everyone else does." Morris hissed through his teeth. Devers is working on this, the man's a bulldog. It will be done soon."

"Mr. Morris we cannot afford to lose momentum, Africa awaits us and there are also the challenges that remain in Europe and Asia." Wa said and the he stood up and continued by saying, "I know that the board has confidence in you. My mandate is to get this accomplished and return the maximum profit while gaining complete control. This comes from the highest authority, do you understand."

"Yes." Drew responded and thought to himself, 'Why does this man feel that he is the only one working to make money for this company? Doesn't he understand that he reports to me?'

"Drew is just as greedy as the rest of us. He'll get it done and quickly." Sherwood said and they all laughed nervously.

"We must be going. Give my best to Gwen."

The three men walked to the elevator which opened upon their approach. Wa bowed, turned and entered. DeMasters waved to Gwen who watch from across the room. He then took Drew's hand. "Tomorrow, eight AM in my office." he said quietly.

"Yes." Drew agreed. DeMasters stepped into the elevator, the doors closed and Morris felt the weight lift momentarily from his shoulders. He felt the impact of a short precocious three year old attach herself to his leg.

"Gramps come see what I did." she said smiling up at him. Gramps put the security problems neatly in a mental 'box' and joined his family smiling.

****

Philip awoke with a start. He had fallen asleep sitting in front of the stack of paper notes that represented Dr. Leopold Jenkins swan song, his final treatise. The progress had been very slow, arduous. He had managed to wade through the first fifteen pages. He understood why Jessica had given up at page thirty five, but he also knew that he had set a course that could not be undone, not if he wanted to keep his job or his new found friend. He started by pushing the papers together and gathering them into a somewhat organized stack.

He looked about the room. It seemed to be a waste to have paid for a room in Dayton when he was only going to use it for a couple of hours. He had arrived at one forty five AM and now it was almost four and he would have to be at the train station soon to catch the five thirty to Lexington Kentucky where he would meet his brother. Philip extended one leg and then the other. He worked them back and forth until they seemed to have regained their full allotment of circulation. Standing and stretching became the next hurdle which was over come in a few moments with a quick stagger to the bathroom. He then relied on a hot shower to revive him.

Roger would be arriving in about three hours. He had to meet him at the station and then they would make the half hour trip to see their grandfather, Old Harry. Standing in front of the mirror Philip studied his face. He was almost thirty five and felt as though his life was slipping away. Where had his life gone?

****

Harry Lee awoke to the repetitive yapping of his Boston terrier, Mugsy. He opened his left eye and peered at the clock that sat on a small smoking stand he used as bed side table. The digital display read '4:42 AM'. He let his left arm fall off the bed and felt the familiar licks of Mugsy encouraging him to get his one hundred and seven year old frame moving. The morning ritual was a challenge but he could not bear to think about not having his loyal friend to keep him company.

In a few minutes he was standing and several minutes later he was dressed and walking on the small strip of grass that was his enclosed yard outside of his apartment. He was fortunate to have access to actual grass that Mugsy could smell, feel between his toes and of course it was the perfect repository for poop.

The sun would be rising above the row of housing that sprawled to the east of Harry's apartment, he thought. When it did, as the first rays would strike the glass of the yard enclosure it would begin to tint automatically, saving his precious lawn from being scorched. Harry walked to the entrance of his apartment and sat down in his lawn chair that was positioned so that he could sit and watch Mugsy roam about his domain.

Joseph Harrington Lee knew the family secrets or at least everyone thought that he did. What was the reason for all the fuss about what happened more than one hundred years ago? The scandal wasn't about the Lees or the Leesops, it was about a marriage his grandfather entered into and John Leesop's failed attempts at elected office due to guilt by association. His wife, Harry's grandmother, also was an innocent victim, her only crime was that she had a father that committed an act of betrayal that played out in a very public and embarrassing way. He was a sex offender, a troubled man that collapsed under a weight of stress and feelings of entitlement. John Leesop had found out about his father-in-law's crime shortly after he met Adelaide, the love of his life.

Harry closed his eyes and pictured the day that his grandmother had told him about his great grandfather. He remembered the sadness in her eyes but he also saw something else, the love that she had for her father. His grandmother was a remarkable person, he thought. Her honesty was penetrating, her loyalty fierce for she defended those she loved with every ounce of her being.

Harry reached into his pocket and pulled out a small rectangular, metal case that measured about three inches long and an inch or so wide. He pushed on the clasp and it opened revealing its contents; two cigarettes and a very small cigarette lighter. It had been a gift to him by his grandmother, it had been her father's.

His gnarled fingers awkwardly manipulated the cigarette to the point of extraction from the case. Once the cigarette was secured between his lips he fumbled getting the lighter out and finally ignited the cigarette. He pulled hard and inhaled deeply. He had years of practice, decades, almost a century and he still enjoyed the sensation of the smoke going in and then being expelled in a slow and steady stream of white that drifted and slowly disbursed around him.

Tobacco use had been illegal in the United States for approximately fifty years, yet cigarettes and other tobacco products could still be manufactured and supplied around the world. These probably had come from Iceland at the cost of more the two IMC each. The healthcare system caused the ban and if Harry were to be caught with just one he would lose his healthcare benefits and at his age that could be a very painful loss.

Mugsy rolled on the grass as Harry watched his loyal companion repeat the routine he had observed him do for the past seven years. This was the fourth Boston terrier with which he had shared his home. Maggie would have loved Mugsy he thought, she loved dogs and as he continued to stare a small tear formed in his left eye.

Why are the grand kids coming now? They haven't been to see him in more than five years, he thought. Harry felt his fingers getting warmer as the cigarette burned. He placed it between his lips and drew its last contribution to his eventual demise. He cough as he exhaled. It would be nice to see his daughter, but she really didn't want to have too much to do with her father instead he had to settle for his son's children, the boys.

****

Philip had the smell of Jessica's perfume lingering in his nostrils. He took his seat on the train and felt an uncharacteristic lurch as the Baldwin 880 high speed shuttle came to life and ascended the bed to its run some one hundred feet above the ground. They were only used in areas where the water table was too high or the ground too unstable but the most enjoyable part about riding the 880 was the view. The cylindrical bullet passenger compartment was predominately transparent, its propulsion mounted on two arms that extended away from the passenger compartment which was suspended at a forty five degree angle below these magnetic propulsion units that ran along the two 'tracks'. These arms extended upward like the wings of a bird. Philip felt that the trip was like that of an amusement park ride.

The train reached a top speed of only about two hundred fifty miles per hour, not intercontinental speeds but fast enough to make it from Dayton to Lexington in about forty minutes. Philip would see the sun coming up in about thirty minutes and that would make the trip worth while for him.

Seeing his grandfather was not something that he had looked forward to doing since the time when he had reached his teens. Harry always smelled bad, his house was perpetually in disarray but most of all Philip felt that Harry did not like him. He felt that Harry disliked everyone in his family except his sister, though she didn't appear to like him very much. This visit was a courtesy for his brother Roger's sake. He asked himself what Harry could have to say that was so important that was not known by someone more pleasant to deal with in the family. It always seemed that secrets were guarded by the least friendly and ill-tempered watch dogs, he mused.   Perhaps the reason the secrets resided with these trustees was that they really had no one interested in what they had to say or wished to be in their company.

The 880 was running at full speed and unlike the other Baldwin Maglevs, the passengers truly had a sense of motion. Philip felt the train bank, as though it were a low flying airplane and a slight tug of g-force pushed his body to the right. He glanced out of the enclosure into the blackness where he could see the scattered lights of houses and commercial buildings. His thoughts refused to land on anything specific, they bounced like a rubber ball gaining momentum down a thought path and then quickly losing that thought as his mind collided with another subject. He went from Harry smelling bad, to thinking about how he hated the smell of broccoli cooking and then quickly he thought about vintage cooking television shows he seen when he was a child.

****

Harry knew that the boys were coming in the morning and if things ran to true to form that they would be on their way home or to where ever by noon. He already was planning what he would have to eat after they left and visualized how much he would enjoy his cigarette soon after eating.   He then thought that perhaps he should get some value or enjoyment from their visit instead of rushing past it like so many things he had done in his life. But he was not able to bring that thought to reality, there were so many things that just didn't seem to be important or interesting.   Why should he have to be bothered?   These family obligations, he thought, were thinly veiled guilt experiences that one felt a sense of true a relief when they were over.

Well, at least Mugsy enjoyed company, he thought. It was good for him, but he doesn't realize how difficult it is to be in the company of those people. Such pretension, they are self-absorbed egotists with no time or concern for others' feelings.

****

Roger's eyes popped open and he wondered what time it was. He had to meet Philip in Lexington at seven AM. If he was late, he would never hear the end of it, he thought. Why did Philip always have to do things so early in the morning? At that point all he thought about was how he would deal with his girlfriend, Gloria. She was upset that he was going and there was a good chance that she would not be living there when he got home. Who would have a relationship with him anyway? For that matter who would have a relationship with any of them, Austin included? Well maybe especially Austin, he thought. The youngest of the brothers crawled out of bed. He saw the dimly lit clock across the darken room. It read five thirty two. It was time for him to really get moving or he would be late.

****

He was Harry Lee and they used to call him 'Light Horse' after George Washington's friend, but then there was Margaret who would with a look and a sneer call him 'Light Weight' on the way to Miss Spear's ninth grade English class. A woman can have so much power over men or boys, he thought. That's probably why his great grandfather had lost his way. Though he had always been told that it was because he had drifted away from the plan for his life. When we know that there is a plan for our lives it makes us seem to be important or valuable and not we just a random collection of atoms struggling to exist in a small fish bowl surrounded an infinitely immense universe, he mused.

Mugsy barked to get his master's attention. Harry reacted by putting his hand on his rounded head. This was a 'Pavlovian' response to years of conditioning; the dog had him trained. Harry studied the horizon, he could see nothing but the roof line of rows upon rows of trapezoidal containers where thousands of people were making their best attempts to live out their lives.

"If mankind could only recognize how unimportant most activities are." Harry said out loud. What passes for amusement and diversion at one time can be socially important and over time gradually becoming modified into something that carries greater significance, even getting to the place where it is the cornerstone of people's lives. It could be sports, it could be religion, and it might even become other people. Where does meaning, true meaning come into play?

****

Philip read Jenkins' hypothesis several times. It was difficult to completely understand. It put forth premise that there were moments in time when all things going forward from that point had the potential to be literally one hundred and eighty degrees dissimilar from the current existence and should a change occur at that point in time the process that time measures, life would take a clearly disparate path or thread. This, simply put, meant that existence, fundamentally speaking, would be moved in the opposite direction.   The analysis of the variables lead Jenkins to define each of these moments in time as an 'Epiphanal Startling', where the fabric of time literally could be changed dramatically. The subsequent theory that altering the variables at such a point would either render the moment as inconsequential or cataclysmal in that the initial time line was destroyed and a new one would take its place.

The battle of Gettysburg, July first, 1863 was determined by Jenkins to be such a point in time. He stated that it was a time in past history that if four variables were altered or destroyed, the time line we currently find ourselves playing out at present would be replaced. This was the process that he seemed be describing and that it was completely viable.   He seemed to be espousing that it was time to throw our current reality onto the proverbial rubbish heap.

Philip shook his head and thought to himself, giving him the opportunity to take a moment and reflect on this. Was Jessica's father on to something? If so, there could be significantly more to life than random events and chance. The convergence that he outlined showed at least one hundred paths that mankind could have traveled that would have changed the world events for hundreds if not thousands of years.

Jessica's image crept into Philip's thoughts once again. It was tough enough to concentrate on work without her soft scent of coco butter that lingered on his hands, its oily film resistant to anything but a very rigorous scrubbing. The fact was he saw her riveting eyes, those brown eyes with blue flecks that sparkled, in everyone. They were windows into such a prismatic soul that was complex yet mysteriously inviting. She had a smile that could slay dragons, a laugh that resonated like a choir that was serenading, he thought. This was so pleasant and yet so excruciating.

There were times when he knew that she cared for him, that she looked at him and wanted him almost the way he yearned for her and then there were those times when couldn't get the emotional validation he needed. He wondered whether she had masked her feelings or was it just his personal issues that manifested themselves like a tenuous branch that he found himself balancing upon. One that swayed or sighed under the psychological baggage he lugged about through every day. Paranoia, whether it was an acute awareness of potential threat or the dark view of all that surrounds oneself, does little to endear us to others. Perhaps that's why she was not involved more, Philip pondered. The sunlight burst forth in a streaming arch as the train banked into its final turn before coming to rest at its destination. Will my brother be on time, he wondered.

****

"Come on Mugsy, let's go old boy- let's get some breakfast." Harry said as pushed himself out of the chair and straighten himself. This will all be over soon he thought, then he would go back to important stuff like taking a nap and having a cigarette, and he smiled as he thought about those things.

In the kitchen Harry felt very much at home. He enjoyed cooking, it had always been a soothing activity that help to melt the day's stress away. He knew that when he was done there was a reward, he could eat what he made and it usually tasted good. It always amazed him how he could grab some seemly disparate ingredients and mix them together into a symphony of flavor. This was always simple fare but it was usually surprisingly pleasing to the palate and the eye.

Harry worked busily getting his breakfast together quickly. He wasn't certain at what time his guests would arrive and he wanted to be certain he had his breakfast done, he wasn't going to feed them. They might linger and take more of his day in whatever nonsense they had on their agenda. While Harry busily worked, Mugsy sat patiently awaiting his breakfast. He knew Harry would feed him and that he would be first to eat, sometimes by accident if Harry dropped food during preparation, but still his bowl would be filled before Harry sat down to eat.

Soon the two companions were silently enjoying their food. It appeared that they were in some sort of race to see who would finish first. Harry's table manners were not much better than the dogs. When they both finished Mugsy licked his bowl clean while Harry took his finger and dragged it across the plate making certain that he got the very last bit of food. "Time to do the dishes old boy." he said as he looked down at the dog.

****

When Philip felt the train stop at the platform he was jolted back to the task at hand. He once again wondered whether Roger would be there and if not when he would arrive. As he exited the train his question was answered. Roger stood on the platform scanning the departing passengers to find his brother. He looked like he hadn't slept in a week, thought Philip.

"Roger, over here!" he called out while raising his hand so that Roger would see the motion and therefore see him.

"Hi Phil, how was your train ride?" he asked extending his hand.

"It was fun, the 880 is an entertaining ride. Have you ever had the chance to ride one?" Philip replied.

"No, I am not as enthusiastic about trains as you are, to me they are a means to get from point A to point B. I am just happy when there are no issues, delays and that I don't have some obnoxious child disturbing me." Roger said reminding his brother of his feeling.

"So how was your ride?" Philip asked.

"Uneventful, perfect, though I can't say that I was happy about what I thought about during the ride." Roger answered.

"Well, let's get this over with. I rented a car I think we can get there using one of those." Roger said as he pointed at a small electric cart that was parked beneath a small kiosk that was magnetically suspended above it. Roger approached it and announced his intentions. The cart acknowledged his request and the two men took a seat facing each other. The small electric cart took off accelerating quickly and maneuvering through the maze of pedestrians that walked or stood on the moving sidewalks.

"We could have walked I guess, but this terminal is very confusing and I couldn't actually remember where I left the car." Roger explained breaking the silence.

The cart came to rest directly in front of the rental. It was a Voltrun 90 exactly like the one that Philip had rented. They entered and the vehicle took off for their destination. Roger and Philip sat silently for several minutes.

Roger wanted to talk about the upcoming visit but wasn't quite sure how to broach the subject. Philip was the first to speak saying, "How do you think we will find Old Harry anyway?"

"I am not sure. I can't even remember the last time I saw him. It must be at least ten years." Roger replied.

"I saw him about seven years ago at Uncle Bob's memorial service. He seemed to be not all there, not too coherent and he definitely did not act friendly towards anyone except Aunt Jayden. Dad told me that he always favored her above everyone else." Philip replied.

"What do you think we are going to find out today? What dark secrets does this man possess?" Roger asked.

"I am not sure we will find out anything. He is such an uncooperative person. Not very easy to talk to, though there was a time when I thought he liked me and I know I certainly liked him- he is partly the reason that I love history the way that I do." Philip stated.

"When did his feeling change?" Roger asked.

"I am not really certain. I started to notice it after Dad and Uncle Bob had the falling out. I don't know if you remember, we were at a wedding and Uncle Bob said some things to Dad that he didn't like and they started yelling at one another. I think it had to do with Dad's job at the time. He was working for the government on some secret project. This all took place when I was fourteen so that would make it 2092 about fourteen years before Uncle Bob died." Philip said.

Roger did not reply. He tried to remember the event but he was only ten years old at the time. All he knew was that he did not see his uncle very much as he was growing up. Austin, and to a lesser extent Philip, raved about him. They portrayed him as god like. He thought that it must have been a contributing factor to the distancing that occurred between him and his father, a sort of jealousy. Roger on the other hand had always been loyal to his dad. There was nothing that his father could do that was wrong. That was until he admitted that there were secrets that had been withheld from him, big secrets. It made him angry that he was not included, that he had not thought enough of him to tell him that his last name was originally not really Lee.

Not being who he thought he always was, now that was something that will take some time getting used to, he thought. He realized that it would take time before he would be able to forgive his father, but he also recognized that it would happen. He felt that he could take comfort in knowing that he was not the only family member that was unaware of the fact that Lee was not originally their name. If Philip had known, or worse yet Austin, then he would really have cause to hold a grudge for a very long time, he felt.

Roger was shaking his head involuntarily while he thought these things and Philip took notice. "What's wrong?" he asked.

"I am just confused about why Dad hadn't told use earlier about this Leesop matter. How could he keep that from us for so long?" Roger said expressing his confusion and frustration.

Philip took a moment and thought of how to best answer a question for he was pondering the answer to that very same question. He finally responded by saying, "I think he must have been embarrassed or ashamed. Besides, you don't know when Dad found out. It could have been recently. There could also be other reasons that we aren't aware exist, things that we can't even imagine." Philip realized that his last comment was a little farfetched but he was trying to mend the fences between his father, the enigma, and his brother, the man that worshiped his father's image, one that was apparently not an accurate picture of the man he was.

Roger did not react to his brother's comments. He continued to focus on the fact that his father owed him honesty. His father had always expected it from him. Why should it be any different when it came to a father's relationship with his son? He considered the fact that his father might be protecting him and that reason might enable him to move past what he believed to be a betrayal.

He looked out the window and saw the row upon row of housing units on each side of the street. He felt like they were passing through an endless canyon of trapezoidal shapes. Their earth tone pigment was designed to give them a feel of being one with the surroundings but it mostly conveyed a feel of sameness; uniformity that offered the dweller little or no hope of individuality.

The Voltrun slowed as it approached the destination. Philip turned to Roger and said, "You know, it's not too late to turn around." Roger looked at him and smiled. This was something that had been said many times by their father when they approached a destination that they were dreading. The car pulled up in front of the building and the doors opened. It was around eight and the heat of the day was already starting to build.

Both men exited the vehicle and walked the short concrete walkway to a door that opened as they approached. They were met with cool air that had medicinal odor, something that was not unpleasant but certainly not a natural aroma. The smell was a tell-tale signature of the presence of the medical facility that was located on the first floor below the six living units that it supported.

Philip and Roger proceeded to the escalator that was directly ahead of them. It was a long ride to the second level which was almost forty feet above the ground floor. At the top of the escalator there was a door facing them across the corridor which stretched out in both directions. That door was the entrance to Old Harry's residence. As they approach a pleasant female voice invited them to state their names which they did. The voice then instructed them to wait.

"Wait, why do we have to wait?" asked Roger not really expecting a reply. They were words spoken out of frustration and as a reaction to a true desire of not wanting to be where he was. Philip looked at him and shrugged. The both men returned their attention to the door, expecting it to open in short order. They heard the yapping of a small dog coming from inside and it seemed to be getting louder as the dog apparently approached the door.

The door opened and there stood Harry. He was dressed in a white tee shirt and gray sweat pants and had slippers on his feet. Between his legs stood Mugsy attempting to act the part of the fierce guard dog but very anxious to make friends as soon as he was told that he could do so.

Harry stared at them for a moment and grumbled, "Well you might as well come inside." He turned and walked back into his apartment, expecting them follow and to shut the door behind them.

Philip motioned to Roger to follow Harry and he reluctantly complied. The two men followed Harry into a dimly lit room where there was a small sofa and two chairs facing it. There was music playing softly but it was not an easily recognizable tune. They waited for Harry to sit and then they both sat on the sofa. Harry looked at them as though he was trying to recognize them. Then he suddenly said, "You are Philip and you are Roger. Where is the other one?"

The two men looked at each other and Philip then replied that Austin couldn't make it because of his work schedule; which of course was a lie since he was not allowed to leave the state as a condition of his parole. Then there was silence.

"Listen son, I know you brother just got out of jail and I guess that he is not able to leave the state without permission, am I right?" Harry kept speaking without allowing them to agree, "I also think he probably didn't even try to get permission, he was always a timid person- not much in the way of intestinal fortitude." Harry stopped and looked at the men. They were in shock. "I think that you boys are a little confused by the old man, but don't be. I might not have as good a memory as I once did but I have never been known to be slow."

"Pop Pop, we just didn't..." Philip attempted to explain.

Then Harry interrupted, "Look Phil, I think that a thirty five year old man should not be calling anyone Pop Pop - how about you call me Harry like everyone else does, okay?" Harry took great delight in keeping people off balance, always surprising them. The reactions he was getting were making his morning go much better than he had anticipated.

"You too ah..." Harry glanced again at his palm where he had written the boys names so that he wouldn't appear to be old and feeble. "...Roger you should call me Harry too. We'll make Austin have to call Pop Pop, since he didn't have the guts to come himself." Harry chuckled and the two men made an attempt to laugh.

Philip asked Harry about his health and several questions about the dog before getting around to the real reason they had come. "Our father told us a couple of days ago that our family's name had been changed. He told us that it had been Leesop but because of some scandal it was changed by your grandfather." he said watching Harry intently for some slight change in his facial expression, but there was none.

"Go on." Harry responded.

"Our father didn't go into details about why this happened and he left us with more questions then he said he had answers. He finally told us that if we wanted to know what had happened we should speak with you." Philip said.

Again, Harry's countenance did not betray what he was thinking and he responded with, "I see." Philip continued to relate what he knew but when he mentioned Christopher Leesop, Harry facial expression changed dramatically. He looked extremely sad.

"He was a great man." Harry interrupted. "We should be honored that he was related to us not shamed by what people said or that he was thought to be a traitor. He was a hero." As the words were coming out of Harry's mouth Roger thought about what he knew about Christopher Leesop and how he was branded a traitor. He wasn't just convicted in the court of public opinion, he was convicted in a military court and executed for treason. This man was no hero and we are related to him, he thought.

Harry stopped and stared at the floor. Mugsy sensed his master's mood change and jumped into his lap and started to lick him. Harry accepted the affection and patted the small dog's head in response.

"You are wondering how I can say that a man is a hero when the government labels him a traitor? You had to know the circumstance that surrounded the trial. He was convicted in place of the real traitor. A man named Girard who worked for the banks. The same people that your brother was attempting to bring down. The same people that had my... your uncle killed." Harry said stopping to think about his son, Bob and how he was such a good boy.

Christopher and Bob were more than cousins they were friends, they were united in a cause that was not so difficult to understand. They believed in the worth of humanity. They were trying to illustrate it, live it, model and project it with every action and fiber of their beings.

"Uncle Bob died fighting in the war." Roger stated simply.

"Why do you think he was doing a second tour when he was not a volunteer?" Harry asked.

"It is every citizen's obligation to service in the military. Unless they have been incarcerated." Roger responded.

"Then why haven't you or your brother here been called to active duty?" Harry said why motioning to Philip who watched him intently.

This did not make any sense. Harry was making Christopher Leesop to be as much a hero as Uncle Bob, maybe even more of one. This was going far differently than I could ever imagined, thought Philip.

"Harry." he said awkwardly still not accustomed to referring to his grandfather as anything but Pop Pop, "Why do you say that Christopher Leesop was a hero? From all accounts that I have read he acted against the good of those very people that you said he was trying to help." Philip paused and waited for a reply but there was none forthcoming.

Harry just looked at him and then changed the subject to the reason the two men had come to see him. "So you want to know why my grandfather changed the family's name." he stated as it were fact and not a question. "What I can tell you are the circumstances that lead to the name change and some of the things that I heard about it from various people, but I can't actually tell you why. The answer went to the grave with my grandfather, he never shared too much with anyone, except my grandmother and my aunt Katherine. They were the source of most of the information that I received. My father was not much of a talker either and if he knew anything he certainly didn't let on that he did." Harry took a breath and then continued.

"My grandfather, John Leesop, was a socially conscience person. He wanted to do right by everyone. He was not cut out for political life even though he was drawn to it like a moth to a flame. He met and married Adelaide Buckingham McGovern in 2014, seven years after Adelaide's father had been arrested. He was what they used to call a sex offender. It was a very messy thing and it costs everyone a great deal. There was a great deal of public attention to these people that were suspected of being harmful to the very young and those that were not capable of defending themselves."

"In those days people that performed these acts were kept in the public spotlight and had a very difficult time earning peoples trust. Their pictures were always available on the computer networks. They were put there so that people could feel safe. That they would always know where the people that did those horrible deeds were. The man that did this was not a Leesop. He was a man that had experienced what he referred to as a rebirth and a transformation." Harry again paused and waited to see how the men would react.

Philip bit, "So why did your grandfather change his name, he wasn't the one that was guilty of the crime?" he asked. Harry took a moment again. He thought it would be great if he could step outside and have a cigarette, but then thought, knowing these boys they would probably turn him in to the authorities.

"You boys have read about the technology overload events that happened during the fifties and eventually how they helped to cause the collapse of much of the computer processing around the world and the loss of most of the information that was stored in those computers." Roger jumped at the chance to talk about his favorite topic.

"Yes we lost and never recovered more than half of the data that was stored, significant computer code, numerous inventions and it set mankind back about forty years in many ways and the data lost, much of it was lost forever. That was as a result of the technology wars that began…"

Harry interrupted, "One of the reasons for the collapse was that man was trying to keep track of too much in a very fragile environment. They became too confident and eliminated a lot of redundancy that had been in place."

"But the Koreans created a virus that was so virulent that it contaminated even their own systems. By the time it was detected the damage was done, there was no recovery possible. It sat dormant so that as back-up systems were brought on line they too were corrupted instantaneously. It was transported to self-contained systems by the use of personal memory devices, they used to be called flash drives or memory sticks. It latched on to anything and in some cases was even introduced by biological means. Nothing eluded it, including those that set it free upon the world."

"But my point Roger is that we had done away with those other means of storing information, like paper. Criminal records were lost at that point and all of the attempts that man had made to keep track of all of the people that could be harmful to society were foiled over the period of ninety days the time the virus was released until it had wiped out everything."

"So McGovern's criminal record was gone. The name change was not necessary. I am still having trouble understanding why it was necessary in the first place." Philip wondered out loud.

Harry nodded his head then continued, "McGovern became a public figure. He was intent on sharing with others the dangers of a lifestyle that had lead him to offend. His mission was to spread a message of truth and love. The redemptive power of confession, but there were a great number of people that did not believe that he had changed and that he was an evil man trying to fool them."

"My grandfather was in the midst of a political campaign when it came to light that his wife was the daughter of this horrible man. The opposition dredged up the past press clippings and smeared him with guilt by association. To his credit he never condemned his father-in-law. He pointed out that they were separate issues and that he should be judged on his merits alone. He took the high road." Harry said and then again paused shaking his head.

"He lost the election but the press did not leave him or his wife and children alone. Maybe that's the reason my father was always so quiet and withdrawn. Finally he had had enough. He moved the family to Harrisburg and changed his name. My grandmother never saw her father again after that. It broke her heart. Every time his name was mentioned she would start to cry. My grandfather, never forgave his father-in-law. All he saw was the ruination of his career and family."

Everyone sat still as Philip and Roger tried to absorb what they had heard. 'What does all of this have to do with Christopher Leesop and Uncle Bob?' Philip thought.

Harry again broke the silence by saying, "I have a copy of the first book that my great grandfather wrote, it is credited as being the reason that the press were so aggressive when it came to their pursuit of his downfall. I can get it if you would like to see it?" Harry said and stood not waiting for their response. He knew Philip would want to see it, he was a lot like him. Harry loved history and so did Philip, they both always wanted to know why something happened.

Roger stared at the floor and the beige carpet whose knap had been crushed and worn. He tried to imagine the events that took place more than one hundred years ago and how they could have relevance today. What was the big deal that his last name had been changed? Would it mean that Gloria would not want to see him anymore, and if it did was that so important? Maybe it was time to move on from that relationship anyway, she was far too demanding of his time. He needed more time for his work, he thought.

Harry returned carrying a book and what appeared to be a journal. "I brought this along too." he said holding up the journal. "It's written in Christopher's own hand. It is a very special piece of work." Harry placed the two books on the table in front of the two men. Roger watched Philip to see what he would do. He had decided that he would look at whichever one that Philip did not take, a gesture done out of courtesy.

Philip weighed the decision as to which book to look at first. If he chose the journal was he not giving enough respect to the memories of his grandfather? He decided to take the book. It was a small book with a dark colored cover. 'My Triumphant Failure', its title was shown with the silhouette man peering through the words. The author's name, J Randolph McGovern, was in small print in the lower right hand corner and appeared to almost be an after-thought. He opened the cover. The book had been read but only once or twice, it still had a very crisp feel to it, though it was clearly very old.

The inside cover was autographed by the author and it was inscribed to his daughter. The ink was slightly smudged but still readable. He turned the page carefully and saw that the book was dedicated to his children. He read quickly through the forward and then into the first chapter. It was an easy read, there was a warm familiar cadence to the meter of the words. They flowed from paragraph to paragraph. The message was a gentle one and it was clear that the person that wrote those words was apparently a very humble self-deprecating soul that was longing for forgiveness.

Philip stopped and looked up at Harry who was watching him intently. "Well, does this answer some of your questions?" he asked with a tone that betrayed genuine tenderness.

"I think it poses even more. How much more can you tell us about Jonathan McGovern?" Philip asked in reply.

Harry looked at Roger who was thumbing through Christopher's journal and then spoke, "I think that there is more substance in what you brother is reading than that which is contained in those pages." He had said that while he pointed his finger at the book Philip was still holding.

"My great grandfather was not the issue. He was an unfortunate man that succumbed to his vices and addiction to pornography and then was caught with his proverbial pants down. He was not an evil man he was a stupid man that was consumed with himself. His son-in-law was a weak man that could not stand the pressure. He would have been a terrible mayor of Philadelphia."

Harry looked Philip intently in the eyes and continued, "He changed the name to make himself feel safer. He didn't do it for anyone other than himself. It was a selfish act but it had little or no consequences. The storm blew over just as it would have if he had not changed his name. He claimed he did it for his family but he did it for himself. His brother did not change his name. Albert Henry Leesop, my great uncle, was as very interesting man, you would have liked him Roger, very much the computer scientist."

The mention of his name caused Roger to look up. He had not been paying attention. He was reading the journal and it had him captivated. There was something very powerful in the message that Christopher Leesop was imparting.

"Pop... I mean Harry, would it be alright if I borrowed this and made a copy. I am sure that I could find a local place that would do it and it would be gone but a few hours."

Philip turned and looked at his brother. What he had found so interesting in the pages of that journal, he wondered. He then turn to see how his grandfather would respond.

"I thought that it would grab you, though I thought Phil here would have been the first to want to see it. I can't let anything happen to it and there are people out there that would like to see it destroyed. I am not sure that it would be safe to make a copy." Roger stared at Harry and he thought.

"I understand your concern. I have an idea - give me a minute and I will know if it can be accomplished." Roger said and then placed a call to his office and asked them to locate a facility where he could rent secure scanning equipment. "That's right five hundred and twelve bit encryption at least." he instructed. "Okay, get them to send it to this address." and his PCU sent the coordinates by longitude and latitude. "How long before it arrives?" Roger looked at Philip and then at Harry. "It will have to do. Thank you for your assistance. Good Bye." The call disconnected and Roger sat back in the sofa.

"Well?" Philip asked.

"I am having scanning equipment sent over, it will be here in about an hour, maybe sooner. The best part is that it isn't going to cost me anything. The company is paying for it." Roger smugly replied. At that time Harry glanced at the clock that sat on the table next the sofa. It was a very old clock that sat under a glass protector. Its hands indicated that it was eight forty two and he thought about how much longer these men would be with him.

"Whatever you do, should someone ask where you received the copy of this journal, you must not tell them that I have it. They will want to destroy it." Harry implored.

"Is there any danger to you Harry?" Philip inquired.

"No, and if there were it wouldn't matter, the key is to keep the journal from being destroyed." Harry responded.

Philip was extremely curious about why Roger wanted the copy of the book. His brother was never one for reading anything that didn't deal with technology or computers. Why now the interest in something that would be considered to be the scribbling of a traitor? This was truly puzzling behavior, he thought as he continued to page through McGovern's book. The book did not resonate with him. There was nothing that he saw that made this book anything special, there was no powerful message. This man was a man who acted stupidly and then repented and claimed that it had changed him. There were so many that had made similar claims.

"Harry, did your great grandfather do anything special with his life other than write this book and apologize for all the harm that he had done?" Philip asked not looking up from the pages.

Harry took a moment and then said, "He was an inspiration to Christopher, or at least that is what I heard. Christopher read all of his books."

"How many did he write?"

"Four that I am aware of, I have two others but was never able to get a copy of the last one that he wrote."

"What were the others about?"

"They were all science fiction works. They symbolically represented man's attempts to understand his existence. They are entertaining but I don't see that they accomplished his intent." said Harry. Harry watched Philip page through the book methodically. He seemed to be reading most of each page that he turned absorbing the contents and moving on to the next page. Harry then turned his attention to Roger who appeared have become stuck on a page; reading and re-reading it as though he couldn't quite grasp its message. Harry wondered what he was looking at and why he was studying it so intently.

Philip too took notice of Roger's intense study as well and then asked, "Roger, what are you reading that has caught your interest?"

Roger looked up with a quizzical look on his face. He had not realized how absorbed he had become until it was pointed out to him. Smiling sheepishly he said, "This is some very interesting work. I hadn't realized what Christopher Leesop believed until now... at least I am beginning to understand. Austin would really enjoy reading this."

Roger stopped talking and his gaze fell back on the page he had been reading. He looked at the words that were written on the page, each carefully penned and skillfully scribed. Christopher had written it in his own hand. This document was unique and he could feel the power of the words resonating within him. Christopher Leesop must have been a remarkable man, he thought.

"Roger, the people with the scanner are at the door, you have to sign for it." Harry's words brought him back to the here and now. He stood and placed the journal carefully under his arm, not wishing to part company with it. He walked to the door and in a moment returned with the scanner. It was a small rectangular case approximately one half inch thick. It was hinged on one side with a small undetectable clasp on the opposite side. Roger fumbled with it to open it and Philip looked at his brother not knowing how to help him. The unit popped open and came to life. Roger placed on the table and began to carefully manipulate the pages of the journal so that they could be scanned.

No one spoke for quite some time. Harry was the first to talk and it was to Mugsy when he asked him if he needed to go outside. Mugsy was always ready to go out and Harry thought he might even be able to sneak a few puffs on his cigarette until Philip offered to join him. The two men left Roger busily copying the journal and headed toward the backdoor to the apartment. Mugsy stood there waiting for them looking up at the handle, waiting for someone to let him out.

Even though the small area was enclosed and it was still early in the morning, the temperature in the backyard was almost ninety degrees. The overhead cover was on maximum tint and the air was being circulated by fans that were part of the enclosed cooling unit. The air smelled of stale smoke and Philip shook his head at the fact that his grandfather continued to smoke despite the risks to him physically as well as costs economically. It made no sense, he thought.

Mugsy ran up and down the grass as the two men watched him. "Harry, thank you for taking the time to see us. I know that we have not always gotten along, for whatever reason. It was great that you shared some of the family secrets." Philip said with a smile.

Harry turned and looked at him. He was searching to see if this comment was genuine. Far too often he had been told things that people thought he wanted to hear and he believed them. It took years for him to finally realize that most people are so self-absorbed that they can't even begin to understand that everyone else has the same issues, fears, hopes and dreams. They just manifest themselves differently. We aren't so complex after all, he concluded. He didn't see anything that would make him think that Philip wasn't being anything but sincere.

"Philip, I have not been able to spend much time in your company, since your uncle died. I began to see everything as a conspiracy and it was difficult not to think that I was the blame for some of the events that transpired. I kept myself distant from the members of the family for that reason." Harry stopped and wondered how much of what he had just said he actually meant. He didn't do it because he wanted to protect the family, he did it because he didn't really like them.

Philip looked at the old man. His posture stooped and he was leaning to one side as though off balance. He had steel blue eyes that burned with intensity, not like that of many older people where they have a dull film that makes them appear sickly. Harry was a survivor. Philip watched him nervously fidget, it was manifestation of the absence of nicotine in his blood stream. He would soon grow more impatient and appear to be angry with the world while it was just his body crying out for a cigarette.

"Harry, if you want to have a cigarette, it won't offend me." Philip blurted out.

The words took Harry by surprise. He didn't expect to be found out let alone have this person tell him that it was okay to partake in an illegal act. He struggled to find the proper response, after all he did not want to give this person the upper hand. He needed to be in control and then it happened. He thought of Christopher and then knew that he had to do.

"Thank you Phil, I suppose it's pretty obvious, the smoking I mean." Harry reached into his sweat pants pocket and pulled out the small case. He wondered if he should offer one to Philip. "I don't suppose you want to join me?" he asked. Philip just smiled and shook his head.

Harry started talking to Philip about Mugsy but soon changed the subject to Christopher. "You know you should read that journal. I think it will change the way you look at life." he said sincerely.

"Is that what is happening to Roger?" Philip asked.

Harry fumbled with his case and extracted the cigarette and small lighter. He mumbled his reply to Philip, "Your brother is just scratching the surface. The next time he reads those same words he will get a whole different meaning. But, yes he is learning."

Philip pondered the statement and then continued, "Are you telling me that there is something more than just philosophy on those pages?" He looked at the old man and waited for his reply but Harry turned his back and began to walk toward the end of the yard, investigating what Mugsy was digging up. He pulled long and hard on the cigarette and the nicotine caused him to become a little light-headed for a moment.

"What do you want from me? This is something that you must figure out for yourself." Harry called over his shoulder.

Philip looked at him, wondering why the old man would not answer a simple question. It was an opinion question, one whose answer would only have value if you assigned any to it. He wondered why does Harry had to play games with people. He seems to be one type of person and then you catch a glimpse of something else. He then pondered how much of what he had told them was true?

"Harry would it be possible for me to borrow your grandfather's book for a few days?"

"You can have a copy- I have several, just not that one that I showed you. It would probably be good if someone else had a good understanding of all that went on." he concluded. Philip looked at him, he was still facing away from him.

"That's the thing Harry, I don't have a good idea what went on, and really wish that I did." Philip replied.

This comment forced Harry to turn and face him. "I know you don't and I am not sure that I can give you what you want. You came here seeking an answer to one question and you found that the question isn't really relevant, is it? Yet you keep on pursuing an answer that won't make a difference. My great grandfather is a small part of a much larger puzzle. I'll tell you that his only significance is that what Christopher has given him. Nothing more. Read his book, dissect it as I have done many times over the past seventy years. The road will end at the same place, at the feet of Christopher Leesop. You will see, it is a journey that will tell you a great deal about yourself." Harry said and turned without waiting for a reaction and concentrated on Mugsy once again. His friend would be there after these men left and moved on with their important lives, he thought. Mugsy would be here to help him enjoy the evening cigarette and then he would be there to lick his hand as he drifted off to sleep.

"Harry, I will take the book and I will read it and I will also read Christopher's journal, he was one of the last to see Uncle Bob before he died, perhaps he could give more insight into him as well." Philip stated.

This man will not understand until he takes to the time to slow down and read the signs, Harry thought. Should he tell him that Robert was only a voice that announced the coming of Christopher and that Robert felt unworthy to be in his company or should he let him discover this on his own? Perhaps he should have another piece of information or two to help in his discovery.

"Would you like to have a couple of letters that your uncle wrote to me? I could let Roger copy them as well, if you would like." Harry's offer was sincere but his patience was wearing thin and he wanted these men to leave and the sooner the better. He had important matters to attend to, like taking a nap.

"That would be great. Thank you." replied Philip.

The two men then exchanged complaints about the rising temperature and Harry called Mugsy to go inside. They returned to find Roger finishing the scanning and Harry excused himself returning with promised letters and a fresh copy of McGovern's book.

Roger scanned the letters quickly and then took two small tubes from another package that had been delivered with the scanner. He transferred the scanned images to the screens and rolled them up and put them into the tubes. After that he proceeded to wipe the memory clean of the scanned images. He then reformatted the storage by copying the operating system back over itself completely sterilizing the scanners storage.

"I probably didn't need to reformat the storage but it just makes it that much more certain that there are no residual images floating around on the equipment. The company that provides these has a top secret clearance but I still don't like to leave anything to chance." Roger explained. He was enjoying the intrigue. It was like a big game to him, he really didn't think that Harry had any reason to be concerned but the journal was interesting and Harry was kind enough to allow him to copy it. Why not humor the old guy, he thought.

Harry took notice of Roger insertion of the screens into the tubes. He wondered how they worked.

"Roger, I have never seen one of those screen things up close before. How do they work?"

Once again Roger came to life. If he could show you something that had to do with technology he was extremely enthusiastic and an engaging a person that you would ever meet, and this was a chance to show off a little. Roger took one of the screens out of its tube and explained the very thin and flexible rectangular screen could hold the equivalent of ten thousand books easily. It was approximately the thickness of three sheets of paper. He showed him how to turn it on and then how you could either hold it one of two ways.

"Harry, if you hold it this way you can, by bringing each of the end together cause the two pages that are being displayed to change, like you were turning the pages of a book. If you are holding it lengthwise you simply turn it over and the next page appears there. They were experimenting with real time downloads of news but decided that people were much more likely to use their PCU for news and entertainment. That is something to see when you are trying to concentrate on the 'real' stuff going on around you." Roger gasped a breath and was about to continue on, but Harry stopped him when he told him that it was impressive but he liked paper better.

Roger again packed the screen in the tube and began to gather all of the pieces he now had. He handed Harry the journal and thanked him. Philip also surrendered the original signed copy in exchange for the new unread version of McGovern's book. It was obvious that it was time to end this meeting. Each of them feeling it could have been a lot worse but they were still not looking forward to their next encounter.

Philip extended his hand to Harry and said, "You know Grandfather, I was hoping that this meeting would be tolerable and I would say that for me it was almost enjoyable."

Harry took his hand and said, "Let's not get carried away." and then he smiled. It was the first smile that Philip could remember seeing on his face since he was a child, and the memory filled him.

It was a time when Philip had been working in his room. He was about ten or eleven years old and was doing his homework. He had come up with an idea of using a panoramic display of historic events surrounding the technology wars of 2056. It illustrated pictorially the effects of the loss of computer systems and how it caused society to come to a screeching halt. Harry found him in his room and watched him from the doorway, thinking he was unobserved but Philip knew he was there. He could see him out of the corner of his eye, he was smiling at him. He must have enjoyed the fact that his grandson had the same passion for history that he did.

"You know Harry, we are not too different you and I." he finally said. Harry smile faded away like the mist of morning, gone without a trace.

"You would think that were true, wouldn't you?" he responded still shaking his hand with a firm grip.

"You are a lot like your mother." he continued "and that is a good thing." He let his hand disengage and turned his attention to Roger.

"Roger, keep those documents safe, please." Roger looked at him and nodded.

"Let's get going Phil." he then said as he too held out his hand and Harry shook it briefly. Harry walked them half way to the door and told them they knew the way out and they should make sure the door was shut behind them.

It was eleven fifteen when they positioned themselves in the Voltrun to take them first to return the scanner and then to the train station to catch the Pittsburgh train after which Roger would finish his journey in Philadelphia. The ride to drop off the scanner went very quickly and Philip and Roger talked very briefly about the encounter. Roger seemed reluctant to talk about his impressions of the journal finally telling Philip that he really needed to read it himself. That shut down conversation between the two brothers until they exited the Voltrun at the train station. Philip looked at his brother and thought, what did we just do?

"Roger, what was that? How do you think that it went?" he asked.

Roger stopped and looked back at him. "It went much better than I expected. He's not such a bad old guy. He is a lot more aware of what is going on than I thought he would be." He then looked at Philip to see if that was the kind of response he was looking for but did not receive the validation, so he shrugged and made a face.

Philip laughed at his response. "It was better than I thought it would be, but it caused me to think about things that I haven't thought about for a long time. It was kind of sad."

Roger looked at the ground and saw his shadow, a short stubby blob gathered at his feet. The heat was oppressive, he was beginning to perspire profusely. "I know what you mean. I thought about Uncle Bob a great deal and even though I didn't know him as well as you and Austin did, I knew that he was a very special man. Let's get inside before my shoes melt." he said half joking.

The two brothers walked the twenty or so feet to enter the train station. Their PCUs instructed them where and when the next train to Pittsburgh was scheduled to depart and they found a cart to take them to it. As they rode the cart Roger talked about wanting to understand what was held within the pages of the journal and that he was sorry that he couldn't explain why he found it so fascinating.

"I think it might be because of what he did. He betrayed his country and hurt a great number of people. And then after reading his words it was difficult to imagine the man that wrote so powerfully and yet with

150

such a gentle message could possibly have done what he was charged with doing and eventually cost him his life."

Philip grasped his brother's dilemma. "It does seem odd that Uncle Bob, a war hero, would be so close to a man that was diametrically opposed to his vision. Their relationship was just as strong the day that he left for his final tour of duty as it was when they were growing up." Philip added.

"Harry misses Bob, like any father would miss his son, but I think he misses Christopher as much if not more. This is very strange. Maybe that is why he is such a difficult man to deal with at times."

"At times?" Roger rejoined with a hearty laugh.

They reached the platform and queued up waiting for the train to arrive. The smell of electricity hung heavily on the platform and Roger and Philip both felt the charges tingling against their flesh.

"There must be an energy drain somewhere. Can you feel the current crawling on your skin?" Philip revealed to Roger.

"Yes, that is one of the bad things about all of this power that's need to run these trains. We have dear old Dad to thank for this." Roger replied.

"Yes, we do. Yes, we do." Philip said as he looked and saw the train silently approaching. They would be in Pittsburgh by one o'clock, he thought and then he could take a nap. He was exhausted.

When Roger walked into his apartment he half expected to find it destroyed and most of his things missing. Instead it was completely clean. Everything was in its place. Gloria must have cleaned before she left, he thought. The time flashed before his eyes. It was almost three, there was probably some sporting event on that he could listen to while he worked on the encryption algorithms that he had brought home to solve or he could take some more time and review the journal. It seemed to be calling to him. He then heard the sound of water running and he then realized that he was not alone. She hadn't left. He guessed his time in purgatory would be extended a little longer.

****

"Devers, are we still on for tonight?" Girard asked as he started the conversation.

"Yes, why?" Devers wondered why Girard would call him let alone ask that question.

"I just gotta call from a guy who asked me if he could trust you. He is someone that I had worked with in the past. He is known for eradicating pests." he said. Girard sounded irritated.

"I am working on multiple problems that require a lot of clean up. I need you for another more sensitive issue. Those people tend to be a little too high profile for your type of assignment." Devers explained.

"Oh, okay - just checking. I did say that he could trust you and you should hear from them... probably tomorrow." Girard said and disconnected the call without any further conversation.

Devers thought that things were coming together nicely. He was beginning to see all the pieces fall into place and he had a plan that would keep the Bank out of the spotlight. All he had to do was find Justin Welsh and get rid of him once and for all. That man had too much information and if he ever used it there would be a lot of trouble for many very powerful people.

"Mr. Devers, Kate Foster here. I just wanted to let you know that Mr. Lee has been stationary most of the day at his home. There was one time when he went for a walk but he did not see anyone or stop to talk. The walk lasted twenty minutes and we made certain that if he interacted with anyone that we were prepared to deal with it immediately. Nothing to report." Katherine Foster sounded a little frightened but she was doing her best to control her emotions. She knew this was going to be her big opportunity and she couldn't let it pass her by.

"Good work Foster. Have a good night and we will talk again tomorrow. Stay with him. Rasputin disconnect."

Chapter Five

Another day at work was about to end and Austin was looking forward to seeing his two friends. Since he had left prison he had times when he felt completely isolated. There weren't many times, but when they occurred it was difficult for him to not feel depressed or angry. He was angry with himself, that he had put himself in the position where he couldn't move about freely and that he had hurt so many people. It was surprising how much he had taken for granted in the past, those things that which he had assumed to be entitled.

Being able to share a night with friends was a major production because it required a meeting with his parole officer and forms to be filled out and of course background checks. He had to report where he was going to be and with whom he would be spending the evening. The burden for such activities was onerous. It was at times like these that he took time to collect his thoughts and pictured some moment in time when he was in prison. Usually that memory was enough for him to recognize that things were much better now than when he was inside.

His workstation was cluttered with many pages of numbers. The financial statements and projections painted a portrait of an anemic company that was struggling to keep up its proverbial head above water. The company's owners were looking for an injection of some much needed capital but the cost for such a transfusion was extremely high. Equity wasn't merely at stake, the cost would be everything of value; corporate as well as personal. The better the accountant's review appeared, the more funds that would be available and perhaps there would be something left of their individual dignity but most likely not. He searched their balance sheet for clues as to how he could show the company in the most favorable light. He landed on intellectual property depreciation, a favorite place to illustrate the potential cash flow that seemed to be lacking.

The time for quitting passed and Austin was still on the hunt for the 'pony'. He stopped and laughed out loud when he thought of a poorly constructed and delivered parable about the two young boys that find a huge pile of manure in the stable of their grandfather's farm. The first boy turned up his nose at the smell and ran out of the stable. The other boy started digging in the pile with glee. When his grandfather asked him why, he replied with all this manure there has to be a pony in here somewhere!

Gina, the woman that worked in the cubical across from him stared at him. What does he have to be laughing about? Doesn't he realize that he works under the worst conditions and for a poorly run company? What does he have to be happy about? While she was thinking about the deplorable conditions she realized that Austin was looking back at her. His smile was lingering on his face and she now wondered if he had been laughing at her for something she had done. Quickly she gathered her things and left without another glance or word.

Austin watched her as she left he was wondering what precipitated her erratic behavior. When he had first started to work for the company she had been somewhat friendly but as he settled into his position she became more and more distant. There were many days when they did not acknowledge the others' presence in any way. His apparent disinterest was confusing to him since she was an attractive woman that was the right age. Perhaps it all comes down to his feelings of unworthiness. Who wants to be involved with a criminal, especially one that was preparing to destroy the economic balance and to take away even more for those who had the least to give, or at least that was how he was portrayed in the headlines. He guessed it was time to leave, he thought but then a column of numbers caught his interest and he found himself absorbed in the balance sheet once again.

****

"How have you been Austin? Are things getting any better for you?" John asked.

Austin looked at his two friends and thought about the past three months and how things had been going. He had been out of jail and had a job, thanks to his father's help, but otherwise he still felt incomplete as though he were waiting for a train but wasn't sure when it was to arrive and where it was going. A hazy veil had been in front of his eyes for the past six plus years. He had an occasional glimpse of something that he believed to be a purpose or direction for his life but no sooner had he felt it come into focus it disappeared as though absorbed by the fog that had enveloped him. "Things have been okay- how about you?" he finally replied.

It had been almost two months since he had seen George and even longer since he had seen John. They were two members of a very small group of people that had stayed loyal to Austin through his incarceration. Why wouldn't they, they were united in the same cause. Each time they had met it was awkward at first, no one wanted to open up the subject of the cause that they knew had drawn them together to champion.

Nobody was sure where to begin, but as John and George began to relax they began to view Austin as the person they once thought he was. They shared similar views about the economic oppression that gripped the country. Austin sat sipping club soda while the others drank more potent beverages. Naturally, the conversation turned to the frustration that gnawed at them all. Today's meeting had a different feel than those in the past. There seemed to be a new agenda and Austin was a little wary, has was concerned about being set up once again. The end result of ensnarement would be a trip back to a very depressing destination.

"No matter what I do, I can't seem to stop being angry. The thought of those few entitled people living in such opulence, such decadence infuriates me." Austin said. The two men sitting across the table just stared at him. Austin instantly felt he may have said too much. Paranoia struck fear into Austin and he knew these men but still wasn't certain that he could trust them. He knew only one thing and that was that he did not want to go back to jail, he thought. As he did he gazed at the table and at the glasses where sweat formed small pools, drenching the coasters that they sat upon. It is warm in here, he observed silently.

John broke the silence jolting Austin back to the meeting. "Austin, where is this going? Just because you spent time ..." His voice trailed off not wanting to hear once again about his prison experience. He had heard it all, 'Poor Austin living in such conditions'. A cause had to have sacrifice. If you were going to do what was right then you had to expect that those that were doing wrong would try to stop you and persecute you. Maybe John hadn't spent the time in prison but he had dedicated himself to the cause, he wanted change and was prepared to do whatever it took to bring it about.

"Look Austin, we are serious about making a difference, about changing this mess. What about you? Are you ready to get back into the fight?" John asked because he needed to know if Austin was willing to help, but not just help, commit himself to freeing the masses from the choking hold of economic slavery.   He thought briefly of his father who had worked tirelessly to provide for his family to preserve the home that had been in their family for six generations only to lose the battle with the banks. The hopelessness that ensued, the despair that gripped them all was nothing compared to emptiness that they all experience when his father passed away.   John blamed his premature death on that brokenness.

"We all have a great deal to risk. The banks are not going to just fold up their tents and go home without a fight- a very dirty fight. The real challenge is coming up with a plan that will work and not just be another irritation, a pebble in their shoe." Austin said this because he felt the way John did when Justin had enlisted him in the cause.   Was the fire he had returning? The only problem with that was the feeling of desperation that accompanied it. The plan they had attempted to execute before had been as close to perfection as they could have envisioned and yet still it failed. They needed to have another strategy or different tactics. There had to be something that they could use to bring down the 'root of all evil' as they saw it.

"Alright, I guess I'm in. How do you suggest that we accomplish this?" he finally replied.   The conversation at the table immediately ceased.   No one had an idea of how to do it, they only knew that it needed to be done.

George mustered up enough courage to throw an idea out that was so from the realm of logical possibilities that he couldn't believe that he was about to say it.

"The best way to eradicate a disease is to prevent it from ever taking hold in the first place."   Both Austin and John looked at each other and then at George. They both wondered what he was he thinking. The banks had been in control for such a very long time.

"Okay George, can you see how we can inoculate ourselves against this disease?" Austin asked.

George then replied "We thought we had that very solution seven years ago when the conversion of currencies was just underway, but that was just another symptom not the disease."

"Where are you going with this line of thinking?" Austin asked and paused waiting for George to further explain his thoughts.

"I think we have to identify the primal source. We must look past all the symptoms, all the results no matter how cataclysmic they are and first identify the disease and then find its origin." George had stated a fairly obvious series of facts. It was clear to all of them that the disease was greed and the origin was prehistoric and engrained in all mankind. If they looked a little further they would see that it was really fear which caused the insecurity that bred the greed. It then led to feelings of entitlement an assumed form of greed.

"Let's assume that we know all the disease is man's greed, his self-centered need to possess and control but you end up at a point where you have to change mankind, that's not a productive exercise to undertake." John interjected.

"Don't you think greed is just a symptom too? Why are people greedy? I think that it's because they are fearful- for many reasons but fearful never the less."

"Where is this leading us? To despair and frustration because we can't change man's nature globally it's a one on one intimate, 'revelationary' process."

Both John and Austin looked at George and said in unison, "'Revelationary'?"

He then replied, "I am pretty certain that the term has been used before and if it's not a real word it should be."

The conversation continued to meander about seeking an objective that could be identified as the next step in satisfying their thirst for retribution, an ambition to balance the proverbial scales of justice. Soon it became apparent that the path they had chosen would not yield the results that they had hoped.   The perfect plan had failed before and opportunity to recreate it was gone forever.   Austin thought if they could only go back in time, and then said it out loud.

George reacted quickly and vehemently stating, "Time travel is not possible. Time is only the measurement of a process; it would be like moving the earth backwards. There is no way to do it – so many people have invested countless hours thinking about it- waste pure waste."

Austin's response came just as quickly, "Who said anything about travel? What if we could find a way to alter the past without having to be there?" He went on to tell the two men about an article that he had read a couple of years earlier while in prison that spoke about the ability to retrace the elements of light thus providing a means of being able to see into the past and they had actually accomplished it. He concluded by saying, "Of course the view into the past was only a couple of minutes, but it did prove that it was possible."

George looked at Austin and then at John. "Okay, if this is possible what would you do? Go back to the moments before the police showed up at your door and drug you out into the street? And then what would you do, warn yourself about the upcoming raid?" The group fell silent again.

"It would have to be some other time or event, our plan wouldn't have worked anyway- even though we were led to think it would.   We need an event that will destabilize the world order and I know just the guy to help us find it, my brother Phil." Austin then said.

****

Philip was again waiting for a call that might never come. The elusive Ms. Jenkins had promised to call him once again and he had again believed her promise. Over the past three months they had seen each other a dozen times and each time there was tremendous sexual tension, innocent touching of hands and a hand full of friendly kisses but nothing more. It wasn't anyone's fault the timing seemed to always be really bad.

Philip needed to get some sleep and turn off his unit, shut out the world and sleep. Relaxing was a lost art, limited to the times when he wasn't working on preparing lectures, exams or his published works. The need to publish or perish had never been more apparent and had been elevated to a new level. The Dean had been in his office daily inquiring about his progress. Who would have thought that failing an underclassman would have had so many political ramifications, he thought. He now needed to be error-less, the perfect professor.

He looked at the notes that he had spread out across his work table. It would be easy to just wave his hand and have the open files close and put themselves away neatly. He had dictated five pages today and yet he still felt there was significantly more to be added to support the arguments. For example, he wondered why would Lee have moved on to Philadelphia, why not turn south and head for Baltimore or Washington?

Jenkins had contended that Philadelphians were wavering in their support of the cause. Their support for continuing the war was at an all-time low at the time just before the battle at Gettysburg and that Philadelphia, while it held little or no military advantage, it was one of the key cities in the north. Additionally, there were no established defensive fortifications surrounding the city, whereas Washington had thousands of soldiers encamped about its perimeter. All Beauregard had to do was fain an attack across the Potomac to paralyze the Union forces and Philadelphia would be in the hands of Marse Robert.

This was an interesting foundation for the treatise that would then go on to have the Union dissolving into two very different countries each of them much weaker and unable to influence the world affairs as it had since the early Twentieth century. Not a powerful economic force but modest participant at the world's table. The First World War would drag on for fifteen years longer than it had without the Yanks being added to the cannon fodder. A corporal in the German army was killed in the unending trench warfare and then there was then no Adolf Hitler to lead the Nazi movement that does not materialize.

There was no way to be certain about the projected outcome but the argument for the weakness of the two countries was very compelling. Weakened by the conflict between them their northern and southern neighbors took advantage as well. England's desire to increase its holdings caused it to expand in the northwestern territories. The states of North and South Dakota as well as Montana, Washington, Oregon and Idaho became part of the Canadian territory. Mexico also took back Arizona, New Mexico and the southern part of California just north of San Diego. The remaining western states split between the United States and the new Confederate States of America. What would the world be like if the United States was not the super power that it was during the Twentieth and Twenty First centuries and would the banks have still been able to have the ultimate control that they have today?

Jenkins' thesis was complex and at times convoluted but the case was adequately made that would support a major shift of power away from the current time thread, the path that humanity was currently traveling.

Time threads were discussed in great detail by Jenkins and it appeared to be the reaction to his consideration of this part of published materials that most people thought him to be a harmless fool. That was except for one government memo that Jessica had circled and indicated was extremely important. The memo was the cover page for a study that the Department of Internal Security had commissioned regarding threats to the Financial Services Markets which his brother Austin affectionately called the 'banks'. They indicated that the Jenkins' theory contained an element of threat to the stability to the financial markets. How could that be? He guessed the government had nothing better to do than commission reports on outlandish theories. Still that report might be interesting reading, he thought.

Philip began to search for a copy of the report and he could not be find it in the files that Jessica had given him to review. He then searched the government archives and the results of that search yielded nothing as well, not even a disclaimer regarding the sensitive nature of the material hence a top secret security clearance. That was odd. Philip decided to call his cousin and see if he could get him a copy of the report. How serious could something as far-fetched as this theory be, he wondered.

An incoming call from Austin message appeared before him. I guess the call to Robert will have to wait, he said to himself. "Austin how are you?"

"Good Philip – listen I need to ask you a question – if you had to pick an event in past history where if the outcome were changed the world as you know it would be completely different, what would that event be?"

Philip laughed and said, "Funny you should bring that up, I am working on a paper that is exploring a theory that the battle of Gettysburg was such an event. Why?"

****

It was a small one paragraph story on page two about a traffic fatality that had Devers smiling. It read that Ms. Fuentes was a pedestrian that was struck by a delivery van in the Georgetown section of Washington DC late yesterday. She was pronounced dead on the scene. Girard really out did himself on this one, he thought. There was no way that anyone could trace this back to the bank, he thought. Now with her out of the way maybe we could get this Welsh thing back on track. It has been almost three months and we have made very little progress if any. The Austin Lee surveillance was as tight as it can possibly be and still nothing, he thought.

On the other hand the situations between the Monks and Hell's Assassins, that was a different story. HA had escalated the conflict to look like a gang war had broken out and it was only a matter of time until Hector G was no longer among the living.   Executions in the prison system were much more complex than they used to be, he thought and that campaign had begun in earnest about thirty days after the initial phone call. It was decided that it would be a gradual buildup of hostilities as to not draw any unnecessary attention.

The Venezuela government was toppled in a silent coupe and the IMC was announced as the currency of the new regime. It had been a good March and now April was off to a great start with the chance to appoint a new CIA liaison, someone that was controllable. It would be great if that could be someone that they already had an established relationship with WBOI, someone that they owned, thought Devers.

Sam tapped on the door and stuck her head into the room. "Mr. Devers, it's getting late and I need to pick up my daughter, would it be alright if I left in a few minutes?" she asked plaintively.

"What is the problem, is everything alright at home?" Devers responded with an attempt at compassion.

"Oh, her father has been transferred to the Chicago office and is attempting to modify the custody agreement. It could end up with Lilly spending half of her life in Chicago." she whined.

Devers held up one finger and then placed a call. "Matthews, Devers here. I need you to help my girl out. She is in a custody fight... Samantha Lewis - hold on. Lewis I am transferring this to you. Tell him what you need - he will help you."

Devers felt powerful when he was able to help the 'little people'. He turned and looked out the windows of his office. All he could see were a few lights of the buildings across the street and the blackness of night. He was waiting for the latest report regarding Austin Lee. He knew where Lee was at every minute of every day. They had high jacked the locator signal of his implant chip and they had boosted the gain so that they could track him up to one hundred fifty miles away. They were working on a means of getting the audio feed but it had been problematic since the pick-up was not sensitive enough to provide intelligible conversation unless whoever was speaking was talking directly into Austin's forearm.

"Mr. Devers, thank you. Mr. Matthews seems to think that everything will work out okay. That is a big relief." Sam said as she interrupted Devers daydreaming.

"That's good news Lewis, now you owe me one." he said with a sly smile and Sam knew what that meant.

"I'll bring you some cookies, I know how much you like them." she replied trying to get his thoughts out of the gutter. Then she remembered that Katherine Foster had just arrived for the debriefing. "Oh, Katherine Foster is here, should I send her in?"

Devers looked at her and then answered "Yes, send her in and you can take off, but we'll talk more tomorrow on how much you appreciate what I have done for you."

Katherine Foster entered the office as Sam left and closed the door. She walked in purposely with her hand extended. This was the third time she had been asked to personally review the Lee surveillance and after each time she felt like she needed a shower to wash Devers' disease from her. Whether it was his leering or his criminal mentality it did not matter, Devers was an evil man.

Devers called her to the meeting so that he could discover what progress they were making toward getting close to Lee. He had devised a plan where he would have a co-worker initially spy on his activities and then eventually gain his trust. To date there had been little progress and Devers was getting frustrated. Foster was a great employee and was quick to do what was demanded of her. She was not Devers' type and even though he enjoyed looking at all women, she was too much like a young boy, no shape to her, he thought.

"Have a seat Foster." he said gesturing toward a cluster of four chairs gathered around a small circular glass table. "Can I get you anything before Lewis leaves for the evening?"

Kate did not want to be there for any longer than necessary. "No thank you sir." she replied. "I have a summary of the recent surveillance." she stated as she handed him a tube with the report enclosed. "I will tell you that we have made some headway in securing the cooperation of Ms. Fanacci regarding the observation and eventual seduction of Austin Lee."

Devers looked at her as though he didn't believe her. "What happened to change her mind?" he questioned her with an intense look that seemed to say, 'Don't be giving me a lot of nonsense girl, I have been lied to by the best of them.'

"We were able to find out some interesting background information that Ms. Fanacci would not like to be known to her family or her employer. We have some very interesting photographic evidence that supports what initially were just rumors of inappropriate behavior and excessive use of controlled substances."

"She's a druggie? That's marvelous, this woman is exactly what we need, someone we can control. Did you approach her with free drugs yet?"

Kate looked at Devers and asked herself, was he serious? "That was not something I thought of as viable plan of action. I thought..."

Devers interrupted, "I am going to give you the names of some people that will be able to make this happen. You are right we don't want to have a direction connection. Great work Foster, now if you don't mind I have to get going. Keep me posted though." Devers said as he stood and extended his hand.

Kate couldn't believe how fast it all went. There was no staring at her body or sneering leers. The only thing that was troubling was the glee that he took when he found out that Gina Fanacci was a drug addict. As she walked through entrance to the elevators she found herself shaking her head. She had to keep the process moving and call the contacts Devers transferred to her. It would at the least make certain that it appeared she was following his orders. What she wasn't sure was that she would be able to get in the business of procuring illegal drugs for someone, even if she were ordered to do so.

She looked at her reflection in the highly polished chrome walls of the elevator. Maybe it was how she was dressed that discouraged Devers, if so she had to remember to wear this 'lucky' suit next time she was called in for a briefing. She placed the call to the first name on the list.

"Hello." the voice said. "Who are you and why have you called?" and then she realized that it was a recording, someone's idea of a joke she assumed. She left no information, the record of her call would be enough. She then placed the next call.

"Who is Katherine Foster anyway?" was the response to her call.

"Mr. uh Julian Williams?" I work for John Devers at WBOI and he directed me to contact you regarding a personnel problem. Are you willing to meet with me to discuss it?"

She waited and then the voice replied, "Tell Devers he still owes me for the last job and until I see the payment there will be no more 'help'." and he emphasized the word 'help' strongly.

"I see..." she began to respond but the call disconnected. Well it was reassuring that Devers treated everyone the same, poorly. She placed the call to the last name on the list and a woman answer. The name was Foon, just Foon. She had not been able to determine whether the person would be male or female.

"Yes, what do you want Foster?" she said curtly.

"John...." but she was interrupted.

"Yes, you work for Devers and he wants me to help you. Okay, here is the deal I will do it but I need fifteen hundred IMC now and another three thousand once it's documented that we have the desired results - plus expenses. Do you understand?" Foon said challenging Kate's patience.

"I understand what you want but do you understand the assignment?" Kate asked.

Foon hesitated and then replied, "I don't know and don't care. This is what I need to have in order to do whatever Devers wants. I need the initial funds deposited to my account before I hear about the assignment. Devers understands how I work. If you have an issue I suggest you take it up with him. I don't want to hear from you again until I have the funds and the assignment. Is this understood?" There was no point in responding the call ended. Devers had some very interesting business associates, she mused.

Before she realized what she was doing she had placed a call to Devers. She had exited the building and was seeking refuge from the heat. It was ninety seven degrees at eight PM and the sun had been down for almost two hours.

'Ah yes April in New York City what a great time of year.' she thought. The heat was bad but the smell was worse. It was like the whole city had body odor, an odor that would not go away.

"Foster that was quick, how long ago did you leave?" Devers teased. "Let me guess Foon wants money before she will take the assignment and other two aren't really interested."

"Foon wants a total of forty five hundred IMC, fifteen hundred up front and the balance on verification that the assignment has been completed. If you knew, why didn't you just have me contact Foon?"

"First of all you need these contacts if you are going to move up in my organization and secondly, Foon is difficult to deal with at times and I wasn't sure if she would even take the call. She must need the funds." Kate listened him, trying to evaluate what the next step should be. "Foster, tell her the funds will be in her account in the morning and that she will have the assignment personally delivered to her by you. Pick up the document at the secure site in the branch closest to your home and then take the train to Cleveland to meet with her. Good work, we will be getting some meaningful intelligence very soon." Again there was no point in responding he had disconnected the phone.

Next she placed the call to Foon, half expecting her not to answer. "Yes Foster what is the problem, didn't you understand the rules?"

"Okay Ms. Foon, or is that your first name? The funds will be in your account in the morning and I will hand deliver the assignment to you in Cleveland by mid-morning. Do you understand?"

"It is just Foon and we will meet at the Olde Town Coffee Shoppe on Fifth at eleven, don't be late I will only wait for five minutes."

Kate disconnected the call before Foon could do so, it was a control issue. Who were these people that were so ill bred that they could not end a conversation civilly, she wondered. Kate descended the stairs to the subway system and felt the relief from the heat but the intensity of the odor increased dramatically.

The first of the colonies of people living beneath the street was looming ahead of her. It was a make shift combination of storage containers, tents and anything else that could be used to create a little private space for those that were unfortunate to have to live in there. Security was at a high level here and there was little need for concern for one's safety because of it. The people that lived there were people that were part of the large number of unemployed that had been struggling to survive for the past forty or fifty years, she thought.

The images took her back to her childhood when her family lived together with her grandparents in three rooms in Charlotte. To her it was a great adventure, until her she found her mother crying hysterically one afternoon and then she realized that they needed to have their own place, that there were too many people living in too close of quarters. She shook the image off and concentrated on the fact that she would be on the train soon and back in her apartment in Philadelphia with her two sons and her parrot Bill.

****

Philip disconnected the call with his brother. He asked a very odd question at very strange time, he thought. Was it mere coincidence or maybe he had heard him talking about the idea with their father or had he overheard a conversation with Jessica? It did seem odd though. He forced himself back to the research and concentrated on tatter piece of paper labeled '1-21-421'. It was outside of the cryptic reference system and he couldn't make too much sense of it. It appeared to be genealogical research on a Brigadier General A. G. Jenkins in Lee's mounted infantry. There was a DNA report also that was badly deteriorated but the summary showed that Leopold Jenkins was a descendant of this man.

Philip scratched his head and smiled and then laughed out loud. Leopold Jenkins was clearly a man of color, a black man. This man was a white slave holder that fought to maintain slavery and southern way of life. He wondered whether Jessica knew this and if she did, did she actually care. It seemed odd that Jenkins would be so intent on illustrating that the South could have won the war and that winning the war would have changed the world. This would be a world changed so that he might never would have had born, or if he was he would have had a much different life. What demons did this man have working within him to cause him to take that direction?

The discovery seemed to energize Philip who continued to work most of the night following the logic trail that Jenkins had laid out. There were reams of computer data models that showed millions of permutations. These were iterations of the time thread as it would be modified during the 'Epiphanal Startling' depending upon the events that were altered. When he glanced at the clock to see whether it was too late to call Jessica to ask her a question about one of the references he discovered that it was almost four in the morning and that he would have to get up in about an hour and half to go to work. He turned to the next section and continued working.

At about five he stood up and went to make coffee. On the way back from the kitchen he took a detour to the bathroom where he turned the shower on and proceeded to get ready for the day. His mind had not missed a thought in the symphony of cognitive discovery played out in four part harmony. He was enjoying the challenge the puzzle that was in front of him and now he had to enjoy the fact that he would be functioning on no sleep for the third time in the last ten days. This pattern would end with a physical collapse, it had happened before but there was no way to avoid it. He was hooked on the endorphin high that these discoveries produced. It was almost orgasmic.

When Philip finished his second class he had a message waiting for him. It was from a Nelson Truax with the Department of Internal Security. It was an odd message that basically told him that he should make himself available to the Department when they arrive at F&M later in the day today. It did not state a time and there was no stated purpose for the meeting. Philip assumed that it was regarding some civil rights research that he had done for the government in the past and suspected that they were looking for more information. Nothing the government did ever surprised him and he did not give it a second thought.

****

Kate walked out of the secured facility at the center city branch office of WBOI. She had placed the tube with Foon's assignment in her bag and was making her way out into the morning crowds toward the closest subway entrance. She was still new to Philadelphia having been a resident for only two months since receiving the promotion to the Philadelphia Regional Security Director. An RSD was a good job, something that most people would welcome, but the drawback at WBOI was working with Devers. She hoped that within a year or two she would have a chance to move out of security and away from him.

She found her way to a staircase that lead to the subway and descended the stairs rapidly. She wondered if she should have brought someone with her to act as back up should the meeting not go according to plan. As she approached the entrance to the line that ran to the central hub train station she became aware that there was no over powering smell like she had experienced in New York. The air was surprisingly fresh she thought, though the walls and floors did not appear to be all that clean. It was not as nice a visual presentation as New York but there was no odor and that was a very good thing, she thought.

The connection from the Pittsburgh train to the Cleveland train required everything to run on time. Should there be any delays she could miss the connection and not make the meeting on time. She was worried that things would not work out. It was in her nature to worry like that. As she turned the corner to the subway platform she was struck by a young boy who was apparently running from three others. She fell backwards and landed on her side. It's a good thing that I am not wearing a skirt she thought as she struggled to her feet. Kate looked at the boy as he too struggled to his feet. He was small and approximately twelve or thirteen years old with short brown hair. His clothes appeared to be clean and well pressed though they were not what would be considered fashionable. That's probably why he was being chased, she thought. When he stood it appeared that he was actually a little taller than she, about five foot one inch. He also must have out-weighed her by forty pounds.

"Are you alright?" she asked catching her breath. He glanced nervously to see what the other were going to do. Kate turned and looked at them. "Is there a problem here?" she asked them. They in unison looked at the ground and then turned and ran off. When she returned her attention to the boy she found that he too had disappeared. She reached for her bag and made certain that the contents were still there. She then remembered that she was on an extremely tight schedule and must get going. She started to jog to the platform seeing that the subway train was about to depart. Kate squeezed through the doors as they were about to close. The transit policeman shot her a black look of disapproval, but then turned his attention to the noise that was coming from the other end of the car.

Before Kate could see what was actually transpiring the transit policemen had one man on the ground and was holding the other off with his light stick. That was what they called the electrically charged tip that was mounted on the end of an extendable wand. It could incapacitate someone in seconds. The man on the ground was foaming at the mouth and was twitching in convulsions brought on by the application of the light stick. The other man cowered by squatting and leaning against the door at the end of the car.

"Don't worry about what is happening here people. Everything is under control." the transit policeman told the occupants in a matter-of-fact tone.

Arrests like this were very common. Kate never assumed that she had anything to worry about, but some of her friends had told stories about people that had been arrested when they were not doing anything that broke the law. There were so many laws that it was impossible to believe that they were innocent, she thought, though there did seem to be a lot of people in jail. She was working on putting some more there herself and she chuckled out loud at the thought. Her career would really take off if she could find and apprehend Justin Welsh. He had eluded the FBI and WBOI for more than seven years.

When the train stopped she became aware of her surroundings once again. The woman standing next to her on the train looked at her and then turned away quickly. She appeared to be someone that was nervous about something. Perhaps she was with those men that were just arrested, Kate thought. The doors opened and Kate quickly exited seeking the fastest way to reach the Pittsburgh train. Her PCU guided her and she soon found herself queued up in one of the stalls awaiting the train's arrival.

****

Roger was gazing at the rows upon rows of numbers. It seemed like an endless stream of code that had no real structure to the uninitiated but he read the patterns like people read a menu in a restaurant, he knew what he wanted and he was quickly paging through to find the exact information that would satisfy his needs. There it was, now all he had to find was the escape logarithm and he could call this project completed.

His phone indicated that he had a call from Gloria. He wondered why she would be calling at that time of the day. Usually she was not even awake before noon because of her work schedule. The need for professional mannequins was great but the hours that they were required to work typically went into the early morning. She didn't typically go into work until Roger had been home for at least an hour.

"Good morning Gloria, I am shocked, you are awake." he said teasingly.

"Roger there was a man here looking for you. He said that you owed him money and that if you didn't pay he was going to break your legs." Gloria sounded frantic.

"What did he look like?" Roger asked nervously, though he knew he did not owe anyone money.

"He was around six feet tall with really dark brown hair almost black. He had very light colored blue eyes and he was dressed in all black, shirt, tie, pants shoes and nail polish too. He was very sinister looking."

Roger started to laugh. "His name is Lawrence, William Lawrence. He is a friend from college. He was always a prankster, I am truly sorry he got you up. Please go back to bed."

"You have some very stupid friends Roger. What's the name of that other one that tries to grab me every time he sees us together? You need to have them grow up. It's not right." Gloria paused for a moment and then said, "You know I love you don't you?"

Now Roger knew where this was going. He would be trapped into saying that he loved her when he wasn't even sure what that meant. "Yes, I know you do, I have to run I am on a deadline I will call you around noon, good bye Gloria."

He disconnected the call and wondered whether he should make a change to his life. He was breaking convention by living with her, but it was her decision to do this. Even though they were not having sexual relations, it was still wrong to be living together. There were times when they had almost broken that taboo as well. There were lots of instances when it could have happened but they both understood what society would have to say about a man and a woman being together before marriage.

He needed to get back to work but he now was thinking about why Willie would be stopping by. He hadn't talked to him since his father died in that freak whitewater accident. The man was a genius though, he thought. If he wanted to get together Roger thought that he should bring his work with him. He could save him a lot of time. He thought about calling him, but just as he was about to place the call his boss called him in to review his latest results and then work just cascaded into his office like endless waterfall of encryption algorithms.

****

It was ten forty eight when Kate turned the corner and saw the Olde Town Coffee Shoppe midway down the block. The streets of Cleveland were deserted except for occasional PT that whined by with the occupants staring out at the foolish person walking in the heat. Kate's air conditioned suit was only partially working since the collision with the young boy. Her right side was cool but the left side from her mid-thigh down was like it was on fire. There was perspiration forming on the back side of her leg behind the knee and the material of her pants was sticking to it.

When she reached the doorway and it opened to admit her it was ten fifty three. She scanned the room but her PCU did not pick up a signature for Foon. There were three people that must have had blocks on their units and it was most likely that Foon was one of them. The biggest problem was that all of the people that had their identification blocked were women. Kate thought about the problem and had two options. One was to wait and allow Foon to make her presence known since she did not have her identification turned off or she could simply call her. She decided to call.

A tall thin woman seated in the back of the shop looked up when the call was placed. She nodded her head and gestured with her hand for Kate to have a seat. As Kate took the seat the woman offered her hand and said, "I am Foon, and you are Foster correct?" Kate did not extend her hand but instead placed the tube that she had been carrying into Foon's open hand.

"I see, we could at least pretend to be polite Ms. Foster. Especially if we are going to be working with each other for a little while."

Kate looked at her and then decided that she could not trust Foon. She was a manipulator, she made people do things and think things that they did not really want to do. Devers had authorized a lot of money to pay this woman, this woman must be exceptionally talented and therefore when dealing with Foon she knew that she had to keep her distance and maintain control at all times, she thought.

"Foon, I am easy to work with and I am always polite. Do your job and do it well and we will have a very pleasant business relationship. Fail and we will not do business again." Kate said with a smile.

Foon toyed with opening the tube and fiddled with it. "Do you know what is contained within this?" she asked gesturing with it.

"Yes." Kate replied though she really did not know the details or the depth that Devers had directed Foon to pursue the objective. Foon continued to stare into Kate's eyes.

"When I have reached a milestone, who should I contact, you or Devers?"

Kate weighed the answer for if she contacted her and there was illegal activity she could be implicated but if she sent her directly to Devers Kate would mostly be back in Washington working on branch security or worse.

"Me." she said. There it was, she was now into whatever crazy plan Devers had put together, hopefully it was not illegal.

Foon seemed to relax upon hearing that she would be reporting to Kate. "Foster, you don't know how happy it makes me not to have to see or talk to that man." Foon said with a smile of relief.

"Yes, unfortunately I do know what you mean." Kate replied and they both laughed. Kate then continued by saying, "I expect that you will give me periodic updates. You can send the files here." She then instructed her PCU to download contact information to a secure message box.

Foon looked at her and then said, "I will." At that point she stood and extended her hand once again. This time Kate stood and took it. It was time to get back to Philadelphia and if she hurried she would be able to make the noon train. She turned to walk to the door and Foon walked with her.

"Where are you headed?" she asked.

"Back to Philadelphia." Kate replied.

"I can drop you at the train if you would like, it is very hot today, as usual." Foon offered.

"Normally I would say no, but I am pressed for time, thank you."

Foon had a PT parked in front of the shop and they quickly got inside. The compartment was cool when compared to the one hundred seven degree temperature that Cleveland was experiencing in late morning. "The forecasted high today is one hundred eighteen degrees." Foon said as she instructed the PT to take them to the train station.

The ride was quick but Kate did have an opportunity to study Foon a bit more. She took note of her appearance and while she was thin she did not appear to be in very good physical shape, perhaps she spent too much time behind a desk or in front of a computer. Her long black hair was not her natural color which appeared to be auburn or maybe even a little closer to red than brown. Kate had thought by the sound of her name that she would be of Asian extraction but it was clear that she was not, possibly Eastern European. The PT glided up to the curb outside of the train station. "Foster, I will be in touch."

Kate exited the PT and turned to reply but Foon did not wait she sped off. She was a very interesting woman, Kate thought as she walked quickly into the station. She would have plenty of time to catch the train but instead of browsing she elected to queue up and wait. While she stood in the stall she wondered if she should open and read the instructions. At that point she still had the ability to deny any detailed knowledge of the plan and wanted to preserve that as long as possible, so the answer was still no.

****

Philip was sitting in his office between classes reviewing the notes he had scribbled down in the last several hours of work the previous night. He had a deadline for publication that had passed and had been given an extension because of the complexity of the article and the fact that it promised to be a truly inspiring piece. The Dean had made it clear that there would be no more extensions and that he had to finish by April fifteenth, a mere thirteen days from then.

He was perplexed because every time he felt he had a grasp of how to finish the paper he invariably found something new that could impact the piece's conclusion. Last night it was the connection between Leopold and his ancestor. He wondered whether it had any relevance to the thesis or was it just an interesting bit of background material that could be filed away for later discussions with Jessica. The interesting point he was now considering was that Stewart's cavalry's absence was one of the key argument for failure espoused by the Southern Apologists. Many contended that Jenkins was not of the same caliber of leader as Stewart and that Lee did not have the confidence in him to utilize his command of mounted infantry as they could have been used.

Jenkins' contended that the changes would have to be targeted at several key moments. He believed that the death of 'Stonewall' Jackson was one of those changes that would have made a huge difference. From a strategic standpoint and much more directly connected was the appointment of Meade as commander of the Army of the Potomac instead of leaving Hooker in place they started to put the odds in favor of Union success. The change of focus from Baltimore and Washington DC to Philadelphia as a military objective along with the tactical events that he laborious outlined made a clear case for the results favoring a Southern victory and the eventual capitulation of the North, not because they couldn't win, but because they lost the desire to do so.

Philip was exhausted and was having difficulty keeping his eyes open. He knew that he needed to get some sleep but wasn't exactly sure when he would be able to do so. He closed his eyes and felt his thoughts begin to slow. He thought about how Thomas Edison had been able to work getting very little rest and that he should use the technique. He would as soon as he rested for just a few more minutes, he thought.

The next thing Philip knew was that he had been asleep and there was someone trying to wake him up. "Dr. Lee, Dr. Lee there are men from the Department of Internal Security here to see you. Please wake up." Philip opened his eyes and saw the security guard in front of him that had been speaking to him.

"Yes, give me a minute. I will be out to see them in just a minute." Philip said rubbing his eyes. He took a moment to organize his work, putting all of the files back in their electronic folders and making a backup that was automatically loaded on his home computer.

Philip came out of his office to find two members of the Department of Internal Security waiting for them. "Gentlemen, how can I help you today?" he asked extending his hand.

Nelson Truax stepped forward and shook his hand saying, "Dr. Lee, my name is Nelson Truax and this Luther Strong. We are special investigators with the Department of Internal Security. Is there somewhere that we can talk?" Philip acknowledged Luther Strong with a nod of the head and then motioned for them to follow him. He took them to the conference room that was located several doors down the hall.

"Can I get you anything to drink?" Philip inquired.

"No thank you." Truax responded and then he continued, "We will get directly to the point Dr. Lee. We believe that you are in possession of some classified information that cannot be permitted to be released to the public. Do you know Jessica Jenkins?"

"Yes I do know Ms. Jenkins, what does this have to do with her?" Philip asked cautiously.

"Ms. Jenkins was in the possession of information that was classified as a threat to National security and we believe that she passed that information on to you. We also believe that she probably did so without informing you of the nature of the information."

"Ms. Jenkins provided me with her father's research regarding a hypothetical thesis. I can't see how that information is considered classified." Philip pushed back slightly but knew that if Internal Security felt it was a threat then it was.

Truax continued asking, "Do you remember seeing a document that had these markings on it?" He held up a screen that displayed the classified symbol on it. It appeared to be on a page that he was trying to get his cousin to procure for him. Now he understood, they thought he already had it.

"Gentlemen I saw a reference to a page that was classified but did not see the actual page nor was it given to me by Ms. Jenkins or anyone else. I am confused though, this theory is only an academic exercise there is no chance of any of it becoming reality."

"I couldn't comment on that sir, I only know that we were lead to believe that you had a copy of the document. Would you allow us to verify that?"

Great, they want to search his office and probably his home looking for a document that he did not have but had tried to get, Philip thought. He did not have a choice but to comply.

"Gentlemen you can look through all of my research material both here and at my home." Philip offered.

"That won't be necessary Dr. Lee. It appears that the paper that we are seeking is still in the offices of our bureau. This apparently was a tremendous waste of your time. I am so sorry we have inconvenienced you." Truax said while extending his hand. Philip looked at them as he shook Truax's hand. There is no way that this was an accidental meeting, this was a warning of some kind. He was supposed to stay away from that classified document and they were letting him know that they knew he was interested in it.

If Philip wasn't awake before the meeting, he certainly was after it was over. His next class was set to begin at one thirty and that gave him a few minutes to eat and to decide what to do next. He was going to find out what made that document so important and the best person to answer that question was Jessica.

****

Roger was getting hungry and needed to escape his office. The work was just going to keep coming and there was nothing he could do at this point except work as quickly and efficiently as possible. The work required perfection, he could make no mistakes and because of this it had slowed his production down considerably. He found himself looking at each solution to the problem three or four times before releasing it as being complete.

Still he needed to get out of the office. He remember that Willie had stopped at his apartment earlier and thought that this would be a great time for him to reach out and see what he wanted. He placed the call to William Lawrence and waited to see if he would answer. There was a strong probability that he would not because Willie was just the type that did not remember why or when he did things or he would ignore you after trying to reach you for days. He was just that quirky and that's why Roger enjoyed him so.

Just as Roger was about to disconnect his voice boomed, "Who is this anyway, and why are you bothering me?"

Willie was in rare form Roger thought. "Willie, its Roger. About the money, I have no intention of ever paying you back." Roger started to chuckle and Willie burst out laughing.

"Roger that is a very good looking cleaning woman you have." Of course Willie never knew where the line was that he should not cross and at this point Roger wasn't so sure he liked someone comparing Gloria to a cleaning woman. No one could talk about Gloria negatively that was his right exclusively and he never complained about her to anyone, in fact most people didn't even know she existed.

"Willie, how have you been? It has been a couple of months since the last time you figured out how to open the door to your place and let yourself out. My guess is there is an APB out on you right now." Roger teased his friend but he was truly glad that he had stopped by to see him. "Are you free for lunch?" he asked.

There was silence on the line and Roger wondered if Willie had disconnected the call. He had once done that and Roger must have talked for ten minutes before he realized what he had done. He was about to ask if Willie was still on the line when he finally responded, "Yes, let's get lunch, the sooner the better. I just realized I haven't eaten since yesterday. Where would you like to meet?"

How about Tony's down off of ninth, do you know the place?" Roger replied.

"You and those artery clogging sandwiches, sounds good, I can be there in about twenty minutes. Is that okay with you?"

"Perfect, I will see you then."

Roger did his best to put things in order so that when he returned from lunch he could start back to work without losing too much ground. The unfortunate thing was that he there was no way to avoid falling dramatically behind.   The work would keep coming even while he was away from his desk. It would have been great if the company would have chosen to find some additional help for him. Perhaps they could take on some of his lesser jobs but he knew that was not going to happen either. Productivity was extremely important and even though unemployment continued to be extremely high there was no indication that businesses would make the concessions necessary to realize the President's goal for running a twenty four hour and seven day per week economy with shorter work weeks and utilizing three people to perform every job of consequence. Roger left his desk dreading coming back to it after lunch but his stomach needed to be filled and the place they were going would do more than an adequate job of filling it.

****

Kate's arrived at her office at three o'clock and at that point she still had almost five hours of work left in her day. When she was finally able leave she made the quick commute without incident and arrived home in time to spend a few precious minutes with her sons before tucking them into bed for the night. Then she had a quick meal, a verbal joust with the bird and was into the bath for a nice soak. This day had been certainly one of 'those' days, she thought.

Kate decided to use the time she had to catch up on some needed sleep. As she lay there waiting for sleep to capture her and take her away from the issues of the day she thought about what had transpired. She had left home at before seven that morning and all she had thought about was finding an alternate way to get Gina Fanacci to help WBOI. She had thought that perhaps they could appeal to her desire to do what was right, but that had not gone well when she was originally approached three months earlier, just before Kate had been given the entire Lee assignment. That was when they had found out that Lee's father was going to use his influence to get his son a job.

They had interviewed most of the staff to see if anyone would be willing to help. There were a couple of people that had stepped forward but for any number of reasons they were not useful. Gina it was determined, after Lee had taken the position, to be the best fit. She had similar skills and was an attractive woman that he might become interested in pursuing. So far video surveillance had not shown anything other than the fact that they really did not get along very well. Lee had tried to engage her in conversations but she had been distant and the apparent increase in her drug usage was probably what prompted that type of antisocial behavior.

She thought about how it was clear that the investigation needed a break through event and that could very well lead to Justin Welsh's capture. She had visualized it before and continued to see herself in the pivotal role in bringing him to justice. They would probably give him the death penalty for all the hardship he had caused. The economy would not be in the miserable shape it was in if he hadn't attacked the Banking Consortium. All of his team had been caught, they were all, with the exception of Austin Lee, behind bars and were not to be released from prison any time soon.

Her husband wouldn't have been sent to war. She would not have to be working as hard as she was if the transition to the IMC had not been undermined by Welsh and Lee. They were evil, selfish men that thought nothing about the people that they hurt and their only concern was to make more and more money for themselves.

As she continued to think about how her husband was forced to be away from his family and that he might die or be disfigured, she pictured him sitting alone. He had been gone for six months and it was likely that he would be gone at least another year or more. The war moved from country to country and continent to continent. At least he was in a combat support role and not was directly involved in the fighting, she thought. Their youngest son would not recognize his father if she didn't make certain to show him video of him repeatedly. Those times were extremely difficult for her to see him and not to be able to tell him how she felt.

****

Austin had just come back from lunch, it was a little after one twenty and he was hoping the day would end. The work had been tedious and he was thinking about his meeting last evening. John and George were so passionate. He was simply frightened about going back to prison. They had that crazy idea about changing time and he even called his brother to see when it would be the time to do it. That was just a crazy notion. Granted he had read that article and they did say it was possible. If only he could remember the scientists' name perhaps he could prove to himself that it was just as screwy an idea as it originally had sounded.

He glanced over to see Gina staring at the cubicle wall. There did not appear to be anything that was noteworthy on the wall but he could not be certain. Gina had been acting even stranger than normal the past several days and Austin was concerned that she would do something that would reflect poorly on him. He toyed with the idea of saying something to her. Unfortunately he couldn't think of anything to say that would appear to be genuine. As he was thinking this she happened to glance over at him and noticed that he had been looking at her. Her eyes seemed to have difficulty focusing on him at first and then she seemed to recognize that he had been looking at her. She almost smiled, or at least he thought she did. He decided in that instant to open his mouth and say something. "Did you enjoy you lunch today?" he asked and immediately felt self-conscience about the nature of the question.

Gina brought Austin into focus and heard him ask the question. She was not sure how to respond and it didn't seem to matter. Her life was not going particularly well. She had lost her mother seven months earlier to a freak accident. She had been extremely close to her and the loss hit her very hard. Her doctor had prescribed a mood elevating drug that was designed to help combat the type of depression from which she suffered. It was effective for a short period of time but she soon fell back into the pit of sorrow. A friend had given her some pills and she was told that they would help her sleep and while they didn't help with sleeping they seemed to make it easier for her to cope. The problem was that she needed higher doses now than she did initially. She was now addicted and she had come to realize it when she asked for more.

"Hello Austin, my lunch was fine. How was yours?" the words flowed but she really didn't seem to have too much control of the tone of her voice or the particular words that came out. "Did you know Austin that I have been working for this company for more than five years and have never taken a vacation?" Gina asked rhetorically. "I can do this job in my sleep." she said with a laugh.

Austin wasn't sure what to say. It was clear to him that Gina was not behaving normally. She seemed to be under the influence of something. What should he do? Should he tell anyone? He came to the conclusion that he should just ignore the behavior and get back to work.

"I don't have the same skill level you do apparently, I find some of the work challenging." he said hoping to transition the conversation to work and then get them both back on task.

"Oh, let me help you." she said standing and approaching him, "What are you working on now?" It went from bad to worse as she tripped and end up falling on him as he sat there.

Austin caught her and managed to avoid grabbing her in an inappropriate manner. She smelled good he thought as he attempted to help her up. Gina regained her composure and stepped back.

"I think I am going to go back to work." she said.   After that she returned to her seat and stared quietly at the cubical walls again. Austin returned his attention to work but found himself glancing at Gina to see if she was alright. During the next hour her attention shifted from the cubical wall to her desk top to finally the work that was on the screens that lay scattered on her desk.

Slowly she became more and more aware of what she was to be doing and by the time their supervisor stopped by to check on their progress she was actively doing her work. Austin noticed during this time that she would glance quickly at him as though she was checking what he was doing. As the day came to a close he wondered if he should make an attempt to speak with her again. He did not want to embarrass her or cause her any reason not to like him. There were enough people in the world that didn't like him, it was best not to increase the number voluntarily, he concluded.

****

Lunch with Willie had been an interesting one. Willie had told Roger that he had been visited by two men from Internal Security regarding his father's work and he was also asked whether he had been contacted by Philip, Roger's brother, regarding research on time thread manipulation. Willie told them that he had not seen Philip in several years. He also said that he didn't know anything about his father's research or even the circumstances surrounding the accident that caused his death. They went on to ask if he knew Senator Sun Ya Yen, and whether he had been contacted by the Senator or anyone on the Senator's staff.

Now this was really a mystery, Roger thought. Willie told them that he did know the Senator but only because he had come to his father's funeral. The Senator was in a body case that performed all of his life functions. Even his speech was generated by the case, an enclosed self-contained unit that kept the Senator alive. They had not spoken again and he had not heard from anyone on his staff. Willie said that the Senator had been on the trip with his father and that he was the only one that survived. The other man was a professor of some sort that lived in Los Angeles.

Roger called Gloria as he was on his way back to his office. He woke her up and told her about the strange lunch conversation. Gloria's response was that she didn't know Philip and then wondered why she had never met the members of his family. He then thought about what motivated him to make the call let alone share personal information with Gloria. She immediately made the conversation about her, when it should have been about him. He then stopped and examined his thought process, he then recalled something he had read within Christopher Leesop's journal regarding where the focus of our lives should be. He wondered at that moment whether he had been too self-absorbed and perhaps Gloria was right.

He planned on calling Philip later after he had left work to discuss the events and to see if it made any sense to him. He had to call Philip because Willie had told him that his name was mentioned by Internal Security. He knew that Philip had been contacted by DIS in the past and had done research for them, but this did not sound like a research request. It sounded like an investigation. Roger then thought of Austin and the probability that he was somehow linked to this. It was bad enough when the government goes after someone that deserves it, but there was no reason for them to go after someone just because they were related to a person that had offended. Guilt by association was totally unfair, he continued to think. Perhaps there was a good reason for them contacting Willie. It seemed that they were focused on his father's research. He then wondered what that was.

****

Philip finished his last class and proceeded to gather his things for the ride home to Pittsburgh. He thought about stopping to see Austin, especially after the conversation the last evening but decided that he should go home and try to get some sleep. He did have one call he knew that he had to make. That call was to Jessica so that he could gain some insight into what was so important in her father's research that it had been classified.

He found himself dosing during the ride home and when the train reached Pittsburgh he had to be awakened by a steward to make certain that he got off the train and didn't return to Philadelphia. The balance of his commute was a short ten minute shuttle ride and a five minute walk in the early evening heat. As he walked he decided to call Jessica. It would be a brief call and then he could get to bed. Tomorrow he would go back to work on the paper. He had to finish it soon. This was getting to be far too much work and too much of an intrusion into how he thought his life should be, he surmised.

Jessica answered the call by asking a question, "Did Internal Security come to see you today?" She seemed agitated. "They were asking about a document and they told me that I gave it to you and that you were going to published it."

Philip listened to all that she had to say and then proceeded to tell her about his encounter. It seemed like they had been on a 'fishing expedition' and when they couldn't find any fish they packed up and left. Jessica told him that they did apologize and that there had been a mistake. It was a truly odd visit and it caused her to think about her father, how he died and how much she missed him. She then started to cry. Philip felt helpless, he wanted to comfort her but could only reassure her that she was going to be alright and that nothing was going to come of whatever they were trying to prove.

"Philip, maybe you should stop working on my father's theory? It seems like there was a reason that it was never brought to light before." Jessica had responded to his desire to help her, but instead of accepting his help she was willing to give up.

"Why do you say that? I thought this was important to you. Besides I have to continue it if I expect to keep my job. The Dean has made it very clear that it must be done and done quickly, there is no time for me to find another subject."

There was silence on the other end of the line. Philip waited to hear what she would say next. Seconds passed and there was nothing said. It was becoming awkward for Philip, he now felt he had to say something. He resisted the urge to speak. He felt that he had to give her a chance to respond to his statement, to tell him what she was thinking and feeling. The seconds gave way to a minute and then a second minute.

Finally Jessica said, "Philip are you still there?"

Philip responded, "Yes, I was waiting for you to say something."

"Oh, I really don't have anything to say. I will call you later. Good bye." and the connection was gone. Jessica's reaction had confused him. She was a woman that had openly shared her inner most thoughts with him but yet when it came time to validate their relationship, she seemed to vanish, and it was then that she emotionally disappeared.

****

Kate was about to start working on the shift rotation schedule for the surveillance of Austin Lee when she received a notification of a secure message receipt. She thought that it must be from Foon, but it was much too quick for her to have made any headway on the assignment. She was going to wait until she finished the schedule but her curiosity compelled her to open the message. It was an audio report. The tag indicated that it was indeed from Foon and that it had been sent at three forty two PM.

Foon indicated that she had made contact with the subject at two minutes past twelve and had provided her with a sample of what was hoped to become her drug of choice. It was significantly more powerful and much more addictive. Prolonged usage would remove a person's ability to resist suggestions and therefore the person would be susceptible to being easily controlled. She indicated that it was a very popular drug in the sex trafficking trade.

Kate played the message three times to make certain she had a thorough understanding of everything that was being communicated. Foon was a person that could say things that might be construed differently upon each evaluation. There was nothing that could have been misunderstood. Gina Fanacci was being manipulated to become the operative they needed to catch Justin Welsh. Kate had to accept that this person was going to be sacrificed for the greater good. She felt sad for a moment but then began to picture how it would be when she apprehended Welsh and how much better off the whole world would be.

Kate went back to work on the schedule knowing that Foon was working hard to accomplish the task that was assigned to her. She was a good asset that was proving to be very reliable. It would not surprise her if she heard from her again very soon. 'Keep focused on your job.' she thought. You have to do it better each day if you are expecting to move up and out from under Devers' control.

****

The day was finally over for Roger. The work that he had done saved his company millions of IMC and it put computing back on the same track that it had been on some sixty years earlier. It was satisfying work for him knowing that he was rebuilding the networks and computing power that had society on the verge of technological breakthroughs in artificial intelligence, nano-computing and intuitive processing.

His next project would be working with thought controlled processors and it would mean that he would be working at one of the major university hospitals to build the processing interface between the mind and the computer. It certainly was exciting for him and there were times when he could not restrain the enthusiasm. It was necessary for him to do so since much of the work that he did was considered highly sensitive and not available for many to see or even know that it was being done. He would be getting his instructions on the new project within the coming weeks as he put the finishing touches on the encryption programs. There were several small problems that he had to address but the workload would be nothing like what he had been experiencing. There would be no more days like today, he thankfully thought.

As he walked to the PT that he was using to commute to his apartment overlooking the Schuylkill River he barely noticed the heat. He was consumed with putting all of the days' pieces into their right places. The next piece of business was to call his brother and talk to him about the day, specifically the Internal Security visit to Willie and the fact that he was mentioned by name.

"Hello Roger, I was hoping that you would call, I need a friendly voice right now. It was been one of those days and to top it off I haven't slept more than a couple of minutes in the past twenty four hours." Philip started the conversation without giving Roger a chance to even say hello. When he had finished talking he had told him about the research that he had been doing, the fact that Internal Security had been to see him and that he had been seeing Jessica. The last piece of information stuck with Roger though he decided to talk about the Internal Security incident since there was a coincidence factor present that could not be overlooked.

"Phil, my friend, Willie Lawrence had a visit from Internal Security today as well. First thing this morning they showed up at his apartment and asked him what he knew about his father's research and then they asked if he knew whether you were in possession of a particular classified document." Roger explained.

"Did they mention me by name?" Philip asked.

"Oh, yes they did. It was odd too since there is no reason that you would have been in contact with Willie. I know you met him once or twice but I don't think you even spoke to him other than when he was in my company. You didn't go to his father's funeral last year did you?" Roger asked.

"I didn't know that his father was dead. How did it happen?" Philip asked. Roger went on to explain about the whitewater excursion and how he was killed along with a professor from California and the other passenger was a senator. As he explained Philip began to become uncomfortable. Now he wanted to know what Lawrence was working on at the time of his death and if there was a connection between Jenkins and the Senator. He needed more information.

"What was Willie's father working on when he died?" Philip asked.

"I am not sure, he had a government contract or grant and it was all very secretive. I am not even sure Willie knows what the project was." Philip thought that it might be the key as to why the Internal Security people were investigating. Maybe they think that Jenkins knew something about the research and that was what they were seeking. It seemed to make sense.

"Roger, can you see if Willie knows what his father was working on at the time of his death, and I'll see if I can find out the name of the senator and contact him."

Roger replied, "Phil, the senator's name is Sun Ya Yen and I will give Willie a call and get back you. I am not sure if you should take this too far. Internal Security is a very dangerous agency. Remember they are the ones that prosecuted Austin."

Philip knew all too well that Internal Security was the agency that spearheaded the prosecution of his brother but they were only acting on the orders of WBOI and the other banks that made up the Banking Consortium. This whole thing could be as a result of their continued concern about Austin and that Justin Welsh fellow that they never caught. I am certain that his eluding captivity did not sit well with the powers that be, he thought. Regardless of what was going on, he had not done anything that was illegal or unethical.

"Phil, what about this woman? How does she fit into all of this?" Roger finally got back to the topic that was most intriguing to him.

"Her name is Jessica Jenkins and her father was Dr. Leopold Jenkins the historian and ..."

"Don't tell me he was the other man that was killed in that whitewater accident?" Roger interrupted.

"Yes, he was. This all sounds very contrived doesn't?" Philip asked.

Roger and Philip discussed the several possible connections, including the element of chance. Perhaps the trigger was his meeting Jessica or perhaps it was the fact that their brother was a known accomplice of Justin Welsh. There were so many possible scenarios but the main point they agreed on was not to do anything that that would be considered illegal. They would contact Internal Security and give them anything relevant or even remotely related to the classified document that they were seeking information about. The call ended with the two brothers saying that they would speak again tomorrow.

After Roger disconnected the call Philip sat trying to determine what he should do next. His head was throbbing and he was certain that he was experiencing a rush of adrenalin that was keeping him from curling up in a ball and going to sleep. In the end though he decided that his best course of action was to go to sleep. He had considered calling Jessica, and then the Senator and finally his brother Austin. The call to Austin was the one that it took him the longest amount time to decide against making. He did not have enough information to make a determination of what to do next. Any call he placed would not benefit the person being called, the end result would be more worry.

****

Austin finished his assigned work for the day. It was getting late and he was feeling tired. The work was tedious and now there was a new element of stress that he had to consider. The person across from him had a drug problem and he wondered whether it could reflect negatively on him. He called his supervisor and informed him that he needed to use the rest room and once he had secured his permission he got up, leaving Gina working at her desk.

There were a number of men in the rest room and the sound of their voices reverberated off the gleaming white tile. As the door closed behind Austin with a whoosh, each of the men turn in unison to see who had entered. Several of them stopped speaking while the others were apparently were unaffected by his entrance.

Austin accomplished his intended purpose and stepped up to one of the sinks to wash his hands. There were only three men remaining in the room. The one closest to Austin nodded hello, while the man drying his hands said, "Hello, Lee how's it going?"

Austin smiled and replied, "Not too bad Charlie, it can get a little tedious looking at all those numbers though."

Charles Long laughed and continued, "At least it's time to go home. Have a good night."

"You too Charlie." Austin responded.

When Austin returned to his cubicle, he discovered that Gina had already left. He was relieved that he would not have to speak to her. He could now determine whether he should speak to his supervisor about what he had seen earlier that day. Telling his supervisor, he thought, would be the right thing to do for everyone. If she has a drug problem then she could get the help that she needed to end her dependence and it would also show he was doing everything he could to walk the straight and narrow path. He decided to act on this before he changed his mind. He cleared his desk and packed up for the evening.

Austin left his work area and walked in the direction of his supervisor's cubicle. It appeared from a distance there was activity so that he might still be working. This would be a good thing Austin thought. He would be able to have a conversation that would not draw a lot of attention. Unfortunately when he got closer he saw that his supervisor was speaking with a tall, pale, thin woman with black hair. He did not feel comfortable in approaching his supervisor when he was engaged in conversation with someone else. Austin turned to leave but his supervisor saw him and called him by name. "Lee, did you need to speak with me about something?" Roscoe Plantiere asked.

"Mr. Plantiere, it can wait until tomorrow, have a good night." Austin replied.

Roscoe thought for a moment and then said something to his visitor, who then turned and left. "Lee come here, lets handle it right now - tomorrow will come and there won't be time. We are both here let's get it handled now, right?" Roscoe tended to repeat things until people acknowledged that they understood and after that he still might repeat it.

"Okay. Mr. Plantiere, I was going to bring something to your attention." Austin said as he walked closer. He stopped about two feet from Roscoe and then lowered his voice so that it could only be heard by Roscoe. "Gina, the woman that works next to me might have a problem." Austin waited to see if there would be a reaction.

Roscoe responded with, "What kind of problem? Is it personal? Is it with you, because I know your father helped you get this job but if you are causing problems... well, we just can't have that."

"No the problem isn't with me. I think she might be using drugs, she was behaving very strangely today." Austin said while lowering his head. He felt bad about informing Roscoe, perhaps he should have thought it through more before acting. This could be a good example of the need to be patient, sometimes he could be so impetuous not giving things enough time to resolve themselves. It was a part of him he need learn to control, he thought.

"Lee, you are a good worker and it was right that you brought your concern to me." Roscoe reassured him. "I will watch to see what I can learn about the situation. I know she had experienced some problems at home. Her mother had died not too long ago and her father is not a very kind man apparently. I need you to watch over her, see if you can become her friend and let me know what comes of it. Okay?"

Austin did not feel comfortable being put in that situation but he needed to make sure that Roscoe was on his side. If he didn't have a job he could be sent back to prison.

"Okay, Mr. Plantiere, I will do my best." Austin said.

"Thanks, Lee. I will make certain that the right people know what is going on and we will make certain that Gina gets the right kind of help once we know for sure what is happening." After saying that Roscoe sat down and turned his attention to other things. Austin interpreted his actions as the conclusion of their meeting. As he walked away he felt that he had done right thing but was a little anxious about his role of observer. He was never very good at reading people. If he had been able to read people he would not have been so easily taken in by Justin, he thought. Then he now wondered why he had not heard any further from Justin, it had been almost three months and it wasn't like Justin to allow anyone or thing to go unattended for too long.

Austin walked to the train station. It was almost seven o'clock and the sun had set and even though the temperature was close to one hundred degrees it felt cooler not having the sun beating down upon him. The four block walk went quickly as he spent most of the time thinking about his new assignment. He tried to visualize Gina and then he thought about Gina and the loss of her mother. What would he have done if he had lost his mother? MacKenzie had been a chief supporter of him while he was in jail. She was the glue that held the family together. He knew that she loved him very much. He suddenly realized that he felt that he did not deserve it.

****

Devers had one more call to place. "Foster, how did it go today?" His voice pierced Kate's serenity, she had just finished her work and was on her way to see her children and finally had a chance to escape the pressures of the day.

"Mr. Devers, good to hear from you. Foon has the assignment and has already made inroads regarding the plan. I expect that she will be able to accomplish the mission very quickly." Kate cheerfully recounted.

"Good. Foon typically does fast work, though the quality of her work can be a little spotty at times. Keep a close watch on her and what she does. Your performance has definitely been a pleasant surprise. The quality of your work is quite impressive. I think you should do very well for yourself, especially if this Welsh thing gets resolved finally. Keep it up."

The connection was dropped and Kate knew not to try to respond. Devers had told her what she already knew. Her next step was to get someone above Devers to recognize her accomplishments. If that happened she could be assured that her next position would be outside of Devers' control and domain.

****

A call came from Nelson Truax. "Nelson my good man, so good of you to call. How was your day?"

"Fine Sir, the team was able to get the plan moving in the proper direction and judging by the calls that were logged there is quite a lot of traffic and confusion regarding this missing document." Truax replied.

"That's wonderful news. Did anyone of them reach out to Austin yet?"

"No, but is just a matter of time. My guess is that Philip Lee will try to reach out to the Senator very shortly and his brother Roger will be contacting Lawrence again." Truax said. Truax went on to report that there would be a lull in their efforts for the next two or three days while they observed the reaction to the inquiry and the actions that were spawned. He conclude with a summary of the next actions which included the careful monitoring of the surveillance on Austin Lee. He indicated that there apparently was some attempt by WBOI security to influence people at his place of work.

"Austin is very important, you must make certain that they do not find any means of hurting him. Do you understand?"

"Yes Mr. Welsh, I do understand and we will do everything in our power to make certain that he is protected along with the other members of your new team."

Chapter Six

Philip stared at the pages in front of him. He felt that the paper was as ready as it could be and that it should go to press. The only nagging issue was what reaction there would be from Internal Security. They had been quiet and everything had returned to a peaceful state after that one day last week. He was finally able to get a meeting with the Senator and he would be going to his facility where he was being treated in Virginia the next day. He had hoped not to go alone but knew that he couldn't take anyone except Jessica.

Jessica had not been very receptive to accompanying him on the visit but she had been much more attentive to Philip in the past week. It was as though Philip, by not pressuring her, had allowed her to come to him on her own terms. Philip continued to show restraint. It was important because he didn't want to take a step backwards as far as the relationship was concerned. He was expecting her to call him that evening and at that time he would ask her again to join him once again. If she said yes that would be great but if not he would drop the subject.

The subject of publication had to be broached as well and it represented an opportunity for a dispute. There had been no mention of it since he told her that it was too late to alter the topic of his publication.

He looked up from the work on his desk to find the room full of students. His class should have started five minutes before and he had not heard the tone nor the students that had apparently arrived without his observation. The topic for the day was Theodore Roosevelt and his impact on the presidency. He wished that the material was easier for the students to relate to but there were some very critical points he wished to communicate and future lessons would be based upon some of that discussion. He pushed himself away from his desk, stood up and began his lecture.

****

Roger and Willie had rekindled their friendship and Gloria was a little jealous.   She didn't mind Willie, in fact she actually enjoyed his lighthearted approach to life.   It was odd that he worked so hard at having fun and joking when there had been so much tragedy in his life. Gloria watched as Roger and Willie worked some computer problem together. It was obvious that Roger really admired Willie and that Willie enjoyed the attention. When Roger looked down at his work Willie took a writing stylus that he had been using. Gloria watched Roger's reaction when he couldn't find it and then watched Willie act as though he was looking for it too.   Then he asked Roger to hold very still and proceeded to pull the stylus from his nose. Roger looked at him in disbelief. "I can't believe that I fall for your antics all of the time." he said.

Gloria laughed at the two of them and they in turn looked at her as though their feelings were hurt. Gloria was having none of it though, these little boys could play their games but it did not mean that she had join in as well. The early evening was her favorite time of the day. It was when she could spend some time with Roger before she left for her job.

That was what it was, a job, not a career that she had trained for or one that she could gain some satisfaction in doing. Instead she spent between five and ten hours standing in one place, as still as possible. Her presence was to call attention to an article of clothing she was wearing or a piece of jewelry.   The job paid well but it was a fad that would eventually lose its luster and then there would be some other way to convince the wealthy to part with their money.

Originally Roger had hoped that by being in his company Willie would be able to give him some insight into the work that his father was doing, but as time when on it became clear that Willie did not know. It was also apparent that he had missed not being in his company. Willie made him feel good and he was a great resource when it came to complex logic problems, there was probably no one better that he knew. He used to think that his father was the smartest man in the world and then he met Willie.

****

Kate was about to leave the office, she hadn't heard anything from Foon in two days but the last information was quite encouraging.   It seemed that Lee had taken an interest in Gina and was engaging her regularly in conversation. The remainder of the report detailed her drug usage and the fact that she was addicted as they had anticipated and hope that she would be. Her daily requirements had outstripped her ability to pay the bill. Soon she would be forced to become completely reliant upon them. She would then do what was necessary to get close to Lee, and that meant anything. The more Kate thought about the situation and the direction that it was taking the more he found herself feeling very uncomfortable.

She was a good person, and wondered how could have she agreed to play a part in the destruction of another person. If she had met Gina she knew she would never have been able to put her in that position. How could she expect Foon to do this and how did Foon live with herself knowing what she was doing. Once again her defense mechanism kicked into gear. She focused on the fact that she needed her job to provide for her family while her husband was away engaged in the war effort. If she didn't do this she would be stuck working with that horrible man Devers and Welsh would be free to ruin even more lives and families like hers. She believed now more than ever that her husband would not be away at war if it wasn't for Justin Welsh.

As she closed her files a secure message was delivered. It had to be the latest in Foon's reports and it might have some critical information that she would relay to Devers and hopefully bring this to a speedy conclusion. She sat back in her chair and stretched. She started to play the message and from the moment she heard Foon's tone, she knew that things were not going well. Foon indicated that Lee had been cordial and while engaging Gina, but she had discovered the reason why. Lee had told his supervisor that he suspected Gina's drug use and Roscoe Plantiere had told him to spy on her, to win her confidence and they would get her the help that she needed.

Plantiere would be a problem, Foon went on to say. He was a well-connected middle manager who had relatives in the government. They were probably using him to keep tabs on Lee as well. If that was true Gina would not be useful to them and they would have to look at some other way to put Lee under surveillance. Foon was meeting with someone later that night to determine the depth of the problem. Plantiere's brother-in-law was regional director for Internal Security and he could represent a significant hindrance to their plans to use Lee to get to Welsh. Internal Security was extremely bad at clandestine operations and Welsh would certainly be able to see any attempt by them to monitor Lee's activities.

Devers should know about this but it would be more meaningful if she had the results of Foon's meeting that was to take place in the next several hours. Bad news tonight or bad news tomorrow would have roughly the same impact. She decided to delay calling him but also decided that if he were to call her, she would share the information. She stood and collected her things and turned quickly walked out of her office. Foon would have good news tomorrow she hoped.

****

"John, why haven't we put this Welsh thing to bed yet?" Fortesque asked plaintively. The disappointed was dripping from his voice. He had backed Devers when everyone else wanted to throw him to the dogs. This was especially true after the last series of Middle East wars, when his aggressiveness derailed the peaceful adaptation of the IMC for the third time. He had cost WBOI over a trillion IMC but he had also saved it much more. He was a two edged sword that an inept handler could end up losing their arm while they were wielding it. He had been cut several times but nothing that did not heal rapidly. "What are we going to do John?" Devers thought for a moment and then went on to brief Fortesque on the recent developments.

"It sounds like we don't know if Lee has been in contact with Welsh, do we John?"

"Sir, I would stake my reputation on the fact that Lee has not been contacted by Welsh in the past three months except for that first occasion when we were woefully unprepared. Since then I have a real bull dog on the case and she wants Welsh as much as we do."

"John, I want to remind you that if this does not get resolved in our favor and in the proper amount of time, that there will be serious repercussions. You have never let us down before and while your methods are found to be distasteful to many, they are effective. I will expect another briefing within the week and I also expect to see some significant progress. Do take care. Good bye."

Devers sat back in his chair. He understood that Fortesque was anxious to make his move on DeMasters, that timing was everything, but the plan that he had put into action required time to execute. If they had allowed him to kill Welsh eight years ago when he had the opportunity to do so no one would not be worried about this today. These people had no guts, they were spineless manipulative weasels that sat and watched the real workers, the doers, get the job accomplished while they reaped the rewards.

It became apparent to him that he needed a drink, in fact tonight he needed as many as it would take to allow him to release the pent up anger and emotions that were barely in check throughout each day. Everyone had left by now, he thought. He would have to get this himself, he thought as he went to the credenza behind his desk and opened it. He found one of several bottles of whiskey that he kept there for days like today. Recently these days seemed to occur with regularity.

He thought about calling Foster and then decided that she would have called him if there were any news, she was good like that. She would do anything to get ahead and that was a good to know. She might have to make some larger sacrifices should things not go well with Foon and her junkie friend. She was driven by the need to provide for her family. If that proved to not be enough he could always leverage her husband in one way or another. She was perfect for the job, he mused.

Devers decided he did not need a glass. Why stand on formalities, he was not entertaining or sipping fine cognac. He was getting drunk, it was what he did. He took a long drink from the bottle and wiped his mouth with his shirt sleeve. He felt the warmth of the alcohol move from his throat to his stomach. Before he had the chance to feel its affects he had another drink. He knew how much it was going to take to put him where he knew he would end up.

****

Foon was very uncomfortable meeting in such a secluded location. There would be no way for her to get to safety should things go poorly. There was no reason to believe that a government employee would act inappropriately but she had been in the company of many people that seemed to be above reproach and then turned into something that was quite different when they believed no one was watching them. Her PT came to rest in front of an older building in Southside Flats near the river. It appeared to have once been a home that was converted into a retail condominium. There were several placards hanging indicated the businesses that were located within. Foon had been told to meet her contact at the For Eyes store. The sign indicated that it was located on the first floor in the rear of the building. None of the businesses were open and the street was empty of traffic and pedestrians.

Foon mustered up the courage and stepped out of the PT. She felt the humidity of the area and could hardly catch her breath. As she walked to the building's entrance she asked herself why anyone would want to live there. As she entered the building a pleasant series of chimes announced her arrival. The sound echoed down the hardwood floored hallway and then bounce off the door to For Eyes. The door was made of what appeared to be oak and had a single frosted glass panel that showed a light source emanating from inside the business. At least there appeared to be someone there, she thought.

The door was unlocked and she pushed it open and entered into a brightly lit room and saw an empty reception desk that was centrally located. Around the perimeter of the room were several chairs and there were several blank video screens that were hanging on the walls. It was clear that the business was not open, but it was also clear by the noises that she heard that came from elsewhere in the shop that someone was on the premises.

"Hello, is there anyone here?" Foon called out hoping that the person would respond. She heard the sound of desk drawers being closed and then footfalls as someone moved toward her.

Emerging from an entrance located behind the reception desk came a small man with a large round head. He was dressed in a white shirt that was far too big for his frame and it came down to his mid-thigh. Foon looked him over. His manner of dress was truly eccentric and she wasn't certain that he was wearing anything on underneath the shirt, a thought she found disturbing. She was startled by his appearance but her countenance never changed.

"You are Foon?" he asked.

"Yes, and you are...?" she replied because she did not know his name.

"It does not matter who I am. Were you followed?" he asked nervously attempting to see behind her.

"No." she said.

"Follow me." he instructed as he turned and walked back through the entrance way.

Foon followed the man into an octagonal shaped room that had doors on each of the walls. The man turned to her and said to her to wait as he walked to a desk that was off to their right. He opened a drawer and took out a key ring and proceeded to the door directly behind the desk and unlocked it. Foon noticed that he was bare footed and again felt that there was far too much mystery involved in this meeting then was necessary. The man gestured for her to follow him again.

Once inside he closed the door behind them. The room was a small one, only about seven or eight feet square. There were two chairs facing each other separated by a small wooden table. On the table there was a pitcher and two glasses and what appeared to be a speaker, something that might have been used a very long time ago. The man walked to one of the chairs and sat down.

He looked at Foon and then said, "What is it you wish to know about our operation at Newstart Incorporated?" Foon was trying to decide whether she should sit. Was this going to be a very brief meeting? She elected to stand, this would enable her to make a quick exit if need be.

"I am working on a surveillance assignment but do not wish to clash with Internal Security. I need to know what their interest is in Gina Fanacci and Austin Lee." Foon asked in a direct fashion. This was the government and she did not wish to get in the middle of a government investigation.

"There is no interest in Fanacci, she is a person that means nothing to us. On the other hand we are watching Lee, he is a known felon and has the potential to be a threat to the country once again." the man replied in a monotone voice.

"Do you have more than one operative in Newstart at this time?" Foon asked.

The man looked at her and said, "Right now we have three people that are engaged in watching Austin Lee. We have been considering adding more since he met recently with two individuals that are currently on our watch list. How many people do you have watching Lee?" he in turn asked.

Foon didn't know the answer to the question. She suspected since Foster was directly involved that therefore must be at least a full team in place which meant there were twenty or twenty five people involved. Now she had to decide in a spit second how she was going to respond. "I am only part of a larger operation. I believe it is safe to say that there is a whole team in place and that would be somewhere between twenty and twenty five people."

The man looked at her and nodded. Foon then noticed that he seemed to be responding to another person's input, someone else was here or at least monitoring the conversation. "It is good that you are telling us the truth Foon." he finally said. "My supervisor indicates that you are well trained, but it is also true that we can see through that training." he then told her that they had been monitoring her with the new Voracity Plus system which the government had been using to determine deception on the part of anyone that the system monitored. She had sensed the right response and done it.

"What is Fanacci to you and your operation." he then asked.

This was a tough one to answer. She did not want to have to explain that they were going to give her drugs in exchange for Fanacci doing whatever it took to get information from Lee about the location of Justin Welsh. "We are hoping to enlist her to win Lee's confidence and ultimately we would hope to find a way to get to Welsh."

The man cocked his head as though he were a dog listening to its master's instructions and not quite knowing how to respond. Time seem to stop as Foon waited for the next question or the reply. Had they detected that she did not give them everything? Had they not seen the Justin Welsh connection? Did they suspect that Fanacci could be a problem because of her drug use? Foon nervously watched as the man continued to listen to his handler.

Finally he looked at Foon and his eyes seemed to come back into focus on what was in front of him. "Foon, this woman was proven to be of no use in that capacity and I would encourage you to abandon your efforts to enlist her, though it is entirely up to you if you wish to expend the resources on a losing cause. Unless there is something else we will consider the matter closed. We are both watching the same individual and we expect that should you find information that Austin Lee is involved in illegal activities you will immediately contact us. Is that understood?"

Foon nodded and then asked a question, "Do you have any current intelligence on Justin Welsh that you can share with us?"

The man turned away from her and there was silence for a short time. "We have information that Justin Welsh has fled the country and is living in Europe. We have enlisted the CIA to take the case based upon that intelligence. They are working on it as of two days ago. It's unfortunate that the Eastern Regional Station Chief died in a traffic accident recently. She would have been a good contact for you to use. The replacement has not been named as of yet. Is there anything else?"

Foon drew a breath and answered, "Yes, you mentioned that Fanacci is not a good candidate for intelligence. Why?"

"I was waiting for you to ask that question. She is a drug addict and even if we were to use drugs as an inducement to turn her out, drug addicts are sloppy and they make mistakes. She is also not Lee's type. He likes diminutive long haired women, preferably Asian. She does not have the temperament either, she is too passive and intellectually not his equal. The best you could hope for is a one night encounter. We think using his empathy and sympathy for her will force his concentration to be less than effective. He will not see the others that are watching him." the man finished.

"Thank you for the information, I will let you know if we discover anything that proves that Lee is dirty." Foon concluded. She then turn to leave by way of the door that she had entered and discovered it had been locked the entire time they were in the room. The man stepped in front of her and unlocked the door.

"Good bye Foon, and good luck."

Foon reached the PT quickly not looking back. She was glad to be out of the meeting. The man was one of the oddest contacts she had had in quite some time. It was obvious that the person he was speaking for was very much aware of Internal Security and their actions but she was not convinced that they were actually members of Internal Security, though they did have access to information and systems that only Internal Security would have. Still, they were far too forthcoming and willing to share. She would have to do some additional checking. This project was getting more costly, perhaps it was time to ask for a raise.

****

Austin had an incoming call from Roscoe. He thought about ignoring it, after all it was eight thirty in the evening and he was home on his time. "Hello Mr. Plantiere." he said.

"Lee, I am calling because I wanted to be certain that you have been keeping an eye on Gina. I noticed today that she seemed a little tired. Is she showing signs of losing her battle with the drugs?" Roscoe asked.

"She has been having a difficult fight but I think she is able to keep up with work and she seems to be trusting me more. Maybe she will listen to me and take my advice." Austin replied. He was not comfortable in his role as a spy and wanted to transition the relationship to one where he could give her counsel and then hand her off to someone that was better equipped to help her.

"Lee, I realize that you are uncomfortable with spying on Gina, but it will only be for a little while longer. Once she is able to trust you then you can point her in the direction to the help that she needs. I don't think it is wise for us to discuss this at work so I will call you for updates. Here is my number should you need to reach me. Feel free to call me at any time. Good night Lee." Roscoe said as he disconnected the call. He had established another opportunity to gain Lee's trust. They were not going to be friends but if he could get Lee to trust him, he could get a better idea of what he and his two cohorts were planning.

Austin looked around his room. He could hear music coming from his sister's room next door. His room was larger than the cell that he shared for the five years that he was in prison, yet for some reason it felt smaller. It had been more than a week since he had asked Philip about events that could change the world. He had talked to him briefly about his paper on the battle of Gettysburg but it didn't seem to have the ability to have the effect that would change the world like he felt it should be changed.

He reached under his bed and pulled out a tube that held the screen copy of Christopher Leesop's journal and a few letters that Uncle Bob had written to his father. He had glanced over the material once but had not spent the time to read it carefully as his brother Roger had asked him to do. He was confused by all that was going on around him. He felt as though he had been sleep walking through his life with no direction or purpose. It was as though he was cast on the winds of chance and now he had been blown to a shore line where there was far too much despair. He needed to find a purpose, his purpose.

He opened the first page of the journal and stared at the neatly formed letters on the page. Christopher Leesop had very good handwriting, he thought. He had fallen back into the habit of not writing and he was not even sure if he could write anything except his name. Except for the time he spent in prison most of this life he had not had to do so. Even in prison where you had to write by hand if you wanted to send a letter he wrote very little and it was a chore to do. He appreciated the letters that he received, far more than the visits, but there was usually a significant amount of time that would pass before he reciprocated. Often he did not know what to say.

He read the first sentence and then stopped. The words hit him. 'The man that is humble and does not seek his own glory is one that will find ultimate reward.' This seemed like a very awkward place to start, especially for a man that was executed for crimes against the state. If he believed what he said, how could he have done such things? The next paragraph began with another statement indicating that those that have suffered loss will be reassured. Again, this man was portrayed as a man bent on revenge against a system that he felt had wronged him and not given him is fair share. These words are not the words of a vengeful person.

'Those of us that are not aggressive and show respect for all life are those that will in the end be victorious in life and death.' he read. What did he mean by victorious in death? When you die, there is nothing. That's the end of things. That is why we have to get the most while we are here. Isn't that what we have been taught, he questioned.

'You, the ones that seek to understand and to do right by all, are the people that understand why we are here. We are here to serve each other.' The words jumped off the page again and echoed through his mind life a vast empty cavern receiving sound that it had been deprived of for very long. This was what Uncle Bob had been talking about when he gave the speeches and what he listened to when he attended the rallies, he remembered.

'When you show kindness, you can expect that kindness will be shown to you, because it will be. You will know the path and if you follow this path of virtue you will receive what you seek. You will be a receiver of great rewards if you are able to help those that intend to do violence see the error of their ways and so stop their violence. Should you be condemned for doing these things, you should consider yourself a person that has done what is right by all. When you stand up under the persecution of those that live exclusively for themselves you are truly to be revered. Your rewards will be great in your life beyond this one.'

He mentioned eternal life and with so much authority. There was no reason for us to think that there was anything more than what we had here and now, Austin thought. That myth was propagated to control the masses so that they would be content in living under the control of those in power. There was no one in power accept the banks and they are just greedy men that want more at the expense of others. Can we just sit here and allow them to take everything while we wait and hope for better times to come in life or in death, he questioned.

Austin continued to read and to think. He respected his uncle but if he believed those words then he must have been confused by all that he had experienced in the war. Watching people die or even killing them must have exacted a heavy toll on him. He then thought about Spud and wondered whether he had seen a man die for no reason other than the fact that he did not follow the rules.

He decided to close the journal and read the letters that Uncle Bob had written to his father. Perhaps they would provide him with some insight as to why his favorite uncle had been deluded by this man that preached impossible things to a group of people that had no hope. How could two men of such different character be united in the same cause? It did not make sense to him.

He pulled the first letter to the front of the screen and read it slowly. It said only that he missed home and that he was glad that everything was going well for everyone. He mentioned people by name, including Austin. Seeing his name in the letter had a disheartening effect on him. He was overcome with a feeling of sadness that caused him to look away from the page.

A few moments later the feeling passed and he then turned his attention back to the letters. This letter did not have any reference to Christopher Leesop or his teachings. The next letter told a different tale. Uncle Bob was clearly agitated by the events at home and spoke about the persecution of his cousin though he did not mention his name. He asked his father to look after him and to see that he was provided for adequately. The letter ended with a statement that he had read earlier. There was obviously a connection, but why, he wondered.

The third letter was a brief one thanking his father for helping his cousin and that he looked forward to coming home soon. The date on the letter was two days before he was killed. It was a shame that there was nothing more. Austin went back to the first letter and searched for unfamiliar names to see if there were someone that was a member of the faith that he could contact and see what was so special that his uncle wanted to protect a criminal. Then he thought, how could he be critical? Wasn't he also a criminal and wasn't his offense similar to Christopher's?

Austin grimaced and thought about what was currently transpiring. Now he was beginning to think the same way that had before he was arrested. What he had been thinking was what he had been conditioned to believe, that what he did was a crime against society and mankind and that anyone that did anything similar was as guilty as he was. The conflict within him raged. He remembered the feelings that he had when he had first met Justin Welsh and how they were going to set things right with the world. These feelings were not too far different than what he had just read.

On the fourth line from the bottom of the page there was a reference to a JW that he had missed the first time he had read through it. Could that be Justin Welsh? Could he have been involved with my uncle and Christopher Leesop? There was nothing that man did or could do that could surprise him. Everything that he had read gave him more to think about. He realized that he was going to have a difficult time sleeping if he did not find a way to distract himself. He needed to find something to think about that was not part of the confusion in his life.

Austin decided that he would seek out someone to talk to in the house. Maybe his mother or father could help to distract him for a little while. In the worst case he could knock on the door to his sister's room and see if she wanted to talk. Pam liked to play games of any kind, and while Austin was not very good at them, he would be willing to risk certain humiliation to gain the distraction he sought. As he descended the stairs he heard his mother talking to someone in the kitchen. That sounded like it had promise and he walked toward the kitchen hoping to find his mother in the midst of making something to eat. Food was another great distraction, and he could always eat.

****

It was getting late and Philip still had not received the call from Jessica. He was beginning to resign himself to the fact that she was not going to call. He had hoped that she would agree to accompany him on his visit to see the Senator in the morning but if she did not call he was not going to reach out to contact her. It was clearly part of her persona, the need to be unpredictable and by doing so she became totally predictable. He smiled as he thought of her and then turn his attention back to the final reading of his work. He would be submitting the document to his editor by Thursday, the day after tomorrow. It would take the editor about a week to make their recommendations for changes and then they would argue a little and the paper would get published by May the fifteenth exactly when the Dean had required it to be completed.

It had been several days since he had last read the paper and it was his intent to allow a fair amount of time to pass so that he could gain some distance intellectually from the material. If he had his way he would have waited a month before coming back to the material. He found that when he read his material after that much time had passed it was if he was reading something that had been written by someone else.

After an hour and a half had passed and he had made a couple of minor revisions, he was ready to leave it alone until it was returned to him by the editor. It wasn't half bad, he thought.

It was still too early to go to sleep though he knew his body and mind would welcome the chance to shut down. He decided to get out the copy of Christopher Leesop's journal and finally see why his brother had been so captivated with it. He had never responded that way to anything he had written. Perhaps he was a little jealous, he thought.

As he read the words he thought about his brother, Austin. This was a man that came in close contact with Uncle Bob and knew him and what he wanted. If Robert Lee was a follower of this man then it appears that he would not have condoned the course of action that Austin and his compatriots pursued. He would have suggested change but he would have worked with each individual to change their hearts. As he read it became apparent to him that Christopher Leesop could not have been the man that they accused him of being. He was far too gentle and too kind a man. It appeared that he did not have a political bone in his body.

The hours rushed by and Philip was absorbed in reading and dissecting it. He attempted to see the logic behind Leesop's arguments but it escaped him. He began to realize that his premises were not built upon logic and current philosophy, but were constructed on faith in something greater than all of us. This was a very difficult position to accept. Philip knew that there was no higher power. He had been taught that man was the culmination of a very random set of processes. That's the reason that Jenkins' proposal was truly preposterous. Chance got us to where we are today and there was no way to find a pattern among the chaotic noise, he thought.

It was the reason that the government's attempts to move society away from 'natural selection' economics was doomed to fail. Man cannot figure this out himself. Time and activity yield results. Christopher

Leesop speaks of, among many other things, order and purpose. He taught that man must reverence what he had been given, he must be a good steward. Philip began to see why Leesop was considered to be a traitor, not for what he did but for what he thought.

Philip stretched and realized that he had been in the same position for far too long. He stood up and requested the time. The pale green display showed that it was five minutes after two in the morning. He had to be up and out of the door by six thirty. It was time to get some sleep. He left everything where it was last touched and headed for his bed. He definitely needed rest and his body agreed with him.

****

The PCU alerted Philip that it was time to get up and begin his day. He was going to Virginia to meet with Senator Sun Ya Yen. It was a meeting that had little to do with anything other than the need to understand if there was more to the death of Leopold Jenkins and William Lawrence then a simple accident. It would be a long day for him because after the meeting he had to return to campus to teach the last two classes of the day and then he was to meet with the Dean regarding the submission of his work. There was a great deal to be accomplished and then there would be a chance to take a little time to relax before final exams and preparation for the summer semester's course outlines. He then thought he might actually have two or three days that he could call his own.

As much as he enjoyed studying the Civil War after the research that he had done preparing this paper he would be glad not to have it in the course catalog for quite a while. He had investigated the battle many times in the past but this time he was compelled to see strategic moves as flaws in a time-line not as elements of chance. Jenkins had managed to reduce a passionate study to a series of movements of the cogs of time. The process of inter-meshing gears were the events that created the time thread in which he lived. He had been shown that time was not a ticking of a second off the proverbial master clock, it was a movement of many different things and it represented man's feeble attempt to lasso the concept. It was an attempt to define something that was infinite; never having begun and never to having an end.

The argument was that if it was a process then it could be reversed and altered. That was what the paper written by Giles Mendez indicated. It was the reason that it was included with all of those papers in the Jenkins' file. The reference to the concept of time thread manipulation was left out of the paper he was publishing. It was not a key element in

Jenkins' research and it would only serve to have those that read his work take it much less a seriously. They would be inclined to discredit it because of what many believed to be an outlandish theory. Philip knew this because that was what he would do.

He was walking out the door when he received an incoming call from Jessica Jenkins. He thought for a moment and then elected to reject the call. He did not need to be distracted today by whatever her agenda was. He knew she was calling regarding his visit. Most likely she would be trying to talk him out of going. This was something he had to do for the sake of the investigation that apparently was underway. He had been implicated because of something she had initiated. It was for this reason that he felt she had no right to ask him to stop, he concluded.

He walked the usual path to the train station. The temperature at this hour was relatively cool seventy five degrees. Even though the sun was just cresting the horizon he could feel evidence of it as he walked in and out of the shadows of the buildings that lined the street. Overhead he saw the construction beginning on the Sky Tran that would be a loop of elevated transportation stopping at the major office and retail buildings throughout Pittsburgh. It was a marvel and Philip thought it was like something out of the futuristic movies that depicted man's technological fate. Of course no one had anticipated that there would be a technology war and that world would take giant steps backward before mankind could once again move toward that bright and shining future, he thought.

Philip had walked past the government housing section every day and did his best to avoid looking at any one that was in that area. It was not that he felt superior to them, it was that he felt that they looked so helpless and sad. He did not need to be brought down to that level. He felt that it was difficult enough maintaining a positive attitude when you had a job and a good place to live. Things were supposed to be better by now, the country was supposed to be adding jobs and helping more people rebuild their lives. Instead it was very much the same as it had been for the past fifteen or twenty years.

As a student of history Philip knew that this pattern had been repeating itself for the past two hundred years. When things got bad enough the people at the bottom started to act on their frustrations and usually the threat of revolution that was the inevitable end to the boiling rage that was typically quelled by concessions. The Twenty First century version of this was amnestied with the legalization of marijuana and other drugs. It dulled the sense of those at the bottom of the economic ladder. It also cost the country in productivity, as a result the New Morality Movement began. It pushed drugs and promiscuity to a place of undesirability for the mainstream of the population. It encourage men to marry later in life, their mid to late forties was considered ideal and women were to marry in the early to mid-twenties for the purpose of child bearing. The New Morality Movement began in the year 2030 and it was now in its last gasps Philip speculated but he was not certain what the next social wave would be.

He would be traveling to Philadelphia and then to Washington DC where he would pick up a commuter line to McLean Virginia where the Second Chance Recovery Center that housed the Senator was located. They had a very strict visitation protocol and that was the reason it took Philip more than a week to be approved for a visit. He was instructed that he would only be allowed a maximum of thirty minutes with the Senator and the length of the visit could be cut short should the Senator become fatigued or agitated.

Philip wasn't exactly sure what to expect. He didn't even know the extent of the Senator's injuries and whether he would find someone that was able to communicate. What did he want out of this meeting? He wanted to know if there was a connection other than friendship between the three men that went on this trip. He had looked into their pasts and found there was very little that tied them to each other on a personal level. Still friendships don't always come into being because of prolonged common experiences, they can spring up spontaneously, he thought.

It was time to think about other things. He needed to be prepared for his meeting with the Dean and he should have some idea of the courses that he would like to teach during the summer session. He decided to review the potential offerings to see what appealed to him. He used the PCU to display the course catalog and started to review the topics. He found himself getting sleepy as he did so he closed his eyes. The images continued to be display as though projected on the black screen of the inside of his eye lids.

****

Austin arrived at work early. He thought he would make an extra effort to befriend Gina that day. She certainly seemed to be lacking focus and direction in her life. He wondered why she had allowed herself to become a drug user. It was considered to be a sign of personal weakness. As he entered the work area he noticed that Roscoe was not at his desk. This was odd since he was usually sitting at his desk working when he arrived, no matter what time Austin arrived. Perhaps he was meeting with his supervisor he thought.

The office seemed extremely quiet and as he reached his cubicle he still saw no one at their workstations. He decided to start working on the assignment he had been attempting to finish over the past three days. He soon became immersed in the tables of information. The numbers fell into place and he could see a positive end to the project and that was something he had not visualized when he had been given it. He smiled and looked up and there he saw that Gina had arrived and was working. He also noticed the there was a fair amount of activity going on around him. This gave him a good feeling knowing that he could become that involved where the rest of the world did not matter.

"Good morning Gina, how are you today?" he said. Gina looked up at him and smiled and nodded. She thought about how helpful Austin had been to her and how she couldn't do what they were asking of her, even if it meant that she would not have the drugs that she so desperately needed. What she needed to do was her job and to hold out as long as she could without using anything. As she tried to do her assignment it became clear that all she could think about was the need to feel better. She fidgeted with her hair twirling it between her thumb and forefinger.

Austin noticed Gina's increased agitation and thought about how he might help her. He placed a call to Roscoe and informed him of his intent to go the cafeteria.

"Gina I am going to the cafeteria, can I get you something?" he asked.

She looked at him and thought. Maybe a cup of tea might help me. Herbal tea can be quite soothing, she thought. "A cup of tea might be nice. If you don't mind? Here... Here is some..." she responded but Austin would not allow her finish.

"Don't worry about it, it is my treat. Do you take anything in it?"

"A little lemon and sugar, please." she said sheepishly.

"Okay, I'll be right back." he said over his shoulder as he departed for the cafeteria.

Austin returned with the tea and gave it to Gina. As she sipped it she seemed to relax slightly and was able to compose herself. Gina turned to her work after thanking Austin several times. She also noticed that Austin did not bring anything back for himself. He explained to her that they did not have anything that he desired. He felt that she was doing a little better and he returned to his work hoping that he could spend the necessary time to finish the assignment that day.

****

The first thing Kate did after she greeted her children and had her cup of coffee was to listen to the report that Foon had left for her. It did not start off positively and when she had finished it was clear that she was not going to have a very good day. She dreaded the next call she would be placing and decided that she should prepare herself for the day in the event she was going to be traveling to New York. She had breakfast with the boys making every attempt at not letting the news adversely affect her mood and the limited time that she had with her sons.

She stepped into the shower and let the water pour over her. It drenched her and then stopped automatically allowing her time to apply soap and shampoo. At the appropriate time it came back on again rinsing her clean. She thought wouldn't be much easier if we could get rid of life's problems the way we get rid of the day's grime on our bodies. As much as she thought about finding a solution she could not. She knew that because the government was involved that there was no way for her to continue the operation the way it was being conducted and be successful.

Lee was going to be under their watch too and that meant that if he did contact Justin Welsh that the government would be there to swoop in and grab him and the reward that she was working to achieve. What could she do? As she dried herself she rehearsed the call to Devers and tried to anticipate every possible scenario including her losing her job. That thought made her shutter. The realization that she might be in a position to lose her job while her husband was away meant that they would have to move back in with her parents, again. She did not welcome that prospect. Her father was a tough man to live with when things were going well. Now that he was ill and her mother was of little help, it was very difficult to spend time any time with him.

She dressed and then got the boys ready for school. As soon as they were out of the door she placed the call to Devers hoping he wouldn't pick up the call.

"Foster, what's the good word?" Devers asked in a cheery voice.

Kate hesitated for a moment and then proceeded to tell him about Foon's report. During the briefing Devers did not say one word. He waited for her to complete the report and then said, "I want you on the next train to New York." The call was disconnected and she knew that she must get moving quickly. She checked the schedule and found that the next train for New York departed in thirty minutes. It would be tight but she could make it if she moved quickly, which she did.

****

Outside of the Second Chance Recovery Center two men sat in a PT waiting for Philip Lee to arrive. They knew he was coming. They were instructed to let him complete his meeting with the Senator and after that meeting, which was being monitored, they would be instructed as to whether they were to pick him up for questioning or maybe more. The tint on the PT was almost black and no one could see in from the outside of the vehicle. It was obvious that someone was inside the vehicle since it was running to maintain the climate control settings.

"What time is he scheduled to be here?" asked the man sitting in what some would call the passenger seat.

"He is due here at ten o'clock. Relax we get paid no matter whether he shows or doesn't show." the other man replied.

"Do you have any idea what this is about?" the passenger asked. The other man just looked at him and the conversation ended. They sat silently waiting for Philip Lee to meet with the Senator.

****

The train station was a five block from the Second Chance Recovery Center and Philip elected to walk. It was a little warmer than ninety degrees but the humidity was fairly low and there was a pleasant breeze blowing under a partially sunny sky. As Philip walked along the tree lined street he kept wondering what he was going to encounter. This man had been under doctors' care since the accident. From the limited amount of information that Jessica was able or willing to share he was paralyzed from the neck down and that the treatment he has been undergoing was designed to restore him completely.

There were a few people out walking and there was also the ever present whine of PTs moving rapidly about. Philip spotted the building ahead and took note of a PT that was parked at the curb. It was odd to see one parked like that and it was also odd to see one with blacked out windows. This was a very affluent suburb of Washington so it may just be some wealthy person's transport waiting for them, he surmised.

The people sitting in the PT also noticed him.

"There he is. I'll let them know he's arrived." the one man said to the other. "He's here, you can begin the recording when he enters the room." he then said to the surveillance team.

Philip entered through the center doors. He was scanned immediately and the green light on the reception panel showed that he was an expected guest. A young women in her early thirties greeted him, "Welcome Dr. Lee we were expecting you and you are right on time. If you would take the door to your right there will be someone to meet you on the other side to take you to see Senator Sun."

Philip did what he was instructed to do. On the other side of the door was another woman that was slightly older but very stunning in her appearance. She was quite a bit shorter than Philip and had a medium build. She smiled at him and extended her hand saying, "Greetings Dr. Lee so good of you to come. My name is Dr. Simmons, I am Senator Sun's personal physician and I have been working with him through this difficult time. Before we go in to see the Senator do you have any questions I can answer for you?"

Philip smiled and replied, "It's very nice to meet you Dr. Simmons. I have one or two medical questions that I am curious about. What is the Senator's prognosis?" he asked.

"He should make a full recovery in another six to nine months." she said proudly.

"That seems remarkable since according to what I read about the accident he is fortunate to be alive let alone return to a normal life." Philip replied hoping to get the doctor to become conversational. The doctor began to tell Philip how the Senator came to them on life support and had been without a pulse for more than fifteen minutes. They revived him more than twelve times during the first two days he was with them. For the past year he has been stable without any incidents.

Philip then asked the key question, "Does he have full use of his mental faculties?" The doctor looked at him and appeared to be searching for the right answer, apparently there was something that was not one hundred percent right here, Philip thought.

The doctor began, "I wouldn't say that he has regained all of his mental faculties at this time. He becomes very agitated when people talk about history for some reason. It doesn't have to be anything specific, but... I'll give you a for instance. Yesterday, one of the orderlies was in the hallway outside of his room speaking to one of the nurses about some personal business, something that we do discourage but where there are people, you know they will sometimes cross into areas they shouldn't. Anyway, he began to talk about the wars and then he mentioned something about the tech war and I could see the Senator beginning to get upset. When he mentioned the world wars he became irrational and started to scream. It was most unusual, but I think he has increased sensitivity that is probably due to all of the medication and the healing technology that he is being subjected to regularly."

"This doesn't bode well for me, I teach American Studies at Franklin and Marshall, I guess I will have to stay off my favorite subject then." said Philip as he tried to make light of comment but the doctor did not appreciate his sense of humor.

She said, "Please do not do anything that will aggravate his condition. These emotional outburst can set his recovery back significantly." Philip nodded his head thinking it was best not to say anything in reply. She looked at him and then told him to follow her.

As they entered the room it was apparent that there was a very ill person within the walls. The lighting was subdued and the white room had an appearance that there was a haze present. In the center to the room suspended using magnetic levitation was a clear platform on which the Senator reclined. He also had what appeared to be identical platform suspended directly over him and he was connected to intravenous feeding and medication tubes, the origins of which were somewhere concealed in the ceiling. It was not clear whether the Senator was conscious for Philip could not see his face which was obscured entirely by a white mask of some sort. It had wires attached to it and the ends attenuated and were suspended, attached to nothing.

Philip followed the doctor as she walked toward the bed. When she was approximately three feet from the bed she said, "Senator Sun, you have a visitor. His name is Dr. Lee. He wants to ask you a few questions, are you feeling up to seeing him?"

A muffled voice responded with a feeble "Yes, how do you do Dr. Lee?"

Philip approached the platform and responded "Very well, it's nice of you to allow me to visit you." At that point the doctor excused herself and left them alone.

"Is the doctor gone?" the Senator asked.

"Yes, she is." Philip answered.

"Good, she means well but she hovers around too much and it is very unnerving. What can I do for you Dr. Lee? Have we met before?"

Philip explained that they had not met and that he was there on behalf of another person that found it too difficult to come. He then told her about Jessica and how she was anxious to have her father's work completed. Philip waited for some sort of reaction, but there was none.

"Dr. Lee I barely knew Leopold Jenkins before the accident. He was there to meet with Dr. William Lawrence, I had simply helped him meet Dr. Lawrence because of a favor I was doing for a friend." said the Senator in a voice that seemed to be fading because of lack of use.

"Oh I see, do you know why Dr. Jenkins wanted to meet Dr. Lawrence?" Philip asked hoping that this was not going to be a complete waste of time.

"It had to do with the research that he was doing regarding time thread manipulation. The funding of which fell under the committee that I was the chairman. That is how I knew Dr. Lawrence, he provided the committee with classified briefings on his research. I really can't discuss the details of the briefings though." said the Senator.

"If it was classified how did Dr. Jenkins expect to learn anything about that? He must have known that Dr. Lawrence would be bound not to tell anything about it?" Philip asked fearing that the Senator was holding back information about how much he knew about the substance of their encounter.

"I can't say what Dr. Jenkins was thinking, like I said, I didn't know him very well." The Senator's reply sounded as though he were getting upset but was endeavoring to maintain his composure.

"Are you able to tell me who referred Dr. Jenkins to you so that he could learn more about the research?" Philip inquired.

There was a period of silence and then the Senator said, "It was man named Jeremy Giles, he was working on a government project at the time and his wife was my aide. We have been friends of quite a few years." The name sounded familiar to Philip though he was not sure where he had heard it before but he knew the name.

"Do you know how I can get in touch with him? Perhaps he can shed some light on Dr. Jenkins and his reasons for wanting to become acquainted with Dr. Lawrence." Philip asked and waited for a response.

"I am not certain, you might try calling my office and asking them if they can get in touch with Laura Giles, my previous assistant and his wife. I am afraid that I am getting a little tired Dr. Lee, so if that is all perhaps you could come back at another time should you have more questions." the Senator said his voice showing sign of fatigue and stress.

Philip suddenly had the suspicious thought that this person may not even be the Senator. He wondered if he should make some attempt to verify his identity. There was no information that he had about the Senator that could not be retrieved from public records, the place where he had learned about him. This was a problem in that there was no personal information that could be used to verify it. There was always DNA, he thought but he would have to get close enough to touch him.

"Senator, may I shake your hand and wish you well?" Philip requested. He did not have anything to lose, after all he could not see any part of the man and while his height seemed to be correct it was difficult to gauge accurately while he was reclining. He was covered with a milky colored sheet that adhered to the contours of his body. The sheet covering was apparently part of the healing process since it too was connected by a wire or a tube to a box that was attached to the underside of the platform.

"If you feel you must, then of course you can." the Senator replied and he slowly moved his right hand out from under the sheet. Philip noticed the color of his skin was a pale blue and his hand was free of hair and was smooth, without wrinkles or creases. Philip approached the platform and reached out to take his hand. He was hoping that there would be some moisture that his skin was secreting or perhaps he could get a small fleck of loose skin to adhere to his hand. This was going to be a challenge, he realized. He grasped his hand and took it carefully. The hand clasp was surprisingly firm though his hand felt cool and clammy. They held the grasp for several seconds. Finally Philip eased his grip thinking he had enough trace DNA to be able to determine with whom he had been speaking.

"Did you get want you wanted?" the Senator inquired turning his head for the first time in the direction of Philip. Philip could not read the comment since the mask obscured the Senators entire face including his eyes.

"I am glad that we had the opportunity to meet." Philip responded trying to avoid answering a question where he wasn't exactly sure what he was being asked.

"I can see by your face that you have. I wish you good luck on your quest Dr. Lee. If you do manage to find Jeremy please give him and Laura my best. I think about them often. Good bye Dr. Lee."

Philip turned to walk away and then stopped. "Do you think your injury was as the result of an accident?" he asked.

"What else could it be? Be careful when you travel down a path like the one you are traveling, you do not know what you may encounter along the way and the destination may not be what your are expecting." At that point Philip recognized that the Senator felt that they had been observed. He also suspected that the Senator did not feel he had anything to hide.

"Good bye Senator I look forward to seeing you again when your recovery is complete. Thank you for taking this time with me."

Philip walked out of the room and back toward the reception area. His visit had been only twenty minutes but it had yielded another avenue to explore. He would talk to Jessica to see if she knew anything about Jeremy Giles and where he could be reached. As he approached the reception area the doctor was there and apparently waiting for him.

"Dr. Lee that was a fast visit. Did everything go okay?" she asked him.

"It went well and I did not mention history at all so there were no problems. I thank you Dr. Simmons for the opportunity to meet with him. Though I have one question before I go if you don't mind. At one point the Senator mentioned that he could see me, though there were no opening for his eyes, how does that work?"

The doctor looked at him and the proceeded to explain that one of the functions of the mask was to act as a conductive light sensor that worked like a camera. "The image that is generated is transmitted to his PCU and he can see it just like you see information and pictures when your eyes are closed. It only works when the object is within a foot or two of the mask. You must have been fairly close to him." she state with a concerned expression on her face.

"I was within a couple of feet I was having difficult hearing him at one point." Philip stated.

"Oh, I should have had you set your PCU to his broadcast channel and then you would have heard fine from any distance. Maybe next time. Will we be seeing you again?" she asked with a smile.

"I suspect that I will be back to see the Senator again at some point. I hope to be able to sit with him and learn his remarkable story. He has gone through so much."

The doctor appeared to be trying to delay him for some reason coming up with additional things to talk about and questions to ask him. She inquired as to his work in a manner that appeared to show she was genuinely interested in it. Then he realized that she was not married and while she was quite attractive she was passed the prime age for having children and that made her less desirable to most men. Philips suspicions were proven correct when she offered him her number, which he took out of courtesy. He was finally able to extricate himself from the conversation by stating that he needed to return to campus to teach the remainder of the day's classes, which was a true statement.

As Philip exited the building to walk back to the commuter station he noticed the same PT sitting in the same location. It was clearly operating since he could hear the high pitched whine of the electric motor running to maintain a cool temperature within the vehicle. It was obvious that there was someone inside but because of the tint of the windows he was not able to see inside. It was almost eleven o'clock and the temperature was flirting with one hundred degrees. As much as Philip wanted to determine who was inside, what he wanted more was to be somewhere out of the heat. He walked purposefully to the station and welcomed the relief of the cool air as he entered the waiting area.

His pulse was elevated and his entire body appeared to be perspiring but soon his respiration began to slow. It was not too much longer that his thoughts returned to the visit. He was shocked by the appearance of the Senator for it was clear to him that this man should have been dead as well. The amount of reconstruction that was being undertaken was truly amazing.

They apparently were growing new skin on his entire body along with the mending of many broken bones. The presence of L-Q87, which he had observed on one of the many drug dispensing apparatus, meant that there had been a transplant of one or more organs and that they were most likely synthetic or created. A medical bill for these types of procedures was unfathomable. He was a United States Senator but there was a limit to what the government would do to preserve the life of its own. He must be receiving private help. He took a moment and reflected on what he had just seen and realized that he might be overreacting to the coincidences that surely must be happening.

Philip placed a call to Jessica half hoping that she would not pick up. He wasn't exactly sure what kind of a reaction he was going to get since he went through with the meeting and was about to publish the paper that she inspired him to write but now was intent on having him reconsider his actions. He waited and then suddenly there was her voice on the line.

"Hello Philip, how did your meeting go?" she asked. Philip went on to tell her that he had seen the Senator and he described in some detail the surrounding. "That sounds like pretty a horrible existence. I don't think I would want to remain alive in that condition." she expressed her feelings clearly.

"I don't know how I feel about it, he does have hope that he will make a full recovery." Philip replied. He then went on to tell her about Jeremy Giles and then asked her if she knew him.

There was silence on the other end of the call and then Philip heard what sounded like laughing. "Philip are you kidding me? Don't you remember? He is the man that was working on the power generation equipment the day you and I first met."

Philip paused for a moment then laughed, that's where he had heard the name before. "Did you know that he was the man that introduced your father to the Senator?" Philip asked expecting her to say no.

Again there was a pause and then she answered in a meek voice, "Yes, I knew him and have known him most of my life."

Philip waited for a moment to digest the substance of what he had heard. "I see... no actually I don't see. Do you know how to get in touch with him now?" he asked in a tone that had gone from affable to one that displayed his growing irritation.

"I don't understand why you are upset just because I didn't share that with you. And yes I can get in touch with him and my aunt any time that I want or need to do so." Jessica responded in an manner that showed that she was irritated as well.

Jessica continued to explain that Laura and Jeremy were her aunt and uncle on her mother's side. Laura was her mother's sister. From Philip's perspective there appeared to be too much information being given, and he suspected there was another agenda and he had not yet uncovered what it was.

"Philip, you must understand something and that is that my uncle told me about you before we met that day. He told me that you ride the Lancaster shuttle daily and that if I wanted to meet you he would make a point of being there to help." Jessica concluded.

There it was, the information that was missing. Jessica had planned the meeting, but why, he thought. "Why did you want to meet me?" he bluntly asked.

There was again a period awkward silence. "I needed someone to help get my father's message out and I saw you at the conference and remembered how impressed my father was with you and your work. You were the right choice once my uncle confirmed that he worked for your father it seemed that it was meant to be and that you were going to be the one to help clear up this mess. My uncle insisted that there was more to this then just research, that I wouldn't have remembered someone just because my father had said that he was good at his job. He was right, but I have never admitted that to him." she said finally.

Now the silence originated on Philip's end. He didn't know if he should believe her. It wouldn't be the first time she had mislead him or deliberately lied to him.

"Jessica, you know how I feel about you. I was smitten the first moment I saw you. I am glad that you wanted to meet me. I only wish I had been the one that had made that first encounter happen." he said to her. He had said words similar to this before and it should not have seemed disingenuous but he was not convinced that her motives were tainted by an attraction to him. She had something else in mind, he sensed it.

Philip left the conversation open to her telling him of the way she felt toward him now but she did not pursue it. She seemed relieved Philip did not challenge her more on the subject. Philip then told her that he was meeting with the Dean and that the paper was going to the editors tomorrow. She seemed to be excited for him and glad that the work was finally coming out for public consumption.

The last thing Philip brought up was the need to speak with Jeremy and whether Jessica wanted to set meeting or should he contact him through his father. Jessica seemed amenable to setting the meeting and then asked if she could be included. Philip cautiously agreed to include her and gave her several dates and times when he would be available. The call came to an end with the two of them telling each other how much they wanted to see the other but no date or time was set for that meeting to happen.

Philip settled into his seat on the train that would take him to Philadelphia. He wondered whether he should place a call to his father and start the process of reaching out to Jeremy Giles through him. He tried in vain to piece together all of the information that he had received. He was now beginning to entertain the idea that his brother Austin may also have been an involuntary player in this ill-conceived drama. There seemed to be too many coincidences and that things were going too neatly to be chance. He knew that life was chaos and there was no structure like the one that was illustrated in Jenkins' theories. Jenkins stated that time was a process and that we constructed a means to measure it so that we could understand our position within the process. This theory was contrary to everything he had been taught to believe.

The problem was he did not know who was engineering the massive conspiracy he visualized unfolding and why it was being done? There were so many possibilities most notably the Banking Consortium led by WBOI or there was also the government lead by the FBI or the Department of Internal Security. The fact that someone thought that Jenkins was actually a threat to national security would be almost laughable if he wasn't experiencing the strange activities that were going on around him. Then again this just could be a series of unlikely happenstance that was part of the random activities of life. After all when given an infinite amount of time you could expect that a group of chimpanzees beating on keyboards would be able to reproduce all of the great masterpieces of literature. Everything was entirely random. He needed more information to prove that there was or wasn't a conspiracy and he was certain that the information would be forthcoming some point in the not too distant future.

****

The train ride appeared to be far too short Kate thought as she was not looking forward to her meeting. As she stared blankly at the screen-scapes her thoughts began to cycle through the various scenarios that she could expect as an outcome for a meeting where she was to justify her failure and explain why they had not succeeded. She pictured herself being fired and told that she must seek employment elsewhere. If that happened she would have to call her parents immediately and begin the slow process of moving back to Ohio. Upon completing the evaluation of her savings and the potential for a severance package, she concluded that she could expect to have enough funds to stay where she was until the boys finished the current semester at school.

As the train came to rest at the platform she found herself thinking that they most likely wouldn't fire her. They would transfer, demote her or worse yet Devers would try to use this as means of getting her to do his bidding. Her mind raced to some very dark places when she thought about what that man might be capable of requiring her to do. She would resign before she would allow Devers manipulate her in any way. There were always options and there could be another job somewhere down the line. Perhaps she should have used the train ride to make calls to see what positions might be available elsewhere within the company or outside of it, she thought.

The walk to the subway was a brief one and while the odor was gut wrenching the temperature was at least tolerable. Hers was a strong determined stride and she intentionally avoided eye contact with the people that lived beneath the city. This enabled her to not dwell on the plight of the unfortunate ones that were trapped in that hell on earth. Her time there would be over soon and in a moment she would be in the world of the rich and powerful.

"I can't lose my job over this- I won't." she said out loud.

Kate entered the building with authority. She was going to control this meeting. It was not her fault that the target they selected was an inferior one and that the operative that was chosen by Devers was incapable of completing the mission successfully. This was Devers' show from start to finish and she did her best to make it work. As the elevator neared the one hundred and first floor her bravery began to wane, she must not let him get the upper hand she repeated to herself. This was what she was thinking as she was shown into his office my Sam Lewis.

Devers was engaged in a call and was waving his arms gesturing. His face was red and it was clear that he was upset about something. He motioned for her to sit in one of the chairs that were away from his desk. Devers' back was to her and she watched him intently. It was difficult to find the good in him. He seemed like evil personified.

She wonder if he was ever married and then thought immediately that there was no possibility of any woman wanting to be with him. She found herself frowning and instantly attempted to correct that expression before he saw her and asked why she was upset. She didn't want to have to lie, even to him.

Devers ended the call and then turned to Kate and said, "Can you believe the incompetence that I am surrounded by? That idiot Larson in the Government Liaison Division has failed to get our nominee in front of the President for consideration. If we don't get the right replacement for Fuentes then all of that..." Devers stopped short realizing that Kate was not necessarily trustworthy when it came the necessary evils of the job.

"Enough of that. How are you Foster? Are you ready to get serious about the Welsh matter? We need one hundred percent from you now."

"Mr. Devers I always give one hundred percent, you should know that about me by now." Kate replied.

Devers looked at her and could tell she was genuinely disappointed when he had implied that she did not give her all for the mission. "Listen Foster this is a very tough assignment. We had a set back once again but we learned some valuable information and I have formulated a new plan of which you are going to be our key operative." Kate looked at him waiting to hear what was next. She was beginning to relax her guard slightly and beginning to feel less threatened. Perhaps Devers was going to be reasonable in his interpretation of the events that took place.

"Based upon your report and the intelligence that Foon has provided you, we have realized the need to find an agent to replace our drug addict and to become close to Austin Lee. We did a profile analysis and there were three candidates that are members of our team that we can trust for such an important assignment. As far as I am concerned there is only one person that I want to go undercover and that is you." Devers said as he turned his back on her once again.

Kate thought about the opportunity of going into the field undercover and was excited by the prospects of watching Lee and uncovering all of his secrets. This could be a fascinating assignment but what about her family, would she still have time for her sons and should it go on for months her husband would be home from the war in two months and then she could be limited in her ability to see him, and she missed him so.

"I am not sure I have a full understanding of what you are expecting of me Mr. Devers." she said and as she did she thought that now she would be able to get to what he really wanted her to do.

Devers knew that she would not want to do the job once she found out the lengths that she was expected to go. The job required that she would do anything and that meant she must act regardless of legal or moral restriction she might feel impede her. She must accomplish the mission without constraint, she must get Lee to tell her what they need to know. Devers continued to stare out the window and there was a period of awkward silence. He thought whether he should try to convince her or if he should play his trump card and get on with the rest of his day.

Kate could not bear the silence. Her mind raced and she began to think about the different ways that Devers could mean by choice of the word 'anything'. That could mean anything within legal and ethical boundaries but that would certainly be something new for Devers to decide to play the game according to rules other than the ones he had put in place.

"Mr. Devers, you know that I am dedicated to my work and I have proved my loyalty but there are actions that I am not prepared to carry out. Those things that are illegal or unethical I cannot, in good conscience, do." she finally said. There, if he wants to play the game dirty he will have to find someone else., she thought.

Devers did not respond to her statement. He needed to hear her divulge all of her limits so that he could push past them at one time. There would be no negotiations and he now knew that he would be able have her comply with the terms necessary for WBOI to get Justin Welsh, dead or alive. He continued to wait for her to speak again and he did not have to wait long.

"Mr. Devers, my family is very important to me and because of that I will not do anything that I feel will compromise my ability to ensure their wellbeing. My husband will be home from the war shortly. If the job requires more sacrifice than I can in good conscience make then I am prepared to tender my resignation." she said giving Devers exactly what he hoped she would say. She squirmed a little in her chair. She was not bluffing, her offer to resign was sincere, but she was also hopeful that there would be a way to keep her job along with her principles.

Devers turned slowly and stared at her. His look was stern and though he was acting out an elaborate scheme he never appreciated anyone that could not be bullied or controlled. "Foster, I don't think you will resign. I do think you will take this assignment and be successful, and you will do whatever it takes and do so willingly." Devers said and stopped again turning to face the window.

This game was extremely enjoyable, he thought and he could play it all day but worked needed to be done and this woman's company wasn't that pleasurable. He wondered how Austin Lee could find someone like that attractive. The intelligence that was provided to him came from an unimpeachable source so he had no choice but to accept it. Besides if the plan did not work we could always use her to participate in any plan to extract information involuntarily.

"Mr. Devers you may think you know me, but I am certain that I will only do things that are right." Kate stated resolutely. She was not going to be bullied into doing something that was outside of her beliefs. That he would think that she was so desperate to maintain her job at any cost caused her to feel anger. She worried that he might find a weakness that he could think that he could exploit and then she would be forced to take the matter to Human Resources or the authorities, something that she did not want to do. Should she do so it could make it difficult for her to get another job and there was little likelihood anything would be done to

Devers. Others had tried in the past to have him held accountable and had not been successful.

Devers had had enough. It's time to get this moving in the right direction. "Here is the situation Foster. Your husband, as you said, was scheduled to return home in two months and eight days. Please note that I said 'was'. As of this morning his tour has been extended indefinitely. Should you not cooperate you can be certain that where he is stationed, now in relation to the conflict, will be modified to a less secure location. Do you understand?" Devers asked in closing.

Kate was shocked. How could anyone do such a thing? "Mr. Devers, I don't believe it, I don't think that you would do such a thing." she exclaimed her emotions choking her words.

Devers sense that she was losing control of her emotions and that was exactly what he wanted to see. "Here let's get him on a call and see if he what I am saying is true. Lewis, get me Army headquarters in Uruguay. In case you didn't realize it that is where we are fighting today." Devers said and he chuckled. Sam Lewis appeared at the door and told him that the call had been placed and was waiting for him.

"Devers from WBOI here. I need to reach a Michael Foster. He is attached to the Reconnaissance Troop, I believe it's the Tactical Evaluation Unit." Devers expected action quickly and got what he expected.

"Foster, hold please I have someone that needs to speak with you. I am transferring the call." he looked at Kate and then instructed Rasputin to transfer the call. "I will give you some privacy." and he turned and walked to the far end of his office again gazing out of the window.

Kate was trembling when the call connected. She hadn't heard Michael's voice in over a month and the messages she had received were always brief and focused on the boys and the need for reassurance that everyone was okay. The connection was very clear and it sounded as though he was in the room with her. There was a video feed available and because she had not seen him in such a long time she was anxious to connect with it as well. The quality was not good but she could recognize him and she instinctively smiled and tears began to form.

"Michael, its Kate."

"Kate how did you manage this? I have been trying to call you for three weeks but because of the security associated with the latest action no one has been allowed to contact anyone at home. It is great he hear your voice. I wish I could see you." Michael said enthusiastically. He had missed his wife and was so glad to hear her voice even though he knew he must give her some very bad news. "Kate, I don't know how long I will be able to speak with you but I have to tell you some news and it's...

it's not good. I have been extended. I can't come home when I thought I could." his voice betraying the sadness that he felt.

"When do you think you can come home?" Kate asked already knowing the answer that she would hear.

"I don't know it is indefinite and I can at least be thankful that I am not on the front lines. The fighting has been going very bad lately. We've lost quite a few men." he replied.

"I need you to stay safe Mickey, your sons need their father home in one piece. A little delay won't matter as long as we can give you a hug and a kiss." Kate bravely encouraged him.

"You are a very special woman, Kate. That's why I love you so much." Michael said fighting back tears. "I have to go, they tell me that the call enables the enemy to target our positions. Take care I will send you a message soon. I love you." Michael said and the line went dead.

Kate stared at Devers through the haze of tears. He was an evil man, even more evil than she could have imagined. "Mr. Devers, how could you do this?" she said to his back.

Devers responded by turning around and with a look of mock concern on his face. "Foster, this is a very serious situation in which we are involved. I need to get Justin Welsh and I am using whatever means that I can to do so. Austin Lee is just one component of this operation but he is the most important one at this time. You may not have to do anything that will make you uncomfortable, we just need to know that if the need should arise where you have to do something extreme, that you are prepared and will enthusiastically complete the mission." Devers replied.

Kate looked at him and then asked, "What assurances do I have that Michael will return safely?" Kate's reply gave Devers what he had expected. He knew he was going to have things work exactly as planned.

"I will have him transferred to a non-combat area as a reservist immediately upon your agreement to accept the assignment and all that is required. When you have completed the mission he will be allowed to come home to you and will be released from any further service obligation. You also will receive a promotion that will enable you to transfer to any office."

"That means that if I am successful next week that Michael would be home then?" she asked. Kate was thinking about the benefits of complying with this man. Devers responded by nodding his head. "And what type of promotion would I receive and in what department?"

Devers was doing mental cartwheels with joy, not only had she resigned herself to the obligation but she was now looking for the benefits. "You can name your assignment, within reason, and you would be promoted to assistant vice president." Devers stated frankly. He could see by the expression on her face that she was being tempted and that temptation was working.

"Okay, assuming I accept this assignment what is our next move? she asked directly.

Devers figured that this would be the area where she might decide to run. "You will be going deep under cover, which will include an identity change. You are going to pose as a successful fashion photographer that lives in Mechanicsburg, just outside of Harrisburg Pennsylvania. We will set you up in an apartment as well as provide you with a car, a Voltrun 122C, something befitting a person of your status."

Kate took in what was said and immediately wondered why the elaborate ruse. She could be put in place of Gina at work and then it would be easy to observe him closely. She also thought about her boys were they going to be included in this masquerade or was she expected to abandon them. As Devers continued to outline the plan it became more apparent to her that she was to become the romantic interest of Austin and that she was expected to make it convincing. As long as she was not to take it beyond what was socially accepted then she would not have to worry about violating her marriage vows. She was formulating questions and Devers' monolog was answering some of them as he continued. Kate waited patiently for him to complete the explanation and when he was finished she planned to ask the questions most important to her.

Devers continued to speak about how this was the only way that they could be sure to find Welsh. Lee himself was unimportant and expendable, whatever that meant. Kate saw the opportunity for more success and did not see a downside yet. Though there were unanswered questions regarding her boys and of course there were always potential illegal activities that had not been disclosed. If she would be able to see her boys regularly even if not every day, this could work. If she was able to get her husband home soon and even if that was delayed at least that while she was working on the assignment he would be safe and away from the conflict and harm's way. This could be the salvation of her life and it could help her to get out from underneath Devers control.

"What about my children, will I be able to have them with me?" she asked when Devers had finally stopped talking. Devers went on to explain that while she had the residence in Mechanicsburg she would not be actually sleeping there. She would spending the majority of her nights in her apartment in Philadelphia with her boys. Because she would be working late a good deal of the time she would have a work schedule as a photographer that started later in the day. She would be also known to travel to New York and Paris so that there would be times when she would not have to be in Mechanicsburg or on assignment on those days and those days she could spend with her family. The more Devers sold the assignment the deeper her commitment became.

Devers said, "You will be working with only one point of contact and that person is not tied directly to the bank, you will be on your own for the most part. After this meeting you will not hear from me until we have received the go ahead from you to act according to the plan you have initiated for capturing Welsh." He hesitated for just a moment yelled, "Lewis, send her in now." To Kate's astonishment Foon walked through the door. She was dressed very stylishly and her long hair had been cut short and it was now a bright shade of pink. "Foon will be your executive assistant and she will travel with you. She will be the one to relay information and reports to us. She has done it many times in the past and she is someone that can and will help you." Kate also knew that she was a master of manipulation and could not be trusted to serve anyone's interest but her own.

"Hello Foon, it's good to see you." Kate said.

"Likewise Katherine Foster, it seems we are to be tied together for a little while longer. This plan that has been devised should work fairly quickly. Did John tell you what you will need to do from an appearance standpoint?" Foon asked.

"No he did not, do tell me what is going to be required?" Kate asked thinking that whatever it was it could not be any worse than what she has agreed to already.

Foon went on to describe that she will be required to wear make-up that would change her appearance slightly. It was able to be removed and reapplied easily and that she would help her until she could do it herself. She would be wearing a dark brown almost black wig that was shoulder length and cut asymmetrically on diagonal angles that would cover her short red hair. Her wardrobe would be provided and when she was in character she must wear those clothes and accessories.

Devers watched the two women sort through the details and then when appeared they had reached point where they were in agreement he interjected, "Alright, Foster good luck we are expecting results. Failure is not an option. You are scheduled to meet Lee tomorrow at twelve thirty it has been arranged that he will be at a coffee shop standing in line when Foon will bump into him. This will call attention to you. At that point, he should be awestruck. You will need to make certain that out of that meeting you make arrangements to see him soon- within two days tops. Remember we need results and we need them fast. One last thing your name is now Melissa Champion and Foon is now Jewels Nile. Lewis has a file and the car will be waiting for you in Philadelphia."

Kate looked at him and continued to wonder why they had chosen her when there were many that would have jumped at the chance to score an easy promotion or a large financial windfall. There was something about the choice of careers and the appearance that was more than reflecting a particular style or type of woman. There was someone in Austin's past that they were trying to replicate and someone that he would be extremely vulnerable to their exploitation of those feelings.

She stood up to leave and with her Foon rose as well. They looked at one another and smiled. It was the first smile she had allowed herself since she left the company of her boys. It was almost noon and she would be on her way back to the office to clean up a few things and then off to prepare with Foon later in the afternoon. They would be spending a great deal of time together.

Foon would actually be living in the apartment to give the illusion that Kate, or should she say Melissa Champion actually resided there. She would enter and depart from the garage and then take an elevator that went directly and exclusively to the apartment. The Voltrun was selected because it afforded the maximum privacy and was used by wealthy people that wanted their identity hidden. The only possible problem would be once she exited the vehicle in Philadelphia but careful execution of normal security protocol would limit any possible exposure. Foon would accompany her most of the time to provide additional protection and to insure that she stayed within the guidelines of the plan.

On their way out Foon suggested that she look at her wardrobe before it was shipped and that she should make a selection of what she would wear for tomorrow's encounter. They went down several floors to a security office that required a high level encryption code to gain entrance. Foster's PCU had already been programmed into the system for access and she was mildly surprised at the efficiency of the group.

When they entered they found themselves in a large open room with several tables arranged randomly throughout. Neither of the women knew where they were to go or where the wardrobe was being staged for shipment. "Perhaps it's already been shipped." stated Kate.

"May I help you?" asked a computer generated voice.

The voice startled both women who looked at one another and then Foon asked, "Where is the wardrobe located for the Lee surveillance?" There was no response.

Kate then said, "This is not very organized."

The voice then responded, "What are you looking for?" Kate asked the identical question and the voice instructed them to go to the illuminated table. At that point a table at the far end of the room became illuminated and as they walked toward it a chute extended down from the ceiling and containers, of what they assumed were the wardrobe, began to slowly descend until they were positioned on the table.

They began to look through the containers at the clothing. The items were definitely not what Kate would have chosen to wear. Many of them she considered immodest revealing too much of her. She struggled to find something that was not too far outside of respectability but had no luck. She turned helplessly to Foon who then told her that she must remember she is playing a part and this was acting. No one would know that it was her if she did the job correctly, and Foon said that she that knew that she would. Foon told her that she should pick the most "un-Kate" like outfit and wear that. The sooner she got used to being Melissa Champion the faster this operation would be over.

Kate reluctantly agreed and as she made her selection she wondered how much more this assignment was going to challenge her in the days and weeks to come. She was certainly going to learn a great deal about herself. Today she had made a decision that could have a fantastic effect on her family and their future. The boys would get their father home, and she would be reunited with her husband. She would no longer have to work for Devers and she would be making more money and have more power than ever before. Not bad for a girl from a little town in Ohio, she thought.

****

Philip was prepared to meet the Dean separately but he also knew that the Dean would not be comfortable unless he had several people in the room to witness the encounter. This was partly done because Wilford Lawless Montague was an ego maniac that needed to be the center of the attention in every venue. The balance of the reasons came down to protecting himself from any air of impropriety or discrimination. Philip was under heavy scrutiny and the University needed to be protected against attacks by powerful individuals, especially those on the Board of Trustees. His hope was that there would be at least one attendee that was supportive of him and his value to the institution.

As he walked through the Quadrangle he noticed for the first time that it was raining. The rain was steady and beat down on the transparent Plexiglas passage ways that enabled students and faculty both to move across campus in comfort and safety. It was a dreary day that had started out with such promise, but he couldn't allow himself to drift to thoughts about anything other than those about the meeting that he was about to enter. He climbed the three hundred year old stairs to the central conference room where he had been instructed the meeting would occur. It was the largest conference room on campus and that meant there were most likely going to be quite a few people in attendance. As he approached the double oak doors, he hesitated for a moment reflecting upon what he was about to do and what he was going to say. The length of his career would be determined in this meeting. It could end today or it could continue indefinitely, all because of Norville Forrest's uninspired and lazy daughter.

As he entered he scanned the room to see who was in attendance. There were at least ten people in addition to the Dean. Heidi Grunthal was sitting at one end of the long rectangular oak table. The room was abuzz with individual conversations and the meeting which had not been called to order was due to start at any moment. Philip nodded to those that he recognized except for the Dean. He walked around the table and offered his hand as they exchanged greetings. Up until this episode they had had a very positive relationship and Philip was considered to be one of the shining stars of the University.

There was one person that he did not recognize but looked very familiar to him, and he assumed that man to be Forrest. There were two members of the board of Trustees as well as key faculty members and a man that he recognized from his national reputation on American Studies, Rubin Vasillio. They are going to make certain that my research will stand up under very significant scrutiny, he thought.

The Dean called the meeting to order and then introduced everyone at the table, describing the purpose of their attendance. When he had completed the introductions he went on to talk briefly about the purpose of the meeting and why it was of utmost importance that what was discussed be held in strict confidence. After completing the opening statement he turned the meeting over to Philip for his presentation of the publication.

Philip began by thanking everyone in attendance and then proceeded to outline the paper that was being presented. He gave a broad overview hoping that those that were interested would ask questions and that if there were none he would welcome the chance to do something other than sit in this inquisition. His presentation lasted roughly twenty minutes and when it was completed no one reacted at first. There was no statement of affirmation or no visible positive or negative reaction, it was if they were stunned by the content of the message.

"Philip that is a very interesting theory but one can't help to wonder about its relevance." the Dean commented.

Philip had anticipated this question above all others. "Why should we bother to view other potential time threads, after all we cannot cause them to become reality?" he asked rhetorically. Philip continued to explain that by first viewing the concept of the Epiphanal Startling one could gain the insight into the potential ramifications for all actions at any given moment. It caused us to think about where we were in relationship to where we wanted to be, or at least where we thought we wanted to be.

The challenges came from all members in the room but nothing more than issues that Philip could address by showing the thought process and the data that backed the suppositions. The questions and expressions of doubts continued for more than one hour and then it seemed as though the group began collectively to support the paper. There was one person that did conspicuously hold to the notion that it should not be published and that was naturally Norville Forrest.

"Mr. Lee, I mean Dr. Lee, did you honestly think that a pipe-dream paper like this is up to the caliber that is expected of this University's faculty?" Forrest asked as he attempted once again to rally support for his conclusion.

"Mr. Forrest, initially when this topic was brought to my attention I had almost the identical reaction as most of the people in this room, yours included sir. Today I have elected not to read the entire paper to you. It is thorough and the research is sound. It does not advocate time travel or time thread manipulation as some have indicated. It does shows, through careful modeling and by using voluminous amounts of data, the conclusions logically. I trust you will see that it is up to the standard that I set for my own works and that it equals or exceeds those set by the University. Dean Montague, I respectively submit the topic for publication and plan for it to be sent for final editing tomorrow, with your permission."

The Dean looked at the attendees and then spoke, "Philip this is a fine piece of work and we will be proud to have it published under our approbation. Good job son." The Dean looked relieved but then caught the look from Forrest who did not seem quite as pleased. He stood up and thanked everyone for their time and contribution and adjourned the meeting promptly.

Philip was approached by several people congratulating him on a great job. Then as Forrest walked by Philip, Philip extended his hand and said, "I am sorry but you look very familiar, have we met before?"

Forrest hesitated and then took Philip's hand. "No Dr. Lee I don't believe that we have. I will tell you that I am impressed by the loyalty of the people that work with you. The good news is that my daughter does not have to have you as an instructor again. I wish you the best. Good day." he said and turned and quickly departed.

Philip started to breathe again and as he walked out of the room he felt a true sense of relief, the burden was lifted. He placed a call to his editor and instructed him that the paper was a go and told them that he expected to see the work back in his hands within three weeks at the latest. The next call he placed was to Jessica who did not answer. He left a message telling her that he still had a job and that paper would go to print at the end of May. For now, though, it was time to go home.

****

Austin wondered why Gina had asked him to go for coffee with her tomorrow but then again nothing that Gina did or said made too much sense to him. He knew that tomorrow would be another interesting day filled with new opportunities to feel like an outcast, and that was something he continually felt. He accepted the invitation in an attempt to be nice to Gina and also because he had to do so. He knew that she was a weak and manipulative person that truly had problems but so did everyone. Look at him, he thought.

Chapter Seven

Austin was awaken by an incoming call. His brother Philip was on the line and wanted to speak to him about some of the things that had been happening to him recently. He wanted to meet for dinner at their parent's house and since that was where Austin was living it would be an easy commute for him. Since he had met with George and John he had decided that the whole idea of carrying on the cause was not a good one to pursue. He had ten years left on his sentence and should he be found guilty of a similar charge he would be spending the majority of the rest of his days on earth within prison walls. That was not a welcome prospect in his mind. It was for that reason that he had been avoiding the calls that they had placed to him and why he had not pursued the conversation he had with Philip regarding significant moments in history. He reluctantly agreed to meet with Philip but he believed he knew where it was all going to lead.

Austin prepared to make the commute to Newstart Incorporated. The train ride to Pittsburgh was not a pleasant one. Austin was beginning to think that he did not like trains. He would rather walk or drive but there was no way that he could drive, he had no car. He tried to block out the people around him. There were always so many people riding the trains those days, people commuting long distances to where the jobs were and living where they could afford to live. This society was a mess, Austin thought. He then thought of prison and came to the conclusion that things were better outside of those walls, though only marginally.

****

Philip was sitting at his desk feeling a sense of euphoria that came from the surrendering of his burden to someone else, in this case his editor. He could now enjoy the next several weeks coming up to final examinations. The summer curriculum was a much easier workload since most students did not attend school during that session. The best news was that he did not have to worry about publishing again until the fall semester. By that time the storm that surrounded this publication would have passed.

He began to think of Norville Forrest once again. The fact that he knew that he had seen him once before at conference or some other formal event troubled him slightly. He was certain that he had seen him before. This was happening to him quite often, forgetting where he had seen people previously. He couldn't be developing memory problems at his age, could he, he pondered. As a result of those thoughts, he spent the next several minutes obsessing over his mental health and wondering if he should seek medical attention. Then he thought of the doctor he had met. Perhaps she would be interested in giving him an evaluation. Then he laughed out loud at the prospect. He really was in a great mood.

****

"Mom I am going to be late for school. Do you know where my book bag is?" Kate's oldest son William, or Billy to his friends, called out from the main room of the apartment.

"Billy I will be right out. Look on the floor in your bedroom, that's where I saw it last night when you went to bed." Kate replied loudly.

She was looking at her wardrobe selection in the light of day. It was quite revealing, nothing a married mother of two should be wearing in public. She had dressed as though she were going to her office so that the boys would not suspect that anything was out of the ordinary. It seemed like it took much longer than it normally did to get them ready and out the door and on their way to school. If she could think of a way to spend more time in the morning with them she would do so, but until she was able to make her schedule into a routine it was unlikely that it would come to be.

She had not yet dressed for her meeting with Austin when Foon announced that she was waiting in the car outside. It was eight forty three in the morning and the drive to Pittsburgh took about three hours so there was a little time to spare but it was not a good idea to be late for a coordinated event like this one. She told Foon she was running a little late and asked her to park the car and come up. Foon begrudgingly complied with her request.

When Foon saw that she still not ready she clearly showed her irritation.   Kate saw that this woman was an extremely intense and apparently did a tremendous job of suppressing her anger that was beneath the surface.   But as quickly as the anger had appeared any trace of it vanished.

"Katherine Foster you must get ready, we cannot be late.   This is a finely orchestrated operation.   You know that the person that we are relying on is hanging on to her sanity by a thread.   If we do not execute our end of the operation she may fall apart and tell him everything that she knows."

Kate looked at her and said, "Foon, my name is Melissa Champion please call me Melissa or Ms. Champion from this point forward and I will refer to you only as Jewels.   Yes, I know that I have to be on time but this wardrobe is a challenge for me.   Can you help get past this please?"

Foon agreed and helped her apply her make-up and to put on the wig.   Once they were done and Kate had seen her reflection she felt much better about the dress.   She looked like a completely different person.   It was doubtful that anyone would recognize her, even if they were standing next to her.   She took a deep breath and put on the dress.   The fabric had appeared to be transparent on the hanger tinted to a mauve translucent intensity and then Foon told her that she could synchronize the dress with her PCU and control the level of transparency from clear to opaque and levels in between.   For day time events it would be advisable to keep the level at where it was, it provided a sense of mystery, she said.   She also told her that color for the dress was an option as well.

Foon had instructed the Voltrun to be available within ten minutes of their signal.   The car responded flawlessly.   It had a double 'AA' priority, and while that was not the top security protocol it was right below the police, firefighters and certain Military vehicles and of course they were right behind people like the President of WBOI.   The car met them at the curb as they exited Kate's building.   In the future Kate would not be dressing as Melissa at her home, all of her wardrobe would be at the Melissa's apartment in Mechanicsburg.

Kate had not seen a Voltrun 122C and when she saw its black color and sleek lines she couldn't help but smile.   With a price tag of over three quarters of million IMC, it was one of the most expensive vehicles that someone could own.   It was equipped with all of the latest technology and was capable of driving at speeds approaching two hundred miles per hour. A trip like the one to Pittsburgh at top speed was roughly the cruising limit for the electric vehicle before it had to be charged.

Once inside the vehicle the windows showed a reflective silver and while it impaired those outside of the vehicle from seeing inside, the passengers could see everything very clearly. The seats automatically adjusted for optimum comfort and the vehicle was off. All traffic made way for the car as it sped through the City at twice the legal limit. All traffic signals functioned in accordance to the vehicles protocol. They had all the green lights.

****

"Mr. Truax is here to see you sir. Shall I send him in now?" the receptionist asked Norville Forrest.

His reply was "Yes, by all means." The office lighting was subdued but brightened as Nelson Truax entered the room. He was followed by his partner who remained a step behind him and to his left. "Good to see you Truax old boy. How are you?" Norville asked.

"I am well sir." Truax replied and then cleared his throat hoping that Norville would acknowledge his partner.

"Oh yes, Barnaby how are you son?" Norville politely included him as well taking the cue from Truax.

After indicating that they should have a seat in a small seating area in front of what appeared to be a real fireplace, Norville offered the men refreshments which they respectfully declined.

"Well tell me what have you to say about the visit Dr. Lee paid to our friend the Senator. Did he have a successful trip?" Norville asked pleasantly.

Truax told him that Philip had seen the Senator and even went as far as to test his DNA to make certain that it was him. He then continued to tell Norville that the Senator had given him the name of Jeremy Giles and that Philip had placed a call to Jessica Jenkins to find out if she could help in contacting Giles.

Norville listened intently with a smile on his face. He was quite pleased with the report. "I can't wait to see Dr. Lee's reaction to the conversation he is going to have with Jeremy. I would love to see that personally." he said with a chuckle. Then he continued, "And what about our friend Foon, was she given the information that she needed?"

Truax deferred to Barnaby who had been the one sent to monitor the meeting Foon had with their operative. Barnaby stammered with nerves, he was not used to speaking with Norville and was intimidated by him and his apparent wealth. After some gentle reassurance from Norville he began the briefing explaining the situation. He finished by saying it was unclear what WBOI would do in response. The last portion of the briefing he spoke about Austin and the fact that he had been invited to coffee with Gina, it was their intention to monitor the meeting.

232

While not as pleased with the results of this portion of the assignment Norville did not allow the two men to see anything but a cheerful countenance. Austin was a delicate piece of this very elaborate plot and if he should be exposed to some truly ruthless behavior on the part of WBOI it could cause him to break down or even be killed. Norville then said, "Gentlemen you have done very well. Please make certain that you both are involved in the meeting this afternoon. We need to know what WBOI is up to regarding Austin Lee. He needs to be protected."

The men left quickly because they would be driving to Pittsburgh from their current location in western Maryland. As they walked to the Voltrun 110 that belonged to Norville's company they both were quiet. They needed to make certain that anything that they said was not overheard by anyone. This Voltrun, was equipped with anti-eavesdropping technology so that they could feel confident when they were inside that they could not be overheard.

Once they were in the vehicle they began to relax as Voltrun sped toward Pittsburgh. It was necessary to drive from this location since there were no trains that were connected to major commuting lines. The rural portions of western Maryland, like many of the rural areas of the country, had not been considered priority as the country had rebuilt its transportation system around the Maglev Train Technology.

Barnaby was the first to speak when he asked, "Do you think that the meeting went well?"

Truax looked at him and replied, "Yes, it went fine. We have a lot to think about regarding today's surveillance, though. Pull up a map of the area and the blue prints of the building."

Barnaby activated the screen display that was embedded in the dashboard of the Voltrun. The panel was then attached to a console that was raised from the floor of the vehicle. The two men were able to study the map and blueprints in three dimensions as a holographic image was displayed above the screen. They discussed the various vantage points and determined where they would get the best results when it came to installing listening devices and cameras. They soon came to an agreement on their respective assignments and they would each be responsible for installing four devices. Once they had decided on the plan they turned away from each other and continued the trip in silence.

****

Austin arrived a work on time, not early as he had been doing since he had been given the assignment to monitor Gina's behavior. As he approached his desk he noticed that Gina was at her desk already working. She looked much better than she had in the previous days.

"Good morning Gina. You look great today. How are you feeling?" he said with a smile. Gina looked up and responded with a good morning and then returned to her work. Austin shrugged off the lack of attention as part of the routine.

He wondered if they were still to have coffee that afternoon. She may have changed her mind and decided that she didn't want to go for whatever reason. Austin decided he couldn't afford to obsess about this, he had work to do. He pushed himself to work on the project he had been assigned. The hours quickly passed and his stomach told him it was approaching the time for it to be fed. Having been interrupted he took this chance to look over to see what Gina was doing. She seem to be working very hard on her project. He requested the time and was told that it was eleven fifty. The plan was for the two of them to have lunch at a coffee shop that she frequented at twelve thirty and he began to think of alternate arrangements in the event these plans did not come to fruition.

"Austin are you still interested in going to lunch at twelve thirty?" Gina asked him quietly. Austin turned and nodded. She in turn smiled and went back to her work. She thought about how Austin seemed so nice and it was a shame that he was involved with those bad people. Even so if she wanted to keep her supply of drugs flowing she had to take him to lunch and after that she would not have to worry about what he did or did not do.

Soon they were walking out of the building on their way to the coffee shop. It was a short walk of less than two blocks from the building where they worked. The sidewalk was enclosed to the street corners at which time they exited the enclosure via a large revolving door that rotated constantly allowing pedestrians to cross in either direction. Gina was very talkative, a sign that she was nervous. She told Austin about her family life up until the time her mother had died. Then she proceeded to tell him about her sisters and brother. They were not close and when her mother passed away they lost touch with one another. She missed not having people in her life.

At one point during the short walk Austin tried to interject some comments into the conversation but it was lost as Gina continued to speak of the pain that she felt. This was a person that had no outlet for those feelings and was taking this opportunity to put into words the many feelings that she constantly repressed. Austin saw that this was a very lonely person and he could relate to her thoughts of feeling alone.

They arrived at the coffee shop at twelve thirty two. The time was being carefully tracked by multiple interested parties. The plan had called for Foon to bump into Gina but Gina was in a state of agitation and was not thinking very clearly. She had accomplished the mission as far as she was concerned and now it was up to the others to make it work. Foon being a resourceful operative and veteran of many of these type of operations was able to come up with an alternative. She simply spilled her drink on Gina while she was seated.

Gina jumped up in shock as the cold drink ran down her back. She turned and glared at Foon who then apologized and offered to have her clothing cleaned. Foon ushered her off to the women's rest room and when she did Kate moved in and began a conversation with Austin. She stood back-lit against the window and Austin could see the outline of her body. She had a slight athletic build and she was a fairly short person though he could not gauge her height accurately because she was wearing high heels.

Kate repositioned herself so that Austin could clearly see her face. It was then that Austin felt his mouth open in astonishment. It was Melinda, or her twin. This was too good to be true and he blurted out, "Melinda is that you?"

Kate at that moment understood the reason for the appearance and responded, "No, my name is Melissa, Melissa Champion and you are?" Austin didn't speak, he was trying to process the fact that there was another woman that looked like Melinda and she was here right in front of him.

He stood up and finally said, "My name is Austin Lee, very nice to meet you." and he extended his hand. She looked at his hand as though she was inspecting it for cleanliness and then took it. Her hand shake was soft and Austin barely felt any pressure, but when he went to withdraw Kate applied a slight squeeze to indicate that she was interested in him.

"Well Austin it seems as though Jewels has caused a bit of a commotion here by spilling her drink. I am certain your friend will be okay." she said with a laugh.

Austin searched for something to say, "You remind me of someone that I used to know." was all he could manage to formulate. "Please would you join me while we wait for them to return." followed as he finally discovered his manners. "You don't look like you hail from Pittsburgh, what brings you to town?" he asked.

"I am here shooting a private fashion show." she replied.

"Oh, are you a model or a designer?" he asked.

She laughed again and said, "No, I am the photographer. I work exclusively in the fashion industry, though I would much rather be photographing other subjects. Let me guess what you do, you are an architect. Am I right?"

Austin wanted to just say yes so that she would be happy but he told her that he was an accountant. She then responded that he did not appear to fit the image she had of an accountant, and asked if he was always an accountant or had he done other things. Austin continued to stare at her and when Foon and Gina returned he barely took notice.

Gina seemed relieved that Austin was engaged in a conversation with Melissa because now she knew she did not have to spy on him again. She could become his real friend not one that had an ulterior motive. As she finished her lunch she was feeling much more relaxed and had withdrawn into her own world, and as such was not participating in the conversation.

Austin and Kate were actively engaged in conversation. Kate used some of her own history and background to fill in the details that were missing from character sketch she had been provided.

She had worked hard at being charming but her intellect was what appealed to Austin. He felt that that she was a very intelligent woman. It was then that he made an unprecedented move and asked to see her again.

Kate was duty bound to accept the offer but wanted to make it a little challenging. She hesitated and Austin took the bait and ran with it. She toyed with him like a savvy fisherman would with a fish too powerful and heavy for the line that he had been using. Finally she agreed to have dinner with him Friday evening at a restaurant in Harrisburg. He was to meet her there at seven.

He asked for her contact information and she indicated that her PCU was not functioning properly. Austin almost asked to see if he could look at it since he had assembled them for four years while he was in prison. She told him that they would just have to trust that the other party would be there. She smiled and stood saying good bye over her shoulder and then she was gone.

****

Barnaby called Truax and asked whether one of them should follow the woman and her companion.

Truax told him, "Stay with her but if appears she may be aware that she is being followed stop it. We know where she will be on Friday and will be better prepared."

In keeping with his orders Barnaby followed Kate and Foon to their car. At which time they sped off leaving Barnaby unable to follow. He was successful in getting the identification transponder to surrender the vehicles information. This was a tremendously valuable piece of luck. Truax was just as busy and just as fortunate. He went into the coffee shop and was able to secure the cups of all in attendance. This would give the means to identify the two women.

****

Upon arrival back at the office Austin noticed that there were several people congregating around his work area. When he reached the cubicle he noticed that Roscoe was there along with two women. Gina had stopped in the women's rest room and was not with him when he returned. Roscoe asked him where she was and when told that she was in the rest room he took off in that direction with the two women closely behind him.

Approximately an hour later a security guard accompanied by a woman that he had seen before, but could not remember where, showed up at Gina's cubicle. They boxed up her personal items quickly.

"What happened to Gina?" Austin asked. The woman turned and looked at him but did not answer. The two left as quickly as they had arrived.

"Mr. Plantiere what happened to Gina?" Austin inquired.

Roscoe answered quickly and firmly, "Don't worry about her Lee, she is being taken to a rehab clinic for detoxification. After that, when she is declared fit, she will be offered her job back here. You did a good job looking out for her." Austin tried to reply but the call had been cut off. He looked at his desk and then at Gina's empty cubicle. He did not have time to waste on worrying about what happened and why, he had a lot of work to do and he was falling behind schedule. He took this type of personal drama in stride, the years he had spent in prison had left a callous on his heart. He needed to be able to move passed moments like this one, he needed to finish so he could leave promptly on Friday, he had a date.

****

Truax and Barnaby met at Pittsburgh's public library. They would have access all of the computing power and identity tracking equipment that they would need there. In the Law Enforcement Section they would be able to scan for DNA and finger prints on the cups and use the encryption equipment to get the data regarding ownership of the Voltrun 122C. As they entered they were required to show identification that they were with a law enforcement organization so that they could use the equipment.   Barnaby showed his Philadelphia Police Department credentials and Truax his FBI badge.   Both of the men were admitted without further questions.

"I think we will be much better prepared for our mystery lady once we find out who she is and who she is working for.   Don't you agree Barnaby?" asked Truax as he placed the cups on a small conveyor belt which ran them through an identification processing scanner.   The end results would be shown on a series of screens located near-by.   Truax went and sat down in front of one of the screens waiting for the results to appear.

Meanwhile Barnaby was seated at another workstation and was interpreting the transponder information.   It showed that the vehicle was recently registered to a Ms. Melissa Champion who lived in Mechanicsburg Pennsylvania and was a professional photographer by trade.   The identity seems to be legitimate except there was a little too much recent information and historic data was spotty and very limited.   Most identifications were the opposite and it was for that reason that he suspected that it was possible that the identification was a fake.

Barnaby's effort then shift to determining if there were some way of discovering whether it was or was not.   The first thing he did was to start with the date of manufacture of the vehicle and from there he traced its shipping information.   Voltrun 122C was a rare vehicle and they were ordered specifically for certain clients.   He worked his way back to the original order to find that it had been placed by Ustra Corporation.   Upon further research he found that Ustra Corp was owned by limited partnership.   The general partner or the visible one was WGB Holdings.   If he had not been familiar with WGB Holdings the trail would have ended there but WGB Holdings was known to be run by a man named Girard, who was connected to WBOI through John Devers the head of the Global Security Division.   Barnaby was convinced that the vehicle was purchased by WBOI and that its occupants were probably tied to it as well.   He continued to work on that basis of assumption and shifted his concentration to the living quarters and if that too could be traced back to WBOI as well.

The results of the identity scan came back and showed that the women were Jewels Nile and Melissa Champion.   The database that the subsequent detail search took him to the same source that Barnaby had been exploring and he too was suspicious by the way the information was presented.   He then decided to attempt to find the date and time of entry of the information.   It would involve a long and elaborate process that would only show him when the information was added and not by whom.   "Barnaby, have you had any luck with your search?" he asked.

Barnaby presented his finding and Truax was impressed. That was definitely a link to WBOI and now they had another place to look for the true identity of Ms. Champion.   Barnaby indicated the residence information had also most likely been altered as well. He had been able to find previous tenant's information that has been confirmed to show that they were most likely living there last month even though the landlord disclosure file indicated that Melissa Champion had been living there for the past six months.

Truax started working on the WBOI employee records files and their identities. He started looking for woman according to approximately age, hair and eye color, weight and height. He came up with a very large sample and sighed heavily when he saw how many files he would have to review. Barnaby took note of the sigh and asked him what was wrong.

"There are too many woman that fit the profile." he complained.

Barnaby made a very keen observation at that point, "I would suggest that you look only according to height first and I would factor the heels out of the measurement. I would say they add at least four inches to her height. That makes her a very small person- five foot at best."

Truax looked at him and smiled a very broad smile. "That's why I like having you around - you can be brilliant at times- truly brilliant."   The search narrowed the list to fourteen women and only one of them worked in security. She was the Northeast Regional Director Katherine E. Foster.

"That's her!" they both said at the same time.   Their excitement caused a stir and a nasty look from the Librarian. The looked at each other and laughed.

"That's great now who is the other one?" Barnaby asked.

With that Truax shrugged and said, "I guess it's not time to go home quite yet."

Uncovering Jewels Nile's true identity proved to be very frustrating. First, it did not appear to be fake. There were no anomalies as they had seen with Kate's identity, this one was constructed by a true artist. They went through every residence and job that Jewels was supposed to have had. They ran the trace back ten years and found no inconsistencies.

"This is very frustrating Barnaby, very frustrating. I know this woman is not who she represents herself to be but she didn't show up in the WBOI database and we can't find anything that would confirm or deny her identity. Any thoughts or brilliance?" Truax joked.

"How about the criminal database? Try the height search.   This woman was right around six feet tall. Though, I am thinking I know who this might be." Barnaby stated.

"Who are you thinking it is?" Truax asked.

"It's the woman that I was communicating through Jubal with at For Eyes the other day. She used to work for Girard but now freelances for Devers, Foon is her name. Though I have no proof."

Truax looked at the surveillance recordings they had of Foon and then compared it to the recording of the meeting earlier that day. They were seeking to apply facial recognition as well as height, weight and symmetry comparisons. What they ended up with was an eighty two percent chance that it was Foon. Then Barnaby noticed a gesture that both subjects made. It was the way that she touched her chin with her forefinger and thumb. It was a unique gesture and that made it conclusive as far as he was concerned. They would have a great deal to share with Mr. Forrest later this evening. They packed up their materials and headed to the car. Once again they remained silent until they had reached the safety of the car. They now knew who, all they needed to know was what WBOI was planning to do.

****

Philip was on his way to meet with his brother Austin at their parent's home. He had called his mother to alert her to that fact that he would be stopping by. There was a pastry shop in Lancaster that made the best Italian cannoli and his mother had a true passion for them. He stopped there and they accommodated him with a refrigerated bag which he paid a small deposit to assure them that he would return it. The train ride was uneventful and while riding he paged through Christopher Leesop's journal once again. He had read it once and now he was studying it. He found that it revealed more each time he read through a section.

Philip had been hoping that Jessica would call with the time that he could meet with Jeremy or, at least, when he could speak to him. He had decided that he would not call her. She would have to call him. It seemed a little childish but he was unsure about her motives and if she expected a relationship with Philip as she had implied in their last conversation, then she would have to put forth some effort. Dealing with this woman was exasperating, he thought.

His thoughts returned to the journal and he focused on a section where Christopher challenged those that were his followers to be prepared to sacrifice as he was going to have to be sacrificed. Philip thought about the significance of the term sacrifice. In his mind he had always saw Christopher Leesop as a self-serving fanatic that was only interested in destroying everything that society had built. He saw none of that in his teachings illustrated in the journal.

What he now saw was a man that continued to point to the good that we could all do for each other. He talked about our need to give to each other that what we were expecting from others, our love. It did not seem to be at all consistent with any propaganda that had he had read about the man. He decided to start to do additional research and if discovered more supporting information it could make a great paper and he needed a subject for the fall publication in his pocket should Norville Forrest continue to be hunting for his head.

He arrived at his parent's home and when he entered he was greeted by the smell of roasted turkey. His mother had apparently had a turkey prepared and brought in for dinner. He was fairly certain that she had not prepared it herself, since MacKenzie was not known for her cooking. MacKenzie heard the door open and wondered who had arrived since she was expecting two of her sons and her husband all of whom were due at roughly the same time though they were all coming from different points of origin.

The other two men arrived at the same time and soon the house was full of conversation and laughter. MacKenzie commented that it would be perfect if Roger had come but she understood he was working on some very important project and it was consuming a good deal of his time and of course there was the mystery woman he had been seeing for so many months too. They continued to eat and joke about various family past events and shared moments. It was a time when they all felt good about being related to one another.

Dinner was over and Philip and Pam cleared the table while Austin talked to his mother about his day. He seemed much more alive and involved in what was happening around him. MacKenzie felt that she was seeing her son emerge from the protective shell he had been hiding in for the past six years. She felt joy as she saw him speak with confidence and with true strength in his voice. This was the Austin she had always known, this was her number one son.

MacKenzie knew that Philip was there to meet with Austin and that they had things to discuss so she made every effort to allow them to separate themselves and discuss what needed to be done. Philip on the other hand was going to make an attempt to gain a meeting with Jeremy Giles through his father and he opened the conversation by explaining a little about his research paper. He talked about Leopold Jenkins and then about meeting his daughter on a train when he had met Jeremy. He then explained that Jeremy had introduced Leopold to Senator Sun who in turn set up a meeting with Dr. William Lawrence. They all went on a white water rafting junket and two of the men were killed.

MacKenzie interrupted, "Was that Willie's father that was killed?" Philip said that it was. He then continued by asking his father if he could have Jeremy call him so that he could answer a few questions that came up as a result of meeting he had with the Senator yesterday. His father told him he would pass the message along when he saw him. Philip thanked him and silently hoped that he would pass the message along in a timely fashion, for his father was not known for remembering to do things when they were supposed to be done.

Philip began to talk about the subject of the paper. He felt that this was a way that he could get the subject in front of Austin without having to spend a lot of time isolated with him and possibly inviting questions from his parents. He opened up the conversation by asking if they would like to learn a little about the paper that he was publishing. The look from his mother was priceless, of course she wanted to learn as much as she could about what her son was doing. Gregory on the other hand had been through a tough day at work and was hoping to not have to concentrate too much on any one thing. Still Philip didn't routinely share anything about his life so he thought it best to take advantage of a rare gift given to a parent of an adult offspring.

Philip started with the statement which defined what an Epiphanal Startling was. His mother than proceeded to ask if he had invented the term because it wasn't something that she had ever heard before. Philip assured her that it was an invented term but he could not take credit for it, the credit belonged to Dr. Leopold Jenkins. MacKenzie nodded showing her understanding and waited for him to continue. Philip continued by explaining that these rare instances in history were so significant because a change of their outcome would cause the entire direction of earth's future to be altered in a dramatic fashion. At that point his father asked if that wasn't true with a great many events in history. Philip responded the events he was talking about were man-made events and have taken place over a very short period of time, hours or a few days.

Gregory decided for purpose of expediency he would not argue the point and he too nodded his head in understanding. At that point Philip started to name several of these events and then he came to rest on the battle at Gettysburg. It was Dr. Jenkins' contention that this battle represented a classic example of the Epiphanal Startling of which he had spoken. Everyone in the room recognized that Gettysburg was indeed a significant battle during the Civil War, but the argument that its outcome would have changed the world seemed to be a difficult one to follow.

"I felt the way you do." Philip responded. He went on to state that a series of very sophisticated computer programs had been developed to model the resulting scenarios and with a ninety two percent chance of accuracy the results for the world being as it was now was very unlikely.

"In fact, the United States of America as it has been known throughout the world these past three hundred and sixty plus years would not be the force that it has been. We would be, in all likelihood, two smaller countries that would never have amounted to anything more than second rate countries. Not bad place to live, mind you, but not like the country that threw its youth into the trenches in 1918. It was during that war the United States became recognized as an upstart world power and that investment of manpower tipped the scales in the favor of the allies." Philip said and then he took a quick break to catch his breath and take a sip of water.

When Philip started talking about Leopold Jenkins Austin had been barely paying attention his mind was stuck on Melissa Champion and their date in two days. But as Philip began to talk about the concept of Epiphanal Startling he suddenly woke up. He woke up from six years of sleep. His mind began to think about what could be if someone could bring that type of monumental change about. He started to remember the passion he once had regarding 'the cause' and while he had a fleeting feeling when he met with John and George it soon passed away. Then he became afraid of what would happen should he get caught again. This was not the sign of someone that had gotten past their problem; someone that had accepted that what they had done was wrong. It was the picture of a fearful uncommitted coward, he thought.

Austin listened Philip intently as he explained the reasoning for choosing the battle at Gettysburg and how the ripples in the time thread would compound in severity as time continued to pass. First there would be a cooling down period between the two new countries. They would lick their wounds and begin to heal. There would eventually be a normalization of relations between them but that would be decades after the war had ended. The first of the major changes would be a renewed aggressive posture by both England and Mexico. Mexico would strike first and it would take back most of New Mexico, all of Arizona, the southern portion of California and the western section of Texas. Canada would then seize control of the Pacific Northwest, Montana, the Dakotas and Minnesota entirely and parts of Idaho, Wyoming and Wisconsin. This would leave the United States of America to be predominately concentrated in the Northeastern section of the continent.

The South would continue on its path as an agrarian society and would not develop the industrial capabilities to rival their neighbors to the north. The rate and the level of that development would be retarded by the lack of diversity in the economy. Neither country would relax their military build-up in fear that the other would decide aggression would be in order. There preoccupation with each other and the trauma that the war had caused proved to be difficult obstacles for the two countries to overcome. When the call to fight comes in Europe, neither country was able to muster enough support for fear that the other would seize the moment and invade them. As a result of the United States not participating in the conflict in Europe the war continues. It is a virtual stalemate and the trench warfare continues with neither side able to gain enough of an edge to claim victory. After fifteen more years of bloodshed a truce is finally struck and Europe's countries realigned.

The delay in a sustainable peace has taken its toll on many lives in Europe. Many of the German's that would have come to power during the next war do not survive this modified war, one of them was a corporal named Adolph. The Second World War does not occur in the same fashion as we know it. The Russian Bear becomes the dominate force and they become the one and only global superpower. Communism becomes the global standard for all countries to emulate.

When Philip stopped talking this time there were no questions, there was only silence. Gregory was tired and wanted to go to bed. The story his son had just told was entertaining, even though it was depressing. He did not see the point in the conjecture since Philip clearly did not believe it to be viable and he could not share his true knowledge or true feeling at that time. It is because of what has happened to us that made us who we are. As a scientist he recognized the need to dream, it fueled the creative spark that was needed to break new ground and discover better ways to do things. Still this type of dreaming, he thought, was counterproductive and it was contrary to what he believed was the true reason and definition of an Epiphanal Startling.

"Philip I am going to have to excuse myself, though this has been fascinating. I wish you the best with the paper." Gregory said. He stood up and left the room hoping to get some time where he could collect his thoughts about his day and put things in order for tomorrow's challenges. Philip said good night to him and MacKenzie and Austin said that they would see him later.

Philip then went on to say that he wasn't certain that the changes would alter the time thread as radically as Jenkins had hypothesized. The power would have shifted from the traditional rich and powerful in Europe to a military backed totalitarian regime. You would be in effect trading one demon for another.

"Philip, could a subsequent event change the direction that the Russia would take in their quest for world domination?" Austin asked.

"Jenkins had a series of secondary scenarios that predominately looked at the effects on the two American countries. I have not reviewed them all but there did not seem to be too many variations that showed much promise for improvement." Philip answered.

That was not what Austin wanted to hear. He had hoped that there was a scenario that would have the world become a better place, not just different. "I would be interested to know if Jenkins had a favorite scenario." Austin stated.

"That's odd, I don't think I recall reading that he did have one that he favored over the others. I wonder if I missed something." Philip reflected out loud. He started to think about the pages that he had not reviewed. There must have been hundreds that he scanned but did not read carefully. Could there have been a scenario that Jenkins favored? He would have to dig through the files again just to make certain that he had not missed something.

Austin and MacKenzie continued to show that they were very interested in what he was talking about so he continued to the next part of the paper and that was the sequence of events that would have to occur for the South to be victorious at Gettysburg. He would have to start with some background information that might be important for his audience to understand. He explained that General Lee had staked the future of the war on a second attempt to invade the North. Lee believed that it was necessary so that the army could replenish itself and that the Union's resolve could be shaken and he believed if they were dealt a definitive blow within their own borders that their resolve would crumble. This represented the South's only real chance of winning the war.

Philip continued to talk about the political climate in the North as well as the willingness of England and France to recognize the South as a free and independent country. They were waiting for the one definitive action that would show them that they were not backing a losing cause. Their confidence had been shaken by the loss at Antietam when Southern carelessness and Northern good fortune won the day for General George McClellan and the Army of the Potomac. True to form, though, he allowed Lee to escape. It was under that shadow that Lee left Virginia and entered Maryland on his way to Pennsylvania.

MacKenzie began to show her waning interest in the subject matter and she decided that she should allow the boys to have their time alone. She stood up abruptly and said, "I have to get up early tomorrow so I am going to get to bed." She approached Philip and bent over and kissed his cheek. "Good Night Philip, you need to stop by more often. I think your work is very interesting and would love to hear more about when I am more awake." she said with a smile. Philip and Austin both said good night to their mother. As she walked past Austin she touched his shoulder and looked down on him and smiled.

Now that MacKenzie had left Austin felt that he could ask some additional questions. He first wanted to know how many variables would have to be altered for the change to come into being. This question was a difficult one for Philip to answer since there were several scenarios that had been referenced and each one had a similar effect. This answer did not seem to be adequate for Austin since he had pressed Philip to outline a scenario that had the highest probability of being successful.

Philip thought for a moment and then pushed back once again. He talked about the loss of Stonewall Jackson as being truly significant. If Jackson had survived the balance of the war may have gone easier for Lee and the South, but his survival alone would not guaranty success. Then Philip changed the line of thinking to include a very elaborate chain of events that would end in a successful Pickett's charge. In this one, while it was a victory the Southern forces, they were at that point too weak to have a sustainable push that was needed for the North to capitulate. The effort to win would hinge upon the first day of the battle, Philip believed, the first of July.

The first step necessary would take place on the twenty eighth of June when Joseph Hooker was replaced by Meade as commander of the Army of the Potomac. Hooker was the commanding general when the Union army lost at Chancellorsville, when with fewer men Lee routed the Union army. By keeping Hooker in place the South would be given a more significant advantage in strategic planning and tactical execution. Philip looked at his brother and wondered why he had developed so much interest in history. Austin had never found history the slightest bit interesting and he had refrained from participation in discussion on every occasion in the past. Rather than ask him about it directly he would wait and see what developed.

The next point that Philip made dealt with was J. E. B. Stewart. The flamboyant general that had a special place in the commanding General's heart, but during this campaign his performance was less then acceptable. He allowed the Army of Northern Virginia to function without its eyes and his participation in the first day of the battle would have had a positive bearing on events that transpired that day. As it was Lee was left with A. G. Jenkins who, aside from sharing his last name with Leopold Jenkins, was a commander that Lee did not have the confidence in his abilities to provide meaningful intelligence.

Philip then proceeded to talk about the Henry Heth's clash with Reynolds west of Gettysburg. He explained that this encounter, on the battle's first day was a pivotal one, and should the Southern forces been able to take the higher ground and hold it they would have been in a strong position to win the battle even without the other changes that were recommended in this scenario.

Austin responded to this scenario in a very enthusiastic fashion. "Do you mean that with the right type of intelligence and the loss of a critical note indicating that Hooker should be replaced that the battle would have gone to the South?" he asked.

"Yes, that's exactly what this scenario's conclusion is."

The next move that was required was the one that would take a significant amount of effort and that would be for General Lee to attack Philadelphia. There were multiple reasons to do this and they all are revolved around breaking the will of the North to continue the fight. Philadelphia was one of the strong holds of antiwar opinion and coupling this action with an even bolder plan would give the South the victory over the North because their desire to continue the fight was gone. There was no historic data to say that Lee would be inclined to attack Philadelphia and there would have had to have been significant incentive to entice Lee to move in that direction.

"The interesting thing about Jenkins' argument is that it does not have to have a probable argument it just needs to be possible." said Philip.

Austin thought for a moment before asking the question that immediately came to mind. If he posed this question Philip may be even more curious as to why he was so interested in an event that could change the world. He decided to ask it, "How could you best influence Lee to make such a move?"

Philip heard the question and while he had an opinion he did not know why such a question arose. This was just a theoretical exercise and nothing more.

"I am not sure what it would take. Why do you ask?" Philip inquired wanting to get to the real reason Austin was so interested. The reaction that Philip saw to his question did not make him feel secure that Austin's motives for asking were not strictly out of curiosity. There was something else at stake here.

Austin felt uncomfortable about telling his brother what he was thinking. It would not be understood. He had only been out of jail for a little more than three months and he was now considering doing something that might be illegal. But was it? There couldn't be a law governing time thread manipulation for if there were that would mean that the government thought that it was possible.

"Philip what if it were possible to influence past events and by doing so change the time thread from that point forward?" Austin finally asked.

Philip looked at him and smiled. "Do you believe that it is?" Philip responded with his own question.

A lot was being said even though no words were directly dealing with the questions that were asked. Philip now suspected his brother thought that time thread manipulation was possible and that was troubling to him.

"Austin, time thread manipulation is not possible and even if it were I am certain that it is something the government would take a very dim view of someone trying to change history. I know you don't want to go back to...." and then he stopped short of saying the word 'prison'. There was no need to state the obvious but there was one thing that he did notice about his brother and that was that his demeanor was much more like it was prior to his arrest, like it was when he was seeing Melinda. Either he has found another woman or he was getting back involved with the cause or both, he conjectured.

Austin heard the concern in his brother's voice and saw the worried looked on his face. This was a man that had remained loyal to him the whole time he was in prison and had been there with his mother when he was released. He had always admired him, though he hadn't realized it until he had told him the last time he had come to visit him while he was in prison.

"Philip, the last thing I want to is to go back to prison. I don't believe that talking about time thread manipulation rises to the level of criminal conspiracy, though." Austin said with a smile.

Philip wondered if he should talk to Austin about what he had been dealing with regarding Internal Security and the fact that there may have been foul play involved in the deaths of Jenkins and Lawrence. There was also the matter of the top secret document that once had been part of Jenkins' research.

"I wouldn't be surprised if there was a law on the books that governs time thread manipulation. I found a reference to it in a paper that was included in the research that I was doing and that paper was classified top secret. The subject was obscured but I received a visit from Internal Security last week and they were inquiring whether I had the document or had seen it. Of course I did not have it and had not seen it either." Philip said hoping that his brother would change the subject and he would not feel compelled to say more about his visit to see the Senator or that Roger had spoken to Willie to see what his father had been working on just prior to his death. The Senator had stated that his work was on time thread manipulation but would not expound upon it. It would be more important now to find out whether Austin truly believed that it was possible and why.

"Do you think time thread manipulation is possible?" he asked Austin.

"I read an article when I was in prison about a scientist that had performed a test of sorts that included the ability to send the image of an object back in time. His experiment only included a small note that he sent to a colleague fifteen minutes in the past. Unfortunately, I don't remember the name of the scientist and I haven't been able to locate any information on the process. It is like the article never existed." Austin flatly stated.

"That sounds incredible are you certain the scientist was legitimate? It wouldn't be the first time someone tried perpetrate a hoax." Philip countered.

"Philip, I know what I read. I believe that what he did makes for some interesting fantasies." Austin's comment convinced Philip that he did indeed believe that there was a way to manipulate time and even if there was not a law that restricted it, the fact that the government had been studying the feasibility could lead Austin into a very dangerous area.

"You know that I only want the best for you and I am a little concerned that this time thread manipulation thing might put you on somebody's list to watch." he said trying to avoid the mention of Internal Security.

Austin studying his brother and then replied, "I don't see that being interested in time thread manipulation is a crime, yet. Though I am sure that if the government thinks there is a reason to prevent it then it will certainly be against the law. And it should be - who wants somebody creating a time thread that could cause them financial loss or even their existence." he said with a laugh.

The two men knew there was more to each other's statements then they were admitting to each other but the evasive dance continued none the less. It had been engrained in them to avoid conflict and confrontation at all costs. It was never stated, it was an observed trait that they saw their father practice continuously. It made a stand on principles almost impossible, and honesty between two people difficult to achieve.

The conversation continued for several more minutes in much the same way with neither man really stating what was on their mind. Finally Austin asked his brother a question that put Philip in a position where he would have to lie to avoid telling him about the situation with Internal Security. He was frustrated and was trying to determine whether he should leave and not answer the question at all when Austin said, "Look whatever you know that you think will hurt me or cause me to get into trouble doesn't matter. I am thinking about why I went to jail and what it all meant. I have been reading Christopher Leesop's journal and Uncle Bob's letters trying to make sense of everything that has happened. If I can figure out a way alter time - legally, I think I have to do it." Austin stopped and waited to see his brother's reaction.

Philip responded in kind. He told Austin of the Internal Security episode and then he went on to tell him about his visit to the Senator and also Roger's attempt at discovering if Willie had known what his father's research had been about. He then went even farther stating that he believed that the deaths of Jenkins and Lawrence were not accidents. He had no proof of it but he did have a very strong feeling that they were killed for some reason and it might have centered on what Austin was trying to discover.

The conversation went on for the next two hours, each man expressing their opinions with passion. Austin wanted to make things right and to get back to a time when people were better connected and had hope of a better life. Philip was concerned that his brother was treading on a dangerous path that had an end that was far too familiar. Philip also thought about the impact that it would have on him, he had invested in Austin. He had placed faith and trust in him. If he went back to prison not only did Austin fail but he felt he had failed as well. At the point of realizing this Philip pushed his conscious thoughts in another direction so he did not have to confront the ugly image that selfishness reflects when one looks closely into the mirror that reveals one's soul. Austin had his freedom to lose but he had already experienced that, Austin's loss would be great but his loss would be greater, thought Philip.

Austin asked questions about the upcoming meeting that Philip hoped to have with Jeremy Giles and while he wanted to be there he did not think that it would be good for him to attend. He was hoping that he could give Philip a couple of questions to ask and if Philip would record the meeting so that he could listen to Jeremy's responses. Philip dissuaded him from wanting the meeting to be recorded and they settled on the plan for Philip to leave his PCU open for Austin to listen to the conversation, this way Austin could hear it as it was happening. If something appeared to be missing or wrong he could actually contact Philip and let him know while the meeting was taking place.

It was decided that Philip would ask Jeremy about the research that was being done and what Jenkins' interest was in time thread manipulation, if any. The only other question that Philip had not considered was the one the last one that Austin requested him to seek an answer, "Did Jeremy know Willie's father before the meeting was scheduled, why did they select whitewater rafting as venue for the meeting to occur and who suggested it?" Austin asked. He speculated that they had set the meeting in the mountainous region of Maine to be out of the earshot of eavesdropping and visual surveillance.

Philip thought that the question was a good one and needed to be asked. Why would anyone set up an initial meeting between three men, all of who were highly regarded in their fields and whose only tie to one another would appear to be their interest in time and the effect it would have on historic and current events. He agreed to ask the questions and then indicated that he had to be going. He had work in the morning and still had a little more than an hour before he would be getting home.

They parted company neither convinced that the other really understood their position and what they truly intended to do. Austin was tired and wanted to get to bed, he had a big day and was beginning to think about Melissa again. This was too good to be true he thought, maybe his luck was finally changing and he could start to put my life back in some sort of order, he thought.

She reminded him of Melinda but there was a big difference that he couldn't pin down. What was it? She looked like her and yet she didn't. She acted like her, but not really. She was intelligent but yet she was actually much more substantial. She seemed to be a more complete person than Melinda ever was. He climbed the stairs to his boyhood room that he had not changed since he took up residence in his parent's home for the second time in his life. It was time to move out, he thought.

****

Philip had been walking for several minutes when he received a call from Jessica. "Hello Philip, how are you? I was concerned when I didn't hear from you after your presentation." she said.

"I did call and I left you a message. The presentation went well and they accepted the paper. It will be published, most likely by the end of May if all goes well. Yesterday was day that I got a lot of things put to rest." he stated hoping she would comment or at the very least show some interest in his trials.

She, true to form let a period of awkward silence continue and then said, "I am glad you were able to get the publication approved. I hope that there will be people that will finally understand what my father was trying to do."

Philip responded, "I am not sure I understand what he was trying to do. My brother, Austin brought up an interesting point this evening and I am going to do some more research, not to add to the publication but to enhance my own comprehension of the thesis. There was so much information and of course there was that report that was missing."

He hoped she had made an attempt to reach out to Jeremy Giles and that was the reason for her call, or perhaps for personal reasons but instead he suspected that she had another agenda and was on a fishing expedition looking for information.

"Thank you for being so thorough in your analysis. I know that is the reason that my father thought you were so good at your job." she replied. "I wanted to hear your voice and see if you were okay. You seem to be distracted or tired or something so I will talk to you some other time. Have a good night Philip." Jessica concluded and waited for him to reply.

"You too Jessica. Thanks for calling. Good night." and Philip disconnected the call. He did not like the way he had behaved. It was childish but he desperately need her to validate his importance to her and once again he received nothing but a token expression of interest in him.

****

"Mr. Forrest are you there?" asked Nelson Truax as his entered his large office. The lights were at a very dim level and the office seemed empty but then there was a stirring from the couch in the corner and Norville Forrest stretched his thin arms and arched his back as he tried to wake himself from the half sleep state where he had drifted.

"Truax is that you?" he asked groggily.

"Yes sir and Barnaby will be here in short order as well. Sir, Barnaby really did a fantastic job today. Without him we would never had made the progress that we did. You should be pleased with his work." Truax gloated.

"Wonderful news. What do you have?"

Truax started with the surveillance and gave a detailed summary of what took place. He showed the video of the encounter with Kate and Austin. He explained that Austin had a significant emotional response to meeting Kate and as a result they could conclude that he was attracted to her. She on the other hand had no emotional response consistent with attraction though her body language and verbal expression were consistent with someone that was interested in the other person. She was acting the part and doing it well. After Truax had completed showing the video images and the emotional sensitivity data he paused.

"That is some outstanding work Mr. Truax, I am pleased with what I see in more ways than one." Forrest exclaimed. He looked at Truax who repeatedly glanced at the doorway. Truax was anticipating Barnaby's arrival and he did not want to proceed further without him being present. It was his work that had uncovered the identity of both women and the connection with them to WBOI. He wanted Barnaby to make the presentation and to get the credit.

"What do you think is holding up Barnaby?" Forrest asked deducing that Truax wanted him there for the balance of the briefing.

"I am not sure sir. If we could just wait few minutes I am certain that he will…" Truax implored but as he was completing the request Barnaby came into the office quietly.

He apparently wanted to enter without drawing attention to himself, but when he saw that both men were looking directly at him, he offered a greeting to them, "Mr. Forrest, Nelson, I am truly sorry I was delayed. I received information regarding where the vehicle is housed and I dispatched a colleague to install listening and tracking devices in it." Truax beamed, this is exactly what he was hoping would happen, Barnaby would prove that the confidence he in him was properly justified.

"Well done Mr. Barnaby, Mr. Truax has provided a good start to the briefing and I expect the next part is your responsibility." Forrest said. Norville thought to himself, this Barnaby fellow seems to be a good recruit for the team. He is intelligent and apparently well connected. Truax has once again proven that he can make good hiring decisions. He watched as Truax turned to Barnaby and made him aware of at what point the briefing had been paused.

Barnaby then proceeded to explain the identities of the two women and how they came to the conclusion. He indicated that the probability that their suppositions were correct was in the ninetieth percentile. He then stated he was confident and that the listening device should provide them with adequate back up should there be any doubts lingering. As he spoke he watched Truax and Forrest to see how they were receiving the information. Was he doing a good job, he wondered. He made every effort to not let the self-doubt he had been living with for the past several years since his partner had been killed dominate his thoughts. He questioned everything that he did, he couldn't make a mistake ever again.

Forrest listened to the balance of the briefing but he had heard enough. As far as he was concerned things were going according to plan. The next phase would include two distinct actions. The first was the surveillance of the 'date' that Austin and Kate were to have on Friday and the second was the monitoring of the meeting between Jeremy and Philip. The only two additional pieces that needed attention at that moment and were not being manipulated into doing what was needed of them were Roger Lee and Willie Lawrence. Those two men were to be needed shortly if the plan was going to be successfully executed.

"This is the extent of our activities Mr. Forrest. Our plan is to move on to the secondary target tomorrow and to monitor Philip Lee's activities so that when the meeting with Jeremy Giles is scheduled we will be there to monitor it as well." Truax said concluding the briefing.

Forrest nodded and the two men left. As they walked out of the office Truax gave Barnaby a 'thumbs up' taking every chance he could to help to rebuild this very insecure man's confidence. They would be working closely for the next several weeks while the plan was being slowly executed. If they did their jobs competently the plan had a much better chance of being successfully completed then if they did not.

****

"Hello is this Philip Lee?" asked Jeremy Giles.

"Yes it is. I see by the identification that you are Jeremy Giles. It is kind of you to call. How have you been?" Philip asked.

"I am fine. I understand that you want to talk to me. My niece called me and asked if I would meet with you to discuss certain things regarding her father. How soon did you want to meet?" Jeremy asked. His voice was dispassionate, it was clear to Philip that he did not want to have the meeting and was doing it as a favor to someone.

"Tomorrow, if you can find the time. I can meet you after work at the Harrisburg train station." Philip was going to try to push him to meet as soon as possible.

"Okay, five thirty in the main concourse." Jeremy responded.

Philip said, "Good, I will see you then." and the call was disconnected. Philip opened the door to his apartment and stepped inside thinking that he that tomorrow he would have a better idea of what had happened to Jenkins and Lawrence and why, at least he hoped so.

Chapter Eight

Willie Lawrence was tired of his latest assignment. It was boring. There was no fun in it at all. He thought about not going in to work and that would be certainly cause quite a stink. Everyone was counting on his genius to solve the problems of the world, or at least their world, as limited as it was.   He sat looking in the mirror that hung over the platform he used for a bed, couch and dining table. The bedding was scattered about in the positions he had thrown them during his fitful sleep. He made several grimaces and then yawned. It wasn't so much that it wasn't fun that made it boring, it was that it was too easy. It was like reading a poorly written mystery novel with a transparent plot that didn't hold your interest because you knew what was going to happen before the author disclosed it. This was flipping boring, he thought.

"The car is here for you Mr. Lawrence." came to him as the automated service contacted him on his PCU. Willie was still looking at himself in the mirror and he tried to ignore the page knowing that it would continue until he responded in some fashion. He heard his father telling him that a real man doesn't shirk his responsibilities and that if he were in the room with him he would be literally pushing him out the door.

"This one's for you dad." he said whimsically and turned and went to the door and walked out to the waiting vehicle.

Once settled into his seat the vehicle slowly at first, pulled off and then rapidly built up speed. Willie gazed out the window but paid limited attention to what he was seeing. He was thinking about his next challenge, what to have for lunch and whether he could sneak away early and attempt to find something to distract him. It was then that he noticed that something about the route seemed different to him.

"Blast, I hope you haven't taken a wrong turn car." he said out loud. The vehicle responded stating that it had been directed to take Willie to the Federal Government building located at Broad and Patterson. Willie wasn't aware that there were federal offices at that location but thought that the government was located almost everywhere so why would they not be located there.

It was not the first time that he had been diverted to a federal office to learn of a project where they sought his assistance. He was mildly curious as to what secret project that they had for him to undertake but he quickly thought that it would probably just as boring as the one that he was currently sleepwalking through.

The car sped along the river drive and he was soon in the heart of the city. The car seemed to be functioning at a higher security level since traffic made way for it and crossing signals all synchronized to ensure timely arrival at the destination.

The building was situated on the corner of a distinctive South Philadelphia neighborhood. Many of the surrounding building had been built more than three hundred years earlier. They were once commercial building with some multi-living residential houses. All had been converted over time to be commercial real estate and lately it appeared that they were being used be either the government or financial institutions. These were more bureaucratic offices, Willie thought. The lower section of what appeared to be a neoclassic style office building opened and the car drove through the opening into a brightly lit garage where there were a number of vehicles parked. The door closed behind them and once it was closed the vehicle came to a rest in a space and the doors opened.

"Welcome Dr. Lawrence, please proceed to the elevator." a pleasant female voice said to him.

The elevator ride was a short one, only a couple of floors. Willie looked at his reflection in the mirrored walls and door. He realized that he was wearing the same clothes that he had been wearing for the past two days, his hair was a matted tangle of brown straw and he had not shaved in almost a week, other than that he thought he looked pretty good. As the doors opened a large man that apparently had his back to elevator turned quickly and stared at him intently.

Willie did not move he waited for the man to instruct him as to what he was supposed to do. The man stood still and continued to stare at him. His green eyes not blinking, his expression not changing. Willie began to feel a little uncomfortable and he moved his fingers nervously. As Willie became more anxious he studied the man intently avoiding his eyes he looked at his clothing. He wore a simple dark patterned suit cut in a traditional style. He wore no tie and the shirt while it had a collar had no buttons or fasteners of any kind. It was close fitting and he must pull it over his head to put it on, Willie thought. His shoes were black and had a slender silver thread that highlighted the seams that had been stitched together to form the shoe. Willie liked the shoes.

"Dr. Lawrence, please follow me." the man suddenly said and turned on his heels and proceeded to walk away briskly.

Willie did not hesitate, he followed him promptly. As they walked Willie noticed that there were many cubicles that lined the walls but they were unoccupied.

"Is this a new location?" Willie asked the man who either did not hear him or chose not to respond.

They continued down a hall that ended at a doorway. The man stopped and stood to the side to allow Willie to pass him.

"Please continue on alone, Dr. Lawrence." the man said and as Willie passed him he heard the man's footfalls as he apparently returned to the entrance of the elevator.

Willie entered the room which was large and sparsely furnished. What furniture there was, was practical in design and function. There were no frills here. The walls were as white as they could be. The floor was the same.

He was in the room alone, there was no one there. Willie glanced about the room hoping to find something to occupy his racing mind but there was nothing to grab his attention. The desk that was positioned in front of the large window had nothing on it except for a very common looking lamp. The view out of the window was of the wall of the adjacent building which was apparently only a few feet away. He walked to the window and looked at the other building. It was simply a wall of bricks that had been painted white and there were no windows that he could see. This was even more boring than his current project, he thought.

He continued to wait for what seemed to be a very long time. Willie decided to call his office and explain that he had been taken to a government office and was meeting with them regarding a work assignment and would be in as soon as they finished the meeting. The call was accepted as business as usual for Willie. He always had a story or there was something going on in his life that made it difficult for him to make it work on time. This time it wasn't a concocted story to provide an excuse for his tardiness but he wasn't quite sure what it was. The government agencies that he had worked for in the past hadn't been this secretive or mysterious. Whatever this was, it certainly was very different.

"Welcome Dr. Lawrence. My name is August Barnaby." Barnaby said walking toward him with his hand extended directly in front of him. Willie reluctantly took his hand. It was large and the grip was a little too firm for his liking.

"Mr. Barnaby why am I here?" he asked directly. It was time to get this moving and while he wasn't looking forward to work he was also plagued by the call to duty.

"Come let us sit down and I will explain the project for which we are requesting your assistance." Barnaby stated as he ushered him to the two chairs that were positioned in front of the desk.

As Willie took his seat he continued to question the fact that this was a government office. It appeared to be too sterile and there was no hint of confusion that was typically present.

"Dr. Lawrence what I am about to tell you is to remain in the strictest of confidence. Failure to maintain the confidentiality of the message can result in criminal prosecution and imprisonment or both. Do you understand?" Barnaby asked.

"Yes, I do but I do not have a security clearance that I am aware of that would warrant being told anything that would be deemed classified." Willie replied.

Barnaby continued without responding to his comment. "Your father was involved in some very sensitive research at the time of his death. It was very important to well-being of the country and the world for that matter. Do you know the nature of his research?" Barnaby asked.

"No, I don't and I don't think that I would be of much assistance, my father and I did different kinds of work. He was a physicist, I am a computer scientist." Willie responded.

Barnaby once again discounted what was said and continued, "The project that your father was working on had reached an impasse due to the limited computing ability available several years ago. Since that time quantum leaps have occurred and we are now able to process greater volumes of data much faster than ever before. We need your services to work with the manipulation of a data stream that is one hundred and twelve to the thirty ninth power in magnitude." Barnaby stated flatly.

The idea of manipulating that much data seem unfathomable. One Hundred and twelve duodecillion was truly an amazing number. Willie was instantly captivated by the magnitude of the challenge. "What type of computer and operating system could parse that much data?" he asked leaning forward in his chair.

Barnaby went on to tell him about the Norwind Hermes class computers that had been recently come into existence. Willie did not even know that Norwind had branched out into computing but was not terribly surprised by the news. The cooling and power requirements must be tremendous, he thought. Willie went through multiple variables and influences looking at the scope of the required resources and was fascinated by prospects of working with such a machine.

"Okay, you have peaked my interest. What type of problem would require that volume of data to be interpreted?" he asked eagerly.

"Do you know what a photolytic element is?" Barnaby asked.

"Yes, I believe that my father told me that it is the smallest component of light, the elements of each of the spectrum of color that make up a photon." Willie answered.

"If you were to analyze data that was collected by photon bombardment of specific area over a fixed period of time you would come up with a number of data elements that equal the figure previously mentioned." Barnaby responded and then went on to explain that the program to analyze photolytic elements would deal with the unique shape that they take on after they have collided with a reflective surface. An interpretation of the absorption of a portion of the photolytes that occurs enables the resulting configuration to be read in concert with the balance of the photon and in turn with other photon so that an image can be rendered. That image can be one of the recent past or one from the distant past.

The more that Willie heard the more he smiled. Barnaby took note of his reactions and Truax who had been monitoring the conversation from another room commented to Barnaby through his PCU that Willie would be joining them, it would only depend upon how fast he could finish the project that he was engaged in completing.

"I am concerned that I don't know enough about the properties of light to be too much help other than some very rudimentary manipulation of the data." Willie commented. Barnaby smiled and told him that he would be joined by Dr. Avery Silcox the preeminent authority on light mechanics to which Willie replied, "Avery Silcox, the Goddess of Light? Wow! It would be amazing to work with her."

At that point Willie asked when he would be expected to begin the work and how he could extricate himself from the current assignment. Barnaby told him in response that his superiors would be contacting his employer and they would arrange a temporary leave of absence that could be anywhere from two to six months depending upon how the project progressed.

Willie thought about the scope of the venture as he rode in the car to work. He was about an hour late but was ready to tackle the assignment with a new found enthusiasm. He had a reason to wrap it up quickly. It was a new challenge worthy of daydreams. When he took his seat at his desk he was already half way through the planning of how he could finish his current project by the end of the week.

Originally his employer would have been happy if he had finished the assignment before the end of the year, but it was April and he wanted to by working on his new assignment in earnest before the end of the month. He sat there moving code from one section to another. He then began moving subroutines to complement the code that had already been constructed. It flowed, it was simple and took time but not thought.

If he could only find a way to generate the code faster, he thought and then he saw a means to do just that. Within an hour he had written a routine that automated the process. He had only to build the parameters and then set it into motion. By the end of the day he knew that he would be almost done with the project and by the next afternoon he could test it with the expectations that he could be done by Friday. He smiled and watched the code assemble. He then started formulating a means of handling large amounts of data. This was going to be a great deal of fun, he thought.

****

Philip had spent the morning thinking about the battle at Gettysburg. His editor had called him and challenged two of the conclusions that had been drawn. He wanted to be able to say with certainty that he had offered the best solution to the challenge that Jenkins had set forth. He thought about A. G. Jenkins and how he really played a limited role in the battle in fact how none of the Lee's cavalry had had a meaningful role and that one of Jenkins' premises was to have Stewart engaged in the battle from the first day and that he had provided meaningful intelligence during the days leading up to the chance encounter on the Chambersburg Pike on the road to Gettysburg.

He was stumbling through the volumes of pages that represented Jenkins' work and came across some of the forecasted results that he had either not noticed before or had rejected as being too preposterous to consider. There were some very unusual symbols on the cover of a group of papers that were held together by metal staples. This was a very odd way to fasten papers together, he thought and while he had read about the process he had never seen first-hand how it was done. There were four staples, one in each corner so that if one wanted to read the contents they would have to tear the paper or remove the staples in at least two corners. It was clear that he had not bothered to look at its contents before and wondered whether it was worth the effort to look inside.

He requested the time from his PCU and found he had a little more than an hour left before his next class was to begin. After taking a deep breath he pulled the papers apart completely. He discovered that there were seven pages within and that they were neatly typed and not in Jenkins' usual difficult to read scrawl. His eyes scanned the words on the first page and when he came to the words 'New Africa' he stopped. The scenario he was reading was one where the South's victory lead to the creation of a new country ruled by African Americans, the slaves that they fought to keep oppressed. As he continued to read it became clear that Jenkins had a fondness for this time thread and it was also made clear during the last two pages that he would be taking the variables with him when he met with Lawrence in Maine.

There it was, the proof that Jenkins believed that time thread manipulation was possible and that he intended to bring about the end of slavery while maintaining a separate country for his race. The effect on modern history was almost identical to that of any of the other scenarios, the only change, and it was a major one, was the creation of New Africa. It was in keeping with Lincoln's initial thoughts regarding a separate country for the slaves. Lincoln during the end of his second term, because he was not assassinated in that time thread, created a secret task force designed to de-stabilize the fledgling country which eventually lead to the overthrow and the seizing of power by the slaves.

The country remained a separate entity and eventually all of the black men and women were forced to immigrate to New Africa. The two countries were allies but maintained a significant distance when it came trade across the borders and the sharing of resources. There were also some difference when it came to the loss of territory. Most of Texas under this scenario was returned to Mexico and the border of New Mexico was shifted north by several hundred miles. The northern territory remain exactly the same.

Philip looked at the pages in front of him and could not believe that Jenkins actually thought that he could somehow manipulate time to make this dream a reality. He must have been going insane, Philip thought. What else could cause a man that was truly brilliant to succumb to such a fantastic illusion? As he shook his head while thinking about the absurdity of the content of the pages that he held in his hand, he looked up to see that his classroom was filled with students that were intently watching his reaction to what he had read. The class was to have started several minutes earlier.

"Open your text to page one hundred and fifty six and we will begin our discussion with the impact on the social fabric that the Technology War of 2052 had on the American way of life." Philip said while he cleared his desk and shifted his thoughts to the lesson at hand.

****

"John, it was good of you to come." DeMasters said invitingly. He had summoned the head of security to find out where the operation stood. He knew that Devers was very close to Lionel Fortesque and that his career aspirations involved the end of the threat that Justin Welsh represented to the currency conversion. He wanted to know what Fortesque knew and whether he could trust Devers. He also wanted to know how viable the plan to apprehend Justin Welsh was. That information would enable him to know how aggressive he would have to be to defend his position within the bank. Fortesque wanted desperately to become chairman of WBOI and Sherwood DeMasters did not intend for that to happen.

Devers knew this was a dangerous meeting but he also knew that he had to work both sides of the aisle. His ability to pick the winning side seemed to be uncanny to the casual observer, only upon careful scrutiny did the fact come to light that he had a two headed coin and he always picked heads to win.

"Mr. DeMasters it is always an honor to meet with you." he said in response to the greeting. Neither man extended their hand, they both knew too well the others agenda.

"Let's not mince words, shall we John. I know you have been working very hard on this Justin Welsh thing for the past several years." he began. Devers cringed when he heard the words 'several years', he knew that DeMasters was prodding him. "This man has been a problem for a long time but I don't feel that he is as big a threat to our overall success as others do within this organization. Please give me you honest assessment of the dangers and the cost associated with either continuing our aggressive pursuit or augmenting our approach." DeMasters concluded with the challenge.

Devers thought for a brief moment and then began to respond, "Sir, it is my opinion that Welsh is a threat because of his connection to the Monks and that if he is not stopped he can dramatically slow the conversion of currency effort that is already significantly behind schedule. The cost to the company, should it choose not pursue him and his associates, would be difficult to economically quantify except that it would be in excess of several billion IMC." Devers completed his opening statement and watched DeMasters' reaction. The old gentleman's demeanor did not change there was no evidence whether he approved or disapproved of what he had heard.

"That is what I keep hearing from everyone. I just don't understand how one man can be so powerful when he does not have the resources behind him like we do." DeMasters responded hoping that Devers would drop his guard a little and share some of what he really believed. Devers all the while kept his emotions and feelings in check as well and did not respond to the statement visually. He did feel challenged and when challenged he typically lashed out but this man was far too powerful for Devers to respond assertively, he knew that he had to watch his conduct.

"Again sir, Justin Welsh has eluded capture for more than six years while both the FBI and WBOI were trying to apprehend him. He has ample resources and many friends. He has much to gain should the IMC fail to become the global currency standard. His ties to the gang are clearly documented and while we have exaggerated this connection at times to enlist support for our effort, the exaggeration was not significant and in some cases has proved to be understatement of depth of the relationship." Devers said but he had not revealed anything more than what he had in the past.

DeMasters came to the conclusion that this meeting was a waste of his time. He did gain one piece of new information. He had wanted to learn what Devers was up to especially how much Fortesque was involved in the process along his head of security.

"John, Internal Security's investigation of the matter might be problematic especially in light of the fact that they have been questioning Lee's brothers and other associates. Make certain that this does not reopen the Jenkins' matter. The Senator is still very much alive and seems to be getting better by the day. We cannot afford too much light on this very dark subject. True?" DeMasters forcefully stated.

Devers showed signs of surprise that vanished almost as quickly as the expression caused his eyes to widen. Lee's brothers were being questioned, how was that he did not know this? He had good sources in DIS and there should have been some indication that they were investigating the other members of the Lee family. This could simply be an attempt to push his investigation in a different direction, one that could have embarrassing consequences, harming him and Fortesque.

He weighed his options and then responded, "I am not aware of any credible investigation that includes other members of the Lee family. I will, however give this matter additional attention. I will assign…"

DeMasters interrupted, "I don't need or want to know what you are doing John. This is your assignment not mine. I only want results that will allow the currency conversion to be completed as quickly as possible."

****

Devers was in the hallway leading to the street when he placed the call to Fortesque. "Lionel, it's John. I just met with DeMasters and he made very interesting statement regarding an investigation by Internal

Security and the Lee family, not just Austin. I have heard nothing about this and I am thinking it is probably nothing but it would be a good idea to run a quick check to see if there is anything to the statement." Devers said completing the message. Fortesque would certainly get back to him if he believed that there was anything to be concerned about. The next call he placed was to Girard.

"Yeah, what do ya want now?" Girard grumbled. Devers went on to tell him about the possibility of DIS investigating the Lees. Girard laughed at him. There is no way that they could be looking at the Lees they were preoccupied with other issues. Only WBOI saw Lee as a potential threat and that was only because of his connection with Welsh. He told Devers to relax and then disconnected the call.

Devers felt better after he heard what Girard had to say. Still, it was troubling that the chairman would go to those lengths to put him off the track. It was also true that DIS had been following Austin Lee, he knew this because of Foon's report to Foster. There may be something that Girard does not know about, though that seems highly unlikely. He thought about it and decided to contact Foon to have her make some discrete inquiries regarding Lee's brothers and DIS. If Girard is slipping it might be a good idea to terminate any involvement with him. He knew a great deal about WBOI's dirty laundry and if he were cornered he might be inclined to share the information with anyone that he thought could help him.

He then placed the call to Foon. Foon told him that there was nothing that she was aware of except the existence of their surveillance of Austin Lee and that was perfectly normal based upon his criminal background. It also was done to hold the parole department accountable should he be up to anything that would be considered a violation. Devers ended that call asking her to be vigilant in her monitoring of Lee and anyone with whom he came in contact. He was impatient for the next phase of the Lee operation to begin with the dinner engagement that was to take place in two days. This should be the end Lee and Welsh, he thought. Within sixty days he should be able to look back on this and smile knowing that he had secured his future while at the same time made a significant fortune in currency speculation. He could retire if he saw fit, buy an island, some women to go with it and drink himself into oblivion.

****

Kate was enjoying her day off with her boys. She had kept them out of school for the day and they were spending time together walking through America's oldest zoo. It was completely enclosed in a dome which covered a portion of the Schuylkill River as well since the Zoological Society had expanded their operation to include an aquarium. The floor that spanned the river was transparent and it appeared that a person was actually walking on water. There were periodic opening like giant holes cut into ice, ice that never melted. This was day where she felt peaceful and was enjoying the lull before the storm that she imagined was about to commence in two days.

She watched her oldest boy carefully look after his younger brother and smiled at the genuine care that he seemed to be showing. The contrast was so severe between this idyllic scene and the brutal chaos that existed working for Devers. The moment was then interrupted by a call from Foon. She wanted to verify that she would be meeting her in Harrisburg tomorrow. They were going to attempt to have an 'accidental' encounter with a news crew that would have her highlighted and give Austin even more reasons to be anticipating the encounter on Friday.

****

Roger saw the notification of an incoming call from Willie. He wanted to accept the call but the project supervisor was informing him that he was about to be re-assigned to a government project. The message he was delivering was long and drawn out. It appeared that he was making every attempt to ensure that Roger did not feel that he was being fired from the project, a thought that would never have entered his mind. He knew he was the best employee the company had when it came to programming and if they did not feel that way he was certain that there were many other opportunities for him to ply his trade.

The meeting ended with Roger not knowing where he was supposed to report to work in the morning. The supervisor had simply told him that he would be contacted shortly and that he was to follow their instructions until further notice. When he was asked how long the assignment change would be, the answer was a resounding 'I don't know'. Roger walked slowly back to his desk. He wanted to know what was happening. Since he was a child he always dreaded situations when he did not know what to expect, when received half of the information necessary to understand the circumstances in which he was involved. As a child he would become anxious and then that feeling would give way to fear which could manifest itself to the point of hysterics, and while he did not react that way as an adult, the situation was still disquieting.

Willie was still so excited about the new project, he had to tell someone and the only person that he trusted and would also understand was Roger. He through caution to the wind and placed another call and this time they connected.

"Roger, you will never believe what just happened to me. I was just given the most amazing assignment with the government. I will be working on the same mission my father was involved in when he died, and the best part is that I will be working with Avery "the Goddess of Light" Silcox. How amazing is this?" he said exuberantly.

Roger smiled a broad toothy smile. He was energized to hear his friend speak with such passion. "That is fantastic. I am really happy for you Willie. No one deserves it more than you do, except maybe me." he added with a laugh.

Willie went on to describe the scope of the project without giving too much away. Roger tried to conceptually grasp the magnitude of the calculations but knew that it was a massive effort but wasn't quite sure he understood just how Herculean the task of manipulating integers of that size would be.

When Willie had reached a point when his enthusiasm started to wane, Roger interjected the news about his new assignment as well. Willie then went on to say that he hoped that Roger was going to be assigned to the same project because he would surely someone that could help him with the monumental task.

Roger again laughed and then said teasingly, "So you need a water boy?"

"That's not what I meant and you know it." Willie responded. He then continued by asking Roger what he knew about his upcoming assignment. Unfortunately Roger could not give him any more than he had received which caused him to once again to become anxious.

Willie detected his friend's anxiety for he had witnessed it before many times. Their friendship dated back to when they were in school together. It continued because they both shared a passion for solving problems and their intelligence complimented the others. Willie assured Roger that he would know very soon what was going to happen and that they would hopefully be working together for the first time. Roger disconnected the call after accepting his friend's encouragement and returned to his desk to finish the day's work. He did not have much time to complete it when he was joined by a man he had never seen before.

"Dr. Lee would you follow me please?" he asked though it was more of a request then a question.

Roger did not move but asked, "Who are you and why are you asking me to follow you?"

The man replied, "Who I am is not important, I am taking you to meet with Nelson Truax the local coordinator of Verne project, you will know soon enough what that means." Roger slowly stood up and followed the man out of his office to the conference room that was locate at the northeast corner of the building. It was there he joined two men that were seated. Neither of them acknowledged him in any way when he arrived as they continued to converse in a discrete fashion.

"Have a seat Dr. Lee we will be with you in a few moments." the larger of the two men said as they turned their attention back to each other. As Roger sat down he strained to hear what they were saying and though they were with only a couple of feet from him the acoustic attributes of the room apparently deadened the sound effectively. Roger spent time focusing on his breathing a technique he used as a teenager to surpress his anxiety when he felt he was not in control. The muffled sound of the two men talking played in the back of his consciousness as he felt himself regain his composure which had been slipping away. 'Why were these men doing this to him?' he asked himself.

"Terribly sorry Dr. Lee, we have been trying to coordinate the implementation of this project from multiple locations. The logistical requirements are complex, which brings us to why we needed to see you. Effective tomorrow morning, and continuing until it is completed, you have been 'lent' to us by your company with the expectation that you will be able to write a series of algorithms that will deal with event permutations in a four dimensional array environment." Truax said.

"I am sorry, who are you?" Roger asked trying to understand what gave them the influence or authority to do what they are doing.

Truax responded, "Oh, I am terribly sorry my name is Nelson Truax I am the Eastern Regional Coordinator for the Verne project. We are a government funded agency and the project is classified. When you report for work tomorrow you will be given a complete briefing of the scope of the project and the information that you need to complete your assigned tasks. Please don't think that you will be given all of the information about the project. You will only be given what you need to know, nothing more. What questions do you have?"

"I have never heard of the Verne project before and I am wondering what you can tell me about it." he inquired.

Truax responded, "The Verne project deals with theoretical influences to temporal scenarios within a controlled environment."

"Time thread manipulation!" Roger replied enthusiastically. "You have got to be kidding. I had read a couple of papers on the subject four or five years ago but since then there has been nothing published. What happened?"

Truax looked at Barnaby and then shrugged. "The lead scientist on the project died in an accident. You will be working with his son, and I believe you know Dr. William Lawrence Jr., don't you?" Truax said knowingly. Willie was right, we are going to be working together on this really cool project.

****

Willie went back to his desk. There were about four hours left in the day and he was going to give it his best effort to finish the work he had planned to spend the balance of the week completing. Tomorrow he would be working on a project that was classified. How exciting was that? Apparently it also was going to require him to break a proverbial sweat to get it accomplished. He brought the latest iterations of the algorithms that he was constructing and ran a test on them to see if they were durable. They collapsed in the thirty fourth cycle and he grimaced. He would have to work late to finish them, but then again he really wasn't expected to finish, he was just supposed to go to work somewhere else tomorrow.

****

When Gloria called to see how Roger was doing she expected him to be at home. She was letting him know that her job required her to be out until well after midnight and that it would be really a big help if he could meet her when she was finished. She did not feel comfortable being out at that hour alone. Roger agreed to do it and would have probably offered to do so without her asking. Crime was escalating again with the latest increases in the cost of food and transportation. At least housing never increased in cost, it was set as a percentage of your income twenty two to thirty one percent. The people at the lower income and the highest income segments used the twenty two percent number and those in the middle the higher percentages. It made little sense to him but then again it made certain that everyone that was working could have a place to live, unlike the period right after the Technology War when the housing market finally collapsed and the government stepped in and nationalized all property and then gave it to the banks to manage and eventually own.

Roger had not shared any of his news with Gloria during the call. He decided to save it for when he met her later that night. She had been surprised that he was still at work when she called him but not shocked. The call had brought him back to the reality that he was not going to be able to complete the project before he left. Most likely it would still be there when he came back. The company did not have the expertise readily available to make any substantial headway on the complex algorithms that he was proficient at coding. At least he had job security he thought with a chuckle as he packed up what he needed for tomorrow leaving the balance of his possessions to remain there, he was certain that he would be back at some point and why move something that he wasn't going to need.

****

Austin called Philip to see if they could resume their conversation. He wanted to reassure his brother that he had no intentions of going down a path that would land him in jail. He had had time to reflect upon the day's activities. He had come to the conclusion that things were different then the last time he was confronted with the need to right the world's inequities. He was not tempted by the allure a siren. This woman was similar to the one that he had obsessed about from the moment he met her until his eyes fell upon Melissa. The difference was that she was more real that Melinda was. Melinda now slipped into his conscious background, still present but the memory was more like a hazy recollection as opposed to a force to be reckoned with daily.

He counseled himself not to attempt to try to impress this woman with his daring acts of what now should be known as stupidity. Winning her over should be done by illustrating his personal qualities of intelligence, honesty, loyalty and integrity. He could not affect the physical packaging except by altering his grooming. He thought that maybe it was time to cut his hair. It was almost to the middle of his back and there were few men that wore their hair that long any more. This was especially true when you considered that the days' temperature were so hot.

The call to Philip ended at his messaging center and Austin elected not to leave one. He decided that it was not that important and there would be other opportunities to reassure his younger brother of his commitment to not make the same mistake twice. He was almost home and knew that his mother would be waiting for him and dinner would be on the table, though it was a good bet that she hadn't made it.

His thoughts then turned to Justin Welsh. Justin had not been in touch with him since that Saturday in Philadelphia. It seemed unbelievable that he would simply drop out of his life once again. This was not the way Justin worked. When he wanted something he typically got it, regardless of the cost. He was not a patient man and the fact that he had not contacted him meant that he had somehow changed. Perhaps he was being more cautious since he was still very much at the top of the ten most wanted fugitives according to the various news reports Austin had seen.

As Austin got off the train he saw a medium built black man standing as though he was waiting for someone. There was something very familiar about him and then he realized that it was someone that he did know. He thought for moment as to whether he would try to avoid him and then decided that he should not avoid speaking to his partner in cards, Jake.

"Jake, is that you?" he called out and Jake's head snapped to his direction. His face lit up and he charged him with his hand out, but they ended up in an embrace.

"Wow man, good ta see ya, great ta see ya! Wow - ya didn't even cut yur hair." Jake said with a smile that seemed to cover his whole face.

"What have you been doing with yourself?" Austin asked.

Jake replied, "A little dis an dat. I was hopin ta ketch ya - I needs a fava." Jake said looking at the ground.

"What can I do for you?" Austin asked dreading the answer he might hear. He liked Jake but needed to keep his distance. Associating with a felon, especially one that was one parole, like they were, was frowned upon by the parole department and with the locators that each of them had installed under their skin there was no way that they couldn't know that they were together.

"Austin, ya know I wudn't ask if it weren't real important but I's gotta find work - ya think ya could point me in a direction where I could fine somethin?" Jake asked with a sheepish half smile. He was truly embarrassed by having to ask.

"Jake, it's not safe for either of us to be standing around too long together. Do you have a number where I can call you?" Austin asked while looking around nervously.

"Yeah, here." he said handing him a small scrap of paper.

"Give me a day or two and I will try to come up with something. Do you need some money?" Austin asked.

"Money I got - the job keeps me from gowin back." he said with a laugh. "Good ta see ya. Yur right bout bein together too long." he said while pointing at his wrist.

Austin said "Talk to you soon Jake - man it's good to see you." They waved as they parted company and each one hurried off in opposite directions.

During the walk home Austin wondered what he could do to help Jake and then he started wondering how he had found him. He hadn't told him where he lived and there was no one that he was acquainted with that knew Jake or for that matter any of the people that were in prison with him. The heat was taking its toll on him as he finished the last two blocks of his commute. He thought about his hair again. Maybe he should cut it, even Jake had made a point of noticing it. Then he could look like he did when he was arrested, a well groomed investment banker that robs the poor to feed the rich. But it was very warm walking around with all that hair, he would wait until after Friday to see how that went. If Melissa liked his long hair he would think about keeping it, but if she had no opinion then it was going to go.

When he walked through the door he found his mother sitting on a chair facing the window and looking out at the street. She seemed distracted. "Oh Austin you are home, did that man find you at the train station?" she asked pensively. Austin looked at her wondering if she meant Jake.

"Did he say who he was?" he asked rather than explaining his encounter with Jake unnecessarily.

He said his name was Jacob Warren and that he knew you, but he did not say from where. I assumed that he was someone you met in that place." she replied still appearing to be upset by the call.

"Yes, that was Jake and yes he knew me from prison. He was hoping I could refer him to someone about a job." Austin responded.

The answer seemed to make MacKenzie a little more at ease. She rose from the chair and walked toward him and touched his shoulder. "You really should think about getting your hair cut?" she said then she walked out of the room presumably to the kitchen.

Austin wasn't sure what he could do to help Jake but he was drawn to try to do something. He was afraid of the consequence of anything that he would do but he also felt that he should try regardless. The image of Jake back in prison was one that he was not comfortable visualizing. It was almost as though he was there with him. Then his thoughts turned to his mother's comment about his hair needing to be cut. It was clear that people had strong opinions about it, much stronger than he had regarding it.

"What do you want for dinner tonight Austin? It's just the two of us, your father has been called into some government meeting and will not be home until late." MacKenzie called from the kitchen. Austin decided to walk to the kitchen while he thought about what to have to eat. Food was such a problem, he could never seem to make up his mind what to have.

****

Philip was standing in the main concourse of the train station. Jeremy was late and Philip was wondering if he was coming at all. This meeting was important to him for he would gain additional insight into the elusive Ms. Jenkins' motives and perhaps find out if there was any reason for him to hope for more than what he had already experienced with her. It seemed that life had taken on an eerie pattern and that he was seeing the number of coincidences mount and a common thread was woven through the various compartments of his life. As he tried to bring them into focus and was almost able to draw the connections, the threads broke and the connections were gone. He almost shook his head as he tried to recapture what he had just thought but he could not retrieve it from his consciousness instead he turned his head and there was Jeremy Giles staring at him. He did not seem half as jovial or good natured as he had on the day when they first met. The lack of a smile on his face, a somber almost concerned look, was the harbinger of a less than pleasant meeting that could be in store, Philip thought.

"Philip, it's very good to see you my boy." Jeremy said while attempting a smile and extending his hand.

"Thank you Jeremy, thank you for coming on such short notice. This has been a very unusual time for me and I am just trying to sort out a lot of details." Philip responded while shaking his hand. "We need to find a place where we can talk privately." he continued.

"Follow me." Jeremy said and he turned and walked in the direction of the interstate train platforms. Jeremy was walking briskly and even though his legs were quite a bit shorter than Philips, Philip was challenged to keep pace with him.

Jeremy led them to the entrance of a platform that was closed temporarily for repairs. The normally transparent doors were tinted to their maximum darkness and they had a mirror like quality reflecting their images as they approached. When they were close, within several feet, the doors automatically opened and Jeremy gestured for Philip to proceed. They entered a large room with many islands of furniture placed throughout. This waiting area was used by general travelers, the first class lounge was up a level and its entrance was visible at the far end of the room.

There was no need to go farther than the first seating area yet Philip walked past several before turning and asking, "Is this okay?"

Jeremy nodded and the two men sat on chairs facing one another. "I was really taken aback when I found out that you were Jessica's uncle. It made the world seem so small at first and then I became suspicious as to the motives for the meeting. Did Jessica come to you to arrange a way for her to meet me?" Philip asked directly. He watched Jeremy process the question and as he did he made several facial expressions that indicated he was not comfortable with answering the question directly.

"I did not set up the rendezvous but I did tell her your commuting schedule, your dad was kind enough to share it with me. I was there to offer moral support if needed. That's all." Jeremy stopped he answered just enough to appear as though he was cooperating.

"I see. Did she say why she wanted to meet me?" Philip asked. He was trying to systematically get answers to Jessica's motives and then he would begin to ask the more important questions about Leopold Jenkins' reasons for the meeting with Senator Sun and William Lawrence.

"Jess, a couple of months after her father died, came to me and asked if I knew anyone that could help her get her father's work published. She was consumed with the idea that his work was important and that she had to get it published for him, to honor his memory. I wasn't working with your father quite yet and did not know anything about you so I told her that I did not. Shortly after that, about a year ago I was having lunch with your father and he told me what you did for a living. He also told me of your passion for the Civil War. That night I called Jess and told her about you. She was so excited and she wanted to find you that night but I told her she needed to take it easy - chill out a little." Jeremy said seeming to relax and fall into his natural way of speaking.

Philip watched him as he continued. "About five months ago she came to me again and asked me to see what I could do to help her set up a meeting. This time she mentioned that she had met you once before at a conference she attended with Leopold. She was distraught and I agreed to help. That's when I asked your dad about your commuting routine."

"It was easy to find out the details once I knew where you originated your commute and what hour you started work. As a result I was able give her enough information to easily arrange a chance encounter and I knew that the train would be the perfect means of doing so. Your dad had also volunteered the details about your love of that technology." Jeremy finished his explanation and seemed relieved. Perhaps this was as innocent as it initially appeared.

"Thanks that clears things up a little. I really find Jessica a very interesting woman. I have grown quite fond of her and enjoy her company a great deal, maybe too much." Philip said with an extremely self-conscious titter.

"She likes you a great deal too Philip." Jeremy volunteered. "She talks about you constantly, I think she is quite taken with you." Philip felt his pulse quicken and then thought that it might be a ploy to keep him off balance and he knew how effective Ms. Jenkins was at doing just that.

"Jeremy the real reason I wanted to see you was regarding a referral you made through your wife to Senator Sun. You apparently put Dr. Jenkins in touch with him so that he could meet with Dr. William Lawrence. That meeting took place on a white-water rafting junket that ended badly. Why did Dr. Jenkins want to meet with Dr. Lawrence?" he finally asked. Philip thought that he was far too verbose in asking that question. He needed to do better on the subsequent ones or he would make it appear that his interest in the information was more than just curiosity.

"I was contacted by my brother-in-law regarding a crazy idea he had that involved the use of subatomic sized light component tracking where the origins of these light elements could enable someone to theoretically see images from the past. This was done on limited scale for the first time in 2092 and then it was done with variation that was even more remarkable in 2108. Dr. William Lawrence, working with Avery Silcox and James Dubin, created a means of being able to insert an image into the stream of light particles that was at the same intensity as the past image light particles, thus inserting that image into that time thread. This was really far out technology. Leopold heard of it, read of it and then he was on to it. It was a way of proving his theory he thought." Jeremy stopped short and then looked at Philip to see if he had understood what he had just been told.

"I thought this was all classified material?" Philip asked trying to get him to continue.

Apparently Jeremy had no problem disclosing what he knew about the project as he went on for the next several minutes explain the fundamental principles involved in the tracing of photolytic components. He explained the equipment used and it seemed as though it was as if he had been a participant in the project as well.

"Jeremy how many times did Dr. Jenkins meet with Dr. Lawrence?" Philip asked as nonchalantly as possible. Jeremy looked at him and opened his mouth to say the word 'once' but the words three or four came tumbling out followed by he really didn't know for certain.

"It seems as though Dr. Jenkins confided in you about the substance of the meetings. Did he tell you what his objective was, what he hoped would be accomplished?" Philip asked. He was now beginning to understand that Jeremy was more of an active participant then he had first thought. He studied the man's round face, his eyes darted from one object of attention to another never remaining long enough for Philip to pick up what he was looking at specifically.

Jeremy had now reached the point where he was nervous about what had been said, Philip speculated. As time passed and Jeremy did not respond directly to the question Philip began to doubt that he would learn enough to be able to see the path that Jenkins had intended to travel.

"Philip that is a very difficult question to answer. I believe that he was searching to change his life and used the theory time thread manipulation as way to attempt to affect the changes that he felt were needed to be made. I was present one time when he and Bill met to discuss the feasibility of time thread manipulation. Bill was convinced that it could be done but they did not yet have the tools necessary. They needed more computing power and they needed more electrical energy in order to make it reality."

Jeremy stopped for a moment and waited on Philips reaction. Philip had been nodding his head in understanding, he resisted the urge to interrupt or speak, it might alter what Jeremy was about to disclose. "That's when they asked me about the research project on which I had been assisting." he continued. Philip then knew that Jeremy was speaking about the research his father had done on the power plants that were being built today, compact tera-watt cold fusion generators.

"I was not able to give them a timetable for completion your father had not had the breakthrough yet. It did not occur until just before they went on the whitewater excursion. We were supposed to meet and discuss the impact of the increase in power generation on the theoretical application of the process. The meeting was scheduled for the day after they were to return from the trip." Jeremy said as he turned his gaze to the floor while slowly lowering his head. Philip wasn't certain whether he was remembering the death of his brother-in-law or if he was feeling shame that he was about to share research that could at best be considered theft of a corporate secret and in the worst case it could have represented a national security issue.

"I can understand Dr. Lawrence's involvement but I don't follow the connection to the Senator. All he did was oversee the funding of the project. Was there more to his involvement than that?" Philip asked.

Again Jeremy took his time in answering. He was weighing everything before he opened his mouth. His choice of word was more exacting, as he explained how the Senator had been interested personally in the viability of the project and been very enthusiastic about what that could mean as far as relief from the woeful economic conditions of the last sixty years. Both the Senator and Jenkins had differed on what changes should be made. It had been considered a moot point until the news came about the power source. It was expected that the computing power would soon follow, which it did.

The time passed quickly and the light that had been streaming in through the narrow windows that ran along the line where the walls met the ceiling was fading and the lighting in the lounge began to slowly brighten. The design was to keep the lighting uniform regardless of the time of day. Jeremy seemed to jump slightly in his seat and then remarked, "This platform will become active in a few minutes and we will have to be leaving. Have I answered your questions Philip? Do you now understand that Jessica was only trying to preserve her father's memory and legacy? She actually doesn't know many of the things that I have told you. It is important that you know them because there will be a time when someone will contact you and ask you questions about the paper you wrote and they will be asking them in the context of time thread manipulation. How you answer them is your business. Me, I have fulfilled my obligations to Jessica, to you, your father and others. Please don't ask me to do this again." he implored.

The two men stood up and as they did the marquee that lined the walls came alive with information on the next arriving train and estimated departure time. Apparently the repairs had been completed.

A woman in a railroad uniform entered through a concealed doorway behind a counter that was rising from the floor. It was time for the two men to leave. Philip was confident that he knew much more then when he had started the meeting but there were some new questions that were being formulated and he had nagging thoughts that his father may have been involved in a cursory fashion when the research was being conducted. Did he know that Jeremy had been letting those men know about the cold fusion development project? Still if he had only told them that it existed and did not reveal corporate secrets he was now guilty of only ruining a surprise.

Jeremy hustled away barely saying good bye. It was then that Philip heard Austin comment, "Good job Phil." He had forgotten that his PCU was open and that he was being monitored by his brother.

"Austin, I will have to call you back later to talk about this. I think we got some good information though." he replied. He heard the PCU disconnect and he turned his attention to the next leg of his journey, the trip home.

Philip still had to take the train to Pittsburgh for his day to be over. He briefly thought about going to his parents, he also thought that he should call that Austin to discuss what had just happened. He decided that it would be the best course of action to go home then he could sit and think about what he can do to fill in the missing pieces. Perhaps he should revisit the Senator at the end of the semester next month, he thought. He continued to walk purposefully toward the familiar platform where the Pittsburgh train would arrive shortly.

An incoming call message appeared and it indicated that it was Jessica. "Hello Jessica, I was just thinking of you." he said.

"Philip, is my uncle still with you?" she asked without saying hello.

"No, we just parted company not more than five minutes ago." he answered.

"Oh, I have been trying to contact him and the call will not go through. I will keep trying. Good bye." and then she was gone. That seemed very odd to Philip and he stopped walking and turned to look back at where he had been. Jeremy had gone in the opposite direction and at the speed he was walking he could be anywhere by now, he thought. Nevertheless, he was considering returning to the platform lounge area and then he would attempt to retrace Jeremy's steps. Then the call came through, "Philip, my uncle is okay but there was a problem. He told me to tell you to be careful and go directly home. Do you understand? I am worried for you, please go directly home." she disconnected the call.

Philip remained still. He knew that the train would be at the platform in a very short time, and he also realized he had to walk quickly if he was to catch that train. But he didn't move, he simply looked in all direction to see if there was indeed any reason to feel threatened. He saw nothing.

****

Willie was studying the components of a photon. He wanted to learn as much as he could before he arrived at work. The Goddess of Light was someone that he had heard his father speak of many times during the last years of his life. He told Willie that she was truly brilliant and that he had never met anyone that was quite as intelligent, that was until he had met him. His father would always find a way compliment him, even when he was drilling him about how important a man's word was and the need to always go to work no matter how miserable you felt.

He held the screen that contained the schematics of several highly sophisticated pieces of equipment that he had never known existed. The first one called a Sympathetic Actuator was a device that read the topography of an individual photolytic component. Apparently, according to what Willie read, the device was able to read the silhouette of the photolytic component which simply stated were the elements of color that made up a photon or dot of light. The photolytic was affected by an impact or reflection from an encounter with an object. Parts of the color were absorbed and that absorption was manifested as unevenness in what would originally have been an almost perfect circular image.

As the photon collided with an object the photolytic components surrendered some of their color and they left an imprint that was able to be read. This imprint was the negative of the reflected image. Each photon was comprised of approximately one billion photolytic components. Willie upon reading this scratched his head, it wasn't that long ago that the photon was thought to be the smallest component the thing that defined light, now it seemed that the photon was the definition of light but the photolytic components were the words that complete the definition.

He then read about the Photolytic Integrity Filter that read the decaying photolytic components and insured the accuracy of the interpretation of the decaying particle. 'Particle?' Willie thought, they weren't particles, they were sub-particles of sub-particles. How were they able to read these things? The description of the integrity of the read was to be able to detect the particles as they aged for three hundred and twenty seven years at rate of ninety seven percent accuracy after that the rate decay accelerated until, at approximately four hundred and twelve years, there was only a three percent accuracy. The paper then added that new technologies emerge every day and that these facts may not be considered to be true at any point in the future.

Willie continued to read and as he did he found himself constantly shaking his head in disbelief. This was the stuff my father was working on six years ago, it was impossible science. It was more like magic. Just when he thought it couldn't get any more outlandish he stumbled on the description of the Photolytic Enhancement Generator. This device was designed to fill in the missing pieces since there would be times when a complete photon could not be reconstructed. The schematic for the design was mind boggling. The programming to achieve the results was incomplete. It was here that he discovered what he would be doing and where his expertise could be most beneficial. He then thought to himself that Roger Lee would be someone that should be working a project like this, maybe not this part but there was so much to do.

He now was looking at the Photolytic Component Generator/Duplicator. This was another device designed to fill in missing pieces and for the first time there was a discussion on harvesting the photon and photolytic components. The surface density and environmental issues were taken into consideration at it was here that Willie saw how truly immense the project really was. It would not only deal with the retrieval of the photons but also the interpretation of that which was found. This device was to allow someone to create an image that could be inserted into the photon stream. It would be as if the item was actually there. It meant that a place in time was to be selected and if time thread manipulation was the goal then scenarios had to be modeled to forecast the change that might occur.

He then started to think of people that could assist him in his design work. He would need a few people that he could discuss the merits of his designs and critique his logic. It was the way he worked. Then he wondered whether he would be able to work that way on this project since it was a government project that was considered classified. As he continued to look at the pages he began to realize that he was not going to be able to sleep. There was too much to think about. His life was getting interesting, very interesting.

****

"Jeremy, what happen I heard that there was trouble?" the caller asked.

"I must have been followed and I thought that I had been so careful. It was a woman, a very tall woman with black hair, I didn't get a very good look at her face. When she realized I had discovered her she took off and I was unable to follow catch up with her." Jeremy replied.

"Do you think she heard anything that you said." he asked.

"I can't be certain, but I don't think that she was able to get close enough to hear. I am not even certain that she saw who I was with because he was able to leave without her apparently taking notice." Jeremy continued. "Philip was very interested in what I had to say. He is starting to put the pieces together just as you said that he would. How involved do we have to have my niece in this? She is bright woman but not very stable, especially since the death of her father. You said that she would be cared for and that we would not need her involvement for the entire time, or has that change?" Jeremy asked hoping the answer would be that she was free to return to her life away from all of the developing intrigue.

"Jeremy, I know how important your niece is to you and to Laura but you must understand that Philip Lee is a very important part of our plan and his willing or unwilling participation must not be interrupted before we have received everything that he is able to do for us. He is captivated by your niece and from what you have told me she is attracted to him as well. Is that not true?" the man asked.

"Yes sir, it is true. In fact, she is more than attracted to him. She explained it to me this way, that it was important for her to not let her feelings for him interfere with the need to finish her father's work. She felt at one point last week that she was going to tell him to stop working on the project and go away with her." Jeremy confided. He was not certain that he should have said what he did because he feared for his niece's safety and he still wasn't certain that violence was not considered a viable solution to problems by the caller. He knew that the people that were following him had no qualms about killing someone or destroying them in some other fashion. His level of distrust stemmed from the method that was used to recruit his services, he was basically blackmailed into facilitating Jessica's participation. He was told how to engineer it and then required to execute the plan all the while being told that Jessica's life was in danger if he did not help.

"Do you think when the time is right that she can be compelled to abandon Philip?" the man asked.

Jeremy wasn't sure about whether she would leave, she was a very determined woman when she wanted to be. "I am not sure, I suppose that it would depend upon what the motivating factor would be. I think if there was a threat of harm to him, she might be more inclined to back away then if someone tried to intimidate her." he had settled on an answer that was probably true, though he had watched Jessica behave erratically in the past.

"That is good to know Jeremy. We have no intention of intimidating anyone nor are we going to threaten Philip. When and if the time comes for Jessica to withdraw from an active participation in our little play then we will find a way not to disturb their relationship, should she still be captivated with Philip. Who are we to stand in the way of love." the man said with a chuckle.

"That's good to know sir. What is it that you want me to do next?" Jeremy asked. He was hoping that he would not have to do much of anything. He did not like being unable to be truthful, especially with his family and close friends. He was trapped in a situation where he was constantly tell half-truths so that he could protect those that he cared about.

"Jeremy that will be all for the time being. We may not need you for quite a while; a couple of weeks or maybe a month. Stay available and we will try to give you as much notice as possible. As always Mr. Truax or Mr. Barnaby will be in contact with you when you are needed. Take care." and the man disconnected the call.

Jeremy got up from his chair the back of his neck was wet with perspiration even though the temperature in the house was a comfortable seventy four degrees. He felt the stress start to leave him and he began to think about Laura and what she must be thinking about all of these secretive calls that lasted far too long. He went to the door which opened as he approached. His home was one of the new generation tract homes located to the northeast, outside of the Harrisburg. He had a very quick commute of less than twenty minutes and it made life almost bearable.

Laura was sitting at the kitchen table reading the news of the day. She did not even glance up when she heard her husband walk into the room. She waited for him to speak. She knew he was under a great deal of stress as of late and her interrogating him as she did when they were younger did nothing but compound the problem, he would withdraw. When he was ready to speak she would be there to listen and offer any kind of support she could.

"Laura, I am sorry about all these calls. The project that I am working on has been all consuming." Jeremy said.

Laura responded, "It's alright Jer, I am sure that it will be over soon and then you can get back to being the life of the party that I married." With that comment Jeremy smiled. It made his day.

****

Kate was trying to sleep but she had done so little that it was hard for her to drop immediately into a comma as she normally did. Her activity level was normally so high and she worked so hard at everything she did that when her head hit the pillow it was only a matter of minutes until she was in the arms of Morpheus.

She was alerted to the arrival of an incoming call and elected to accept it since she was having difficulty sleeping. "Katherine, its Foon. Did I wake you?" Foon said.

"Hello Jewels, how are you?" Kate said with a smile. "No, you didn't wake me, has there been a development?"

Foon went on to explain that she had been on her way home to the apartment since she was living there to give the impression that it was Kate's residence. She spotted Philip Lee talking to a short man in his fifties who when he saw that she was watching them took off after her. She ran and got lost in the crowd. She did get his picture though and was transmitting it to Kate so that it could be run through recognition protocols to determine who he was.

Kate thanked her for the observation but then cautioned her that it might just have been innocent. She said that she was not aware of any investigation that included Philip Lee but that Foon should ask Devers if they should include him in their surveillance based upon what they discovered about the man that was meeting with him. Foon was after all the primary contact for communications with Devers and WBOI, though during the past two days Devers had placed calls directly to Kate and it seemed as though he preferred speaking to her over Foon.

Kate went on to explain that they might then be able to determine why he behaved the way that he had. Foon wished her a good night and reminded her that they were to meet tomorrow at the apartment to discuss the logistics for the surveillance that was going to be conducted on Friday.

Kate said good night and then once again tried to close her eyes and sleep, This time she began to think about the operation and what she might have to do on Friday to accelerate the Austin's attachment to her. Then she forced herself to think about her husband and the fact that he would be coming home as a result of her sacrifice and then she began to feel resentment starting to build. She jerked herself to the sitting position and then felt the flood of emotions begin to surge and the next thing she knew she was crying and desperately trying to muffle the noise in her pillow so that the boys would not hear her. This was not what she wanted out of life.

Chapter Nine

Thursday had passed and nothing of consequence had occurred in Philip's life. He had heard from Jessica three times during the day which he thought was very odd but other than that there was nothing worth noting. He was once again sitting on the train this time he held Mitchell's 'We Lost It All', on his knee. The book was considered to be the best resource for understanding the depth of the impact the Technology War had on the quality of life. Philip had read it once when he was in college studying for his master's degree but had forgotten the level of human suffering that the war had spawned.

The train ride continued as he prepared for his first class. He ascribed to the philosophy that all he had to do was be prepared to discuss the material that was to be covered that day. That was usually more than enough to out-pace the class. The day's lesson was to summarize effects of the critical information that cost tens of millions of people everything. This was a time when people rioted and Marshall-Law was instituted. The automobile industry that had been limping along for more than twenty five years completely collapsed taking with it the insurance industry which impacted banking and investment communities and the ripples that it caused in the collective economic sea were staggering. Many banks failed, and when they felt insecure they accelerated repayment of their outstanding notes and the snowball took off down the hill at the speed of light. Businesses from all sectors then failed.

The violence led to the creation of a new empowered Department of Internal Security ('DIS'). Not one like the one that had existed during the terrorist paranoia of the late Twentieth to early Twenty First centuries, but one with the ability to arrest, convict and sentence within days after someone was apprehended. The only recourse for a person that was convicted was an appeal through the regular court system but no one dared overturn an Internal Security conviction.

These same powers existed today because once a law was put on the books no one seemed to be motivated to ever rescind it, they simply add another law that might contradict the first one and then it's up to the courts to figure out what it all meant and what the intent of the legislature was when they drafted the original bill. Philip read his notes one more time and shook his head. He wondered what the Founding Fathers would have to say about the state of 'the land of the free and the home of the brave'.

The pattern for such legal confusion had been established almost from the beginning of the country, but like a computer program that was continually patched without concern for the impact the patch had on the fundamental structure of the design, it would eventually break down. Philip decided to use that day's lesson to concentrate on the break down and what that meant to the average person attempting to eke out a living.

It was clear to him that he did not fully grasp the level of desperation that most people felt. He came from a stable family, his father and mother had always been together. Gregory had been a good provider and made certain that his family did not do without. Still Philip knew what the others were dealing with on a daily basis, he saw it in the faces of so many that he passed as he traveled to and from work.

****

Willie was waiting anxiously for the car to pick him up for work. He wanted to get started on the new project and he wanted to meet Avery. He thought how exciting it would be to be able to write the code that interpreted actual history, to see the past as it truly occurred. His mind raced through many different scenarios and then came to rest on the possibility that this was only to be look back in time that was meant for only a minutes or even hours. He could see advantages of that but he also found it less inspiring and less challenging. The hope that he had was linked to being able to go back and see the past in such a way that might he have been able to stop the accident that killed his father.

The page came alerting him that the car had arrived. He was out the door before the message had been completely conveyed. Willie saw that the transport was a PT and not his usual Voltrun. As he entered he found that there was someone already inside the vehicle. He had seen the man before and therefore assumed that he was part of the project.

"Good morning Dr. Lawrence, my name is Barnaby and I will be escorting you to the work site. Please feel free to ask any questions you may have since we will be together for the next hour and a half - approximately." Barnaby said warmly.

Willie nodded and then they were off, pulling away rapidly. There were a fair number of PTs on the streets at that hour as many were using them for their commute or to travel between their work assignments.

The PT weaved through the traffic and came to rest outside of the train station. Barnaby instructed Willie to follow him which he did. They boarded a train headed to Harrisburg, instead of being seated in the general section. Barnaby took Willie to a compartment that was set up as an informal meeting room. Inside they joined three other people that apparently knew Barnaby but were unknown to Willie.

Barnaby announced, "Dr. Jun, Dr. Phelps and Dr. DeMarco, this is Dr. Lawrence he will be working with you all in assisting Dr. Silcox with the project, his specialty is sophisticated computer simulation modeling on a macro level." They turned and smiled at Willie who in turn tried to do the same. They had not be conversing with each other prior to Willie arriving and they did not begin after Willie had arrived. Each of them seemed to be involved in their own thoughts and theories and that some-how reassured Willie that these were people that were serious about research and their jobs.

Barnaby sat in one of the chairs away from the group and Willie sat in the one next to him. At that point Barnaby began to share details on each of their traveling companions, though Willie knew of two of them by their reputations within their fields of expertise. The group had impeccable credentials and Willie thought that it was truly remarkable that they would all be working on the same project. It was becoming clearer to him that this project must have been extremely important to invest these types of resources.

After Barnaby had completed telling Willie about his traveling companions he turned away to stare at the screen-scape. Willie began to construct a model that would be the basis for his program. He soon became lost in the complexity of the process and when the train halted at the station he, like the others, had to be told to follow Barnaby to their next transportation point.

The small group walked briskly to a train platform that was located outside of the main station it was a place that seemed to be not often used. When they arrived at the platform there was a train parked there. It was almost as though it was there exclusively for their use but that did not appear to be true judging by the number of people that were in the two cars that Willie could see. There were far too many people to be going to work on this project, he thought.

Barnaby lead them to a third car that was partially full of people. It appeared to be a cross section of the general population. The only part of the population that was conspicuously absent were children, everyone was an adult. Willie took note of the way that several of the men were dressed. Their attire was that of manual laborers while others were dressed for work in a clean room environment. At this point Willie assumed that the train would be making multiple stops.

Several more people slowly worked their way to seats in the car and it was almost filled before the chime sounded indicating that the doors would be closing. Willie looked up from his work for a moment to see through the transparent doors, what appeared to be a familiar face in next car. Could that be Roger, he thought, but he could not be sure.

"Barnaby, do you know if Roger Lee is working on this project?" he asked.

Barnaby looked at him and said, "But of course, he has a different responsibility and you probably won't see him much unfortunately. I know that you two are good friends."

The train's doors closed and it soon left the platform. It descended into the blackness of the tunnel and soon the familiar screen-scape displayed a sunny idyllic day in the Pennsylvania countryside. Willie once again turned his thoughts to the design of his program. He was consumed with the idea of handling so much data at one time and created repetitive cyphers to enable him to deal with the data elements in a manageable format. He defined an element then used that element as part of the definition of another macro-element which was comprised of the initial element and a string of other defined elements which created a sort of short hand with which he could manage the data. Then he placed the macro-element to a multi-dimensional array which in turn enabled him to then numerically illustrate the topography of a photolytic component. He had created the foundation for the format within hours of being given the assignment now all he had to do was code it and test it.

The train emerged from the tunnel into the brightly lit day. It slowed noticeably and soon the screen-scape was gone and replace with a view of the countryside. Willie did not recognize the area. It was very rural and there were few houses and those that he saw seem to be abandoned. There was no human activity at all that he could see. The sight was so curious that he abandoned work on his design so that he could discern the nature of his surroundings.

The train continued to slow and then came to rest. Several of the people on the train clearly had the same reaction that Willie did, one of confusion. Where was the city, or for that matter the station, Willie wondered. It was clear that others had traveled this route before because they seemed content as they sat in their seats.

Willie turned his attention to the windows on the other side of the train. He could see several poles that were evenly placed which indicated to him that there was at least something other than countryside on that side of the train. The answer became apparent when the chime sounded and the doors opened. A rush of hot air filled the cabin and some of his traveling companions let out audible groans at the unpleasant encounter with the elements.

The train's occupants filed slowly out into the heat of the day. There was no shade just a barren platform that was a little longer than the train. Willie noticed that the line did not go any farther. He also noticed that there was a road that appeared to be the width a single vehicle. There was also a bus that was parked near the far end of the platform and the train's passengers were all walking toward it. Willie began to be concerned about whether there would be enough room when he saw the bus that had been sitting there pull away. As it cleared the platform another bus appeared to emerge from the ground and it was soon filled and then another one came and took its place as well. When the line had reached a point where Willie could see the place where the buses originated he saw a concealed underground garage that was capable of housing several buses. As the final bus emerged Willie saw the cover slide into place to conceal the garage. He was relieved to finally be seated in the cool comfort of the bus and as he settled in he saw the train pull away and then take a spur which lead to an underground terminal which it would be stored until it was needed again.

The bus convoy followed the road until it ended in an intersection with another road. They made a right turn and followed the road briefly until it entered into a wooded area. At that point the buses stopped and again Willie maneuvered himself to see what was happening and what they would do next. The bus in front of the one that Willie was on pulled forward and then slowly sunk from site. As it did the bus that he was on pulled forward and shortly it too began to descend. The seven buses had been lowered into an underground tunnel.

The descent was a short one. Willie estimated that they were only about sixty or seventy feet below the surface. The bus drove off of the elevator and then proceeded down a narrow dimly lit tunnel. They continued on the path for several minutes and then the tunnel opened into a large dome shaped receiving area where the bus stopped and its doors opened. The occupants stood up in unison and began to exit. Willie stood as well anxious to see what was ahead of him. The people seemed to sort themselves, those dressed for construction took a path that lead away to the left. Those attired in clean room garb went to an escalator that descended to another lower level. Willie looked for Barnaby but he seemed to have vanished from sight. He wondered where he should be going but then he saw Dr. Diane DeMarco and thought he would follow her, which he did.

DeMarco walked down a corridor that was off to the right of the terminus and Willie had to walk briskly to keep her in his sight. He continued after her and as he walked he saw spotted Barnaby who was walking just ahead of her. It was then that he felt confident that he was headed in the right direction. The corridor was wide enough for six or seven people to walk abreast and it was comfortably lit, not too bright nor dim. Willie noticed that there were no doors and they walked what seemed to be several minutes before a doorway came into view.

It appeared that some of the people working in this wing exited through that doorway into what appeared to be a fairly large room Willie noticed as he walked past it. On the opposite side of the corridor another doorway came into view and several more people exited through that doorway. Willie did not look inside he had temporarily lost sight of DeMarco and Barnaby. The people in front of him exited through another doorway and at then could see them directly in front of him.

There were only six people left walking in the corridor and Willie recognized five of them. The sixth was a mystery but he was certain he would learn who they were when the time was right. The corridor ended and they entered a room that was brightly lit and whose walls, floor and ceiling were a startling white, there was no color except that which was provided by the inclusion of the people in the room.

Willie stopped walking when he entered, though the others continued to walk further into the room and then they turned to face the middle of the room where a holographic image was displayed. It was Avery Silcox and she welcomed the team and told them that they would be shown to their work areas momentarily. She then indicated that she wished to have meetings with Dr. Diane DeMarco and with Dr. William Lawrence shortly after they were situated. She indicated that she would come to their work space. She wished everyone a good day and then the hologram was terminated.

Barnaby approached Willie and said, "Glad you kept up with us. Follow me Dr. Lawrence and I will show you to your work area." Willie followed behind Barnaby, he was extremely excited about the upcoming meeting with Avery Silcox and he wanted to find out what he would have at his disposal with which to work on the problem. His questions were answered quickly as soon as he entered his work area he saw the computing power. There was an octagonal array of displays suspended from the ceiling. It rotated slowly enabling Willie to see all of the programs that were being executed. It was obvious that work had been done ahead of him and that he would now have to rethink some of his original thoughts should he find that there was another path that the creator had taken. He recognized the work, the signature so to speak, it was his father's hand that he saw.

****

At the same time Willie was being shown his work area Roger was being shown his work area and it was equally impressive. He did not need quite the same intensity as far as processing power as Willie needed to complete his assignment but his program was to be uniquely challenging in that number of historic variables governing scenarios or time threads that were not realized was mind boggling. The interpretation of events was at times the product of intuitive guessing as much as it was that of probability motivated conclusions. He had not had the time to fully appreciate the scope of the project since it had only been revealed to him upon his arrival. He was pondering the entry of data and how that could be condensed meaningfully into mathematical symbols.

The predictive analysis was not a new process it was used by corporations as they attempted to provide the winning design in order to secure the rights to manufacture and market a product. The difference with this design and that of a commercial product came down to the vast number of variables. Because of this the program could only be constructed to deal with one scenario at a time. That meant that in order to compare scenarios that multiple programs would have to be constructed and then a governing program would then compare the results and show the consequences comparatively. Each scenario required that hard coding was necessary to ensure that all variables were processed correctly. This made copying the program almost useless and it would therefore only be done with certain sections of the program's code. This would save a minimal amount of time, but it saved time nevertheless.

Roger surmised that he would be constructing several programs to forecast scenarios and then once he completed them he would then have to harvest the data using the comparative analysis program. He, like Willie, was supercharged with enthusiasm. It was as if he had been given the best possible gift. One that he opened and was enjoying but like most gifts he wanted to share his enthusiasm with someone and there was no one available at that moment. He felt that he was going to burst, so he let out a huge whoop and pumped his fist in the air. Security came to his assistance and he sheepishly explained what he had done and why he had done it to people whose expression did not change and that could not have cared less about his state of mind, only caring for his physical safety.

****

Kate was dressing at Melissa's apartment in Mechanicsburg. The encounter with Austin was hours in the future yet she found herself thinking about what she should wear and finally she decided to try on different clothing in an attempt to be certain to have the right outfit. Foon had not arrived from her errand and Kate was nervous and would have welcomed the chance to talk to this enigmatic woman that was becoming a friend despite her attempts to not allow it to happen. There was something very genuine about her and despite the training she had received in manipulation which made Foon very difficult to read as person, there was a wholesome goodness about her.

She received notice of an incoming call. It came in on her personal line which meant that it had to do with a member of her family. The voice on the other end was automated and it asked her to stand by for an important transmission.

"Mrs. Foster, is that you?" the male voice asked.

"Who is calling?" Kate responded not wish to surrender information to any one prior to understanding to whom she was speaking.

"Mrs. Foster, this is Major J. E. Calster I am with the Intelligence Corp." Calster said assuming it was Kate.

"What can I do for you Major?" Kate responded.

"Mrs. Foster, Your husband Michael was captured by a group of hostiles yesterday evening. At this point we have every reason to believe that he is in good health and that we expect to hear their demands very shortly.

Kate felt as though someone had an unexpectedly punched her in her abdomen. "What, he was removed from the combat area! How could something like this happen?" she yelled back involuntarily.

"Mrs. Foster, your husband and five others were in a rear echelon encampment far from any conflict, in fact they were all scheduled to be moved out of country within a few days. Unfortunately these types of things happen all over the world. We have an excellent track record when it comes to retrieving our people and bringing those that perpetrated the act to an early demise." Calster stated directly.

Calster went on to tell Kate that they would update her regularly on the status and then she thanked him for the call and disconnected.

Within seconds she had place a call to Devers, trying to find the most emphatic way of saying that 'all bets were off'.

"How are things going Foster?" Devers answered.

"Not good, not good at all. My husband has been captured by some 'hostiles' I think was how it was put and I am ready to tell you to take this assignment and shove it!" Kate exploded into the phone.

Devers was silent for a moment and then came back at her, "Listen, if you want out, then I expect your resignation on my desk. You will be done with WBOI and if I can have an influence, you will not work again in any meaningful position. You cannot simply walk away, this operation is built upon you. I did not know about your husband, the last I heard was that they were taking him out of the blasted country."

"What went wrong? I need answers. My boys need their father. You made me a promise, and you can't expect me to honor my side of the agreement if you won't honor yours." Kate responded tearfully.

Devers knew that he had her it was just a matter if he wanted an ally or just someone that he could push into doing his bidding. He elected to try to win an ally. "Foster, I will look into this personally and will bring into this everyone that I can. I will call the new CIA liaison and have them make it their number one priority. I will also find out what idiot drug their feet in getting your husband out of harm's way. You have my word, we will do everything to get him back safely." Devers said his voice cracking with emotion. He had played this role before and found it to be very compelling especially when it came to women.

Kate thought about her situation and she felt that she needed Devers as long as there was hope of getting her husband out safely. She did not believe that he was emotionally on her side but she did believe that he needed her to do her job. She also knew that he was ruthless and that she would not be able to secure employment easily if he were to 'black list' her.

"Okay Mr. Devers I am counting on your help and you can count on me to do my job." she finally replied and disconnected the call. Devers had been ready to continue the conversation but when the call went dead he was relieved.

The next call he placed was to Girard.

"What?" Girard answered.

"This is Devers I need you to fix this situation with Michael Foster." Devers directed.

"What situation? The last I heard was that he was scheduled to leave the country tomorrow." Girard responded.

"Someone took him. Find out who and get him back. Then deal with whoever took him. I don't want to hear about them ever again." Devers said and disconnected the call. What else could go wrong with this operation? Lee's brother or brothers may be getting involved, Internal Security is playing around in our investigation and now this.

"Lewis." he bellowed and Sam appeared at the doorway poking her head inside.

"Yes Sir?" she inquired.

"Lewis I need you to get that thug at HA on the line for me as soon as possible. Those people are supposed to be doing a job for us, instead all they are just another group of thugs with their hands in our pockets." he said not meaning the rest to be more than a commentary on his frustration about the lack of progress in the war against the Monks. Sam had left without responding and placed several calls in an attempt to comply with Devers' demands.

"Sir, I have Little Pete on the line do you wish me to connect him?" Sam asked.

Devers took the call "Little Pete, what's going on with are friends the religious fanatics. I would have thought we would have seen them suffering more than they have been so far."

"Devers, knock it off. We are doing what we are paid to do. This takes time, providing you want it to look like a naturally occurring phenomenon. If not we can nuke 'em tonight." Peter Gnonst said with a laugh.

"No, it has to appear as though it occurred out of rivalry between two gangs and cannot have anything that leads back to me or the bank." Devers pushed back. "This has to move faster. There are plans that are on hold until this war breaks out in earnest. Move it along. Find something to cause it come to a head now, not six months from now." Devers continued. Gnonst listened and then told Devers that they would push things into high gear and he would be back to him early next week. The call concluded and Devers was very frustrated. His people were not doing their jobs and this was going to cost everyone and he did not want that list of everyone to include himself. He walked the cabinet behind his desk and removed the bottle. It was early but he needed it and then again anytime was a good time for a drink. If he drank enough quickly enough even Lewis would look good to him.

****

Kate pulled herself together and began to try various outfits, some of which were barely enough to be considered clothing at all. They were certainly not what she would have elected to wear, not as a married mother of two young boys. She was supposed to set a good example of modesty so that they did not expect women that they encountered later in their lives to dress inappropriately. She wanted her sons to respect and value women as they should, as their father had done. She was not exceptionally thrilled with the age differential that was set as society's norm she was twenty one when she married Michael who was one month shy of his fortieth birthday. The change in thinking regarding marriages had forged much more stable relationships and the divorce rate had plummeted to less than twenty five percent of all marriages down from the all-time high of eighty percent during the 2050s. Now her forty nine year old husband was a kidnapped victim and she could be a widow at the age of thirty.

She tried to keep her mind on the assignment and as such started to think about Austin Lee. It had been important for her to visualize him as the consummate evil doer, the man that was going to bring about the end of society and bring harm to her family. Now when she pictured him she saw a thirty nine year old man that was kind and soft spoken. He was well educated and had an engaging smile. This was a man that she would have looked at on the street and thought to herself if she wasn't married he might be the kind of man that would be worth pursuing. This of course was a dangerous way to view him she thought. He was a known associate of Justin Welsh, who was the man responsible for the economic chaos that people were living through. Then she wondered whether she even knew what Justin Welsh looked like and would she be able to identify him if he were with Austin when they met.

When Foon returned she knew instantly that Kate was under a great deal of stress and she assumed that it had to do with the upcoming operation. She saw her standing at the mirror wearing a dress that was clearly not appropriate for daytime wear and even in most evening venues would have been considered far too immodest to be worn by most women, but then again her character was not most women.

"Katherine, don't stress about this meeting. Austin Lee is already in love with you. You could show up wearing coveralls and a clown nose and he would be still worshiping at your feet." she said with a smile.

Kate looked at her and burst into tears and then blubbered incoherently about her husband and the kidnapping. After three times through the story, Foon finally grasped the problem and attempted to reassure her that Devers would fix it because it was in his best interest to do so. Kate finally pulled herself together enough to think about the upcoming meeting and asked if the dress she was wearing was a good one for the date. Foon looked at her and then told her that the dress left absolutely nothing to the imagination and then asked her if she remembered her days when she was courting and how it was always a good thing to leave the man wanting more.

****

Avery Silcox approached the Willie's work area slowly. She was not looking forward to this meeting. She had always admired Willie's father but they did not agree on significant elements of the project and it was likely that Willie once he saw his father's work would most likely want to continue in that vein. If that was true there would be a battle of wills and she was confident that she would win the battle but might ultimately lose the war. Her long grey hair was pulled back in a casual knot on the back of her head. She wore glasses though it wasn't clear that she needed them. Most thought she did it to appear studious and so that she could peer over them with a look of disdain that she apparently had practiced and perfected.

"Dr. Lawrence, Avery Silcox." Avery said as she entered the room extending her hand. Willie looked up from his work and his mouth dropped open.

"Dr. Silcox it is an honor to meet you and even more so to be working on this project with you. Thank you for the opportunity." Willie enthusiastically said while pumping her hand with a little too much zeal.

"Please call my Avery." she said and then tried to get him to let go of her hand which he did so reluctantly.

"Okay, you must then call me Willie." he replied.

She nodded and then said "Willie, I knew your father very well and he was brilliant man. I know that you are equally gifted and he bragged about your intellectual prowess repeatedly. I will go right to the heart of my concerns about your assistance on this project. Your father and I differed on the approach to one key element of the topographical mapping of the photon and it represents a key part of this entire project. I need to be certain that you will endeavor to see my side of this argument. I am not foolish enough to believe that I am always right but I also have the ultimate responsibility for this portion of the project and I am the primary interface to the project leader and the other component teams. Please work with me on this one or it will be a very difficult time for all of us."

Avery did not wait hear how Willie felt about the statement, she knew he would have his own opinion and what she had said would not matter significantly but she still hoped that he would be objective which is all she ever wanted from any of her colleagues. She turned and left Willie's work area.

Willie watched her leave and as she did she made one additional request of him. "Willie please get me your initial assessment within twenty four hours. It is great to have you on board." she said over her shoulder and was gone.

This woman was amazing he thought. If she were only a little younger he would ask her to marry him, but hey he might even do that anyway, he thought with a smile. She was brilliant. He said to himself, let's see what she was talking about and he began a comparison between the father's notes that he had discovered and the formal statement of direction published by Avery.

After about an hour he had discovered the conflict and saw it to be as she had said; the theories were diametrically opposed. He then reduced it to layman's terms when he said that you either read the photon or the photon's shadow, the imprint left on the surface after collision. His father had contended that the photon would be the only true way of determining what the image that it impacted resembled but the problem was the harvesting of the photon and the data that would need to be interpreted was exponentially greater than the huge amounts that they already had to consider. It represented what Willie saw as a flaw in his father's approach.

He then looked Avery's approach and discovered a significant flaw in her thought process as well. It involved the dissecting of a photon mass (a surface that had been bombarded by photons over time and how they, according to Avery, established a bond that was magnetically forged, though the term and properties were not magnetic). This bond represented the potential for corruption of the photons that had adhered to the surface. These then would be suspect when being read and therefore useless. Neither of the two proposals worked.

Willie saw the problem differently than the two that had made their proposals. Each one, it seemed, was intent on being right and not really interested in solving the problem. Unfortunately he had lived through many an academic battle that was focused on winning the argument without concern for the truth or what was correct. He decided that he had to have a better understanding of the properties of photolytic elements and started reading Avery's published works on them.

Several hours passed and he felt he saw the glimmer of a solution. It was predominately Avery's solution but there was a twist that he had borrowed from his father that seemed to provide the way around the stalemate and a way to let Avery feel that she had won, almost.

Since Willie had done most of the primary design work of his programs during the commute to work he felt that he could explain it all to Avery and get the project moving along at a rapid pace. He placed the call to Avery who answered promptly.

"What took you so long?" she asked. "I will be right there."

Willie seemed a little confused by her assumption that it would take him so little time to solve such a complex problem. She of course was kidding him but Willie did not know her sense of humor nor did he ever seem to know when others were kidding. It was as if he was the only one allowed to joke about things.

Avery arrived at his work area within minutes of their conversation. She was very anxious to see what he had discovered in such a short period of time. Willie dispensed with the greeting and went directly into his explanation and conclusions regarding the difference of methodologies, he then set forth his solution and followed up with the design that he had devised during his commute.

Avery looked at him and said, "And I thought your father was brilliant. Willie this is fantastic work. How did you do this so quickly?" Willie then explained how he had found the problem and then how he had read her papers on the properties of photolytic components. He then resolved the issue using the de-stabilizer element equation that his father had created when he was supporting the solution that clearly would not work.

Avery smiled at Willie and then asked, "How soon will you have a model that we can test?"

Willie wasn't sure since there was such a large volume of code to write and while most of it did not require extraordinary skills it was time consuming and tedious work. It could take me a week, may be more he thought and then replied, "We had better plan for at least two weeks."

Avery looked at him and said, "You have a team of eight skilled programmers working for you and it's going to take two weeks? I think that one week should be more than enough time." Willie didn't know about the programmers, it was his first day.

"Avery, I am sorry I didn't know that there was anyone else other than me working on this part of the puzzle."

Avery laughed and said, "I know, you need to take yourself a little less seriously. I enjoy a good laugh now and again- especially at some else's expense." she said continuing to chuckle. Willie looked lost. "Follow me I will introduce you to your team. They are very excited about working with you. Many of them knew your father and admired his work. I think they will even be more impressed than I am that you are already so far into the project.

****

Austin walked into the parole office building. He hoped that Jake would be on time. This the one place that they both could be at the same time and no one would think anything about it. He spotted Jake standing talking to another man but as soon as they made eye contact Jake walked away and stood near Austin. The geo-positioning tracking was not elevation sensitive and as far as anyone knew they could be on any of the twenty floors in the building. It was the reason that they felt comfortable being there and could afford to spend ten or fifteen minutes talking.

As he handed him a slip of paper he said, "Jake I found someone that might be able help you get a job. Give this man a call. Don't mention my name but mention that you know Justin. That should be enough to get him motivated to help you."

"Austin, ya'll rite. Thanks - I has somethin for ya here." Jake said handing him what appeared to be a glove of some kind. "It's for blocking the trackin thing. Ya neva know when ya needs somethin like dat." Jake looked at him and smiled. "I miss playin' cards which ya." he said.

"Jake that was the only good thing about being inside for me." Austin responded. "We better get going. I will call you in a couple of days to see how you made out. Take care my friend." The two men shook hands and part ways, each walking quickly away and not looking back. Austin felt sad and tired of the nonsense and then once again he got angry.

In a few moments Austin was able to turn his attention to the date he had with Melissa and he thought that it would be a good idea to get there early, he didn't want her to have to wait for him. He tried to remember exactly what she looked like but couldn't. The only thing he kept visualizing were her eyes. She had such depth of character he thought, not like Melinda, who while she was stunning to look at did not have the apparent intelligence that Melissa had nor the complexity that lurked below the surface. She seemed to have conflicting elements to her and it was almost as though she were two different people he thought. Still she was beautiful and intelligent and was willing to spend a little more time with him. Now the big question was why?

Austin arrived at the restaurant approximately an hour before he was scheduled to meet Melissa. He tried to make it seem like he was only there to ensure that she did not have to wait for him, but he finally admitted to himself that he was very anxious to see her. He had not had a romantic feeling for anyone in more than five years and even then looking back at his relationship with Melinda he was not certain whether he was involved out of a sense of obligation. He had made a commitment to her and was going to honor it no matter what happened. Still he was attracted to her physically and he began to think about the time they had spent together and the experiences that they had shared.

"I wonder where she is now?" he said out loud. The people around him did not give a second thought to someone talking out loud, the PCU generation expected it.

There was someone else that had arrived well in advance of the meeting. Nelson Truax was evaluating the environment so that he would have the best vantage point. It was at that moment that he spotted Austin standing among a group of people that were enjoying cocktails prior to their meal. Austin was among them but clearly not with them. He seemed awkwardly trying to blend in but was not succeeding. Truax thought that this was an opportunity that could not be missed.

He walked to the area where Austin was standing and ordered a drink. He then turned to Austin and said, "This is going to be a great night." Austin turned and looked at him wondering if he was talking to him and when their eyes met he knew that the remark was directed to him.

"I sure hope so." he responded.

"I have a blind date and it's my first one. My friends tell me that we are made for each other. I certainly hope so." Truax continued. Austin looked at him and wondered why he was so talkative. It could be his personality type but he seemed far too disciplined to be prone to free self-disclosure. His time in jail taught him to view such encounters with a jaundiced eye.

Truax continued to talk about his evening and the fictitious encounter that was to occur before Austin's date arrived. He would was endeavoring to elicit a sympathetic response when it was revealed that the blind date did not arrive. Unfortunately a women, that had apparently been drinking too much, found Truax to be a legitimate prospect and sauntered up to him asking him where he had been all of her life. This disruption caused Austin to retreat and the engagement was over, but Truax did manage to activate Austin's PCU so that it would enable him to hear the conversations between Austin and Kate.

After a short time Truax was able to convince the woman that there were much better opportunities elsewhere and he escaped to a suitable vantage point to wait for the evening's events to unfold. His actions, however, did not go unnoticed. Julian Unger watched with curiosity to see if Truax was someone that he needed to be watched. It seemed clear to him that Truax was working for someone that was interested in Lee but did he work for Internal Security, WBOI or some other interested party? He placed a call to Girard and asked him for back up. He shifted his attention to following Truax knowing that Lee would not move until the date actually began some thirty minutes from then. Foon had told him that they would arrive exactly on time.

Soon Truax began to sense that there might be a problem. A short balding man had left his seat in the restaurant and moved to another that gave him a vantage point of his activities. It was clear that WBOI had someone watching the operation as well. Truax placed a call to Norville and requested guidance. The reply was a direction to leave and monitor the meeting from the car since the PCU was active he would be able to know what they were talking about and doing. He would also know where they were doing it. Seeing what was transpiring was optimal but not critical especially if it compromised the operation. He then said he would try to dispatch Barnaby who might be able to take over direct observation. After receiving his orders Truax promptly prepared to leave the restaurant.

Unger was not sure what to do. Should he follow Truax or not? He called Girard who told him to follow him to determine whether he was part of an observation team or not. Unger got up from his seat and walked to the door. Truax saw him from the corner of his eye and realized that he would have to make his departure look genuine. He then decided to return to the restaurant's bar area. This move made Unger look foolish as he had to stop and find something to do while waiting to see what Truax would do. Truax found the woman that had engaged him earlier and she was standing alone attempting to find the best marriage prospect that was available. Truax smiled at her and she walked up to him. He then whispered in her ear and the two of them left the restaurant arm and arm. Unger then decided that the need for further observation was pointless and returned to his seat.

Truax and his new friend ended their journey together when he dropped her off at another restaurant several blocks away. He was confident that she would find someone to distract her. He then circled back to a parking space around the corner from the restaurant and waited. He did not have to wait long because a familiar voice informed him that he was approximately twenty minutes away and would be there to assist in the surveillance.

"Thank you Barnaby, it's good to know that you are going to be the eyes of this operation." he replied.

****

Avery had made plans to leave work early, but it seemed that Willie's discovery was altering them by the minute. Willie had apparently started his team working on the coding and was already seeking a means of automating the coding even further. If he could achieve what he had expressed as his objective then they would be able to test the program's effectiveness tomorrow afternoon. It appeared that Willie had no interest in sleeping or eating until the assignment was well under way. The enthusiasm was contagious and she witness the entire project group increase its effort to achieve the new milestone as quickly as possible. Perhaps her group would be able to finish their piece of the puzzle in time to be able to offer assistance elsewhere on the project, but she was even certain what 'elsewhere' was.

Avery decided to visit with Willie one more time before she went home for the evening. As she walked down the hall to his area she noticed how many people were still at their work areas and how intent they looked. She smiled and then thought about how she had been worried that adding the young Dr. Lawrence would have had disastrous effects. Instead Willie had been the catalyst needed to ignite the project and get past the roadblock that stale thinking often imposed. When she arrived at Willie's work area she found him talking to someone over his PCU.

"Wow Roger that is so exciting. I am really happy for you. You have to see what we are up to here too. What you have told me gives me additional insight into the scope of this project." Willie said looking up to see Avery. "I have to get going, where are you working maybe we can get together later." he continued and held a one finger to let Avery that he would be off the call in a minute. "Great! I will try to figure out where that is. I will see you later, good bye."

Avery then said, "You are not supposed to be in contact with anyone outside of our group regarding the nature of this project. In fact that is the reason you are sequestered here, to prevent security leaks from occurring. Who was that you were talking to just now?"

"Roger Lee, my oldest friend, is working on simulation programs, he is the top guy in his field." he replied.

"Dr. Roger Lee is your friend? He is working on the simulations here. Did you know that he was here?" she then asked.

"Yes, I saw him on the train but lost track of him when we got on the buses."

Willie then went on to tell her that he believe that there were four teams working on different components of the project. He suspected that three were housed here and that the one did not require the tremendous use of resources that these three groups did but was still equally important.

"What do you think these groups are?" Avery asked partially out of the desire to put him in his place and secondly to possibly learn what the intent of the project was.

"The first group is the one that is not here. They are the group that determines the objective which then selects the Epiphanal Startling point. Once their work is done the second group which is the forecasting group takes over. It utilizes some of the same technology of the third group which is the simulations group. The fourth group is ours we are the discovery/delivery group, we plant the seeds for the manipulation to occur.

Avery stood facing Willie with a look of incredulity. It was impossible for him to have known the structure and purpose of all the groups involved in the project, yet he did as she understood it. How did he gain this insight, was he told more than she was regarding their mission or was he that brilliant. Had his father told him the details of his work? "How do you know this?" Avery finally asked.

Willie smiled at her and said, "I guessed and you just confirmed that I was right." and then he laughed. "I am going to see how the team is making out and then start this new code generator. It will need to run for nine or ten hours, but when it's through, we should be able the test the model and find the holes and shortcomings by this time tomorrow. Once that is done we can sit around and wait for everyone else to catch up." Willie said smiling and chuckling. He knew that they were a week or more away from being close to completion and that assumed that everything he was implementing was capable of functioning as designed. That had never happened before, and he wasn't counting on happening now. He was just enjoying the role of 'mad scientist' and genius and he would laugh all the way to the first problem.

"Good night Willie, don't work too late. I will see you in the morning and I am counting on you to deliver on your commitment." Avery said as she turned and walked away. She thought that he was never going to keep this pace up but she also knew that the momentum would not slow for at least a week, maybe two and that would be enough time to have the majority of the work done. This was a good day.

****

Austin saw Melissa enter the room. Behind her was Foon acting in her role as Jewels perfectly. She made certain that Kate was seen by everyone in the room and that they knew that she was an important person. Unger saw her and he spent in inordinate amount of time evaluating her total appearance. She was a distraction and he was being distracted. While he watched her Barnaby moved into position directly behind him and hijacked his PCU. Now they would know to whom he was reporting and what they were planning. Barnaby thought this man couldn't be a professional but he was wrong. Unger was a professional, his specialty was not surveillance, but it was extermination. He was there to take care of extraneous pieces that might come up during the operation.

Kate saw Austin but did not let on that she had spied him. She wanted Austin to come to her. Every action that she would take was choreographed to spawn a reflect action which would take Austin further into the web constructed for him and him alone.

Austin could not breathe when he first saw her. She was even more beautiful than he had remembered her to be. He tried to move toward her but his legs would not cooperate. Others in front of him tried to gain her attention, she ignored them. She was there for him, he needed to act. This seemed to be enough motivation because he lurched forward and took several steps. "Melissa, it is very good to see you again." he said holding out his hand.

Kate turned her attention to Austin and smiled. Her whole face lit up and she tried to dampen the broadness of the grin but she was having difficulty. He looked good. Even with the long hair, he looked good. "Austin, nice to see you as well." she said taking his hand. She grasped it firmly and then released slightly and tighten it again monetarily. Another subtle goad to drive the unsuspecting cattle forward.

"I have a table waiting for us." Austin then said as he turned and lead the way toward a table centrally positioned in the room.

He had secured the table on a rouse but he had been trained to gain advantage in all situations and his days as a vice president, and investment banker stood him in good stead when it came to moving in affluent circles. He could elevate the charm and wit to levels that few could master. Austin felt the ghost of those days awaken for the first time in years.

When the waiter came Austin took charge and directed the service and ordered for them both. He had requested that honor which had been bestowed upon him. Kate had not been accustomed to being in the company of a man that had interacted with the rich and powerful. She was playing a character but she had no experience to draw upon and as such she remained quiet. Her quiet behavior led Austin to doubt his impact on her, that he was losing the magnetism that originally had drawn her to him. He worked harder and as he did so, the more she withdrew.

She was intimidated by him and in awe at the same time. This was a man like no other she had met. He had a soft and gentle side that appeared to be governing his personality at times and then there was a calculating demeanor that was prevalent at other times. It was difficult for her to ascertain which was the real man and which was the facade.

She fought to be more assertive and gradually began to participate modestly in the conversation, and at that time Austin began to soften his efforts to impress her having gained some confidence that she was not disinterested in him.

Austin began to sense a feeling of sadness within Kate. He could see it in her eyes and then in her body language. She slumped slightly rounding her shoulders inward. He could see her fighting the sadness with a brave front but he was taught to read people and to uncover what they were all about. This sadness was not a natural state for this person he thought, it was something new that she was attempting to work through.

"Melissa, are you feeling alright? There seems to be something troubling you." he finally asked after the waiter had finished placing their dinner plates in front of them.

Kate didn't need to be challenged about her emotional health. She had good moments and bad moments and she was at a point where talking about Michael was the last thing she needed to do if she wanted to stay in character.

"A very close friend has been kidnapped by hostiles during his service in the war. I just found out about it earlier today. I am worried for him and his family. He has two children, two boys." she said fighting with tears that were forming in the corners of her eyes.

Austin looked at her and then said. "I understand your concern and sadness. I lost my uncle in combat. We were very close. It was the main reason that I did some of the stupid things that I did during my life. Is there anything I can do to help you or his family? My father has many friends within the government, perhaps they could bring additional pressure to bear. I don't know... This type of situation makes you feel very helpless... so alone." Austin trailed voice trailed off. He reached across the table and took Kate's hand offering it a reassuring pat. Kate looked at him through the blur of tears and then quickly turned away.

They both sat toying with their food, neither were hungry and those observing the date might come to the conclusion that things were not going well. That conclusion couldn't be further from the truth, in fact they were going too well from Kate's perspective. She was touched by this man in a way that she had never been touched before and Austin saw a beautiful intelligent woman that was strong willed and his equal.

"Melissa you are the most interesting woman I have ever met." he said sincerely.

Kate should have been doing internal cartwheels with this revelation that she had ensnared Austin Lee, direct contact of Justin Welsh and ticket to her husband's return and her promotion, but it was bitter sweet.

She found herself wanting to stay with him and hear more so when the time came to leave, she stayed. It was her choice to make and it was supposedly based upon the direction that the operation was headed but the operation was on course and still she stayed.

Austin told her of his Uncle Bob and of his time in jail. He told her why he had been arrested and who had been in charge of the operation. He held back nothing except for the connection to Christopher Leesop. He had not fully digested that piece of Lee history and decided that he would tell her if the time was right at a later date. She also talked about herself in general terms but gave insight into her personality and character that would enable him to see who she was at her core. She liked what she saw in him and he liked what he had learned about her. Austin did sense that there was much more to learn and that she was hesitant to disclose it for some reason, but it was their second meeting and first official date, he couldn't expect much more.

"I would really like to see you again Melissa." Austin stated. Her response was to be 'call me and we will set something up', but she simply asked, "When?"

They arranged to see each other on Sunday at the Philadelphia Zoological Society. Kate smiled not for any other reason but that was where she had just been with her two boys. They found reasons to extend their time together, little excuses that enabled them to talk about one more thing. Austin was taken with her beauty and she was taken with his soul. It was a match that no one would have believed possible and doomed to fail because of the underlying theme of lies and deception.

Foon took Kate by the arm and lead her out into the night. It was still in the nineties and the humidity was unbearable. She squeezed her arm tightly to illustrate her displeasure and frustration with Kate's performance. Finally when they were far enough away from anyone to hear she said, "Katherine what were you thinking. You had him two hours ago. This is to be a slow seduction and the reason it is done that way is so that when the time comes to pull you away the devastation will be complete. He will be a broken man and we can use that man to get to Justin Welsh. Do you understand?" Foon asked emphatically.

****

Barnaby joined Truax in the car after watching Unger leave and follow the two women. He was to make certain that he did not follow Austin. "You can't make these kind of evening up." he said as he took a seat next to Truax.

"So true my friend. That man Unger is a dangerous one, I ran his background and he has been a suspect in at least ten homicides. His primary contact has been, you guessed it, Girard. Now that is one bad man." Truax said.

"I know we are supposed to make certain that Austin Lee remains safe but how important is that to the overall operation? I can see where most of the others fit in, he doesn't seem to be doing much of anything."

Truax understood his partner thoughts and only wished that he would keep his mind on doing the job and not what the job was supposed to accomplish. "Barnaby, we are only soldiers doing what we are supposed to do. I can say this and this is only between the two of us, Austin Lee is a misdirection, a decoy that will keep those that might want to stop the project from going ahead looking in the wrong places. Norville just wants to be certain that he doesn't get hurt in the process.

****

"Unger what are you telling me?" Girard demanded.

"There was no one there that represented a threat to the operation. The only one watching the meeting was me." Unger repeated firmly.

"Okay, they will be doing this again on Sunday in Philadelphia make certain that you are close by in case there is a problem. I will have another operative as the eyes on the scene." Girard finished his statement and ended the call. He debated whether he should call Devers and then decided that he had enough of that wind bag for the week. He would give him a debriefing on Monday or Tuesday.

Girard's car pulled into the parking space that was reserved for him. The unit scanned the area for signs of life and identified three people that were within a one hundred meter radius of the vehicle. Two of the people were walking away from the area while the third appeared to be stationary and partially obscured by a large truck that was parked on the street. Girard hesitated before giving the open command to the car. He wanted to be certain that the individual was not a threat. He had many enemies, some of whom claimed to be good friends that worked at WBOI. Their relationship was tenuous at best, like a leech attached to a rabid dog, neither of the parties felt secure.

The person did not move. Girard started to feel anxious, he was not in a good position should this be an attempt on his life. He could not muster a good defense and was not in a position to go on the offensive. As much as he did not like to call for help, he believed that he had no choice. "Yeah, there is someone that could be a possible threat and I need it checked out." he said.

There was no reply but within two minutes there were three armed men that converged on the location where the person was standing. It turned out that it was a woman hoping to make a little money providing personal services. The guards informed Girard who then exited the car and approached them. He looked at the woman who was apparently in her mid to late thirties. Her clothing revealed much of her thin frame and he could see that they were extremely worn. Girard nodded to the men and they departed. The woman stood there looking at him and tried to smile though she was clearly shaken by the experience.

"Here." Girard said as he handed her a one thousand IMC note. "Go home and think about your life. You can do better." Then he handed her a card and told her to call the number in the morning, there might be honest work for her.

Girard turned as the woman left and did not say a word but walk away. Perhaps she will turn her life around or she will use the money to buy drugs or drink herself into oblivion, everyone needs a second chance, he thought as he rapidly walked to his building and entered.

Once inside he knew he was safe. No one could penetrate the defenses, though there had been two times when individuals did try to do so. He rode the elevator to the top floor which opened directly into his apartment. The lighting came up to a pleasant level, the sound of jazz music filled the air at a respectable level and he could smell his favorite food being prepared in the kitchen.

"Hi Dad. How was your day?" his daughter Jayden yelled from the kitchen.

"Hello there Jay - it was okay, how was yours?"

Girard went to his room and took off his black jacket and then removed the weapon that he carried mostly for his own protection. He placed it in the gun safe that was concealed in the wall. As he closed it and put it away for the evening he thought about a day when he wouldn't have to carry such a thing. He was getting tired of all of the intrigue, he wanted be able to live in peace and comfort. He had to have comfort and that meant more money. That requirement meant more time with WBOI and Devers. It all would be over soon, very soon.

Jayden met her father in the living room and gave him a quick hug and peck on the cheek. "You look like the other guys won today." she said with concern.

"No, you should have seen them." he replied with a smile. As he looked at her he thought that she was so much like his sister it was almost frightening. Thank goodness she did act like his ex-wife, there would be no living with her. "I smell meatloaf." he said. All Jayden did was smile. She turned and went toward the kitchen. He followed behind her so very glad to be home.

****

Willie found Roger but it was in his work area and not at his home. He was finishing a call that he had placed to Gloria and he was returning to the problems that were stretched out before him. Initially he had thought that the requirements for data manipulation would not be so daunting but it was now clear that they were a great deal larger than he had envisioned. His first task was to create a program that would enable a scenario's starting point to be input and then used a check against the projected time threads. He was not even sure what the starting model would look like. Were the variables limited in numbers or was a very complex situation where multiple effects would have to transpire, he wondered. He worked drawing images of how saw the program flow and where he encounter a road block or dead end he drew a box with a question mark in it. There were a lot of those boxes on the pages that he had been illustrating.

"Roger, are you still working?" Willie asked in amazement. "It is only the first day, you can't expect to have the problems solved already." he had continued.

Looking up from his work he smiled to see his friend and then said, "It seems that Avery called my boss and was bragging about how much progress her team had made today and so..."

"Now wait a minute, all I did was do what they asked me to do, and I can't help it if I am a genius." he said with a laugh. Willie looked at his friend and realized that there was no animosity he was just as driven as he was to do his best. He also knew that Roger was brilliant and that if anyone in the facility could out shine him it would be the man that was struggling in front of him now.

Roger continued to work and Willie sat down. He began to play game through his PCU that was displayed as holograms that only he could see. The game required him to build a series three of pyramids that were rotating at different speeds. Each pyramid was constructed with twenty like colored smaller pyramids. The game was a race against the clock. The longer it took the faster the rotation until the pyramids spun so fast that they blew apart scattering out of site of the player. Willie played it because it was like a mountain to a mountain climber, 'because it was there'.

"Have you ever heard of Adria Constantina?" Roger asked not taking his eyes from the work.

"Yes, she is a time theorist, one of those people that thinks about the nature and structure of time. It is a little too intense for me. I am not sure I understand the whole time is a process model any way." Willie said and then he grimaced as the pieces of the pyramid scattered before his eyes. "This game is maddening." he went on to comment.

Roger looked up and then back to his work. "She states that time is a creation of man so that he can understand the processes that go on around him. Because life is a process it can be reversed and even stopped." Roger stated with little emotion since it was all channeled into the project front of him. He said the words but did not fully grasp the concept. If the theory was correct then the process was perpetually in motion. It had no beginning and no end but continued forever. The question remaining was did it repeat itself or was the process so large that it approached infinite in scope and grandeur.

The project's intent was to prove the theory of process. The interception of a point in time and modify the results in a fantastic fashion. The change would be so significant that the current time thread would be forever modified and that what was now, would be something entirely different. Roger's team was to take the defined moments, identify the changes and forecast the results. The project had been on-going for more than ten years and there was a lot that had been accomplished but when compared to what had to be done it represented less than five percent of the effort.

Roger had assimilated the data and seen the course he needed, his epiphany, and it would be startling if he could accomplish the task within his life time let alone the weeks that he had been told that he must deliver the results. He finally looked up from the work to pay attention to his visitor for the first time since he had arrived an hour earlier.

"This project is huge. I don't know how you got yours under control so rapidly but every time I feel that I have a grasp as to how it could be done another variable throws all the work out the window." Willie looked at his friend and resisted the urge to poke fun or make a joke.

"This is the first day, you haven't had the problem for more than ten hours. How long did the people that had the problem before you work on it? Years! We are a lot of alike and this I know, you will have this well under control within a couple of days - a week tops. Maybe you need to step away from it and let your subconscious work on the problem while your body rests and you check your eye lids for holes." he concluded with an attempt at levity.

Willie's words echoed in his head as he continued to mull over the scope of the project. He thought about asking for his help and then decided that he should work on it for a while before he gave up and admitted that project was larger than he could handle.

"Do you know exactly where we are?" he asked Willie changing the subject.

"We are in a small town in rural Maryland. Someone said its name but I can't seem to remember it. I think it started with an 'M'. Why?" Willie replied.

"It seems very odd for a government installation to be this isolated, not entirely improbable but it is very odd. I have worked government projects before and they relied upon enhanced security and technology to maintain secrecy not isolation like this." Roger explained.

"What are you saying?" Willie asked.

"I am not sure that this is a government project. It might be something else." Roger said. "I am not much for conspiracies and I don't suffer from paranoia it just seems really odd, that's all." he continued.

Willie looked at him and then told him to get some rest. He was going to call it a night and attack the problem refreshed tomorrow, even though he was confident that he had made extraordinary progress today.

"Good night Willie. It was great to see you and thanks for stopping by. I might be calling you in the next couple of days if this doesn't start to make sense." Roger said.

Willie then replied, "Good night, remember you are the best at what you do. No one can do it if you can't. I mean no one." He then turned and walked away.

Roger turned his attention back to the project. Over the next several hours he began to see that the need to hard code the starting point was imperative. There was no way to elegantly select the starting point or to model a starting point by inserting variables into the code as data entry points or fields. You had to know where the journey was to begin before you could determine how sophisticated the program was going to be. He didn't know the beginning so it was almost impossible design anything that would be meaningful. That discovery did not stop him from continuing in his design in fact it fueled his enthusiasm. He now was able to construct discrete sections of the code. These in turn lead him to the creation of robotic code generators that would replicate the code the appropriate amount of times. When he finished the creation of one of these robots he felt that he had finally accomplished enough so that he could get some sleep. It was four thirty two in the morning, his PCU informed him, and that would mean he could get two or three hours of sleep.

He thought about using the technique that Thomas Edison had used to work at the frenetic pace that he had done when attempting to find a suitable filament for the electric light bulb. Edison would hold two or more books in his outstretched hands while seated and when he drifted to sleep his hand would loses their grip on the books. The action would cause him to wake and as a result would feel somewhat refreshed. It enabled him to work almost around the clock. Roger thought he would give it a try and three hours later he was awaken to the first of his team arriving to get an early start on the day. "Roger, did you stay here all night?" they asked.

"Uh, yes." Roger replied sleepily. So much for the story about Edison he thought.

"Did Dr. Culpeper arrive yet?" he then asked.

"No. He is not in yet, but he usually does not come in until around eight or eight thirty. What can I do to help this morning?" Uta Lung asked.

"Dr. Lung, you can look over this section of code that has just compiled and see if it there are any errors. If you find them please set traps and isolate them. Let me know what you find. Okay?" Roger asked rhetorically since he knew Uta was a competent computer scientist.

"Yes Dr. Lee." she replied.

"Please call me Roger." Dr. Lee sounds like my father or my older brother." he said. "Alright Roger, please call my Uta." she replied.

"Very good. Let's get to work."

Roger continued to work on the code that the robots would generate. It would have to be tied into a series of repeating test that would ultimately determine the outcome that a specific action would have on the time thread. A weighted probability would be determined and that would then be fed into another program that would compare a number of possible alternatives. The cut off for consideration would have to be arbitrary or there would be no way to limit the number of variables. He elected to set the limit at one, one millionth of a percent probability. Since he could not chose an infinite number and expect the program to ever produce a result.

Horatio Culpeper arrived at his work area slightly before eight o'clock he was hoping to get some of the backlog of paperwork handled before the crush of the day's activities began. He sat down and sensed that he was not alone. He was correct in his feeling because when he looked up he saw Roger.

"Good morning Dr. Lee or should I say good evening?" he said noticing that Roger was still dressed as he had been when he arrived the day before.

"Dr. Culpeper would it be possible to get Dr. Constantina to come here. I believe I know how we can get this project moving quite a bit faster." Roger said ignoring the need to be socially correct or cordial.

"Dr. Lee, I understand your enthusiasm but Dr. Constantina is not someone that is inclined come to visit with us just because we think that there might be a way to move the project along more rapidly. We have a fundamental design flaw and without a fix for that problem there is no need to waste her time." Culpeper responded. He had been with the project for the past four years and knew that there was a flaw. He had worked feverishly to find it but he was unable to do so. Bringing Roger in to help was just another attempt to find a way past the problem, to solve it.

"Dr. Culpeper, I believe that I have found the flaw and I also believe that I have a solution that will enable us to move the project forward rapidly. Please, I can only validate the theory if I am able to speak with Dr. Constantina. Her theory on time as a process is an important element of the answer to the problem." Roger implored.

"Explain it to me. If it has the remote possibility of being viable I will make the call to get her here." Culpeper replied firmly.

So Roger began to explain the discovery that it was impossible to begin the project without knowing the starting point. It was like trying to solve an equation that had no known variables, it could not be done. You couldn't even simulate it because there were too many variables to enable you attempt a solution. It was a simple explanation that had been not considered due to the construction of project as discrete elements that worked independent of one another until the project leader determined the time was right to share only the information that was needed at that time. Secrecy had caused the project to stop dead in its tracks.

After just a few minutes Culpeper raised his hand as if in surrender and placed the call. Apparently after hearing from Culpeper Adria agreed to come to the facility.

"Dr. Lee, it is apparent that you and Dr. Lawrence are the breath of fresh air that this project has needed. I appreciate your dedication. How can I help you?" Culpeper asked. He couldn't believe how simple the solution was.

"Dr. Culpepper, thank you I have Uta working on checking the validity of some robots that I wrote last night and I was just about to assemble the rest of the team to assign a series of test algorithms for them to debug. If all of this checks out and I am left alone for a couple of hours we might be able have design that should meet the objective. What you can do for me is to review this document and schematic and see if the flow is correct. I would also appreciate some help on the coding of this."

he said as he handed him a hand drawn diagram of the program that would select the most likely scenarios and extract them for comparison.

Culpepper starting pouring over the information that Roger had left him. He smiled as he looked at the work. Where had this man been for the past four years we could have had the project completed by now. I guess things are done for a reason. We sit and wait for the cogs of process to come and rotate into position so that life can move forward. He thought about how Adria Constantina had illustrated time as a gigantic mosaic in one of her analogies and that mosaic as viewed by us as those that are part of it appears to be a series of blobs of color and meaningless shapes. Once we can step back and see it, and history affords us that opportunity we can discern the pattern the image of what has happen and can in some cases see what will transpire.

Adria would arrive on Sunday in the afternoon and he would have a great deal to show her he hoped. Roger had given him reason to once again hope that they could find the solution to the problem that they were once facing. He also hoped that with Adria's blessing that the project leader would give them the information that they needed to move forward. Would he do it, give them the information that they needed? Did he even know what the answer to the question was? Only time would tell, but he also thought that perhaps he should have the project leader here as well, he would need to know what they were up against and better it should be explained by others, especially since he had been the one to insist that Roger become a member of the team.

****

"Norville here." the voice answered.

"Mr. Forrest it is Horatio Culpepper calling I did not wish to disturb you but I believe it will be necessary for you to come here tomorrow and meet with my team and Dr. Constantina, who is coming here as a result of a breakthrough by Dr. Lee." Culpeper said but did not ask.

"I will join you. What time do you want me there?" Norville asked.

"Sometime after three PM Sir." Culpepper replied.

"Great, I will see you then. This sounds like we are making progress finally. Good job Dr. Culpepper." Culpepper felt good about what he had done. It was his job to get the resources working for the good of his portion of the project and that's what was done. He turned his attention to the schematic that Roger had given him. He realized that he needed to get others involved as well. He called in two assistants and delegated each a third of the project retaining a third for himself. He asked them to return in an hour with their opinions and the corresponding code.

****

Kate awoke to two sets of eyes peering down at her. Her sons had been awake for quite some time and they had tried to be patient but they had reached their limits. "Mom, do you know what time it is?" Billy asked.

"No, I don't Billy but I am sure that you are going to tell me." she said with a sleepy smile.

"It's almost nine o'clock and you promised that we were going to do something fun today." Billy said sternly.

"Alright, you boys get ready for the day and let me do the same." she said pulling herself up and swinging her feet to the floor. The boys quickly scampered out of the room so that their mother could get dressed. They knew that if they let her alone she would move much faster than if they were there pestering her. While she ran a comb through her hair her thoughts turned to Michael who was being held hostage, but they did not stay there. She started to think about Austin and pictured his eyes. As she realized where her thoughts had gone she tried to jolt herself back to something relating to her home and family, but she saw the remnants of a smile that had formed in response to picturing Austin and she then felt guilt.

Chapter Ten

Philip had spent the night working once again. He found it was easier to do that then to obsess over Jessica, which was something he had been doing as of late. He had been pouring over the Christopher Leesop journal again, this was the fifth time he had been through it and though it was a very short journal of less than two hundred pages it took him days to read it each time. The style was not easy to read and the subject matter was unfamiliar, not that he hadn't read philosophy before but this was something different. He had supporting texts open to try to frame the work in historical context but that did nothing but confuse the meaning of the material even more. Each time he read it, it seemed that it revealed a new concept or thought. It was a building block that rested on the understanding of the previous readings, and this was a kind of progressive revelation.

Christopher Leesop would have been an interesting man to meet, he thought. He still didn't quite see why my brother was so taken by what he had read. This was just a man who felt that everyone was important and that our obligation was to care for each other. Then he noticed something in a book written by Ivan Suchmanzki where Leesop claimed a connection to supernatural events and beings. This was probably what Roger found so interesting. Roger really enjoyed fiction especially science fiction and those books that described supernatural events.

He guessed Roger liked to suspend reality like the rest of us. Roger's distraction was this type of stuff and his was Jessica, he thought. Then he could not believe that she managed to become part of his thoughts once again and what he had been thinking about had nothing to do with her or anything closely related to her.

He pushed her back into her compartment and went back to his study. He had the whole rest of the weekend to work in a sleep-deprived stupor toward what end he did not know, he just knew that he needed to understand more than he currently did. He continued to read Suchmanzki's paper on the philosophical influence of Christopher Leesop. He was intrigued by Suchmanzki's conclusions that there was more to Leesop than a simple fanatic self-absorbed philosopher that one might view him as when a person first began to read his teachings. He was clearly apolitical and that conclusion went against the case that the government had made that he was treasonous and therefore deserved to be executed.

Philip then did a search to determine how many people had been executed for treason in the past fifty years. There had only been one, Christopher Leesop. He then expanded the search to one hundred years and received the same answer. When he took the search out to two hundred years and he found a second person and his crime was that he had murdered one hundred and fifty three people. This seemed almost unbelievable that the government would find this man's behavior would warrant execution, especially in light of the fact that the evidence of his treason was circumstantial at best. His conviction rested on the testimony of a few individuals all of which had been found guilty of a variety of crimes and each benefited from testifying against Christopher.

He then turned his attention to a speech that the President of the United States gave in 2084. The speech was a very unpopular one and the speech writer was a young man that was fresh from college and was credited by many as the influence for the tone if not the message. His name was Christopher Leesop. He read it once and then went back as was his custom and took the speech line by line evaluating the content and the strength of the message.

My fellow citizens of these United States of America, I thank you for allowing me to come into your home this evening and to share with you what I have learned in the past several hours. We have all been anxiously awaiting some good news that we can pin our hopes upon. Ever since that day almost thirty years ago when our great technological based civilization came to a sudden and painful halt, we have been working diligently to recover from the loss of vital information and computing capacity that we have relied upon for a very long time.

Unfortunately, this is the time for us to consider drastic options so that we can begin a very long process that will shift our economy to a new and more progressive direction. We have for too long wasted our resources trying to replicate what we all believe to be the natural course of how the human race became what it is today. We have evolved through trial and error.

We have used our finite natural resources in the same natural selection, based upon the survival of the fittest. Natural Selection Economics is wasteful and this a time when we can ill afford to waste much, yet we continue to do so. It is for this reason that we seek your commitment to change this. Not in some radical fashion but in a virtual fashion, like we use in the modeling of any scenario.

The time is right while our computing infrastructure continues to be rebuilt that we take advantage of a great opportunity to construct it in such a way that it best prepares to handle the future. We have been given this opportunity for a new beginning and we can now avoid being stuck dragging old antiquated technology with us as we grow to face the challenges that now confront us.

We have lost many of our manufacturing jobs to a glut of products being offered and to the confusion of our marketplace. This cannot continue. To create jobs we are going to shift our emphasis away from global markets and concentrate on healing our country and its people that have been ravaged by the past forty five years of economic struggle. It is time to move forward not backward trying to recapture something that can clearly never be again.

How will we accomplish these things? I am sure you are asking yourself that very question right now. I know that I did when this idea was put forth to me several months ago. At that time a proposal was given to me that recommended a radical shift of thinking. We would still function as a free market society but some fundamental changes were necessary so that we could actually grow beyond what we always believed we could become.

The first shift will be in how we conduct our business. Just by changing one component of that we can radically help ourselves, especially those that find themselves without employment. We will shift our business operations to a twenty four hour platform. This means that all businesses will be open around the clock. There will be no time that America sleeps.

*These increased hours of operation will put millions
back to work. While we have a need to grow food we have
not been an agrarian society for a very long time, yet we
have persisted with the mind set of our early history. We
are being forced to change and this is a change that should
have taken place a long ago. To facilitate this change,
businesses that move rapidly to adopt the new mentality will
be given tax incentives and in some cases stimulus packages
will be created to help fund the transition.*

At this point Philip stopped reading and thought about the parts of the speech that he had read. This was not the first time that he had read or heard the speech, it was historic in its significance, infamous in a manner of speaking. It was also not the first time that a twenty four hour economy had been called for since President Ansterman had also challenged business to move in that direction.

The thing that drew him to the speech was the speech writer, it was Christopher Leesop he was twenty years old and had just graduated from William and Mary. He was considered a bright and shining star at that point in his burgeoning career, he was destine to do great things which was evidenced by the fact that he was called upon to write such an historic speech. There were many that could have been brought into assist the President but they picked a twenty year old genius with no political connections to write it. Why?

The first part of the speech did little to reveal any of Christopher's philosophic ideals. There wasn't anything that would lead a person to believe that he would become the person that had written the journal and there was no indication that he would become the treasonous brigand that he was purported to be. Philip continued to read hoping to find additional insight into what made this man who he was.

*Forty years ago the automobile and the housing
industries fueled this economy. Today the automobile
industry is but a shell of its once greatness. Home
ownership has been replaced with a secure right to good
housing for all and while we have not totally gotten this part
of our plan completed, ninety seven percent of all
Americans are living in improved housing and we plan to
reach one hundred percent by the year 2087, just three
years from now.*

Philip stopped and thought about how that part of the promise. It still had not been fulfilled, there were about five million homeless in the country or about one and half percent of the population. And it has been almost thirty years since that promise was made. He turned his attention back to the next part of the speech which seemed to have had slightly different tenor.

> *I know that this difficult and that we asking a great deal of sacrifice from so many of you. What may not be clear is that we are attempting to do this in a just and compassionate manner. We owe it to our fellow citizens that all of the needs of each and every one of us are met. These are not wants or desires but the needs. We don't expect that this will make many of you happy since we have been a 'want' based society for so long, always expecting more. It is time for us to change our thinking. To look at each other and to extend a hand to those around us that are in need.*
>
> *Many of you have lost a great deal. Others have not suffered as great a loss. Think about this, if a poor man and a rich both lose one hundred dollars, who has lost more? It is the same amount of money but the impact on the quality of life is so much greater on the one than the other.*

It was at that point that he stopped. It was as if the speech had been written by two different people or at the very least from two different perspectives. President had given this speech when he was 72 years old. Philip now wondered if he was still alive and if he might be able to speak with him regarding the speech, and he knew just who he could call for help.

"Luther? It's Phil Lee. How are you doing sir?" Philip had asked as he connected the call to Luther Washira. Luther was the Under Secretary of State in the Vumalt administration and he was a good friend of his fathers, in fact they had been friends since the sixth grade. This was a man that Philip respected and admired for his integrity and loyalty to a fault.

"Phil Lee, I was just thinking about you and your Dad the other day - what a coincidence. I am doing well enjoying my current work assignment. How are you son?" Luther said in a strong voice.

"I am good, the whole family is good now that Austin is home finally and things are starting to get back to a little more normal." Philip responded anticipating that Luther would ask about everyone and he did want to get to the heart of the reason he called sooner rather than later.

Philip listened to Luther talk about his life and his garden and he responded to his questions about his work and the family. Philip enjoyed speaking with him and if he didn't have the desire to solve this latest puzzle he would have been glad to engage in a long discussion on any topic that Luther found interesting, but he was on a mission and wanted to uncover vital information.

"Luther, do you recall the speech that the President gave in 2084?" Philip finally asked.

"That was the 'Change the World Speech'. That was political suicide for the poor man. It was a fine speech until he took that severe left turn." Luther said.

"Do you know who wrote the speech?" Philip asked.

There was a pause and then he replied, "It was written by three different people but the infamous section was written by your second cousin, but I suspect you already knew he had a hand in it." Luther stated directly.

Philip then went on to explain to Luther the nature of his question. "How could Christopher Leesop have fallen so far?"

Luther responded, "Christopher was a gentle soul and did not fall so far. The claims that were made against him were not founded. There was no evidence to support the charge of treason and yet he was convicted and was executed. There is another interesting element, look how fast the execution occurred after conviction. No one has ever been executed that quickly except during times of war and I am not talking about some currency conversion inspired conflicts. He was dead within seventy two hours after the sentence was pronounced, there was no possibility of appeal. Wouldn't you say that was odd?"

Clearly Philip had struck a nerve with Luther. He had never realized that anyone felt that Christopher had been treated unfairly until very recently.

"Luther it seems like you feel that Christopher Leesop may not have been treated fairly. Did you think that the part of the speech, and I am assuming that you mean where the President says that sacrifice was not uniform that the poor were forced to shoulder too much of the burden, was a reflection of what Christopher was then or a foreshadowing of what he was to become?" Philip asked.

"My goodness Phil you are interested in learning a lot about your cousin. Why the sudden interest?" Luther asked. Philip then went on to explain his visit to see his grandfather and the information that came from that meeting. He told Luther that he had a copy of the journal and Luther then interrupted, "Phil, you can't let anyone know where you got that and you shouldn't even tell people that you have a copy. That is very incendiary material, combustible beyond your wildest imagination." There was an air of urgency and anxiety to his forceful comment.

"Luther I know that the journal's existence is not something that should be made public. My grandfather warned us of the need to keep it in confidence. You said that there were three people that wrote that speech who were the other two?"

"The President was the final author and he made a few changes as I understand and then there was the now Senator Sun. It is unfortunate what happened to him, though I understand that he is on the mend finally." Luther said.

"Senator Sun? I have met him regarding another matter, and yes he is on the mend. It was a terrible accident."

"What accident Phil? Jenkins, Lawrence and Sun were not supposed to survive. Uh, I've said too much- you know I am getting up in years - ask your father he will tell you how you start to get a little confused when you get older." he said with a chuckle.

"Luther, you can't just make a statement like that and not expect me to push you for the detail. It's important, I know Jessica Jenkins and I have published the details of her father's theory, not completely but enough to raise some interest if there is any reason for interest to be raised. What was the reason for their deaths?" Philip asked.

"It has nothing to do with Jenkins' and Lawrence's theories on time thread manipulation and 'Epiphanal Startling' or his misguided use that phrase. It has everything to do with Sun's connection to Christopher and the movement." Luther replied. "If you want to know more about this asked your father or the Senator. This should not be discussed further. Do you understand?" Luther asked.

Philip believed that Luther was telling him that he felt that there was danger in continuing the conversation. "I understand... I think." he replied. "Was Jenkins a follower?" he then persisted in asking.

"No, but I said that. That is all and if you won't respect my request then this conversation is over." Luther said forcefully.

There was silence and the Philip said, "Luther I will not ask anything about this again. Thank you for what you have shared with me. I still do not understand but know that I have to seek answers elsewhere. It was great to have the opportunity to talk with you. We should get together and share a meal sometime soon."

"No thank you Phil, I think it would be wise for us not to see each other for some time. Take care and give my best to your family. Good bye." The line went dead and Philip finally realized that he had done some serious damage to his friendship with Luther.

The connection that his encounter with Jessica had put in motion had come full circle back to his family and the meeting with his grandfather. His father had suggested the meeting and was it possible his father was involved in this situation as well. Bob was his brother and Christopher was his cousin, perhaps he too was not so much a mainstream follower as he had always represented himself to be. His mother might be the best person to speak to about this and he planned to go to see her Sunday afternoon. He also wondered whether he should reach out to the Senator once again now that he had more questions that seemed to take the whole purpose of meeting in a completely different direction. Luther had stated, not implied, that those men were killed because of some involvement with a movement that was affiliated with Christopher Leesop. That was a staggering revelation, one that he had not foreseen or anticipated. Then there was Jeremy, the man worked with his father and he knew all three men. I never thought to ask him about Christopher, this is far too confusing and he really longed for the days when my biggest problem was whether he should pass or fail Ms. Forrest, he thought.

****

The project had moved forward with a quantum jump to the next series of challenges. Willie was running the tests on his model and was awaiting an interface to be created for the photolytic harvester that was scheduled to arrive on Monday. This would give everyone a complete look at whether the ability to accurately harvest, read and then interpret what was read was feasible. Willie had arrived a little before six in the morning to begin the long process of testing the programs that he had designed and written. He anticipated that if it went well that they would complete the test cycle in roughly nine and three quarter hours. That would still give him a good bit of the day to fix any design flaws that were not major.

Willie wondered whether Roger had been successful in his assignment. He certainly had the ability and the drive. He just needed a bit of luck. Just like he had experienced when he discovered the nature of the problem by seeing the flaw in the thought process that was used. A fresh set of eyes often revealed the obvious flaw, the large gaping hole that everyone that had been working the project had been walking around thinking that things were supposed to be that way.

He smiled and then started to think about the next phase. He would have to design a self-calibrating measurement array and was not sure where he would get the data. Avery Silcox seemed the only one that would have such information and if she did not there could be another stumbling block. He requested the time and discovered that it was still far too early to place a call to Avery. He would have to wait. He would need illustrate that he could be patient, something that was a projection of his intent and not an ingrained element of his being.

****

Roger placed a call to Willie to let him know that he had also had a break through and that there was going to be an opportunity to meet the world's preeminent time theorist later tha day, but Willie did not answer. It wasn't that Willie was ignoring the call or even that he had been notified, but since their connection and meeting a damping field had been activated that prohibited calls being completed, this was true with all calls in and out bound. The project had become extremely viable once again and security had to be maintained.

The two men, each absorbed in their work and anxious to see results worked at a pace that could not be sustained by a marathon runner. They felt the urgency and they needed to gain results now and not tomorrow. Nothing specifically had been said by anyone of them regarding the need to move the project along at a rapid pace but there was a feeling that fed their own compulsions to solve problems rapidly. It was feeling of a need to compete, not with some other person, though that did arise from time to time, but to compete against a standard and to rise to it, be the best and fulfill the mission.

Roger was preparing his model so that once the date and event was selected he could then, with the help of his team, begin to hard code the variables necessary to forecast the ripples that would occur in the time thread. He set the tolerance level at what he felt was a reasonable sensitivity but he would naturally have to confirm those setting with Adria when she arrived later.

The thought of talking to a time theorist was disquieting though. He was not sure whether he accepted the premise on which the entire argument rested; that time was man's attempt to define a process quantitatively. He then requested that the time be displayed continuously, with updates every tenth of a second. The numbers rolled on and on in front of him. He sat motionless. He was waiting, wasting time. There was nothing to indicate that he was involved in anything and that his actions made no contribution to anything, there was no process that could be measured, time was just passing. How was it possible to reverse the process and change the past? This seemed to be so much nonsense.

The challenge was being able to work with the sheer volume of data necessary to derive a solution. It was a huge puzzle, a maze of tremendous complexity. He sat wondering if this formula that he had fashioned was going to hold up under the multitude of iterations that were necessary yield a single permutation of which there would be millions. Current operating systems could be paralyzed and processing speed were woefully inadequate. He had the theoretical answer to the problem and the structure under which it would function but he did not have the means to execute it and no idea how to find a way to do so.

****

Willie was coming to much the same conclusion as Roger. The computer equipment that he was working with was not up to the rigors of the calculations that were required. During the first test the system crashed four times within the first five minutes of operation and when he sought to determine the amount of code that had been executed he found that roughly forty seconds into the execution of the start command the system began to thrash and then it became locked and when it was unable to extricate itself from the thrashing the system failed.

Willie thought that he had been told that there would be adequate processing power and now he found it necessary to contact Avery and ask what they were going to do to solve the problem.

"Avery, we have a problem and it is one that I cannot overcome with slick 'rabbit out of my hat' programming." Willie stated as though Avery had been party to all of his thoughts leading up to the conclusion that he had reached.

"I know, it will be handled within the next three hours. Go have some breakfast and come back then, you will be pleasantly surprised." Avery said and disconnected the call. What a narcissistic twit, he was so good at what he did but like his friend Roger Lee they both had egos the size of the moon and can't see past the games that they choose to play and what they mean to the regular folk. Of course who are the regular folk, certainly not me, she mused with a chuckle.

****

The morning was passing slowly for Austin. He had wanted to leave to go to Philadelphia at six thirty but considering that he was not meet Melissa there until shortly before noon that would have been foolishness.

He pictured her briefly, but his attention did not stay with her physical appearance as it had with so many other women that he had encountered in his past. He thought about her laugh and then he thought about her speech pattern and the way she assembled her words to express herself. This was different, he thought as he caught himself in the midst of his reflections. He checked the time and it seemed that time had stopped or was moving at such a slow pace that he could not feel it passing.

****

Kate was preparing the boys for their day that they would spend with friends. She had been promised to be able to spend more time with them but she found that as she managed to spend more time with them, she found herself wanting and needing even more. She held on to them as though they represented the only true connection to who she thought she was. Her husband Michael was somewhere in the world but no one knew where and there had been no further communication. This was a very odd thing since Americans were always taken for leverage or for money, and neither had been requested. She thought about him very briefly and then her thoughts shifted to her day with Austin and as she walked through the room and past the mirror she caught a glimpse of herself in the mirror, she was smiling once again.

She was schedule to rendezvous with Foon at ten forty five to plan the surveillance, since Foon would not to be present, it would give the illusion of the date being an opportunity for them to get to know one another better. Foon was certain that they had been watched at the restaurant but was not able to identify who specifically it was. She told Kate that there might have been as many as three men or more. She also had said that she wasn't certain what interest they represented, it could have been Devers checking up on them for all that she knew. It was not outside the realm of possibilities for Devers to do such a thing, she thought. It was time to start to get ready, this day was going to be an interesting one.

****

Jubal Clevers was a man that had always been for hire. He was just as happy working for one side of an issue as the other. He had been working in that retail front for so long though. He knew that what he was doing was important to establish continuity, he was frustrated by the fact that he was in place for eight months doing nothing more than endless eye glass fitting and having only one meeting that had any intrigue to it at all. The only exception was the meeting he had with the tall black haired woman with the strange name that he couldn't remember. It was good that he was being called to do something more meaningful, surveillance had always been exciting and this time he was going to be at the zoo watching two people. His assignment was to simply observe who was observing them and to report back the details. It was simple enough but it was still much better than sitting in that dreadful shop waiting for some to call him to action.

Jubal stood waiting in the heat of the morning. It crept down his throat as he breathed in the morning air. It was going to be very hot today, he thought, not the kind of day that he welcomed being outside but a job was a job and he needed this one to preserve his sanity. He scanned the empty streets of center city Philadelphia. It was Sunday and there was no one in town. Philadelphia for all of its efforts had never been able to generate an interest in seeing the nation's second capital on Sundays unlike it sister cities scattered along the eastern seaboard.

The Voltrun pulled up to the curb and its rear passenger side door opened with a rush of cool air greeting him as he climbed inside.

"Good morning Jubal, pleasant day huh?" Barnaby asked with a smile.

"Not so bad as some, Mr. Barnaby." Jubal replied as the vehicle quickly pulled away.

"I don't believe you know Jubal, Mr. Truax this is Jubal Clevers, he has been manning our operation in Pittsburgh for the past several months.

"Good to meet you Jubal." Truax responded.

"Do you understand your assignment today?" Truax asked him.

"Yes sir. I will let you know who is watching them and any other activities that arise."

The Voltrun approached the Zoological Society complex and came to rest near one of its entrances.

"Good luck, keep in touch with us hourly, even if there is nothing to report, we want to make certain that you have them in your sight at all times. Understood?" Truax asked.

"Yes sir. Very good I will be speaking to you within the hour." Jubal said and with that he exited the vehicle and walked through the entrance.

Once inside the zoo he found a suitable location to position a camera he then planted and activated it. He repeated the procedure at all of the entrances and then activate facial recognition protocols so that when the subjects arrived he would be able to find them and begin the operation. He then sought out a refreshment stand and sat under the tinted climate controlled dome watching a male peacock demonstrate to win the attention of a coy pea hen. Jubal watched apparently mesmerized by the drama unfolding before his eyes. It had been years since he had taken the time to sit and watch anything then he wasn't being paid to observe.

The alert flashed in front of his eyes and the indication was that Austin had arrived at the northeast gate. Jubal was up and moving as quickly as his short legs could stride. He was moving very rapidly and his actions drew the attention of others that were present to observe. Foon saw him and at first did not recognize him but then it came back to her. The man with the shirt, she thought. The little weasel of a man that spoke to Internal Security or at least someone that claimed to be Internal Security. What was he doing here and then she saw Austin and she knew that he was shadowing him.

She thought about calling Kate and letting her know and then decided to contact Devers. The call with Devers was brief and he indicated that Girard would be in touch. She didn't have to wait long. Girard instructed her to upload his image so that he could determine the next course of action. The call ended with Foon not knowing what was going to happen. She decided to get into position where they had agreed that Kate would take Austin after they had met. She wondered who else would be there to observe this and what did they expect to happen. Foon was there for security, they weren't expecting Justin Welsh or Austin Lee to suddenly become violent, they were hoping that someone would show up that worked for Welsh and would lead them back to him eventually.

Kate arrived exactly on time and behind her lurking in a crowd of Asian tourist was Unger. Girard had asked him to observe the surveillance and to be prepared to follow his instructions to the letter. He knew he had to locate the individual that was spying on their operation, he just needed to identify him without being discovered. He knew that Foon was aware of the individual and their location but he was under no circumstance make Foon aware of his presence. At that moment Girard sent him a message detailing his location and his description. Unger spotted Jubal standing near a kiosk attempting to look as though he was engaged in some activity there.

Unger made the determination that he must tag him so that in case he wanders from his view he will be able to locate him at any time. He removed a pen from his pocket. The pen served three purposes; it acted as a writing implement, both on paper and on electronic medium, a silicon based trace gel propulsion device and a neural paralyzer that could kill a person within seconds from a distance of twenty feet. He rotated the barrel to the appropriate setting and approached Julian from behind.

When he was within ten feet he pointed the pen by rotating his wrist and raising his hand parallel to the ground. The action was not natural but did not draw attention, it was subtle. A small click indicated that the gel was dispensed and the audible tone he heard through his PCU confirm its successful placement. He continued to walk past never getting within seven or eight feet of Jubal and he was clearly not observed by him.

Girard had asked him to report back on his observations and to also attempt to determine whether there was anyone else that was watching the couple or possibly the man that he was observing. Surveillance like this could become very complex very quickly. Unger knew that he would have to be aware of his actions being detected by others including Austin and Kate. So he kept his distance and watched the movements of his quarry from a far.

Jubal called Barnaby and indicated that he was observing the two of them and had not detected anyone aside from him that was watching them. He was then instructed to make certain that he was not observed and that he should check in in an hour or sooner should there be a development.

Unger intercepted the call and recorded it. He forwarded the call to Girard and asked for instructions. Girard told him to continue to watch to attempt to locate the individuals that were directing Jubal. The cat and mouse game continued. Girard had suspected that Jubal was being directed and the recorded call confirmed that fact. He was obviously there to look for those that were monitoring the couple not to watch the couple themselves. He also knew that this was a sign that either the government was involved or Justin Welsh was trying to determine whether it was safe to contact Austin Lee. He impressed upon Unger the need to be extremely cautious and then disconnected the call.

****

Philip continued to work up until the time when he prepared to go to his parent's home. He was trying to find a way to ask his father some very awkward questions. No one had been completely honest with him, he thought. Everyone seemed to have their own view of the situation and some of that was perspective while some of it was subterfuge. The more he looked at what Christopher Leesop was teaching and what he did with his life the more he was convinced that his conviction and death was not warranted and in fact not justifiable. He didn't agree with his teachings but that was not enough of reason to persecute the man.

He packed up his notes and the copy of the journal and headed to the train station. He intended to spend the time on the train trying to find a diplomatic method of asking the questions. He was accusing his father of being involved in something that was considered by the government to be illegal. It was going to be a challenge but perhaps it wouldn't be as difficult if Austin and his mother were both there. This was a spontaneous trip he had not called ahead and thought that it would be better that way. There would not be much time for everyone to speculate as to why he was coming.

As the train moved him closer to the destination he still had not come up with any way to soften the questions. He was about to give up when he received a call from Jessica. It was a welcome distraction and since he had not spoken with her in several days it might be that Jessica missed him. "Hello Jessica, how are you?" he asked.

"Philip where have you been I have been trying to reach you?" she asked frantically.

"I am on a train to Harrisburg, perhaps the service was interrupted by the magnetic field." he explained.

"Oh, I was worried, I haven't heard from you in several days and wondered what you were doing to stay out of trouble." she said more calmly.

The Jessica was surprisingly talkative and every time that Philip sought to end the conversation she found a way to keep him on the phone. It was a pleasant distraction for him since he had been obsessing about how to handle the questioning of this father and he found himself still engaged in conversation as he was climbing the steps to his parents' home.

The cool air that greeted him as he entered was very welcome. The house's interior was bathed with the filtered sunlight and had a golden glow caused by the light passing through the ivory curtains that MacKenzie had prided herself in procuring at such a bargain.

"Hello!" Philip called out and listened.

He heard someone stirring in the kitchen and walked toward the sound. "Philip is that you?" his mother asked.

"Yes Mother it is I." he replied.

"What a pleasant surprise. How are you? Is everything alright?" MacKenzie asked.

Philip assured his mother that everything was in good order and then was surprised to learn that she was the only one at home. "Where are the rest of your roommates?" he asked.

"Oh your father was called into work and Pam is out with friends and Austin... well I think Austin has a date." she added with a smile.

Philip looked at his mother and then asked, "When is Dad coming home, I need to ask him some questions."

MacKenzie didn't know when Gregory was coming home. He had left early that morning saying that he might be home in the evening or if things did not go well it might be a day or two before she would see him.

She was used to this happening when he was doing an installation and that what he had told her he was doing. She told Philip that she wasn't exactly sure but he was welcome to have dinner with her and should he not come home until Monday or Tuesday she told him she would let him know that you wanted to talk with him.

Philip was disappointed and wasn't sure what he should do. He had no real friends that he could share what was troubling him. Of his brothers Austin was most likely to be the one that would listen, Roger would see it as a game and problem that needed to be solved.

"Where is he working, do you know?" he asked his mother. She replied that all she knew was that it was a power installation for some new computers. Philip nodded his understanding and then changed the topic to dinner. They mutually agreed to order Thai food and sat down and waited for it to be delivered. The conversation was light and about current events and the miserable weather.

****

Gregory Lee walked behind the line of cargo movers that were carrying seventeen multiple tera-watt generators. These units were to be installed to power the latest super computers and the respective cooling towers, which were even more critical than the power required for the computer itself. The job would take several hours and it would mean that he would be required to be on standby in case the installation did not go as planned. While he waited he hoped that he would be able to find Roger so that he could say hello. Instead of seeing Roger he ran into Willie.

"Dr. Lee, what a great surprise, but I guess it shouldn't be, considering what is being installed here today. How are you sir?" Willie asked.

"I am fine William it is good to see you. Have you seen Roger?" Gregory inquired.

"I saw him last on Friday evening. He was working late and was a little frustrated at the progress he was making. I did talk to him yesterday and this morning. He is doing much better but we both had encountered the same problem which I understand you are here to help fix- the computing power." Willie answered with great detail.

Gregory was hoping that Roger was close by but Willie did not volunteer his location. "Can you tell me where I can find him?" he asked.

Willie smiled and then realized that he might want to see Roger as opposed to check on his condition. "If you follow this corridor back the way that you came and when you reach the central hub walk directly across and down that corridor for about two or three hundred yards you will find his work area to the left. When do you think the systems will be on-line?" he asked Gregory.

"We should be ready to test in about four or five hours. Until then I have very little to do after the initial test of the power up sequence which will be starting in about ten minutes, I have to get going. Good seeing you William. Good luck today." Gregory wished him well and turned and walked briskly to catch up with the people that he had been following.

Willie placed a called to Roger and when he didn't accept the call he elected not to leave a message. It will be a surprise, he thought and then he returned to work. It was time to assume that everything would perform according to the design and it was now necessary to work on the extractor program and that required that Avery give him some additional education on the characteristics of the photolytic components. It was necessary to learn the rate and nature of decay over how long a period of time. This would enable him to build a model that could show the age of the particle and like aged particles in close proximity could be used to create an image.

"What will cause the photolytic component to break down?" he asked Avery on the call that he placed to her.

"Well, the residual of the impact with an article would degrade primarily because of time passing. Environmental factors, with the exception of gamma ray bombardment have little effect on the photolytic component. There are so many variables that go into the interpretation of a single photon and how it has been influenced by the collisions that it has had. They bounce about leaving traces of themselves behind until they are finally absorbed after a specific number of impacts with the right substances. The darker the color the more of the attributes of the photon are absorbed. Pure black absorbs it all, but there is no pure black. There is always something that is radiated back."

"When we harvest photons and their photolytic components we are looking at virgin data. These are things that have never been seen by anyone, for if they were then they would not have been able to be retrieved." Avery said and then continued to explain about angles of refraction and photolytic silhouettes and Willie typed feverishly to incorporate what he was hearing into the code he was writing. He had the harvester's interface code and the fact that it would present the photons one at a time, gave him the chance to determine what had happen to them, approximately how old they were, and how far they had traveled.

The more he thought about the complexity the clearer the solution seemed to be. Avery continued to elaborate and suddenly Willie interrupted, "Can you get me a core sample of earth from the target area?" There was no immediate response, just silence. Willie thought that the line had dropped. "Hello, Avery are you there?" he finally asked.

There appeared to be a sigh and then, "Yes Willie I am here. Don't you think it might be a little premature for the core sample? You have not written the interface yet." she pushed back at his request.

"Oh, but that's where you are wrong, I think I have the interface written and maybe even a little bit more. How soon could we have the core?" he asked again.

"Willie if you have done what you say you have, then any core should be adequate and I can have a suitable test core with in forty eight hours." she responded.

"Suitable test core, do we know what we would be looking for in that suitable test core? We could assemble data and tune the results to fit any scenario but if we have one defined then we can determine whether we have success or not." he emphatically stated. Willie wasn't opposed to the idea of using a test core he just want to be certain that it would be worth testing.

Avery bit her tongue and then slowly replied, "It is our contention that we should not use a sample that will yield results that can be disputed because of inadequate means of documenting the events we are attempting to witness. It is for that reason that we have selected a core that involves a high profile event that was recorded for posterity. It is a suitable control and it will give us the means to adequately test what you and your team have done." Avery concluded and disconnected the call.

Willie was satisfied assuming what she had said was true. She was the authority on the properties of light and he could not argue the mechanics but once he grasped what was going on and could transform it into code it was under his control and guidance. He then wondered if Roger was having as much fun.

****

Roger wasn't having fun at all. He was stressed about the upcoming meeting and whether his program would withstand the rigors of a test that would approximate the scope of the project, whatever that was. He had been seeing technicians coming and going for the past several hours. It was apparent that the team was installing, hopefully, the computing power necessary to accomplish the mission. He was thinking that the power requirements for such processing capacity had to be staggering and he thought of his father and his work. He looked up from the chaos on his desk to see his father standing above him smiling with his arms crossed.

"Roger you look like you have seen better days." Gregory said seeing that his son had finally acknowledged his presence.

"Dad it's a surprise to see you, though if I had been thinking properly I probably should have guessed that you would be here overseeing the power installation for the new computer. It's very good to see you. You know Willie is here too?" he rambled.

"Yes I know, I saw him and he told me how to find you. Do they let you have coffee or breaks or something?" Gregory asked.

"They had better, I am running this part of the project and that should count for something. Give me two minutes with the people working on this section of code and then we can find ourselves a quiet place to talk for a little while." Roger said rising and then leaving Gregory standing alone in front of his desk.

A few minutes later Roger came back followed by two people dressed in white coats and black trousers. The woman was talking to someone on her PCU and the man was watching Roger intently.

"Here is where you need to concentrate. Try to open this up as much as possible so that when we get the scenario we don't have to spend hours imputing data. I think this hauler that I wrote should provide for some intuitive help, try implementing it in sections twelve, nineteen and forty three. Also I am not against looking for other tools, if you have something laying around in your bag of tricks this would be a really good time to bring it out and see if it may help us. Plan on not getting a lot of sleep over the next couple of days." Roger instructed them.

"Will do Roger." the man said and the woman nodded and then they turned and left. Roger led the way and Gregory followed. They were off to the cafeteria to sit down and have something to eat and talk. Roger had been trying to find a way to let his father know that the anger he had felt about him withholding information about his lineage had gone. He had not been able to hold on to any anger in recent times. It was an odd situation but his life as a whole seem much more tranquil. He generally had a feeling of contentment. That was predominately true except when it came to the project, he found that there was no way to be content with the level of pressure that was being brought to bear from unknown sources. This project seemed to have far too elevated importance to be a simple research project. There was purpose here that no one seemed to know or understand.

****

Unger had been following Jubal for more than two hours and it was clear to him that there was no one else that was observing Kate and Austin. There was also no way to determine where Jubal's contact was located and who it was. They never used names and the information that was given was very brief and it went through an encryption server that gave the impression that the signal was coming from at least twenty different location all of which were probably incorrect. Because of this Unger placed yet another call to Girard.

"Sir, there has been no progress and I have not been able to gain any insight into who this man is working for. Do you think he might be persuaded to volunteer that information under the right circumstances?" Unger asked hoping Girard would set him free to interrogate Jubal. The response was, 'no and to be patient'. That was not Unger's strong suit, he wanted to act and to act now.

Jubal seemed to be drifting from reality into a dream-like state. He was bored by the assignment. He thought there would be some excitement or there would be more action, instead he watched two people talking while they sat on a bench for what appeared to be hours. There wasn't even a way to get a vicarious thrill from sexually charged actions or contact. Their conversation revolved around social issues and wars. He forced himself to get up and move a little. If they moved he would find them. Perhaps someone would come and kidnap them, then there would be some excitement. He called Barnaby and told him of his plan to walk around. There was no response and he took that as passive agreement with his plan.

When Jubal stood up Unger's head snapped as though he had been awaken from a deep sleep. He watch Jubal move away from the two of them and then duck into a small service corridor. If ever there was a chance to snatch this man this was it, he thought. Unger had never been known for his ability to follow orders and had been in trouble many times for acting without thinking. This was another chance to be true to his character as he stood up and walked directly for the service corridor. As he turned in there was Jubal standing in his way talking to someone on his PCU. Unger thought for a split second and then grabbed his pen and rotated the barrel and with one continuous motion fired the neural paralyzer and Jubal slumped to the ground immediately and was dead within seconds. Unger knew enough to leave the area and considered abandoning his assignment but elected to see if anyone would come to claim Jubal's body.

Unger withdrew to an area about one hundred yards from the service corridor. He could see it plainly and if someone approached it he would have ample time to determine what he should do. He continued to watch as many people walked past the corridor but no one entered. As he watched he attempted to maintain surveillance on the couple as they continued to sit on the bench and talk. If they should move he would be torn between maintaining the surveillance and possibly finding out for whom Jubal had been working.

Foon spotted Unger leaving the corridor and when Jubal did not re-emerge she thought that Unger must have done something to incapacitate him or worse. She wouldn't risk being seen by Unger because if he had done violence then there was nothing that could rule out him doing the same to her. The man had a reputation for recklessness and apparently had proved himself to be that person once again. Foon decided that she would call Devers and let him know what had happened.

The call was brief and Devers did not betray any feelings one way or another. The next call that he made was to Girard and there was more emotion displayed in the tone of the call.

"Girard what is that idiot that you have working for you up to now? My person on the scene says he may have killed the person he was tailing is that true?" Devers asked. Girard replied that he did not know but would find out immediately and call him back.

The situation was deteriorating quickly, Unger wanted to leave the zoo and put as much distance between him and the dead body as possible but Girard had instructed him to stay put and watch. There was nothing that could be done now but to see if Jubal had back up and if they would come to investigate his lack of communication. This meant that when Austin and Kate got up and began to walk away that Unger had to hold his position and wait. Foon would be responsible for the additional surveillance. It was clear to everyone that Unger had made a huge mistake.

Austin walked closely to Kate and their hands touched as they moved their arms in contrast to their strides. At one such pass Austin gently took her hand and she did not resist. They walked aimlessly around the Zoological Society. They had been with each other for more than three hours and neither one of them could tell if asked what they had seen.

Kate began to get nervous regarding how she was going to end the date. They had made so much progress on getting to know one another and it was obvious that he was attracted to her and she gave him signs that she was attracted to him. The unfortunate thing was that she was actually attracted to him and that made her feel guilty. They continued to walk and it seemed that the conversation flowed from one topic to the next and there was always something interesting in what he had to say about it.

They walked to the Reptile House and Austin asked her if she had any interest in going inside. Kate as a child had been interested in anything that moved and had more than two legs. She enjoyed looking at the creatures and trying to see the similarities that she believed that we shared with them all. Whether it was the fact that they had two eyes or they exhibited what appeared to be reasoning powers, it was interesting to learn about them and then tell somebody, like her father what she had learned. She nodded approval and they went inside.

Foon could see that Unger was beginning to get visibly agitated and it was clear that he would have to be relieved of his assignment. The day was not a good one and Girard had two men on route to his position and he hoped that Unger would remain until they arrived. There was still no sign of anyone that had any interest in where Jubal was located. She saw no movement of any kind that would indicated someone searching. This was extremely odd. If there had been an agent down in her operation she would want to know what had happened and why. The people that Jubal worked for apparently did not care enough about him and his part of the operation to investigate his disappearance. What a pity, she thought and she hoped that she would never work for such a callous group of people. And she thought that Devers was bad, and with that thought a smile came to her face.

It was getting late and Foon began to think that Kate didn't have a graceful way to end the date. She would have to come to her rescue, but it would have to wait until Unger was safely out of the area and the other two men were in position. That meant another fifteen or twenty minutes of making certain that Unger did not do something even more foolish then he had already.

The time passed slowly. Then suddenly there was a commotion near the service corridor and it appeared that someone had discovered Jubal's body. This was more than Unger could handle and he turned from his position and started to walk away. He did it slowly at first and then began to gather momentum and soon he was almost running from the scene. Two security guards that were responding to the report of the apparent discovery spotted him running and took off in pursuit.

The ugly event was about to become even uglier. Foon called Devers again asking for direction and he once again did not respond. A call came in from Girard saying to make certain that Kate and Austin were not aware of what was transpiring. She was directed to get them out of there and told that Unger would be dealt with by the men on route. Foon acted quickly calling Kate and telling her to end the date quickly but don't forget to set another one either tomorrow or the next day. It was important to keep the intensity building.

"I really must be going, this has been a very nice day." Kate told Austin. She did not feign disappointment, she did not want their time together to come to an end.

"Melissa it seems like we just sat down to talk and now I see that we have been together for almost four hours. Next time we should allow more time if it is going to pass so quickly." he replied.

"What are you doing tomorrow evening?" she asked.

"I work until five and then I am free." he replied.

"Meet me at the train station in Harrisburg in the main concourse at five thirty and I'll have a surprise for you." she said and smiled. She then raised up on her toes and kissed his cheek. "I will see you tomorrow." she continued as she turned and walked away.

Austin was not sure what had happened and why the day's events had ended so abruptly but he was going to see her tomorrow and there was going to be a surprise. That alone would keep him occupied with thoughts of Melissa. His attention was drawn to a man running and being chased by two security guards. As he turned to get a better look he saw a crowd had gathered in another area and it appeared that someone was injured since there was a medical team present. For a moment he thought about going to see what had happened but he decided that it would be best to let his curiosity not be satisfied. He wonder if anything could be gained by going there, could he help or would he be just another inquisitive spectator that was seeking some perverse thrill? He turned and walked toward the exit.

Unger knew they were gaining on him and he did not have the stamina to continue the sprint much longer. He reached in his pocket and pull the pen out and glanced at it as he ran. There was one charge left in the neural paralyzer chamber and he could either use it on one of the security guards or himself. He didn't have a chance to make the decision. He felt the sting.

Unger tumbled head first to the ground bashing his head into a bloody mess as he his lifeless body skidded to a stop. The two men that had been waiting for him simply turned and walked into the crowd that had been gathering. They soon separated and went for two different exits. One took up the surveillance of Austin as he found him waiting for a train. They both boarded the shuttle that took them to the main train station. The man would stay with Austin until he reached his home. His assignment was to determine if anyone was following his target. There was no one that fit the profile.

****

Gregory and Roger parted company after spending an enjoyable hour talking about computers and their power requirements. It was clear that their relationship was returning to the same level that it had been prior to the revelation of the family history.

Roger had forgiven his father and as they parted company he told him, "Dad, I want you to know that I have forgiven you. It doesn't matter why you didn't tell us about our family history. It's just not that important. I wanted you to know that."

Gregory looked at his son and then said, "Thank you. I have always been proud of you and I should have not tried to shield you from something that you didn't need to be shielded from at all. The interesting thing is that I had entertained the notion of changing our name back to Leesop several years ago. That would have shaken things up a bit." Gregory smiled and squeezed his son's shoulder and turned and left.

Roger thought for a moment about what his father had said and then was interrupted by three of his team members, each with an issue that needed immediate attention. The coding was going well but there were problems, not significant ones, but problems none the less and they needed to be addressed by before three o'clock when they would be challenged with the scenario that they would have to build into the program.

****

Willie was pacing in his work area awaiting the final connection of the new computer system. They were in the middle of the power up sequence and it would be available for use as soon as the operating systems were loaded. He decided to walk into general work area where most of the staff working on the project had their workstations. As he entered the area he noticed that there was a lack of activity. The programmers seemed to be grouped together talking and joking.

Two of the programmers on Willie's team saw him enter. They watched him as he walked through the area and as he did it was clear to them that he was not pleased. His facial expression betrayed a look of disappointment that yielded to a look of anger. They took this as a sign that they should be engaged in some other activity but there was nothing that they could do until the computers came back on line. This was a welcomed rest from the frantic pace that they had been working at since Willie arrived.

Most of the people that were working on this project had been involved with it for more than a year. Some had been working on this problem since its inception, seven years ago. Those that had been with the project for an extended period of time had seen this level of enthusiasm quickly wane when obstacles were encountered showing the participants the true scope of the project. They were certain that Willie too would hit a wall and then it would be back to the status quo.

Willie joined a small group of programmers that were conversing and as he joined them he noticed that their demeanor changed. They had been smiling and joking but now were quiet and reserved.

"Are we ready for the test?" he asked the group. They answered affirmatively in unison. "Good." he responded. He wasn't certain what to say or to do next. He stood there as the group attempted to have a conversation. He watched and listened but it was clear that they did not welcome his companionship. He continued persist in his attempt to join the group and did not show any signs of leaving when they were interrupted by Gregory Lee.

"Dr. Lawrence, may I have a word with you please?" Gregory requested.

"Yes of course, Dr. Lee." Willie responded and the two men withdrew out of earshot of the group.

"Willie, we are just about to restart the computers. The first time through the cooling system failed due to power fluctuations. This is a very sophisticated piece of equipment and I am hopeful that we have found the problem, but if not it may take several hours to isolate the failure. I thought you should know." Gregory concluded his statement with a reassuring smile.

"Is there anything I can do to assist you?" Willie offered sincerely.

"No.... oh yes, call Roger and relate the news to him. I must be getting back to this. Thank you for your understanding." Gregory concluded.

Willie called Roger and told him of the status of the installation. It was almost three and Adria would be arriving to discuss the scenario and how it was to be input into the system. Roger explained to Willie that he still had a great deal of programming to complete before the system would be needed for a meaningful test. He then told Willie that they had not had the opportunity to stop and catch their breath. He also told him he was concerned for the people that were putting in all the time that they were. They needed some down time so that they could recharge themselves. Willie told him that he understood but thought to himself that these were young driven people and they need to be able to work at the level that the job requires. Roger seems to have shifted his priorities, he thought.

Roger continued to have his team work on the final coding sequences in preparation for the loading of the scenario which was to occur in the next hour or two. He received a call stating that Adria had arrived and that there would be briefing in the main conference room in half an hour. He wondered why there was a delay but did not give it too much thought. He wanted to be ready to go when given the information. He also thought it wise to bring at least two additional staff members so that they would have a complete appreciation of the task at hand.

****

Norville was forty minutes away from the installation. The whine of the finely tuned engine betrayed its alien nature. This internal combustion engine powered vehicle was a unique beast. There were very few left outside of museums and most of them were built in the early part of the previous century. This one was built at the end of the Twentieth century and had a pedigree that would make most royalty envious. It had been owned by the husband of the Queen of England and then by the Shak Kilanmani Ghortami the then richest man in the world and now it belonged to Norville Forrest.

The trouble with owning a vehicle that runs on gasoline or alcohol was finding a way to secure it. There were very few places where it could be obtained and none of them were one hundred percent legal. Still he wouldn't drive any other vehicle it was just too much fun running through the eight speed transmission on roads that were not designed for speeds above thirty or forty miles per hour, he was pushing the car to do more than ninety. It had a top end of almost two hundred miles per hour and a mere seven inches of ground clearance. The Italians certainly knew how to build a fine sports car and the color, of course it had to be red, he mused.

****

Philip and his mother had just ordered their dinner and were waiting for it to arrive. They heard the door open and in walked Austin. "Austin, I didn't expect you until later." MacKenzie said.

"Hello Mom, hello Philip. How was your day?" he asked not directing the question to either of them in particular. He didn't want to have to explain his date he just wanted to have the night end and the next work day past so that he could see his Melissa at five thirty.

"Now if only your father would come home, it would be a perfect evening." MacKenzie continued.

****

340

The conference room was almost full. There were many people that Roger had not seen before. He assumed that they had been traveling with Adria but then again they could be working on other aspects of the project. In front of each of the seats at the oval shaped table was a tube. The contents of it were most likely the subject of the briefing. Roger was curious but he also noticed that no one had touched theirs yet.

An older women with long grey hair pulled back in a pony-tail entered the room. She looked about and smiled and nodded her head to several people. "Dr. Constantina, you may have this seat if you like." Horatio said standing and offering his seat.

"Thank you Horatio but I think that one of these young men should be the one to stand." she said looking at Roger.

"But of course Dr. Constantina you may have my seat." Roger said and stood promptly.

"Thank you young man, I don't believe we have been introduced yet. You are?" she asked.

"My name is Roger Lee, I am working on the scenario selection programming along with a team of about twenty programmers and analysts." Roger replied.

"Lee, are you Philip Lee's brother?" she asked.

"Yes and Gregory Lee is my father." he responded.

"You have quite an illustrious family, and there are several more of note. One in particular that has made a remarkable contribution to our tiny planet. But this is stuff that can be discuss at another time and place. Today it is all about you Dr. Lee and your brother Philip and of course your friend Dr. Lawrence. You have the spot light. Even your father, who I believe is working here today is not in the spot light like you are. This is the chance for you to be a beacon to us all, much like the Lees of the past." Adria said finishing with a knowing look which she shared with everyone in attendance.

"Dr. Constantina we are only servants in this great project, you have to point us in the right direction." Roger replied.

"Thank you Dr. Lee, Roger is it? Roger where would you like me to start?" she asked.

"In the beginning. At what point in history we are evaluating the time thread? What is our objective?" he asked.

"So you want the beginning and the end and then you will fill in the rest? That is excellent, that is exactly what your portion of the project is to do. This is the throw away portion of the project because once its results are learned there will be no reason to hold on to it any longer. It is like you have been asked to invent a disposal drinking cup because you are thirsty and you need something to hold your beverage and once you have invented it and created it you throw it away. This is so indicative of our society, the way everything is meant to be consumed and discarded. The program you write and the results of this program cannot be used again that is the primary difference were as many of the things that we think are disposable can be used again and again. Everything else that we have laid our hands upon has been able to be reused and appreciated for its value. We do not have to waste what is not ours to waste."

Adria completed her monolog and then turned her back on the people at the table. She waited to hear them start to talk and then she quickly swiveled her chair so that she could catch them in mid-sentence.

"What do you have to say about what you just heard?" she asked.

"Do you think that the old lady has lost her mind? I will tell you this, it is likely that I never had one to lose in the beginning of this journey called life. We measure our lives by the ticks of a mechanized device that enables us to predict where we are in our journey around the sun. It is through this process that we see our purpose and in this context we try to give it meaning and substance. We mark it but because the process is indefinable when we use our limited intellect our attempts to label it define it as something that it is not." she paused again, waiting for those that were listening to mull over what had just been said.

It was like they eating a tough piece of tasty meat and having to chew it repeatedly to get the full flavor and the advantage of every nutrient from it. They were almost reluctant to swallow it as they might not have savored its true value and substance.

When she stopped speaking there was silence. Everyone wondered what had they just heard. Then Adria broke the silence once again by saying, "As you probably guessed I am stalling. The meeting was delayed initially and was supposed to start about ten minutes ago but the project leader has not arrived as of yet so we have to be a little patient. But this was a good example of process measurement. The time we are spending here, the way we look at it as the seconds are ticking by. When if you examine it from another perspective there is rabid activity the likes of which I am sure you experienced over the past day or two. The cogs of a machine meshing to move us forward to the fulfilling of our designed purpose."

There was a small commotion that originated somewhere down the corridor leading to the conference room. A number of people were heading in their direction and there was quite a bit of loud talking. The group of people came around the corner of the corridor and into the line of sight of those in the conference room. A tall elderly man was flanked by several people on either side as well as two or three that were trailing behind him. This must be the project leader Roger thought.

Norville entered the conference room expecting to see only three or four staff members, instead he saw almost twenty. It was too large a crowd for what he had in mind to discuss. They were going to reveal a good deal of the plan today and that information was needed by only a very select few. He knew that the morale of the project was at a high point and he did not want to dampen it by making people feel as though they were not worthy of receiving the briefing. These people were all used to being at the top of their class and have always been made to feel special. All eyes were fixed upon him.

"Norville it is great to see you again." Adria greeted him.

"Adria, are you boring these people with your time equals process theories?" Norville responded rhetorically. "People my name is Norville Forrest and I am the illusive project leader. I am going to ask that we have two meetings. The first meeting will be with just the senior department heads then each of them will have a staff meeting and I will attend each one of those. There is one thing that I am good at and that is attending meetings." he said with a laugh.

The room was soon cleared and that left only six people behind, three from the installation and Adria, Norville and one of his associates. Culpeper, Roger and the project security chief Bonnatu and they sat on one side of the table while the others sat on the opposite side.

"This is a little better." Norville stated. "There is only one person that I haven't met as of yet but I know by reputation. Dr. Lee, it is a pleasure to meet you. I know your brother Philip, though I dare say he doesn't care for me much and I also known your brother Austin from an encounter several years ago, I always thought he was one of the brightest men I ever met." Norville continued speaking.

Roger nodded and replied, "It is nice to make your acquaintance."

"Please open your briefing material and we will begin the summary of the mission and the selection of the point in time that we wish to use as our tipping point." Norville instructed.

"Excuse me sir, what is a tipping point?" asked Roger.

"For our purposes it defines the point in time that we are trying to affect and by doing so cause an Epiphanal Startling as defined by Jenkins and illustrated in the recently published paper by Dr. Philip Lee."

Adria then added, "Please take a moment and read the critical mission summary located on the top of the second page. When you have finished reading we will begin our discussion and answer any relevant questions that pertain to the time for completion of the mission."

Roger took the screen out of the tube and selected page two and began to read the statement. It was two paragraphs that indicated that the purpose of the project was to first determine whether time could be accurately 'rewound', and viewed using technology that had been identified as potentially viable. That technology was the reading of the components of light and the residual deposits of those components and the altered photons that are present after a collision with an object occur. The process was called Shadow Construction and it saw the activity of light as a part of the process of which time was constructed.

The second paragraph indicated that should the viability exist there was to be a selection of an event to test this theory and that event should be significant as to change the outcome of the world as we know it. Roger mulled this point over, and came to the conclusion that in a sense they would be building a device that put in place a means to launch our own obsolescence. What would possess someone to want to obliterate their own time thread, and commit suicide by un-creating themselves. Perhaps he had misunderstood the meaning of the paragraph or there was an alternate answer to the questions that it posed.

"Mr. Forrest, I am not certain I understand why anyone would want to initiate the actions that would cause the second paragraphs mission to be accomplished. Isn't that equivalent to taking your own life?" Roger asked.

Norville looked at him and smiled knowingly, "Roger, this is an exercise that is designed to prove a theory it does not state that it will be implemented and there is no proof that it actually can be implemented." he stated.

"But sir, the simple fact that you are trying to do this thing doesn't make any sense to me." Roger replied.

"Let us continue to provide the background material and then we will see if there is a reason for us to proceed with the project. I think you will come to the same conclusion that I did. It is an important project." Norville stated.

For the next half hour Norville talked about the sorry state of the world both from a physical standpoint as well as a spiritual standpoint. He spoke of the hopelessness of the human condition. He lost Roger shortly after he started. Roger was there for one reason, to see if he could do the job. The puzzle was the most complex one that had ever been created and he had to solve it, it was that simple. It didn't matter what they did with the results. He didn't believe that time could be manipulated but he did believe that man could create predictive scenarios that could be tested and found to be valid and the likelihood of them coming into existence was governed by the rules of probability. Those rules were being refined with this process and it was there that he found the reasons for hope and a reason to work to solve the problem.

Norville then asked the group to look at the second section of the briefing. This was where the starting point would be. He asked that they begin to study the attached document and that they would have the opportunity within the next week to review the scenario with the author of the paper. Roger looked at the paper and saw that his brother Philip had written it. It dealt with the battle of Gettysburg and the theory that Jenkins had put forth that a different outcome would have meant a different world today.

"What we are going to find out is where exactly this starting point is and what certain actions can be taken to disrupt the existing time thread. Once we have done that we will need accurately predict what the effects those changes would have on today's world. If there are changes, what are they?" Norville asked rhetorically though Culpeper attempted to start to answer the question but stopped when Norville stared at him in disbelief.

Adria looked at the group and saw that there was little hope that she would be to speak to them about the theory of time as a process that she had devoted her life to refining its definition. She saw her mission at this point was to get the group focused on the input of the starting point into the computer model and after that to begin to test the durability of the design.

Norville went on to state that the initial premise was the same one that was created several decades earlier when they enabled the manufacturing process to utilize predictive programs and was therefore encouraged to move away from pure natural selection product development. After a period of time the term evolved into the what was called Natural Selection Economics which encompassed all aspects of the economic system including; financial services, manufacturing, infrastructure, and consumer satisfaction. All of the development of future products was to be done using these predictive tools. The designs had become more intricate and the effective useful range had been expanded from five to fifteen years, with a goal of being able to expand that even further. The results had enabled designers to leap-frog over interim designs which would have occurred in natural development and thus saving money, time and resources.

If they were to be successful in the predictive programming that was required to successfully fulfill this project's requirements the ancillary effects on product and services development would be monumental. It would be the type of residual impact that the space program had on the development of computers and a myriad of consumer products during the second half of the Twentieth Century, he concluded.

At that point Adria took over the briefing and was explaining the reason for the selection of the particular point in time. There was a need to select a moment that would have a dramatic effect yet would be one where there would be a controllable amount of variables. There were many other points that could have had the same type of impact but would require too many secondary events to consider them tenable. What was needed was an event that could be altered and once altered would require a minimal amount of secondary interference to alter the time thread dynamically.

"You mentioned that my brother would be joining us at some point to enhance the details that we already have to work with from his published paper. I have not completely studied it but there does not seem to be an identified starting point. The paper, more or less, gives a general suggestion of some key elements for change. Who will make the decision on what that point in time is?" Roger asked.

"I have made that decision already and you and I will discuss that after the meeting since this information should be shared with as few a number of people as possible. We are seeking unbiased results, not ones influenced by an agenda or prejudice." Adria replied.

"At this point I suggest that we adjourn and start the individual staff meetings. Roger your meeting will be the last one conducted, security will be first followed by the general operations meeting. They will last about a half hour each. This will give you and Adria enough time to work through the details and should make your staff meeting even more meaningful." Norville instructed.

It was at that moment that each PCU received the same announcement, that there would be a delay in going live with the new computer system due to cooling systems issues. The programs would not be tested today. This information caused Norville to instruct the group by saying, "Well it seems like everyone is going to get some much needed rest. I suggest we delay everything until tomorrow and send everyone home. We will reconvene in twenty four hours."

Chapter Eleven

The rest would do him a lot of good, he thought. It hadn't taken much convincing to get Roger out of his work area and into a shuttle and then on to the train. His final destination was his home in Philadelphia where he was looking forward to some much needed down time. He was teetering on a narrow edge of disinterest in the project. He wanted there to be an elegant solution to an academic problem. They were making this far too real for him, that it was actually considered by the people that sat in the room with him as viable. It was good to be out of there for a few precious hours, he thought.

His arrival at home had its share of drama. Gloria was so happy to see him that she cried. That reaction cost him a great deal of sleep and he wondered whether it was time to change his living situation. No one should be that dependent upon another that much, he thought. Still he smiled every time he thought of her and he was already missing seeing her while she sat across from him at the breakfast table. She was sharing her activities of the past several days and while they may have sounded very similar to other experiences she had shared previously, they nevertheless seem to be somewhat captivating. He found himself listening intently to what she said and asking questions that illustrated his awareness of the conversation's direction and content.

He thought about calling Philip to see when he would be joining them and then he wondered why his father had not mentioned it to him. Perhaps Gregory didn't know and he decided that he would ask his father later if he saw him. He was certain that his father had not had a peaceful night and time to reflect as he had. When there are power problems with computers, especially the size and complexity of the one they were implementing, any variance or inconsistency could be catastrophic and apparently was.

Gloria finished sharing and turned her attention to Roger and she asked him about the project and how it was proceeding. Roger wasn't certain how much he could share with her and counted on his ability to bore her with technical details about the project. This would cause her to take the conversation in a different direction, something he had mastered over the time he had known her. Apparently it worked because Gloria began to ask questions regarding when he would be home next and whether they could go to dinner sometime soon. Roger assured her that the project would be over within a couple of weeks and that he would come home as often as he could. He stood up and went to his room to get himself ready to depart for work. He entered and sat on the bed and it was then that he realized that he didn't want to leave Gloria, he was going to miss her.

****

Austin had arrived at work an hour early. He had not slept well and he had hoped to talk to his father about what was happening. There was reason for him to be concerned for when he was arrested he had been consumed with the thoughts of Melinda and now it was Melissa that was creeping into his consciousness repeatedly. It happened when he least expected it. She was taking over his thoughts and feelings and he did not want to lose control. He wanted to share his concerns with someone that would not judge him, and his father had become that person as of late.

That had not been true before his arrest but something had changed Gregory or perhaps he was the one that changed, it wasn't really very clear. His father wasn't available and his mother, while she would listen, she would also worry and he did not wish to cause her any added pain, she had suffered greatly when he was in jail and that was more than enough. This day was going to be a long one, he thought.

****

Philip received an early morning call from Jessica. She sounded distracted and kept asking him if he was alright and that she wanted to see him soon. He finally agreed to see her but his feelings had been changing toward her since he had found out about her connection to the Jeremy and that their chance meeting had little to do with serendipity and was more of a contrivance. Still her physical appearance had left its mark indelibly on his hippocampus and when he closed his eyes and heard her voice and her image filled his thoughts.

He left his apartment at the same time as he had every morning. This time he was met by two men. They stood on either side of him after verifying his identity. They told that he was to go with them.

"Where are you taking me?" Philip asked.

There was no reply as they pushed him into the waiting Voltrun. Once inside the vehicle their demeanor changed. "Dr. Lee we are taking you to a secret facility where you will be asked to assist us with some very critical research. Your brother Roger is working on this project along with your father, though he will only be involved for a very short time. Any questions you may have will be answered once we arrive. Please sit back and try to enjoy the ride. We will be going through some very scenic areas in West Virginia and Maryland." the one man told him and then he turned and looked out the window.

****

Gregory had been working through the night with his team trying to find the source of the power fluctuations. The problem had been isolated to one of the new transforms and its oscillating generator interface. It was necessary to compensate for the draw-down of the power to insure uniform power availability to the cooling agents and the draw exceeded the capacity of the interface to regulate the power within the tolerance of the equipment. His team could not find the cause within the equipment but rather than waste any more resources he had requested another unit to be sent and it was due to arrive shortly after ten that morning. If the replacement performed properly he could expect to be on his way home in the early afternoon, something he would welcome.

****

Kate was sitting with her boys and explained to them why she would not be home in the evening and that they would be taking tomorrow off from school so that they could do something fun together. Theo, the youngest, seemed distressed by the news that his mommy would not be there at night but when he was told that he would be going to see Grandpa and Grandma and that they would take him to get ice cream he became enthusiastic about the adventure. She told them that she would see them in the morning and that she loved them very much.

As they walked away to go to school she had a sense of 'aloneness' that chilled her. These were her children that she was watching walk away from her, what if this were the last time she would see them. She fought the urge to run after them and began to work on an intellectual solution to the feelings she was experiencing. She was reacting to the report of the news that two men had died yesterday during the operation did not make her feel safe. Foon had explained that Unger was a person that she would not have selected for the job since he was known to be unbalanced. Foon's words did little to comfort her, she could have easily been the target of Unger's irrational behavior. At that point she started to think about Michael and that he was not there to protect her, to care for her. He promised that he would always do that and he hadn't.

She then realized that she had no one that she could truly confide in that would not judge her. The only person she could think of that had the characteristics that she needed to be her confidant was the person she was trying to ensnare in the WBOI web. How could this man be the evil person that he was portrayed to be. She felt alone and abandoned.

She was awaken from her thoughts of despair by an incoming call from the Army.

"Mrs. Foster? This is Major Goodman with the US Army Tactical Corps I am calling regarding your husband."

"Yes, this is Kate Foster. What is wrong Major?" Kate replied with concern.

"There has been no change to his status other than to say there have been no demands for a ransom which is the normal course of action in these situations. It is for that reason that we thought it best to let you know that there is very little chance that your husband will be recovered alive." the Major stated with little feeling.

"How can you say that, do you have any proof that he is dead?" Kate replied her voice growing louder and more shrill.

"Mrs. Foster, we don't make these calls to people without careful thought and investigation and while there is still reason to hope, the likelihood of this situation coming to a positive conclusion is remote at best. We have a great deal of experience in these matter. I can tell you this that we also have a great deal of success in bringing the perpetrators to justice and to a quick end. And yes I understand that this does not help replace your loss, it does however help to curtail the activity for a while and does save lives." the Major said.

"This can't be the end of this. I want to speak to someone who is in charge. Now!" Kate screamed.

"I am in charge Mrs. Foster, but if you want to speak to someone else I suggest that you contact the State Department, they might be able to give answers that I do not have. I will send you a name and contact information. I know this is a trying time and you have our deepest sympathy." he said and disconnected he call.

Kate received the contact information and considered placing the call but first she elected to contact Devers. He promised her a positive resolution, this was not what she had agreed to at all.

"Mr. Devers, this is Kate Foster, I am calling to let you know that the Army has given up on the idea of recovering my husband alive. They believe that he is already dead. Please call me a soon as possible. Our agreement has been broken and I am not certain I wish to continue with this." she said as she left the message and then terminated the call in hopes that he would respond. It is possible that he already knew and did not take the call knowing what it was about, she thought. She then placed the call to the State Department.

Barbara Keith answered the call that had been placed to Yesseh Jaumter by Kate. She indicated that she was familiar with her husband's plight and that they were working through all channels to find him. They had not given up trying nor had they given up hope. The military was much more scientific in their approach and they always responded according to historical data which supported their reason to contact her and advise her of the situation as it stood at this time. Barbara then went on to tell her that she should make that office her primary contact from this point forward and that someone would be in touch with her regularly to update her on the progress of the retrieval.

The use of the word retrieval seemed to give Kate some hope but this was also a public relations office and they would do everything they could to make things seem as positive as possible. Still it was a reason to hope and she needed to think that her children would not be fatherless, it would devastate them. She took a few moments to collect herself and then determined that she must go through with tonight's scheduled meeting. Austin had become completely attached to her, she thought and this was going to be a decisive point in the operation. She felt confident that he would tell her what he knew about Justin and his location. If he was involved in anything at this time she would be able to begin to extract that information from him. She, unfortunately, was not convinced that he was involved in anything other than trying to put his life back together after being in prison for five years.

****

"I want this completely clear, Michael Foster is not to be harmed. Do you understand?" Truax said emphatically to Juan Garza who was standing no more than two feet from him with a very menacing look on his face.

Juan replied, "Mr. Truax we understand that Foster is not to be harmed but once we surrender him to our business associates it is out of our hands. They can get very enthusiastic."

Truax sensed the tension but did not care whether Juan was upset or not by his comments. "I will state it again. He is your responsibility and if something happens to him it will be considered your fault. The consequences for that failure will be yours and you will pay the price." Truax said directly and with no emotion. The threat was not his voice it was his words. Juan had to know that Foster had further value to the Norville.

"You tell your Mr. Welsh, or is it Forrest, I get confused easily these days, that we will do our best to make certain that Foster is kept safe until he is needed. You have my word." Juan said with a sinister smile. The others in the room moved closer to Juan as a sign of unity and strength. Truax, who was alone, but gave no indication that he was intimidated by the action.

"Good I am glad you understand how important this is to Mr. Forrest." Truax said and turned and slowly left the room. His next action was to call Norville Forrest and assure him that Michael Foster would be protected.

"Mr. Truax that is reassuring. We don't need further complications in this area. It is important that sometime next week that Mr. Foster is reunited with his wife. By that time she will be totally confused and we should be able to use her to our advantage. It is clear that WBOI does not have any idea what is going on at this time and we must maintain the misdirection for next sixty days, after that it won't matter." Norville said.

"What should we do for Jubal's daughter, her father was her only living relative?" Truax inquired.

"Money seems hardly enough, but it's all we can do at this point. I am glad that Unger's people took care of their problem themselves. It had to be either on Girard or Devers' orders, and I believe that the order came directly from Devers." Norville shared.

"I suspect we can use that to our advantage at some time in the future sir." Truax speculated.

The call went on for a few more minutes and Norville gave Truax his assignment for the next two days. He was to enlist Barnaby in creating more miss direction by activating Austin's two friends, John and George. They would be pulled into a meeting with a known member of the Monks and they were to work on getting Austin to meet with him as well. This would give Devers and his group plenty to think about.

"It would be helpful if Kate Foster could be the source of the information about the meeting between the two men and the Monks." Norville stated.

"I could contact Juan and have him set up the meeting and ask them to invite Austin to join them. It must be on a day when he would have to choose between meeting with Mrs. Foster and them, because we know what his choice will be sir." Truax said offering a possible way to have Kate find out from Austin about the meeting they were attending.

"Good idea, Mr. Truax, have him also give them a meeting place with the hopes that they will convey that to Austin too. This will make certain that Devers' people will be at the right place." Norville replied.

"One more thing make certain that Juan has adequate security, I don't want Devers' people hurting anyone." he added.

"Yes sir."

Norville disconnected the call and was pleased with the events as they were unfolding. Now if his team could somehow get the computer installation successfully completed the project could move forward with the next phase of critical tests things would be perfect, he thought.

Norville left the room where he had spent the past several hours. He was hoping to find a way to avoid being the first person that Philip Lee saw when he arrived. Barnaby and another man had been escorting him to the facility and had not given him much information other than it was a matter of great importance. It was clear that he was going to be very suspicious once he saw Norville, the man that wanted him fired. He was the man that put him in the position to write a paper that just happened to be on the very subject that time theorist Adria Constantina had selected as the point at which time thread manipulation would occur. That time that was to be the Epiphanal Startling that Jenkins had predicted. This was far too coincidental for him to accept it as simply that.

He decided to let Philip meet Adria alone and then meet with his brother so that they could refine the selection point and begin to interpret the data that was produced by the programs. This was assuming the computer was functioning properly. Perhaps it would help if he saw his father while he was here as well, Norville thought. He decided that he must meditate on that point and with that he went back into the room and shut the door and locked it. This was the key to every step of the process and he was not going to break faith with his routine.

Barnaby disturbed his solitude with an incoming call that indicated that they were within a few minutes of arriving at the facility. He instructed Barnaby to take Philip to see Adria in the Forecasting Laboratory, once he had been briefed by her Barnaby was to get Roger to be included in the meeting as well. After Barnaby had invited Roger to attend the meeting he was to then come to meet with Norville. They would discuss the next several day's activities and the need to be certain that Austin Lee did his part in maintaining the misdirection.

After disconnecting the call Norville returned to his meditation as he had spent hours in reflection over this project and had received a clear understanding of the path that he was to follow regarding the implementation of the time manipulation protocol that was being designed. It was important that he knew that he was on the right path and that the steps that were to be taken to change the course of time were done in accordance with the purpose, the true destiny of mankind. Man was not put here in this place to concentrate all his activities on himself but he was put here to work in concert with those around him. Norville had become what was once was called a 'true believer'. His path was certain and his motives pure, at least in his mind.

****

The Voltrun approached the point where the tunnel opened into the passages below ground level. The entrance way opened just enough to allow the vehicle to enter and Philip felt a little uneasy despite the fact that going underground when riding on trains was a common occurrence and something that he had experienced many times. They descended to the main concourse level and when they arrived at the terminus they were met by two people. Barnaby got out of the vehicle with Philip while the other man remained in the Voltrun which pulled away slowly.

"Dr. Lee, please follow me. You will be meeting with Dr. Constantina in the Forecasting Lab conference room." the young woman in the white coat said in welcoming manner.

"Mr. Barnaby you will also follow us please." said the older man in the tan jumpsuit. He appeared to be a security operative though Barnaby wondered how secure the facility was if someone of his stature was responsible for the safety of the people associated with the project, he seemed almost feeble. Barnaby nodded and gestured for them to lead the way. The older man took off at a surprisingly fast pace and it was a challenge to keep up with him. They continued down the long corridor and came into the Forecasting Laboratory main work area. There were several people working on different aspects of the project and they did not acknowledge the presence of the new people. They had seen so many come and go it was taken for granted that there would be visitors in attendance on a daily basis.

Adria was looking out of the glass walls of the conference room and saw that Philip had arrived. She was not looking forward to this meeting because of her encounters with Roger. She assumed that Philip would be similar in deportment. Another narcissistic one-dimensional boob was not needed here, she thought. It was obvious that brilliance was one thing, social ineptitude was quite another. We have too many of them here on this project, though Roger was nowhere as difficult as his friend Willie, Avery truly has a monumental task in keeping that ego in check. Were these people raised by wolves, she mused.

Philip saw the woman peering at them from behind the glass. It was Adria Constantina, he had recognized her from her photograph in one of the papers in Jenkins research. So this what it was about he thought, more of the time thread manipulation nonsense? This was truly getting tiresome. He followed his guide into the room where he was introduced to Adria and offered him a seat. The others left the two of them alone.

"Dr. Lee I am pleased to meet you. I have read your paper and was impressed by its candor. It seems that you are a little skeptical about the possibility of time thread manipulation and in fact I will go as far as to say that you don't think that the past can even be viewed. Are these proper conclusions on my part?" Adria asked.

"I would say that I don't believe that what you contend might be true, I would say more accurately that it is a difficult premise to accept, but you are fundamentally correct." replied Philip.

"Fair enough. We did not bring you here to discuss whether you think what we are doing is viable. We brought you here to help us determine whether it is. To do this we have been made aware that we need to have a definitive starting point. A position in time from which we can begin to model the results. If we are successful in determining that and then controlling the interpretation of the time thread we might be in a position to ultimately answer the question of whether my hypothesis is correct or it is just another random attempt to make sense of our existence." Adria said.

Philip looked at her intently and was about to speak but she then continued. "I am going to invite someone to join us that will help us select the precise moment in time. While we are waiting for her to join us I want you to think about the date June 29, 1863. We can start from that point and move forward in time. I believe that we will settle on a date that will range from June twenty ninth, thirtieth and July first. It will be an interesting forensic exercise for you and I do know that you enjoy discussing this period in American history. My nephew was in one of your classes and spoke very highly of the way you conducted the class. He said that you brought the period to life for him. That is a high compliment to any teacher I believe."

"What is your nephew's name?" he asked, as he was curious.

"It doesn't have any relevance to what we are about to do Dr. Lee. I mentioned it only to assure you that we accept you as an authority and that by helping us you will receive some benefit as well." Adria answered with surgical precision.

Philip shifted in his chair and glanced out the glass to the work area where ten or more people were working intently. He recognized one of the men as someone he had seen at his father's work place. He then suspected that there was power equipment being installed and that it was possible his father was on site.

"I was wondering if my father was here by any chance?" he asked.

Adria nodded in response and then said, "He is working on installing the power generation equipment for a new computer system. I am certain that you will be able to say hello to him at some point later today."

Philip began to think about the dates that she had mentioned. It was a vague request and he was not certain what it was that he was to identify. He thought about significant events and pictured himself watching the activities unfold. It was evident that should he view this question as it related to Jenkins' work that he should concentrate on the activities of the Confederate troops.

His thoughts went to J. E. B. Stuart who was conspicuously absent from most of the battles events and with cavalry being the primary means of reconnaissance of the day, he had left the Army of Northern Virginia in the dark fumbling toward its eventual demise. He was not certain that any one actually knew definitively where Stuart was on any of those days. They had his testimony and there was some evidence to support some of his activities. If he had been doing what he had been commissioned to do there would have been the opportunity to reduce some of the Confederate losses, especially on the first day. Though if he was to choose a starting point to occur within those three days it probably would not involve the flamboyant Stuart. However if it were possible to move the date back and consider the twenty seventh of June it would then be possible for his actions to have an impact on the battle's outcome. Philip thought that Stuart was too far from the balance of the army to be of use providing intelligence or fighting support.

Avery joined the two who she noticed were sitting in silence when she arrived. "Avery I would like you to meet Dr. Philip Lee, and yes he is related to Roger and Gregory for that matter. Please have a seat. It is important that Dr. Lee understand the type of data that you will need so I thought an explanation of the process that you will be working with would be helpful." Adria said to Avery.

"Dr. Lee I am Avery Silcox, Dr. Lawrence and I are working on a program that interprets effects on the components of light when they collide with objects. If you will allow me to illustrate the process I think we can get the background material out of the way quickly and then begin to look at choosing the right place in time. I say place in time because the topography will play an important part in the selection of the time." Avery said and then she went on to explain the process and how the light components were evaluated and as such their age and number of collision can be interpreted with relative ease.

"Please look at this recording of the Hershold experiment where they were able to display past images using a collection of photons which were broken down into photolytic components. Each one of these represents color within the photon. What happens on collision is that a portion of these particles is absorbed by the item with which it had come in contact. As you can see in the illustration on the screen that the surface of the particle is changes. The changes indicate what color that portion of the object were at the location of the collision. You can see by the playing back of time images that there is an almost ghost like shadow formed as the figure moves from one place to another. We use the term 'trail' to describe and define this effect. The term comes from the 1960's subculture whose members had used hallucinogens and witnessed the residual images as they moved. There are almost an infinite number of positions that are between point A and point B but we have produced a formula that determined that roughly one hundred fifty two thousand positions per centimeter provides for the appearance of a seamless image." Avery explained in great detail.

She continued on to speak of angles of deflection and this is where it became apparent that the location of the event in time must be in a place where the topography was suitable for deflection and the harvesting of the photolytic components. At that point a list of the types of desirable landscape were given. It was surprising to Philip that the only areas that were consider useless were areas where construction had occurred or that were in close proximity to magnetic fields such as the ones that the subterranean trains generate.

To illustrate the available sites Avery displayed a grid of all of the train lines in central Pennsylvania and northern Maryland. It showed that Gettysburg and the corridor between it and the other cities such as York had not been included in train construction as of yet. The plan to do such work was scheduled for later in the fall. At that point the area would be rendered useless as far as this project was concerned.

"If I understand correctly you are looking for an area where there has been no development done and that there are no train lines." Philip asked to be certain he had not missed any of the fine points.

"Yes that is correct. There are other aspects that we would like you to consider and that would be the time of day. It depending upon the time of day our best imprints will occur from the bouncing of direct sun light off of an object. There for those activities that occur during the hours of nine and eleven o'clock in the morning and two and five in the afternoon that represent our best times to be seeking results." Avery added.

"Now I understand the challenges associated with making a selection I am curious to know why you did not use one of the references in my paper. I know that you have read it and apparently are using it since this whole scenario is based upon what Leo Jenkins was attempting to put together along with William Lawrence senior. What is wrong with the outline that you have?" Philip asked.

Adria looked at him sternly and then replied, "Dr. Lee the general information that you outlined in your paper could be considered a starting point, similar to finding a good place to sit at the beach. You know the beach you want to go to and how close you want to be to the water but when it comes down to choosing the point where you wish to plant your chair, you are very specific, you are only able to do it in one spot. True?" Adria asked.

Philip felt like a fool though he didn't know why. This woman was an extraordinarily forceful personality. It is no wonder that people believed in her theories, they are afraid if they didn't they would be considered an idiot, he thought.

"Okay, since you are looking for a precise moment in which to start I will have to give that some thought. I have always been of the mind-set that the battle was lost by the South in three different ways. The first being a break down in the command structure, Robert Lee was too soft hearted a man when it came to his leadership. He expected the loyalty that he showed to them and unfortunately it was not returned in certain instances. This isn't to say that his general officers were disloyal, they just did not have the rabid enthusiasm that he had counted upon such as that was exhibited by 'Stonewall' Jackson. "Pete" Longstreet and A. P. Hill were fine generals and good tacticians. John Bell Hood was as good a replacement as you could hope to find to take Jackson's place but none of his general corps brought the leadership and instinctive soldering that Jackson did." Philip said and then paused.

Avery was bored, you could see it in her eyes, on the other hand Adria was impressed with his ability to 'spin a yarn', as she might call it.

"Dr. Lee if you don't mind I am going to release Avery from her obligation to remain here with us. I think you have a solid grasp of what she needs us to provide her. Should something come up that confounds us we certainly can give her a call. Run along my dear." Adria said. Avery stood and Philip responded as a gesture of courtesy, she expressed her thanks for his coming to meet with them and wished him a safe trip home.

Philip sat down and looked once again at Adria. He was not sure why he should participate in this event. "Please tell me why I should feel compelled to help on this project? There seems to be an agenda that has not yet been revealed. I am not certain that this project is what it is represented to be." Philip said.

"Dr. Lee this project is exactly as it is represented to be and that is an attempt to alter a time thread, the one on which we currently traveling. It is not what some of the people that are working on it believe it to be. It is not meant to make their lives better or satisfy their need to solve complex puzzles, though just because we have different perspectives and desires does not mean that we are not united to achieve the same end. You may see this project as an attempt to prove a theory. I am seeing this this project as the only opportunity to set the course of our journey in another more positive direction. That is why it exists, for no other reason. Please continue with what you were discussing before, I find it very fascinating." she said.

Philip felt he was being pushed in a direction that he did not wish to travel and he most certainly did not agree with the ultimate outcome. What was so wrong with the way life was at this time. The climate was being slowly repaired and more and more people were returning to work. Life was becoming almost bearable for the vast majority of the country's population.

"Why do we have to change it in such a dramatic way? Things are finally starting to improve." he replied.

"Really? Do you really believe that the fact that almost twenty five percent of the population are in prison illustrates how a proper society should function? If the people are that troubled that they have to be restrained and isolated from society, doesn't society have to take a good hard look at the conditions that created this antisocial subclass of citizens?" Adria asked.

Philip looked at her and then thought of his brother and then his uncle and then finally the cousin that he had never met.

"You make a strong point. I am concerned that it just might be premature, that we have not seen the results of all of the changes that have been made." he countered.

"Why did your brother do what he did?" she asked.

Philip thought for a moment and then answered, "He felt that the currency conversion was going to place the world's wealth in the hands of too few. The results of that action would be less and less freedom for the people of this country and the world."

"Was he right?" she asked.

That was a very hard question for Philip to answer. He loved his brother but he also disliked the results of his actions and the affect that they had on his family, especially his mother. There was embarrassment to all of them but she lost contact with her oldest son. She was not able to see him without having to go through a humiliating ordeal.

"My brother wasn't as altruistic as you may think. His behavior was prompted by his need to impress a woman. I am not saying that he didn't agree with the cause, I am just saying that he would not have gone as far as he did if it were not for his interest in impressing her." Philip explained.

"Yes, you are probably able to relate to that, aren't you?" Adria said knowingly. Philip wondered if she was just assuming that he had similar experiences or if she knew about Jessica.

"I am not sure what you mean by your comment." he replied.

"Philip, please can we turn this discussion back to something that is more interesting?   You had indicated that the generalship of the Confederacy was not what it once was and that was a key contributing factor.   Does that mean that we should be looking at the battle at Chancellorsville as starting point and the ability to save the life of Stonewall Jackson?"

Apparently that was enough of a distraction to force Philip to engage in the conversation. "It would be a very good place to start but it would also mean that Gettysburg may never have happened at all. It is not clear that Lee would have visualized the plan if he had Jackson with him. The campaign to invade the North was a desperate attempt to force capitulation and may have worked if they had been successful at Gettysburg. People were getting tired of the cost of the conflict and both England and France were looking for excuses to recognize the new country. They were dependent upon the supply of cotton and saw many other economic advantages as well." Philip stated.

"So then we should abandon trying to keep Jackson alive and stay with the scenarios that have been outlined in your paper. What were the other factors that you mentioned?" Adria inquired.

"The next biggest factor I believe was suitable intelligence. If there had been a way for Lee to understand what he was facing then I believe that the proper emphasis on specific objectives would have occurred. The starting point should focus on the need to get information to Lee that he will find credible and would have provided him with advance knowledge of specific events. I do find that I am only inclined to provide accurate information and I am not inclined to provide misinformation to the Union forces." Philip said.

"Where would you start then?" Adria asked not sure where Philip was leading the discussion.

"I would start with one event where the added intelligence could would set troop movement and strategic positioning into motion. You must remember that Robert Lee was a very cautious man, an engineer by education and a career officer that had built his reputation using his analytical skills. He thought and prayed very hard over every decision he made and would not take intelligence offered from anyone other than what he deemed to be a reliable source. Credibility would have to be constructed and tested before he would accept the information as being valid contribution to the decision making process."

"I understand so do we need to change the target range of days? Perhaps we should go further back in time?" Avery asked as she was thinking out loud.

"I believe that moving the target date slightly could be advantageous. It won't be necessary move it by more than a few days, historic record provides the perfect place to introduce a source that will be considered unimpeachable. Are you familiar with the story that General John B Gordon, a brigadier in Jubal Early's division told regarding intelligence that he received from a fourteen year old girl in a bouquet of flowers?" Philip asked.

"No, I am not. When did it occur and where?" Adria asked.

"It took place in York Pennsylvania on June the twenty eighth. What would have to done would be a substitution of the intelligence information from the information about troop fortification in and around Wrightsville to show the anticipated track of the Union forces which culminate in Bufford's encounter to the west of Gettysburg on July first. The source of the intelligence would have to be J. E. B. Stuart and the letter would to be a very good forgery as Lee knew his handwriting having received numerous reports and correspondences from him over the years." Philip told her.

Adria looked at him intently and then asked additional questions regarding the location and whether or not there had been construction and could they verify a specific location. Philip answered that he did not know about the construction but he had done a little research on the subject and had been able to verify several key things about this snippet in history.

The first thing he did was make certain that it actually had happen and he did this by meeting with several people that claimed to have ancestors that had participated in the event. Once he had received believable testimony which included the young girls name, date of birth and other key pieces of biographical information he sought for additional physical proof. The diary entry of a Kathleen O'Sullivan of York Pennsylvania outlined a very mysterious meeting with a man named William Harper who was reported to be an unemployed drifter that was a later arrested and convicted of espionage. Harper's meeting with the girl may have been something that was sordid and the girl was apparently manipulated into helping him with romantic ovations. Philip indicated that he did not follow up on that element of the research but the diary entries were disturbing to read at times.

As he spoke Adria became convinced that this man held the key to providing them with enough information to intelligently select the point at which they needed to 'jump off'. He had spent months of his life with Leopold Jenkins materials and was an expert even before he had commenced the formulation of the thesis. She continued to listen to him speak about how he had uncovered the information and then he revealed the most stunning of his findings.

"I have three pages of her actual diary at home and it is for the dates of June twenty fifth, twenty seventh, and twenty eighth. They indicate where she picked the flowers and that is where Harper had given her the note. If she was honest in her recording of the events then you will have the exact spot and time at which you can begin the process." Philip said proudly. He had definitively found a solution to an extremely difficult challenge and he was the only person that could have offered that solution. No one to his knowledge had ever done research on this particular piece of historic trivia. He then laughed when he thought, 'why would anyone want to know this stuff?' It was good to know that he could not always take himself seriously, he thought.

Adria had heard exactly what she wanted to hear. "Philip, you don't mind if I call you Philip because I only call people by their first names if I like them and think that they are fundamentally good people. I think that you have identified exactly the point for which we had been searching and it was located thanks to you and you alone." she said smiling at him. The smile made him feel good.

****

Willie was pacing and could not control his nervous behavior no matter how he tried to apply the techniques that he had been taught since he was a very young boy. Each time a new tragedy had struck Willie found it more difficult to recover from the anxiety and high stress situation, especially ones where he had created the stress, those were extremely difficult for him to maintain control. The idea that the project could be delayed because of a lack of computer processing was not acceptable to him. He wanted to scream he wanted to find the person responsible and tell them they were incompetent. He believed that things needed to be made right and soon.

Gregory Lee was in the process of listening to his unit manager explain when they could expect the power to be stabilized. What he heard was that the draw from the cooling towers was extremely erratic and fluctuated in ranges that drew the power down faster than that the regulator system could compensate for the draw. This caused the computer to sense a failure and it initiated a shut down. The problem was not the design of the power systems but it was brought about due to the very unusual design of the cooling towers.

"What do you suggest?" Gregory asked. The man looked at him with blank expression. That did not give Gregory confidence and he wanted to pack up and go home today, not spend another day underground dealing with this problem. "Do we have another generator?" he asked.

"Yes sir, we actually have two others." the man replied.

"Great, let's wire a second generator to the computing system outside the cooling tower power loop. Give each one their own discreet power source and that should solve the problem." Gregory told the man.

"Yes sir, but that will take some time to do sir and we need to be certain that the power fluctuation module will continue to work with a second generator in the grid." he replied.

"I know there are issues but it's the only way we can get this done without having the cooling tower technology replaced and that could take…. a very long time." Gregory stated. "Get going, now!"

****

Barnaby was instructed to get Roger and bring him into the conference room where he could join the meeting that Adria and his brother had been having for almost two hours. Roger reluctantly left his work area feeling he could be spending his time getting the coding done that was to be used to import historic data into the an array for processing that was almost too large to imagine. Every time he had thought he had accounted for all the variables necessary to make a predictive calculation, he found another one and the snooper program he had written was doing its best to add every little jot and tittle to the process. There was so much to consider when trying to predict what will happen next, he thought.

Roger spotted his brother before Philip noticed him. He knew that he was going to be joining them but was not certain when and it was a great thrill knowing that his brother was also working on the project. The only person missing now was Austin but he knew that he had nothing that he could bring to this project. Roger walked through the door smiling.

"Phil, I am glad you could join us. We need you to get us going in the right direction." he said extending his hand.

Philip was not completely surprised to see his brother, this was the type of project that would have intrigued him and he had been told that he was working on it. The need to create a program that so sophisticated and required such elegance in design that if Roger had known about it he would have found a way to participate even if he was not sought after to work on it. He was also certain that his brother had been recruited, just as he had been and that there was no coincidence, everything had been planned. The question that was unanswered was who the person that was pulling the strings, the person with the agenda?

"Roger, I knew there had to be someone with some computing expertise behind the scenes. The next thing you will tell me is that Willie is here as well." Philip said. He knew that he was, Adria had mentioned it and only had said it to feign ignorance.

"You couldn't keep him away. Dad's here working on the power for the new computer, I got a chance to see him for a while yesterday but he has been working very hard trying to solve a huge problem today and I haven't seen him at all." Roger said.

"Roger, Philip is here to help us to select the starting point you have shown us that we needed so that we may begin to model those elements that must be changed to ensure the proper end results. He has come up with the exact starting point we need and I am going to ask him to summarize it and then I would like you to provide him with a list of variables that you will need in order to successfully input the starting point into the program." Adria said.

Philip gave Roger the overview that Adria had requested and he provided him with additional information that he thought would be enhance his brother's understanding of the precise moment in time that he was recommending. Roger paid close attention to what was said and as Philip approached the end of the explanation he asked a question that while not germane to the immediate problem was something that he had begun to recognize as a need for the success of the project as a whole.

"Will you be working with us during the testing phase?"

Philip looked at his brother. He hadn't realized that he had been given a choice as to whether he would participate. For some reason he thought that this was a government project and that his participation was mandatory.

"I assumed that I would be working on the project as long as I was required to be here. If my participation is optional I believe that this will be the last time you will see me engaged working toward completing this project's objectives." Philip answered his brother directly.

"Phil, it would be a big help to me to have you here. We will be modeling the impact of actions on the time line and when we encounter the next decision point I would like to have an informed opinion as to where to go from there." Roger replied.

Adria simply watched the two brothers discuss the project on personal terms. Each one was participating for their own reasons. She had known that there might be need to employ additional leverage to keep Philip engaged.   If Roger failed to convince him to remain and actively participate then Norville could be quite compelling even though the circumstances of their first encounter were not pleasant.

"Roger, haven't you wondered why we are all involved in this project? Doesn't it seem unlikely that a group of people would be assembled to change the course of history in such a way as to alter the current power structure? I would say that if Austin was involved in this project then there would be no doubt as to who the author of this mystery is." Philip asked rhetorically.

"Phil, I am here because this is the biggest challenge in programming I have ever seen and it is certainly larger than anything I could have previously imagined. You are here because you are an expert on the time period that they need.   What does all of this have to do with the overthrowing of the banks and Justin Welsh?" Roger asked him.   He needed to understand how he made the connection.

"Gentlemen, you are both right.   This project has been created to change the world and with that change will come a shifting of power. The power will no longer be with the banks, but that is a byproduct, it is not the purpose. The purpose is to improve the human condition. We are all here for our own personal reasons. The primary reason I am here is to prove my theories on time and process. Roger is here to prove that he can solve the biggest puzzle that man can envision at this moment. Leopold Jenkins wanted to create an African American country by using the split of the two countries and an eventual revolt that would create an opportunity for the black man to live in dignity and peace." Adria said and stopped and gauged Philip's reaction to the statement about Jenkins. "Yes Philip that was left out of the information that you were given." she said not knowing that Philip did have that piece of the puzzle.

"Adria, are you telling me that I was recruited for this project just as everyone else that is here was enlisted?" Philip asked.

"Yes, and you should not look harshly at those that were involved in the seduction, they were recruited as well. We all play a part in a very complex series of events that culminate in this moment in time, the place within the process of life." Adria stated.

"It is interesting that you used the term seduction." Philip responded with a sneer.

"Oh come now Philip, the young woman was the perfect means to get your attention unless we could have found a way to have a train compel you to participate. She was seeking someone to help her heal from the pain of the loss of her father. You were perfect because you were able to give her what she needed a means to validate her father's existence. She loves you for it, more than you know." Adria replied. "You must recognize that we are all interconnected in some fashion and those connections occur as part of this grand process called life."

Philip was not convinced that he should continue helping them. He thought that he would finish the day and give them what he could for his brother's sake but he did not appreciate being manipulated and being thought of as a cog within a very large machine. He knew that as long as his father was here that he would have means to leave so long as they didn't use force to detain him.

Roger saw Norville approaching and did not react to his arrival. He wanted to get the most out of his brother's visit and the background information that he had received was important the successful modeling of the scenario. There were numerous data bases to which he would need to be interfaced and he was in the process of making a list of the ones that he had not been aware of prior to the meeting.

"Philip are the archives at the Cross University Information System accessible using the UTRA protocol?" Roger asked.

"Yes and you can use that method when you interrogate the Pennsylvania State Archives System as well." Philip replied and then as he was about to continue speaking he saw the reflection of Norville as he was entering the room. He slowly turned and their eyes met.

Norville smiled but Philip did not return the smile. "Doctors Lee how are you today?" Norville said looking first at Roger and then again at Philip.

"Good Mr. Forrest. Philip has been giving us exactly what we need. Now if our father can solve the power problem we will be ready to begin a very long arduous task of testing the theories." Roger said.

"That's great, thank you Dr. Lee. When I was told that you would be the perfect man for the job I had my doubts. I know your family very well and I saw you as being very resistant to working on something that did not have a direct immediate bearing on you and those that you care about." Norville stated.

The comment went to the heart of what he felt about Philip's unwillingness to help others if he did not feel it benefited him. It was an attitude that he saw when he witnessed Philip's failure to assist his brother Austin when he reached out for help before he fell into the conspiracy. Philip loved Austin but only so much. Philip also loved Jessica and this was the area where they would have to see if he had changed, he thought. We need to see if reading his cousin's journal has had the impact that it has had on Roger or even Austin.

"Dr. Lee we do very much appreciate all that you have done. I am certain that you have some questions that you would like to ask me and I will ask that Adria and Roger give us the room for a little while so that we can speak candidly. Do you agree?" Norville asked.

"Mr. Forrest I really don't think there is much to gain by going through the situations of the past. Let me finish helping my brother and then I can be off and you can finish your project." Philip replied.

"But Dr. Lee we need you to work with us for at least the next several weeks. We have very tight time constraints, or should I say process constraints." he said as he looked at Adria and smiled. "Please allow me the chance to enlighten you and when that is completed and if you should still wish to leave I will have a car take you home immediately."

Philip felt that he had only one answer that he could give that would preserve his image as a fair and open minded individual, it is an image that he has cultivated and did not wish to tarnish.

"I am always seeking new information and am open to learning whenever possible." he reluctantly complied.

Adria and Roger excused themselves and left with the understanding that he meeting would continue after Norville and Philip had the opportunity to clarify some information.

"Philip you must understand that this plan has been in effect for a very long time, roughly six years, and that there are people that have lost their lives as a result of this effort. I would like to start by first apologizing for enlisting into the program the way that we did. It would have been far better for all of us if we were able to come and ask you to participate or even to order you to do so out of a sense of duty, but we both know that you would not have responded favorably. Things have to be done on your terms, don't they?" Norville asked him without showing any emotion or condemnation, for he was stating fact.

Philip looked at him and nodded but said, "I am not an unreasonable man, you make it seem that if you don't ascribe to this fantastic cause that you are somehow not doing the best..."

Norville interrupted asking, "The best for whom?"

"I am not alone in thinking that we must take care of ourselves first before we can be concerned about any other's well-being. I have a history of helping people, including both my brothers and of course Jessica." Philip responded almost as if he were pleading.

"No one has accused you of being a bad man or one that does not work well within the confines of society. You are like the vast majority. That does not make you evil or bad but it doesn't make you who you could be. Were you put here to do things only when it was convenient to do them?" Norville asked.

"Take a look around at the people that you pass every day. Are they as blessed as you are or is it easier to not see them and to continue on with a blind eye to the fact that they do not have what you have, they do not have what they truly need." There was no reply. Philip was trying to understand why this man sounded so much like he was reading Christopher Leesop.

"When I started this cause to change society the reason for changing it was all about me. I wanted to avoid my financial loss that would have occurred because of the adaptation of the one world currency, the IMC." Norville said staring at the floor. "Six years ago a group of high spirited young men lead by an old, foolish and greedy one took on the banking system in an attempt to stop the conversion of the currency. Everyone except that old fool went to prison for their actions, they all paid a very high price. The old fool was left to think about what he had done and what could have been different. Philip we have actually met more than once before. Your brother Austin invited you along to a party that I gave at my home. It was about eight years ago, I think and it was only a very brief meeting since Melinda was behaving poorly and Austin elected to leave abruptly." Norville said and then waited for Philip to remember.

"Justin Welsh, you are Justin Welsh." he finally said. "I knew you looked familiar when I saw you at school. I just could not remember where I had seen you before. So this is the new plan, the one where you stop the banks from taking everything?" Philip asked. Philip saw that Norville was disturbed by his question.

"Do you understand what will happen if we are successful Philip? There will be nothing that is as it is right now, all will be changed. There is a significant likelihood that people that we know will not be alive. That many people will not be born in the new time thread. It is believed that people that emigrated to this country during the end of the Nineteenth and early Twentieth Centuries would not come here and if you were the product of a marital Union between whose parents met here there is little chance that they you would have come into being. I am such a person, you are not." Norville finished speaking and waited for a response.

"Why should I help you? You have indicated that I am selfish and self-centered and that I would need a reason to help that served my purposes. I can think of nothing that fulfills the requirements." Philip stated and prepared to end the conversation.

"What about Jessica? Do you care enough for her to put your own interests aside or better yet are you able to understand that someone's best interest may in turn serve your best interest?" Norville asked.

"What does Jessica have to do with this? She was apparently used to be gain access to me and you apparently then applied pressure to my employer so that I would have to write a paper and it coincidentally happened to serve your interests. I am almost certain that you have something to do with Senator Sun's medical treatments since there is little possibility that the government would have gone to such great lengths to keep him alive. I don't know why some of the things that you have done were done but I can certainly see that you had a hand in many activities surrounding my life as of late. It is not a comforting thing to discover that you are simply a pawn in a much larger game." Philip stated indigently.

"Philip are you so blind as to not see that all of us are just simply very small pieces in a very and large complex puzzle. You may not see existence like Adria does, but you must admit to your relative importance or should I say lack of importance." Norville countered.

"Jessica became involved as you know because she was trying to fill a hole in her life, a large gap created when her father died. I owe her father a great debt. I have attempted to help to fill that hole but I am not able to do so. So far there has only been one person that has come close to meeting that need and that is you."

"If what you say is true, then my place in this melodrama is at her side not here helping you find the perfect places in time so that you can destroy the current time line." Philip said.

"Why do you think you are able to fill that hole Philip? It is not your staggeringly good looks nor is it your tender nurturing personality, it is your intellect and your ability to help have her father's life mean something other than the lunacy that it has been credited to have been built upon. Even now the paper that you have published has reflected poorly on his image. It has placed you in a position where you are highly regarded because of the construction of the paper, which was masterfully done, but it deflected the all negative imagery to Leopold Jenkins while the positive light was cast ever so brightly on you Philip. It is only a matter of time until Jessica sees this and then you will no longer be her knight in shining armor but another carpetbagger making his way to success on the back of the black man." Norville punctuated the statement with a small tap of his fist on the table.

There was another period of silence as Philip thought about Norville's comments. They were not true, he was simply trying to manipulate him into continuing to help with the cause, to provide them with the meaningless pieces of historic trivia the likes of which he had stored in his head like a squirrel that has hoarded so many nuts that he can't even recall where he hid them all.

"Philip don't you see that the only way you can hold on to Jessica is to follow through on her father's work?" Norville asked.

"If she cares about me as a person and not someone that is trying to be her father then she will understand that this is a dangerous project to be associated with and I am not willing to risk my career and reputation over something as frivolous as this is." Philip stated.

"I see, so as far as you are concerned Jessica's feelings are to cater to your ego. Is that what you are saying?" Norville asked, but before Philip could answer he continued. "Philip this could be your last chance with her. I know the woman and I know what she needs at this time. I also believe I know how you feel about her and what you are feeling does not match the words that are coming out of your mouth. She is on her way here, today and I believe that if she does not find you here she will take news very badly." Norville said thrusting the issue back into Philips lap.

"Why would you bring her here? This is not fair..." Philip whined.

"Philip she is part of this and if you want to help her heal, you will stop thinking about yourself and start thinking about others; Jessica, your brothers and all of the people that this will help." Norville said and then he stood.

"I think you need to think this through and I will call the others back so that you can continue to work through today's issues. If you decide not to stay I will make a car available for you in about two hours, that should be enough time for you to have helped Roger and Adria and still get you out of here before Jessica is due to arrive. Okay?" Norville asked.

Philip nodded and Norville turned and left the room. Outside he encountered Adria who looked at him with inquiring eyes.

"You have him to work with for the next two hours, beyond that I do not know what he is thinking. I tried to appeal to the one thing that might be able to penetrate his fear but I am not certain that his feelings for her are strong enough to overcome the paralysis from which he suffers." Norville explained.

"I do hope he decides to join us, it would make things quite a bit easier." she said.

Roger walked back into the room and saw that his brother was deep in thought. He wondered what Norville had told him, he also thought that it would be so much easier if his brother cooperated and help them with the problems.

"Philip I can't tell you how much I appreciate what you have done today. It has made finding a solution to this puzzle a reality, thanks." Roger said sincerely.

"Roger do you know who that man is?" Philip asked.

"Yes, I know who he is and I know what he is doing. Do you honestly think that there is chance that he can manipulate time and change history? I know that I don't think that the efforts here will yield that result but what I do think is that we will make some amazing strides in computer processing. The impact on human kind will be amazing. I believe that we will see improvement in all aspects of society, just like what happened during the 1960's with the space program. The return was not in the trips to the moon it was in the other technology that was developed and how it help improve the quality of life for so many." Roger said.

"When did you become such an altruist?" Philip asked his brother.

"I don't think I am being altruistic I believe that I am doing what is needed to improve things not just for me but for everyone. Who knows, I could decide to get married and want to have a family and when that happens I can't see leaving this mess for my children to clean up, a mess that I refused to do anything about fixing." Roger said.

"You have a long time before you should be thinking about marriage, but I see your point. I suppose I should consider staying and helping you for a while." Philip said with a weak smile. "But only if we can see some results out of the information I gave you earlier."

"That shouldn't be a problem, if our father ever gets the power stabilized I will be able to show you what you gave us and what it means from a programming standpoint. I have had team working on coding since you started giving me information. At this point we have about thirty percent of the data input that we need and the corresponding coding is about twelve percent completed as well. If I wasn't certain that it would crash the existing computer I would run the simulation as it exists just to show you how awesome this process really is." Roger said beaming.

****

John had received a message from Juan regarding a meeting to take place where they would outline the new strategy for destabilizing the Banking Consortium. This meeting was to be in several hours and he requested that both George and Austin attend the meeting if possible. Juan made a point of stressing that it was important to attempt reach out to Austin and impress upon him how important his presence would be.

"Austin this is John, I was hoping that we could get together this evening for a little meeting. One of my relatives is in town just for tonight and it would be good if you could meet him I think you both have a lot in common. Call me as soon as you get this message. Thanks." John said and he disconnected the call and then placed the call to George who indicated that he would make the meeting.

****

The call to Austin had been monitored and Foon called Kate to let her know about the attempt to reach Austin regarding a meeting. She was confident that Austin would not attend but did not want to tell anyone that she believed that he would choose her over any meeting.

"Mr. Devers we have reason to believe that there is going to be a meeting between two of Austin's friends and a representative of the Monks this evening. They are attempting to have Austin join them but Austin is scheduled to meet with me. What action should I take?" Kate asked.

"Do nothing, if he cancels then we will follow him and if he doesn't we will monitor the meeting regardless. Keep me aware of any developments, we need to find Justin Welsh soon, time is running out." said Devers who disconnected the call only to place another to Girard to inform him of the meeting.

****

"So what do you want me to do? I think that this surveillance is getting us nowhere. I have this feeling that we are being shown what we want to see. Are you sure that this guy Lee is going to lead us to Welsh. Welsh is no dummy, ya know." Girard told Devers.

Devers did not want to hear Girard's opinions he just wanted results and not high profile attention like the operation had received the past twenty four hours.

"I need you to follow the leads that we have and not worry about whether they appear as though they are going to yield results. I know that Welsh has his hand in these events and it is just a matter of time and we will get the break that we have been waiting to see materialize. Let me know what happens." Devers said completing the call.

Devers turned and stared out the window. What if Girard was right and the Lee connection was just a distraction meant to keep their attention on someone that was not even remotely involved in whatever Welsh was scheming. Was that even possible? No, he thought, it wasn't possible, Lee had been such an integral part of his past operations and there was such a substantial effort made to get him released, that he had to be important.

****

John and George were concerned that Austin had not returned their call but they also knew that he had to be very careful since there was a good chance that his conversations were monitored. George decided to give Austin one more chance to join them. He called and when Austin did not accept the call he left a message stating that he was going to be at the Berlini Club having a drink with friends and that he should come out and join them. Now Austin had the information as to where they were meeting and if he could be there he would, George was certain of that.

Austin had received both of the messages and understood that both men were telling him about a meeting that most likely had to do with some plan that was being hatched to undermine the banks. He was past that cause now, he had been tempted to join the last time that they were together but it did not seem to make sense any longer. He was more concerned about people and their feelings and helping those people that he could have a direct impact on their lives. He felt that helping someone like Jake would be a much better course of action, he was someone that did not need to go back to prison because he couldn't find a job. There were thousands of people like Jake. He knew that there had to be more that could be done and if he could help even one person it would make his life seem more meaningful. He decided to share this with Kate when he saw her. He sensed that she would appreciate what he was doing.

He then thought about returning George's call, he had been a good friend over the years but he decided that all that would accomplish was to get his blood pressure elevated and the conversation would end badly. It would be in his best interest to focus on the positives that he could accomplish if he set his mind to it. He decided to go to his room and read. He knew just the thing that would help to keep him following the right path.

****

Kate was nervous, she wanted it to be later than it was. This could be a big day, there could be clues as to where Justin Welsh had been hiding and perhaps this man from the Monks would lead them to him. She also envisioned that Austin would no longer be directly involved in the operation and perhaps he could be eliminated from the surveillance all together. Then she wondered what she would do regarding her feelings for him. She was drawn to him, he was someone that was worth having in her life, so long as he wasn't doing illegal things. She was thinking that she was now a free woman, no longer married since her husband was for all practical purposes dead. Those thoughts caused her to feel guilt and sadness. Her sons would no longer have their father in their lives or the hope of ever seeing him again. How could she emotionally push aside her marriage of nine years and forget about all Michael had sacrificed for them, giving his life for his family and country.

****

Juan took his wife and son into the bedroom of their small apartment. He looked at them both and said to them, "I need you to understand what I am about to tell you and that there is no way that I can change things. Okay?" They both nodded their heads and Maria eyes betrayed the fear that she anticipated with the next words to come from his mouth. "Maria, I have to go to a meeting in two hours, at the end of that meeting I am to be arrested. I will be put in jail for about a week and then I will be released. It is important that I know that you and Humberto are safe, so you are to go to your sister's and stay there until I get out. After this is done we will not have to worry about too many things any more. I love you both very much and if I could do things differently I would. Please trust me, okay?" he finished and looked away trying to regain his composure.

Maria stepped forward and hugged her husband tightly. "Juan you know we love you and we will be waiting when you are released. Humberto give your father a hug too." Maria instructed the boy. Humberto put his arms around his father's waist and hugged him tightly fighting tears, not wanting to show his father his fear and the pain of the impending separation.

Juan stroked his head and then freed himself from the boys embrace and bent to look him in the eye. "I am very proud of you son." he said with a smile. "Take good care of your mother."

****

"Whatever you do, no one is to be hurt as a result of our actions. Is this clear? We do not use the same tactics that WBOI does. We do not kill people without having a reason." the captain said to his team of six men and women. Each one was dressed in the brown uniform of Internal Security and they didn't know why they were given the tip to act upon but they were certain that the source was credible and that they needed to become more active in the war on terror now that WBOI appeared to be acting with impunity. They could not tolerate an independent entity conducting their business at the expense of the safety and well-being of the country's citizens. The team gathered their belts including their weapons. Each team member knew their assignment and they also knew that there would be risks.

"Remember there is a high probability that WBOI or their agents will be present at least in surveillance, should we identify the two men that were seen leaving the scene at the Zoological Society then we should be prepared to apprehend and detain them for questioning. If they use force you are authorized to respond in kind using the minimum necessary to ensure your safety and that of the public and your team. Good luck." the captain said and turned to tend to his gear.

****

"The operation is scheduled to commence in one hour and forty minutes. You must have your crew in place so that this can be recorded in the best possible light." Worster told his photo-documenter.

"I will be on the scene in thirty minutes and no one will know that we are recording this until they see their faces on the news." Milton replied.

"Okay, I will see you an in about an hour. This should help the ratings a little and maybe get me some better assignments." Worster said ending the call.

It was a good thing that Internal Security was seeking to improve the public image otherwise this operation would have been executed without so much as a whisper of what was to transpire. Worster was unclear as to why he received the call but it did not change the facts that he did get the call and it was through an official outlet, not some back door where you could simply be a pawn in someone's political battle. This was an attempt to show the public that murders like the ones at the Zoological Society would not be tolerated.

****

Kate stood waiting at the train station for Austin to arrive. His train would be at the terminal within the next five minutes and she felt her heart pounding in anticipation of the evening. She was taking him to her apartment, that was to say Melissa's apartment. Foon had coordinated an evening meal and the time together was designed to provide her with another opportunity to deepen his commitment to her and she was to attempt to find out if he had been in contact with Justin. If he had been in contact that would be the break that the surveillance was supposed to generate. Kate's intuition told her that Austin was not directly involved was continuously the center of her thoughts. She wonder whether it was just wishful thinking because she found him attractive. She lifted her small frame on her toes to see a little better down the rail bed. She thought she heard the sound of switches actuating, which was the prelude to the arrival of the train. She was right, it suddenly burst into view. The evening's events were about to begin to unfold.

****

George arrived first and decided to sit at the bar. He did not order an alcoholic drink instead elected to have sparkling water that was served a half a degree above the freezing point. If he drank it fast enough it felt like small razor blades dragging their way down his throat, he thought. He instead sipped it, the cold numbing his mouth quickly. It had its desired effect of lowering his body temperature which was elevated due to his time outside. John had chosen the place because it was always very crowded and there were at least seven exits that could be used in the event that they would have to leave quickly. There was no reason to suspect that they would have any problems this was a preliminary contact, a dry run so to speak. Other meetings would take place after they became comfortable with each other and each time it was hoped that they would be able to share more information.

George saw John arrive. He made no attempt to get his attention, he watched as John moved through the dense crowd. He noticed that John took a moment to appreciate the beauty of a woman that was standing in his path. He then pushed past her smiling. George was trying to see if anyone appeared to be interested in John and his movements, and from his vantage point there did not appear to be anyone watching.

John spotted George and worked his way toward him, stopping periodically to see if there was anything unusual about the people in the crowd. It seemed like a typical night with a great number of people milling about drinking and attempting to find some place where they could recover from their day.

"Hello George, is our friend here yet?" John asked.

"Not to my knowledge. Never did hear from Austin, I suspect that the woman he is seeing has distracted him. It is so typical of his level of commitment." George responded. George felt a tap on his shoulder and turned to see Juan looking at him.

"Good evening Mr. George and Mr. John, how are you two gentlemen this fine torrid evening?" Juan asked.

"Torrid? That's a good way to put this weather." George replied with a smile. Juan did not return the smile, he was preparing himself for what was soon to happen.

The two men that had been at the Zoological Society were standing on opposite sides of the room. They were the back up to another team of three that was located near the three men. It was the man closest to the main entrance that spotted the Internal Security team member enter and when he went to alert his team members he felt the stick of a sharp object in his ribs. He turned and saw another Internal Security team member standing next to him with his weapon pressed against the man's ribs at point blank range. There would be no chance to warn anyone. He placed his hands on his head and awaited instructions.

The primary team noticed that there was something wrong when they lost contact with their back up and before they could understand what was happening they saw three members of Internal Security rush forward to the bar area where George, John and Juan were standing and they grabbed the trio, put them in restraints and ushered them out of the building. The team attempted to disburse in hopes of getting out of the club without being detected but there communications equipment gave them away and all three were apprehended as well.

"Milton did you get all of that?" Worster asked hopefully.

"Oh yes, the best scene was when they popped the first guy. They actually shoved a weapon into his rib cage. I got a great close up of his facial expression when it happen. I have no idea who these people are but I am sure you can sort all of that out. The video will be in your mobile file within the next couple of minutes. I am going to go home and put my feet up and wait for the praise to come rolling in from our management group. That is the best stuff so far this month, maybe this year." Milton replied.

"Good work, I will call you later after I have had a chance to put it to bed." Worster said feeling very happy with the results.

****

Foon was standing on the street outside of the club. It was very hot and she did not want to be there but something had made her feel uncomfortable about going inside and when she saw the Internal Security team come out of the club with eight prisoners she thanked her intuition for keeping her from harm's way. "Katherine, that party that Austin was invited to attend, well it was crashed by some Internal Security people and they arrested eight people and I think five of them were ours. I will call you later. Oh and I will leave the call to Devers for you to make. I value my hearing." Foon's message was clear.

****

Austin sat down on the couch after the two had eaten. The conversation during the meal was light and each one related a couple of amusing anecdotes from their childhood. Kate had struggle to find two since most of her memories were not fond ones. Her parents had a strained relationship and she always felt that she was the cause of the turmoil in the household. Austin found the conversation with the meal to be uplifting and he felt that he was getting to understand Melissa a little bit better. After they had finished they moved to a sitting area that surrounded a small circular pool which had at its center an oscillating fountain that was bathed in changing colored lights. The water played a melody on a series of resonating bars that lined the pool and as the water made contact each bar it sung out its tone in a quiet whisper. It was soothing to watch and to hear.

"Austin, what are you thinking?" Kate asked.

"I was just about to tell you about an invitation that I received earlier today. Two men that I know have been attempting to get me to participate in a plan to overthrow the Banking Consortium and they were meeting with a person tonight and wanted me to attend the meeting. Needless to say I didn't attend, I value our time together too much and I am not that person any longer. I don't want to overthrow anything, all I want to do is help people reach their true potential." Austin replied.

"What about that man that should have gone to jail but didn't, Jason, uh... what's his name, was he involved in this meeting?" Kate asked.

"I don't know. I haven't seen Justin Welsh for a long time and I don't really have any desire to see or hear from him at all. I don't think what he was trying to do was the right thing. Though perhaps he has changed and we all deserve a second chance, or maybe more." he said with a chuckle.

"Melissa, I am done with the illegal activities I am dedicating myself to helping to heal those that are in pain. I am not sure what my next move will be but I am confident that the opportunity to help will be shown to me when the time is right." Austin said. He searched Kate's face for some sign of approval and all he saw was confusion. She did not know what to do with the information that he had just given her. Now she was certain that Austin Lee was a blind alley in the search for Justin Welsh.

"Oh, I promised you a surprise, and here it is." she said revealing a small black box she had been concealing in her hands.

"What is it?" he asked.

"I hope you like it. I just wanted to give you something that told you how much you mean to me." she said as he opened the box and revealed a small platinum pin with his initials A. L. It was the type of gift that one gives someone when you are trying to impress upon them how much you care for them. Austin was stunned.

****

"Roger, it's your father. I have some good news, you should be able to start your computer simulations in about an hour. I suspect that is a mixed blessing since the simulations that you are developing are bound to take a significant amount of processing time to complete." Gregory said advising his son that the power problem had been fixed. He did not tell him that they had used a second power transformer to accomplish it and that there was more power being generated in the facility then it took to operate the city of Baltimore. Still he was relieved to have solved the problem. During the conversation he learned that Philip was at the facility as well. Gregory was pleased but not surprised. He told Roger to pass a message to Philip that he hoped they could get together and talk about a few things as soon as possible.

"Dad, the first simulation is a comparative one that will run the against the current time line and the second run will utilize the data from the new scenario and compare the variances for a period of one day, one week and then one month. The end result should give us a large number of modeling opportunities. The time to run the first compilation is roughly seventeen hours. So I am going to send most of the people home along with Philip. I think if you two travel home together that could give you a good deal of time to talk through any issues that might be on either of your minds." Roger said while looking at Philip. Philip gave him the thumbs up and they made plans to meet in two hours to depart for home.

Chapter Twelve

"Gregory did you see the news? There were arrests made yesterday evening at a club in Pittsburgh. The two of the men were local businessmen and the third was a reputed member of a criminal gang called the Monks. It also seems that they caught the two men that were responsible for the murders at the Philadelphia Zoological Society this past weekend. My there hasn't been this much excitement in a very long time." MacKenzie said.

Gregory looked at her as she continued on with her commentary about the state of American society and the lack of compassion for our fellow man. As he looked at her he was reminded of what it was that had drawn him to her those forty years ago. His thoughts were interrupted by Austin joining them.

"Good morning Mom, good morning Dad. Did everyone have a good night sleep?" Austin asked.

"I slept great because your father was home. Did you hear about the terrorist that were arrested yesterday in a club in Pittsburgh?" MacKenzie said as she then repeated what she had said to Gregory.

Austin couldn't believe that George and John had been arrested. He watched the story unfold on his PCU and it seemed almost surreal. The event looked almost staged and poor George and John looked so frightened. He knew that he had to help in some way. John had a wife and a child and George had a fiancé. They would be in shock and would need as much help as could be found. So often there was no one to help the people left behind. He felt helpless and needed to find a way to help.

"Dad can I speak to you alone for a moment?" he asked. MacKenzie smiled and got up from the table and excused herself. She knew there were times when the men needed to talk and she tried not to take it as a personal affront, she saw it as a chance for Austin and his father to work on some problem together. As soon as she was out of earshot Austin asked his father for his help. He explained that he knew George and John both. They had invited him to the meeting and he had declined, he was not going to involved in illegal activities, he was tired of hurting people, he only wanted to help now.

"What kind of help do you want from me?" Gregory asked.

"I don't think it would be wise to reach out with direct help to the men, but they have families and loved ones and if there is some way we can reach out to them and give them some support we should do it." Austin said.

Gregory looked at his son and thought about the ordeal that they had gone through when he was arrested. The public humiliation and shame that they had felt. They were assumed to be just as guilty as Austin was in the minds of many of the people that they knew. Vilification was a term that no one should have learn about through first-hand experience.

"I know a couple of things that we can do and I know someone that you should include in this mission and that is the woman that just left us alone." Gregory said.

He then call for MacKenzie to join them and Austin shared the story once again, this time he prefaced it with the fact he had hurt his mother so much that he did not want to have her concerned that he might be doing something that would cause her more pain. MacKenzie grasped his hand and told him that originally all she ever wanted for her sons was their happiness, but in the past years she had modified that to reflect what she felt was a more appropriate desire for their need for contentment accompanied by a sense of fulfillment. She saw this blossoming within him and she was very proud of him.

"Austin if you can get me their names and contact information I will reach out to them and I know some women that would welcome the chance to comfort those that are in pain." MacKenzie said.

Gregory too offered to do what he could and said that he had one individual that he knew that would help. He planned on calling him later in the day.

"Thank you both, I am not sure how active I can be in this area but I need to do something too. Dad do you have any suggestions?" Austin asked.

"I suggest that you meditate on it and I believe that you will discover what you are supposed to do." he replied.

Austin thought about the advice and promised to do just that. He rose from the table and went to his room to prepare for his day at work, but before he did he sat and quietly reflected on what had happened.

****

"Mr. Devers this is Kate Foster I have to report that our operation in Pittsburgh last evening was an utter failure based upon what I saw in the news and from what Foon has told me of it. I also did not have the kind of success with Austin Lee last evening that we were hoping to attain." Kate said and waited for the screaming to begin, but there was silence. Kate had spent the better part of the night tossing fitfully in her bed trying to determine whether she should not include what Austin had told her in her report to Devers in the morning. She came to the conclusion that she would tell him. There was a good chance he would think that he was just being secretive and that they should continue the operation, a thing that Kate very much wanted to do.

She also thought about the possibility that the feelings that she had for Austin were nothing more than a displacement of the feelings that she had for Michael and that she should not be fooled by a false attachment that was based upon an attempt to cover the feeling of loss that she was surely experiencing. More introspection yielded no clear feelings of loss that were based upon her needs, only the needs of her boys.

"Foster the operation did not go well last night but there is a very big positive in its results. It could force Lee to have to reach out to Welsh since his friends are now trapped in prison on some trumped up conspiracy charges. This actually could finally be the break we were looking for in the surveillance. Now what was so terrible about your conversation with Lee?" Devers asked.

"Lee told me that he has not been in contact with Welsh for a long period of time and he had no intention of contacting for anything. He was not interested in participating in any illegal activities." Kate told him.

"You haven't been doing your job. Your job is to make him want to reach out to Welsh for whatever reason. Find a way to make him want to impress you like he did with that Melinda woman. That is why we made you in her image so that he would want to please you just as he did with her. Do you think he was some radical political social activist? He was just some horny man trying impress a beautiful woman. He will do the same with you. Do your job Foster." Devers said emphatically. The words rang in her ears.

"Alright Mr. Devers I will continue to move him forward to contact Welsh. While I have your attention, have you heard anything regarding my husband's status?" Kate asked. Her question was met with silence, she wondered whether he was even on the line since his habit was to make statements and to disconnect the call. She then heard a sigh and Devers cleared his throat as he emitted a low guttural sound.

"Foster we have not been successful in getting him back as of yet. I receive updates daily on the situation and as soon as I have news, regardless of what it is, I will inform you. You have my word that we are doing everything possible to ensure his safe return. I must be going. Keep your eye on the objective, we must find and apprehend Welsh, he is the key to everything, the end to all of these wars." Devers said as he disconnected the call.

Was Welsh really the key to everything, she wondered. If Austin wasn't the evil man that they portrayed him to be by their own admission, is it possible Welsh was just as innocent? Kate's doubts were beginning to overwhelm her and she needed to focus on the safety of her family, her boys. If Welsh could be apprehended and the war did end perhaps Michael would be returned as well. She repeated those thoughts a number of times until she began to formulate a plan to ensnare Austin and compel him to reach out to Welsh for help.

****

"Gregory it was good of you to call. What can I do for you?" Norville inquired.

"It seems as though two of Austin's friends were arrested last evening and he is concerned about their families and he wants to help them." Gregory responded.

"I see. There are a lot of innocents that get hurt in these situations. What do you think I can do about this?" Norville replied with a question. He had already taken steps to ensure that the families would be provided for while the men spent the next five to seven days in jail.

"Whatever you can Norville. I understand that you make decisions based upon what is best for the cause but there are people's lives involved and isn't that truly what the cause is about?" Gregory asked rhetorically. "I just wanted you to know that MacKenzie will be contacting some of her friends to reach out and provide comfort for those that were affected. Do the two men know their purpose in this event?" he asked.

"No, they don't and they probably never will. I am hoping that the experience will cause them to modify their approach from this overt revolution nonsense that they have been espousing and cause them to evaluate their circumstance as a more ephemeral challenge. They must begin to look at that solution as a change of man's heart and not his financial status." Norville said.

"Easier said than done Norville. I am sure that Austin will appreciate anything that you can do to lighten these people's burden. On another note are the two computer scientists happy with their new toy?" Gregory asked.

"Oh my yes. Roger was especially please and I must say proud of his father's accomplishment. I do thank you for your effort, we all do." Norville replied. He then went on to explain that the results of both test should be apparent within the next several hours and that it appeared that Philip had also had a change of heart and would be returning to help for the foreseeable future.

Gregory had already known Philip's intent as they had spent more than an hour together talking about the mission and his involvement. He had told Philip that he had been working with Justin for the past four years ever since he discovered that Justin was a follower of Christopher Leesop, something that he had become shortly after Austin's arrest.

Philip had told his father that he was confused by the situation and that he did not have strong conviction to want to help the cause. He felt that helping Roger was important but he explained that there had been so many activities that had taken place, each of them meant to push him closer to participation in helping the cause. He then told his father of his desire to help Jessica and the responsibility that he felt for her well-being. Gregory appreciated his son's feeling and told him that these orchestrated events were not the work of just one man, they were the events that were predestined to goad him into following the course his life was meant to follow.

Philip could not believe what heard coming from his father's mouth, it was as though he was reading the journal to him. The discussion then became entirely focused on the teachings of Christopher Leesop and Philip tried to make the discussion an intellectual debate and all Gregory did was counter with practical application of his teachings. Philip saw clearly that his father was a changed man. He wasn't exactly sure when this had happened but it must have been as a result of Austin's arrest and the separation from him while he was in prison.

The call ended with Gregory thanking Norville and the assurance that something would be done to help those that were suffering. Gregory walked out of his study and toward the kitchen. MacKenzie was making calls in an attempt to bring as many of her friends to help as she could manage. She saw Gregory approaching and knew that he was getting ready to depart for his day at work. He had not been in his office in several days and that usually meant that he would be working late. It was for this reason that she told her friend that she had to call her back and ended the call.

"Come here." she said as she pulled him close to her.

They embraced and kissed. They found comfort in each other's arms and a reassurance that life was as it should be. "I know you will be late this evening, just try to take it easy. There will be plenty of opportunities to solve problems tomorrow as well." MacKenzie said with a smile.

"Have I told you that I love you lately?" Gregory asked.

"All the time, just not with words so much." she said.

"Have a great day Kenzie." he said and turned to leave.

"You too old man." she said with a laugh.

****

A car was waiting for Philip when he arrived in Lancaster. When he started to explain that he would be missing from his classes for the next several weeks, the Dean simply smiled and told him that they understood and that he should not worry about anything. Most of the students would be relieved that he was not there since two of the courses that he taught this semester were required and the students were only there because they had to attend the class in order to fulfill the basic degree requirements. The other courses were predominately independent study now and he had only to meet with them once a week. He shifted the meeting times so that he could continue to attend those meetings and insure that the students received the proper attention.

Before he knew it he was on his way to Maryland and knew that he would not be back on campus until next week at the same time. Perhaps the project wouldn't need him any further by then, though he suspected that there would be a great deal of information that they would need from him. As he settled in his seat for the one hour plus journey he thought about the brief encounter with Jessica last evening. She seemed so thrilled to see him, much more than he could have imaged and when she discovered that he would be staying on to assist with the project she couldn't stop smiling, that was until he told her that he would be leaving for the evening. It was a disappointment he did not want to experience again. She said that she understood and that she would be back to see him in two days and that she hoped that they could spend a great deal of time together. This did not seem to be the person that was so difficult to understand just a few months ago. Perhaps he was over thinking the situation. She had been under a great deal of stress, we all have been he thought.

The name on the road sign indicated their arrival at Magdalla Maryland, population two hundred thirty four. Philip believed there were at least twice that number residing in the subterranean project center. He thought that this was an interesting little town that betrayed no evidence that there was even a rail line that came to an end which should have enabled it to grow. It was obvious that it was not supposed to be noticeable and that it was not supposed to grow in size or attract attention. This was in an innocuous location that was something other than what it appeared to be.

"Great to see you Philip." Roger yelled out across the large room, at which point everyone working stopped to see who had arrived. Philip waved hello.

"We had a fantastic success as far as the programming goes and as soon as I can get Adria here we can start to look at what happened and plan our next move." Roger enthusiastically reported.

"Good, maybe this will be an easier task than everyone initially thought." Philip replied optimistically.

"No way brother, it looks like it is going to be even a little more difficult than I thought but I can visualize how we can do it and that makes it exciting." Roger said beaming.

"I will need a moment to freshen up and then I will join you in the conference room." Philip told his brother.

Fifteen minutes later the three were together. Adria did not know what Roger was going to say about the test, she had been in meetings most of the morning regarding additional resource requests which were summarily rejected. "What do you have for us Roger?" she asked.

Roger began with a brief summary of the process so that everyone understood how the base line had been determined. He explained that he had the entire world history's events reduced to mathematical statements. These statements, billions upon billions of them were to be used as check to validate assumptions based upon probability of occurrence and 'plain old dumb luck' as he put it. This process was not as daunting as it might appear since most of the data had already been up loaded during the past thirty years as part of the recovery from the Technology World War. If the war had never occurred the likelihood that they could be sitting here at this stage of the test was very remote.

"So, if I understand what you have done so far is to upload all history from the period of time that we are influencing forward ending with today's events?" Philip asked.

"That's close but we actually loaded the complete history that we have and that dates back to about the year 1424 at this point. The reason for this is the more data we have to utilize, the more likely the prediction will be closer to being accurate." Roger replied.

After he finished with this element he explained that a program that applied the predictive element was run against the change that was made to the time thread and the results were measured on an immediate, twenty four hour impact as well as one week, one month and one year to see what the effect it had on the time thread at those times. If the effect was significant the program would be run again on a decade by decade study to see the trend as it unfolded.

"So what happened Roger? The suspense is driving me to distraction." Adria asked anxiously.

"The change that was introduced by adding a suitable forged document giving Robert E. Lee valuable intelligence had an immediate impact that showed tremendous potential but because there were no subsequent actions the outcome of the battle was that the South did not prevail but instead the battle of Gettysburg did not have any real significance." Roger stated.

Philip then stated that when they had been discussing the likelihood of this message being successful it would have to be followed up with a series of actions. The movement of J. E. B. Stuart's cavalry would have to occur twenty four hours sooner and it would have to be in support of Ewell's portion of the first day's offensive. Also, it would be necessary to have Longstreet believe that his forces could win the day by acting swiftly and not by his usual slow and deliberate approach. He needed to be more like Stonewall and take the battle to the enemy and not wait for the enemy to come to him.

"Philip that is exactly what we expected would be necessary. We anticipated that there would need to be anywhere from five to twenty independent adjustments that would have to be made to create a sustainable time thread alteration. Our next step is to discuss the changes that occurred and to determine the next change point and then run the scenario again from the beginning. We will then compare the result with the initial iteration and determine whether the point we have selected and the action associated with it are in keeping with the objective." Adria stated.

"Adria that means that we could actually defeat the changes by whatever we elect to do on subsequent alterations?" Philip asked.

"Philip, that is most definitely true. It would not be uncommon for this to occur if the programming performs like that which has been used in the manufacturing sector to simulate product evolution." Adria replied.

"The challenge is at multiple levels because you must be able to interpret the data that you have received as it relates to the projected time thread. Once you have accomplished that you must guess, for lack of a better word, what change or changes will yield the best result that will eventually produce the outcome that you are aspiring to achieve." Adria elaborated.

"Guess?" Roger asked rhetorically. "We are scientist here, we hypothesize!" he said with a laugh. They all joined his laughter which it became a much funnier event then it should have been as a result of the significant tension that had been building because of the weight that each step represented. Any opportunity for release was welcome.

After they regained their composure Roger started to review the results of the test. It seemed that the change had caused Lee to accelerate troop movement northward toward Gettysburg via the Emmitsburg Road. This movement created an imbalance and the Northern units under Reynolds were unable to compensate for the influx of troops and the apparent flanking maneuver that occurred as a result of that action. The Union troops withdrew to the east and established a perimeter that they held until the Hancock could position the balance of the seven Corps at his disposal.

This created a stalemate that put Lee at disadvantage and fearing the rumor Pennsylvania Militia providing addition reinforcement from Harrisburg Lee elected to retreat back into Maryland to fight another day. The results of the war were the same, but they were delayed by one year and that came about because of the fall of Vicksburg and the failure of England and France to recognize the new country. The South lost once again.

Philip listened to Roger's summary and it made perfect sense as a potential scenario. Roger completed his review by stating that it had a seventy two percent chance of being the outcome. At that point Philip suggested that two things be considered, one would be to consider destroying the orders that name Meade the replacement for Joe Hooker, the general that had lost at Chancellorsville, and thus have a leader that was not as competent as Meade, or change the substance of the note and move Stuart's cavalry forty eight hours earlier to a position where they could engage Buford. The first day was to take place as it did just make certain that the Seminary Ridge was taken by Ewell's troops and that they get the high ground. That enabled Longstreet to fight the battle as he wanted to do so, defensively.

"Phil I think your original starting point is an excellent one and that we should hold the line and continue to jump off from that point. How can you move Stuart's cavalry to support your plan of action?" Adria asked. Philip thought for a moment and he pictured the man. He was flamboyant and he wanted to be the center of attention. He also could not resist the invitation of raiding the Union supply lines.

"We could give him faulty intelligence that would lead him to the place we desire him to be by allowing him to believe there was a cache of Union booty there to be plundered." Philip told the two with eager enthusiasm. He hadn't thought about the characters as people in a long time. This was the stuff that made a book like the 'Killer Angels' come alive for people that did not know the conflict or the historic figures.

"This sounds like a good place to begin the second effort. We will make two changes in the subsequent time thread after our initial change. How long will it take to make the adjustment and to run the test Roger?" Adria asked.

Roger paused for a moment and did some very quick mental calculations. "I will need to know how many variables will be added specifically. It sounds like three changes each with multiple variables such as specific time and location and the item or item or actions that are the catalyst for the change." Roger replied.

"Philip when can you have the specific information that Roger is looking to insert into his program?" Adria inquired as she bounced her attention from one Lee brother to the other. Then she said something that seemed to be completely out of character, "You boys don't need a referee, handle this and get back to me before you push the button. I just want be able to say that I knew what you were doing. Of course if you need me I am only a call a way." With that she rose from her chair and walked out of the area leaving Philip and Roger looking at one another.

"That was odd." Roger said.

"Very." Philip responded and then began to detail the changes he was suggesting. He reached into his briefcase and pulled out a tube that had contained all of the maps of the campaign that he was able to locate. Stuart's precise location could not be determined due to the fact that he was not following orders during the days that lead up to the battle. He was interpreting the directive given to him with his own agenda as the primary motivating factor and not that of the commanding general. Since he was later killed in action he did not have the opportunity like Pete Longstreet to justify his actions and to deflect blame in other directions.

Philip took the mention of Longstreet as an opportunity to add a bit of information that would he would later use as the basis for another alteration of an element of the time line. He went on to say that he was not implying that Longstreet was not a fine general, but he had moments, like most men, when he was less than convinced that a course of action was appropriate. It was widely believed that the level confidence that one has in a plan can be, in large measure, the determining factor of whether it can be successfully executed. Any doubts that he had during the battle could have made success that much more difficult to achieve. That lack of confidence in the offensive nature of the campaign had him moving more cautiously then Lee had hoped would have been the case.

The maps Philip provided outlined the most likely location of Stuart's cavalry and it was decided that a large wagon train of munitions was suitable enticement and would get Stuart to move to the desired location. The intent was for him to emerge on the left flank of Buford's cavalry at the instant that Heth's division encountered them. This would reduce the level of losses to Heth's division and put them in a position to push the Union back. To support the flow of the battle it was also determined that Ewell would be given additional incentive to move his troops more quickly to join the fight. These two pincers should enable the Army of Northern Virginia to control the better ground and an opportunity to highlight Longstreet's strength as a defensive strategist.

Roger looked at Philip and said, "This looks like a good test to me. Let's give Adria a call and see what she has to say about it." Philip smiled and nodded. He was still trying to think of other variables that might, if introduced, yield even more favorable results. They had come up with four changes and each one had very special location, time and items that had been defined. They sat facing each other not saying a word waiting for Adria to arrive and give her blessing to the test criteria.

Adria took several minutes after listening to Roger give a summary of the events that would be altered before she responded. After that she asked a question that she had asked before but had not received an answer. "How long will it take to input the data and make the appropriate changes to the code and once that his completed how long will the program have to run before we know what the results are?" she asked.

"It will take about an hour to input and code and then about three hours to run. Once it has run we will need another half hour or so to put the output in readable form. All total, a little less than five hours." Roger replied.

"Get going and we will meet back here at four o'clock to discuss what we found. I am hopeful that we can get another run done today. Philip start thinking about your next potential changes. See if you can guess the conclusions that the system will reach." Adria said with a smile.

****

"What are we supposed to do with these three men? We have no evidence linking them to anything. While two of them clearly know each other, the third man, the alleged gang member, doesn't know them and they don't know him. The only connection we have is what we were told by the anonymous tip." Freidman said.

"We can hold them for a couple of days but I am inclined to let them go now. The good news is that we do have the two that killed the man at the zoo and the other three are somehow linked to them because of their communication gear ties them together. I want to charge the two with murder and hold the others and see what happens." Logan replied offering his opinion regarding the operation.

"Okay we will let the three go and keep the rest. If nothing else it will irritate the people at WBOI since I know that there is a connection with at least two of the people that we picked up. The killers have been known to associate with Girard and he has a connection with Devers at WBOI. I am not certain what they think they are doing over at WBOI but it is time for them to understand that they do not run national security and if they get in the way and we can prove it, they will be in jail just like anyone else that breaks the law." Friedman said agreeing that they should release George, John and Juan.

Processing took less than an hour and the three men were on their way to the respective homes no one saying a word to the others. It was quite clear to George that this was the end of his radical days, he thought to himself wondering how Austin was able to endure five years of that humiliation, he was there less than fifteen hours and he knew he never wanted to experience anything like that again. His wife and child would be a welcomed sight and hopefully she would find a way to be understanding and forgive him for any pain that he may have caused her.

Juan stopped at a small convenience store on his way home. The owner was a friend, or more accurately said, he was a brother. He acknowledged Juan and asked if he could be of assistance. Juan asked to use his PCU and the man offered his glasses to him without hesitation. "Maria, its Juan. I am out, it went much better than I thought it would. I will be home within the hour. I just wanted you to know." he said and then he turned to the man and asked for his code so that he could disconnect the call and leave the message.

"Esperanza." he said. Juan smiled at the man and ended the call.

"Bueno." he said and walked out into the heat. It did not seem to be quite as uncomfortable knowing that he was on his way to his home.

****

Devers was not certain what he should do now. This was the first time in his recent memory when an operation had gone so poorly. They had been set up and Girard had foolishly used the two men that had killed Unger at the Zoological Society just two days earlier. The others that were present had ties to the security team at WBOI and Internal Security would be able to link them to the two men. The only action that had worked well was the one taken to keep the information about a possible connection to WBOI out of the public's view, but it was just a matter of time before something more would have be reported about the apprehension of the two men that had been charged with Unger's murder.

Devers had to act quickly and decisively, should he not make the right move his position within the bank might be at risk. "Hilman, this is John Devers at WBOI calling. How are you today?" he asked.

"John, I think I know why you are calling. Can we sit down over lunch and talk about it?" Hilman Scott inquired.

"That's exactly what I had in mind. Where would you like to meet?" Devers asked.

"How about I come to your office and you have your lovely girl Samantha get us something special to eat. I do so enjoy seeing her." he said with a little too much enthusiasm.

"Sounds like a perfect lunch to me. Let's say in two hours?" Devers responded.

"Great, I will see you then John. Tell Samantha that I am counting on seeing her." Hilman said but Devers had cut the call off not wanting to hear the man's voice. He is a pig he thought.

"Lewis!" Devers called out to her. Sam appeared at the door, poking her head in as she was accustom to doing. "Please come inside." Devers said.

His motive was to see how she was dressed and whether it would be enough of a distraction to Scott. He was a little disappointed in that she was not dressed as provocatively as he had hoped.

"Lewis, I need a big favor and I mean a big favor. Are you up for a challenge?" he asked.

"Sir, what do you need me to do?" she asked warily. Devers then explained that Scott was coming from Internal Security and that there was a need to make him as happy as possible. Sam did not need or want him to elaborate. She had literally fought off Scott's advances on two occasions and was not anxious to have to do it again.

"I am going to be sick and leave Mr. Devers." she said.

Devers sensed that he did not have the means to bully her into helping him so he resorted to offering her a bride. She respectfully turned down his offer for vacation time and even a raise in salary. This was not going to be easy. He then asked a final question, "What would it take for you to make Hilman Scott a happy man?"

Sam looked at Devers and then she looked at the floor. There was one thing that she wanted more than anything. She wondered if she had the courage to ask for it. If Devers turned her down she would have to tender her resignation it would be the only course of action she could take. She took a deep breath and then said, "Yes, there is one thing. I want to be transferred to another department, outside of the Security Division." There, she had said it.

Devers had not anticipated that request. He thought that Sam had liked working with him in the Security Division, it was where the power was and he was a very powerful man and that in turn made her a very powerful woman.

"Lewis is that what you really want? You have a good job here and I could get you more money and even a promotion." Devers asked her and then offered her more.

She held firm to her request for the transfer. She sensed that he was in a very difficult position and that if there was ever a time when she could manage to succeed in gaining the transfer it appeared to be now.

"Alright Lewis you can have your transfer if Scott leaves here a happy man and I manage to convince him to keep WBOI out of the investigation that is surely about to happen. I would suggest that you find more alluring attire if you hope to be successful in your mission." Devers acquiesced.

"The transfer will take place immediately, tomorrow. Are we agreed?" Sam pushed for a commitment.

"You will be transferred within one week. That is the best that I can offer. Take it or leave it and you must succeed. If not you are here indefinitely. Agreed?" Devers said firmly as he was not powerless and while he knew he had to accommodate Sam, he still had the ability to say no and let the drama proceed according to a more evolutionary path.

Sam excused herself and ordered lunch and then left the building to do a little last minute shopping. Devers had suggested that she modify her attire and had offered to pay for her clothing, so she elected to take advantage of the situation. She felt liberated for a few moments and then she came to the realization that she had to survive the next several hours with Hilman Scott, the man of a thousand hands and leering eyes.

The fact the Austin Lee was not at the meeting was weighing heavily on Devers mind. "Rasputin, call Girard." and the call was placed immediately. Girard saw the incoming call and did not want to have to listen to Devers one more time.

This was the third time he had called today but if he didn't take the call it would only get worse, more calls and then the screaming when he finally did connect with him. "What do you want?" he answered.

"I think we might have to de-emphasize Lee. There is something that is in the works but I don't think he is anything other than a distraction." Devers said.

"That's what I tried to tell you weeks ago, remember?" Girard responded.

"We have to leave Foster in place otherwise we may lose whatever advantage we might be able to gain. Do you agree?" Devers asked.

"Yeah, Foster has to continue. I think I might have an idea as to how we can bring Welsh out into the open. Give me two hours and if you could meet me it would be good- I prefer not having this going out over the air even though I know it's encrypted." Girard said.

"We will have to meet in about four hours. I am doing damage control with Internal Security for the next several hours. Same place as usual?" Devers asked.

"Yeah, I'll see you in about four hours." Girard said disconnecting the call.

Girard went to the window of the small office he had been renting as part of the inter-gang war covert operation. He saw two members of HA standing in the street two stories below. They were either intoxicated or were mentally impaired or both he assumed as he watched their erratic behavior in the heat of the day. These people are not worth the time we invest in them, he thought. Still they were what he was given as soldiers in a very deadly war. The Monks were so much more formidable then these violent thugs, they executed missions with precision and discipline, it was fortunate if the HA members remembered what was needed to be done to successfully complete a mission. That wasn't true if there were drugs or women involved, then you could count on them to be enthusiastic participants. The plan he was developing needed foot soldiers and these were the only foot soldiers he had at his disposal and as such they would be used. Fortunately the assignment had a woman involved and because of that he could count on them at least remembering to show up.

****

Devers took a moment to catch his breath as he saw a solution developing for both his immediate and long term problems. This could work if Girard's plan was credible. Unfortunately his teams have been very ineffective as of late and that could be because he was working on a mission that was being controlled by external forces, he thought. He also has that group of Neanderthals that were enlisted to start the war with the Monks, a war that they are doing their best to lose. It was all going to come down to Lewis' charms and Girard's plan. At least there were actions they could take to affect the outcome, he thought.

****

Kate was trying not to think about Austin and what was likely to happen should they decide to eliminate the surveillance. She would have to sever all ties with him and probably wouldn't be able to offer any explanation. It was her job and she had not anticipated what had transpired. When she took the assignment her only concern was getting her husband home and apprehending Justin Welsh. Now she didn't care if they apprehended Justin Welsh, for all she knew Justin Welsh didn't exist. Her husband's return was not likely and her boys would be without a father.

"Foon, its Kate. Have you heard anything about the operation? Am I still a go for this evenings meeting with Lee?" she asked.

"Katherine, you are running this operation. Haven't you spoken to Devers?" Foon asked.

"Yes, and he told me to stay the course. I also know that you speak to him from time to time and I wanted to know if you have heard anything to the contrary." she replied hoping to illicit some new information.

"My last conversation with him was about an hour ago and he didn't tell me anything other than he was expecting to be entertaining Hilman Scott for lunch. I do not envy Sam Lewis, he has harassed her on many occasions. I know you know what a pig Devers can be but this man makes him look extremely chivalrous and a gentleman in all situation." Foon explain.

"I don't think I would enjoy meeting him." Kate responded.

"I have met him and it was not a pleasant meeting." Foon continued. Kate asked Foon to meet her later just prior to the time she was scheduled to meet with Austin. She indicated that she wished to talk about how the operation might be headed in a different direction. Foon agreed to meet her.

****

Roger stared at the results of the test scenario and shook his head in disbelief. This can't be, he thought. There has to be a mistake somewhere in the code. He thought it best to re-run the code and set traps to 'compartmentally' run sections of the code to determine if they were performing correctly. The exercise would mean that they would suffer a two hour delay, but if the results were identical then it would mean that they were significantly farther along in the process then they could have imagined they would be.

The changes instituted had cause a ripple so large that the projected outcome of the war was significantly changed. It was not definitively determined that the South had won the war but the time line one year out had England and France providing both economic and military aid to the new country. This would have meant that the South had been recognized as a viable country and the spirit of the North was surely damaged.

The next step would be to run five year projection along with two decade projections to determine whether the results were indeed conclusive. Roger want to tell his brother that he had done an extraordinary job but it could be for naught if it did not hold up on the second run through. He placed the call to Adria explaining that there would be a delay and that they would meet two hours later than originally planned. She was disappointed but understanding, after all they were in uncharted territory and were writing the procedures as they went along.

Philip decided to take the extra two hours and attend to personal affairs. He had been remiss in making his payments for his commuter pass and his housing. He had received notices several days earlier threatening to suspend his rail pass. It wasn't that he did not have the funds, it was that he just didn't seem to remember to take care of those things. He also decided that he should make his PCU payment at the same time since it would be due at some point and this way he wouldn't have to worry about it later.

After he had taken care of the insuring his ability to have a roof over his head, travel and communicate he decided to contact Jessica and see if she remained as enthusiastic to speak with him as she was yesterday. It would not surprise him if she did not take his call. He was used to that behavior. One day it appeared that she could not stand to hear his voice and the next she was desperate to see him. This could be explained by the fact that she felt guilt in bringing him into the project without providing him a truthful basis of understanding. It made sense so long as there were no more wild oscillations in her temperament as it related to him. As the call was going through he wondered what he would do if she did not answer.

"Philip is that you? I am so glad you called I was just thinking of you and wondering what you were doing. Are things going okay? Is it still good that I am coming to see you tomorrow?" Jessica gushed.

"Yes, I am fine and very much looking forward to seeing you tomorrow. I had a few moments and I was thinking of you so I hope you don't mind that I called?" Philip asked though it was obvious that she was pleased to hear from him. They would spend the next hour talking about nothing in particular apparently just content to be talking to one another.

****

Willie and Avery had the results of their second round of tests and thing seemed a little clearer but they were not able to replicate what had been accomplished six years earlier using the controls that had been set in place. They had more powerful computers and what appeared to be superior programming, yet they had not been able to take the twenty minute step back into the past. Willie was getting more frustrated by the minute. He knew that what he had created should be working and he could not locate the source of the problem.

One of the technicians that had been standing by watching Willie become more frustrated decided to risk the potential backlash and interrupted with a question, "Are we sure that the initial test used harvesting technology or did they perhaps cheat a little and collect the photons directly? That wouldn't be much more difficult than using a video camera to record the event." she said.

Avery replied, "Could it be that simple? Are we building our platform on a substandard foundation?" she asked. "I hadn't thought to look there. Let's get out the documentation and see what they really did and not what we have assumed they did."

They spent the next hour dissecting the documentation that accompanied the images of the test itself. It was during the third reading of a subsection on controls that the truth finally was discovered. The scientists had taken a very big short cut. They did not utilize the harvesting technique that the team had been using as the basis for creating its model for testing. The blame for the failure rest with Avery and while no one was accusing her of being incompetent it was clear that she had missed a very key element having accepted the work of her predecessor as being thorough. She was clearly embarrassed.

Willie spoke first saying, "I cannot believe that these so called scientist were so intent on proving their hypothesis that they cheated. How are we to know if harvesting is even possible?"

"Harvesting is possible, I have done it and under extreme circumstances. The methods that I used were different than those that my colleagues had employed but it is now apparent that they were never able to make it work. Give me an hour and we can reconvene, I will have a plan as to how to move forward and recover from this significant setback." Avery said as she stood and turned to leave the room.

"Avery. This is not a significant setback if you have a means of accomplishing the same results utilizing another process. Can I do anything to assist you at this time?" Willie asked.

"No Willie there is nothing that you can do to assist me with what I have to do. You can however extract all of the coding that deals with the Harvester Interface and highlight its locations so that when I give you the new specifications we can be prepared to execute this as quickly as possible. As it stands we are looking at a delay that will be a minimum of two days possibly as long as a week." she said shaking her head and continuing to leave.

Willie called the team together and explained what had happen. They were visibly disappointed when they heard the news. Willie then praised Judy Wolpart, the associate that had asked the question that lead to the discovery of the nature of the error. He made the assignments for deconstructing the interface and explained that there would be a need to insert new code but there was no way to forecast how much would be required and where specifically other than the obvious interface locations. Once everyone was comfortable with what they were to do Willie adjourned the meeting. His last words we, "I expect a status report before each of you stop work for the day. Good luck."

****

Norville walked into Roger's work area expecting to see a flurry of activity as he and his team worked on the next time thread changes. Instead Roger sat in solitude watching his screen as the program ran through the final executions of its intricate code.

"Hello Roger. Where is everyone?" Norville asked. Roger startled by the words jumped slightly and then regained his composure.

"Oh hello Mr. Forrest. The team will be meeting in about an hour. I re-ran the program to make certain there were no errors. That action caused the meeting time to be delayed for about two hours."

"Oh, did you have a small set back?" Norville asked displaying mild curiosity.

"No, quite the contrary, the results were actually too perfect which usually indicates that there was some error on initial input. I reloaded the appropriate data and checked what I could prior to making the decision to re-execute the code. I started that little more than an hour ago." Roger explained trying to maintain a calm demeanor all the while wanting to do handsprings across the floor.

"It sound like your team is doing very well. I am glad that you have a few moments while you are waiting for the code to execute. Unless I am mistaken there is not much you can do unless and error is flagged or you the there is some failure or another, you have the next hour free. Is that right?" Norville asked.

"Yes Mr. Forrest I am just here pacing the floor like an expectant father." Roger replied with a chuckle.

Norville smiled and then continued. "What I am about to discuss with you is extremely sensitive material and no one can know about it. I mean absolutely no one." Norville said with a very serious expression on his face.

"I understand Mr. Forrest I will certainly keep whatever we talk about in the strictest confidence." Roger replied.

"Good, and please since we are going to be working with each other and I hope will be friends please call me Norville." Norville said warmly.

"Fair enough." Roger replied.

"Have you ever heard of the project 'Good Hope'?" Norville asked.

"No, it doesn't sound familiar." Roger replied.

"Let me tell you a little about it. It is a great story. Two years ago while a several astrophysicists were researching potential solar systems that might sustain life they made a fantastic discovery. They found a planet roughly fifty two light years from us that could sustain life. That was an amazing find, but it gets better. The solar systems is roughly three billion years old and significantly younger than our system." Norville could see that Roger had already anticipated the nature of the project.

"That's right, we are going there. The preliminary phase of the project got underway about six months ago and the scope is being defined. It has been determined that our journey to this planet will have to be on a grand scale. We will be building a ship that will house several thousand people." Norville waited to see Roger's reaction.

Roger, who was processing the information as rapidly as he could looked at him and said, "I want to go. I want to be part of it."

Norville who was not at all surprised then said, "We thought you might. So we will be in touch with you after you finish your work here.

They agreed to suspend conversations until after the Roger's involvement in the project was no longer required. Of the technology groups his would be the first one that will finish its work. Once effects of the changes had been forecasted and the program had been successfully run, there will be no need for his group to be actively involved with the project. The only thing that could cause him to be needed after that was the occurance of a catastrophic system failure and the likelihood of that happening was very remote.

****

Before Avery returned to Willie's work area she requested a private meeting with him. She indicated that she had reached a point in her research and she needed the opportunity to discuss the ramifications of the next phase of the process. Avery said that she felt that if there were an open forum there would be too many opportunities for debate to occur and since some of the team that was in place had allegiance to the theorists that had done the original experiment, there was the possibility that an argument would ensue. Any disharmony at this point could set the schedule back even further.

Willie agreed to meet Avery privately and made it a goal to have his area cleared of all team members. He reassigned his part of the time specific tasks to ensure a speedy recovery from the problem. Avery's people would not normally have cause to be in his area but he made certain that it was clear and that they were not to be disturbed. When Avery arrived she came in and sat down immediately. She looked tired and seemed to be teetering on an emotional break.

"Willie, I have the solution and it's going to take us a lot of effort to implement it. The entire interface was based upon the specifications for the extraction being accomplished using a subatomic laser knife to separate the layers of photons. The process does not work. The laser is too, for lack of a better term, 'thick' and it tears the photons, destroying the possibility of reading them. When I had done my research I used a micro burst electron wave emitter. This device causes the photons to vibrate apart and they are captured by an oscillating magnetic ribbon and then transferred to the induction film to be read." Avery had shared this with Willie assuming he understood all that she had said.

"I am sure what you are telling me is a viable solution, the interface, I am assuming, as it is written is useless and the new interface must be constructed using an entirely different technological platform." Willie replied letting her know that he grasped most of what she said but there were some gaps in his understanding.

Avery went on to explain the process in very specific detail and soon Willie began to visualize the interface and how he could marry the new technology metric into the programming that he and his team had constructed.

"I think I finally have it Avery." he said.

"I don't think I want to have my team involved in the implementation until the first run of test is complete. At that point I can illustrate a functional model and there will be little room for argument and revolt." Avery declared.

"Revolt, there can't be that much passion about a process that doesn't work." Willie said.

"I hope you are right. There are some very loyal technicians in that group and no one wants to think that they have wasted years of their life in pursuit of a false solution, an untenable cause." Avery replied and in doing so made it clear to Willie that his team would be working on this project with her only for the next several days as they managed to get the interface functional.

"I am going to send my people on a three day holiday and when they come back we can show them how well everything is working. Who knows maybe we will be done with whole thing." Avery said with a laugh.

Avery's team took the news with enthusiasm and left thinking that the cause of the delay was due to programming of the interface and not that the harvesting technique was not viable. As soon as they had left Avery and Willie called his team together and explained the problem in detail. Willie had devised a means of interpreting the magnetic ribbon that would ensure the integrity of the capture. The risk of overlapping photons or having them missed placed in sequence was very real but could be remedied once there topography was digitized. They could at that point place a sequencing tag on each fragment until it was aligned and using a process similar to that of a virtual programmable loom they were able to run these strands of photons back and forth on a carrier. Once the thread had been secured the tags could be reused and only two sets of tags would be needed for the entire process. "Jacquard would have been proud of me." Willie exclaimed after giving his discourse.

Avery commented on the fact he had managed to reference Jacquard and that it was truly inspiring and then she laughed. Willie smiled and never lost his place in conveying the message.

The team left energized and was ready for the work ahead of them. Willie hoped that they had the endurance necessary to complete the task because the challenges on the interface were truly daunting in his estimation. He was settling into his next design challenge when Norville arrived in his work area. He was looking for an update and had just come from Roger's area where they were interpreting the results of the past run and very optimistically believe that they had made a quantum leap ahead in there portion of the project.

****

Roger looked at the two summaries and the results were almost identical but the fact that they were not identical was troubling him. He was used to formulas where one plus one always equaled two, not two point one the first time and two point one, one the next iteration. It was very close and he needed an opinion as to what he should do. His natural instinct was to want to take the program apart and see what caused the variance. Was it an anomaly or was it something more significant a fundamental flaw with the design that would cause unpredictable results.

When Adria arrived to review the results she saw a man that was deeply stressed by something. It caused her to immediately conclude that things were not going the way that he had hoped they would go. She sat down at the table in the conference room quietly. Roger looked up at her and smiled a thin smile. He had three tubes in front of him and it was apparent that he was waiting for Philip to join them. Adria wondered what was delaying Philip and was about to ask Roger if he knew where his brother was when Philip entered the room.

"Why the long face brother?" he asked. He had learned through the years that his brother often saw problems and challenges that were not necessarily as severe as he envisioned them to be.

"I will do my best to explain the situation, though I am not certain what has happened." Roger said.

"Just tell us the results and what you see the problems are and we will sort through it together. Okay?" Adria said.

Roger went on to explain that when he ran the program the first time the results indicated that the trend toward success was at eighty one percent. "That's right eighty one percent." he reiterated.

"That is phenomenal. I can't believe that the results were that good!" Adria exclaimed.

"Neither could I so I ran the program again. I wanted to see if we were getting false results." Roger told them.

"What happened on the second run?" Philip asked.

"The results were almost the same. That's the problem they were not exactly the same." Roger said with the frustration apparent in the tone of his voice.

"How far off was it?" Adria asked with a smile.

"The first run was eighty one point six seven percent and the second run was eighty one point six four percent. That amount of variance is statistically valid and a problem don't you think?" Roger went on to further explain.

"Roger, the results are better than perfect. If you run that program a thousand times it will not yield exactly the same results because of the time that as transpired since you had run it last. As more time pass from when you ran the program initially things have happened. You are always comparing the new time thread to the present one that is the reason that it can never be the same." Adria explained.

"But the start and end time within the program are constant and the program should only deal with those specific variables." Roger argued back.

"Did you disengage the system clock?" Adria asked.

"No, I can't do that, the program will not have a valid ref... oh, I see." Roger acknowledged the gap in his thinking.

"This is fantastic. I didn't believe that we would be at this point in the simulation for several days if not longer." Adria exclaimed. "Where does the simulation start to show signs of inconsistency?" she asked.

"It is here, right after the charge made by Hancock's forces to the position that Longstreet's Corps held on Seminary ridge. It was almost a mirrored action." Roger stated.

"This is perfect, it is exactly the way I would expected the equation to be balanced." Adria continued. "When the processes of life culminate in there is a discharge of huge amounts of energy, such as the loss of life that took place on July the third, it is inevitable that the equal intensity discharge will occur. Men died on that day and it did not necessarily mean that the same men died in the new time thread, just that a large quantity of them did." Adria said resolutely.

"That makes no sense. You act as though this process that you talk about has rules under which it has to function, like that of the physical universe. There is nothing that supports this conclusion." Philip stated skeptically.

Both Roger and Adria looked at Philip and then at each other. To them the argument made sense there was an order and a balance. Life was set in motion like a spinning top and each wobble and dance that the gyrating dreidel performed was contrived, known in advance and it each movement must precede the others that are designed to function in series and those that were concurrent must be synchronized or else there was nothing. Life was not chaos and it was not meaningless.

Philip didn't want to argue about mysticism, he want the project finished so that Jessica would be free from the demons that currently haunted her and that his brother and these other people could get on with their lives and stop living and working on a fool's mission. The best course of action was to agree with them and sit back and watch the circus performance take place.

Philip decided to nod as though he was following their thoughts and believed what Adria was preaching. The message had a very familiar ring to it though, it was like he had heard some of this before. It must have been when he was talking with his father, who also seemed to be mesmerized by the predestination philosophy that Adria was chanting.

Roger interjected that there was need to start to determine whether another change to the modified time thread should occur at the time of the charge on the third of July. Also he suggested that once the determination was made that another run should occur prior to the insertion of the variable into the program for periods of five and ten years in to the then projected future. Adria agreed with his plan and then they both turned to Philip for insight into the change that would be needed at that junction.

Philip stated that it was important to have Lee prepare for the movement toward Philadelphia. This was the action that would accelerate the end of the war. As far as he knew from what the results of the scenario that had been constructed it had indicated that the war under the new time thread went favorably for the South but it was still not clear that the South won their separation from the Union. It was for that reason that a plan would have to set in motion events that would have the Army of Northern Virginia move on Philadelphia on the July the fourth, attacking the city on the fifth.

"Why is it so important that they head for Philadelphia instead of Baltimore or Washington?" Adria inquired.

"One of the largest anti-war factions was located in Philadelphia and the city, like New York and Boston, carried tremendous stigma. It was the second capital of the Union and the seat of freedom. There were virtually no protective fortifications and it would open up options to go either north to New York or south to Baltimore and Washington. I believe that the absolute best solution would be a minor assault on Philadelphia and a capturing of the rail lines and then the movement of a large portion of the army by rail south striking Washington and ending the war within three weeks."

"None of this was in Jenkins' paper." Adria complained.

"No and none of the changes we have used so far have been either." Philip contended.

"Jenkins' wanted a different result, he had a different agenda. In his scenario the South fights for several more years and then when both sides are beaten to a pulp like punch drug pugilists of old, the end result would have the black man in the position to finally have his country. The Confederate States would be the place that Lincoln envisioned when had wanted to move the black man back to Africa, Jenkins wanted him to have this country below the Mason Dixon line." Philip concluded.

Adria then replied, "Jenkins' scenario was the one that was approved as the mission. I don't know if we can use an alternate scenario. It was believed that his scenario would cause all of the changes necessary in

European history that will enable the Banking Consortium to never become the force that it is today."

"I don't think that Jenkins' scenario would yield the results you are looking for at all. The only way the banks do not gain their prominence is for the communist movement to be empowered and take their place. I firmly believe that they are just another form of evil." Philip responded.

"I am going to make a call. Proceed as though we are going to follow Philip's scenario. Based upon what I am seeing it appears that it is a superior solution." Adria said and she rose and exited the conference room.

She placed the call to Norville who was in the middle of trying to understand why Avery had taken all their previous work and discarded it in favor of another method of photolytic harvesting. Initially it seemed to him it seemed like an ego driven grab for control of the project but he was slowly being shown that the technology that was originally specified was inadequate for getting the results that they needed. Because he was being challenged by Avery when Adria called he was less than receptive to the idea of discussing changes to the objectives as they were originally designed. Adria convinced him to meet with her and the team after he had finished with Avery and Willie. She went back to the meeting and watched Philip talk about how he planned on influencing Robert E. Lee to send his forces to Philadelphia.

Philip went on to explain that when they arrived in Philadelphia the Confederate forces would commandeer rail transportation and use the Philadelphia Wilmington Baltimore Rail Road to convey a large force to Baltimore. After securing the city they would then take the B & O line into Washington DC arriving north of the capitol. In addition to this movement it would be important to have general Beauregard's corps to move north to demonstrate as though they were about to attack Washington across the Potomac this should cause the Union army to remain in its then current defensive posture and those troops that were arriving from the Army of the Potomac's encounter at Gettysburg would be thrown into the defense of the Capitol in a supporting role.

It would take the Army of Northern Virginia almost two full days to march from Gettysburg to Philadelphia. During that time the Union Army would be expecting them to turn south attack Baltimore and the on to Washington. The attack on Philadelphia will completely confound the military strategist since they do not see Philadelphia as having strategic importance. The reason for that was there was no military force located there and it was not the decision making location that Washington was.

Adria listened to the case that Philip made and it was very compelling and his early conclusions had proven to offer better results than the plan that Jenkins' had put forth in his theory. The only point that concerned her was whether the creation of an African American country was a necessary to ensure that the subsequent events unfolded as needed.

Norville walked in as Philip and Roger were working on crafting the intelligence that would be used to convince Robert E. Lee to move the Army of Northern Virginia to attack Philadelphia. This information would not be added to the program until the next iteration. It would be two or possibly three days before it could be tested and if so Philip had mentioned that he would like to spend the time working at Franklin and Marshal. He would be able teach a little and work with the independent study groups to ensure that everyone was preparing for their final exams that would take place in the middle of next month. Adria caught Norville by the arm before he sat down and lead him out of the room.

Adria proceeded to tell Norville of Philip's contribution and how he had made the very strong case that the Jenkins' scenario was flawed and would not yield the desired results. Norville listened carefully and deliberately avoided interjecting any opinion before she had finished. When Adria had done she had made it very clear that she felt that Philip had offered the proper solution and she asked that they be allowed to resume the tests with the scenario Philip had constructed. She awaited Norville's reaction and answer with some level of apprehension.

"Adria, our concern is to get to the specific end not to worry about the intermediate steps. If you think that Philip's scenario will get us there and get us there quickly I am one hundred percent with you." Norville said with a smile. "Let me hear what he has to say first hand I am certain that it is one heck of a story." He then turned and walked back toward the conference room.

"Norville, that was far too easy. I always thought that you were completely committed to the Jenkins' scenario and yet you abandoned it with relative ease. Why?" Adria asked.

"I just sat for two hours defending a process that does not work. We always believed that the group that conceived of the Photolytic Harvester was employing technology that they had tested and we found out recently that they miss-represented the technology's viability, it doesn't work. I think that is what you have just told me about Jenkins' theory, it sounds similar and I trust you and your judgment. The team members are brilliant and Jenkins' was focused on accomplishing something that was not a necessary part of our plan. The fact is that I am not sure now that we would have been able to reach the objective following that path. Philip has shown us a path that seems true and is on course for success. We will see where it goes. Right?" Norville said and then entered the room.

"Okay Philip, tell me how you have been able to put us a week ahead of schedule?" Norville asked with a big smile.

****

Girard called the two HA men into his office. They smelled bad, like day old beer and sewage and neither man had shaved in some time. They were very noisy as they walked in and sat down without securing permission or an invitation. These men were not the type that he would have chosen for this task or for that matter any task that did not involve violence. Still they had to look menacing and they certainly did look the part.

"Here is what you are to do. If you do not follow these instruction to the letter you won't have to worry about following any instructions in the future. There is no room to mess this up. This woman in the image that is being displayed on your PCU is to be abducted in front of this man. You are to cause this man a moderate amount of pain during the abduction but you are not seriously hurt him or by no means kill him. Do you understand?" Girard said directly.

The two men laughed.

"Do you understand what I am telling you?" Girard asked again. They laughed louder and then stood up and approached Girard in an attempt to intimidate him. That was a mistake. Girard took a weapon from his pocket and shot one of the men in the head. He dropped to the floor the smile still frozen on his face. The other man attempted to attack Girard and Girard simply trained the weapon on him and he stopped immediately. "Do you understand what I am telling you?" Girard repeated again for the third time and this time there was no laughter.

"You made a mistake doing that Girard." the man said and with that Girard shot him in the head as well.

"Marty get in here I have a mess for you to clean up." Girard said and then, "Get that guy Bone Man or whatever his name is, for me and have him get over here right away." Marty came through the door and saw the two men dead on the floor.

"The man's name is Bowman and he will be here in about twenty minutes. What should I do with his colleagues?" Marty asked.

"Leave 'em. I think they will make a great conversation piece. Don't you?" Girard said with a smirk.

"Oh yes I couldn't agree more. Do you want me to call in some additional support in case things get a little ugly?" Marty asked.

"No that won't be necessary. I think Mr. Bowman will be a reasonable man once he understands the big picture." Girard replied.

"Don't forget your meeting with Devers." Marty reminded him.

"Yeah, how could I forget a meeting with that man." Girard responded with a laugh. He sat down and tried to avoid looking at the two bodies that were stilling laying where they fell. It was very difficult to concentrate on much, they smelled as bad as they did while they were living, Girard thought.

Bowman arrived with two men that looked very much like the two dead men laying on Girard's office floor. His expression did not change when he saw the bodies but the two men with him assumed aggressive postures. Girard thought that it might have been a good idea to have back up after all and that perhaps he should start paying more attention to Marty's advice.

"What happened here?" Bowman asked.

"Nice to see you again Mr. Bowman. These business associates of yours were asked to perform a job and did not show the proper respect. You understand that it is important to be respectful in our line of work, don't you?" Girard asked as he grasped the weapon in his pocket. He was fairly certain he could kill two of them before they could get to him but if Bowman had a weapon he was certain that he would not be able to kill him before he could get off a shot.

"We have a job to do. It is a simple job but it requires that specific things happen and also that certain things don't happen. I asked your associates if they understood and all they could do was laugh. Then they thought it would be entertaining to try to intimidate me. That is not something that happens." Girard said plainly and with no emotion.

"Mr. Girard I am sorry that these idiots behaved so poorly, it looks as if they got what they deserved. What service can we provide for you?" Bowman asked.

Girard offered the men a seat and something to drink. He had Marty remove the bodies and as he did Girard began to explain the operation. It involved kidnapping Kate Foster while she was in the presence of Austin Lee. They were to assault Lee but not cause him serious injury and by no means was he to be killed. At that point in the conversation he asked if the men understood and they all said they did. The operation needed to occur within the following three hours but they were not to proceed until they received confirmation from him. The men agreed and stood up to leave.

"Mr. Girard, in the future do not take it upon yourself to discipline my people, we police our own. We don't take too kindly to people that act aggressively toward any of the brothers. This is your one warning, we will not be so understanding next time. If you have a problem with any of the brothers you call me. Do you understand?" Bowman asked.

Girard turned and looked away. "I will certainly give you the courtesy in the future, Mr. Bowman, assuming I am given the opportunity. Good luck I will be calling you within the hour."

****

Devers saw the time and was not pleased that Hilman Scott was still in his office, though it did not surprise him. Sam had been flirtatious and had kept him in a very good mood, but he had not yet agreed to bury the problem and it was almost time for Devers to leave so that he could meet Girard. He did not want to have to call Girard and postpone since Girard could decide to not meet with him which was something that he had done in the past.

"Hilman, I need this favor. Are you going to help me? We have made your time here very enjoyable. Have we not?" Devers asked.

Scott looked him and then he leered at Sam. "I would be inclined to help you if I was able to see things more clearly." he said with a wicked smile forming on his lips.

"I have thought that I made our position very clear, but I will..." Devers started to say but was interrupted by Scott.

"That's not what I meant. Samantha does that dress have a means to adjust its transparency?" he asked knowing that it did. Sam looked at him and blushed. She knew what he wanted and she also knew that it would be cost associated with her freedom from her position within the Security Division and under Devers' control.

"Yes it does. Why do you ask?" she asked coyly.

"May I see the controls?" he asked in return. Sam looked intently at Devers to make certain he understood that he would have to honor his commitment.

"Lewis I need to step out of the office for a moment to make a call. Please know that I really appreciate you keeping Mr. Scott company while I am gone and that the matter we discussed earlier will be taken care of tomorrow." Devers said leaving the office.

Sam understood that he expected her to cooperate with Scott but that he would be back before things could get out of hand and that he would honor his commitment to her. She took a deep breath and handed the controls to Scott who took them excitedly. Scott began to immediately play with the dials and it was soon clear that he had changed the visual settings to the minimum opaque setting. It was if she was wearing nothing in front of him.

Devers came back within two minutes and Scott was standing very close to Sam but not touching her. Devers could see that he had her dress setting at the minimum but when he realized that Devers was in the office he returned them to the maximum setting quickly.

"John, I think that your people, the three of them, will be released within the next several hours. It's obvious that they have done nothing wrong. As for the other two men, you have told me that you did not know them and as a result they will stand trial for the murder or murders we are not quite sure they did not kill the other man as well." Scott said.

"Thank you Hilman, the families of these people will appreciate that, as do I." Devers said.

"Samantha it was wonderful seeing you. You made my day. I hope to see you again soon." Scott said.

"Thank you Mr. Scott. I am glad that you were able to see what you needed to see." she said looking at him intently. Scott felt that she was not as enthusiastic about the episode as he had been.

He turned to leave the office and finished by saying, "John, you can send someone to pick your people up by seven. Okay? And please don't let them get caught in anything like this ever again because the cost next time will be significantly higher. Good bye."

"If it's alright with you sir I will be leaving. Where do I report to work tomorrow?" Sam asked.

"Lewis please take the day off tomorrow, paid of course, and I will have someone call you with your new assignment later in the day. I don't suppose there is anything that I can say to make you change your mind?" Devers asked sincerely.

"No, I am going to go home and take a long shower and hopefully wash the memory of today off of me. I will await the call. Have a good evening Sir." Sam said as she turned to leave.

"Thank you for your years of good service. I will miss you. Good night and good luck." Devers said as she walked away. Sam never looked back or acknowledged his comments. She now had to let the realization of her knew freedom sink into her consciousness.

Devers walked out directly behind her and he took an express elevator to his awaiting car. The Voltrun 190SC with its high priority clearance sped through traffic and soon was in front of a small cafe in the Bronx. He could see Girard sitting at one of the tables and with him was Marty. As he entered Marty stood and left the table leaving the two men to talk privately. It would not be a long conversation if it ran true to form. Girard hated to spend time talking, he was more interested in doing.

"Devers you are late." Girard said gruffly.

"I was delayed fixing that fiasco in Pittsburgh. Your people, the two men that took care of Unger are not going to make it out of this without doing some time in prison. I will make sure that it is the least amount of time and that they are compensated for their trouble." Devers said directly.

"Sounds fair. Here is the next move that I think will get us back on track. I am going to have two HA morons kidnap Foster in front of Lee tonight. They are going to beat Lee but not injure him severely. That should result in Lee reaching out to either his friends within the Monks or to Welsh directly. It should give us an active trail that we can begin to follow and find out what Welsh is really up to now." Girard stated and when he finished he took a long drink from the glass that was in front of him.

A waiter started to approach the two men but Girard looked at him and as their eyes met the young man realized that he was not needed and turned and went back to the kitchen.

"It seems like a good plan except for one possible wrinkle. What happens if he simply contacts the authorities? Based upon what Foster has reported the man is afraid of his own shadow and doesn't want to go back to jail under any circumstances." Devers countered.

"If he contacts the authorities Welsh will know and will come to the rescue. You know he was working behind the scenes to get Lee out of prison. He contacted him the day of his release, he can't help himself. He thinks of Lee almost as a son. I don't see how this can't be a winning situation so long as the HA guys do their job well. Oh, that reminds me I had to eliminate two of them for being stupid and you may hear about it but I had no other option, it had to be done." Girard added.

Devers thought for several minutes and Girard, being used to Devers and his methods of problem solving, simply sat waiting for the results of his cognitive machinations.

"Okay, I like the plan, but not tonight. Do it tomorrow evening and I want adequate back up to ensure that HA doesn't screw it up. If we hurry it then we can make mistakes and we have been plagued by them lately. I don't think we should alert Foster, and I don't want her to think that this is anything but genuine. We can use this later to our advantage." Devers said.

"What about Foon? Should we tell her?" Girard asked.

"No, not until after Foster is abducted." Devers said as he stood up.

"Good luck tomorrow keep me updated." Devers then said.

"This will get much better results than what we have been getting. You will see." Girard said as Devers left.

Chapter Thirteen

Philip had contacted Jessica to let her know that he was not in Maryland and would be traveling to Lancaster. He was hoping that they could spend some time together in the afternoon as they had planned. Jessica seemed enthusiastic about meeting and suggested that they meet in Harrisburg for an early dinner and perhaps they could go to a holographic theater for some entertainment. They agreed to meet and both began their days looking forward to seeing the other that evening.

When Philip arrived at school he was greeted with an onslaught of eager students and curious faculty. Morgan seemed frazzled and was not able to put together a complete sentence as he greeted Philip. It was obvious that he was glad that Philip was there for he could use the help. Philip could not help but smile at the chaos that surrounded him, it was a familiar sight and one that he always seemed to enjoy. When everyone else was panicking he could always remain calm and watch the events unfold with keen interest and a sense of amusement.

When there was a lull in the bedlam he took a moment to check his messages. There was one from a Dr. Simmons and at first he could not place the name but then he recalled that she was Senator Sun's personal physician. He wondered what she could possibly want.

In addition that message there were a number from various students and two from the Dean. He elected to delay returning Dr. Simmons' call until after his first class. He was curious but not so curious that he wanted to ruin his morning's fun with his classes. This type of call could only mean more drama. He heard the warning tone alerting him that the first period classes would begin in three minutes. He quickly left the office

413

and headed for the classroom, how would it look if were late after being absent from teaching for the past week. He entered the room to a full classroom as the tone chimed indicating that the class had begun. It was good to be here, he thought.

****

Juan was on a secure link to Venezuela and he was frustrated at the poor signal strength. He was having difficulty getting the message through and it was extremely important. Michael Foster needed to be moved once again and this time he was to be smuggled into the United States. This was a delicate operation and one that was going to require much more finesse than his people were typically capable of providing. He did have the best men working on the job and he was hopeful that it would be accomplished without a mistake. He could not afford to have him captured or hurt in any way. If only the Monks had experience in smuggling drugs or currency it would have been a helpful skill set they could have exploited but there was no such experience to call upon, he thought.

They would have to be certain that Foster was unconscious during the entire trip since he might have made noises that would have caused him to be discovered. The transport carrying him would be arriving at the intercontinental train station in Bogota Columbia in several hours. It had left San Cristobal late the night before and had been driving non-stop in order to meet the train at its departure time of three in the afternoon local time. The man on the other end of the call assured him that they would meet the train on time and that he would be loaded into a freight container that was filled with bananas. Juan disconnected the call and immediately placed another call to his contact in Laredo Texas, the point of entry of the trans-continental train service into the United States. The train was due to arrive at eight that evening after making two stops along the way.

Juan needed to be certain that the container would be allowed to pass through customs and he needed to provide them with the information of where Foster was to be sent next on his journey that would have him arriving in Philadelphia within three days. Once he was in Philadelphia he would be given to Truax to handle and the problem would no longer be his. He could go back to running the resistance operations in South America which was why he was recruited so heavily by the Monks. With a PHD in International Affairs from Princeton University and fluent communications in four languages, Juan was a formidable adversary on the battleground where WBOI typically fought. The political alacrity of an individual was the best weapon that one had when trying to combat the conversion of currency in a foreign country.

The cloak and dagger gambit was not his strength and he did not enjoy the high drama that always seemed to accompany these types of activities. It had been ridiculous that he had to be arrested and considered a common thug. The group that was running this operation was involved in very intricate manipulations in an attempt to stay ahead of both WBOI and the Government. He enjoyed a challenge but these types of challenges were a little too stressful. He was looking forward to getting back in a room full of politicians and convincing them that it was not in their best interest to convert to the IMC.

People outside of the Monk's organization had a very different view of what they did. Yes, there were times when they operated outside of the law and that was a reflection of their efforts to derail the currency conversion which was a subset of their larger objective which was to end the bank's choke hold on mankind. Even those that were allies did not fully understand what their mission was, and for that matter there were many foot soldiers that did not have the same insight and saw the Monks in the role of a traditional Latino gang.

The transport arrived at the terminus and the coffin shaped box that held Michael Foster was removed and placed among a group similar boxes, each bearing the symbol of the Brazilian Food Cooperative. BFC was the number one exporter of fruits and vegetables in South America and their containers were rarely inspected since they were considered above reproach. It had cost dearly to bribe the Operations Supervisor to enable this box to be inserted into one of the holds of the seven hundred cars on this train.

The biggest challenge was to get the box loaded, once it was safely inside it would not be disturbed until it was off loaded in Texas. The two men that were responsible for making certain the box made its way on to the train paced nervously as the automated insertion equipment moved down the line lifting and positioning each of the boxes into a slot in each car. The equipment was weight sensitive and each box had to be within a specific weight range for it be loaded without human intervention. The unit methodically approached and when it grabbed the box holding Foster it hesitated for a moment. This did not appear to be a good sign. There was a small whine and then an arm extended with a reader attachment. It scanned the label on the container and then was retracted. There was another whine and the unit slid the box into place. The two men looked at each other and smiled and then turned and walked away. They were finished with their part of the operation.

****

Austin was working on another attempt to find a favorable presentation of the very disappointing quarterly financial statements. It was clear that the company was not in good financial condition. As part of his exercise Austin created a model to forecast the state of the company in five years. The results of the model showed the company to have negative value and that the number was significant, so much so that Austin then developed a model to show when the company would cross over into an untenable cash position. The answer he discovered was four months. That was much faster than he would have thought possible and he then checked his calculations to determine if an error had been made.

He took a moment and collected his thoughts. He had a job today and that was all he really needed to worry about. There would be things that were much more pressing then the fact the company for which he was working was in serious trouble and needed an infusion of capital at the very least. Austin continued to work to find the source of the problem but the more he peeled back the layers of the financial statements the more confusing they became.

There was something that was not quite right he thought. He decided to run the same projection he had just completed against data that was twelve months old. When he completed the exercise he got a startling result. The company should have been out of business seven months earlier. There was capital that was being infused into its coffers though it was not in the form of sales revenues, debt or equity compensation. There was no explanation as to where the funds had come from and then there was another odd thing that he found. There was a drain on funds that also could not be explained. He thought that it was time to take his discovery to his supervisor and hopefully he could shed some light on what was going on with the books.

Roscoe Plantiere sat at his workstation monitoring his staff's activities and had stopped his casual observation and took a more attentive look at what Austin had been doing. It seemed as though Austin had discovered the heavily guarded secret, that the company was receiving and disbursing funds outside of its normal business operations. It made the company look anemic and it was therefore of no interest to serious investors nor did the banks spend any time considering it as a company worth following. The architect of the corporate structure was careful to do just enough to keep everyone mildly disinterested.

Now Austin had stumbled onto data that could be considered a red flag to others if he were to voice his concerns outside of his immediate chain of command. He would have to speak with him should Austin fail to contact him by the end of the day. It didn't take that long because as he looked up he saw Austin's head above the cubicles heading in his direction. Where to speak to him was the next challenge. He did not want others to become suspicious since it was clear that they had the same information as Austin for a significantly longer period of time and had not spotted the problem.

"Austin I was just going to call you. Let's you and I go to the break room for a moment. I want to talk to you about what you have found." Roscoe said.

Austin was mildly surprised that Roscoe had known why he was coming to see him but he also knew that everyone's work was monitored. As they walked Roscoe told Austin that he was very pleased with his work and the company appreciated all that he had done to help with the very difficult situation.

"Substance abuse problems in the workplace are fairly rare these days." Roscoe said. "Most people that are working are just happy to have a job and the level of screening that is done before hiring a person catches most with tendencies toward that type of problem. It is still a very large problem in society as a whole though. Don't you think that it is?" he asked Austin.

"I supposed so, I see a lot of people frequenting bars and clubs and they are not there drinking sparkling water. Though I had the super cooled sparkling water and that is an amazing drink because it lowers your body temperature so very fast." Austin replied in an attempt to be polite and relaxed.

The break room was empty as Roscoe had known that it would be. There were no scheduled breaks at that time and anyone that wanted to leave their area, except to conduct business, must seek their supervisor's permission and that included rest room breaks as well.

"Well I see you found out that the company is involved in the movement of external funds through its accounts. It is an attempt by the management team to help prop up another of their corporate interests so that it can be traded at a significant profit. I don't have to tell you that what they are doing is not one hundred percent ethical, but it is within the legal limits of activities." Roscoe explained.

Austin listened to what he had to say and did not comment. The explanation may have fooled a financial analyst with lesser skills but Austin knew that what was being done was not legal and there was no way that the types of transactions that were being done could help any business look more favorably financially.

"I am not certain that is what is going on here or at least it is not what I discovered. Perhaps you would like to see how much money we are talking about." Austin responded.

"I think that might be a good idea. Prepare a report outlined what you have found and have it on my desk by this time tomorrow. I will review it and take whatever actions are appropriate. Thank you for your diligence and your hard work Austin. We are very fortunate to have you working for us." Roscoe said and he turned and left the room leaving Austin who stood trying to determine what he should do next. He decided that he should go back to his desk and dig deeper to uncover all of the issues for if he was to prepare a report, it should be comprehensive.

When Roscoe returned to his desk he placed a call, "Mr. Truax it seems that Austin Lee has uncovered the financial inconsistencies." he said and then he disconnected the call. It was a brief message but it conveyed the nature of the problem and it was enough to get Truax working on a solution. Roscoe went back to monitoring the work of the employees and hoped that there would not be anything as trying as what he had already uncovered.

****

Roger's work area was very quiet. Missing was the low murmur of people working on programming problems. Instead there was a periodic low tone emitted when the executed code attained a generational milestone and iteration of the program. These represented years in the first phase of the test but then they were changed to reporting at five year periods and then decades. The scenario was to evaluate the conditions of the time thread after a fifty seven year period of time had been processed. If at the end of that time the program had reached one of three possible end points it would be considered a success and the testing would proceed to the next level which would be to evaluate the results based on a one hundred and twenty one years of time passage. If that proved to be successful then the test would be run to bring the scenario to the current date and one hundred and twelve markers were to be evaluated. The success of the program would be determined by how many of the critical markers were met.

The final test would be to project fifty years into the future. The final test results did not have markers the results were just to be interpreted. If the results were favorable then the scenario would be handed to the extraction team and they would be responsible for locating photolytic components necessary to achieving the start of the process and all subsequent introduction sectors. Once the project was surrendered to the

Light Team the need for future simulations would only occur should the harvesting of photons in a specific areas proved to be limited or unable to occur at all.

Roger sat and listened for each tone and once he had heard one he began to look at the results that had been produced. He would not be able to determine what level of success they had attained until the program had run completely but he did have a sense whether they were headed in the right direction.

The time passed slowly and he began to think about the entire project in wich that they were participated and the completing of the first section. He did not understand how the rest of the project could be successful. He understood that Willie and Avery were working on a means of extracting and reading photolytic components and he could see how that was to function. He also conceptually grasped the ability to graft an item into the created image. Then there came the breakdown in his ability to see how that inserting a forged element into the image would cause previous activities to spontaneously change and therefore alter the time thread permanently.

He saw this as being similar finding a fossil of an extinct creature and thinking that if you modified the fossils of dinosaurs by taking a chisel and altering the shape of the features of the fossil and expecting that to affect the actual animal's appearance several billion years ago. Roger just could not grasp how it could be done. He thought about contacting Willie to see if he could explain how it could work. Perhaps he was missing more information about the project. There really was no need for him to understand more than he already did. He could deliver exactly what the project called for him to complete without understanding or knowing what else would transpire.

Roger placed a call to Willie who was in the middle of a very sensitive transition. The adaptation of the code from one original interface to the new process and equipment was not proceeding rapidly. He felt as though with every action that he had taken there were more problems being uncovered. Willie wanted to talk to Roger but he just couldn't do it then.

"Roger, I am sorry I am really in the middle of a very serious problem. I will call you back soon." he said and disconnected the call. He knew Roger would understand, he had done the very same thing to him on numerous occasions. It was the nature of their personalities and their mutual desire to solve problems at the expense of everything else around them.

Roger decided that he would call Adria and see if she could give him some additional insight. The call went unanswered. He was now left with no one to talk to about his need to understand the project completely. He then started to think about the results of what would happen if the people that were alive today living in the current time thread. If they were of a lineage that was resident in the United States prior to the beginning of the Civil War then there was a chance that they would exist in the new time thread. If they were not, then there was a more significant chance that they would not. He thought about his lineage and felt confident that he would exist if they were successful. His thoughts then turned to Gloria and whether she would exist in the new time thread. It wasn't clear to him whether she would exist or not. He did not know enough about her ancestry. Now he wondered whether these changes would benefit him and his situation. These thoughts got him even more disturbed because he did not know whether it would make his life better or worse.

The tone interrupted the spiral of thoughts that had taken him to a very dark and dreary place of depression. He studied the data that was created by the second iteration. The effect of the changes on the time thread seven years after the date of the introduction of the changes. It seemed that changes had occurred as Philip had predicted them. There were two countries on the continent and they both had apparently been weakened significantly by the war and their attempts to rebuild their respective countries.

The president of the United States was George McClellan. Lincoln had not been re-elected and McClellan was in his second term. There were a lot of detail that had been produced that Roger did not feel inspired to read about. He wanted to return to the thinking about whether he was doing the right thing by helping to fulfill this mission. Norville had offered him a position on the Good Hope project and that seemed to be very appealing. But again the thoughts of Gloria entered his consciousness, what would happen to her if he left and went into space? What would happen to the space project if this project was successful? There was only one person left that he could call.

"Hello Roger, I didn't expect to talk to you until I came back to work with you in two more days. Is there a problem?" Philip asked.

"Yes and No. The simulation is running very well and your assumptions had been right on the mark. George McClellan became the Union president defeating Lincoln who did not win a second term." Roger said.

"That is very fascinating I can't wait to see how the whole thing works out. But I suspect you didn't call to congratulate me on doing a good job. What is troubling you?" Philip asked.

Roger started by explaining that he had doubts about the project and he knew that Philip did as well. He stated that he was concerned about what would happen in the event the project was successful. At that point in the conversation Philip laughed.

"I don't think there is a remote chance that this project will work. I do think that as you illustrated earlier that society will benefit from it though.   There will be the opportunity to weigh our decisions and see what will come about should we follow a particular path.   It will help to reduce risk of rapidly depleting our limited resources and should improve the quality of life for everyone. That's what I see happening as a result of what you and Willie are doing." Philip told him reassuringly.

That was just the right message at the right time for Roger to hear. He then told Philip about the invitation to work on another project that would take him away from the family, possibly forever. He saw it as a great chance to do something that would help a great number of people. Philip listened to him and then assured him that he should follow the path that he saw as the right one and should not worry about what others thought about his decision. Those that love him will want the best for him even if that means they will be without his company.

Lastly he brought up Gloria and he mentioned her for the first time by name. He did not know if he could leave her behind and he asked Philip what he would do under the circumstances.

"You are a little young, according to the customs of the day to entertain marriage but if you believe that you should spend the rest of your life with Gloria, then you should listen to what your heart is saying to you." When Philip had finished Roger thanked him though he gave no indication what actions he would take.

Philip had provided Roger with exactly what he had needed at that time. If he had spoken to Willie he would have gotten more depth of understanding regarding the process and it might have convinced him that the project could be successful. That conversation would have made him anxious and he never would have been able to speak about Gloria to Willie at all. Willie knew Gloria and he liked her but he had expressed to Roger several times that he was wasting his life spending time with just one woman. This was especially true of a woman that was not his intellectual equal, but that was where Willie was wrong. Gloria was every bit his equal on many levels, she was just not oriented toward working with technology. She was a social scientist and if there were room in her field she would be working in it. Instead she was doing what she could to survive.   Then Roger realized that he was defending her in his own thoughts against an imagined attack by Willie, he smiled and went back to the reading the data. There had to be something interesting buried in the volumes of information that the program had been producing.

****

Kate had gone back to bed after she had sent the boys to school. She had been perpetually exhausted and couldn't recall the last time she had felt rested. It was difficult for her to do what she was doing today, sleeping late. The boys needed her and once she was up with them there did not seem to be any reason not to continue to do things until she was needed for the surveillance of Austin Lee. The past two weeks had been difficult with late nights dedicated to trying to win Austin's confidence and affection. It was clear she had done both but there did not appear to be anything else that she could get from him. Austin was not a viable link to Welsh as things stood. There would have to be another tactic that could be employed to get Welsh, perhaps through another contact but all of that would take even more time and she was not sure she had that much stamina.

She forced her eyes open and called for the time to display. It was three thirty in the afternoon, she had been asleep for eight hours. She had slept five hours before she had gotten up at six with her boys. That meant that see had thirteen hours sleep out of the last twenty four. She wondered why she still felt so groggy. She needed to get ready since she was to meet Austin in Harrisburg at five thirty. After a quick shower she began to feel a little more energetic and when Foon called to tell she was on her way to pick her up. She was ready for a late night and hopefully some progress, otherwise she was intent on telling Devers that they should take the operation in a different direction.

Kate was on the street when Foon arrived. Foon seemed to be in much better spirits than she was usually. "Hello Foon, you seem to be in great mood. I guess you are having a good day." Kate said.

Foon replied, "Katherine this is an important day for me. I am going to be seeing my brother after I drop you off at the train station in Harrisburg. I have not seen him in almost eight years."

It was obvious to Kate that Foon was enthusiastic about the prospects of seeing her brother. Kate had not known that Foon had a brother and for that matter Kate did not know much about Foon's personal life at all.

"That sounds wonderful. Is he older or younger than you are?" Kate asked.

Foon smiled and then replied, "He is my twin brother but to be one hundred percent accurate he is seven minutes older than I am."

Kate smiled back at her. "Do you have any other siblings?" she asked.

"No, it is just my brother and I. Our parents are both deceased and we have no other family." Foon replied. After that there was a brief period of awkward silence. Kate did not know what else to say and Foon was not inclined to volunteer any additional personal information.

The car moved quickly along its appointed route. It was approaching the time that she was to meet Austin and it appeared that she would be late in arriving. "How late do you think we will be Foon?" Kate asked.

We should arrive approximately five minutes late." she replied. Kate decided that she would not call Austin to let him know that she was going to be late.   The uncertainty would have a positive effect on his dependence on her and she thought that it would help to cement the bonds between them. She also liked keeping him guessing, it made her feel a little powerful and in control.

****

Austin stood at their meeting place. He was early as he was each time that he was to see her. It was always suspenseful and he felt his blood pressure rise as he stood sheltered from the heat of the day, staring out of the windows of the train station. He knew her vehicle by sight. It was easy to spot since there were not that many of those in service in the Harrisburg area. His glasses showed the time. She was due to arrive at any moment and his pulse quicken in anticipation.

As he looked out the tinted windows he noted that the concrete apron appeared to be seamless and was a very stark white. This made it highly reflective and difficult to look at for any period of time even through the tinted windows. The drive to the station ended in a horseshoe shape with two lanes, one that could be used for dropping off and picking up passengers and the other used for moving traffic.

He looked down the multi-lane drive that fed the horseshoe. There was no traffic. It seemed amazing to him that the roadways were continuously maintained for the relatively small number of vehicles that they served. The buildings that were on either side were the typical office buildings of the day. They were fifteen story brushed steel finished buildings with no apparent windows. The windows had the same appearance as the building and were designed to reflect light and heat from penetrating the interior. All in all it was a very sterile appearance and one the Austin had come to treat as common place.

Austin was so intent on seeing Kate's vehicle arrive that he failed to notice the five men that were loitering near him. The two of the men stood at the door ready to grab Kate as soon as she stepped from the vehicle were dress in a silver cooling suits with collarless jackets that were considered stylish by many younger people. Two other men sat in a small cargo van that was parked in a service parking space roughly fifteen feet away. One of these man was small in stature and was sitting at the back door ready to open it and to subdue Kate once she was placed inside while the other sat toward the front of the vehicle and watched for potential trouble. Each of these men scanned their surroundings to make certain they knew what variables they would have to contend with when the time came to act. They all nervously watched for the vehicle.

The fifth man was dressed in the colors of the Hell's Assassins. He was a tall man at almost six foot seven and easily weighed three hundred and fifty pounds. His face was scarred from the numerous physical encounters he had been involved in as an enforcer for HA. He had his red hair cut very short since he had learned over time that having long hair gave your opponent another piece of leverage in a fight. He wore a black leather shirt with their red emblem on his left breast. It was a very distinctive patch and no one had any trouble recognizing the Letter 'H' on a forty five degree angle with the letter 'A' using the right leg of the 'H' as its starting point the with the cross piece a silver pitch fork. Most people gave the wearer of these colors a wide birth when they saw them on the street.

Bowman had instructed them to wait for the vehicle to depart before they grabbed Kate unless the vehicle did not move prior to her entry into the building. Under no circumstances was she to enter the building. When she was taken they were to allow Austin to see her being forced into the vehicle before he was to be attacked. The man nearest to Austin who looked like a member of HA was responsible for making certain that Austin did not get outside to interfere with the van's departure. He was to make it clear to Austin that HA had taken Kate without telling him verbally. The colors that he wore and his overall appearance conveyed that message clearly.

All eyes widened as the Voltrun stopped at the curb and Kate stepped out. The men inside tensed and Austin started toward the door. Foon delayed the departure to be certain that Austin was waiting for Kate. Kate had walked ten of the twenty five feet distance to the building before the men burst through the door and grabbed her. Austin upon seeing her exit the vehicle moved to the door and was trying to greet her, but he was stopped by the man in the HA colors who pushed him easily to the ground. As he sat on the floor he witnessed the two men dragging Kate toward the van. He could see that she must have been screaming but he could not hear a sound.

When Foon saw what was happening she immediately exited the vehicle to help free Kate from the abductors. As she stood up one of the men reached under his jacket and pulled out a weapon and pointed it in her direction. She ducked down to avoid being shot. She then open the doors and got back into the vehicle with intention of following the men that were taking Kate.

When Austin saw Kate being pushed into the van he attempted to get up and past the man that was blocking his way. This was the first time that he noticed the emblem on his shirt and he slightly hesitated out of fear. No sooner had he gotten to his feet when he was pummeled by a series of blows to his torso and then to his face. He tried to react and protect himself at the same time he looked for a chance to strike back but his reaction time was too slow in comparison to that of his attacker. He was once again on the floor face down and could feel the pain of repeated kicks to his back and side. Then when the foot of the man struck his head he lost consciousness, everything went black.

Foon watched the van speed away and instructed the car to follow it. She was reluctant to contact the authorities but felt she had no alternative. As she placed the call a priority call came in cutting off her outbound call.

"Foon, back off." Girard instructed her.

"They just took Katherine Foster, I cannot just back off." she replied.

"It's part of the operation. We needed to force Lee into doing something and this will do just that. You need to set up surveillance of him and let us know what he does. Right now he is out cold on the floor of the train station and the authorities are on their way to attend to him. Get there first if you can and make certain he doesn't say the wrong things." Girard told her.

"Why didn't you warn her before you did this?" Foon asked.

"The fewer people that knew the better. Besides, there is some concern that she would have let Lee know what was going to happen. It is fairly obvious that she has developed feelings for the guy." Girard told her.

"That wasn't fair, she would never have compromised the mission. Katherine is a professional and would do what was right." Foon responded. She instructed the vehicle to break off the pursuit and to return to the train station. "I will do as I am told. When can I speak with Katherine?" Foon asked.

"We are not going to tell her about this for a day or two. Check back with me tomorrow and I will let you know when you can speak with her." Girard told her and disconnected the call.

The Voltrun arrived at the train station and the entrance to the drop off was blocked by an emergency vehicle. Foon could see that they were attending to Austin and that she would not be able to gain access to him. She instructed the vehicle to return to the apartment in Mechanicsburg where she would hopefully be able to collect her thoughts. As the vehicle began to pick up speed she remembered the meeting with her brother. She would be late and she could not miss seeing him this time. It had been so long since they had were able to be together and there was no telling when they would be able to see each other in the future. She gave the vehicle its new instruction and then she attempted to see how the news outlets were treating incident at the train station. On her first cycle through the reporting channels there was no mention of anything.

Foon was not the only one that was anxiously checking the news outlets. Girard was hoping to hear what Austin had told the authorities. There had been no news of any kind indicating that there had been an incident at the Harrisburg Train Station. Girard called Devers and asked him if he had heard anything through official circles. They had a group of HA that were ready to claim the assault as part of the gang war that was allegedly taking place. Devers indicated that all was quiet and that there was nothing being reported except for the dispatch of the medical unit to the train station. Perhaps Lee was unconscious and they did not know what had happened.

****

Austin was trying to hear what people were saying around him. There was a flurry of activity and he tried to speak but he could not utter a sound. He had a tube running down his throat and there was the sound of a respirator hissing in the background. His head hurt a great deal and his stomach was unsettled. It reminded him of a day when he first was put in prison and one of the guards had thought that he had said something about his wife, that was a head injury that had taken him three weeks to recover from its effects. He tried to open his eyes but he could not seem to make his eye lids function. Then he thought about Melissa and what he had seen. Who was going to rescue her, if he died no one would even know that she was gone. Then he remembered that Jewel had been there and she saw the entire kidnapping. He was confident that she would contact the authorities and that they would be working on the getting her back safely.

"Has he regained consciousness?" the Internal Security Station Chief asked.

"Not as of yet, sir. Though they expect that it will be within the hour." Yost replied.

"Mr. Yost I expect a full report on this attack as soon as possible. The best we have right now is that someone that belongs to HA was responsible for the beating of this man who is a Monk, though we are not certain that it is a gang related attack." Scott stated.

"Mr. Scott we will have an answer for you as soon as possible. We are also tracking down a lead that indicates that a kidnapping may have occurred as the same time. Surveillance shows a woman being forced into the back of cargo van and there is also a witness that pursued the van in a Voltrun 122C." Yost added.

"That's a rare vehicle for this part of the world. I want you to find out who the vehicle belongs to." Scott concluded.

"Yes sir." Yost responded.

Yost ran a quick check on the vehicle and discovered that it belong to Melissa Champion but there was something odd about the ownership transfer, so he did the additional research to see who had the vehicle manufactured and the pedigree showed its parent to be none other than WBOI. He then using the images captured from the train station security feed was able to run the recognition program and identified Foon, a known operative employed by WBOI on a consistent basis. The image of Kate was not clear enough to establish her identity. The only thing left to do was to interrogate Austin and Yost stood outside of the treatment room waiting for the doctor to give him an update on Austin's condition.

$$****$$

Devers sat still and listened to the report from Girard. The operation had gone as well as could be expected though there were clearly some elements that displeased him. The location that was selected was a very public venue and there would be a lot of surveillance. If Internal Security were to get involved he would be entertaining Scott again and this time he did not have Lewis to help him. He would have to get a replacement for her immediately, he thought.

The only people that could be tied to WBOI were Kate and Foon but just because WBOI personnel were present and in this case one was abducted, did not mean that WBOI had done anything wrong. It was to appear that Kate was undercover as part of their investigation and must have been abducted by HA as a means to get to Austin, a member of the Monks, and that would be his story should he be asked to explain. Girard finished the briefing by saying, "HA did a good job this time. Though I am not certain as to the whereabouts of Foster or her condition at this time. I will alert you to any problems but otherwise assume that all went according to plan."

"We will see where this takes us. Hopefully Lee will reach out to Welsh or Welsh will attempt to help him recover Foster, if either of those scenarios play out we will have had a successful operation. Call me with any meaningful updates." Devers said and then disconnected the call.

****

"Mr. Truax how are you on this splendid day?" Norville asked upon receiving his call.

"Sir, I have some very bad news." Truax responded somberly.

"Go on." Norville replied.

"Austin Lee has been severely beaten and the WBOI operative that had been attempting to gain his confidence has been abducted by what appear to be members of Hell's Assassins." Truax said.

"How did this happen? Weren't your people in place to stop just this sort of thing?" Norville asked in an accusatory tone.

"Sir we were not in place when it occurred. The woman had just arrived and we were not in a position to render assistance." Truax stated with no attempt to deflect blame.

"Mr. Truax, I am very disappointed. This is exactly the kind of tactic we had spoken about several times. After WBOI realized that Austin was not a direct participant they would attempt to use him as means to discover our plans." Norville said.

"I apologized sir, the intelligence that we had prior to the surveillance today was not correct. We were out of position and I offer no excuse for the failure." Truax stated sincerely.

"Do not be hard on yourself Mr. Truax, this is what happens when the game gets out of the control of one of the participants. WBOI woke up and realized it did not know what was happening and Devers is not a stupid man. Arrogant yes, stupid no." Norville said reassuringly.

"What is our next step sir?" Truax asked.

"As much as it pains me to do this, Austin must be the one to take the next step. We must wait. If he asks us for help, we will deal with that challenge at that time. Until then I suggest that you and Mr. Barnaby come to Maryland while we wait to see how things develop. Oh, and Mr. Truax thank you for your efforts. I am confident that this situation will resolve itself in our favor. Good bye." Norville said.

"Good bye Sir, I will see you soon." Truax replied.

Norville thought about Austin and wanted to know if he was seriously hurt. He suspected that there was an attempt being made to use his attraction to Kate as a means of finding out where Justin Welsh was. Norville chuckled to himself and thought about the fact that Justin Welsh was no more. At this point he wasn't sure if the kidnapping of Kate would have an effect on the plans to re-introduce her husband into her life. That would be determined in the next several days and today had enough challenges to overcome, he thought. He decided that the appropriate course was of action was to meditate and he looked across the room at Adria who was conversing with another associate and said, "Adria, excuse my interruption but I will rejoin you in an hour or two. If you need me feel free to call." He stood up, not waiting for a response and then he left to find a quiet place where he could free himself of the burdens of the day.

****

Class was about to end and Philip had another message displayed on his PCU indicating that Senator Sun wanted to speak with him. This time the message came directly from the Senator and not his doctor. He had intended to return the Senator's call but had seen it as more of a nuisance then something that had importance. He stood up and told the class that he would see them on Friday and dismissed them a few minutes early. When the last straggler had left and he was certain that Morgan would not intrude, he placed the call to the Senator curious to see why the Senator had been trying to reach so urgently.

"Dr. Lee it was good of you to return my call. I only wish that I had been able to reach you sooner. We might have been able to stop what has already happened." the Senator greeted Philip in a surprisingly strong voice.

"Senator Sun it is good to hear from you, your voice is much stronger then when last we spoke. What is it that could possibly been prevented?" Philip asked.

"Your brother Austin has been injured in an attack that I received information about only this morning. I attempted to contact you so that you could find a way to warn him." Sun told him.

"What?" Philip said loudly. "When did it happen? Who is responsible?" he asked. The Senator then went on to explain the details of the assault and when it had occurred. He also told Philip that he was told that WBOI was behind the attack and kidnapping.

Philip listened and then asked, "Who is this woman that my brother has been seeing? What do you know about her?"

"She is the Mid-Atlantic Director of Security for WBOI and reports to John Devers. She was recruited for the operation with the hope that she could have her husband returned from the war zone quickly. She has two sons and currently lives in Philadelphia. Her assumed name is Melissa Champion. She was selected because the physical resemblance to Melinda and please take note the name as well. It was contrived so that Austin would fall in love with her and they could use him to get to Justin

Welsh." Sun said and finally paused to catch his breath. It was obvious that he was beginning to tire.

"I can't believe that these people will not leave him alone. He is not involved in anything remotely illegal, and as far I know Justin Welsh has not been in contact with him." Philip responded.

"That is where you are wrong. Justin did contact him when he first left prison. He offered him a chance to become active in the project that you are working on right now. Austin turned him down." Sun said with even less apparent energy.

It seemed that the Senator had a very reliable source for information about his brother and how he related to the project. The Senator could have given him more of an indication of what was going on when he visited him less than a month earlier. Instead the revelation came about in small doses and it was given as though there was a need to make his awareness occur according to a specific timetable, too soon and the plan did not work.

Philip thought about the fact that most of what had transpired occurred outside of the control of anyone or anything. It was mere coincidence and nothing more, he thought. No one could orchestrate the huge number of variables that were being theoretically manipulated. It was a poor attempt at subterfuge and nothing more. "Senator, are you alright?" he asked.

"It is difficult for me to sustain the level of enthusiasm that I once had, but thanks to a great deal of work and financial resources I am making significant progress." the Senator replied.

"What can we do to help my brother?" Philip asked.

"There is nothing to do at this time. I suggest you visit him at the medical center and encourage him to be less than cooperative with Internal Security. It is important that WBOI intentions are fully understood and that they feel that they are in control of the situation." Sun stated.

Philip was not certain he agreed with the idea of keeping the government from learning what was happening. He did understand that it would be a potential threat to the project in Maryland and that could derail all of Norville's plans. He suspected that the Senator and Norville were tightly allied and that Norville had used the Senator to communicate the information about his brother to him. The interesting thing was that he could not understand why he would do that. Norville had been communicating freely with him and why would Norville allow Austin to be hurt, it made no sense.

"Philip I know you want to make certain that your brother is safe. He will be safe if he stays away from the project and those associated with it.

Your brother Roger will be leaving the project shortly and so will you. I can tell you that there is the very strong chance that as this project gets closer to achieving its desired end that those that have been watching it with mild amusement will take a very serious interest in it." Sun said and then the call was dropped.

A stuttered tone indicated the loss of the signal and Philip sat for a moment trying to determine whether he should try to reconnect the call. His decision was made for him when Morgan came into the room whistling. "Things have been busy in Harrisburg today. There was an assault and a kidnapping. They haven't released any names but the video surveillance of the event was like something from an old gangster movie." Morgan said.

"Was anyone hurt?" Philip asked.

"The one man was beaten pretty badly by a member of Hell's Assassins. They showed his mug shot from a previous arrest and he looked like a really mean man." Morgan related.

"Morgan I have to get going in a little while, can you cover my evening class for me?" Philip asked.

"Absolutely, who do you think has been covering for you while you are involved with that secret government stuff you have been doing? Don't worry about it Phil. Have a good night and I will see you tomorrow." Morgan said.

"Thank you Morgan, I do appreciate you helping out the way you have. It should make your resume a bit more impressive too." Philip said with a smile. "Have a good evening and I will see you tomorrow morning, early. Could you do me one more favor and schedule meetings with all of the independent study students for some time in the next two days?" Philip requested but it was certainly more like a directive, after all it was Morgan's job to do things like that.

"Absolutely. Good night Phil." Morgan said again.

Philip exited the building and into the heat of the day. He decided that he would call his mother and see if she was aware of what had happened to Austin. He placed the call but his father answered instead. "Dad, where is mom, is she alright? Have you heard about Austin?" he asked.

"Your mother is shaken up but is otherwise fine. Yes, we heard about an hour ago. I thought that you might be working and we did not want to disturb you. Your mother and I are at the medical center now. We have not been allowed to see him yet. He regained consciousness about ten minutes ago and the authorities have been with him since then. Your mother is quite upset as you might imagine." Gregory said, the strain evident in the tone of his voice.

"I just heard about ten minutes ago and I am on my way to the medical center. Is there anything that I can do?" Philip asked.

"No, just be careful in your travels. Poor Austin, even when he does everything right he always seems to find himself in the middle of a storm." Gregory said.

"Dad I have some other news about this situation but it is best if I wait until I see you to discuss it." Philip said directly.

"Of course I will tell your mother you are on your way. Please try to reach out to Roger and let him know what is going on as well. I don't want him to feel that we are keeping something from him. You know how he reacted the last time that happened." Gregory said with a forced chuckle.

"Tell mother I will be there as soon as I can and I will call Roger soon. Perhaps he will want to come there as well." Philip stated.

"I will, take care Phil. We will see you soon." Gregory said and disconnected the call.

Philip placed a call to his brother Roger who did not answer the incoming call. It was likely that he was busy working and ignored the call. What he did not know was that Roger was on another call when he received notification of the call from Philip. He was listening to Norville explain what had happened to his brother Austin. Norville made a car available for him and he accepted the offer. Once the call ended he immediately called Philip back.

"Phil did you hear what they did to Austin? I can't believe the vendetta that they have against him. Do Mom and Dad know?" he asked barely waiting for an answer.

"Yes, they are at the medical center. I just spoke with Dad, he asked me to call you and let you know, but I guess you found out from Norville, right?" Philip assumed.

"Norville called me about twenty minutes ago and asked me if I had heard the news. He was very disturbed by the actions that were taken. Austin has nothing to do with what is happening and has no means of giving them what they want from him. This just makes me angry Phil. It is not fair." Roger said loudly, his voice building in volume a reflection of his emotions and the accompanying boil.

"Roger it is important that we remain calm and don't do anything that will cause Austin or anyone else further injury. I received the information from Senator Sun, he says he tried to warn me about the upcoming attack. If that is so, then he has a different contacts than Norville does. It appears on the surface that Norville did not see foresee this event. Yet everything that has taken place to bring about our participation in this project has been carefully contrived or at least foreseen. Did you ask him if he could have done anything to prevent it?" Philip asked.

"I don't think this is the time to being seeking to find the conspiracy Phil. I didn't ask him because the thought never crossed my mind. Norville cares about Austin and doesn't want him hurt." Roger replied.

"Norville is all about making certain that Norville's objectives are met. Austin is a part of that plan. He has used him as a distraction and part of a miss-direction. Did you know that Austin is seeing a woman and that woman works for WBOI, and she is married?" Philip asked Roger knowing that he probably did not know these things.

"How would the Senator know in advance about the attack on Austin? And I don't know anything about any woman that Austin could be seeing. I only know that there was someone kidnapped at the same time Austin was assaulted." Roger said.

"The news reporters are saying it was a gang war related attack since Austin was a member of the gang while he was in prison." Philip said as he continued to provide more information to Roger.

"This is a very confusing situation and I am fairly certain that it has been done because of WBOI's desire to capture Justin Welsh." Philip concluded.

"Yes, I know that they are after him." Roger agreed.

"Norville could turn himself in for the good of the cause. It would take the spotlight off of the resistance to the WBOI control and it would enable the project to be completed without anyone knowing that it even existed." Philip stated to Roger.

Roger listened to his brother's remarks and thought that they had value but he also knew that Norville's financial support enabled the project to continue and without it the project would die. The vast majority of the people that made up the four teams were being paid significantly to participate and the costs of the computer system and related power equipment was far beyond the means that any one person was able to afford. Even if the money were not his, he was the conduit through which it flowed into the coffers that provided for all aspects of the project. The likelihood that the project would continue without him was remote and not exclusively because of funding. As Roger thought about the reasons that the people were involved in the project he realized that it all came down to either money or egos, and the egos of the people involved were huge. It also seemed to him that maintaining a balance and keeping people's personal agendas in line with the ultimate mission was probably a more monumental task than funding the project.

"Roger are you still there?" Philip asked after a significant amount of time passed without hearing from his brother.

"Yes, I was thinking of what you said and I don't believe that this project could continue without Norville. I believe that it would wither and die without the funding he provides and the diplomacy that he employs to ensure that all of his narcissistic playmates behave themselves." Roger stated emphatically.

"What would be the harm if the project did fail? It is not going to succeed as they envision it. We have already spoken of that, haven't we? Weren't you the one that was concerned if it did succeed that all of the people that you knew would no longer be living?" Philip asked.

What Philip had said was true, Roger had felt that way. But when Philip had explained that there would be no effect on the current time thread and that there would be tremendous advantages to improve the quality of life for everyone it had made a great deal of sense. That explanation had changed his thinking, and it had further enabled him to understand the Christopher Leesop's journal. If what they were doing could have that type of positive affect he must see it through.

"Philip think about what you are saying. Remember back to our conversation and how the results of the programming and forecasting will enable us, all of us, to move forward to the next level of growth and development. You read the journal didn't you? You realize that this is not about you or me, it's about us, all of us." Roger said passionately.

Philip decided that it was not appropriate to go further at this time. "Are you going to see Austin?" Philip asked.

"Yes, I am in a car as we speak. Norville made it available to me." Roger replied.

"Good I will see you soon. We can talk about this more at that time." Philip said.

"I think that would be wise. Good bye Phil. Tell Mom and Dad I will see them soon." Roger said and then disconnected the call.

****

Kate was feeling tremendous anxiety. The hood that covered her head made it difficult for her to breathe and she was certain that the men that had abducted her were working for Justin Welsh and that he was going to eliminate her from the operation. She found herself thinking about her boys and took some comfort in that they were with her parents. If she did not return to them they would have a life similar to hers and for that realization she felt sadness.

She then pictured Austin as she had last seen him. He was being kicked repeatedly by that large man and then she started to study his appearance. He wore a black shirt and there was a red emblem. He was a member of HA and then she thought and they were not affiliated with Justin Welsh, they worked with Girard who worked for Devers. These were people that were supposed to be on my own team, she thought.

The binding around her wrists was very tight and her fingers were beginning to feel numb. If these men were working for WBOI they were hoping that Austin's attraction to her would cause him to do something foolish, possibly reach out to Welsh or take matters into his own hands. At that point they could put him back in prison, and work on other ways to ensnare the elusive mister Welsh.

The van pulled into a driveway of a house in the historic section of the Philadelphia suburbs. The house belonged to a person of substance and wealth. Its large brick facade was partially obscured by ivy. They followed the small off shoot from semi-circular drive that lead to a free standing four car garage. The door to one of the bays opened and the van pulled in and stopped. Kate felt the vehicle stop and then heard the door open. She heard voices but they were muffled by the hood and while she was still nervous about the situation that had transpired her anger was growing having deduced that she was being used and they had not thought enough of her to advise her of the plan.

"Get out Mrs. Foster." she heard one of the man say loudly. She wasn't certain how she was supposed to do this while she could not see and her hands and feet were bound.

"How am I supposed to get out? I can't see or move," she said as loudly as she could.

"What did you say?" the voice asked, and then the person laughed. At that moment they pulled the hood from her head. It caught on her hair and when they yanked it off some of her hair went with it, it hurt.

Her eyes slowly adjusted to the light. It was very bright inside the garage and she could see two cars that were in the garage along with the van. There were two men that were standing directly in front of her and one of the men grabbed her feet and cut the restraint so that he could get out of the vehicle. Her hands were behind her as she slid on her bottom to get out and on to her feet.

When her feet touched the ground another man grabbed her by her arm pulling her up to a standing position. It seemed that they were going to maintain the charade and Kate was weighing whether she should play along.

The man that had helped to her feet told her to stand still and he cut the bindings that held her hands secured behind her back. She instantly began to have feeling return to her fingers and she worked her hands together to promote the circulation.

"We are sorry for the inconvenience Mrs. Foster. We were hired to kidnap you so that it would appear as though you had been taken by a member of our gang in retribution for your involvement with Austin Lee. He is currently resting in the Hershey Medical Center in stable condition." the man explained. "We cannot answer any more questions other than the one you are most interested in the answer. We do not know when you will be able to leave here." the man said anticipating Kate's next question.

"Who is in charge of this operation?" Kate asked. "You do know that don't you?" she continued.

"Yes of course I do, but I am not at liberty to say." the man responded.

"It is either under Girard or Devers' direct control. Which means that Devers is still the top man, though you may not know it. I need my PCU activated. Stop blocking the signal." Kate demanded.

"I don't have the authority to do that Mrs. Foster. I will make a call and see if there is anything more we can do for you at this time. In the meantime please follow that man there and he will make certain you are comfortable while you wait." the man instructed her.

Kate was lead from the garage to the house entering through a rear door that allowed entrance to the kitchen. She was met with a refreshing cool blast of air and the pleasant smell of freshly baked cookies. She immediately realized that she was hungry, remembering that she had not eaten since the breakfast she had shared with her sons. A small woman with large eyes and a gaunt countenance greeted her with a sickly smile. She apparently was the cook for the house and was working to prepare dinner.

"Mrs. Foster you will be joining us for dinner but can we get you something to eat now?" the man escorting her inquired.

"No thank you, I just want to go home to my children." Kate responded.

"Yes, of course you do and I am sure that you will able to leave here very soon. Please continue to follow me." he said leading her through the kitchen and out into a hallway. They walked for a few moments and the came to a doorway on their right.

"Please if you would be so kind as to wait in here. Are you certain I can't get you anything? Something to drink? Water?" he asked again.

"I'll have some water then and I do want to talk to Devers right away." she finally said.

Kate entered the room and saw that it was brightly lit and furnished with antiques, some of which were probably more than three hundred years old she thought. Whoever lives here definitely was financially secure, most of the houses like this were destroyed fifty or more years ago to make way for more standardized housing. It was done so that most people would not realize that there were still individuals that controlled most of the wealth and power. The country had come dangerously close to economic revolutions three times in the past one hundred years. Each time it reached a critical juncture there were concessions made to apportion a little bit more of the wealth to the majority of the citizens. The only problem was that the amount that was apportioned was dramatically overstated while at the same time the total of the wealth controlled by the wealthy minority was conversely understated.

The average person was never permitted to see the person who lived this lifestyle, it was never highlighted or promoted by the government or the news reporters. It would be too harsh a reminder of what once was and could never be again. A dream that all could live as kings if they were to just worked as hard as they possibly could. Some realized the fabrication and found another way using exploitation or even illegal means to gain the jewels that were being dangled in front of them. Kate wonder what the person who owned this house had done in order to possess it.

Bowman stood in what would have been referred to as the study of his home waiting for Girard to respond to his request. The call came in just as his temper began to flare. These arrogant fools at WBOI think that they are so much more than we that do their bidding are, he thought.

"Devers told me that she can go home tonight and that he would talk to her in the morning. She is not to speak to anyone except her family and no one is to know anything about what happened." Girard instructed Bowman and disconnected the call.

Bowman shook his head and thought if they weren't paying him so much to do these stupid things he would take great joy in hurting them. He walked to the room where Kate was waiting.

"Mrs. Foster, you will be able to go home very soon, in a couple of hours. I have been told to tell you that Mr. Devers will be calling you in the morning and that you are not speak about this to anyone and are to avoid contact with everyone but your family. Are we clear?" Bowman asked.

"Yes." Kate said and then asked, "By the way, whose house is this?"

"Mine, why do you ask?" Bowman replied.

"It's very beautiful and very tastefully decorated." Kate said.

"Thank you. We will place a call to your associate within the hour and as soon as she arrives you will be able to leave. Please make yourself comfortable until then." Bowman said then turned and left.

****

Girard called Foon to instruct her from where she could retrieve Kate. The call was a brief one and when he had disconnected the call he wondered whether the operation had been worth the effort. He was even more convinced that Austin was a blind alley and that Welsh was involved in other activities and was perfectly happy that WBOI was focused on Lee. It wasn't his place to worry about the effectiveness of any operation so long as he was fulfilling his commitments and honoring the spirit of the agreement. The surveillance that he had been involved with Lee was only a part of his assignment but as of late it was a part of the assignment had been become disproportionately large. WBOI had made an error in assuming that Welsh's plan was identical to what it was before.

Girard reflected upon the entire operation from its inception. He recalled that they had uncovered the plot that Austin had been working to accomplish quite by accident and they had been extremely fortunate to stumble on to Melinda Royce when they did. Melinda hated all men and she enjoyed torturing Austin and whenever she had the chance to hurt him deeply she took it. Melinda gave them every bit of information that they needed to take down the operation. She was trusted by everyone because Austin trusted her.

Melinda was a card that he hoped they could have played again, but Devers was insistent that he had a better way of getting to Lee. Apparently Melinda also hurt Devers and that was quite a Herculean task, he thought. Girard decided that he would head to Hershey Medical Center to personally check on the surveillance and to see if there was any attempt by Welsh to contact Austin. He was also interested to see how Austin was going to respond to the events of the day and whether he enlisted the aid of the authorities or reached out directly to either the Monks or Welsh.

"Devers, I am going to Harrisburg to supervise the operation personally. Have you heard if Lee had cooperated with the Internal Security team that was on site?" he asked in order to be better prepared for the visit.

"No, as far as we have been able to determine he has not said anything to DIS and they are apparently a little disturbed by his silence. They have threatened him with revoking his parole." Devers said.

"That sounds like something that I would do." Girard replied.

"Get up there and see if you can encourage him to reach out to his friend." Devers said.

****

438

Philip arrived and found his parents still waiting to see Austin. They had been told that he was in stable condition and that he had sustained two broken ribs and a concussion. Internal Security had been with him for almost two hours and they apparently were frustrated that Austin had not been more helpful. Philip looked at his mother who sat helplessly staring in the direction of the treatment room where Austin lie.

"Philip." she said and burst into tears. She stood and grabbed Philip tightly and sobbed into his chest. Gregory appeared to be stunned and sat quietly his eyes darting from one point to another, never remaining on any target for more than a few seconds.

"Mom, it will be alright. He is going to be okay from what I have heard so far. Have you been able to see him yet?" Philip asked.

"No, we have not. They apparently feel that he is not cooperating with their investigation." Gregory replied. MacKenzie looked at her husband and she seemed to be telling him to limit his opinions. Gregory got the message and changed the subject to a detailed description of Austin's injuries. The conversation did little to help MacKenzie's outlook.

When MacKenzie finally let go of Philip he elected to see if he could convince the Internal Security people to allow them to see Austin but before he did he asked about his sister Pam.

"She is staying with friends, she doesn't do well in these types of situations. They remind her of the day of Austin's arrest." MacKenzie said. Philip excused himself and approached the nursing station and requested a meeting with the agent in charge.

"I am sorry you will have to take a seat." said the nurse instructing him to wait until they were ready to allow Austin to have visitors. Philip retreated from the station and found a private location where he could place a confidential call. He had not given up the attempting to see his brother.

"Acorn, place call to Senator Sun." he said under his breath. The call went through and a woman's voice answered the call.

"Dr. Lee I believe that the Senator is unable to take your call at this time. May I be of assistance?" the woman asked.

"I was hoping that the Senator could help me with a problem I am having. It seems that my father and mother have not been allowed to see their son, my brother who was assaulted earlier this evening." Philip explained.

"I am aware of the problem. It is almost eight and there are limited options available but I will see what we can do and if necessary will call you back." the woman said and disconnected the call.

Philip thought about who else he could call. Perhaps a call to Norville would be in order, after all it was because of his plan that Austin was in this situation. He had left that conversation to Roger and they clearly had different ideas as to what was best for Austin and for the society as a whole. Roger would be there within an hour and at that time it would make sense for the three men to sit down and see how they can best help Austin and keep him safe. He knew that his father did not know about the woman that Austin was seeing but he was fairly certain that Norville did. He really did not care at all about anything other than making certain that his family was protected. The next step was to determine what it was going to take to protect them.

****

Foon arrived at Bowman's home and as she pulled into the crescent shaped drive the door to the home opened and Kate appeared. The car had barely stopped when its door opened to admit her. She threw herself into the seat and the door closed as the Voltrun started off.

"Katherine it's very good to see you. I am surprised that they let you go so quickly." Foon said.

"Thank you for coming to get me. I will be glad when I get home and can hug my boys." Kate said as she finally allowed her guard to drop ever so slightly.

"I will have you home in about fifteen minutes. Have you heard whether the plan worked?" Foon asked her.

"No, the man that owns that house did not give me any information. It's obvious that he was working for Girard though and that makes Devers the real villain here." Kate said.

"That is always the case. Katherine I want you to know I had nothing to do with this stupid action. If I had known, you would have known, and I think that is why they didn't tell me. They did not trust me, but they also did not trust you and that surprises me. Devers prides himself on knowing the people that are involved in each operation. It is clear that he does not know you." Foon said sincerely.

"I didn't think that you knew anything of the operation. This had all the sophistication of the mess at the Zoological Society. I had been told that HA was working with WBOI on destabilizing the Monks efforts to fight currency conversion but this operation shows me that they are more involved and apparently have their hands in many different operations. They are violent thugs and you can put them in one thousand IMC suits of clothing and multi-million IMC homes and they are still thugs." Kate said indigently.

The car pulled up to her apartment building and she called her mother to let her know that she would be there in a few minutes. She then turned to Foon and asked, "Do you know how badly they hurt him?"

Foon looked back at her and shook her head. It was not the kind of response that meant that she didn't know but it was the kind of response that showed her disappointment in Kate's interest in Austin.

"Katherine, you must leave this alone. Move on and away from him. You still have a husband, leave it alone." Foon said quietly.

"Do you know anything or not?" Kate asked again.

"Yes, he is alright but he has a couple of broken ribs and a concussion. The bigger problem is that Internal Security has been interrogating him for several hours and they have threatened to send him back to prison."

"Well if they send him back to prison that will certainly get him out of my life." Kate said with a sardonic laugh she turned and walked toward the building. She thought that this would be so typical of the way her life had gone when she found something or someone that seemed to be special, everything except for her boys.

On the way up in the elevator she called Foon who answered, "Katherine I am…"

"Don't worry Foon I will see you tomorrow and thank you again for picking me up and for being my friend. It means a great deal. Good night." she said.

"Good night to you too Katherine Foster. You are a good person and I will see you tomorrow." Foon said and disconnected the call.

****

Philip walked back to the waiting area only to find that his mother and father were not there. He looked around to see if they had stepped into the hallway or if they were standing at the nursing station, but he could not see them. A voice called out behind him, "I don't know who you called Dr. Lee but they certainly acted quickly. Your mother and father are in with your brother now. Unfortunately he is limited to only two visitors at a time so you will have to wait to see him." the Nursing Supervisor told him.

"Thank you for the information I am glad they had the chance to get to see him. My mother is very concerned." Philip replied but the she had already turned and walked away. The call to the Senator must have worked.

Roger stepped from the car into the climate controlled walkway that extended when his car arrived. He felt very important for a moment. He normally walked or road trains, and he did not have the same enthusiasm for trains that Philip did. He then thought that no one in the world had the enthusiasm for trains that Philip did which caused him to smile. As he walked several people took note of his smile and some returned it but many more looked away quickly as if it was a disease that might be caught and they too would have their faces contorted in that hideous expression. That thought caused him to smile even more.

He was feeling a sense of relief that Austin would be alright and that it might be possible to get through the day without anything more going wrong. That is when he remembered that he had not called Gloria and he knew she would be at work and would be unreachable so he set an alarm to call her at one o'clock, the time she was scheduled to depart for home. As he approached the nursing station he saw Philip sitting alone in one of several chairs that lined the wall. He seemed to be absorbed in thought, so typical Roger thought as he approached him.

"Hello Roger, you made excellent time I see." Philip said without looking up.

"Phil, have you seen him yet?" Roger asked.

"No, only two visitors are allowed at time and Mom and Dad have been with him for the past half hour. I am just glad they were able to get in and stop the interrogation that Internal Security had been putting him through." Philip said looking at his brother for the first time and extending his hand.

"You might be interested to know that you have been extraordinary in your predictions of what was going to happen when the variables were implemented. Would you care to guess what happens twenty five years out?" Roger asked light-heartedly.

"I'm not in the mood." Philip stated soberly.

"Neither am I. I was just looking for some sort of distraction." Roger replied. After that the two men sat in silence until their parents emerged from the room.

"He is going to try to get some sleep, but if you want to see him for a couple of minutes, they said it would be alright." MacKenzie told her two sons.

As they walked passed she reached up and touched Roger's face gently and smiled. The two men walked into the room. What they saw was Austin, his face swollen and discolored from the beating. He was wired with an electronic stimulus sensors that were designed to accelerate healing. His eyes were open but it did not appear that he recognized them.

Roger was the first to speak. "Austin, it looks like you've managed to become the center of attention once again." he joked while trying to keep a smile on his face. Austin did not respond, he seemed heavily sedated and on the verge of losing consciousness. Philip motioned to Roger that they should leave and he turned to walk out. Roger stayed and watched his brother, it was reminded him of the day when Austin was arrested seven years ago. It was a difficult day then, it certainly was a difficult day today, he thought. Then he too turned and followed Philip out.

Philip was speaking with Gregory when Roger walked out of Austin's room. MacKenzie had left to go to the rest room and it seemed the perfect time for the three of them to discuss what should be done in response to the attack on Austin.

"I don't know this woman that you are speaking about but if what you say is true then Austin is in a very bad predicament and Norville maybe the only one that can get him out of this mess." Gregory replied to Philip.

"Dad that is exactly what WBOI wants us to do. To reach out to Norville and get him to surface, then they can extract their pound of flesh. I don't think that insisting that he help is a good course of action." Roger interrupted.

"Unfortunately, Roger is right. I think Norville would certainly be put a vulnerable place, though I don't care very much that he is considering he left Austin exposed this way, but once they apprehend their most wanted man, Austin would be expendable and he will end up back in prison or possibly worse." Philip warned his father.

"What do you suggest?" Gregory asked.

"I believe that Senator Sun may have some way of helping though I am not exactly certain what his agenda is. At one point I felt he was tightly aligned with Norville and I am certain that Norville is paying for his treatment, but he knew of the attack and tried to warn me hours before it happened. Norville did not know that it was about to take place. I think if he had known that he would have taken steps to protect Austin. I am certain of that. He needs Austin to have a high profile and with an appearance that he is capable. The fact that he was vulnerable and was easily hurt means that he is not a key player in this drama. I think they suspected it and they used the attack today to validate that assumption." Philip explained.

"I will go to Virginia tomorrow and meet with the Senator in the morning. After that I will rendezvous in Maryland and we can try to position things so you can get out of there Roger. Your work is almost done, you only need another two weeks of simulations and the project goes into the hands of Avery and Willie." Philip instructed them. He explained that Norville had asked him to stay with the project through the harvesting process. It would be important to select the right locations and his insight into the area would be important to the success of the harvesting of the samples.

Gregory agreed that it would be better for Austin if Norville were not brought directly into the situation. He then told his sons that he had received a very odd request from Norville earlier in the day. He asked him to meet a man at the train station in Harrisburg tomorrow. Once they had met he was to take the man to meet Austin. He was assured that there was nothing illegal or unethical that was being done. Norville assured him that Austin would be helping someone that he knew by facilitating their meeting. Both men looked at their father and then each in turn cautioned him. They tried to impress upon him that when it came to Norville nothing was as it necessarily seemed.

At that moment MacKenzie returned having stopped at the cafeteria to pick up some drinks and snacks for her family. She offered each of them each a drink which they accepted not wishing to hurt her feelings. For the next several minutes they spoke of Austin's injuries and MacKenzie committed herself to return first thing in the morning. It was decided that everyone would return to their homes for the evening and would check in with MacKenzie in the late morning as to Austin's condition. Roger seemed anxious to leave and when they indicated they were departing he made a quick exit. He had a long ride ahead back to Maryland. Philip elected to stay in Harrisburg for the evening.

It was one o'clock and the car was winding its way over the back roads of northwestern Maryland. "Roger, what are you doing up at this hour?" Gloria asked eagerly.

She received the answer that she had hoped for, "I wanted to hear your voice." Roger said. "How was work?" he asked.

Gloria started to tell him about her day but paused and then asked, "Is Austin okay? Are you okay? I am so glad you called I have been worried about you all day." she said in rapid fire succession. Those were the words he had wanted to hear.

Chapter Fourteen

"There would need to be two teams created to retrieve the samples, but before we do that we need to have a site visit. This should be done with Dr. Philip Lee and Dr. Adria Constantina as well as the technical coordinator for the harvesting project as well as the Insertion Team." Norville told Willie. This was the first time that Willie had heard of the Insertion Team and he had questions.

"Who are the members of the Insertion Team?" he asked.

"They are not your concern. They will be following the protocol that has been established by the other two teams. The first team lays the foundation and it must be flawless. After that your team must replicate the precision and perfection. The execution done by the Insertion Team is the most dangerous part of the process but it is also involves far less precision. The Insertion Team will not be arriving until Roger and his team have departed." Norville explained.

"So there will be a time when I meet these people?" Willie asked.

"Of course you will be working with them during the transition from the theoretical to the practical execution of the process. You will, however be finished with your participation in the project before they execute the final phase of the project." Norville informed him.

Willie was slightly disappointed but he understood that this was like most of the projects that he had worked on in the past where he was required him to play a very discreet role and once he had completed his assignment his services were no longer needed. Most times he did not know what the rest of the project entailed. This time he knew what the goal was and he wanted to understand how they were going to accomplish it.

"I am very curious as to how this is going to all be pieced together. I understand what Roger's team is doing and the importance of Adria and Phil Lee to the support of that end, they give you the locations that you are going to attempt to make the alterations. That is then handed off to our group who is responsible for extracting the exact images of the sites that have been selected. We literally replay the images until we have the exact point where the change is to be implemented. And here is where I start to lose my ability to see how it's all going to work." Willie said hoping that Norville would provide him a few clues as to what would happen at that point in the process.

"Willie when the time comes I will share more of the process with you. I am not certain you will ever be given as much information as you would like, but I am confident that you will have a much better grasp of how all of this is going to work within the next five or six weeks. Our target date for execution of the final phase has been set, and it is the first of July. The two hundred and fifty year anniversary of the start of the battle of Gettysburg. You my friend are only the third person to know that information." Norville said proudly through his smile. He cleared his throat and then told Willie that he had to prepare for his next round of meetings.

"Thank you for your time sir." Willie said standing and preparing to leave. He was disappointed but somewhat optimistic because he had been assured that he would have a greater understanding of the process very soon.

"Willie there is one more thing before you go. I would like to offer you the opportunity to work on a project called Good Hope after you finish here. Roger has already agreed to sign on to it and I can't think of a better addition to his expertise than you." Norville said cautiously.

"I know of the project sir but I am not certain that it would be something that suits my skills." Willie replied.

"Really, I would have thought that you would have welcomed the chance to go into outer space." Norville responded. Norville looked at Willie and wondered whether he was reacting this way because he did not receive the type of disclosure he had hoped for regarding the project. Willie was a temperamental talent and while there were a tremendous number of positive attributes, there was also the matter of his moody behavior and penchant for loud outbursts. Infallible was the illusion that he attempted to perpetrate, he had flaws, perhaps only a few but he did have flaws, Norville thought.

"Let me think about it, Norville. There is an element of appeal to the whole concept and it would be challenging. I just don't like the idea of leaving forever." Willie finally added.

Norville understood that feeling. He was not certain that he could pack up everything and leave, not looking back and being able to see the others that you had left behind. "I understand how you feel, my boy." he finally said.

Willie turned and left to go back to his work area. The project had been moving ahead slowly due to the fact that the new subroutines that created the interface with the new harvesting systems had to be radically modified and the results were that the data handling was significantly more complex than was required by the earlier version of the process. While he had written the original program he found that he could only use bits and pieces of what had been done before. He had been spending fourteen or more hours a day trying to resolve the challenges associated with the code. He felt exhausted but his enthusiasm did not wane. He could see the conclusion of the code sequence and saw the solution, it was simply elegant he thought.

****

"The Senator is not accepting visitors Dr. Lee, I don't care if you were speaking with him yesterday or not." Dr. Simmons said firmly. She was not as friendly as she had been on the previous visit and Philip had thought that it must have been her that had intercepted the call last evening.

"Please, I ask that you speak with him and see if he will see me. I am in need of only ten minutes of his time and then I will leave." Philip implored. Dr. Simmons cocked her head to one side and gave him a quizzical look.

"What is so important that you drove here on a work day unannounced to see a man that you barely know?" she asked him.

"It has to do with the safety of my brother." Philip said.

"Very well Dr. Lee I will see if the Senator can and will accept your visit for a short period of time. If he agrees to do this you must promise me that you will leave promptly and never return again." she hissed through her teeth, an action that was done to illustrate her sincerity as well as to avoid having the message overheard.

Philip watched the doctor exit. He was not certain that he would be allowed to meet with Sun and if he was to meet with him he was not exactly sure what he would learn. He was nervous and started to pace slowly. He started to force himself to think about the rest of his day. He would be in Maryland in a few hours and then he would know how much longer he would be involved in the project. Roger had told him that he would only be involved for a week or two more and he hoped that his involvement would even be shorter. He planned on seeking out Norville for an answer to that question. He thought about Morgan and how much he had improved in his instructional technique in the past several weeks. It's amazing how much we grow when given the opportunity. He then thought about growth and an odd passage from Christopher Leesop's journal jump to the forefront of his conscious thoughts.

> *'There was once a man standing by a pool of water. His feet were planted in the ground as though he was a tree or a large plant and the water fed him and nourished him. The man did nothing to receive this sustenance but he was the recipient of this hidden resource. Soon others came and also benefited from the life giving waters. At some point the pool of water began to drain because the numbers grew too great to support those that had come. The others that came later began to leave to find another resource and soon the man that was first was the only one that remained.*
>
> *He then wept as he saw that there was no more life giving waters and with his tears the pool began to fill again. Soon there was more water than there had ever been. If the others had been patient and waited they would have discovered that the man was the original source of the water and that they were only to wait for the gift of life to be given to them, and never to thirst again.'*

"Dr. Lee, the Senator has agreed to see you. Please follow me." Dr. Simmons said with a smile. Once again she was my friend, Philip thought. As they walked the doctor made small talk and when they reached the Senators room she gestured for him to go inside.

"Perhaps this time you will call me." she said handing him her card as she had done the previous visit.

"Uh, yes, thank you." Philip mumbled his reply as he entered the room.

The room's configuration had been changed since his last visit. The Senator was on what appear to be the same platform but it had been inclined to about a seventy degree angle and he was not wearing the mask. Philip had trouble focusing on the details of his face, it was as if it was covered by a thin layer of gauze or mist but he could not discern what it was. He had difficulty keeping his eyes trained on his face for that reason, it was disquieting. As he approached he noticed that the Senator's eyes were closed, perhaps he was sleeping, he thought.

"Dr. Lee it is good to see you again." the Senator said.

"You as well, Senator Sun, you as well." Philip replied.

"Was your brother seriously injured?" the Senator asked.

"Yes, but nothing that is life threatening, he will make a full recovery. Thank you for asking." Philip answered.

"That is the reason that you are here, your concern for your brother?" Sun inquired.

"Yes, but I think that the problem is broader than just my brother and his safety. Is the project the key concern?" Philip asked.

"No, the key concern of those that are pursuing your brother is revenge and to kill a philosophical dream." Sun responded.

"A philosophical dream? The only concern I have witnessed is an obsession with destroying the Banking Consortium by disrupting the conversion of currency. That is being done an attempt to reshape society by changing the past." Philip said while shaking his head.

The Senator appeared to choke and then he coughed and emitted a high pitched wheeze. The noise startled Philip but he soon realized that Sun was laughing. It was obvious that Philip had said something he found humorous though Philip did not see any humor in anything that he had said.

"Don't you see the irony of your statement Dr. Lee?" the Senator asked after he realize that Philip had been offended by his reaction to what was said.

"Dr. Lee I meant no disrespect. I find the concept of changing the present by rearranging the past laughable. The project has merits but they are in forecasting events not altering time threads. We used your brother Roger's programming to foretell the attack on Austin. It was done at the behest of an interested party, one that thinks a great deal of Austin's sacrifice for the cause." the Senator explained.

"Senator I love my brother and I want him to be safe but he has made no sacrifice. He got involved with the Justin Welsh because he was trying to impress a woman. He got himself involved in this mess because he was involved with a woman. This one is even worse because while the other one set him up for financial gain, this one is married and is working for WBOI for the sole purpose of using him as a means to get to Welsh. WBOI is not a very good intelligence gathering group because they should have known the person they were attempting to use had no capacity to provide them with what they were seeking. Now that's irony Senator." Philip state emphatically.

"You are missing the lesson Dr. Lee, but let's deal with why you are here. You brother needs to be safe guarded and you wanted my advice or assistance. True?" Sun asked.

"Yes, what can be done to insure that Austin does not end up back in prison or dead?" Philip asked directly.

"There is little chance that Austin will be put back in prison and a very small chance that he will be killed as a result of the scheme that has been concocted to keep WBOI away from the project in Maryland." Sun answered.

"Why don't I believe you?" Philip asked. "I am not certain what your reasons are for being involved in this. At times I think that you are working to forward Norville's cause and other times I think that you are working against him." Philip continued.

"Very good. I am working to serve my own interests as are you. We are probably the only two that have unadulterated motives. The others are predominately working for their own reasons except there are hints of greed or altruism mixed in for good measure. I don't trust people that behave like that, they are too erratic and they may do something that does not suit their needs but those of others. Your father and your two brothers fit that mold." Sun said.

"They don't realize that there are many people that want to do them harm and they need to worry about themselves more." Philip agreed.

"So are you telling me not worry about my brother Austin?" he asked the Senator.

"Yes and no. It is likely that he is going to suffer from great emotional stress that will cause those around him to worry." the Senator said.

"Where are you getting all of your information?" Philip asked.

"I already told you how we did it and you chose to ignore what I said. It comes from your brother Roger's latest programming effort. It is exactly what we were hoping it would be. A means of accurately forecasting upcoming events in enough time to actually be able to do something about them." the Senator repeated.

Philip did not completely understand how Roger's program was able to predict the future if it was only using scenarios from the past.

"Dr. Lee please understand this is the only reason that I and my colleagues supported this ridiculous project. There is no way to go back but there is a way to control the future and we now have it, or I should say almost have it. Your brother when he completes the exercise that he is doing will have created the perfect forecasting program. It will give a significant amount of power to people that have been biding their time while these bankers were getting wealthy and powerful." Sun continued to explain. It now was becoming clear that Sun was in league with several others that were manipulating Norville who was manipulating many others.

"Who are the others that you are your associates?" Philip asked.

"I think it is time for you to leave Dr. Lee. It was so good of you to come." Sun said his voice beginning to sound faint.

"Why won't you tell me who they are? Are they all within the government?" he asked.

"It doesn't matter who else is involved. Just know that your family has been a tremendous help to us all and you all will soon be released from your bond. Good by Dr. Lee." Sun said as Dr. Simmons came in to escort him out of the room.

"Senator Sun who is it that you are working with or should I say for?" Philip asked as Dr. Simmons tugged on his arm to leave placing the finger of her left hand to her lips instructing him to be quiet.

Philip left without causing any more commotion. He had gotten some information that he did not have before, but just as had happen every other time he had sought information he seemed to always receive incomplete or misleading data. He now knew that there were at least four different agendas being pursued and that did not include the many subsets that each individual had for wanting the objective to be completed. As he sat on the train on his way to Baltimore he found himself again thinking of Christopher Leesop's writing.

> *'On a Tuesday morning three men and three women met at a crossroads. Each one was headed to the place of their birth and none of them were born at the same place. Seated by the side of the road at that crossroads was a man who knew the way that they must travel. He turned to the first man and said you must travel down this road until it ends. He then said exactly the same thing to each of the travelers.*
>
> *The last one upon hearing that she had been given the same directions to a place that was a different destination then the others asked the man "I am not going to the same place to where they are traveling yet you have told me that I should go and follow the same road. How can I expect to reach my destination?" she asked.*
>
> *"You will reach your destination when it is time to reach your destination. Each must travel the same road for a time. It shows us that we are alike, created the same. What we do when we reach the point when we discover this determines whether we will fulfill our purpose." the man replied.*

"How will I know when I have fulfilled my purpose?"
she asked.
"How is it that you do not know?" the man replied.'

Philip concluded that he needed rest and that Leesop's fables, as he had been referring to them, were nothing but the cryptic ramblings of a man that was mourning the death of his cousin and best friend. Why everyone that had come in contact with them thought them to be something unique and special was very much like the loyal subjects in the parable of the 'Emperor's New Clothes'. He thought about the story of how a charlatan duped an emperor into thinking that he had spun a magnificent suit of clothing out of ethereal thread when he had, in fact, simply taken his money and the thread did not exist. The Emperor's subjects not wanting to feel stupid or to disappoint the emperor agreed that clothing was truly beautiful. The Emperor was indeed embarrassed on the day he wore the clothing in public when a child yelled out that he was wearing no clothing exposing the ruse.

A simple solution to the meaning of all that Leesop espouses was that it was nothing but nonsense, Philip thought. He then continued to think that he must keep those thoughts to himself because it seems like everyone in his family with the possible exceptions of his mother and sister were convinced that the man had tremendous insight into the human condition.

When the train arrived in Baltimore, Philip was tempted to transfer to Lancaster and spend the rest of his day teaching. There seemed little point to finishing his commitment to Norville and his brother, after all the project was just a rouse to get programming to predict the future. He and Roger had spoken of the benefit of using the programming he developed as the initiative but it was the not the primary reason, it was not meant to be the objective. Leopold Jenkins and Willie's father had died thinking that they were working on a program that would change the course of human history. Jenkins wanted a black Confederate States of America and William Lawrence Senior just wanted a better world. Then you have Norville trying to make amends for the pain that he had caused people when he, acting as Justin Welsh, put his closest friends and associates at risk and they all ended up in prison.

The car was waiting for him outside of the train station. Its presence gave him a feeling of importance. People valued him so much that they would have this vehicle waiting for him to insure that he arrived where he was needed at the appropriate time. Again these feelings precipitated another recollection of a Leesop journal entry. This time he pictured Christopher sitting on a stone wall speaking with several people and as he did he called each of them by their entire name. The story he told these people became the backdrop for the lesson that was being taught that each one of those people had value and someone that was purported to be of such high esteem would know the lowest in his circle by their whole name and intimate details of their beings spoke to the importance that he placed on them as people, and as his friends.

Philip felt his whole body jerk as he pulled his thoughts away from the Leesop teachings. This was not right, he thought, I should not be giving this nonsense any more of my time. He turned his attention to the scenery as the car made its way through the late morning light. The trees that lined the road casting long shadows in their path. It was a beautiful day, he thought. The sky was a brilliant blue and there was not a trace of a cloud. The horizon to the south and east had the familiar greenish blue haze showing the pollution ring that surrounded Baltimore, but to the north and west there was no evidence of poor air quality, just the blue of the sky.

****

"When Phil arrives he will be so impressed. The results of the modeling could not have gone better." Roger told Adria.

"Our next two tests are critical. If they go as smoothly as these past three, then we will be ready to start scouting for locations for harvesting. If they match our scenarios then we can consider our work done." Adria told him as she reached across the table and grasped his wrist affectionately.

"Adding you and your brother to the project has saved it from certain failure. Thank you." Adria said sincerely. The older woman smiled at Roger with a motherly smile that he recognized as the same type his mother had shown him when he had made her proud of something he had done.

"I think we should include Norville in our meeting when Philip arrives." Adria suggested. She was hopeful that Norville would allow the scouting to commence while they were running the next two tests. That way Roger's team could be allowed to leave as soon as everything had been validated. She then could begin to prepare for her next assignment. The most challenging part of the project. The part of the project that only four people knew existed and only one of them actually grasped its significance.

Philip Lee would understand it, she thought. He would not approve of it, but he would understand it. The next group that would be coming to the facility would be a small team of six, they will be added to Avery,

453

Willie and four technicians. Philip Lee should remain, but it will be his decision whether he remains with them. Norville will do what he can to convince him to stay. The items of change must be made to appear authentic enough so as to cause the people that interact with them to assume them to be accurate and true.

****

Gregory met the man at the train station as he had been told. He was a tall thin man with a very gaunt face. His had very dark circles under his eyes which were covered with a thick film. The man's jaunty gate indicated that he had restricted movement for some time and he was being shepherded through the crowds by a short Hispanic man sporting a thin mustache and a Monk's patch on his face.

"Are you Gregory Lee?" the Hispanic man asked.

"Yes." Gregory replied.

"This is Michael Foster, you are to take him to meet your son Austin. Further instructions will be following. Oh, yeah, have a nice day." he said with a smile and then turned and left Michael in Gregory's company.

"You seem to be in some pain, can I get you anything?" Gregory asked.

"No, I am not to talk to anyone until I get to meet your son." Michael said. "Please don't walk too fast I am having a little difficulty keeping up." he continued.

Gregory was confused but he also knew that there was a reason that Norville had directed this man to meet with Austin and Norville had been a good friend through the years. He walked slowly keeping pace with Michael, keeping close enough so that if he happened to stumble he would be able to offer some assistance.

They reached the terminus where they could board the shuttle to take them to the medical center. Gregory wondered if he should have Michael seen by someone at the medical center when they arrived but then decided that that decision would be entirely up to Michael. The main objective was to get him to meet Austin for whatever reason. Hopefully it would become apparent when they arrived.

****

Kate's call earlier in the day with Devers was nothing more than a five minute pep talk. He had told her that she was still the key operative and that this part of the operation had to take place as it had so that it would appear to be real. There would be no possibility for it to look staged.

Devers then told her to stay home with her children for the next several days while things sorted themselves out and that when it was time for her to be re-inserted into the operation she would be notified.

After the call she had contacted Foon and advised her of the conversation with Devers. Foon indicated that she had heard from him as well and was told to stay alert to anything that happened but do not actively engage without being told to do so. It seemed that they were both being told to sit and wait for the time when they were needed.

Kate did exactly what she was told and she was waiting for her boys to get home from school so that she could enjoy their company. The panel above her sofa was displaying multiple images. Some were entertainment while two others were news feeds. The sound for the images would play through her PCU if she need one of them to be selected. At the time Michael's image flashed on the screen it was muted.

There he was, her husband, alive and while he looked beleaguered, he appeared alert and was most definitely alive. Her mouth dropped opened and tears began to well up in her eyes to the point where she could not see clearly. She finally activated the audio feed through her PCU. There was a significant amount of noise as reporters talked over each other and pummeled him with rapid-fired questions.

She was saying to the screen "Where is he? Where is he?" she implored and as if her request was being honored the location appeared in the crawl along the bottom of the projected image.

"Live from Hershey Medical Center Harrisburg Pennsylvania." Then she saw him, Austin in the bed behind her husband, his eyes swollen shut from the beating. Standing next to him was his father Gregory who had his hand on Austin's shoulder.

Michael turned and said something to Austin who nodded his head in agreement. Michael then said "I want the people that are holding my wife to release her now. It is bad enough that I was kidnapped but to do this to her is unconscionable, our sons need their mother." Michael said, his voice weak but message discernable.

"Why are you hear at this location?" a disembodied voice inquired.

"I was rescued because of this man and he gestured to Austin. Through his friends I was set free after being kidnapped in Venezuela almost a month ago." Michael said.

"Now I have heard that my wife has been taken, it is just not fair." Michael continued and his emotions got the better of him as he broke down and wept.

The reporters then turned their attention to Austin but Gregory intervened stating that, "Austin is in no condition after the assault that took place yesterday and that assault took place several feet away from where Mrs. Foster was abducted." The images split and there was a feed that showed the assault and kidnapping, while another feed showed Austin's arrest for the currency scandal, and yet another feed that showed her biography as the Northeast Regional Director of Security at WBOI.

Kate was overwhelmed. She was relieved to see that Michael was recovered and that he would be back in the boy's life, at the same time she we distraught that Austin found out that she had been lying to him and that he would believe that the feelings that she had for him were a masquerade, which until this time she had been telling herself was true. She would not be able to see him anymore, and she felt a sense of loss.

****

Devers saw the news feed and he could not believe that it had been done. Austin Lee was no longer a man that was outside of the law, he was a man that helped those that were oppressed and lost. Kate's cover was destroyed and they were no closer to finding Welsh than they were before Lee was released from prison. His first thought was to put him back in prison and start over again. The next thought was to call Girard and see what he was going to do about this. Girard had to be the source of the problem, he thought though he had only done what he had been instructed to do. Girard had also warned him that too many resources were being spent on a very questionable lead. He had always insisted that Austin Lee was not the proper conduit to Welsh and that Welsh was not the proper conduit to solving the bank's problems.

At that moment his chief concern was making certain that the bank's image did not suffer. A plan of action had to be determined regarding the return of Kate and an explanation as to why she was in Austin's company, a known felon. He needed to disclose elements of the operation to Internal Security and to the local authorities as well. Lewis would have been the perfect person to handle such a task but she was no longer available. Her replacement was due to arrive within the hour and so he decided to wait and see what skills they had before determining who would deliver the information to the various parties.

Devers anticipated multiple calls from various concerned executives within the bank. As a result of this he elected to be proactive and make the calls to those to whom he owed allegiance. The first call he decide to make was to Fortesque, and it was the most difficult one to make for John Devers actually liked, respected and admired the man. Each time he had failed him in the past he had come away feeling as though he had dishonored his own father. He knew that he had to have an explanation and a plan of action for the call to be a productive one. The reasons for the failure were still not clear and the plan of action was not completely formulated but if he did not make the call and waited when he did finally speak with Fortesque it would not be at all pleasant.

"Sir, I am sure that you heard the news." Devers said.

"Most definitely John, I assume that you have an explanation." Fortesque replied.

"Yes, a partial one. We are still attempting to understand what had happened and why. I can tell you that there is minimal chance that this will reflect poorly on the bank. WBOI's image will remain above reproach." Devers responded.

"That is what I expected from you, but I also expected that this thorn, Welsh, would be out of our shoe by now. Why is he so difficult to find? This has been going on for more than seven years and it does not appear to be any closer to being resolved then it did when we started." Fortesque demanded as the volume and pitch of his speech was increasing and Devers knew that he must find something positive for him to focus upon.

"Sir, the operation was altered because Lee was not providing us with what we had hoped as a connection to Welsh. We elected to use Lee's attachment to our operative Foster as leverage for him to either reach out to Welsh or have Welsh come to his assistance. It appears that Welsh has come to his assistance, it surprised us that he had been so intimately aware of our operation and that he had apparently been responsible for abducting Foster's husband. We are still wondering why it was executed the way it was but believe that Welsh has made a tactical blunder that we can utilize to find him. His actions have become public and that will attract the government and we can use this to our advantage." Devers explained.

"I don't want to know any more at this time John. This is your last chance to get Welsh. If you don't succeed I will not be able to stop the board from removing you from your position. I do not want that to happen. Do not fail me." Fortesque said and disconnected the call.

Devers made several more calls each one he offered a positive solution, stating that they had caused Welsh to act and to act in a very public way. He had said it so many times that he was beginning to believe it himself. Girard's call came through just as his new executive assistant's arrival was announced. He hesitated for a moment then accepted the incoming call. Girard might have a positive resolution or at least a strategy that might help defuse some of the tension that was clearly building.

"Devers I think it is time to put Foster back into the game. She can run into her husband's arms and you can be the one that rescued her. We will now have to appear that we are going to war with HA, and the bank must portray an image that it has never condoned any activities of the gang's that have terrorized the citizens of our country, or something like that. You follow where we are going with this?" Girard said.

"I like it, we look like heroes, better still let's get DIS involved. We will have a joint raid on the house where she is being held. We won't tell Bowman what we are doing. This way when it goes down there will be a likelihood that the ones holding her will be killed or injured. That will add more credibility to the story." Devers instructed.

"I think you will be making a mistake if you don't tell Bowman, otherwise if he is implicated and not killed I am pretty sure that you and I will both be going down with him." Girard warned.

"Bowman won't support us if we have his people implicated or injured. We need to have this plan completely thought out and executed within the next several hours. Call me back when you have a better idea." Devers said and disconnected the call.

"Send her in." Devers bellowed.

"Mr. Devers this is Virginia Smithson, she has been transferred from Asset Management Group to fill the position that Samantha Lewis had as your executive assistant." Grouper said.

"Smithson, how long have you been with WBOI?" he asked.

"Sir, I have been with WBOI for seven years and have always wanted to work for the Security Division, specifically in your office. This is a great opportunity for me and I intend to make every effort to be successful." Smithson said.

Devers liked what he saw. This was an attractive woman that was in great physical shape, a pleasing demeanor and she was apparently looking to move ahead in the organization. This was someone he could manipulate and control.

"Are you married?" he asked her.

"No sir, I am not and currently I don't have any real prospects." she said with a coy smile.

"Grouper will show you to your work area and then he will get you started on learning the layout of the Security Division. We will get together later today or tomorrow to review my expectations and your list of duties. Welcome aboard." he said.

She looked at him in a puzzled fashion. She had expected him to want to interview her immediately and based upon what she had heard about him, she expected him to make some gesture that was inappropriate or comment that was offensive. Nothing of the kind had happened. Perhaps he was not as bad as she had been warned that he was.

Devers watched her leave and he couldn't help but smile. Smithson was going to be a lot of fun to have in the office, at least for a short time, he thought. It is unfortunate that this Welsh nonsense would consume most of his day. As he turned to look out the window into the cloud that obscured his view as he received a call from Girard.

"Okay here is what I suggest Devers. You don't bring in DIS and you have it look as though HA simply surrendered her to WBOI. I would then hold a press conference stating that members of a local faction of Hell's Assassins had kidnapped her thinking she romantically linked to Austin Lee a known member of the Monks. Once they had discovered that she was a WBOI operative they made arrangements to leave Mrs. Foster in the custody of WBOI security. WBOI has handed over all information about the incident to the Department of Internal Security's Regional Director Scott and will work closely with them to apprehend all those responsible for this crime. You will most likely be asked what Foster was doing with Lee and I suggest that you make it appear as though it was an ongoing operation and that she was attempting to gain intelligence aimed at foiling a plot to subvert WBOI's efforts to assist in the currency conversion efforts around the world. Or something like that." Girard said.

Devers thought about what had been said and it was the least offensive way to get it done and save face on all sides. "Okay, that is our plan. I need to have public relations on board for the press conference and we can have this done within the hour." Devers said thinking out loud.

"Devers, I think you should be the one that holds the press conference. If you are the point man the situation can be controlled. The PR guys will make it seem like it was a day at the park and everyone is now good friends." Girard responded.

Devers did not like to be in the public eye but he saw the merits of Girard's thinking. "Good point Girard, I will give it some thought. I don't want any of your people with ten miles of this. I think we should meet later tonight, I need some attention paid to another issue that has been brought to my attention." Devers said.

"Okay, ten o'clock same place." Girard said.

****

Kate was contacted and told to report to the Philadelphia office where she would be met by Devers and the two would drive to Harrisburg where she would be reunited with her husband. She scrambled to make arrangements for her sons to be cared for by her parents, dressed quickly and was on her way to the office in under an hour. Things were happening very quickly and she was told that Devers would brief her on route to a press conference that was going to be held at the Hershey Medical Center where Michael was undergoing both a physical and a mental examination to assess the effects of his ordeal. As she stepped into the building she was met by two Security Division agents. They quickly escorted her through the lobby and into a small corridor that lead to the parking garage access. Here she found a platinum Voltrun S400 limousine and Devers was inside waiting.

"Foster it is good to see you. Have a seat we are on a tight timetable." Devers said as the doors opened. Kate got in and the doors closed immediately and the vehicle moved forward easing from its position of rest to high speed travel with very little sensation of motion for the occupants.

"Mr. Devers, how did all of this come to happen?" she asked still trying to sort out how she felt about the events that had unfolded. Devers did not answer the question, instead he briefed her on what was going to be said at the news conference and how she was to respond to questions that were asked.

"Foster you have done good work and as soon as we can wrap this Welsh thing up you will have your request for a new assignment approved." Devers said in closing.

Kate listened to everything that was said and did not comment at all. She knew what was expected of her and if she wanted to get out from under the control of Devers she would have to do exactly what he dictated. The balance of the ride the two people sat silently absorbed in their own thoughts, neither person enjoyed being in the other's company but the Union was born out of necessity and would remain in place as long as there was a mutually beneficial reason to have it that way.

****

Austin sat in his bed at the medical center with two Internal Security agents watching him intently. They were assigned to make certain that he did not attempt to leave. The position of DIS was that Austin, because of the association with known felons, had violated the terms of his parole and should be remanded to the county jail while he awaited a hearing to determine what should ultimately be done with him. They had not applied restraints but it appeared to him that it was just a matter of time. His parole agent would have the final word but it was certain that he would be influenced by Internal Security's presence.

He heard the commotion outside of his room and saw a group of news reporters scamper down the hallway past his door. The past twenty four hours had been extraordinary. He had watched the woman that he loved get kidnapped and while she was being abducted he was beaten. This morning he was introduced to the husband of that woman who it turned out worked for WBOI and most likely was attempting to use him in some way. He thought that maybe it had to do with George and John who had been arrested but somehow he knew it came down to his relationship with Justin Welsh.

Melissa was just as bad for him as Melinda had been. WBOI had made certain that they found a woman that he would have found irresistible and they did. He had met her poor husband that had been abducted by members of the Monks, which meant that Justin was somehow involved in that. Why didn't he just let Austin know what was going on so that he would not have made such an emotional investment. He felt the pain in his chest, his heart was most certainly broken.

He forced his concentration back to the door and there was Michael Foster standing in the doorway looking at him. Austin thought that he looked awfully old, though he imagined that it was only the conditions under which he had been living. First he was in the military and secondly he was a prisoner under what Austin thought must be terrible conditions.

"I wanted to thank you Austin, away from all of that circus." Michael said.

"I really didn't have anything to do with it." Austin said.

"We are both pawns in a very complicated game that is being played." Michael replied.

"Please don't for a minute think that my motives were pure, I didn't know you existed until this morning. I didn't know your wife's true name until I heard it at the new conference that was staged here today." Austin stated.

"Yes, I know but you did not contradict anything that was said, even though if you had it would have gone better for you. I think you did that because you care about how others would be treated and some of those others are my family. I thank you for that." Michael said.

"It would serve no purpose to have you hurt any more than you have been already. You and your family have been subjected to too much." Austin said and then continued, "I know what those that are fighting this war of money and power will do to those that do not serve their purposes. They will push them aside or worse."

"I know, the wars that we are fighting now are all about currency conversion and have nothing to do with the people that live in the countries that we attack. My job was to plan strategic offenses that were aimed at inflicting as much suffering on the people without harming the infrastructure of the country. The assets needed to be protected, the people were expendable." Michael said.

"You sound like my Uncle Bob." Austin said.

"Robert Lee was your uncle? Then you are related to Christopher..." Michael said but he was interrupted by the reporters that had discovered where he was. He turned abruptly and without saying another word attempted to lead them away from Austin.

The reporters streamed by following Michael down the hall all except one that lingered at Austin's doorway. She was one of the lesser known news reporters from a syndicated feed that had a very small viewer share. This would be just the type of story that they would pursue, the off-beat less politically sanitized, a story that would evoke theories of conspiracy and intrigue.

"What did Mr. Foster have say to the man that was trying to steal his wife?" she asked Austin with a sneer.

"He wanted to thank me for helping to have him freed from captivity." Austin said keeping to the story as it had been presented.

"Oh, he didn't mind that you were dating his wife?" she asked again.

"The subject did not come up. Perhaps if the news reporters had not arrived it would have been discussed. He did not seem angry, and you can quote me." Austin said and mustered his best smile through the pain of his swollen face.

"I will be back later. Perhaps I can convince you to tell me what you really think about this situation. Rumor has it that you may be going back to prison soon." she said with a chuckle and then turned and walked away.

The press conference took place in the lobby away from where Austin was recuperating. Devers stood before the reporters and read a prepared statement that indicated that Kate had been turned over by members of the Hell's Assassins once they realized that she was not a person that was affiliated with their rival gang the Monks. He went on to tell them that Kate had been involved in an on-going undercover operation as a representative of WBOI security and was meeting with Austin as part her assignment. He then added that they could not divulge the details of this operation other than to say that they were working with Internal Security and have appraised them of the operation as it has proceeded.

The questions that were asked allowed Devers to amplify the position that WBOI was only acting in the public's best interest and that Internal Security was working diligently to apprehend those responsible for Kate's kidnapping. After Devers had finished answering questions Kate took center stage and recited her lines impeccably. When she was finished there were no questions. The public relations representative of WBOI that had been on the scene guided the two people away from the press to avoid any unwanted or inappropriate questions that might be posed by those that operated on the fringe of news reporting, the ones that sought more sensationalism than fact according to many.

The next event in the program was the reuniting of Kate with her husband and that was to be conducted after they were both briefed as to what they could say regarding the events that transpired. Michael's briefing took place with PR representative of WBOI leading the session. They instructed him that he must repeatedly state how grateful he was that WBOI and the CIA had been successful in engineering his release and that if it wasn't for criminals like the Monks and Austin Lee he would not have been kidnapped in the first place. He was then told that he needed to state that he was proud to have served his country and glad to be back with his family.

As they spoke to him Michael thoughts drifted to memories of what he did in service for his country. The strategic selection of targets designed to yield as much terror and pain as possible. It was their intent to break the will of the people, the resistance to the new order. How he could be proud of doing that, he thought. It was during those thoughts that he was pulled back into the reality of where he was and the nature of the people that were standing in front of him.

"And of course should you deviate from the guidelines established, you and your family's reunification could be a drawn out process, one that could take a very long time. Oh yes, and then there is also the matter of the balance of your tour of duty and where you will be spending that time. We know that you will make us all proud Michael." the public relations woman said.

Kate's debriefing was similar to Michael's with one exception it was done by Devers and it took less than two minutes. He told her that she was to stick to the script and defer all questions to him. She was to be the dutiful wife that was so happy to have her husband home. It was at the end of the instructions that Devers said something that hurt her to the core.

"I don't care how you really feel about Lee and I know that you care for him deeply. He will not be getting out of this situation unscathed and whatever happens to him is not your concern any longer. Do you understand that if you interfere it will invalidate any and all agreements we have and you will have lost me as a friend and that is something you do not want to do. Is that clear?" Devers asked.

"Yes sir." Kate replied quietly.

When Kate saw Michael across the room it was as though she were seeing a long lost friend. She was filled with emotions but there wasn't that burning romantic feeling she had hope would spring forth when she saw him. She saw the father of her children and a man that she loved. He appeared to be extremely tired and had lost weight. He also looked very old, much older than his years. The stress of what he had been doing had clearly taken its toll on his body.

She saw him smile broadly when he recognized her, since she had changed her hair color and style to accommodate the operations requirements. There were tears that formed in his eyes as he walked slowly toward her, he was still experiencing mobility challenges from his long term of restricted movements. The news reporters pressed closely to them as they met in an embrace. Kate felt safe in his arms, Michael felt as though he had finally made it home as he temporarily lost his composure and the tears streamed down his face.

The reporters smiled, they knew they had a great human interest piece and many thought about the bonuses that would be paid. It was a good day to be a reporter. Then it happened the joy of the reUnion was interrupted by a shrill female voice that asked the nagging question, "What about Austin Lee. Does he deserve to be going back to prison?" Several turned looked for the source of the question and Devers pushed through to answer.

"Of course he does, look how he caused these people so much pain and suffering. I think there should be an investigation as how he was allowed to be released so early on what was clearly a treasonous offense." Devers bellowed emphatically.

The majority of the reporters then shifted their attention to Devers but the voice asked again, "What about Austin Lee, Mrs. Foster, does he deserve to go back to prison?" Devers searched the crowd for the source of the voice and made eye contact with two of the security agents that bracketed the group, he made a face that they knew meant they should get rid of the nuisance.

Again Devers answered the question finishing with, "Haven't these poor people been through enough without you hounding them with meaningless questions." Unfortunately that last remark did not sit well with the entire reporting group.

They all began asking the same question and one yelled out, "Why won't you answer the question, is there something more to this than what WBOI wants us to know?" That question activated the security agents who pushed forward and began to make a way for the Fosters, Devers and the public relations representative to leave.

Once they were free from the crowd Devers turned to the security agents and instructed them to make certain that none of the reporters were allowed to leave the building without meeting with the public relations representative.

He then said to the public relations representative, "Fix this now."

Everyone knew what they expected to do. Devers looked at Fosters and said, "Follow me, we will find a place to wait this out. It shouldn't take more than an hour to resolve. That will give you an opportunity to arrange your transportation."

****

The meeting was almost finished and Philip was encouraged to hear that Roger's team would be no longer be needed after the next two tests were successfully completed. He believed that there was little reason for him to continue to work on the project after Roger had finished. What could they possibly need him to do after the theoretical scenarios were proved to be correct? The only thing Roger had to do prior executing the program which tested the final solutions results, was to code a minor event change that Adria and Philip had to approve. This would determine the point of insertion and the exact specifications of the change.

The validation subroutines had determined that the result could be optimized by altering the time considered variables in one of three locations. The location points were being assembled for consideration and while the four people waited the topic of the future involvement was broached by Norville.

"As you know Roger and his team should have their portion of the project completed within a little more than a week. Adria you are going to be with us until the end and that leads me to you Philip. For the success of the project we are requesting that you remain with us until the last week, at that point it will be your option whether you want to continue with the project to see its conclusion or to leave." Norville stated and Philip expected that this would in the form of a request but it was stated as a matter of fact.

"I don't see why you need me after Roger's group finishes." Philip replied.

"We will need to talk about that a little later but it's clear that we do need you." Norville said. At that moment a tone resonated in the conference room and Roger glanced at the workstation suspended in front of him.

"Here are the three locations and the suggestions for what can be done."

That news was a welcome distraction from what promised to be a confrontation regarding Philip's future participation. The first change that was suggested was a modification of cavalry assault on Philadelphia. It was recommended that Jenkins cavalry and not Stuart's unit lead the assault. Stuart would then move to cut off communication lines between Philadelphia and Baltimore thus allowing the Confederate troops to more effectively penetrate the Union lines. This suggestion had immediate appeal to Philip and for reasons that had nothing to do with the project. He could show this is a means of impressing Jessica with his attention to her ancestor's well-being.

The second suggestion was regarding the use of a dispatched messenger to have General Beauregard's troops demonstrate on the banks of the Potomac across the river from Washington in an attempt to freeze the Union troops that were located there in the positions that they had held. This would ensure that the assault from the rail station just north and west of the Capital would have a significantly better chance of being successful. This was an element of the original plan that Philip had presented but the timing of the dispatch and the nature of the communication was different than originally proposed. The messenger was to be dispatched immediately after Reynolds' Charge. That seemed to be a relatively easy change to be accomplished. The fact was that the message that was to be sent would also have to be altered to say specific things which include the date on which Beauregard must move his troops and the nature of the feint.

The final suggested change dealt with a modification of the terms for surrender which Philip had not anticipated as being important to progression of historical events. It was suggested that the South demand a cash settlement to compensate it for the losses incurred during the two and half years that they were at war. The settlement would go a long way equalizing the two countries which would be important so that the United States did not become extraordinarily powerful and attempt to reunite the Union at some point in the not too distant future.

After considering this recommendation as well Philip concluded that all three changes should be made and made according to the suggested methods. Adria agreed and Roger looked at both of them and said that he would see them in eight days when the programs had run and the data was ready for interpretation. He then picked up his work and headed to his work area and to his team to make the last assignments of the project. As he walked out of the room he looked back and smiled at his brother. "Philip thank you for all your help. It has made all the difference." he said.

The other two individuals at the table sat for a moment quietly. They were waiting for Philip to make his first statement so they would know how truly difficult it was going to be to compel him to stay with the project to the end.

"There you see? I have made significant contribution. What more do you need from me?" he asked resolutely.

"We need you to be with us when the real challenges occur." Norville stated.

"What real challenges. Do you know where I was this morning?" he asked.

"Yes, you were with our good friend Senator Sun. How is he feeling? Much better I hope, it has cost us a lot of currency to repair him and make him whole again." Norville replied.

"The Senator told me he had been using Roger's programming and it enabled someone to predict the assault on my brother that took place yesterday. He claims that the programs that were developed were the sole reason that he and others supported the project. Sun does not believe that you will be successful and neither do I." Philip said.

"Its troubling news to hear that Senator Sun's people had access to the programs that your brother so skillfully developed. Apparently there is someone in our midst that is working with him. I won't say for him because the Senator is not that bright nor adept at devising a plan that could go undetected by anyone with moderate intelligence." Norville said.

"What do you suggest we do?" Adria inquired.

"Nothing. Philip, do you think your brother could be the leak?" Norville asked bluntly.

"Absolutely not. How can you ask such a question after all he has given to the project?" Philip responded indigently.

"My feelings exactly, but it could be one of his staff or it could be Willie Lawrence. Dr. Lawrence knows the Senator far too well I fear." Norville stated.

"I think the only way that you are going to understand the project is for you to see the entire effort. Until now you have known about two of the three pieces and that makes you as well informed as anyone about the project with the exception of four people. Those four people know that there is another group that will be involved in the project shortly after the first phase of the project is completed. The group will be responsible of the execution of the final phase of the project. Only three people know details about the final phase and of those three only one knows the entire scope of all aspects of the project. That one person is me." Norville stated.

"If Willie has been sharing things with the good Senator then the Senator has as much information as he did when Leopold and William were alive and working with him." he continued.

"The Senator and those with whom he is working have only an incomplete vision of the possibilities of our project. It is a woefully deficient picture of vehicle of change." he concluded.

"You can't actually believe that you can alter history by inserting false images into the elements of light. It makes for a good parlor trick but it's not a real solution." Philip said.

"You are right, you can't just alter light patterns and expect history to change, but you can use those light patterns to locate the magnetic signature of the physical form at that point in time." Adria interjected. "What Avery and her team are doing is finding those entry points, their results will initiate action but will not be the catalyst for change." she stated.

"Why would you want to change things that would eliminate so many people that exist today?" Philip asked.

"We need a better world to live in Philip. Look around you, the earth is overheating soon there will be no way for us to survive. They tell us that it is being fixed, yet we are really doing nothing to fix it. We have an economic system that strangles the life from all those that work under its oppression. What does a banker do for us? They provide capital for investment and building, but who are the real risk takers? They are the real overhead." Norville explained. "Philip I was one of those bankers, I wanted to stop the conversion of currency not to help mankind but to enhance my financial empire. Justin Welsh died six years ago since then Norville Forrest has done everything he can to make the debt he left behind right." Norville said.

Philip looked intently at Norville and wondered whether he actually had expected him to believe that drivel that he just espoused.

"What will your role be in the new time thread? Will you be the president or better yet the king?" Philip asked cynically.

Adria looked at him and shook her head. "Norville will have never been born. He won't exist, for that matter neither will I." she said.

"I have been told that I will be able to live in the new time thread going forward, since there will not be what some have referred to as a spatial contradiction. It will mean that I have nothing but the clothing that I will be wearing and no idea whether I will be able to survive or not." Norville said to Philip.

"How do you know that you will not be part of the new time thread?" Philip asked.

"Everyone on the project has been advised if they were not going to be part of the new time thread. Most of those working here are not. We notified them about two weeks ago when Roger finished the first round of programming. People like you and Roger have a place in the altered time thread and that is why you were not notified, no one that is going to be part of it was notified." Norville explained.

Philip could not believe what he had been hearing. Norville and Adria both knew that they were not part of their altered future yet they were seeking to make the change regardless of the impact on their personal lives. His family was going to survive and be part of that future and then he remembered Jessica.

"What about Jessica Jenkins, is she part of the new time thread?" he asked. Norville looked at Adria and then at Philip.

"Jessica is in the new time thread at this time. We are not certain that will hold based upon the changes that were just made to the program scenario. With A. G. Jenkins cavalry being assigned to lead the assault on Philadelphia there is always the chance that he will not survive. If he dies then Jessica may not be included. If that is the case we will offer her the chance to be with us in the Control Center which is shielded from the alterations. The problem would be that you will most likely not know her and you cannot be included because you exist as part of the new time thread and should you attempt to occupy the same location then both versions of you would be instantly eliminated." Norville stated.

"We must eliminate that variable from the test." Philip said.

"I think we need to wait and see the outcome before we determine whether we should eliminate the variable." Adria responded.

"What about Roger's girlfriend, uhhh...?" asked realizing for the first time that he did not know her name.

"Gloria is also going to be fine." Adria said with a knowing smile.

Philip took a breath and then said, "You are still assuming that it is going to be successful and everything points to its failure. It is unfortunate that I am now thinking that I have to stay to tell you I told you that it would not work! That and to..."

"That and to safeguard Jessica Jenkins, am I right?" Adria interrupted.

"Yes, that is what I was going to say. I will stay for a little while longer, though I am not committing staying through the duration of the project. Do you understand?" Philip asked in a tone that was almost as though he was pleading for them to allow him to leave. He wondered why he felt this burning sense of obligation to help these people.

****

The news reporters had all left, or at least it appeared that they had departed. They all had deadlines for their respective news feeds and Austin Lee would once again be the villain while the poor people at WBOI were victims of his plans to destroy their lives and those of everyone in the United States. Austin felt extraordinarily alone. He would be released from the medical center tomorrow and his fate would be decided. The thought of going back to prison didn't seem so bad when he compared it to the pain he felt as a result of the Kate's betrayal. Still he could not bring himself to hate her, when he thought of her an involuntary smile crept across his face.

"Wat ya have to be smiling bout?" Jake asked the question which was accompanied by the usual cackle. Austin looked up and saw Jake standing in the doorway smiling. He was dress like an orderly. "Like dees clothes? I bought 'em just fer yew." he said and laughed again.

"Jake what are you doing here?" Austin asked.

"I am here to git yew out." he said this time with no laugh.

"No, that is not the right thing to do. I am not going anywhere. I didn't do anything wrong this time Jake. The truth has to come out and I am prepared to go back to jail so that it does." Austin said. "It is good to see you though. You are a true friend and exactly who I needed to see at this very moment." Austin said with another smile.

"Come on man dis ain't right. We could have some fun runnin from dees boys. Make em werk fer der money." Jake said laughing again. This time Austin joined him and the two men laughed until Austin could not stand the pain that it brought him because of his broken ribs.

"You better get going before they figure out that you aren't where you are supposed to be." Austin said and pointed at his wrist and the implant.

Jake held up his arm and Austin could see the shield like the one that he had given him. "They think I'm four miles away from here." Jake said slipping out of the dialect he had cultivated for so long. "Take care Austin. Call me if you change your mind and or if you want to talk." Jake continued.

"Take care Jake, better put the jive back in your voice, never know who is listening." Austin said. "Good bye my friend."

No sooner had Jake departed when Austin had another visitor. This was a man he had never seen before but Austin recognized that he was extremely wealthy and apparently very powerful. He was accompanied by two other men one of which was apparently a security guard and the other was a man of significance as well but clearly he deferred to the other man.

"Mr. Lee, I have been anxious to meet you for some time. Do you know who I am?" Fortesque asked.

"No, I don't know you. Should I?" Austin asked.

"My name is Lionel Fortesque, I am Vice Chairman of WBOI. The man behind me is John Devers Senior Vice President of Global Security for the bank." Fortesque replied. "I decided to pop in and see you on a whim Mr. Lee. You have been a serious problem for our business for many years now and we now have to decide how we are going to address it once and for all. Please understand that this is not a personal decision and has nothing to do with anything other than business. You should understand that, you were at one time considered to be one of the bright and shining stars in the world of finance until you fell into that association with that heathen Justin Welsh. It is very simple now, you can help yourself immensely or doom yourself to life behind bars or maybe worse." Fortesque said.

"I am prepared for prison once again if need be Mr. Fortesque but I can tell you straight out that I do not know in what Justin Welsh is involved and I have not been in contact with him." Austin replied.

"We know these things that you are saying are true, still Justin is very fond of you and has made many efforts to keep you from harm's way, including that stunt he pulled with Michael Foster. That was truly brilliant and almost worked if it hadn't been for the quick thinking of Mr. Devers here." Fortesque said.

"What do you expect me to do?" Austin asked.

"I expect you to help us lure him into a trap." Fortesque said.

"Why would I do that?" Austin asked.

"To save your mother and your family the shame of seeing their son go back to prison for the rest of his life." Fortesque said plainly. "Think about it. Mr. Devers will have Mrs. Foster contact you tomorrow for your answer. You will work with her to ensnare the elusive Mr. Welsh. Nice chatting with you." Fortesque said and he turned and left. Devers gave Austin a long hard stare, Austin had seen that type of stare before from men in prison that were so frightened and yet were making every effort to convince themselves that they were tough. Austin responded with a smile.

****

Kate and Michael did not speak for a very long time while they rode the train to Philadelphia. Neither knew what to say. Michael had been quiet during the press conference and he resented the arrogance of Devers and the lies that were told. He thought that Austin Lee has done nothing to deserve the persecution that he had been receiving and he now wondered how much his wife, the mother of his children, had been a participant in that effort.

It was Michael that broke the silence when he asked, "What did you think was going to be gained by persecuting that man?"

Kate did not know how to answer his question. Should she tell her husband that she only did this for him and her family or should she tell him that she thought catching Justin Welsh was worth going to extraordinary means to find him? Either of those were partial truths and there was one more motive that kept her involved in the mission when she had the chance to get out, she cared deeply for Austin. It was caring that transcended simple compassion for another human being, she wanted to be in his company. She felt as though that it was where she belonged.

"Michael, I am so glad that you are home, the boys have missed you so much." she said.

"Kate, I thought of you and the boys every day and there were days that I thought that I was not going to ever see you again. Why did this happen to me, to us?" he asked rhetorically but Kate felt she needed to give him and answer.

"This has been about money, it is all about money and power." she replied. Michael looked at her and nodded.

"That's why it's so wrong what they are doing to that man. If they can do it to him, they can do it to anyone of us at any time." Michael said.

Michael had been changed by his experience. He seemed more aware of those around him and their needs, he was less self-absorbed. She saw him as being kind, and that was never a word she would have used to describe him before he had left her to serve in the military. It was certain that he was a good father and loved his family but the extent of his love had ended there.

He must have been broken by the experience she thought, now he was no longer focused on what had once mattered. Perhaps he would not be as good a father and provider, she wondered. Yet another part of her felt strangely drawn to him because of these changes. While he said things that seemed to display a weakness in character, there was a reserved strength present as well.

The balance of the train ride they spoke of the boys and how they had changed, their likes and their dreams. They held hands and Kate longed to reconnect with him and to purge all of the past weeks from her thoughts. As she attempted this her thoughts returned to Austin who she pictured laying battered in the bed at the medical center and to the statement that Devers had made saying he would make certain that Austin was put back into prison. It seemed as though Michael wanted to help Austin and she knew that she did not want him to be in prison. All she knew for certain was that she wanted to see him again.

****

"Adria, I am not certain that we should be on such an accelerated pace." Norville said after he was finally able to interrupt her twenty minute soliloquy.   "That phase of our project has significant risk of exposure and the details of how we can do this clandestinely are not available to us at this time." he continued.

"Norville, we have better than ninety percent likelihood that the test will yield the results that we are seeking. I am asking that we send out the scouting teams a week early and begin the process now. Every day we wait there is more of a chance that we will be discovered and then it will be a race to the end." Adria implored.

Philip had been listening to Adria's arguments regarding the sending out of a surveying parties to each of the ten sites where the extractions were to occur. He was not clear as to the danger in doing this since it seemed that most of the sites were heavily traveled tourist spots where it would be easy for small group of people to spend time gathering preliminary data and images and this is what caused him to ask, "What makes these people so different than the people that would normally be in these areas? These are tourist areas and there are lots of people poking around looking at odd things."

Norville breathed a heavy sigh and then turned to Philip.   "Philip unfortunately you have not seen the equipment that these scouts must transport with them. We had envisioned using a utility repair vehicle so that we could disguise some of the activity but we have been having difficulty securing the vehicle and won't have it for another two weeks. And yes Adria, I know that we cannot wait another two weeks!" Norville responded.

"What is the downside if we do it now Norville?" Philip asked.

"If we are detected and the information gets to the two groups that would be motivated to stop us; WBOI and Internal Security, then we would have to work at an accelerated rate and most likely would have to be prepared to move our operation at a moment's notice." Norville replied.

"Progress has been made on the mobile facility and it is almost be ready for occupancy. If it isn't then the whole project is in jeopardy anyway." Adria commented. "I believe that it is time to move forward and out into the light. We cannot remain in the shadows very much longer. When we step out into the light we will have a very few moments when we are able to stand and enjoy its warmth and radiance before we must begin to run. It will be necessary for us to have our steps planned well in advance with a means of changing the plan should they begin to anticipate our next move." Adria told them.

Then Philip asked a very meaningful question, "What about the Senator and the program that he has, will he be able to out think us?"

"The bigger question is not whether he can do it but whether he is motivated to do it." Norville responded.

Adria had not heard what Philip had told Norville in confidence but since they were now planning to move forward with the scouting phase and it was important that Adria knew the risks.

"We should tell Avery and Willie so that they can be aware of the problem." she said.

"We have to assume that someone in that group was the source of the leak to the Senator. I believe that Roger's company in this meeting is very much needed. What do you both think of the idea that Roger would modify the code so that it gives a false results? We could herald it as the latest most accurate program?" Norville asked them.

"I think it would give us a little time that we could use to our advantage. There is one more possible action that could give us a significant advantage and that is if we used the program ourselves to feed another program that would provide us the most unlikely alternative solutions. This program could provide us with a significant edge and allow us to keep several steps ahead. The only problem is that we will need to have a small team dedicated to interpreting and running these programs." Adria replied.

They decided that Roger needed to be included in the meeting and Norville called and requested his presence. Reluctantly he arrived since he was absorbed in preparing the program for execution which was to take place within the next several hours. They briefed Roger on the plan of action and then made the requests regarding the programming.

"I will have to have the program modification done before I execute the test in order for it to appear to be what we are representing it to be. This will take several hours and I will have do it without anyone else being involved. We don't know who is providing them the programming." Roger stated.

****

He returned his call faster than Gregory would have imaged. "Dr. Lee I was distressed to hear about your son's plight. It doesn't seem fair, does it?" asked the Senator sympathetically.

"You know that he had nothing to do with any of this. Norville has been using him as a decoy and the horrible thing is that I knew and did nothing to stop it." Gregory said.

"I believe that we can find a way to protect him and keep him out of prison." the Senator said.

"I don't think he will go along with what they have asked him to do Senator. He doesn't believe that he can do it." Gregory said with an air of desperation in his voice.

"Let me place a call and see if I can have this problem go away Gregory. Your family has made a tremendous contribution to Norville's project and to our country as a whole. The least that we should be able to do for you is to help you keep your son out prison for a crime he did not commit." the Senator said and then disconnected the call.

Gregory sat in his den at his home listening to his daughter and wife argue about what time she was to return from the evening adventure with her friends. Pam was old enough to be out without her mother's permission and MacKenzie normally had no issues with her daughter's social activities but Austin's assault and possible return to prison had her extremely sensitive and she was attempting to protect someone that really did not need her protection.

The door slammed and the discussion was over. It was obvious that they did not part on the best of terms. He then heard the door open and MacKenzie yell out to her daughter, "I love you and have a good time!" To that end MacKenzie always tried to part company on a positive note and closed each conversation with an affirmation of her love for the other person. She had not told Austin that she loved him before he was arrested and it was her several days before she was able to look him in the eyes and say it to him. It had deeply troubled her.

****

"Chu it is time to release Mr. Austin Lee from his debt to your employer. Can you arrange a meeting with my old friend Sherwood so that we can discuss the best way to end this tragedy?" Sun said.

"Yen you are asking far too much from us. You know the internal battle that rages within my company and Sherwood is under attack from Fortesque who is using that dolt Devers to execute his sophomoric plan." Wa responded.

"Believe me the programs that we have received as a result of the work done by the Lee family will enable us to find the proper course of action to eliminate any resistance and threat from the your Vice Chairman and his subordinates. With your permission I will run the program to determine a course of action and will be prepared to present it at the meeting. I think that if it can be brought to light that Fortesque and Devers were trying to use Austin Lee to further their own agendas, then we can put together a strategy where we all win." the Senator said.

"Very well, I will contact Sherwood and attempt to schedule some time for a meeting with you for tomorrow morning." Wa replied.

"Thank you my friend and have a good night." Sun said ending the call.

When Wa heard the call disconnect he hesitated contacting DeMasters. It was not the type of conversation that Sherwood enjoyed having, it represented conflict and Sherwood disliked conflict. This attribute was inconsistent with the profile of a man who dominated and crushed all of his competition. It was always done at high altitude where he did not have to see the carnage, he could convince himself that the results were not as devastating as they invariably were. He was not convinced that there was enough of a benefit to their position within the bank to allow Austin Lee to go free, but the Senator had been very helpful especially now that he had secured the Augur program for them. His plan had been flawless thus far.

"Mr. DeMasters, I am terribly sorry to intrude upon you but I have a matter of some importance. Senator Sun is requesting a meeting for tomorrow morning that will outline a strategy that will remove your adversaries and put you in solid control of all aspects of the bank's operations. And yes, that does include the Security Division." Wa said and then continued to outline the balance of the plan.

DeMasters never said a word until the end of Wa's briefing. "It sounds like the Senator is acting as a good friend to many people. I am intrigued. Eight o'clock sharp, but it must be a very brief meeting." DeMasters instructed.

"Very good sir, I will set it up." Wa replied.

****

"Mr. Truax please come to the Section A conference room." Norville requested. He then turned to the three that were sitting around the table discussing the deployment of the scouting team and said, "Mr. Truax will be joining us momentarily he will be providing logistical support for the three scout teams that I have decided to use. Originally we had planned to use one but the more exposure we have the more likely we will be detected and our location will be discovered."

"Is there time to find three team leaders that are familiar with the process and the requirements that must be met?" Adria asked.

"Oh, I think I have three leaders that are more than qualified. We have Charles who was to lead the scout mission and then we have you Adria and we have Avery. I can't think of two more qualified leaders to head up the other teams. We will have Philip able to watch all three sites via video link which allows him to be in three places at the same time." Norville said confidently.

"You are assuming that Philip is participating." Philip interjected.

"I thought it had been decided." Norville replied.

"I supposed that it has as long as you provide me with a way to make certain that Jessica Jenkins comes through this okay." Philip said.

Norville looked at Adria and then said, "Candidly, no one knows how people will be after the change, all we know is the general course the world will be heading." Norville explained.

"That's not good enough Norville you have the ability to know and if she is not, then I have the ability to make changes to assist her, that is my condition for continuing." Philip said emphatically.

Roger looked at his brother and said, "You seem a little different Philip. You need to be more careful that journal might be having an effect on you too." Philip looked at him perplexed and Roger return to his work with a smile, then said, "Don't worry brother, your secret is safe with me."

When Truax joined the group they worked out a plan for deploying the scout teams within four days. It was at that point that Norville mentioned the problems that would be encountered should they attempt to visit the last site. This was the only location that was outside of the Gettysburg and York corridor, being that a decision to pursue financial compensation would have to have been made in Richmond and made by Jefferson Davis.

This was discussed briefly and it was determined that it should be excluded from the project and removed from the current program run because of the likelihood that they could not find a location that was not influenced by magnetic energy from the numerous rail lines that converged in Richmond. There was also the fact that the time frame at which this was to occur was far outside of the time when the other modifications were being made and because of all of these factors the tenth site was officially eliminated from the project.

It was not as aggressive a plan as Adria had hoped for but it was far more aggressive then what Norville had been prepared to support prior to listening to the time theorist. It was clear to him that they would be under a great deal of pressure as soon as they dispatched those teams. They would have to be functioning at peak efficiency and prepared to change any and all aspects of the plan to ensure that the ultimate goal was achieved.

On July first 2113, two hundred and fifty years after the first shots were fired at Gettysburg Pennsylvania, the Army of North Virginia was poised to re-write world history. Even Robert E. Lee, the eternal optimist when it came to his troop's performance, could not have imagined what this would mean to all people around the world.

****

The meeting at eight the next morning between Senator Sun and Sherwood DeMasters took place in a small hotel located in the historic district of Washington DC. The hotel had served as a temporary residence for several then future presidents including Abraham Lincoln. They met in a small room on the first floor whose oak floors squeaked and groaned under the weight to their footsteps. The Senator arrived in an ambulance and made his way into the room on a gurney while DeMasters exited from a vintage Mercedes Benz limousine the likes of which had not been seen for more than seventy years.

Within minutes of their shaking hands DeMasters had agreed that Austin Lee would be publicly exonerated at the expense of Devers and Fortesque. It would take several days to engineer all of the elements and it was also agreed that Lee should remain at the medical center until the announcement had been made public. DeMasters was pleased that he would be able to rid the bank of Devers who had been a liability for a very long time. His next call was to Drew Morris to express the opinion that Devers was out of control and that it was important to understand where he stood regarding a possible replacement for him.

"There are several people that I would consider very suitable replacements. I will have a short list prepared in the event it is proven to be necessary." Morris replied to the statement.

When the call was over Morris realized that Devers was in very big trouble as far as DeMasters was concerned. He was not clear whether Fortesque could save Devers' position or for that matter whether Fortesque had enough support among the board members to even maintain his own position. It was going to be an interesting next couple of days at WBOI, he thought. It was clear to him that he should not align himself with anyone other than the Chairman at that time, though it would be prudent to understand if there was movement in the bank to support Fortesque and Devers and if so how powerful was it, he thought. He then decided that he needed to make some calls.

Chapter Fifteen

The sun had not completely cleared the horizon and the temperature was surprisingly cool for a day in early May. The smell of rain was in the air and tail end of the storm was barely visible as the thunderheads crept northeastward. Gettysburg was a small city caught in a time vortex. It appeared to be stuck in the late Nineteenth Century except for the absence of horse drawn transportation. Adria and her team traveled through the center of town heading westerly until they encountered Buford Avenue, which had been named after the resolutely tough cavalry man that was a key contributing factor to the delay of the Confederate advance and the reason that the North was able to secure the 'good' ground that they were able to occupy. If the project was successful this road would no longer carry that name, she thought.

They made the soft right hand turn following the road which would soon experience a name change to Chambersburg Highway. The yellow and blue van moved slowly passed the office buildings and scattered residences. It was painted as a utility vehicle the same as the other two scout team's vehicles were. Each one was equipped with specific photolytic detection equipment, several small digging implements and particle beam bore that could be calibrated to accuracy of .0012 micrometer. All of this was powered by a suitcase sized cold fusion generator and this was the device that would be the challenge to conceal from watchful eyes.

The van had been equipped with shielding but it was only able to mask the unit when it was functioning at thirty percent of maximum power output or less. The activities in which the scouting teams would be involved with at times would have their generators running at or near one hundred percent capacity. Their signature would be detectable by a casual observer scanning the power grid, at a distance of five hundred miles and their location identified within five centimeters. It was for this reason that the sequence and timing of the use of this equipment was extremely important. They would coordinate usage so that they were all using the equipment in the same fashion for the same duration. This would give anyone watching the need to make a choice and assuming they had limited resources that they could dispatch to investigate they would have to choose between locations and that would give the teams a bit more time to fulfill their mission. The decision process would most likely require the individual monitoring to contact their supervisor and they, in turn, would decide what to do. That could give the teams an extra ten or more minutes before they would have to shut down and change their location.

Adria continued to look out the windows as the van moved forward at a very slow speed. This was customary for utility vehicles that had been dispatched to solve an energy leak or other potentially hazardous situation. There was little traffic on the roadway and as the sun climbed higher into the sky the landscape became more vivid and alive with color. The green grass and the shimmering reflections from the puddles of water that were left by the rainstorm that had quickly vanished. The tranquility was disturbed by the incoming call from Avery in one of the other scout vehicles.

"Adria, isn't this so much more fun than sitting inside those white sterile rooms beating your head against the unsolvable problems that we seem to solve every day?" Avery said with a laugh.

"Yes, I find this exciting. Though I hope that it doesn't become too exciting." Adria replied with a smile.

"I heard from Philip a little while ago and he indicated that the first coordinated power event will be in about an hour. Are you close to the designated location?" Avery inquired.

"Yes and no. It's all relative we are within a mile and half of the location but sometimes I feel like we are not making any progress in getting there. I have never been in a slower moving vehicle." Adria said out of frustration.

"You will arrive at roughly the same time we do. I estimate that I have about thirty minutes of preparation in order to be ready to go at the designated time. We are planning and doing as much as we can prior to powering up the bore." Avery said.

"Don't forget to take a lot of pictures from many different angles." Adria reminded.

"Thanks mom, I will make sure I eat all my spinach too. I will call you in about an hour. Good luck." Avery said and then disconnected the call.

Philip was looking at the three viewing screens that had been mounted in front of him while the two women were conversing. Each of the displays was a holographic projection that occupied about nine cubic feet. He played with the controls so that he was familiar with changing the vantage point. It was important that he did not cause the others to be delayed in executing their assignment because he was fumbling with technology he could easily have mastered given a little time. He watched the viewing portal that was focused on Avery as she sat riding in the vehicle. He rotated the cube so that he could look over her shoulder and see what she was doing. It turned out that she was doodling on a screen and had drawn a picture of a cow and of a dog. She animated the dog and had it scamper around the screen. It was quite clever and entertaining, Philip thought.

Philip then rotated the cube so that he could see her face from the front. He then caused the image to be magnified to the degree that he could see the pores of her skin. Once he had done that he checked the view from both profiles and looked at her image and then the background checking the depth of field to determine how much clarity he have from both perspectives. He then switched the feed to the other two scout teams to make certain that all they were functioning as well.

Roger had walked in the room and silently watched his brother operate the controls. The technology was adequate for what they were about to do but it was not comparable to that what was found in the holo-theatres that he had attended. He did notice that the resolution, when viewing a subject close up, was quite impressive though and perhaps that was why they were using those particular units.

"I just finished the program modification that will enable us to anticipate what anyone using the predictive programming will be assuming our next action will be. When I was young I used to fantasize about writing really amazing computer programs that could solve all of the problems of the world. Never in any of my fantasies did I dream of anything like this." he said.

Philip looked up from his work and replied, "Yes, this is definitely beyond what I would have thought would be necessary for someone to be able to survive in this world. It has come down to the point where we have to be aware of what others think we are going to do so that we can do something that they would never have imagined that we would do." Philip thought about what he had said and how ridiculous it sounded and that made him smile.

"Just think, we are working on a project that may change the world." Roger said.

"I hope that if it does change the world and that change is for the better. Change is typically nothing more than something different. It is not necessarily better, it may not be any worse, it is just different." Philip replied.

****

Austin was awake and he felt he should make an attempt to get out of bed. He was home for the first time in five days and it was good to sleep in his own bed. He had been transported home late the night before in what could only considered a clandestine operation. It was clear that no one was supposed to know that he was no longer at the medical center. He rolled over and out of the bed ending up on his hands and knees. Reaching up for the bed to steady him he slowly rose to his feet. He was in pain but most of his difficulties were due to stiffness from being immobilized for the five days. When he reached his feet he arched his back and stretched his arms upward with his figures touching the eight foot ceilings.

"Good morning mother." he said catching MacKenzie by surprise.

"Austin, it is so good to have you home. How are you feeling? Sit down I will make you some breakfast." she said in rapid fire succession.

"I am a little stiff but I think I am doing okay. Is Dad home?" he asked.

"No, he went to work about two hours ago. He had missed a lot of time and the company was beginning to get a little impatient with him. I am sure everything will be alright though, especially since you are home now and we don't have to worry about those people trying to put you back into prison." MacKenzie said reassuringly.

"I am not certain what happen." Austin replied. MacKenzie then pulled up a chair next to him and began to explain that there had been a story on the news indicated that several members of WBOI had been working outside of the law and that they had used him and others to try to further their own careers and fortune.

"Two men were named as the primary culprits, Lionel Fortesque and John Devers. There was also talk about the woman, Katherine Foster and her role in their plans." MacKenzie concluded.

Austin sat and listened to his mother as she explained everything from her perspective. Her commentary included a statement that included "... those awful men are finally going to get what they deserve." Austin felt a sense of relief but it was clouded by thoughts of Kate, his Melissa, and what was to be done to her.

"Did you hear if anyone was being charged with any crimes at this time?" Austin asked.

"Oh yes, I heard that there were to be indictments that would be announced at a news conference later today." she said.

"Do you know what time they will be announcing them?' he asked trying not to appear overly interested.

"No, but I am certain that it will be in time for the evening commute's news updates." MacKenzie replied.

****

Fortesque and Devers were sitting in the hotel room that Devers had reserved. He did not want to attempt to go home or to the office fearing the news reporters, and those sharks smelled the blood in the water.

"Lionel, what are you thinking?" Devers asked.

"I am thinking that Sherwood is a sly old fox and I may have underestimated him slightly." Fortesque said with a chuckle.

"I don't see this situation as very amusing." Devers said reacting to Fortesque's apparent frivolity.

"John, my boy, this is all part of the game. Sherwood must be feeling threatened to take this to the level that he has. He must therefore be desperate and desperate men make mistakes and when he makes that mistake we will take him down and things will be as they should be. What I need to do right now is find out where the board stands on this little bit of scandal. My suspicion is that no one is happy that the dirty laundry is out in the open." Fortesque replied to Devers apparent disquietude.

"What can I do to help at this time?" Devers offered.

"We need people that we can assign the blame to this problem. Because of the way that it has been framed by the press, we cannot expect the public to embrace, at least immediately, that nothing was wrong. I believe that there are two likely candidates and they are your good friend Mr. Girard and our lovely protégé Katherine Foster. I suggest you work on plausible explanations that implicate these people solely in the manipulation of poor Austin Lee." Fortesque strongly suggested.

Devers was uncomfortable with having Girard take responsibility since Girard had a significant reserve of information that could implicate most of the senior management within WBOI going back to the Christopher Leesop matter.

"Sir, Girard will be a challenge to implicate. He has a great deal of knowledge regarding the past indiscretions of many of the senior management as well as the majority of the board members. If we don't have his cooperation then he will most likely make this a very ugly affair." Devers said.

Fortesque knew all of this and that was the reason that he wanted Girard out of the way. Devers did not understand that it had to be accomplished and everyone needed to be protected except for DeMasters and any of the board members that were not in line with the what would be the new regime's agenda.

"There is no compromise here John. If you are not up for this task then we will have to find someone that is. Do you understand?" Fortesque replied staring intently into Devers' eyes. "You will think of how it can be done and you will execute the plan and all things will return to the way that they should be. Should you execute this assignment with the alacrity, a way that I know that you are capable of performing, then I don't see why the Vice Chairman seat couldn't be filled by the man with whom I am having this conversation." Fortesque said placing his hand on Devers' shoulder. "I need to have some one that is loyal in that position and who would do a better job for me than the man that helped me rise to the leadership of this institution." he said finishing with a smile.

Devers now understood that Girard had to be eliminated as a future threat. He was a loose end and needed to be cut off. Katherine Foster was just a poor unfortunate casualty and would be the easiest to eliminate by discrediting her and her family. The Girard situation required a great deal of thought and planning. Unfortunately there was not a lot of time to be given to these either situation. He needed people he could trust and that was going to be a big challenge.

****

"Yes, that is an exact transcript of the conversation that Devers and Fortesque had not more than five minutes ago and if you compare it with the Augur Program's forecast you will see that they are almost identical. Please look at what the results will be should he not act." the Senator said.

"Senator, you have out done yourself. We need a game plan right away." DeMasters replied.

"It will have to wait until I upload the latest version of the software. My contact has informed me that it has even greater accuracy." the Senator replied.

"There is no time. Upload it after we get a plan in action. We can certainly use the better program at some point in the future, but for now let us continue to keep the advantage that we have. How do you think they are going to go after Girard?" DeMasters asked.

"According to what we are seeing, they will most likely kill him and Devers will also be assassinated at the same time. The assassins will be from Hell." the Senator replied.

"That would not surprise me at all. Please do me one favor and look into whether there is any advantage for us protect Mr. Devers in this process, at least for the time being. I want to look at all options as quickly as possible. Thank you for the insight and I look forward to our next conversation. Please make it soon. Good bye." DeMasters said.

Senator Sun turned to Dr. Simmons and instructed her to run the program that was currently loaded. There would be plenty of time to upgrade the program in the next several days. Right now the importance of helping DeMasters retain control of WBOI was of paramount. The group in Maryland could continue to work out their meaningless details for their doomed project. It was clear to him that they were not close to anything that would remotely effect his plans for controlling the future of the marketplace and the trillions of IMC that were at stake.

"Who will we be following sir?" she asked.

"Let's start with Mr. Devers and see if we can develop a scenario where Devers is able to be used as an ally." Sun said.

"I am not certain how we can do that." the doctor replied.

Sun took a moment to think and then instructed Simmons to run the program with the current scenario in place. This would give them a baseline that could be modified. Within half an hour they had the complete scenario following Devers from an hour in the future until he was killed in a raid on Girard's office. The resulting death would end the investigation and Fortesque would most likely survive the assault, but with minor correction he could be left in the position of power that he currently had with little or no effect on DeMasters. The plan that Fortesque had in effect would not yield the results they were hoping to achieve.

Sun then instructed Simmons to insert an event were Devers receives notification of Fortesque's intent within the next three hours and the program was again run to predict the future outcome. The results yielded a very surprising event. Girard and Devers took it upon themselves to arrange for Fortesque to have a fatal accident. With Fortesque gone the blame could be easily transferred to him for the conspiracy. The threat would end entirely.

The Senator then asked to see Kate Foster's time thread and how she would be affected by the change that was inserted. It predicted that she would be absolved of blame and would continue to work for WBOI though outside of the Security Division. Upon hearing that Senator asked

Simmons to extend the program and look for an intersection with Austin Lee's time thread. The results would take another hour to compile and they continued to work refining the Devers time thread manipulation, they only had a couple of hours to accomplish the changes.

After Sun and DeMasters spoke it was agreed that Devers should be enticed to change sides. The conversation would have risks and the predictability of its success was even, the resulting action could be positive or catastrophic and it was for that reason that Sun and Simmons were running alternative scenarios in the hopes of having a back-up solution that would favor them. If Devers did not go along with the plan he would have to be eliminated so that he could not divulge the source of their forecasting. The plan would involve enlisting the help of one of Devers' trusted operatives, Foon and the motivating factor would be her desire to help Kate Foster.

****

When the call came through Foon did not know what to make of it. It was a WBOI prefix but she did not recognize the name or the number. She paused before answering wondering if it was the right thing to do. The voice on the other end of the line was a welcome one indeed.

"Foon, it is Kate Foster I need to meet with you soon - where are you?" Kate said.

"Alright Katherine I will meet you in an hour outside of your apartment building." Foon said.

"Thank you, it is very important." Kate replied.

Senator Sun's aide, Lewis Kuzundi, arrived at the Foster's apartment twenty minutes before Kate was scheduled to meet with Foon. It was important that Kate understood what was about to happen and that if she wanted to survive these next two days that she needed to do everything she could to enlist Foon's cooperation and to make certain she did exactly as she was asked to do. The briefing took place quickly and Michael and Kate listened to what Kuzundi had to say and when he had finished they each looked at one another to see how the other felt about the information they had received.

It wasn't hard for them to believe that Kate was going to be held up as being responsible for the operations direction and failures. It also wasn't hard for them to believe that Girard was being slated for termination, but what was difficult to understand was why Senator Sun and Chairman DeMasters were going to try to save Devers and how that would help her.

"Mrs. Foster it is important to understand that there is information that I cannot share with you. If I did you share it and something were not to go as anticipated you could be held legally responsible for not acting on information that could have avoided a crime being perpetrated. As it stands now you do not know anything of the kind." he said.

Kate understood the need to follow the direction of Kuzundi and while she did not want to help Devers, she did take comfort in the fact that if she did her part and everyone else did theirs, she would still have a job and it would not be in the Security Division.

"When you meet with Ms. Foon, you are tell her that she must get Devers to agree to meet with me within the next two hours or things could go very badly for many people." Kuzundi said.

"I understand, but Foon is a very independent person and will not be easily convinced to follow others' direction unless she can see a clear advantage in doing so." Kate responded.

"Take this screen with you and show it to her. I think that when she sees this and hears the message that you have for her that she will comply." Kuzundi stated and handed a tube to her. "Good luck Mrs. Foster." he said.

Kate saw Foon seated in the Voltrun. She thought that it was odd that she was still using the vehicle since the operation had been terminated, at least that was her understanding. The passenger door opened as she approached and she got in and sat down. The door closed and the car pulled away.

"Hello Foon." she said.

"Hello Katherine. What was so important that we had to meet like this?" she asked.

"I need a favor from you and your help. Please take a moment and hear me out." she said.

"I will listen to what you have to say but I probably won't be able to help you Katherine. They have put you in a very bad position and it is one that I cannot see a means to escape the fate they have in store for you." Foon said sadly.

"I have been approached by an aide to Senator Sun and he has told me of a plot to have Girard and Devers assassinated within the next several hours. It is important that you get a message to Devers so that he can meet with this man and save his life." Kate said sincerely.

"Why would you want to help that man, especially after what he has done to you and your family?" Foon intently responded.

"Please take a moment and watch this." said pulling the screen from the tube.

The message began to play immediately. It outlined what Kate had told Foon initially and then went into details about how Kate was also at risk. This was something that Kate felt was possible but Kuzundi had not told her that in their meeting. Foon's expression changed upon hearing that her friend was at risk of being harmed further.

"You can turn that thing off. I will talk to Devers and make him understand that he must meet with this man. Where will the meeting be?"

"Mr. Kuzundi will come to Devers' office in New York in two hours. He can see him or send him away. It will be his decision." Kate said.

The Voltrun stopped in front of Kate's apartment building having circled the block several times while they spoke. "Katherine I will talk to you soon. Please know that I am your friend. I have only said those words a very few times, so it's important that I keep my friends healthy." she said with a sad smile.

"Thank you Foon. You are a very good friend and I am so glad that we met." Kate said as she stepped out into late afternoon heat. She turned after walking several steps and saw Foon looking at her. They waved at each other at exactly the same moment and then both smiled. There was some good that came from just about any experience if you just knew where to look for it, Kate thought.

****

Norville sat quietly next to Philip and Roger as they observed the scout teams methodically make their way to the appointed locations. Each of the scouts would have three stops to make during the two day excursion and the operation would be finished at exactly the same time that the program completed its cycle and that meant the following day would be the decision day, the day they decided to move ahead or to fall back and regroup. It was important that they acted quickly when operating the equipment at or near full power capacity as they risked detection by any of the government agencies that might be monitoring power utilization to detect criminal activity, fraud or unauthorized use of products or services.

All systems seemed to working well and there was a nervous energy present that promoted significant banter among the various team members, laughter abounded as they seemed to find most topics amusing. The most entertaining element was apparently the uniforms that they were wearing. The bright green cooling suits were the standard issue of the utility companies and while they promoted visibility they did not attract attention. One of the woman stated that it did nothing to flatter her form and the other women agreed which lead to comments about modifications that would be necessary to make the clothing more appealing. The discussion became more ridiculous as the men started to voice their opinions on what they would like to see the woman's clothing to be like.

The Alpha Scout Team arrived at their location. It had gently sloping terrain and only a few isolated building scattered about the landscape. There was no sign of movement either on the roadway or from any of the buildings. The van had pulled off the road and parked on the ground, there was no shoulder for disabled vehicles to use. The team started to busy themselves with gathering their equipment and tools together. The first order of business was to erect signs indicated that the utility company was at work in the area.

Horatio Charles climbed out of the back of the van. He was getting too old for all of this physical nonsense he thought. Norville had assured him that the younger people would be doing the physical work and he would only have to make certain that they did it right. That was before they split the operation into three teams and when they anticipated having enough shielding to keep their activities from being discovered. So much for the plan as it was presented to him six months earlier, he thought. They even had a new extraction model and the programs that they were using were completely different than those that were originally supposed to be used.

He would responsible for the extraction of the core samples, all twelve of them at each site. They had about an hour's worth of preparation needed before they could use the bore. Once they started to operate the bore there was no question that they would be vulnerable to detection.

The other member of team moved rapidly into their positions as he checked his communications link with the Command Center where Philip, Roger and Norville were working. Everything was as it should be and he moved the robotic arm that hoisted the bore from its resting place inside the van. Soon the tracked bore was on the ground behind the van and the holographic controls appeared in front of his eyes. He took a small disk shaped controller that was mounted in a recessed slot on the bore's main body. Squeezing the disc between his thumb and forefinger activated the controls and by moving his hand position he toggled through the various command menus until he reached the mobility selection. A quick squeeze of the controls selected the mobility controls and after that the movements of his hand then controlled the forward motion of the bore.

He took the telemetry reading from the predetermined coordinates and dispatched the bore to that exact location. Once it was there the unit stopped and awaited further instruction. Horatio instructed the bore to anchor itself and it did so by extending three arms from the main body rapidly appearing like telescoping spears that had been shot from some sort of weapon. The pointed tips embedded in the ground penetrating roughly eight inches into the earth. It would be almost impossible to move the bore after it had secured itself in this fashion.

The bore rotated its tracks so that the rectangular main body could be lowered and come to rest within a micro millimeter of the surface. The sample area would almost the size of the entire main body or three feet by six feet. The sample was to be taken at four different predetermined depths and then unit was to move first to the right three feet and then to the left six feet and the procedure was to be repeated for each of the movements of the bore. Each of these positioning was to be the same size and that would in turn represent a sampling of fifty four square feet and would give the group enough data to determine whether the area would be viable as a final location to be used.

The team took electromagnetic amplitude measurements and continued to perform the other samplings that had been required according to the procedures that had been developed by Avery and Willie. The time passed quickly and soon they were approaching the time when they were to activate the bores. The program had been downloaded into each bore so all Horatio had to do was to locate the initiate section on the menu and squeeze the disc.

"Horatio my good man, are you about ready?" Norville asked startling Horatio a little as he was running through the mental check list to be certain his team performed as they should.

"Give the word and I will initiate the program." he replied

.   "Good stand-by we are checking with the Bravo and Charlie teams to see if they too are on schedule." Norville answer him in a cheerful voice.

"All set everyone. You may commence in ten seconds. I will count us down." Norville said to all three teams and began to count backwards from ten. Roger sat looking at the power monitoring feed that he had intercepted from Internal Security's systems. It was not illegal to intercept the feed, he just couldn't do anything with the information that he received, which would be a crime punishable by a fine or incarceration. There were two locations where power utilization was shown in yellow otherwise the board was green. When they initiated the bores program the display should show their locations in red. This was the indicator that they were concerned about as it was a definite warning that unauthorized power utilization was occurring.

The sound of the words "... two, one and go." echoed in Horatio's ears as he squeezed the disc and watched the bore spring to life. A bright glow shown around the seam where the main body of the bore and the ground met. It was not a light that caused any pain to look at and it took Horatio a minute to realize that the light was not coming from the main body of the bore but from the ground as the extractor removed the layers of photons and their photolytic components from the earth. The entire process would take roughly fifteen minutes. At that point they would be finished and able to move on within the hour. He glanced at the time counter that showed in the right corner of his PCU display and wondered when they would know if they should expect company and if so when they would arrive.

Roger saw the indicators for the three locations go from green to yellow to red within three minutes of the beginning of the process. That was a substantially slower response than he had expected, thinking that the locations would be shown in red within seconds. It was plus six minutes and there still was no indication of any adverse reaction by the observers. Then something unexpected happened the screen went blank for a moment and the system slowly recycled. It took roughly five minutes for this to happen and another two minutes for the indicators to once again show the areas of the scout expeditions to be red.

"How much longer will the units be functioning?" Roger asked Norville.

"About three more minutes I think." Norville responded, "Are you hearing anything that would cause concern?" he then asked.

"No, quite to the contrary. It is as if they believe that the power signatures are anomalies and they are attempting to clear them from the system.

It was at that moment that the screen went black once again and when the images returned there were no red indications on the grid.

"We learned something very valuable today. The people that operate these sensor equipment are not confident in its accuracy or dependability. We were very fortunate, but I am not as confident that the next time we will have the same results. Let's get our teams moving to their next assignment." Norville told the two men.

"The data is coming in now and I will get working on parsing it so that it can be evenly distributed to my team. We should have good idea how successful this first phase was by some time tomorrow afternoon if all goes well." Roger said.

"I feel as though I am a fifth wheel at this point. Haven't been much help so far." Philip said.

"Philip, you will be needed trust me. These first sites were the easy one's next set should present some challenges that only you can help us over come." Norville said reassuringly.

"Phil let's go get something to eat after I meet with the team. The cafeteria is open for another hour and then we will be stuck. Norville would you like to join us?" Roger asked.

"No thank you Roger. Though you could bring me back a cup of soup and crackers along with something to drink. If you wouldn't mind?" Norville replied.

"Not at all." Philip said.

The two brothers walked to Roger's work area where they found his team standing together talking nervously. Then Roger noticed that among them was Willie who upon seeing Roger took an uneasy step backward and then called out, "There is the man of the hour, or should I say men of the hour?"

"Hello Willie, I am surprised to see you here. How are things going with your part of the project?" Philip asked.

Willie chose to ignore Philip's question instead he made a few joking remarks that did a good job of entertaining those that were working on Roger's team.

"I hate to be the task master but you will find your assignments at your work areas waiting for you. We are under an extreme time constraint and there will be a tremendous amount of data that will be in need of processing arriving within the next several hours. Do not plan on getting much rest during the next two or three days." Roger said trying to maintain an enthusiastic atmosphere. The group turned dutifully from their brief revelry and walked briskly back to their work areas leaving Willie, Roger and Philip alone. When they were outside of earshot Philip again asked his question to Willie.

"Phil, I was bored with what we were doing and needed a little fun. The intensity level is extremely high. The programming seems to be moving ahead at one minute and then five minutes later I feel as though I am getting nowhere. I have never had such a difficult time doing anything in my life." Willie said exasperatedly.

Philip looked at Willie as he spoke. He appeared to be genuine and while it was possible that he was indeed the connection to Senator Sun and whoever were his compatriots, it did not seem that he would be disloyal to Roger, his oldest and closest friend. Philip found that he had a very few people that were what they represented themselves to be. When this was done, he hoped that he would be able to trust people again, to be able to count on them to be what he thought they were.

"What seems to be causing you the most difficulty Willie?" Roger asked.

"The interface with the extractor requires that each photolytic element has to be analyzed and the topography of it mapped and then compared to a data array of each type of element. The comparison yields the interpretation of the age and make-up of the element and it is then fed through a filtering program that enables us to display the results. The mapping is working adequately but somewhere in one of the subroutines there is a flaw that causes the results to be overwritten periodically. What happens is…" Willie said.

Roger interrupted by saying, "The pattern buffer then yields a false result."

"Exactly, and I have not been able to find the problem." Willie responded.

"Maybe a new set of eyes would help, but I understand why you needed to walk away. I do the same thing when I have hit a wall." Roger said sympathetically.

"I do the same thing when I am writing, I get up and go do something that is completely unrelated. It throws the problem into my subconscious and there it gets worked on while I move about trying to find something to distract me and take some of the pressure off." Philip added.

Roger had suspected Willie as much if not more than Philip had and his excuse sounded far too neat to be genuine. The fact that Norville had also suspected him precipitated the decision to keep him out of the way while the scout teams were gathering their sample even though his team would be involved in the processing and interpreting the data once it was handed off by Roger's team.

Roger also knew that Willie had spoken with the Senator within the past couple of weeks and that made him a prime candidate for being the person that was providing the Senator with the programming. But when he looked at Willie he knew that he had not told the Senator anything, it wasn't him. There was something that told him that Willie did not do it.

Willie finally left to go back to his area and work through his frustrations leaving Roger and Philip to make their way to the cafeteria for some food. As they walked Roger said to Philip, "You know Willie didn't contact the Senator."

Philip looked at him and then replied, "Yes, I think you are right."

"Who else could it be?" Roger asked. Philip just shook his head. The two made good time walking to the cafeteria and there were people milling about so that any further conversation on the subject would have to wait. "Do you think Austin is alright?" Roger asked.

"I haven't heard anything in days. It would seem that they have decided to delay any action for a while." Philip answered.

"Your brother is at home and they are looking into charging two or three senior managers at WBOI for fraud and criminal mischief." a young man standing behind them interrupted. Both Roger and Philip turned to see the young man and did not recognize him.

"Who are you? And where and when did you hear that news?" Philip asked looking down sternly at the man.

"My name is Mort Hancock and I heard it where everyone else heard on the news-feeds this morning. Your brother was found to be just a pawn in an elaborate hoax." Morton said as he extended his hand to both men.

"You are the leader of the next phase?" Roger asked.

"I am the operations officer, Norville is the leader and there will be such a small number of team members at the end a more likely title would be the man that is responsible if anything goes wrong." Morton replied with an engaging smile.

"Very nice to meet you. I didn't think you or your team would be here for another few days. It was my understanding that my group would be clearing out before yours came to take our place." Roger stated.

"It's just me and I am here because Norville wanted me to see the teams at work to get an idea of what we might be up against when we are working under some pressure." Morton replied. Philip wanted to know more about Austin and his situation. He decided to play a news feed as he waited for his meal to be prepared.

It was as Morton had said, Austin had been sent home from the medical center and there was an active investigation into several WBOI senior managers' activities. It did not make sense. How did Norville manage to get them to do this? Philip decided that he would ask him when they returned, and that reminded him that he was to get him soup and crackers with something to drink.

"Thank you very much Philip. It smells appetizing." Norville said while watching the progress of the scouting teams.

"Norville, had you heard the news about Austin?" Philip asked. Norville did not immediately answer. There was a period of awkward silence, Philip decided to wait and let him answer.

"I did hear that he was home but I am not certain what happened. I am also not certain that he is out of harm's way completely. That is why I did not mention it to either of you." he answered quietly. The look on Norville's face betrayed his foreknowledge of the events or at least that is how it appeared to Philip. What game was this man playing now, he wondered.

"Norville it seems odd that the authorities would take this path without some significant pressure brought to bear and there are few people influential enough that would be willing to do something like that due to the personal risk that was very real." Roger stated after he too had drawn a similar conclusion to Norville's reaction to the news of Austin's release. Philip sensed Roger's anger building. Roger had little tolerance for people that were not forthcoming and he had been very patient with Norville but it was almost at its end.

"This was not my doing Roger." Norville said choosing his words carefully. "I only wish that I had the influence to be able to do something like that, but I don't." he continued. Norville was struggling and it was apparent to both men as they watched him try to convince them that he was not responsible for the events that had unfolded.

"Do you take me for a fool Norville?" There is no one else that has the interest in seeing my brother free that has even the remotest ability to influence his fate. How can I work with you if I can't trust you?" Roger said as he turned and walked away quickly.

"Roger…" Norville said but it was too late he had already left the room.

"Philip you must understand that I do not have that kind of power."

"Don't you?" Philip responded. "And if you don't who does?" he then asked.

Norville took a moment to answer, he was again carefully framing his reply. "It would have to be someone that was inside of WBOI or was working for the government." he finally answered.

****

"Lewis Kuzundi is here to see you sir." Virginia Smithson said while standing in the doorway to Devers' office.

"Tell him I will be with him momentarily Smithson." Devers replied. He then walked to his credenza and withdrew the bottle of whisky that was perpetual part of his office accoutrements, took it out opened it and drank directly from it, no need to stand on formality. This meeting was going to be an interesting one based upon what Foon had told him. She also told him that his life depended upon it and that statement was the true motivation for him accepting the audience. He had several security officers on standby waiting for his command should it be needed.

"Alright send him in Smithson." he bellowed.

"Mr. Devers my name is Lewis Kuzundi, I am Chief Executive Assistant to Senator Sun and I appreciate you taking a few moments of your precious time to meet with me." Kuzundi said while extending his hand.

Devers rebuffed the hand shake and gestured to the seating area and said, "I am a busy man and you have some valuable information for me. Let's get right to it then."

"As you wish." Kuzundi said settling into one of the sofas, while Devers remained standing. "We have access to next generation forecasting tools that enable us to see specific events that will occur to specific individuals within a controlled time frame. The events that have occurred in the past twenty four hours regarding Austin Lee have been set in motion because of the results of one of these forecasts. It is because of the subsequent ripples that we have come to you to offer you some valuable information." Kuzundi said and when he completed his statement he smiled.

"What information? Like I said I am very busy and do not have time for games and coy behavior Mr. Kuzundi." Devers asked sternly.

"I realize that you are in impatient man but Mr. Devers if I don't give you background information you will not be inclined to accept it as being accurate. I will continue now. There is a ninety three percent chance that when you go to perform the operation to eliminate Mr. Girard later this evening, that while you are watching the events from the hallway outside of his office, you too will be assassinated along with Katherine Foster and her family." Kuzundi said and once again smiled when he completed his message.

Devers looked at him in disbelief and at that moment decided to sit in the sofa directly across from Kuzundi.

"That is preposterous. We have no plan of operations to have this Mr. Girard you are speaking of to be assassinated and even if there was one I would certainly not be anywhere in close proximity of such an event." Devers replied in a steady voice that he was attempting to control with all of his might.

"Please call Mr. Fortesque or better yet when he calls you within the next ten minutes and instructs you as to how the operation is to be conducted I believe that upon hearing those instructions you will be more inclined to believe what I am telling you." Kuzundi replied cordially.

"You are telling me that Lionel Fortesque is going to call me and give a directive that will instruct me to kill another person? You do not know Lionel. Now I know you are wasting my time." Devers said starting feel that this was just a hoax to get him to act foolishly and was most likely a plan that DeMasters had devised. "I must ask you to leave now." Devers added.

"Please allow me one more moment?" Kuzundi asked.

"Sir, have you been monitoring the conversation? Yes, I understand, thank you." Kuzundi said to the person on the other end of the call. "Mr. Devers the call you are going to receive will convince you that I am telling you the truth. I am going to leave since there is a ninety percent chance that you will do exactly what is necessary to preserve your health and well beings. I know that you do not wish to harm Mr. Girard and based upon what we have learned, his survival will be assured as well. Oh, in the off chance you elect to disclose this information to anyone they will probably have the same incredulous attitude that you have displayed, so I would think first before you speak to anyone regarding our conversation. Thank you and good day." said Kuzundi who stood up and walked to the door.

The door opened as he approached and Smithson blocked his path. He moved to the right and she then called out to Devers, "Sir Lionel Fortesque is calling, should I put him through?"

Kuzundi turned to see the look on Devers face. Devers gestured for Kuzundi to return but he shook his head and left smiling.

****

Norville and Philip sat quietly. They watched as the teams made their way slowly to the next assigned location. This was going to be the biggest challenge for two of the three teams. Determination of the exact placement of the bores would be made at the site, on the spot. There would be no way to make a determination where to place the bore until there was visual reconnaissance of the area. Scout Team Bravo had the most challenging assignment of all. They were headed to York Pennsylvania to a meeting place that could very well have been destroyed by construction. Of the nine locations that were being scouted this one had the greatest potential for impacting the time thread most favorably, it also had the greatest potential of being unusable.

Scout Team Bravo was Avery's team and she had been very optimistic about the data that had been collected at the first site. The magnetic readings were far better than she had originally hoped that they would be. That feeling lead her to doubt their chances of having a success at this difficult location. They would be arriving in York two hours before sun down and there would be a significant amount of activity in the area where they were headed.

The Cottage Hill District had been a favorite area of development many times in the past two hundred years. It had been the site of the Cottage Hill School which was a school for girls from the South whose parents were seeking for them an education north of the Mason Dixon Line. It was here that Kathleen O'Sullivan, a young girl of fourteen, met a man, William Harper, who provided her with a letter and map of troop locations. She would then deliver this message in a bouquet of flowers to General Gordon.

They knew the date and Philip had been able to determine an approximate meeting place on the campus of the school. They had used

Roger's program to help to refine where the meetings had taken place. It was hoped that the area along Codorus Creek had not been developed like every other square foot of the area had been. The van moved slowly toward the destination and like each of the other scout teams it was several hours away from being able to determine whether the day could be deemed a success.

****

The Power Grid Monitoring Unit Chief arrived at the station feeling like this was just another one of those simple problems that his paranoid group of subordinates could not muster enough courage to call it an anomaly and move on to the next trial. When he walked through the doorway into the main control room there was pandemonium playing out before his eyes. "What is going on here?" he said loudly, to which he received no immediate response. He waited for a moment for someone to see him but the crew was apparently too absorbed in what they were doing. "What is going on here!" he yelled this time and there was immediate silence and all eyes turned to him.

"Sir, it seems we have either a system problem or there has been an unauthorized power utilization at three different location in south central Pennsylvania." the section manager said while walking up to greet the Unit Chief. He then described the events that took place several hours before and the steps they took to identify the problem.

"How long did it last?" the Unit Chief asked.

"Approximately fifteen minutes and when we reset the system the second time, it vanished." the section manager replied.

"I see, and nothing has happened since then?" the Unit Chief continued to question.

"No, nothing. We have been running as many diagnostic test as we can without doing a complete system restore. I have hesitated doing that since it will take us out of action for ninety minutes." the section manager replied.

"It appears that you have done everything you could within your authority to determine whether it was a ghost or a very serious infraction. I will need to see the recording of the event and will make the decision if we are going to do a purge and cold restart. Where can I have some privacy so that I can review this?" the Unit Chief inquired.

After spending several minutes viewing the recordings of the event the Unit Chief was no closer to understanding the nature of the problem then the members of the crew that had witnessed its occurrence. He was faced to decide between two courses of action; the first being to initialize the system, which would mean that there would be a period of ninety minutes when they would not be able to monitor activity throughout the region or the second alternative, and the one that protocol dictated be followed, was to contact the Department of Internal Security. While the second action would be the most prudent at this time, it meant surrendering their jobs to another agency and if there was no threat and this was simply a computer problem it would be very embarrassing to him. His motto was to take ownership of the problem and fix it.

****

The van carrying Scout Team Bravo approached the city limits of York and slowed even more as it continued its journey through the quaint city. York had been not included in the rail expansion thus far and there was a significant number of commuter buses and PTs that were on the streets. The population had been increasing in recent years since WBOI had placed a large call center that was responsible for customer service activities for the northeastern part of the country. They were the largest employer in the region, with almost twenty two thousand working in the sprawling campuses that ringed the center of the city.

Housing had been plentiful until the recent growth spurt with an average person able to afford to live in a single detached home. Many of these homes had been built before the Civil War, an irony that was not lost on Philip as he surveyed the city through the cameras mounted in the van. On the horizon there was evidence of construction and he could see that the familiar trapezoidal silhouettes against the brightness of the cloud covered sky.

"Avery how far are you from the objective?" Norville asked. Philip and Norville sat quietly together not knowing what to say.

"I will go look for Roger, the teams are going to be in position shortly and we will need him to monitor the power monitoring activity." Philip said getting up.

Norville just nodded in response to his statement. He was as much upset with the two brother's as they were with him. Their reaction to the release of their brother and the suspicion they had was unfounded and he resented being the object of their suspicion. It would be necessary for everyone to put their differences aside for the next several days. There would have to be a way for them to make peace and move on with their assignments. Norville struggled to find a way to put the accusations out of his mind. The Lees had reason to doubt him because he had kept much from them but he never was disloyal and he always had done his best to protect them even when it was not clear he was working for their best interest.

Roger followed Philip slowly into the room. "Norville, I want to apologize for losing my temper. We need to work together, and I made a commitment to the project that I am going to honor. We will talk about Austin and that situation when the teams have completed their mission and before I pack up to leave. Okay?" Roger said sincerely.

"Thank you Roger. You are an honorable man. We will have that talk at that time. You too Philip if you want to be included." Norville said with a sense of relief evident in the tone of his voice.

"Absolutely." Philip said.

"Good, where are the teams located?" Roger asked.

"Alpha and Charlie are at their target locations and are preparing for the bore deployment within the next thirty minutes. The Bravo team is still about ten minutes from the location and once they arrive it will be some time before they are ready to deploy the bore." Norville said.

"Philip we are going to need you to give us the guidance necessary to locate the optimum location to take our samples. Have you determined how you can best assist them?" Norville continued asking Philip for more information about the location and what landmarks might be available for them to use. Philip nodded and began looking at his notes once again to see if he had somehow missed a potential lead that could make this part of the exercise go more smoothly.

****

"I think we are going to have to purge and initialize the grid." the Unit Chief said. "Prepare for an accelerated restart." he told the Section Manager. The crew went to work preparing for the initialization. Because they elected to use an accelerated restart the time the grid would be out of service would be roughly seventy minutes instead of the ninety minutes that the process normally took. The routine message was sent out to the off-site monitoring facilities that the system would not be available ninety minutes. This was the last command that was initiated before the system was powered down.

****

"I can't believe it!" Roger exclaimed.

"Can't believe what?" Philip asked beating Norville to the question.

"They have shut down power monitoring for the next ninety minutes." Roger replied.

"Could this be a trick?" Norville asked.

"No, I don't think so. From what I know about the process this is the step they would take if they felt that they system had been acting erratically. I think that because the signatures were not present when the system came back after the restarts that they were concerned that they there might be a computer problem. This is faulty logic but I have worked with enough government agencies to know that they follow protocol and this would be the next step prior to contacting Internal Security." Roger explained.

"We have a great window of opportunity, let's not lose it. Philip please contact Avery and tell her that she needs to move quickly and I will tell the other two teams to start using their bores as soon as they are ready." Norville said.

Avery, upon hearing the news told her team that they were to move as quickly as possible to get the bore out of the vehicle. The challenge of find the right location would be the only thing that would slow them down she thought. As the van moved down Cottage Hill Road Avery positioned the cameras within the vehicle to view the area along the creek where the rendezvous had allegedly taken place. Philip watched the images that were being broadcasted with the cube split into three segments one for each of the cameras. He was looking for a specific tree that Virginia had written about in her diary. It was under that tree that she had received the letter and the map that she would later pass to the general. Ever so slowly the van rolled down the narrow winding road.

The area had been developed so often throughout the years it was difficult to determine whether they would be fortunate to find a tree or the location of where that tree may have stood. Elm trees have been known to live for several hundred years and this particular one would be very distinctive if it had not been felled in during construction during the early Twentieth century. Each tree that the camera imaged was run through recognition software to determine its type and age. The trees that had been see were poplars and they were all less than forty years old.

As the van meandered the serpentine road it encountered a fairly sharp bend and there was a plaque that indicated that they were on the site of the school and later the Gas Works. Philip asked if they could find a place to pull off the road and get out on foot to look for the tree or evidence of where it may have been. Avery responded that they would look for a suitable place to pull the van off the road and then they would all begin to search for the tree.

"Your best bet to find is within a one thousand square foot area that is located very near to your location. The strip of land that abuts the creek is where we hope to find it, if it was not there we have no hope in finding it since the area has been developed so many times and construction and demolition will have obliterated the all evidence that could allow us to discover its location." Philip said.

"It should not take us very long to search the area, I will leave one of my people with the vehicle to unload the bore should we be fortunate to use it. How are the other teams fairing?" Avery asked.

"Charlie team will be finished with their assignment in about twenty minutes and Alpha will be done in about forty more minutes if we are lucky." Norville interjected.

Philip watched intently as the Avery lead the small group to the specified coordinates. The strip of ground was about twenty feet wide and fifty feet long. They fanned out so that as they walked they could see almost every square inch of the ground. They were looking for evidence that would betray the past existence of that fabled elm. There were two men in addition to Avery that were searching. One of the men was a magnetic field specialist that was carrying a magnetic signature detection device. He swept the wand back and forth in front of him as he watched the display that was integrated into his PCU.

"Lars are you getting anything on the MSD?" Avery asked.

"There are two very faint signatures. This area has not had a great deal of human traffic for a very long time, the readings indicate a hundred years or longer. We may be able to look for signatures that date back two hundred and fifty years and see what we come up with if you like." Lars responded.

"What about vegetation? Can you search for the magnetic aura of a tree?" Avery asked.

"Yes, but not that long ago. The best I could hope to pull in would be about seventy years after it had died." Lars answered.

"Let's hope this tree was standing until recently. As you can see there is not a tree in sight." Avery stated.

****

"John, you know what has to be done regarding Girard and I want you to handle it personally. I don't mean that you have to be in the same room but I want you there to offer tactical support and to encourage the men. Also just think how good it will look that you were there to apprehend the man that cause majority of the problems. The public relations group is putting together an entire piece on the history of Girard's activities for the past twenty years. Anyone that views that will understand just how much a menace the man has been. John this needs to be done within the next several hours. I will have Fortuna call you and coordinate the operation." Fortesque said finally finishing.

Devers responded that he would do whatever he thought was best and disconnected the call. The next call he placed was to Girard telling him to come to his office immediately.

Girard was sitting in Devers' sofa within ten minutes of the call. Devers explained what had happened and what he believed was the only course of action that could be taken. Lionel Fortesque had to be retired permanently and it had to look like it was a natural occurrence or a suicide. Devers asked Girard what he thought would be best.

"Suicide, he can leave a note that will take full responsibility for all actions and get you and Foster out of the limelight." Girard said directly.

"Alright we will need a note and what type of suicide would be appropriate for Lionel? Poison? Hanging? Gunshot to the head?" Devers asked getting more agitated as he continued to think about the prospects of murdering a man who had been his mentor and a friend for more than twenty years.

"He would be a jumper, I think?" Girard said clinically.

"I don't know about this it seems that it is becoming more difficult by the moment." Devers complained.

"Devers this is only going to work if you are involved and I mean on the front line. You will have to be the one to get us inside and once we are there I will take over." Girard insisted.

"It will only be the two of us involved, we cannot risk telling anyone else what we are about to do." Devers told him.

Girard nodded and then said, "Let's get going this needs to be accomplished and then we need to provide ourselves with alibis so that there can be no question that we were not involved." Girard said as he stood up and straightened his shirt.

"This program that Senator Sun has would be extremely useful to possess. Perhaps tomorrow I will take a trip to Virginia to see how neighborly the good Senator can be." Devers said.

"Wait." he then told Girard. He went to the credenza and pulled out the bottle, he offered some to Girard who simply looked at him in disbelief. He then opened it and took a long pull. As returned the bottle to its place he commented, "My supply is starting to get a little low. I believe I will tell Smithson to get me more."

Girard and Devers walked silently to the elevators. Devers had never been this involved in the death of anyone, though his orders had precipitated the death of several people throughout his tenure with WBOI. This was a new experience and he was uncertain that he was up for the task. Time will tell, he thought. At that moment he turned to Girard and asked him, "I need a reason to be stopping to see him unannounced. Any ideas as to why I am visiting him after he had given me very specific orders?"

Girard did not respond and they took the elevator to the parking garage where Devers car was waiting. Devers was becoming agitated and it was clear to Girard that he was not comfortable with what they were about to do.

"You need to make him want to invite you into his office. There will most likely be two or three people there and they will have to be encouraged to leave the area. These people will be the most likely source of any blow back to us. They will have to be encouraged to leave before we arrive or they will have to leave with you and... that's it. We will go up together and I will get off the elevator on the floor below and take the backstairs. You will have to get to that door and open it for me. After you meet with Fortesque you will leave ordering his people to leave with you because he is so distraught. You will take the elevator to the ground floor and request a security team be dispatched to your location. Wait in the lower lobby for them and once they arrive brief the detail leader slowly and carefully, explaining that you were concerned for Fortesque's well-being. The rest you will leave to me."

Devers nodded in agreement. At least he wouldn't be there when Fortesque would be forced to jump to his death.

"I will tell him that I am having trouble with the concept of being at the location when you are eliminated. I will be able handle this." Devers said more for the benefit of convincing himself then Girard. The Voltrun maneuvered through traffic quietly and efficiently. They soon arrived at the Seven Eighty Third Avenue the location of Fortesque's office. The security beacon communicated with the parking garage entrance and they were allowed proceed.

The call from Fortesque came in quickly, "John why are you here and not waiting for our call to proceed?" Fortesque asked.

"Lionel I need to speak with you in person. I guess it's a case of the nerves or something but I am having a problem with being at the location when we resolve our problem. Can you spare a minute or two old friend?" Devers asked in a wavering voice. It was clear to anyone that knew John Devers that he was emotionally distraught.

"Oh, by all means, I completely understand your nervousness. Please come up." Fortesque said kindly.

Girard reached into his pocket and withdrew a small hand gun. It was a fifteen shot military pistol designed to be concealed in the palm of one's hand. It fired explosive rounds, each one no more than a millimeter in diameter. The copper colored weapon was very light weight and very deadly. The weapon was self-aiming and would correct small target acquisition mistakes made by the user.

"You should take this in case he decides to remedy his problems in a different manner." Girard told Devers.

"I hope it doesn't come to that but you are thoughtful to give this to me." Devers said.

"Thoughtfulness has nothing to do with this, if you are dead then so am I." Girard said plainly.

"Let's go." Devers said.

****

"Avery we need to make one more sweep before we give up on this site. We have about twenty minutes remaining until the monitors come back on but it's critical that you move quickly, we cannot have just one location show up. Power monitoring will notify Internal Security." Norville said.

"Very good we are making every effort to find this location, but it is not looking very promising." Avery replied. Having replied that they would make every effort she turned to the two men and told them that we had scan the area one more time and if they found anything that look promising to let her know immediately.

They walked about fifteen feet when one of the men noticed an indentation in the ground that was elliptical in shape and about three feet across. "Dr. Silcox over here please." he called out.

Avery spotted it and bent down to look closely "Bring that magnetic signature reader here please. Hurry we don't have much time." Avery said impatiently.

As he approached with the reader the technician had a big smile. "I think this is it Dr. Silcox. The data reads as an elm that was standing here up until about fifty five years ago, and it was over two hundred years old at that time." he said.

"Great bring out the bore we have to get the data now." Avery barked.

"Avery it is great that you found it but you don't have much time. Our estimates are that you have maybe ten minutes and that you will need at least fifteen." Norville said.

"We are doing this and we will be out of here before they get a true fix on our location. We have worked too hard on this to not be successful." Avery said firmly.

"Move quickly and if there is anything we can do from our end we will do It." Norville replied.

****

The Unit Chief sat patiently reading a letter from his daughter who was away a college. She was telling him about her classes and to his chagrin her new male friend. She described him as young and eager to learn but all the Chief could think about was that he was eager to take advantage of his daughter. He glanced up from the letter to see the count down on the rotating pyramid screens showing four minutes and twelve seconds. This would hopefully put this mess to rest and he could go home and enjoy a nice bath to ease his painful joints.

The people in the control room became more animated as the time to restart approached. If there were any more indication of unauthorized power utilization he would have to contact Internal Security immediately. All he would need was an accurate reading as to the location where the power utilization was occurring and they would have a team at the location in minutes.

****

Five more minutes was all that they needed when Norville's call came through.

"Yes, I know we will be able to shut down in less than five minutes and everything is packed up and ready to go. We will be on our way out of here in about eight minutes." Avery said before Norville had a chance to speak.

"Avery it's more important that you don't get caught, the grid will be back on line in less than two minutes. Shut it down now!" Norville insisted. Avery looked at the bore and the meter it showed three minutes and twelve seconds to completion.

"I am going to wait the three minutes Norville and I swear to you that we will be alright." Avery insisted and terminated the call.

****

The counter had reached zero and the displays were coming up in an orderly fashion. Each grid indicator cycled through from red to yellow and finally to green. The huge board that took up most of the wall in front of the workstations where the monitoring agents worked was flashing predominately green and yellow. There were only six or seven grids that had not refreshed from their original red color. The Unit Chief asked the

Section Manager whether any of the locations were the ones that had shown red before. His answer was no.

"How much longer should we wait?" he asked the Chief.

"The cycle will be complete in less than one minute if there are any sections still showing red get me the exact coordinates so that I can provide them to Internal Security." the Chief responded.

"Yes, sir." he replied as they watched the remaining red lights turn to yellow and then to green.

"Shut it down now, we are done. Quickly, quickly, we need to move out of here now!" Avery said in a tone that conveyed true urgency. They were done and the bore was moving slowly back to the van which was open and ready to accommodate it upon its arrival. "Norville, we are getting ready to move out. Please let me know if there is anyone on the way." Avery implored.

"I will, so far there have been no calls placed to Internal Security. That does not mean that there aren't going to be any or that we may not have detected them. Keep moving and let me know when you have left the area and are on route to the rest area." Norville requested.

****

The call placed to Internal Security was answered within twenty seconds during that time the remaining indicator that had be showing highlighting that somewhere in York Pennsylvania there was unauthorized power utilization changed to yellow and then to green. The entire map for the northeastern section of the United States was green.

"Rogers, Internal Security what is the nature of your emergency?" the agent answered.

"This is Unit Chief Lonugo at the Northeast Power Monitoring Facility, I have to report a red light in York Pennsylvania. It has, since I placed this call, gone to green but there is something odd going on in Pennsylvania and we would like your assistance to determine if there is criminal activity or a threat to national security." the Unit Chief stated.

"Please hold sir." Rogers responded.

The call was transferred three times before Director Scott picked up saying, "Hilman Scott here, how can I help you Chief?"

"Director we have been detecting short duration unauthorized power utilization in south central Pennsylvania and are requesting a field investigation by Internal Security as soon as possible."

"Please give me the background." Scott replied.

The Unit Chief went on to explain the events that had taken place over the past several hours and that because of the nature of the detection protocol dictated that computer malfunction be eliminated, which it had with the last test. There was a marginal residual positive that lasted three minutes beyond the time that it should have cleared from the system.

Scott listened to the entire narrative and then said, "Good job Chief you and your group have been very thorough, I will be assigning a team to this immediately. I am relatively sure that whoever is doing this is testing our system before they go into full production. We can use the next two days to locate them and discover their intent."

"Thank you Director. I was hoping that you would see it for what it was and not just make it seem like we at the Power Monitoring are suffering from paranoia." the Chief responded.

"Glad to be of service I will have agents in the area within the next two hours. You will hear from the agent in charge when they are in York to get as much detail as possible about the site. Good night." Scott said.

"Good night Director Scott." the Chief replied.

****

"Norville we are about twenty minutes away from the rest area. Any activity from Internal Security?" Avery asked.

"They were called and it appears that they will be on site within the next several hours. We will have our work cut out for us tomorrow. I want to have a strategy conference call at six tomorrow morning before you head out to the final sites. Roger has an idea that would make it difficult for them to track you accurately, we just want to think out the impact a little more before deciding whether we should implement it or not. Have a good night and please limit communication I am certain that there will be people listening." Norville said.

Avery responded, "We had a great day and it was almost perfect because the data we collected should make the rest of the project go that much smoother. Good night Norville, please tell Philip and Roger thank you."

"I will, good job and you are right we had a great day. Good night." Norville replied and ended the call.

****

The elevator stopped at the floor below the top. It was floor 99 and it was owned by the small brokerage company that occupied it entirely. Accessing the stairs would not be as easy as Girard had hoped because he was met by a security guard as he stepped off the elevator. "I am here to see Mr. Kearns." Girard stated directly.

"Mr. Kearns, is not here was he expecting you?" the guard responded resting his hand on his stun pistol.

"Yes of course. Why would I be here at this hour if it was not for an appointment? Can you call him? Maybe he is running late." Girard responded aggressively.

"I will call him. What is your name please?" he asked.

"Lionel Fortesque, I have the offices on the floor above." Girard replied.

"Very good sir, would you like to have a seat?" the guard inquired politely.

"No, but could I use your rest room? I have been experience some stomach problems throughout the day." Girard asked.

"It is in that direction down that hall second door on the right." the guard said pointing to the corridor to Girard's right. The stairway entrance was at the end of the hall and Girard walked quickly, when he reached the door to the rest room he stopped to see if he was being observed but he was not. He made his way to the doorway and entered the stairwell and made short work of the stairs. He found the door was propped open and he entered cautiously. He heard voices as Devers was ordering the people to accompany him to the lobby. The tone from the elevator rang out and then he heard the doors close and it was quiet.

Girard walked to the reception area and then he slowly entered the inner office. He had expected to find Fortesque at his desk but did not see him at first. He walked toward the rest room door that was located behind his desk and then he saw him lying on the floor motionless. He reached down to check his pulse there was no evidence of a pulse. As he stood up he heard the tone of the elevator open and heard the sound of men's voices. It was then that he knew that Devers had set him up. There would be no chance to surrender, his best bet was to try to make the stairwell and somehow get back to the offices below. Unfortunately there was no way to do that without going through the men that were going to kill him. He knew it was over. He been outwitted by that weak drunken fool, how could he have been so stupid, he thought.

Chapter Sixteen

The six o'clock conference call was brief and to the point. It had been decided that the three teams would stagger their usage of power. Alpha team would be first and five minutes prior to completion Bravo team would initiate their bore protocols followed by the Charlie team five minutes prior to Bravo completing their mission. Alpha would move locations and would initiate a fourth power usage for ten minutes and would commence five minutes prior to the Charlie team completing their mission. After that all teams were to return to the rest area where they would abandon their equipment and return to Maryland using the PTs that would be waiting for them. There would be two people to each PT and they were not to take a direct route to the facility but were to go by way of Harrisburg, Pittsburgh and Philadelphia which meant that return trips would take up to five hours.

Norville gave them a quick but inspired speech about the good that they were doing for all of mankind and then the communications were severed not to be reinstated until the first team was set to initiate the power sequence and then only to alert them as to Internal Security activities. The exposure time for an individual team was roughly twenty two minutes and the initiation of the second site should cause Internal Security to hesitate in their pursuit for up to five minutes thus giving each team a good chance to meet their objectives.

"Good luck everyone and remember that we are doing this for everyone who lives on this planet." Norville said as he turned to Roger and Philip and crossed his fingers.

****

The press were there in great numbers. How often did they have a murder to report about especially one with a prominent WBOI executive that was involved with gangs and subterfuge? Devers was there speaking about how he had been manipulated by Fortesque and how Girard had been working with him. They died in a gun fight killing each other before the security forces could apprehend them. Devers handed each a one tube full of the nefarious deeds that Girard had actually done and there were links to Fortesque both real and created to make it appear that this high level scandal had exposed all that were guilty and those left would have to work hard to repair the banks credibility and image.

The banks credibility and image was not greatly tarnished. The people were amused by the scandal but the public had a short memory about things like this and it wouldn't be long before everyone had forgotten Lionel Fortesque and Girard.

Devers was now in position to pursue the job of president as long as Drew Morris was promoted and there was no reason to suspect that he would not be promoted. As soon as this circus was over he was prepared to return to his office and sit back and plan what would be the next step in his career. He thought that a call to Drew Morris was probably in order, perhaps lunch with him and DeMasters. He must have a value to DeMasters since they made a point of letting him know about Fortesque's intent to have him killed. That reminded him that he must contact Kuzundi and find out more about the program and how he could get a copy of it for his business and personal use.

****

Internal Security had positioned five agents in the center of York. They were equipped with technology that would pick up residual power signatures. They were also armed with video surveillance warrants that would enable them to retrieve any recorded images for a twenty four hour period within the city limits of York. They had an open line to Power Monitoring and as soon as any area were to go red they were to be dispatched to that location immediately. The briefing that had occurred earlier did not yield a specific location and as a result the city was divided into five zones and each man was methodically driving on all the roads of the city of York. They were seeking a residual signature of power utilization and as the morning wore on there was an air of frustration that was present as they did not find what they were seeking.

At ten minutes past eleven, on Seminary Ridge in Gettysburg Battle field, Alpha team initiated their bore's programming and the power indicators went from green to yellow and finally red within a four minute timeframe. The team in York was alerted to the detection and two of the PTs carrying DIS agents moved rapidly toward Gettysburg. They were nineteen minutes away from reaching the city limits and they would receive exact coordinates while they were on route.

The race with Alpha Team and DIS had begun and the hope was that within nine minutes the next team would begin to power up their bore for its assignment. Bravo Team was ready and in position in a field just off the Emmitsburg Road where it been determined that Lee had stopped on route to Gettysburg. It was here that the forged papers from J. E. B. Stuart would be presented to the Commanding General. This site was roughly seven miles from the Alpha Team site. They were standing by and ready to proceed in less than two minutes.

"Bravo you must perform your operation flawlessly, as I know you will. Bon chance." Norville said them encouraging them to keep to the plan.

The DIS agents were approaching the city limits of Gettysburg when the exact coordinates of the power utilization were communicated to them. They were approximately nine minutes away from reaching the location when they were informed that another hot spot had been detected. They were informed that the new site was roughly thirteen minutes from their current location and with that notification the PTs came to a stop. The agents called request clarification and they were told to hold position temporarily. Within two minutes they were back moving again, one agent was heading to the original site, while the other was directed to the new location.

Two of the units that had remained in York were activated to join the hunt in the Gettysburg area. They had just gotten underway and each was headed to one of the two sites to assist the agents that were on route when the first site went to green and the agent on route had not reached the site where the power usage had been detected. As he approached the site he saw no evidence of any activity whatsoever and there was no residual power signature present. He was then instructed to proceed to the second site and because of that there would be four agents converging on that location. The Unit Chief saw what was developing and decided that it would be appropriate to redirect at least one agent back to the first site to determine if they could find the source of the power or gain information about the person or persons using the generator. He made his request through channels and shortly after that agent that was originally dispatched to that location was instructed to return to that site and begin an investigation. The supervising agent believed that three agents would be more than adequate to handle the second incident.

"Avery you have three agent converging on your location and the first one will be there in roughly seven minutes. How much time do you have left before you can power down?" Norville asked anxiously.

"We are ten minutes away from being able to pack up and leave." she responded.

"Charlie Team will be going live in less than five minutes that should give you a minute or two but not much more. I will see if there is anything else we can do. If they arrive don't shut down and keep the data stream coming we don't want to lose this opportunity." Norville instructed her.

"I agree, I had no intention of giving up until they pull the plug." Avery responded.

"Roger is there anything you can do to help them?" Norville asked.

"I can try to send them a few false reading but there is danger in doing that, they may be able to trace it back to our location." Roger replied.

"Norville, let me call someone that might be able to at least slow them down." Philip interjected.

"Who would that be?" Norville inquired suspiciously.

"Senator Sun." Philip replied. "That would be very dangerous Philip though there is someone you could call that would help a great deal, your father. He could power up multiple generators up and down the east coast." Norville replied.

Philip thought immediately about the repercussions and how it could put his father and the whole family at risk. He immediately imagined the impact on himself and his mother. "I don't think I can ask him to do that, especially with what he and my mother have recently gone through with Austin." Philip replied.

"I agree I think I can set up a cascading loop of false positives that will not be traceable to our location for a very long time." Roger said.

"On second thought I agree, I don't think we should involve Gregory either, he has done enough for the cause already. Roger explain to me how this will work." Norville said.

Roger initiated the cascading loop and the board at Power Monitoring lit up red intermittently. It was obvious to the Unit Chief what was happening and he would have directed the DIS agents to stay on their course but it was not his decision to make. He alerted DIS as to the situation and then recommended a course of action. DIS responded by halting the agents and as such bought the Bravo Team a little more time, but not too much. DIS command elected to have one of the agents continue to the location and the others were to maintain their position until it was determined what was the best course of action. While they were discussing tactics the Unit Chief was implementing a new security protocol which effectively locked Roger out of the system.

"We are now officially blind." Roger said.

"Is there any way we can help our teams?" Norville asked plaintively.

"No, they know we have been monitoring them and they have enhanced the security so that I cannot gain access. You should let the teams know the status." Roger replied.

Norville contacted all three teams and then asked Alpha Team to stop and initiate the power generator for three minutes and then move quickly to another location and re-initiate the power generation within eight minutes. "If we are fortunate this will confuse them enough to have them stop chasing us for a few minutes while they attempt to understand what is afoot." Norville instructed.

"That is our best hope. Bravo is about five minutes away from finishing Charlie Team has begun their power sequence in a few moments they will have three sites from which to choose." Roger said smiling. The smile was not returned by Norville who looked deeply concerned.

"Norville there is still no sign of any DIS agents and we have less than a minute to go. Have you heard from Adria regarding the status of their assignment?" Avery asked.

"No there has been no word and I deliberately not contacting her. She can get flustered when put in high stress situations and this definitely qualifies as one. When you are done get out of there as quickly as you can. Drive a few miles and then power the generator up again and do so for the next five minutes, that should give DIS enough to think about while Adria is finishing up her mission." Norville said.

"Okay, we are finished and the bore is being loaded into the vehicle. We will be out of here in two minutes. I will call you when we stop next to offer the diversion. All data will be transmitted within the next five minutes so I would say at that time we have a successful mission." Avery said with slightly less tension in her voice.

Adria saw the DIS agent approaching from the crest of the hill he was two minutes from their location and they had four minutes to finish their mission. It was not going to end well she thought. "Norville, its Adria. They have found us and will be with us momentarily we will still have two minutes worth of work to accomplish before we can shut down." she said. There was no answer. "Hello are you there?" she asked.

"I am here. I am so sorry Adria, we desperately need you for the final phase of this project and I will get you out as soon as possible." Norville replied.

"We did very well today and I am hoping that the documents that I have will allow me to keep the unit running for the full term." Adria said.

"Maybe we will be very fortunate and they will accept the documents and let you go with a warning." Norville said hopefully.

"Not likely. They have just arrived I will leave the line open so that you can hear what transpires." she replied.

Roger initiated a link with the Charlie Team bore and displayed a counter that showed that there were two minutes and twelve seconds left until the until would be able to be shut down. The video link was active and they could see Adria speaking with a man in a silver cooling suit with the Internal Security crest on the right breast. Adria handed him what all assumed was the forged authorization for the use of the power generation equipment. They had altered the display on the side panels of the van to show the name Norwalk Scientific Research, a research company that Norville used when he wanted appear to be performing government sanctioned work.

Roger, Philip and Norville watched intently as Adria argued with the man who had demanded that she shut down the power generator. With one minute twelve seconds left Adria moved toward the bore and then turned to the man and asked if she could speak to his supervisor. At that point the DIS agent pulled a weapon from his pocket and pointed it Adria, who gasped in horror.

"Please don't hurt me, I will power the generator down." she said imploringly and as she said that the bore shut down. The cycle had been completed.

"Now all we have to do is get her out of there safely, along with that sample data." Norville said as he noticed the arrival of two more of the agents. The one agent appeared to be in charge and he took the agent that had arrived first on the scene along with the documentation aside to apparently decide what to do with Adria and her team. They seemed to be slightly confused by the document.

"Why was this document not registered through proper channels?" the agent asked Adria.

"I thought that it was. I am only a field technician and I only do what I am told. We are doing preliminary work for the transit system. Trying to determine whether the ground is suitable for tube construction or if elevated rail will be the best solution." Adria replied. Using the connection to Norwind was sure to add another level of confusion. The company was so large and had so many departments and divisions it was likely they wouldn't be able to give them an answer for days. While they were discussing what to do the last of the data was transmitted and the mission was almost complete.

"Adria we have all the data. Great job. Please be patient we will get you out of this somehow." Norville assured her.

"Philip what do you think is going to happen?" Norville asked him.

Philip looked at him bewildered and said that he did not know. How could he know what was going to happen?

Then Roger perked up. "We have a way to find out and to possibly influence the outcome, the program that the Senator altered so that it could predict the future." he said enthusiastically.

"Can you make it work?" Norville asked.

"I wrote the program. If I can't make it work then you should have fired me long ago." Roger said confidently.

Roger worked quickly creating a scenario that duplicated the current situation and executed the program. By the time he had the program running the agents had decided to place Adria and her team in custody and to confiscate the van and its contents. The program began to catch up with the action that were occurring in real time and then it began to forecast results. It forecasted the traffic conditions and the phone call that one of the agents received from his wife leaving a message that she would be late getting home from work.

The events did not seem to have much to do with Adria and what would happen to her until the time line reached seven hours in the future. A call would be received from Senator Sun's office inquiring as to who they have apprehended and once he learns of the situation he indicates that Adria must be considered a threat to national security and that he was sending a team to investigate the computer systems and power generation equipment. DIS was to make all of the information that they had collected about the episode available for the team when they arrived at the Harrisburg field office.

Roger then inserted the variable where Adria and the team were released before that call was received by DIS. A list of scenarios was created. They included some very far-fetched plans that would have had little or no chance of success but one of them did appear to be viable.

"Take a look at this." Roger said to Norville and Philip.

"The program has given us a plan that might enable us to get them out custody before DIS surrenders them to Senator Sun's people." Roger continued.

"A call could be placed by someone posing as an executive of Norwind Corporation explaining that there had been an oversight and that the permit petition had not been properly executed. The person that would have to be called would be Hilman Scott and it would be advisable that an attractive woman placed the call. Wait one minute..." Roger stopped in mid thought and punched in some other variables and then stared at the results.

"That's even better. An attractive woman goes to Hilman Scott's office and presents him with the application for permits and seeks his help. Scott has a weakness for women and he is a lecherous pig but it can be used in our favor." Roger said and then stopped to wait for a reaction.

Norville was trying to process the information and come to a conclusion that would be good for everyone on his team. He could not come up with an answer that did not have some negative results for someone.

"Is there no other way?" he asked.

"According to the program there are limited options. This scenario has a forty two percent chance of being favorably resolved. The others are twelve percent or less." Roger replied.

"How about getting them out after the Senator takes them into their custody?" Norville asked seeking alternative. He was could not bring himself to put another person into a situation where they would be at risk as well and it also was not appropriate compel someone to use their sex to achieve the desired results.

"I will have to do some quick modifications. How far out would you like me to take this?" Roger asked.

"As far as we have to insure that we are not putting the project or others at risk. But we must also do this as quickly as possible for Adria and her team's sake." Norville said and the looked at Roger who was staring at him quizzically.

"I know, I am asking the impossible once again, but you keep delivering results. You have spoiled me." Norville said with a smile. Roger returned the smile and turned back to the program.

"What about Jeremy Giles?" Philip asked. "Do you think that he could help in some way?" he continued.

"Who is Jeremy Giles? Wait is that the man that works with Dad? How could he help?" Roger asked.

"I don't think he could help but Roger please put him into the program and see if he can be of some assistance here." Norville answered.

The addition of someone like Jeremy Giles required a download from the central computer files and his profile information was added to the equation in a matter of minutes. Roger waited while the program recompiled and then he executed it once more. The results were startling. Jeremy Giles could solve the problem if he were to enlist the help of his wife Laura. Laura would simply have to ask the Senator to release them and he apparently would do this favor for her because of their long standing relationship.

"I don't believe this. Philip how did you know?" Roger asked. Philip just looked back and smiled.

"Very good idea Philip, I wouldn't have thought that there would be that much leverage but apparently there is." Norville added.

"I think I know just the person to reach out to him for us." Philip added.

"Give her a call. If she doesn't want to do it, I will reach out to him." Norville said.

"It's nice that you two know what is going on here. I feel as though I am trying to understand a conversation that is being spoken in a different language. I hear familiar sounds and think I have got the basics only to find out I don't know what is being said. When you have an opportunity I would be interested in learning what just happened here." Roger said.

"Jessica, how are you?" Philip asked.

"I am fine Philip, how are things going with the project?" she asked in return.

"Things have been going pretty well but we did encounter a problem and need your help." he said directly.

"Oh, what can I do?" she responded. "We need you to reach out to Jeremy and have him contact Senator Sun to ask a favor." he continued to explain.

Jessica listened to what Philip had to say and then awkwardly responded, "I am not sure that he will help you but I will give him a call right away. I know that it is important that the team get back because several of them are to be working on the final phase of the project." she said. Philip took note of the fact that Jessica seemed to be very much aware of the project and if he had not been conditioned to trust absolutely no one, he may have been surprised. As it was, he took the statement in stride and stored the information for later possible use and anticipated that he would eventually see the relevance of the statement at some future time. He had become aware that life was nothing more than a series of progressive revelations, a discovery he had made while reading that journal.

"Philip when are you coming to see me?" Jessica asked.

"It depends upon the how it goes. I would like to say tonight but I think tomorrow is really the best guess at this point. Can I call you in a couple of hours and we can make plans then. Okay?" Philip asked.

"That sounds good. I will be calling you back shortly, perhaps you will have a better idea then." Jessica replied.

"I have to be going. I will talk to you soon though. Good bye." Philip said.

Jessica replied, "I miss you. Good bye."

Philip continued to listen to see if she was still lingering and then he said, "Good bye Jessica, I miss you too." There was no reply, then there was an audible click that indicated that call had been disconnected at which he smiled.

****

John Devers was sitting in his office feeling very smug. He was confident that his position with the bank was now secure. There was one lingering question and that was why he was chosen to be saved. "Smithson!" he yelled. When she appeared at the door he immediately told her, "Get me a list of security subcontractors, we need to have alternative resources."

"Yes sir, right away Mr. Devers." she replied and disappeared behind the closing door. He knew that he would have to work hard to replace Girard as well as to work on finding a new 'friend' within WBOI, Drew Morrison seemed like the most likely candidate. They had worked well together in the past, he thought. Perhaps lunch would be the best way to begin the courtship.

****

DeMasters had two things that he wanted done today. He had to get a copy of the software program from the Senator and he needed to tie up the Devers loose end. He would need some help with both items and wasn't sure where to go to get it. He then thought about how Morrison was assuming that he would take Fortesque's position and if the board met in the next five minutes he would probably be the Vice Chairman for lack of any other viable candidate. Perhaps he should be Vice Chairman, he pondered. This was the exact reason he needed that software now, he concluded. DeMasters walked out of his study and into the large foyer that acted like the hub of a wheel for his enormous house. The steward was waiting for him there and looked attentively as he approached.

"Good morning sir." Lubner said.

"Good morning to you Franz. I will be going out today, around noon I think. Please have a car for me then and I will need you to contact Mr. Morrison and ask him to meet me at two sharp at his office." DeMasters instructed him kindly.

"Very good sir. Will there be anything else?" Lubner asked. DeMasters waved his hand and Lubner turned on his heels and departed to complete the assignments.

"Good morning Senator, so nice to hear your voice. I trust that all is going well today." DeMasters said.

"Sherwood I am doing well today. The doctors tell me that I will begin the next phase of my physical therapy next week and should be walking again very soon. I have been blessed by your kindness." he said and then paused before continuing and stating, "I was hoping to not have to call you on this matter but I received a call from a personal friend asking me a very large favor. I am going to grant the favor, but that is not the reason for my call. This person was contacted by a member of a team working on the project that spawned our software miracle, Augur. I am convinced that they are about to attempt to initiate a process to bring about an Epiphanal Startling and they are going to do it very soon." the Senator said.

"Senator you told me once, emphatically I believe, that what they were attempting to do could not be done. Have you changed your opinion?" DeMasters asked firmly.

"Absolutely not, but if they go through with the project it will bring about a great deal of unwanted attention." the Senator replied.

"Well you do make a very good point. I suppose something will have to be done about it. Please leave that to me." DeMasters said.

"There is one thing that you can do for me if you would be so kind. Please provide me with a copy of the software, I think that it would be a good idea for my people to have a copy of this as well." DeMasters stated.

"But of course, I will make certain that you have a copy within the next twenty four hours." the Senator said graciously.

"Thank you Yen, you have always been an honorable man. I appreciate all that you have done to help us and will not forget your friendship. Good bye." DeMasters said and the Senator replied in kind.

"Doctor please make certain that you copy the software and send it to Mr. DeMasters at the WBOI sometime before tomorrow afternoon. Make a copy of the older version, we have not had the opportunity to test the new version that was sent here and I wouldn't want Mr. DeMasters to receive an untried product.

"Senator, I did have the opportunity to test the program and it has what at first seem to be enhancements to the code, but it was also tampered with in such a way that it was not going to generate the correct predictions. It seems someone discovered that we have the software. They must have realized that the problem would be discovered and that we would revert back to the original software." Dr. Simmons said pensively.

"Doctor, they were trying to slow us down, that is all. They thought we might be interested in stopping their fantastic folly, time thread manipulation another science fiction dream." the Senator said.

"The odd thing is that they are going to such great lengths to complete their mission. It might be a good idea to get a better understanding of what they truly think they can accomplish and what it will mean to our interests if they somehow can do it." he said thinking out loud.

"What do you suggest we do then Senator?" she asked.

"We should assign one of our operatives to investigate Dr. Constantina and at the very least follow her to the facility where she is working." the Senator directed.

"Do you have a particular person in mind for the assignment?" the doctor asked.

"No, surprise me." he said with a chuckle.

****

"Drew, its John Devers calling. I was hoping that we could have lunch today. I think there is a great deal that needs to be discussed in the wake of the deaths of Lionel and Girard." Devers asked politely.

"John thank you for calling, because if you hadn't I surely would have called you. Lunch might be a little too soon. How about dinner instead?" Morrison asked in return.

"That would be good. Where shall we meet?" Devers asked.

"How about the Boardsmen's Club?" I haven't been there in ages and I think it will offer us a great deal of privacy, no questions asked there." he said with a chuckle.

"Very good, say seven?" Devers replied.

"Seven it is. I will see you there. Thank you for calling John, do take care." Morrison responded confirming the meeting.

"Smithson!" Devers bellowed.

"Yes sir." she said appearing at the door.

"I will need a private room at the Boardsmen's Club at seven this evening. The parties will be Mr. Morrison and me." Devers instructed her.

"Yes sir, I will get it done for you. Sir, you received a call from Chairman DeMasters' office. Would you like me to get them back on the line for you?" she asked.

"No, I will handle It." he said turning back to his work. This should be an interesting call, he thought.

****

Adria sat in a white, six by six, room. She was tethered to the small desk and found it very uncomfortable sitting on the hard disc stool that levitated above the floor. Her shoulder length gray hair seemed to levitate as well lifting slightly off her shoulders as though she was charged with static electricity. The temperature was a little warmer than what would normally be considered agreeable to most people. She felt beads of perspiration forming on her back that began to slowly trace a path along her spine. It was obvious to her that they were setting her up for interrogation and that these minor discomforts grouped together and left in place for an extended period of time, heightened ones anxiety.

The door opened and a young man wearing a silver cooling suit entered. He looked at her and then silently reached down and undid her restraint. The cool air from the outside filled the room, a refreshing and energizing breeze. The man turned and walked out of the room leaving the door open. The light in the room was turned off and at that moment it became clear to Adria that she was to leave the room. She stood up and straightened herself. She had been seated in the one spot for over an hour and she had lost some of the feeling in her left leg. Her foot felt as though it was a useless extension of her leg but after a moment or two of standing and moving her leg, she began to regain enough feeling that she felt that she could walk without stumbling.

She entered the hallway and looked in both directions, there was no one in sight. Wondering which way to go she noticed a small flashing light at the end of the corridor and elected to go in that direction. Upon reaching the end she found a door on either side. She tried one and it was locked, but the other one was open and she went inside. The room was fairly large and there were chairs arranged together in small groups. Seated in one of the groupings were the other three members of her team.

"Are you all alright?" Adria asked as she approached them. Everyone responded that they were but it was not clear to her if they were telling the truth. Adria sat in an empty chair close to the group. Everyone remained silent, it was though they were waiting for something or someone but Adria had no idea if that was the case. After several minutes she stood up and went to one of the four doors of which there was one on each wall. She tried it was locked. She tried each of them until on her third try the door opened. Once it was open the others stood but did not move closer. Adria looked out into the hall and saw another of the blinking lights located about two thirds of the way toward the end.

"Come on team, let's get moving." she said she moved through the door. The other slowly followed. As she approached the blinking light she noticed an opening on the right. Through that arch way was another corridor and at the end of it was another light blinking directly above a door.

Upon opening the door they were met by a short woman wearing a silver cooling suit. She smiled at Adria upon seeing her and then said, "Dr. Constantina. My name is Audra Lucy and I am an aide to Senator Sun. I will be accompanying you out of the facility and once we have cleared the perimeter you are free to go."

"Thank you Ms. Lucy." Adria responded. The young woman's round face lit up with a very large smile of appreciation and Adria thought to herself, 'what a pleasant young woman'.

"You are most welcome. Dr. Constantina you will find a case inside the bus that will be taking from this place. I was told that it was an important item." Audra said.

The team followed Audra through a maze of corridors until they reached a platform where a mini bus was waiting for them. In the back of the bus they found the collection module from the bore unit. It housed the photons that had been extracted in their raw form. The fact that this had been provided to them made them feel that the mission could be viewed as a complete success.

The bus went from the detention center to the Harrisburg railroad station where the team was instructed to exit the vehicle and go where ever they wanted to go. There was no explanation given to them as to why they were released nor were they given any special instructions regarding their apprehension. They were simply free.

Once inside the train station Adria called the team members together to ask them what had happened while they were separated. Everyone had basically had the same story to tell. They were asked what was the purpose of the generator utilization and what specifically did they do. There had been no extraordinary pressure brought to bear but they there were multiple versions of the same questions asked in an attempt to find any inconsistency within their story. The two and half hours they were in custody was not anything like what they were prepared to endure and as such everyone seemed to be in fairly buoyant spirits.

As her team waited for the train, Adria placed a call to Norville and let him know that they were on a train bound for Lancaster. The first question that Norville asked was regarding the collection module and Adria replied that it was in her possession. Norville then told her that he was glad to hear that they had been released so quickly and that he would have Mr. Truax there to meet them to discuss how best to transport them to the facility.

"Adria, there is a significant amount of data that needs to be interpreted and I am counting on you and others to get everything perfect for the final phase. Willie will be happy to have something to do now." Norville said.

"Yes Norville, I will be glad to get back into the lab to work on this part. Field work and I have never been very good friends." she said with a laugh.

Roger and Philip showed their emotions. Jessica had come through and contacted Jeremy who in turn had contacted the Senator and whatever that was said had yielded a positive outcome.

"Gentlemen, you both have earned a few days off. Very good work. The computers are going to be working assembling the data for the next two days. Let us reconvene here on Thursday morning at eight. I think we could all use a little time away from this. Don't you agree?" Norville asked.

"There are things that I could be doing to keep the project running smoothly." Roger said.

"Roger you have a very short time left with us. If all goes well in the next three days you will be saying good bye to us by Saturday. Take the time off, enjoy Gloria's company I know that she has missed you and you her." Norville insisted.

"I know I am going to enjoy getting back into the classroom." Philip added.

"Well there is nothing keeping us here so I will see you both Thursday morning. Have safe travels." Norville stood and walked out of the room where they had been working for the past thirty six hours.

"It is time to go home Roger." Philip said as he also stood up stretched and placed his hand on his brother's shoulder. "Good job little brother." he then said with a smile.

"Let's go, I'll ride with you as far as Lancaster." Roger said. "I wonder what time Gloria is finished working tonight?" he then said.

"Call her and find out." Philip said with a smile. He knew was going to call Jessica and thank her and also tell her that if she really wanted to see him, that he could see her tonight. He was hoping that she would.

****

"Hello old friend, I think it's time we meet again." DeMasters said.

"I believe that would be possible. When and where?" the voice replied.

"Could you be available later this evening?" DeMasters asked.

"Yes, perhaps a nice out of the way late supper? I know a great little pub in Manayunk, I am not coming to New York. Never could stand the place." the voice answered back.

"Send me the name and address and I will meet you there at nine." DeMasters said reluctantly.

"Very good, I look forward to seeing you again." the voice said and then disconnected the call.

DeMasters called for Lubner and instructed him to have a car ready for him to be in Philadelphia for a meeting at nine that evening. He also instructed him that the car should pick him up at home.

"Very good sir. Would you like me to have your things laid out for you when you return?" Lubner asked

"Yes that would be good, thank you Franz." DeMasters replied. DeMasters was facing a very interesting day, he decided to take a moment and collect his thoughts by doing some reading. He went to his bedroom and found the tattered book on his nightstand where he had left it the night before. He had started reading it only a few days earlier but after reading it he had so much clarity and felt so good, he was content. The Senator had sent it to him, saying that it was his only copy and that the Senator would like to have it returned when he had reached a point where he felt he had gotten all that he could out of its lessons. He knew little about the author just the scandalous accusations some of which were created by his very own company and could even be attributed to him. Still it was worth reading and it seemed to have a soothing quality that he needed, reading it seemed quiet the rattle of all of his past transgressions. He had a few minutes that he could devote to reading and then he would dress for the event filled day at hand, he thought.

****

Devers finished the morning rehearsing what he was going to say to Drew Morrison. This was a pivotal meeting he thought, one that would determine his fate with WBOI. He had to portray himself as a loyal employee that would support the Chairman and Vice Chairman in any and all activities. He had Smithson in and out of his office frequently. Most of the time it was to gain answers to questions that were necessary to ensure his proper level of preparedness, but other times it was to simply look at her. He found her very pleasant to look at and thought that as much of an asset Lewis had been, Smithson was the perfect replacement. He then thought of Hilman Scott and how he would be drooling over her the moment he set eyes on her, another great reason to have her as a member of his team.

Smithson was at the door again and this time it was not because she had been summoned.

"Sir, there is a woman calling and she will not give her name. Should I have the call traced and disconnect it?" Smithson said.

"No put it through, I think I know who it is." he said.

"Mr. Devers, it is Foon. I wanted to let you know that I have picked up some very interesting intelligence that I thought you might be interested in reviewing. It has to do with your number one person of interest." Foon said.

"Fine, send it over and we will talk after I have seen it." Devers responded casually.

"No, I want to meet you and show you personally and I do not trust talking any further about it now." Foon replied.

"This is going to be a difficult day to do anything like that..." Devers said.

Foon interrupted saying, "I can meet you in the coffee shop located in your building in one hour. It will not take very long. Trust me, this is vital information."

"Okay, I'll meet you in an hour but you will have no more than a few minutes." Devers acquiesced.

"I will see you then." Foon replied.

What could this woman possibly have uncovered that was so important? Still, she has been very useful in the past, he thought. Its only ten minutes of his time and he could get a cup of coffee and see that voluptuous female behind the counter. Perhaps she will be wearing something truly provocative today, it's always good to get the heart pumping with a little adrenalin, he thought giving himself permission to think about some of the more tempting images that he normally buried because they distracted him from his mission.

Today, was a strategy day, there was nothing on the immediate horizon that threatened him or the bank, with the exception of Justin Welsh and for all he knew Justin Welsh no longer existed. Perhaps that was what Foon was going to tell him. He sat back in his chair and put his arms behind his head, like he had seen his father do so often, and then he laughed out loud.

****

Drew Morrison waited in his office for the call. It wasn't due for another hour but yet he sat staring at his desk absorbed in the holographic images that were displayed on his PCU. The stock value of WBOI was stagnant after the company shares had dropped twenty two percent when the news of Fortesque's death was released and that was the response to the prophetic undulations that occurred as the speculating marauders attempted to interpret the future value of the world's largest bank.

Drew wondered if he should liquidate his other investments and buy shares now, what was about to happen could be a needed shot of adrenalin into the stock's arrhythmic heart. He decided that he it was the appropriate course of action and there was no way that he could be accused of being involved in deceptive business practices, that which was one time referred to as 'insider trading'. His complicity was at a far graver level than profit made with inappropriately obtain information, and if he was going to be put in prison this was not the most dangerous or obvious activity he had been engaged in pursuing. He placed the call and lengthen his position by four million shares, roughly one billion IMC. Should the stock return to its value prior to the scandal he would make more than one quarter of a billion IMC, he thought.

****

Foon sat in the coffee shop waiting for Devers. She had arrived more than fifteen minutes early and was nervous about the meeting and the risk that she was taking. She placed a call as she had been instructed to do and the person on the other end simply said, "Proceed." So she ordered a coffee and waited for Devers to arrive. She had been instructed to keep her PCU active so that the conversation could be monitored and that if at any time the operation was to change she could be told to abort or make whatever modifications that were called for by her handler.

Devers walked into the coffee shop and immediately went to the counter. The woman that he hoped to see was not there, and the young man that was working was very nervous and stammered as he took Devers' order. After significant effort the order was filled and Devers, in his usual gruff fashion, berated the man, who as he was being dressed down, looked down at the floor with tear filled eyes. Devers finished, turned and, with a sneer on his face, moved toward the table at which Foon was seated. He proceeded to sit at the table next to her with his back to her.

"What was so important that I had to be pulled away from urgent bank business?" Devers asked sharply.

"Mr. Devers we have received intelligence from a credible source and it is believed that Justin Welsh is working on a project that will, if successful change the entire world." Foon replied directly.

At that point Devers turned around to face her, his face contorted with anger. "What do you mean?" he demanded loudly attracting the attention of the two people that were in the shop in addition to the young man behind the counter.

"Welsh apparently is working on a time thread manipulation protocol that will enable the user to change the current time thread and replace it with a different present and naturally future." Foon replied calmly.

"Is this a joke." he responded with a laugh. "Do you know how many fools have wasted their lives, their time on such a meaningless exercise?" Devers said continuing. "This is the so called important news that you have brought me. I thought you had more sense than this Foon my dear. You disappoint me."

"Mr. Devers I will point out two things that concern those that have have been monitoring the situation. The first is that there is a program that is now being used called Augur predicts the future of a specific elements in time through a finite distance into the future; days, weeks, months and in some cases as long as a year. This program is very accurate. This was developed as part of that project. The second piece is that during the last forty eight hours three teams lead by Welsh have successfully collected data that would instrumental in making this project a reality." she said betraying very little emotion.

Devers at that moment got up from his seat and joined Foon at her table. He sat down and fidgeted with his coffee cup for a moment and then looked at Foon and asked, "Where is their facility located?"

"We believe that it is in the northwestern section of Maryland. An agent is currently following a one of the teams in hopes that they will lead them to the staging site.

"I need to know when you have that exact location. I do not for a minute believe that they can do what you claim they are working toward but I do know that if I can catch Justin Welsh, that my position in WBOI will be secure for many years to come." he said smiling his sardonic grin.

Some commotion occurred as the door to the shop opened and the voluptuous woman entered. The word 'now' appeared on her holographic display and she knew that this was her opportunity. Devers turned to look at that woman and at that moment Foon waved her hand briefly over his coffee cup. Her ring released a microscopic drop of Elmendorf's root extract that dissolves in the blood stream within seconds only after changing the brain chemistry to cease sending electric impulses to the heart. The results were an apparent fatal heart attack and within one hour after being ingested there was no trace of it left anywhere in the body.

When Devers had brought his attention back to Foon she was sitting quietly looking at him.

"She is quite attractive, Mr. Devers, isn't she?" she asked.

"Who are you talking about?" Devers asked as though he had not been quite noticeably gawking at her.

"The young woman with the big breasts that just came in the door. The one you were looking at so intently." Foon said.

"I don't know what you are talking about." he rejoined but then turned and glanced at her and then returned his attention to Foon saying, "Yes, you are quite right she is very attractive." he responded. "This sounds like a great opportunity to finally catch up with Welsh." he said.

Foon nodded in response and picked up her coffee and had a sip. Devers responded by doing the same thing and his fate was sealed. "I must be going Mr. Devers. I will call you with the latest developments. Good bye." she said standing and extending her hand.

"Good bye." Devers said but he did not look up from his cup. He was too busy thinking of the glory that he would receive when Justin Welsh was finally apprehended. Foon hesitated looking down on him. She felt pity for him and though she found him repulsive and was relieved that she would never be called by him again, there was an element of sadness as she realized that this man like all others was doing what he thought was his best. She turned and walked away when she reached the door she looked back only to find him leering at that poor woman once again. He is getting what he deserves, she thought.

"Good work Foon." the voice said. "Stand by for your next assignment. I will contact you tomorrow regarding how we can move forward and capture Justin Welsh once we have that intelligence on where he is located we should have him in custody by week's end." the man continued.

"I will await your instructions and contact you when I have received the intelligence information." Foon responded. The line went dead. Now she needed to be exceptionally wary since she would be the next target after they no longer needed her services. The trip home would be a long quiet one but at least she would be comfortable, they had not asked for the car back so she continued to drive it. It made her feel independent, though when a call came for her to act she knew that she had to do whatever she was instructed to do, and you could hardly call that freedom, she thought.

****

Adria and her team arrived in Lancaster and inquired where they should rendezvous with their ride to the facility. Norville's response was evasive and it was clear that the team could be being used as a means to discover the facilities location. Their release had been far too easy to be anything other than that.

Adria called Norville again and this time she indicated that she understood the dilemma. "Norville, I do understand what we are up against. I think it would be good if we all went home for the day and regrouped tomorrow. I will contact you later." she said. There was no response but she understood that it was the right thing to do.

"All right lady and gentlemen. We are to proceed to our homes for the evening and I will call each of you later tonight and let you know what we will be doing tomorrow. I shouldn't have to say this but please keep what we are doing to yourself. No one else can know." she said emphatically. The team acknowledged what she said and they all stood for a moment not really wanting to say good bye. Each one of them had come close to losing their freedom earlier and they did not give into to the fear and temptation that accompanied their brief incarceration. They felt unified in purpose and that by walking away from each other that the bond of unity would somehow break.

"We are still together and we overcame adversity today. Tomorrow we will do the same. Get some rest, you have earned. Thank you." Adria said.

She turned and walked to the train that would take her to New York and then home to New London, Connecticut. She was carrying the case that held the photons needed for the mission to be finally considered successful. A man approached her carrying a silver case. It was then that she recognized him, it was Truax. There collision looked to be accidental and both dropped their cases. Truax activated the image altering feature that changed his case so that it appeared to be the same as the one Adria was carrying. When he picked up her case he caused it to change form and color as well. The exchange was made like a magician uses sleight of hand to trick his audience.

She collected herself and continued on as though nothing had happened. Adria thought that it hardly seemed worth going home because of the time and distance that she had to travel but she really did welcome the idea of sleeping in her own bed. That was something that she had not done in several months and it may be something she may never do again, she suddenly realized.

****

"Roger, I have just heard from Adria, she has understood our concern for her being followed and she and her team are going home for the evening. Perhaps it would be best if they were to return after you have had a chance to review all of the data, say Friday." Norville said.

"That sounds good. If all goes as I believe it will I will have all the results of the data that was collected and the project will be ready to be handed over to Willie after we have one more meeting to review our findings." Roger replied.

"I will miss you but Good Hope will be getting the very best and that is what is needed now to get the project off in the right direction. You know that it is a very large and long commitment?" Norville said fatherly.

"Yes it is but Gloria and I have talked in over and this will be a chance for both of us to do something very meaningful. She is actually going to be able to use her education for the first time since she left college." Roger said with a laugh.

"That could be dangerous." Norville added and joined in the laughter.

Philip walked the hallway back from a short trip to the restroom. He came upon the two men laughing and the contagion effectively transformed his face from a stern countenance to a smile and then he added a small chuckle for good measure. He had no reason to be laughing but it still felt good and the release was welcomed.

"What is so funny?" he finally asked. Roger explain what started the laughter and in the translation from the experience to story a good deal of the grounds for mirth were lost. Still everyone continued to smile.

"Gentlemen, this has been a great day. We accomplished all of our objectives and all of our teams are safe. We still have a slight edge in that no one that realizes what we are up to is taking us very seriously and those that are hunting Justin Welsh, the man who is no more, do not quite know where to search. That will change I believe in the next several weeks." Norville said.

"What are your plans for the next phase?" Philip asked.

"Philip we will be reducing the number of people at this facility to the four members of Willie's team and the final phase technical team, about fourteen people. All others will be working at different sites. Those new sites will be the final staging points. There are also a manufacturing facilities that have become operational and they will, over the next five weeks, make the units that will be installed at each of the sample locations where we extracted photolytic elements during the past thirty six hours."

"Of course once all of the photon storage devices have arrived Willie's team will initiate the harvesting process with the hope that once that process is complete we will be able to see where exactly we must insert our magnetic influencers into the time thread." he continued to explain.

"In six weeks a team of twelve people will move into the Control Center and will be there for the final three weeks of the operation. That will bring us to the first of July 2113 and the day the world changes." Norville said reverently.

Both Philip and Roger looked at each other and then back at Norville who said, "Thank you. Without you and those in your family before you this would not be happening. You have done a great thing."

"Norville, I have one question, if Roger is going to continue to exist but will be in a different time thread why is it so important that he go to work on this project in which you have encouraged him to participate?" Philip asked.

"It is important to continue on as if everything will remain the same. While we are confident that what we are doing will be successful, we are not the ones that control all aspects of our actions. Our ability to make choices is governed according our conscience and that conscience is governed by something else. The destiny of our actions is predetermined but we do not know what that outcome is. As the events unfold we make decisions based upon our determination of what we are being led by and the destination that it represents." Roger responded.

"That sounds like something from that blasted journal." Philip rejoined.

"It is." Norville answered.

"You too?" Philip asked in amazement.

"Yes, your father shared it will me when I approached him about the power generation equipment several years ago. It has made all the difference in me. My reasons for doing this have changed, originally it was my self-interest but now it's something completely different. It's about saving all of those people that live from minute to minute either anesthetized to control the sense of desperation and pain or the anger and rage that manifests itself in criminal behavior that spawned the multi-trillion IMC business that the prison industry is today. It is not about the possessions, the currency or the power. It is about the only valuable things in this world, those with whom we share our common experience." Norville said sadly.

"You are telling me that you are doing this for those people that we see in the homeless camps buried under the streets of our cities and those people that can't earn a living because business will not recognize that we have only a finite amount of true wealth and resources. The fact that they won't recognize that a program like the one Roger created will enable the system that the President stated as the direction we should follow would truly work is mind boggling."

"We are in a position to, instead of having companies bring products to market they can bring ideas, and those ideas could be run through that program and the most favorable outcome could be determined and the company that presented the idea would be awarded the contract. The workforce would not change just the name on the business door. Annual reviews would enable that direction to always be fresh. We have cheap power and superior computing once again with all of the dead weight gone. This is the dawning of a new age, even if the program does not work." Philip said.

"They say people won't accept it, that they need to have choices. There are choices but things cannot carry the weight of the human purpose, we are more than mindless animals that need to be entertained. We are here for a reason and that reason involves us all." Norville said.

"What will this new present look like? Will it be a world where anyone will be interested living?" Philip asked.

"That is a good question and one that will be answered within the next two weeks as we continue to put all of the pieces together. Philip I know you have said that you will stay with us for a while longer and that is a great blessing to us but your presence in the final minutes prior to initiation of the process could be prove to be invaluable. There is the likelihood that we will encounter things that may have to be changed as we move through the process." Norville said and then he ended by saying, "Please think about it."

"I have been thinking about it. My conditions for staying with the project have not changed. As long as Jessica is safe and you can prove it to me, then I will continue with the project until such time that it does not make sense to continue, and I suspect that means I will be here when you turn out the lights." Philip said.

As much as he did not want to like Norville, he could not seem to avoid being taken in by his fatherly manner and winning smile. It was no surprise that Austin had fallen prey to this man's wild schemes and now here he was doing the same thing. The only difference was that there was no law being broken and whether they were successful or not, no one would even know that anything had been done.

"Philip as much as I enjoy having you here I think you can have the next two days to yourself and we will reconvene on Friday." Norville said.

"That sounds like a good idea. I will see you on Friday Norville." Philip said and stood up and left for campus and then after a few hours catching up on his work he planned to leave for home and hopefully the chance to see Jessica. The semester ends soon and final exams and papers would consume him in the next several weeks. It seemed that he would not be called upon to be actively involved for a short period of time and he welcomed the opportunity to fulfill his obligation to his students and the school.

"Acorn, call Jessica." he said as he exited the facility

"Hello there stranger." she said.

"Stranger? I have seen you or talked to you every day for the past two weeks! Talked to rather more frequently than seen, I must admit but I am not..." Philip replied.

Jessica was laughing and interrupted by saying, "You are such a serious man. I have missed you."

Philip did not know whether to apologize or tease her back. He elected to move to the reason he had called and asked, "How would you like to meet my parents tonight?"

There was an audible gasp on the other end of the line and then a nervous laugh accompanied by her reply, "Uh... that would be nice. Where did this idea come from?"

"This is my version of spontaneity. My parents have been wondering who I have been seeing and I also thought that you might like to meet the infamous Austin Lee, my older brother." Philip replied.

"Philip this is a very big step, in case you don't realize it. You are sending me a very serious message. Is that what you are intending to do?" she asked.

"Uh, I suppose I didn't think of things in that light. I am sorry if I put you in a position where you felt uncomfortable." Philip replied quietly.

"You didn't put me a position that I haven't been thinking almost from the time I met you. I know you and you don't always see things the way everyone else does. This is a step toward commitment and its one that I am ready to make with you. That is why I asked." Jessica responded sincerely.

Philip thought about what Jessica had just said and then questioned his intent. Was this a simple gesture or was it the fulfillment of the cultural 'next step' of their growing relationship? He wanted her in his life. She distracted him from his work and he could not imagine her not with him.

"Yes, it is what the gesture implies." Philip blurted out and the sound of the words as they echoed forth was almost as much a surprise to him as it was to her. There was no sound on the other end of the call and Philip wondered what he had done wrong, how he had miss-handled another interpersonal interaction.

Finally she responded her voice choked with emotion. "What time would you like to meet?" she asked.

"Are you alright?" he asked in return.

"I am fine. I am better than fine. It's been a long time since I have felt this happy." she replied.

"Oh. Can I come and pick you up at around seven?" he asked.

"You don't have to come all this way. I can meet you." she said.

"It will give us more time alone together." Philip said.

"In that case, yes please come and pick me up." she replied.

They spoke for a few more minutes about their days and then completed the call with how much they were looking forward to seeing one another. After the call disengaged he quickly called his mother and asked permission to bring Jessica to diner with him. MacKenzie agreed immediately and then asked what he would like for dinner.

"Surprise me mother." he said. He told her when to expect them and she replied enthusiastically about the possibility of meeting someone that had stolen one of her sons' hearts. The call finally ended and Philip continued on his journey back to school. He took that commuting time to prepare himself for the bedlam that he was certain that he was going to face. He had not been in class in quite some time and with the regularity that he had hoped. Still the administration had been very supportive, mostly because Norville Forrest was one of their most generous benefactors and key member of the board of trustees.

****

When Devers returned from his meeting with Foon he had many thoughts swimming in his head. He saw his potential role as heir apparent to the chairmanship with the world looking at his successful apprehension of Justin Welsh being the key to that inevitability. As he walked past Smithson he smiled thinking that she would be an ideal candidate to share his future fortunes. She was unattached and ambitious. What that meant to him was that he could manipulate her and eventually control her. The foundation for all sound relationships, he thought.

"Smithson I will need you to come in to my office when you have finished what you are doing. There is no hurry but I want to review my itinerary, please bring my schedule with you." he said as he entered his office.

Devers puttered about his office. He had difficulty concentrating on any one thing and as he sat down in his chair he thought about the fact that his rapid paced life style must be catching up to him. Perhaps it would be appropriate to take some time off. Maybe he would invite Smithson along, he thought. He gazed at the reports that were displayed above his desk. He could not determine what they were and what he was supposed to do with them. He felt his pulse quicken, he then started to become anxious and began to perspire. Smithson arrived in the room and immediately asked if there was something wrong. Devers waved his hand and told her to sit.

"Smithson there are going to be some changes around here very soon. If all goes well with my meeting this evening I will be named president of the bank. This could be a big opportunity for you as well." he said in a befuddled manner.

"What could it mean for me?" Smithson asked with a sly smile.

"What could it mean for you? What do you think?" he said abruptly.

"I mean what would do you have in mind for me to do?" she responded confused by the tone and the question.

"I want you to earn it." he said directly.

"Am I not doing what you want me to do? Am I not doing a good job?' she replied her tone betraying irritation.

"You need to do more, to meet all of my needs. If you will do that, you can have whatever you want." Devers said plainly. Smithson did not believe what she had just heard. He had openly told her that she would have to give all of herself to the job, which meant to him.

"That is something I had never considered before Mr. Devers. I will need some time to think about it." she replied.

"You can think about it while you are clearing out your desk. If you are not interested in this then I will find someone that is." he told her firmly.

Smithson felt trapped and she had always felt that she could manipulate men using her appearance and winning smile, but this man was not to be played with she discovered.

"Mr. Devers, I need this job and I like working with you. Is there no way that you can give me a day to think about it?" she pleaded.

"I have said all I am going to say on the matter. Give me my calendar and get me human resources on the line before you leave." he said.

She stared at him in disbelief.

"They will find you a position somewhere in the bank possibly." he then added.

She turned toward the door and opened it thinking that he would call her back telling her it was all a mistake, but there was no sound. At that moment she turned back and said to him, "I have thought about it and I am ready to do whatever you want from me, whenever it is that you want me to do it."

He did not respond to her offer. "Mr. Devers did you hear me. I will be glad to serve under you for as long as you want me to do so." she said again. She approached him and saw that he had a small amount of drool coming out of the corner of his mouth and that his eyes were filled with panic. Suddenly his head whipped backwards bouncing off the wall that was behind the sofa where he had been sitting and he slumped over dead.

When the medical team arrived they pronounced him dead. Devers was not liked by very many people and the news of his demise spread quickly throughout the company. Drew Morrison, upon hearing of his death dispatched a forensics team to evaluate the state of his records and to seek out any information that might damage the bank or him personally. He the then called DeMasters to advise him of the death of their guard dog.

"What should we do?" Morrison asked DeMasters.

"Do? We should reveal the information that we have that puts Devers as the architect of the death or Fortesque and Girard. That he was the master mind behind the framing of Austin Lee. We tell the truth. It will get the company out from under this attack that it has been suffering from ever since Devers got on this campaign to get Welsh at the expense of everything else of value." DeMasters stated clearly.

"Yes Sherwood you are right." he replied.

"How did he die?" DeMasters asked.

"They think it was a heart attack. He went quickly." Morrison responded.

"Well it's good that he did not suffer long. No one deserves that especially someone that had been so useful to us in the past. He was a friend." DeMasters said sympathetically.

"Sherwood, he was a person that could not be controlled and was pursuing his own agenda. If that included looking out for the bank's best interest then so be it, but if not... well he did not always do what was best for us." Morrison responded firmly.

"That is very true but some of his work was extremely beneficial and he was someone we could count on to do the ugly, dirty jobs that came up from time to time. Do you have in mind a replacement?" DeMasters asked.

"I was thinking that Katherine Foster would be a good selection. She was a loyal operative and she will not go off and try to fulfill her own agenda." Morrison replied.

"That has a good public relations ring to it. It is a very big job though. Is she capable?" DeMasters asked skeptically.

"I believe that she may be. Only time and experience will tell for certain. We can always replace her it if doesn't work out." Morrison said reassuringly.

"That is so true. I think you need to contact her and have her come to your office tomorrow. We will meet with her and offer her the position and her first assignment." DeMasters replied.

"What would that be?" Morrison asked a little bewildered.

"To investigate Devers and to bring all of the dirty laundry out into the open. I think you should have Samantha Lewis attend that meeting as well." DeMasters said.

"Good idea Sherwood. I will talk to you tomorrow then. Please try to have a good rest of the day." Morrison said warmly.

"Drew you may here from me later tonight. I have a very interesting meeting that I am attending and I might need to call you late. Would that be alright?" DeMasters asked.

"Absolutely, call at any time." Morrison replied.

"Have a wonderful day old friend." DeMasters said.

"You too. Good bye." Morrison said and then he disconnected the call.

****

The call from Drew Morrison surprised Kate. She had been on administrative leave pending the completion of the investigation into the Austin Lee operation. She wasn't certain that the meeting that he requested with her was anything more than another of the endless debriefing on the nature of the failure of the mission. The shocking element of the conversation came to light when she was told of the death of John Devers. Her reaction was not what she had anticipated, her emotions were a jumble of jubilation and pathos. Such was a sweet and sour emoticon that she struggled to sort through as she did what she always did in life, put things in their proper place.

Her time with Michael had given her a chance to reacquaint herself with the man that she married. It also had become clear to her that she had married him because she thought it was the right thing to do. She liked him and he had a good heart, something that he had illustrated in his caring for her and all of those touched by the recent scandal and that included Austin. She also realized that if she would have met those two men at exactly the same time in her life that she would now have chosen Austin. She loved him and he consumed most of her waking thoughts, even usurping some of the space that had firmly been held sacred for her boys.

This realization meant nothing to her. Her life's direction had been cast and there was no reason to hope for anything other than what she was supposed to do. The presence of Austin had to be eradicated from her conscious and subconscious thoughts and feeling. She was committed to Michael because he was committed to her and their children. Her promise was to honor and obey and it was made until death. Yes, love was part of that promise and she did love him as one would love a brother but not with the burning passion she knew she had within her but was buried deeply.

Michael was playing with the boys. They all looked so happy. She wished that she could join in the joyful games but all she could do was watch as a tear silently rolled down her cheek.

"What is wrong?" Michael said as he took note of his wife's apparent pain.

"Nothing, I am just so glad to see you and the boys enjoying yourselves. It is a true blessing to have you home again." she said. Michael apparently accepted her explanation and went back to playing with the boys. Kate stood up and left the room. She knew she needed to regain her composure and find the fortitude to project a positive image. It would get better, it always did, she just needed to have patience and the pain would pass and life would return to the plain of contentment.

****

Philip and Jessica traveled the forty minutes it took to get from Jessica's home to Philip's parents' house engaged in conversation that was charged with an enthusiasm that was reminiscent of that experienced by a child when they were anticipating a great adventure. They both accepted the importance of this introduction for what it was and there was little doubt that anyone in attendance would not appreciate its importance as well. Philip told her that he planned on spending as much time with her as she would be able to tolerate over the next several days. After that he would most likely be very busy and not able to sneak away to spend time with her for as long as the next two or three weeks. They would be able to call one another and if he could get a way he most certainly would do everything he could to see her.

Jessica was still reeling from the prospects of meeting Philip's parents. She saw this as a great opportunity to have a family life again. She missed her father so much and though she had lost her mother a long time ago, she still thought of the little things that she had done for her as she was growing up. Rather than dwell on the loss she was choosing to concentrate on what was happening now. This had been an important lesson that was learned, she had been taught it repeatedly by both Jeremy and Laura. They spoke of the need to rest in the moment and not in the past or in the future. She did not understand at first but when Jeremy shared his journal with her and she began to read it everything then began to make sense.

MacKenzie bustled about the house coordinating the arrival of the meal that she had ordered. She may not be much of a cook but she certainly could put a good meal together in short order, she thought. The food service delivery personnel moved throughout the house quickly. They were very familiar with MacKenzie since she had used their services once or twice each month for the past several years. They all knew each other by first name and there was no standing on ceremony or protocol that would inhibit the interchange between them.

MacKenzie liked people and people, for the most part, enjoyed her. They saw a whimsical enthusiasm and a genuine caring for the needs of others that shined through her every action. As she was moving from the kitchen to the dining room she heard the front door open. Could they be here this early, she wondered and changed direction, only to meet Austin as he walked in the door from work. The look of puzzlement on his face was almost comical, she thought and she attempted to find something clever to say. 'Happy birthday', was all that came out.

Austin thought for a second and yes, it clearly was not his birthday.

"Mother you do know it's not really my birthday." he replied seriously.

"Yes dear I know, I was there when you were born." she said smiling.

"So why the invasion of the caterers? What is the special occasion?" he asked. MacKenzie then explained that Philip was on his way there and he was bringing a girl will with him.

Austin rallied his enthusiasm and replied, "That's great! I am very happy for him." He looked at his mother to see how she received the words that he had said. Did she accept them at face value or did she read that they were ever so slightly disingenuous prompted by the envy that he felt? Philip, his younger brother, had found someone that he felt was worth bring home to meet his parents and marriage could not be far behind. He thought of his relationships, the last two had been complete failures, he loved the women, or at least thought he did, especially the last one. There was no hint from his mother that she had detected anything other than a sincerest wish for his brother's happiness.

Gregory, Jessica and Philip arrived at the same time and walked up the onto the porch.

"Jessica, it is very good to see you again. It must be six or seven months since I saw you when you came to visit your uncle." Gregory said.

"It's very nice to see you Dr. Lee." she responded extending her hand.

Gregory took her hand and then replied, "Please call me Greg or Gregory. Dr. Lee is not working this evening."

"Alright Gregory." she replied.

Gregory held the door and they proceeded inside. Philip held his breath not certain how his mother would react. He knew that her emotions would be in charge and that she might cry, giggle or just not quite articulate a coherent thought, but she would certainly do nothing to communicate anything but a warm welcome.

"My dear it is so good to meet you." MacKenzie said and instead of offering her hand she reached out and touched Jessica arm all the while beaming.

"Mrs. Lee it is an honor to meet you." Jessica said quietly.

"Please dear, call me MacKenzie or Mom, those are the only two names I answer to." MacKenzie said welcomingly.

"Okay, MacKenzie, you have a beautiful home." Jessica replied looking around her, her eyes stopping on Austin as he entered the room.

"Hello, you must be Jessica. I am Austin, Phil's big brother." Austin said with a smile and a half wave.

"Austin, it's very nice to meet you." Jessica said taking note of his thin build, tall frame and very long hair. This man was not like Philip, there was something different about him, and she sensed it.

The next two hours were filled with lively conversation and a great deal of eating. MacKenzie had ordered an abundance of food never wanting to be put in the position of feeling that someone did not have enough to eat, that usually meant that there were plenty of left over snacks to be had in the following days. Finally, when everyone had insisted for the third time that they had had enough, MacKenzie relented and stopped attempting to cajole them into consuming more food.

They adjourned to the sitting room to enjoy some coffee and to continue the conversations. Philip had a passive involvement in the discussion which seemed to him to be very superficial. He thought that it was good that the conversation stayed light and airy, they did not need to go down the path to the subject of Austin's incarceration or the project in which he was involved. He had just settled into a chair that was facing the sofa where Jessica, MacKenzie and Gregory were sitting when Gregory decided to stir the pot and make the conversation more meaningful.

"Your father was a great man Jessica. I did not have the opportunity to meet him but your uncle spoke of him often and I had read one of his papers on the Native American people, there was such insight into a very terrible situation." Gregory said.

"My father had a true gift as a writer and he was extremely compassionate when it came to the plight of others." Jessica said with pride. Philip watched to see if she was becoming uncomfortable and even though he had no plans to offer assistance he could at the very least know what she may be experiencing so that they could talk about it later. There was no evidence that she was uncomfortable and he continued to stay removed from the conversation.

"Philip you met Leopold did you not?" his father asked. "Yes, I did at a conference in New York. It is also the first time that I met Jessica, though the meeting did not have the same impact on me that our second meeting did." he replied with a smile.

"I have never understood why anyone would study history. It was extremely boring to me when I was in school." Gregory went on to say.

"We have three boys and only one went on to follow in his father's footsteps." MacKenzie added. "Austin is the financial wizard and Philip is the professor." she said with a laugh.

"Why did you elect to study history?" Jessica asked Philip.

"Because I knew it would lead me to you." Philip responded and all of them laughed.

"I'll tell you why I went the route of financial services. It was so I could be with the winners. I thought that the banks had all of the money and power and I wanted to be with all that money and power." Austin said.

"That changed, didn't it?" Gregory added.

"Yes, I am not even sure when. There was a time when I thought it was when Uncle Bob was killed and I started to see that there is only a finite supply of money and power. If you have more than others, the source of that wealth came from them. You were taking from others so that you could have more." Austin said sadly. "I think about all of the people that gave so much so that I could have my elaborate junkets and expensive meals. Things, they are just things, entertaining things, but they are still things." Austin concluded. There was a period of awkward silence that fell over them like a somber fog. The direction to take the conversation back to the land of lively banter was not clear.

"You asked me why I chose history." Philip began. "I chose it because it was the only way I could make sense of why I am here. It illustrates how I am one more rung on an evolutionary ladder that leads to the next stage of mankind. That my contributions on that ladder, what I do with my time here, strengthens mankind and improves the human condition."

"Do you still feel that way now?" Gregory asked. Philip knew the answer to the question, he just did not want to say it out loud.

****

DeMasters arrived promptly at nine at the restaurant and he did not want to be at this meeting for very long, for if he was there for a long time it meant bad news. He exited the limousine and walked slowly to the door. It did not open automatically for him, he had to push it open and as he entered he noticed that the temperature was not quite as cool as he liked to be. There was man standing at a podium that had a small dim light. He had an open book of paper with names written in it, some of which were scratched out.

"Good evening sir. Do you have a reservation?" the man asked politely.

"I am meeting a friend." DeMasters replied.

"Oh but of course, you are Mr. DeMasters. Please follow me." the man said and turned and led DeMasters through a small dining room where every table was occupied.

"The food must be very good here, all of your tables are filled." DeMasters said making conversation.

"They are every night sir and the food is excellent." the man replied. They went into another small dining room that was very much like the one they had just left. Like the first one, all of the tables were occupied. The man stopped in front of an ornately carved door and opened it, gesturing for DeMasters to enter.

"Enjoy your meal Mr. DeMasters." he said.

DeMasters attempted to tip the man using his PCU but he soon discovered the man did not use one. Then then reached in his pocket and pulled out a Ten IMC note that he kept for emergencies and handed it to the man, saying "Thank you."

"Sherwood, I see you were able to find this place. How good it is to see you old friend." Norville said standing and extending his hand.

"Justin, or should I say Norville, you haven't changed a bit in the past few years. It is truly astounding. What is your secret?" DeMasters asked with a smile and laugh.

"Sit down, and let us get the food order out of the way. I think you are the one that requested this meeting and though I suspect that I understand what you want to know, I would like to hear it from you just the same." Norville said.

"Very well, let's order and then we will get down to business while we wait for our food. I only hope what you tell me doesn't put me off of my appetite. The food here smells very good." DeMasters replied.

They ordered according to Norville suggestions and when the waiter left them alone DeMasters came to the point of the meeting bluntly, "Can you do what Jenkins was trying to get Lawrence to do?"

"Yes, and more. We can change the entire time thread, rewrite history." Norville responded. DeMasters looked at his old friend in the eye and then sighed a heavy sigh.

"You are not going to go through with it." he stated.

"And why not?" Norville asked in return and then continued by saying, "Because you are telling me not to do it?"

"No, it makes no sense to do it. Everything that you have done with your life will be gone." DeMasters replied.

"Not just the things that I have done but I will never have lived." Norville said in response.

"Don't you remember? We had an arrangement. I am not going to ask you again. If you do not change your plans. I will stop you and this time I won't look the other way when it comes to having you locked up." DeMasters said his voice getting louder with each word said.

"You do what you have to do old friend but I don't think you can stop this now." Norville stated calmly.

"We shall see. I really don't think I have much of an appetite now. You will understand if I don't stay." DeMasters said as he stood to leave.

"I am sorry you see it this way Sherwood. Have a safe trip back to New York and we shall see shortly which one of us is right." Norville rejoined.

"Good bye Justin. I hope for your sake that we can stop this." DeMasters said, and he turned and walked out of the room.

Norville sat alone thinking about the meeting and wondering what he should do to help safe guard the project. He then realized that there was nothing to do since there was no way that they could know the location of their base of operations. Everything was secure at this time.

DeMasters, on the other hand when he was safely sitting in his limousine placed the call to Drew Morrison. "Drew my boy, this is Sherwood. I am sorry for the late hour but I just got some very bad news in the meeting that I just came from attending. It seems that Mrs. Foster will be involved in more than the Devers matter. I need you to meet me in the office first thing, say seven, and can you please contact that man Scott over at Internal Security and our contacts at the FBI we will need them in our office to meet with us at eight thirty at the latest." DeMasters said.

"What is wrong? I thought we had our problems behind us with Fortesque and Devers out of the picture." Morrison responded.

"No, they had us focusing on the wrong issue. Now it's time to get focused on the right one. Get some sleep because you may not be getting much in the coming days. And one more thing call Mrs. Foster and have her get that Foon person to come to our offices for a meeting after the one when we brief her. That Foon person can be very helpful." DeMasters said.

"Yes, I know. Sherwood, I will get this done." Morrison said in an encouraging tone.

"I know you will. Good night." DeMasters said and disconnected the call. Now if he could only find something to eat, he was famished, he thought.

Chapter Seventeen

Philip had been sitting in his office at school working on the composition of the letters and documents that were to be inserted into the time thread. He was to provide the nine documents along with samples of the hand writing of those who were supposed to be the authors of them. It came down to understanding how the men thought and turned phrases. Some of them were highly educated with a bent toward flowery eloquence, such as J. E. B. Stuart, while others, like 'Pete' Longstreet, were more direct and simple in their style but strong in their clarity and intent. The audience was also of a particular concern since they would have to believe that the person who signed did indeed author it. General Lee prided himself of knowing his men and was suspicious of any conclusion that was drawn other than one that seemed right to him.

The work moved slowly, but it was research and this was what Philip enjoyed about his vocation. He looked for the clues that revealed who these people really were. This was an exciting element about the project, the one part that he had not allowed himself to indulge himself in was the fact that he would really like to see these people in action, the real men making those decisions both good and bad. The men that had come before them were the lower rungs on the ladder of life.

The last meeting they had had taken place several weeks before and at that meeting Roger had made his last appearance as a member of the team. Philip wanted to contact him to get together to have lunch but he had heard that he had already become immersed in his new project and had little time to socialize. Perhaps a call later would be in order, he thought. Avery and Willie were wrapping up the loose ends of their section and were about to go on a brief sabbatical while the tech team began their two week assignment which included the assembling of the nine 'Yom Assimilators'. The units were named after an animated character from a mid-Twentieth Century television program. The character Yom used a device to go back in time to view history and to ensure that history went according to how it was supposed to be with often humorous results.

The Yom was a remarkable design. It was a self-contained magnetic impulse reader which was driven by the photolytic component model created from the extracted material which were fed through the interpretive matrix, the creation of Avery and Willie's team. The design was primarily that of William Lawrence senior's though he worked in collaboration with Dr. Johanas Spruce and Dr. Tira Irving. Those two were the primary technical assistants for the assembly, testing and implementation of the Yom units. Another key member of the assembly and testing phase was Dr. Gregory Lee since these units drew incredible power and several of the tera-watt generators which he designed were necessary to power each of the nine units. They had been working twelve or more hours a day for the past two weeks preparing the units for the testing that would occur in the not too distant future.

The magnetic signature theory was collaboration between Avery and Adria. Each bringing their insight to bear on the problems of interaction with the past. Reading an interpreting light represented the means of being able to view the past but to interact with objects and people from the past there was a need to place the item in the actual position in the process not its reflective shadow. Those that had read the original theories did not have the opportunity to see the problem as distinctly and were viewing the solution as limited to the utilization of light.

Philip looked that the date and it the display showed that it was Monday June fifth and the start of the three week count down to the final date of Saturday July first, 2113 the two hundred and fifty year anniversary of the start of the battle of Gettysburg. The date had no special meaning to the success of failure of the mission, it was the symbolic value that made it significant. He had three more days to refine the 'forgeries' as he liked to call them.

He continued to struggle with two of the documents. The most difficult one was the message from J. E. B. Stuart to Lee regarding his position and the positions of the Union troops. The wording had to be correct and the tone of the document had to be perfect. This man adored Lee and Lee felt like he was one of his sons, a prodigal one at times but nevertheless there was a close bond and Lee had to believe that Stuart had been the author of the document.

For a moment he visualized himself in the tent where Stuart was supposed to be bivouacked and he saw him hunched over a small smoking stand that he was using as a desk. There was an oil lamp hanging from one of the tent poles and it swayed to the warm breeze that filled the tent in rhythmic sighs. He started the letter:

> *'My Dearest General,*
>
> *I, your humble servant, wish to apprise you of a fantastic opportunity that we have discovered in our relentless pursuit of the unpredictable enemy.'*

He went on to provide General Lee with the Union positions and movements. It would be those positions and movements coupled with the acceleration of Stuarts movements away from his treasure trove of captured wagons and in support of the initial day's assault that would put the Army of Northern Virginia in the superior tactical position. He continued to evaluate the use of each word and how he envisioned the overstated Stuart would have framed his message.

When he was confident that this was done in accordance with Stuart's manner, he then had to issue a strong order to Stuart from Lee that would compel him to be where he needed him to be. The timing of this letter and the one that was sent to Lee were roughly the same. Each of these letters offered the opportunity for them to be discovered to be fake. Crafting the letter to Stuart in the proper fashion could limit the chances of him bringing the letter to Lee's attention and when Lee congratulates Stuart on his brilliant contribution there was ample reason to suspect that he will accept the accolades without correcting any details. He would have, after all, be acclaimed to be a hero that he always knew that he was. There will be inconsistencies that will never be resolved but there was little doubt that many will not look too carefully at them, Philip believed.

****

Kate was about to enter the building and officially claim her office. She had been promoted to Senior Vice President three weeks earlier during the whirlwind of activity that surrounded the deaths of two high level WBOI officials and the death of one of their key operatives, but she had maintained her office in Philadelphia. She had assembled a team which included several of her operatives from the District Office as well as her reliable friend Foon who had attended the meeting that followed her meeting with DeMasters and Morrison when she was offered the position.

Foon, as always, was a tremendous help and Kate relied upon her a great deal.

During those weeks she had uncovered a great deal of information that damaged both Devers' and Fortesque's reputations and it seemed to have a cathartic effect on the company as a whole. The stock had rebounded from its all-time low and was once again in line with its true economic value. As expected Drew Morrison was named Vice Chairman and a relatively obscure Senior Vice President from the Hong Kong Bureau was named President. Wa Li Chu had been responsible for real estate holdings and was not considered by many as a likely candidate. It was to him that Kate reported and while she was not certain that he liked her, she liked and respected him.

Her continuing challenge was to find Justin Welsh and her last meeting with Wa had been exclusively focused upon finding him before he was able to execute his plan. Today, after a great deal of complaining and effective nagging she was to learn all of the details about the plan. Previously all that she had been told to that point was that sometime during the first week of July Welsh was going to attempt to topple the financial system. Wa had told her that DeMasters was very concerned that Welsh would succeed in bringing down everything, that word everything stuck as though he actually meant everything and not simply the bank.

As Kate road the elevator to the one hundred and first floor she felt a sense of awe, this was her first real day as the official Senior Vice President of Global Security for the world's largest bank. She had been promoted above and before many that may have been more deserving, still she was there and it was not certain for how long if she did not apprehend Justin Welsh before the month of June ended. The elevator doors opened on to the Security Division operations floor. There were many people walking rapidly caring screens and other devices. They certainly looked busy, she thought.

Kate search for a familiar face and she found one standing at the reception desk, it was Wa and he looked angry but Kate had never seen him when he did not look that way.

"Good morning, Mrs. Foster. I assumed that you would like to understand what will be expected of you in the next two weeks. That is why I am here, to make your assignment crystal clear." Wa said.

"Good morning to you Mr. President, I appreciate you taking the time to meet with me so that I can be certain that I do everything I can to accomplish the mission." Kate replied.

"Good, where should we meet?" he asked. She then became aware of the fact that she did not know if she had an office and where it was located.

Smithson saw Kate enter and was waiting for her to notice her but because of Wa she was not able to make eye contact. "Mrs. Foster." she said loudly. "Please follow me to your office." she then continued and when she was certain that Kate and Wa were in motion to follow her, she turned and lead the way to the corner office. It was not the same one that Devers had used, the entire control center had been moved two floors and this office, while quite a bit smaller than Devers' office, was still large enough to reflect her status within the company.

Kate placed her briefcase on the desk and then offered Chu a refreshment which he declined. "That will be all Virginia." she said dismissing Smithson so that she could discover what brought the new president to her office.

"Congratulations on your new position sir." she said and then gestured that they should sit on the chairs located near the window. The view was impressive, it was a clear day with the sun still low in the east and the floor to ceiling windows enabled the viewer the chance to observe unobstructed vision of the best that New York had to offer. Wa waited for Kate to be seated before he sat down.

"There is a great need for urgency and I am prepared to explain to you why. This cannot be shared with anyone, including your husband and especially that woman Foon. We are not certain that she can be trusted." Wa said as he began to explain the plan and the events that would take placed as they believed they would to occur. They were interrupted by the Smithson who indicated that Senator Sun had just arrived with his apologies for being late for the meeting.

"I wasn't aware that the Senator was invited to the meeting." Kate stated.

"What he has to offer is a very important piece that will enable you to visualize the entire puzzle." Wa replied. "Have him come in please." he continued.

The Senator entered lead by Smithson. Upon his entering Wa stood and bowed respectfully and the Senator replied in kind. He then turned his attention to Kate and said, "Mrs. Foster it is very good to meet you. You have received a very good report card from my associates, they say you are honorable and diligent in your pursuit of the truth."

"Thank you Senator Sun. I am curious to understand why a United States Senator representing the State of North Carolina is here in New York to talk about Justin Welsh." she replied.

"You will come to understand in very short order." the Senator replied. He and Wa both waited for Kate to sit and then they joined her.

"How much have you shared Chu?" the Senator asked.

"I was just getting started." he replied.

"Good. If you will allow me I will give this some historical context and then we can continue by answering any questions, and I am certain that there will be many questions." Sun said with a smile and a small chuckle.

"I am listening." Kate replied in a very serious tone, she did not see the humor or the irony in what the Senator had said but most of all she did not trust him. She knew that he had been involved to some degree with the arrest of Austin and might have been working with Devers regarding her kidnapping or even her husband's abduction.

The Senator spent the next twenty minutes or more explaining the background involving Leopold Jenkins, William Lawrence Senior and Justin Welsh. He spoke about the accident where the two men were killed and where he was seriously injured and was very close to death. It was at that time that he began to speak about the time thread manipulation theory that Jenkins and Lawrence had constructed. He then explained that he and his colleagues did not believe it possible but they saw brilliance in one aspect of the project. It was in a program that would forecast events with uncanny accuracy. The program was now named Augur he explained and both WBOI and the Senator have working versions of the program as a result of careful monitoring of the project. Three weeks ago Sherwood DeMasters met with a very reliable source that indicated to him that the time thread manipulation project was viable and that they were going to set it in motion sometime during the first week of July. The effects of this process, if it is successful would be the end of everything that we know. Life will be replaced by an alternative time thread and many of the people that we know will cease to exist.

Kate listened carefully to what the Senator said and at times she had to suppress an urge to laugh out loud at the sheer implausible nature of what he was describing. There had been so many that had speculated on time travel and when that was proven to be impossible they migrated to other fantastic theories about time. She had read some of the ideas expressed about time as a measurement of the process of life and that any process can be reversed given the right tools. The author of that article was a woman scientist whose name escaped her recollection. She marked her recording of the Senator's explanation with the hope of coming back to identify that person. It could be a key to understanding what was happening here.

The ability to forecast the future was a different story all together and if they had an accurate tool, much better than industry was using today, it could mean that the promises for a better life for everyone could be possible. These and other thoughts went through Kate's mind as she listen to the Senator. It was difficult at times keeping up with what he was saying but it became clear as he finished his briefing that he was still very skeptical that Justin Welsh would be successful and that he was using the Augur program to prove that and to find those that were involved.

"At this time, who do you know is involved in this plot?" Kate asked directly.

"We know that aside from Justin Welsh these people are believed to be involved in the plot: doctors Avery Silcox, Adria Constantina, Philip Lee, and William Lawrence. There are numerous other low level people but these are the key people that represent the heart of the conspiracy." the Senator stated.

"Philip Lee, isn't he the brother of Austin Lee?" she asked noting the connection.

"Yes, he is the brother of Austin Lee but we have no reason to believe that Austin is currently involved in this latest attempt by Justin Welsh to undermine the fabric of our society." the Senator concluded.

Kate looked at the Senator to see if he had concluded his briefing. There was an awkward period of silence and then Wa interjected, "Thank you for taking time from you busy schedule to provide us with all of this much needed information. I am certain that you have helped Mrs. Foster."

"Thank you for allowing me to be of service." the Senator said rising slowly to his feet. "Mrs. Foster it has been a privilege to meet you. Your husband was a brave man and gave a great deal of himself in service to his country." he continued saying, "Might it be possible for us to have a word in private. I promise I will not take much of your time." He smiled graciously and then bowed to Wa.

"But of course. Mr. Wa could you excuse us for a few moments as I walk the Senator to the elevator." Kate said.

"But of course Mrs. Foster. I will wait here. Please remember that time is of the essence and we need to act quickly if we are to thwart this plan." Wa said reminding her of responsibilities and where her allegiance was to lie.

Kate walked the Senator to the elevator. The waiting area was unoccupied and the Senator took that moment to look at her and said, "If they are successful in achieving this 'Epiphanal Startling' thing that they are attempting your life will change significantly. You will still be alive, I took the liberty of running the program to determine the fate of several people of interest to me. Your husband however will cease to exist as will your children. There will be someone that you know and care about that will be alive as well and it seems under that time thread the two of you are together. It was his time thread that I was evaluating when you came to my attention. I wanted you to know this." he said. At that moment the door to the elevator opened and several people emerged.

"Thank you Senator, I understand and appreciate the information. I will have to work doubly hard to ensure the correct outcome." she replied. She watched the door close all the while thinking about what the Senator had said.

"What did the Senator want to tell you in confidence?" Wa asked.

"He told me my fate if we were not successful, that my husband and children would cease to exist. It is very sobering." she replied.

"That is odd that he would do that. There must be another motive, perhaps he is trying offer you additional incentive to complete your work." Wa responded apparently more for his own understanding than to offer Kate any elucidation. Kate on the other hand was not thinking about reasons she was seeking to suppress the thoughts that had started to take over her consciousness, the thought of a time thread where she and Austin were together. It was making it difficult for her to begin to formulate a plan to stop the impending plot from unfolding.

Wa began to offer suggestions as to how they should proceed but stopped short of ordering her to perform any action. After several minutes of volunteering his input, he stopped and asked her what she intended to do. At that point she stated that the first order of business was to put each of the suspected members of the plot under surveillance as quickly as possible with one exception and that would be Dr. Adria Constantina, she would able to provide them with an understanding of the process. It was for that reason that Kate felt that she should be apprehended and questioned. She also felt that it would be appropriate to contact Internal Security even if it meant that WBOI would be taking a secondary role in the initiative to stop the ES, as she referred to the 'Epiphanal Startling', from occurring.

She then asked Wa if he would like to place the call to Internal Security and handle the interaction between the two entities. Wa looked at her and then smiled. It was the first time he done so since she had met him that she could remember.

"That is a very good utilization of all of the assets that you have at your disposal Mrs. Foster. I am impressed." he stated. "I will contact Internal Security and that will enable you to run our operation unimpeded by them. Please do not waste what is being given to you." he concluded.

Wa stood up and turned to leave as he did so he turned around to face Kate when he reached the door. "Mrs. Foster, I was not a supporter of your promotion to this position, I thought you were too young and inexperienced but you have demonstrated to me that you are very capable and I believe that I may have been wrong in my initial assessment, please continue to prove that to be the case. Good bye and good luck." he said and turned and left.

Kate felt that she should have responded to him but did not believe it to be appropriate to follow him out. She had to get moving on her plan and show some solid results if she was to lead the team to stop the ES.

"Virginia, please come in here." she instructed Smithson. The door opened immediately and Smithson entered, she was ready for anything that Kate had for her to do.

"Please assemble a team of twenty operatives, and have them in our conference room within the hour." Kate told her.

"Yes Mrs. Foster. Is there anything else?" she then asked.

"Yes, do you still have the name of Devers' contact with Hell's Assassins?" Kate then asked in return.

"I don't know, I will check." she replied.

"If you find it place a call to that person and let me know when you have them on the line. I want to talk with them." Kate said.

"Yes of course." she replied and looked to make certain that there was nothing more she was to do.

"That will be all." Kate said dismissing her.

Her day was going to be extraordinarily busy and she felt the need to call Michael and alert him to the fact that she would be coming home very late, even though she had no idea exactly how late she would be. After making that call she began to work on the list that Smithson provided her of the operatives that would be attending the briefing and she did her best to match their skills and knowledge to one of the people that they were to locate to determine what they were doing exactly and where they were doing it.

As she performed the evaluation it became increasing clear to her the magnitude of the task at hand. Should Justin Welsh be successful in changing not only his life but the lives of everyone, causing people to no longer exist, the life that she had worked so hard to achieve would have been for naught. She would have different things and different memories, memories that would include Austin as the only consistent factor in her life. If she only had time to think about that and what that meant, but her job was to preserve the present and protect the interests of her employer.

****

"Mr. Lee, you don't know me, though I suspect you know of me. My name is Sun Ya Yen, I am a United States senator and friend of your father." the Senator said introducing himself.

"Yes Senator my father and brother Philip have spoken of you. What can I do for you?" answered Austin.

"I am going to give you information but we do not have time to explain all of the background. Your brothers have been working on a project in Maryland that involves time thread manipulation, the ability to change past events and as such influence the future. I only tell you this because if they are successful then your life will intersect much differently with someone you care about deeply. This change would mean a much different present for you and her." the Senator said calmly.

"I don't understand, why are you telling me these crazy things? Is this a prank?" Austin asked as struggled to keep his emotions barely under control.

"I assure you that this is no prank. I ask you to call your brother Philip and speak to him about what he is doing and then you will know what you must do." the Senator said and then he disconnected the call.

Austin sat for a moment thinking about what he had just heard. It was unfathomable, he could not make any sense of it at all. It was if he had entered a room and joined the conversation between two intimate friends where it was assumed that everyone had the same level of background and understanding, which unfortunately was not the case. His next thoughts centered on whether he should waste his brother's time to explain the call that he had just received. His curiosity bested him and he made the call.

"Phil, it is Austin. Can you spare a moment to talk?" he asked meekly.

"Sure, I always have time for my big brother." Philip responded with a laugh. He was in a good mood. He felt that he was ready to surrender the documents to the team for insertion into the Yom's imagers.

"I just received a very strange call from Senator Sun, he told me some very unbelievable things about a project on which you and Roger had been working." Austin said.

"Really what did he tell you about the project?" Philip asked.

"He told me that it involved time thread manipulation and that if you were successful it would change my life for the better." Austin replied.

Austin wondered if they had been disconnected since there had been no reply or reaction to his statement. It took a few moments for Philip to find word that he felt would offer his brother understanding but still not incite him to action, and want to be directly involved.

"What he told you is true. We have been working on a project that could if it is successful change our lives. Whether it is for the better is hard to say." Philip said breaking the silence.

"This is not the way that you normally behave Phil, what happened. You don't participate in things that change the status quo. Is what you are doing illegal?" Austin asked.

"If you remember our previous conversation you yourself said that there are no laws governing time thread manipulation. Legally, we are not doing anything for which we could be put in jail. That will not stop some people from doing whatever they need to do in order to prevent us from moving ahead with the project." Philip replied.

"The project? You are acting like Roger, that this is some puzzle that needs to be solved. It is about the lives of people, people that you know and for whom you care." Austin said passionately.

"Austin, it is for those very reasons that I have to do this. Your life will change and the lives of our mother and father will be better. The life of someone that I care about very much will also be positively impacted, her father will not be dead as he is now." Philip said calmly. "You see there are so many bad things that have happened that can and will be corrected if we succeed, so many mistakes undone. Uncle Bob will not be dead." he finally said those words that he knew would resonate and touch his soul.

"Phil, your attitude is quite a surprise to me. You had always been the prim and proper brother that did things according the way that they were supposed to be done. What happened to you?" Austin asked in a subdued tone the emotion having been wrung out of him.

"I don't really know. I suddenly discovered that there are events that are more significant than my History 101 class, and I never thought that I would ever make a statement like that." Philip responded with a chuckle. "I want to do something to help others, to make a difference in the events that are transpiring. It all comes down to realizing that in order to love one must be prepared to do whatever is required to reflect that love." Philip said and he then waited for Austin to respond.

A moment passed and then Austin replied, "I have read that somewhere and I suspect that you have read it as well."

"Yes, I suppose I have and just didn't realize the effect those words were having on me." Philip said.

"Phil, what can I do to help with your project?" Austin asked.

"You can stay away from it, the closer you get the more likely you will draw attention to it. The solution is very close." Philip replied.

"I understand but when the time comes and you need me, I will be there to help. I know that that time will come." Austin responded resolutely.

"I know that you want to be there. If this does not work and you are involved you may end up back in prison for at the very least a parole violation." Philip replied.

"I understand the risk. Did Uncle Bob understand the risks of what he did?" Austin asked rhetorically.

"Very well, I promise you if we need you we will call upon you." Philip answered. They were about to continue their conversation when Austin's phone indicated he had an incoming call. He excused himself and told Philip that they would talk soon and then disconnected the call at the same time accepting the incoming call.

"Austin, it's Kate Foster." Kate said announcing who she was and hoping that he would not immediately disconnect the call.

"Hello Kate, I am going to struggle a little with your name, I think of you as being Melissa. How have you been?" Austin asked sincerely.

Kate could not believe that he was being so gracious, so willing to extend forgiveness to her for her betrayal. "I have been okay. My life has been a whirlwind of activity and I had been meaning to call you and apologize to you." Kate said slowly and deliberately.

"Your apology is accepted. I know that you had a job to do and I also know that WBOI was using your husband as leverage to force you to do what you did. Even though it was just a mission for you, I sensed that you communicated a great deal of your inner thoughts to me during the time that we were together. I believe that I met a person that was kind and caring, a person that wanted to do what was right." Austin rejoined.

Kate had placed the call in an attempt to discover where Philip Lee was located. It would save her team significant time and effort if they could simply go to the location and begin their surveillance. Now she was confronted with a situation that would cause her to once again take advantage of Austin. This was not a well-conceived plan she thought as she labored to formulate the next sentence.

"I appreciate your thoughts. Austin, I felt a real connection with you. It was a difficult assignment and this call is an even more difficult one for me to place. I have to ask something and the real reason for this call is to ask you where your brother Philip is at this time. He is involved in a project that could destroy a great many people's lives." Kate said hoping that an honest statement would be effective in persuading Austin to help her.

"Kate, I understand that you have a job to do and that it must involve my brother in some way but I cannot help you." Austin said directly.

"Cannot or will not?" Kate asked in a tone that considerably harsher than it had been earlier in the conversation.

"I cannot. I don't know where he is." he replied.   The stress monitoring of the call depicted a high probability that Austin was telling the truth. Kate's holographic display also prompted her with additional questions to ask him that might help in extracting more information. She elected not to use them.

"Austin, thank you for taking my call. I must tell you one thing before I disconnect and that is I do think of you as someone I would like to call friend. You are a very gifted man and I admire you very much." Kate said her voice trailing off at the end of her statement.

"Kate it was good to hear your voice once again. I have but one regret, that we did not meet under different circumstances, perhaps then we would have been good friends or possibly…" Austin said stopping in mid-sentence. "I wish you only the best, for you and your family Kate." Austin said.

"You, you don't understand Austin." Kate said.

"Yes I do." Austin replied.

"Then how could you say the things that you are saying?" Kate asked showing a slight glimmer of emotion.

"Those things are said out of love for you. I love the complete you, that means the things that you love are important to me too; your children, your husband and all of those truly meaningful things in your life." he replied. "I think that you should say good bye now Kate, I sense that you are going to say something that you may think you mean now but may regret later. Good bye." Austin said and disconnected the call.

As Kate spoke she realized that he had ended the call. She needed to take a moment and collect her thoughts and return her focus to the mission. Austin was a remarkable man and she felt sadness when she thought about not seeing him. She spoke to herself saying that spending time thinking of Austin and picturing him and his smile was a luxury that she could not afford. There was no way that she could allow herself to expend the energy or waste time in that pursuit. She had less than thirty minutes to prepare for the briefing and there would have to be results shown quickly.

It was clear to her that her job security hinged on stopping the event from happening. Then she thought for a moment and came to the realization that WBOI was unable to stop the event from transpiring everything would change. If it occurred as it had been anticipated there would be no knowledge of her failure and her life would be completely different. Still she had to make every effort, if not for her job, for her children lives.

The briefing began simply enough, she dispensed the assignments and told the operatives that they were to provide hourly updates and that the individuals assigned to finding Adria Constantina must immediately inform the office should she be found. She would be then taken to a location that would be named at that time, but under no circumstances was she to be brought to this office.

"It seems that there is not a great deal of information to assist us in locating these individuals. This process could take weeks before we get a solid lead." one of the operatives commented from the rear of the room.

"We do not have weeks, we have today. I expect results. Is that clearly understood?   If you do not feel that you are capable of doing the job, we will find people that are." Kate said firmly.   There was a low murmur and then the room became completely still, the message had been communicated.

"Very well, I expect to hear your first reports within the hour. Dismissed." she said and left the room ahead of everyone in attendance.

****

Mort Hancock's PTU slowly approached the Buffalo Fabrication Company's main gate. It was a large sprawling facility that covered more than sixty two thousand square yards and Morton estimated that it contained at least ten building. Most of the building were at least fifty years old and it appeared that the main building and two others may have been closer to one hundred years old. There was a guard shack at the gate and when the vehicle stopped an older man popped his head up and peered at him from behind the grimy glass windows of the shack. In a few seconds he appeared to recognize Morton and then waved a halfhearted wave while opening the door. He then disappeared from sight once again. Morton then instructed the PTU to proceed and it entered the compound following a meandering course until it came to rest in front of building number seven.

The shift supervisor appeared at the doorway and greeted him with a smile. "Mr. Hancock it's very good to see you sir. How was your trip?" Lou asked.

"Fine Lou. How have you been?" Morton asked this question even though he knew that Lou would want to explain everything that he had going on in his life. Lou did not fail to disappoint, he explained to Morton how he had been having intermittent back spasms for the past several weeks and that his wife had made his favorite diner the night before. As Lou spoke Morton smiled and nodded his head.

As soon as he saw the opportunity he interjected another more meaningful question, "I see. How is the project coming along?" Lou put the same amount of detail into his explanation of the project's status as he had in describing his life. Morton listened intently not interrupting at all, he was confident that Lou would cover every detail of the undertaking.

They began to walk toward the shop floor while Lou continued to update Morton on the project's status. The briefing was proceeding well until Lou said, "We are about three days behind on the build date right now due the absence of the magnetic core couplers that you had requested as part of the specifications. Apparently the only company that makes them received orders for a total twenty seven including the three we ordered and they are having difficulties meeting the demand."

"These units must be ready to ship by June twenty second at the latest. Will that be a problem?" Morton asked.

"It all depends upon those parts. We are continuing with the rest of the build but we will reach a point where we cannot go further unless the part is here and ready to be installed. You do realize sir that the part has to be 'seasoned'?" Lou asked.

"How long does the bombardment have to take place before the unit is ready of installation?" Morton asked in response.

"No less than twenty hours, but it should be twenty four according to the specifications." Lou responded.

"Well that gives us three days to finish this. Your people are very good Lou, they will just have to be at the top of their game to meet the deadline." Morton replied.

"If there is a way to meet the deadline, we will do it, sir." Lou said with a smile. He then proceeded to show Morton the progress and this was the first time that Morton had seen the unit in an almost completed form.

The Yom was an amazing piece of machinery, thought Morton. It was the roughly twenty seven cubic yards in size. It appeared to be black when viewed from one angle and it had a camouflaged pattern when viewed from another. There were several men busy working on the different parts of the unit.

Lou looked at it and smiled again. "This is an impressive beast." he said. "Watch this."

He ordered the men to step back and he initiated the entrenchment protocol. Four particle beams emerged from the top of the unit on each of the four sides. They were suspended by an arm that had an elbow joint that enabled them to pivot. Their purpose was burn a trench roughly two yards deep on all four sides of the unit and to do this in less than a minute. They simulated the trenching process and then the side panels of the unit were extended, the purpose was for them to be inserted into the trench and as they were they would also be extended to a height of nine feet above the ground's surface.

Once these steps were completed a dome like apparatus that housed the magnetic core would be elevated to the height of the walls. When that was in place the unit would be ready for activation and the Yom would then be called upon to find and interact with the residual magnetic signatures of the past. This was only simulated at this point but the unit appeared to be performing according the designed specifications.

"It looks great Lou. You and your team have done very well. Now all we have to do is get you the parts that you need to finish this 'beast' as you put it." Morton said.

He now had to see where the other assembly facilities stood regarding their progress. He hoped that they had received their parts and this delay was only affecting the Buffalo plant. Morton waited for Lou to finish his statements about the quality of their workmanship before he excused himself to place a call to Norville. It would be best if Norville were made aware of the challenge and he could assist him in contacting the other eight facilities.

"Norville it is Mort. I have some good news and some not so good news. The not so good news is that the supplier of the magnetic core couplers is not delivering their products claiming that they have too many orders to fill at this time. It seems that our requirement for twenty seven of them is beyond their manufacturing capacity." Morton said giving Norville the opportunity to hear the problem directly without the social trappings.

"Morton, that doesn't sound like very good news. What do you need me to do?" Norville asked.

"Please contact the supplier and apply as much pressure as you can on them to make their deadlines and also call three of the assembly sites and see if they are having a similar problem." Morton replied.

"I will do that, which sites do you wish me to contact?" Norville asked in response.

"The two Florida sites and the one in Texas. I will call the other five sites that are located closer to the drop ship point." Morton answered.

"Good job, Morton. I will call you later to give you an update on my findings. Good bye son, and thank you for your hard work and dedication." Norville said fatherly.

During the two hours both Norville and Morton contacted all parties and were assured that the build deadlines would be met. The magnetic core coupler manufacturer had already shipped half the units and the balance of the pieces were to ship within the next forty eight hours, which would have them arriving in time for all sites to be able to complete the assembly on time. Each unit was to be shipped to a warehouse that was within two miles of where it was to be installed and made operational.

With the news that the Buffalo unit would be shipping within forty eight hours Morton located Lou and shared the good news. Needless to say that news was met with great enthusiasm. Morton took that occasion to take his leave and as he exited the plant the old man gave him another halfhearted wave.

****

"Dr. Lee, this is Tira Irving and I am on the line with Johanas Spruce, you have never spoken with either of us but we are hoping that you recognize the names." Tira said with a nervous laugh.

"Oh yes, Dr. Irving and Dr. Spruce, I know your names very well." Philip replied.

"Good that saves time with introductions. We will need you to come to our location to review the end results of the items you have had us prepare. We are concerned that the material that these images are being placed on is authentic as well." Tira explained.

"When would you be able to see us?" Johanas asked.

Philip thought a moment and then asked, "Where are you located?"

"We are located in Cincinnati Ohio. It's about a four hour train trip since you have to change trains in Columbus." Johanas replied.

"I can be there tomorrow morning. How long will the session take?" Philip asked.

This is when Tira decided to rejoin the conversation and told him that he must be prepared for it take almost the entire day. An argument over that point ensued after Johanas stated that he did not believe that it would take more than two hours. Philip listened to them as the intensity of the dispute grew.

"I can be there in the morning and I will free my schedule for the whole day and if it only takes a few hours I will have the benefit of having some much needed time off." Philip said hoping that his remarks would end the dispute.

Unfortunately, while they acknowledged his comments the two combative souls continued the verb pugilism for it was far from simple sparring. "Where am I to go tomorrow?" Philip asked. The address materialized on his PCU and neither of them missed a syllable.

Once free from the bickering Philip placed two calls, the first was to Jessica to invite her to diner, and the second was to Morgan to instruct him what need to be done in preparation for the summer term that was starting in two days. He was looking forward to seeing Jessica but he knew that this might be the last time that he saw her for a while if at all.

He still wasn't certain about her future in the new time thread. Since he existed in the alternate time thread he could not be present in the Control Center when the new time thread was being constructed. Those that were in Control Center were those that had no future, they would theoretically be protected and since they did not exist there would be no way that they could encounter themselves. Philip guessed that he would simply go home after the last pieces of the puzzle were put in place and wait.

Tomorrow's meeting might be the last one to require his involvement, but he did not actually believe that. He felt that Norville would be calling him and asking him to take one more look at the time thread projections as they related to the days that they would be influencing. He would be leaving from home shortly to rendezvous with Jessica and from there he would make the trip to Columbus where he intended to spend the night.

****

Kate's team had been calling their reports on time. There had been little success in locating their assigned targets with the exception of Philip. He turned out to be the easiest to find since he was at his home. The call to Austin wasn't necessary but Kate still needed to make it, she wanted to hear his voice. Kate had learned from the briefing paper that had been sent to her that the event was to be centered on a modification of the outcome of the battle of Gettysburg. She had immediately sought out the date that it occurred and surmised that the target date for execution of the plan would most likely be July first, the two hundred and fifty year anniversary of the commencement of the battle. It made sense to her that they would want this to happen on that date. The problem was she still did not understand how they planned on accomplishing this manipulation. If only she had been more attentive in science class, she thought.

****

"Dad I need to talk to you about something." Austin said opening the conversation on a serious note.

"Go ahead son. What's on your mind?" Gregory responded.

"I want to help we the project. I need to be involved." Austin said. Gregory looked at his son, he saw the pain on his face and the trouble that must be tearing him apart from within.

564

"There is not much that needs to be done. You would be putting yourself at risk for a very small contribution. I would advise against it." Gregory said sincerely.

"Dad, I had a dream and I was sitting in a hallway in front of two very large oak doors. I was waiting for some people to come that were trying stop the project from being completed. I need to be there." Austin said. "I have decided that this is the course of action I must follow. It is the right thing to do." he continued.

Gregory looked at him and then lowered his eyes. He had known that Austin would follow a course that would take him away from them, he just wasn't certain what that course was to be.

"I know you feel strongly about bringing down the established economic system but this isn't the way to accomplish it, and you are not needed." Gregory pleaded with his son.

"Were you really needed in this project Dad? Couldn't one of your technicians have done just as well as you did?" Austin asked calmly.

"It is not the same. I am old, and no one will put me in jail for what I did. You could go back to jail or worse." Gregory responded his voice shaking with emotion.

"I know the risks Dad but this is still the only course of action that I can follow that makes any sense to me. Please don't think that I do not love both you and Mom and have not been grateful for everything you have done for me, because I have. I need you to explain this to Mom because I know that I cannot and that she will be so upset that it might temporarily cause me to weaken my resolve." Austin said.

"I cannot tell your mother, you will have to do that. If you are unable to maintain your resolve then perhaps it wasn't meant to be done." Gregory said shaking his head. "Will you listen to Justin if he tells you not to do it?" Gregory asked and without waiting for a reply placed a call to Norville using the home's antiquated phone.

"Hello Gregory, good of you to call." Norville said cheerfully.

"Norville, Austin has made a decision that he wants to participate in the project." Gregory said bluntly.

"That is very serious Gregory. Have you tried to discourage him?" Norville asked in reply.

"Yes, but he told me about having a dream and that he was seated in front of two large oak doors and the reason he was seated there was that he was protecting the project from those that want to stop the project from going forward." Gregory told Norville candidly.

"I see. You don't know this but what you are describing is the location of the Control Center. I am not certain what this means, but there is a strong possibility that Austin is supposed to be with us. I certainly did not envision this happening and if you can persuade him to the contrary please do. That young man has been like a son to me. You have been very fortunate Gregory to have him and the other two men as your sons. They are…" Norville said the emotion preventing him from completing the statement.

Gregory disconnected the call and turned to Austin. "The doors that you saw in your dream are the same doors that the Control Center is located behind. Norville thinks that perhaps you are supposed to be there." Gregory said resigned to the fact that Austin would be going and that he may never see his oldest son again.   "This time, if you are arrested and are sent to prison I will come and visit you. I promise." Gregory said while looking intently at his son who simply stared back at him silently.

****

"Norville I want you to meet Rush Thompson, he is providing us with the final transport and placement of the Yoms." Willie said introducing the small squatty man with very large hands.

"Mr. Forrest it's a pleasure to meet you sir. I have my team standing by for a deployment at zero four hundred hours on one July. All units will be in place by zero five hundred and ready for activation." Rush stated abruptly.

"Mr. Thompson, you come to us highly recommended and we are expecting a flawless mission. What type of vehicle are you going to using to deliver the units?" Norville asked.

A big grin formed on Rush's face as he said, "Well Mr. Forrest about three years ago I was at an auction where the Olds Corporation was disposing of their air mobile transports and I happened to buy a dozen or so of them. That's what we will be using."

"The LA104? Those were considered to be extremely dangerous to operate.   In fact all of the Lighter than Air series from Olds were condemned as failures and technologically impractical." Willie said directly.

"Yes, they were technologically impractical. Why do your think we are still driving around on the ground? They are not unsafe and they are fine pieces of machinery that can do amazing things, such as depositing a piece of hardware at a location that no other vehicle that can haul can reach, and on this mission there are two locations where that is most definitely true." Rush replied.

Norville looked at the man and then at Willie and said "Willie, I think the man knows what he is talking about. Please give him the logistics documents so that he can work out the details of his final plan."

****

Philip walked into the restaurant and saw Jessica sitting with her back to the door. It reminded of their first encounter at the train station in Lancaster. Unfortunately the woman that blocked his way came to mind as well. He smiled as thought about Jessica and how beautiful she was. This night had to be a special night, it might be their last together. He had no assurances that she would be part of his life going forward. The events that led up to their meeting revolved around the project, it brought them together.

Philip walked up to her silently and he hoped to surprise her but when he was within two feet she turned quickly and startled him. Apparently she had seen his reflection is in the gold mirrored tiles that lined the wall. That's why she was so confident sitting with her back to the door, he thought. Jessica laughed and Philip blushed and smiled. He leaned forward that kissed her cheek, the smell of coco butter struck him. She hadn't been using it recently, it reminded him of some of the most pleasant nights that he had spent with her. As he sat down he noticed an envelope on the table and she had one hand resting on it.

She asked about his day and his trip to see her, but it was clear that she was distracted. Jessica fumbled the envelope before finally handing it to Philip while saying, "I should have given you this before, but I didn't understand it until this morning after I woke up from a dream. My father did not invent the term 'Epiphanal Startling', in fact the entire concept was borrowed and enhance scientifically from a short speech given by a man that was later executed as traitor. His name was..."

"Christopher Leesop. I dreamt of him last night. Did you?" Philip asked his voice betraying his amazement.

"No, I dreamed about my father, we were sitting by a small stream and he told me that this man, Christopher Leesop, was the true light, the way to understanding of why we are here. He assured me that I was going to be fine and that we would see each other soon. He also told me that you loved me and that you were willing to sacrifice everything for me, but you were not be the one that was chosen for that task. I am not sure what he meant but I do know that I love you and that I needed to tell you that right now!" Jessica said with her eyes reflecting the emotion that resounded in her words.

Philip stood up and then got down on one knee saying, "Jessica I love you and if you will have me please consent to marrying me and soon!"

"Yes Philip." she replied smiling while reaching forward and touching his cheek.

During the next half hour they talked about the wedding and how many people they would invite and what would be the best location at which to perform the ceremony. Once there was a lull Jessica asked Philip to share with her his dream that he had mentioned. Philip tried to direct the conversation away from his dream. He felt that it was a private matter and most likely had nothing to do with anything.

"Philip it is important that you learn to share more about what is going on inside that fabulous head of yours." she said in an attempt to show him that she was aware of what he was doing.

"You are right. At the very least if I don't want to share I shouldn't mention it in the first place." he said. Jessica did not respond but waited for him to continue. He finally realized that he would have to share it so he began by saying, "First I would like to say that it was very odd that I had a dream like this, I don't normally remember dreams. This dream was like any conscious experience, there were no disjointed or fragmented behaviors. It was as if the events had actually happened."

Jessica nodded and then said, "They were my feelings exactly."

"You and I were riding horses on a beautiful spring day. Everything seemed so natural even though the only horses I have ever seen were either in pictures or at the Zoological Society. The day was perfect, brilliant blue sky and there were yellow flowers mixed among the green grass. I could smell their fragrance in the air and felt the gait of the animal as he walked slowly. We approached a small stand of trees and a man emerged from between them. In the background I heard the murmur of a small stream that lay just beyond the trees. The man, dressed in white robes, raised his hand and called out saying, "Greetings Philip. We have been given a glorious day today."

He then explained that he pulled on the reigns bringing the horse to stop and then asked the man, "Do I know you?"

He replied saying, "I have known you since you and your brother Austin were young boys playing in your father's house."

"'Who are you?' I asked." Philip continued.

"My name is Christopher, we are related you and I. Would you and your wife Jessica sit with me follow awhile, I have something to tell you." he replied." Philip said telling the story slow and deliberately.

At that point Jessica interrupted by asking, "Did he really say your wife?" all the while smiling broadly.

Philip replied with a reassuring nod and then continued the narrative of the dream, "We followed him to the bank of the stream and sat on several large boulders that were polished smooth from erosion.

"You look well Philip. It has been a very long time since I saw you last. I am hoping that will change once you have experienced the events that are going to take place very soon." he said. "I didn't think of him as being dead, I knew that he and my Uncle Bob were very close and that I knew that my Uncle Bob was somehow alive and I accepted it without question, even though I know that he was killed in the war."

"What will be happening soon?"

"You will be involved in an attempt to alter time as it has been. You will succeed but not in the way that you were expecting and the cost to you will appear to be great, but it must happen this way for all to be healed. Everyone will see and they will learn." he said.

"I don't understand." Philip said that he replied.

He replied, "Yes, it is as it should be."

****

Adria had been talking to people all day about prophetic dreams that they had been having. She was beginning to suspect that this was a ripple prior to the event and that meant to some degree that the project had been successful. She wanted to share this with someone but she could not decide who would give it the proper amount of weight. It was important but it gave no indication that the outcome would be as they all hoped it would be.

Norville would make it out to be a huge sign of success, Avery would see it as just another event that substantiated her theories, Willie would say that it was nonsense unless he had had a dream and Philip would be confused by it, but of all the people he was the best candidate to see the event for what it was. They were on the verge of manipulating the life's process and this change was beyond their ability to grasp its true meaning. It was at that point obvious with whom she would share the information.

****

Philip was at the train station and had just finished telling his parents and brothers about his upcoming marriage. He left Jessica in tears, she did not want him to leave but he had to meet with the bickering doctors in the morning where he would be assisting them in the completion of the magnetic objects that that would be inserted into the time thread by the Yoms. He was headed to Columbus to spend the night and another night in a hotel with little or no sleep and yet he was feeling extremely energized by the events of the past several hours. And he wondered how all of this had come to pass.

His thought were interrupted by the incoming call from Adria. After a quick perfunctory social salutation she told him the reason for her call.

"So that's what it was. ." he replied.

"The dream I had was a foreshadowing of events to come, even though the dream was pleasant it did have an ominous pale to it."

"So you experienced a dream as well. That is amazing and it confirms the hypothesis since I am not in the future that we are attempting to supplant and I did not dream." Adria said.

"This must be difficult for you knowing that you will no longer be part of... well, life." Philip said uncertain as to how to respond to someone that knew that very shortly they would cease to exist.

"I will be protected by the magnetic field during the shift and it is believed that once it has occurred when I emerge from its protection I will still be alive, but what that life will be like, I do not know. I could have no memory and literally be as someone that was just born that very day, having to be taught everything. I could recall all or part of the event. Either way my life will be different than it is at this time." Adria said elaborating on what she believed the options to be.

"What about the Control Center, it will have no place in the new time thread and if it ceases to exist don't you run the same risk?" Philip asked.

"Yes, that is possible though we are using an escape pod to exit and it will throw us clear from the Control Center before the total collapse of the magnetic field. There is also the possibility of phase distortion which would mean we would stuck in the previous time thread and won't be able to escape it." Adria said while she answered his question with more information than he was prepared to take in.

"You are meeting with our two combative electromagnetic physicists tomorrow morning. If you can keep them from spending hours arguing about every small insignificant detail you may be able to extricate yourself from their tedious infighting within two or three hours. If not you will be with them all day and still may not accomplish what should have taken a very short period of time." Adria said giving Philip a warning of a condition that he had already anticipated existed.

"Do you believe that the dreams are visions of our life under the alternate time thread?" Philip asked.

"Most definitely. They are images of events that are taking place now under the alternate time thread." Adria replied.

"How do you explain the apparent knowledge that Christopher Leesop had of the events that were about to take place and his statement regarding the sacrifice that must be made by someone that is close to me?" Philip asked.

"That is a very good question and I don't have an answer. That man has been an enigma since he first opened his mouth three years before he was finally silenced by the powers that be." Adria replied.

"Wasn't it the government that executed him?" Philip asked.

"Yes, they pulled the trigger. The man they should have executed was killed very recently and those that were instrumental in engineering the crimes have also been killed. It is fascinating how this has played out. If you are aware of the facts and are perceptive you will see that there appears to be order here that the casual observer finds to be chaos." Adria said waxing a little too philosophic for Philip's attention span to handle at that time.

"I must be going Adria. Thank you for the call, and the news is very exciting indeed. I feel a little bit like I did when I was a child waiting for the family to go on a trip, anxious with anticipation and a little nervous about the outcome. Please take care and I will see you in Baltimore next week." he said.

"Good bye Philip, please be careful and also don't share the subject of our conversation with anyone, including Norville." Adria responded.

"As you wish. Good bye." Philip said and disconnected the call. He decided that when he checked into the hotel that he would not do any work. He would go to sleep, he thought about the changes that his life was going to make and the fact that he would have a whole new set of memories. It was hard to believe that he would be married to Jessica regardless of which direction life took him. He was still not convinced that this was really going to work.

****

"Mrs. Foster we have the subject in sight now. He has just entered a hotel in Columbus Ohio and we have determined that he has a reservation for short shuttle trip to Cincinnati at seven thirty six tomorrow morning. There has not been any phone activity since he had the conversation with Dr. Constantina and we were unable to determine her exact location but it appears that she was located somewhere in eastern Connecticut." the team leader of the Philip's surveillance reported.

"Keep watching him. It appears that, based upon the transcript of the call to from Adria Constantina that he will be meeting with two key individuals tomorrow and that we should plan on interrogating them after he leaves them." Kate told him.

"Yes Mrs. Foster we will maintain the surveillance. Should be apprehend Dr. Lee as well as the two individuals with whom he is meeting?" the team leader asked.

"No, wait until Dr. Lee has left the area before you move on the location. We do not want to arouse any suspicion that will cause him from deviating from his rendezvous with the others that we are seeking." Kate said explaining the instructions so that there could be no misunderstanding. Philip was the only one, of the people that they had identified, that they had been able to locate and follow. He represented their best chance of finding the location of the time thread manipulation equipment and the conspirators, especially Justin Welsh.

****

Philip awoke from a very peaceful sleep. It was a tranquil sleep with only once exception, he had another even more vivid dream. This time he was sitting at his home waiting for his brother Austin to arrive with his wife and child. Jessica spent most of the time preparing a meal and straightening their home in anticipation of the guests' arrival. It was a domestic scene like one that he had read about in his studies of the Nineteenth and Twentieth centuries. There was no vast array of technology just a simple residence with an aura that engulfed it. He had awaken smiling.

Soon he was making his way to the rail station and would be on the shuttle to Cincinnati for the brief trip to see those two colorful doctors. He mused at the thought of them bickering the entire day away, and if he did not feel he could be using his time better, he might even enjoy the banter and the comic relief that it surly would provide. He arrived at the station and was sitting comfortably in his seat waiting for the train to depart. The trip was less than twenty minutes and he would barely be able to get anything accomplished, still he was conditioned to take advantage of this time to do something productive. He decided to review the summer curriculum and to be sure that would be able to cover the material during required during the next eight days, the last eight days of June.

Philip did not notice the man and woman that entered the train at the last moment before its departure. They walked on to the train together and yet they sat in different rows apparently bracketing him. The woman sat in a seat several rows in front of Philip while the man was seated several rows behind him, both were on the opposite side of the aisle. Philip took note that there were very few passengers on the train and he thought that it was odd.

The short walk from the train station was relatively pleasant. There were misting systems that were used to cool the side walk areas. It was technology that had been abandoned by many cities in lieu of enclosed walkways. He turned down the small street the stopped at the river's edge. The small colorful building seemed to be unoccupied but the address, which was clearly displayed, was the one that he had been given. He climbed the two cement stairs to the door and as he approached it opened.

"Dr. Lee, is that you?" a male voice called from within.

"Yes, it is. Dr. Spruce I presume." Philip replied.

"Oh yes, that is me. Tira, is mucking about somewhere, please call my Johanas." Johanas replied.

"Only if you will call me Philip." Philip said in response.

"Very good Philip. Uh, were you followed?" Johanas asked.

"I really don't know. I don't think so, I just didn't give it much thought." Philip answered.

"Oh, I see." Johanas said not knowing exactly how to respond.

"You didn't think that people would be interested in you?" Tira asked as she entered the small room where the two men were standing.

"Tira, this is Philip." Johanas said attempting introduce the two of them and distract Tira from becoming fixed on Philip's failure to observe his surroundings properly.

"Do you know how much trouble this could cause if he was followed and they came bursting through the door and took everything we have been working on for the past three years? It would be what?" she asked Johanas.

"It would be a disaster." he responded rolling his eyes.

"Not just a disaster if could mean the project would fail." she continued on telling him while berating him and staring intently at Philip.

"Can we get started then? If they are going to break down the door any minute, we must certainly work diligently to complete our work." Johanas said sarcastically.

"You will be the death or both of us you old fool." she said and turned and lead the way to the laboratory.

Philip watched quietly while the two scientists worked. They were manipulating their work stations' controls which apparently had something to do with a large transparent box that was suspended above the floor, presumably by a magnetic field.   Within the box there were four small spheres each one attached to a rod that was embedded in four opposing sides of the cube.

"Okay, Tira its time to produce the first document. Please introduce the image matrix and don't forget to wear your protective goggles, the last time we did this you couldn't see for three days. Philip if you wish to watch you will need to wear goggles as well." Johanas said pointing to a peg board that held four sets of goggles. Philip retrieved three pairs and gave each of them a set. He noticed that Johanas had a pair on a chain that he wore around his neck, but he accepted the goggles that Philip had given him and he thanked Philip for them.

Philip watched the center of the cube and as an object appeared to take shape being assembled out of nothing but magnetic energy. It became more and more realistic in appearance until it looked like a piece of paper that had J. E. B. Stuarts flowery script scrawled across it.

"Is the color of the paper authentic?" Tira asked, but Philip did not respond.

"Dr. Lee is the color of the paper authentic?" she asked again. Philip now realized why he had been invited to their laboratory, to authenticate the created forgeries.

"It appears to be from where I am standing but if I could see it closer I will be able to say for certain." Philip replied.

There was a moment when Philip was not certain what was going to happen. The two doctors started bickering immediately at the noise level of almost a whisper. The only words he was able to discern were 'containment' and 'burn'. Neither of these two words filled Philip with a feeling of confidence and security.

Then Johanas said loudly, "Very well."

Johanas then walked up to the box and opened it using an access that Philip had not noticed. Johanas, without any protection on his hands reached into the box and carefully picked up the item that had formed within. After removing it from the box he held it away from his body and moved toward Philip.

"You were right Tira." he said. "There are no real ill effects in handling the document. Though I must admit the sensation on my fingers is rather odd, almost like all the nerve endings are extremely sensitive." he continued.

"I must try this." Tira said quickly walking to Johanas and touching the document.

"You are right. There is a very odd sensation when you come into contact with the document. I suspect that is because that there is less matter than what normally goes into fabricating something like it." she said. "It's not like the substance modification that we are working on for the GH project, if we end up with a finished product like this I suspect we will be put in..." Tira said and then stopped realizing that Philip may not have the security clearance to know about Good Hope.

"Yes quite right." Johanas said with a smile.

Philip looked at the letter. The coloration and texture were exactly what he knew to be authentic looking. "This is remarkable. I would suggest one thing and that you are going to have to have this folded. Will that be a problem?" Philip asked.

"Let's see." Johanas said giving Tira a quick look. He then took the paper and folded it. The paper remained folded as it would have if it had been made of wood pulp and not magnetic energy.

"What happens when you unfold it?" Philip asked. Johanas got a puzzled look on his face and then he unfolded the paper. It went back to the original appearance. "That will be a problem." Philip said.

"It will have to have memory. The fold marks will have to be retained, otherwise it will not appear to be real. Can it be torn or destroyed?" Philip said and asked.

Tira and Johanas listened to Philip explain why the document would have to have all of the characteristics of the original substance. They then excused themselves and left the room. Philip decided that the day was going to be a long one and that he had to prepare himself for a long ordeal of struggling with the bickering doctors and their challenging each other. Philip looked at the paper sitting in front of him on the desk. It was a remarkable accomplishment he thought. If the others are this good then we will have no problem fooling the intended recipients. He decided to touch the paper to understand the feelings that they had expressed. The sensation was odd but not painful, though he imagined that it would be difficult to tolerate over an extended time period. After that brief sensory stimulation he decided that it would be best if he made some positive use of his time. He was just about to retrieve the syllabus of his summer class when the two doctors returned and Tira was holding another piece of paper.

"Would this be serviceable?" she asked handing the paper to Philip. It too had the same sensation but it appeared to be worn from use. There were fold marks, there were smudges of the ink and that looked like dampness had been introduced because there was a visible water stain on one of the corners.

"This is exactly what we need. Was it created like this or did these occur as a result of handling?" Philip asked enthusiastically.

"We engineered it to be influenced by handling based upon the specification that we had received. There was a problem the document after being subjected to the harsh environment would break down and become illegible and we decided to make it more robust and durable." Johanas said explaining the reason for the first paper document.

"This is exactly what we need. It is perfect. The paper was not durable it broke down and was destroyed. We need our forgeries to behave in exactly the same way." Philip said praising their efforts.

They took a moment and looked at each other. "We could have been done with this project two days after you gave us the final copy and specifications. Please let's make haste and review the other eight documents and then we will prepare the imaging modules for your to take with you." Johanas said.

The review process went smoothly. There were a few modifications of text that Philip decided upon seeing them on paper needed to be made. He also had sealing wax and a signet ring impression added to the correspondence from Lee to Longstreet directing him send Jenkins and his mounted infantry to Philadelphia. By the time that Lee and Longstreet would have time to discuss the matter, the plan would have been executed and this method of presentation would ensure that Longstreet took the directive as authentic and the need to execute it quickly imperative. This change took approximately two hours to affect and all of the documents had been approved before it was time for lunch.

Philip inquired if they wished to take a break to eat lunch. Tira leaned toward Johanas and whispered something to him and he replied, "We would like to finish this now." and walked to a cabinet and removed a shiny metal frame that was a foot square. Philip saw that there were nine of these and surmised that they were the imagining modules that were to be inserted into the Yoms. He watched Johanas place the frame on the work station and then he took the first pristine document and placed in the frame. Philip noticed that the frame was adjustable in all of its dimensions and Johanas carefully aligned it so that all sides touched the document. After that he took a thin web of wires and laid over the front of the document. The web instantly adhered to the frame and once that was done Johanas turned the frame over and installed another web on that side as well.

After this was accomplished the frame was inserted into a protective sleeve and that was placed in a small slotted case. Philip watched the process intently. He was unaware that he would be transporting these documents and he began to get nervous as he thought about the prospect of being caught carrying them.

"If someone were to stop you and inspect these you have a button on the case that is located here. Push it and the documents cease to exist. At that point all you will be carrying is a little bit of metal." Johanas said while pointing to the small concealed button and smiling at the prospect of someone inspecting the empty frames.

Philip was walking back to the train station carrying a small case filled with the results of his research and the technology invented by the Tira and Johanas. They seemed anxious for him to leave but he was equally eager to depart. The time passed quickly and he was soon approaching the train station. It was at this time that he received a call from Norville instructing him to be prepared to surrender the case to a young woman that he would be encountering in just a few minutes. She would have a duplicate case and would bump into him and she would handle the exchange.

"Take the case that she gives you home with you and don't worry about anything more, your work is done." Norville said in closing.

Tira and Johanas were in the custody of Internal Security before Philip had received the call from Norville. They had managed to destroy all evidence of the project and what remained was their work on the classified government project. A project that had benefited greatly by the technological breakthroughs that they had made.

When the exchange of the cases was made the surveillance team split their assignments and alerted Kate as to what was transpiring. They were broadening their understanding of the network and Kate rapidly called in resources from the pursuit of the other individuals to apply them to the surveillance of the woman courier and Philip.

The young woman met Morton at the train station in Baltimore. He inspected the case and its contents briefly and then smiled at her and told his daughter that she had done well. He gave her a quick hug and a kiss on the cheek. He was uncertain when and if he would see her again since he was one of those people that would not exist in the new time thread.

One of the operatives that was shadowing the young courier heard her refer to Morton as dad. He felt that this information should be shared and he placed a call to Kate. Kate upon hearing this decided that they had to allow the girl to continue without being detained. The contents of the case were the primary concern and the individual that had it. They had identified the girl and were convinced that they could apprehend her at any time should it be deemed appropriate.

Morton felt that there was something wrong. He sensed that he was being followed and knew that he would have to find a way to get the case into another's hands as quickly as possible. He called Norville and alerted him of the situation and Norville did not seemed to be phased by the news.

"Morton, my boy, the contents of the case will be installed in the appropriate units when they have been tested tomorrow. You will be the one that will install them. I will help you lose the people that are following you, just do as I say." Norville said encouraging him to remain calm. Norville instructed Morton to get on a train bound for Philadelphia, when he arrived there he should look for a group of people that would be gathered in front of the coffee shop located in the main concourse. He was to mingle with the group who will alter his appearance while creating a diversion. Then he should take a train back to Baltimore, during that train ride he would receive additional instructions.

The diversion had worked and Morton was able to lose his surveillance. The surveillance had gained an advantage in that they were able to identify him and they began to systematically search his place of business, residence and all know location of relatives. It was just a matter of time before they would be able to re-acquire him and put him back under surveillance.

Kate and her team were working efficiently and supporting the Internal Security group that was in charge of the operation. During the briefing that had taken place earlier that day it was determined that a series of unauthorized electric power usages were determined to be part of the plan that was underway. They could be the sites that the conspirators were going to deploy their machines that would change the world forever she thought. The data that Internal Security had provided showed three general locations but there could very well be more. The locations were in and around the small city of Gettysburg Pennsylvania and Kate had dispatched a team of twelve agents to do investigative work. The day ended with the team having made some solid gains in intelligence gathering but there was still a long way to go and they were running out of time.

Chapter Eighteen

The next morning, June twenty fifth, 2113 was a beautiful day, Morton thought. He had slept soundly, and had not dreamt at all. His day was going to be a very full one and once it was completed he could go home and see his wife and two children for the first time in almost three weeks. He was going to meet with Rush and the two men would travel to each of the nine storage locations where the Yom units were being house. This was final testing day and after the tests the imaging frames would be installed and the units would sit dormant until they were activated on the morning of July first. This was the first time that Rush would see the Yom and he would have to be confident that he and his team could deploy these units within the window of opportunity that they would have available to them.

"Good morning Mort. Are you ready for a busy day?" Rush asked extending his hand.

"Good morning Rush. It is a beautiful day and I am ready to get this project to the final phase.

Let's get going." Morton replied. The two men walked to the street in front of the hotel where Mort had been staying. As the approached the curb a Voltrun 110 stopped and the two men got in. Morton was carrying the case with the documents. He would not be able to relax until the last one was installed in its Yom. Rush was an incessant talker and Morton was able to focus on his responsibilities not being burden by having to invent small talk.

"We are going to be visiting the units in the order in which they will be activated. This will mean that we are not following what would appear to be a methodical pattern. It will also help us to determine if we are being observed." Rush said as they approached the first warehouse. The building sat alone in the middle of a large parking lot. There were no vehicles at the location at that hour and they used a key card to open the gate and enter. The Voltrun maneuvered to a parking place just outside of the storage unit's entrance. The two men exited the vehicle into the heat of the morning.

"Are you going to be placing the units in series or concurrently?" Morton asked Rush.

"We have nine transports ready and waiting. All of the units will be picked up and installed at their locations at the same time." Rush answered.

"This will be a lot of fun. I like precision exercises and I enjoy watching the results of well-coordinated plans being executed to perfection." Rush said to punctuate his desire to do a good job on a difficult assignment.

When they entered the storage unit they immediately saw the Yom. It had one glowing red lamp that let them know that its security field was in place and active. "Please don't approach the unit until I have deactivated the security system." Morton told Rush.

"I understand that these units are equipped with a magnetic field that will burn a man to a crisp in seconds if he comes in contact with it." Rush said in response. Morton looked at him and nodded.

Morton entered the code and disarmed the unit for the final time. "When you pick these units up next week the security system will be active they will exit the building and will enter your transports under their own power. They have no offensive capability they are passively protected by the magnetic shielding, as long as you and your men understand to stay out of their way there will be no problems." Morton said as he removed the hatch and prepared to insert the magnetic imaged document into the actuator. Once the document was accepted by the Yom, Morton initiated the integration sequence. The unit indicated that it had accepted the imaged document and was poised to complete its next instruction when it was received. The test was a success.

"So that's it?" Rush asked.

"Yes, we have completed the test sequence and the unit is working according to design. All we have to do is send the arm control command and the unit will be tamper proof. The only command that it will obey is the next phase initiation command and that can only be sent by one system and only sent once. After that nothing can stop the unit from performing its tasks. After it completes the next phase there will be a request made by the unit to proceed. If that request is not responded to within thirty minutes of the request it will initiate the procedure without the acknowledgment being received. Like I said, nothing can stop this after the next command is given." Morton said soberly.

"What about destroying these things. Can that be done?" Rush asked.

"Nothing short of a nuclear blast with have any impact on the unit and the blast might not work either." Morton said.

"What about an EMP?" Rush asked.

"The unit is built upon magnetic resonance technology and using an EMP would simply strengthen the bonds of the defensive shield and have no impact on the internal workings of the systems." Morton said.

"Who designed such a thing?" Rush asked in awe.

"Several people, including me." Morton answered. Rush looked at Morton but did not say anything more. They returned to the Voltrun and proceeded to the next storage facility to perform the same operation.

Before it was noon they had completed testing and arming seven of the nine units. They were in transit to the eighth unit when Morton received a call from Norville telling him that doctors from Cincinnati had been detained by Internal Security. Norville warned Morton to very careful with the remaining units that were to be installed and to make certain that they were not followed. Morton had been very cautious and Rush was a professional and knew how to avoid detection. When they finished the eighth unit the anxiety level increased. Morton felt how close they were to completing his portion of the project which was more than five years in the design and implementation planning.

The ride to the ninth unit's location took a meandering path and the storage unit was in converted Twentieth Century barn that had one time been used to dry and season the tobacco crop. Its wooden slats could be pivoted outward though they no longer provided ventilation, merely an example of how the barn was used during that time period. Because of this feature and other aspects of the old barn it had become an attraction for tourist.

At lunch time on a pleasant early summer day there were a handful of people milling about, some equipped with photographic equipment which they used to document their travels. The Voltrun parked in front of the entrance to the storage facility but Morton hesitated in exiting the vehicle as he observed several people that were close to their location.

"What do you think about all of these people being here? I am not too concerned that the unit will be harmed but if someone were to determine it was here they could make it difficult for you to get it out of here." Morton asked while providing information as to his concern.

"Mort, if someone wants to try to stop me from doing my job they had better be well armed and looking for a good fight. I won't let a little resistance stop me from doing what needs to be done. That's why you folks hired me." Rush said defiantly.

"Okay Rush, let's get this one set up and so we can go home and enjoy a couple of days off." Morton said with a smile. The two men then exited the car only to be confronted by a young boy that was running from one group to another group of the people that were there. He apparently was trying to impress everyone with how fast he could run and how much he knew about barns.

"Mister, do you know that this barn was built in 1958 and was used for curing tobacco until 2033 when it was converted into commercial storage? I wonder what type of things they store in a place like this. Do you know mister? What they store in a place like this." the young boy asked Morton.

"No son I don't. I think it would be a good idea to ask your mother a question like that." Morton replied. The young boy looked at him and then turned and ran to the next group of people and repeated the same speech loudly. Morton and Rush walked deliberately to the entrance of the storage facility and went inside closing the door tightly behind them. This unit like the others appeared to be in good working order but when it came time to introduce the image the unit it did not perform correctly.

Morton looked at the Rush and said, "Apparently there is going to be a small delay in getting this unit operational." He then walked over the base of the unit and reached down to the seam where the two panels met the base and pushed on a small circle that was barely visible. The button popped out and Morton turned it counterclockwise. An arm extended from the top of the unit with a small box attached to it. The box was locked with a combination that Morton entered. When he had entered it the box slowly opened and inside was a keyboard and several odd looking tools.

"I am going to try to reset the unit. If this works then we can proceed if not I will be forced to take some of the components apart to determine the nature of the failure." Morton told Rush.

"What can I do to help?" Rush asked.

"This is really a one person job at this point. Please keep watch on the people outside. We don't want to attract too much attention." Morton said.

The re-start did not clear the problem. It appeared that one of the circuits was not closing properly and if there was a need to replace a part, it could be a problem that they could not overcome. All of the parts for these units were custom made specifically for the units. Morton ran the diagnostic program in hopes that the unit would indicate what part was malfunctioning.

"Rush, I need you to help me with the diagnostic read out. When the display on your side of the unit flashes tell me if there are lamps that illuminate on both sides of the panel." Morton said to Rush.

"Okay. I am ready when you are." Rush replied. Morton initiated the diagnostic procedure and the lamps on the right side of the unit came on but the left bank flickered and then went dark. "The lights on the right side are on but the left side flickered a couple of times and then went out." Rush reported. Morton smiled, he knew the problem and he could solve it. It was just going to take an hour maybe a little more to do so and he told Rush his conclusion.

The air flow within the storage facility was not very good and the temperature had risen from a tolerable eighty degrees when they first arrived to a little more than ninety two degrees. The perspiration was flowing like a steady stream and the salt residue stung Morton's eyes as he put his head down to attach the cover before initiating the test sequence once again. He elected not to run the diagnostic protocol before the test since if this didn't work he was going to have to take the whole unit apart and inspect all of the components.

"Step back Rush, I am going to try to do this again." Morton said while he straightened up and stepped away from the unit. He initiate the image acceptance procedure and waited as the unit sprung to life and within a minute he knew that things were working as they should.

Rush sat quietly during the ride to Harrisburg. He was thinking about the next step and about how his team needed to perform. He broke the silence after he had reached his conclusions and developed the final pieces of the plan that would be executed in a little more than one hundred hours.

"I think I have the deployment plan worked out, but do have one question. How will the units know when we've arrived?" Rush asked.

"They will extricate themselves from the storage units at exactly zero four thirty and each of your transports will have a transponder that will act as a homing beacon to the unit. You are to place the transponder in the center of the cargo hold. The unit will secure itself." Morton said.

"That sounds easy enough. I suspect the storage facilities won't be in too good of shape after the units have 'extricated' themselves but that's not my concern. I have to deliver them precisely and on time." Rush replied.

"The locations are marked by pulsing signal emitters and these will activate at zero four thirty seven and will broadcast for only four minutes. That gives you eleven minutes to load the units and arrive at the location. Each storage facilities is less than two miles from its corresponding target location. Your travel time should be less than two minutes and the load time will be less than five. That gives you some time to stop for a cup of coffee." Morton said with a smile.

"Yes, and a doughnut." Rush said with a laugh. "This is going to be fun." he added.

****

It was almost midnight before Kate was able to start to clear her desk and begin the commute to her home and family. The children hadn't seen their mother in three days. She had been in the house when they were asleep, arriving after they went to bed and departing before they awoke for the day. Fortunately Michael had been there for them and they were getting reacquainted with their father, a good thing she thought. The call came just as she was about to walk out of her office. "Kate Foster here." she answered.

"Mrs. Foster we have reacquired Morton Hancock, he has just arrived at his home." the female operative said.

"Very good. Did he still have the case with him?" Kate asked.

"We saw him carry something into his house. We are not exactly certain what it was." the operative replied.

"We must be prepared to follow him and disrupt what he is involved in as soon as possible. Let me know when he moves again." Kate said disconnecting the call.

****

Norville heard the chimes of the grandfather clock in the living room ring out sounding the quarter hour. The question of what quarter hour sprung to mind. He did not wish to sleep, he did not enjoy sleeping now that did not have dreams. He had none for the past two weeks and while he knew that the end of this journey was almost at hand, he wondered if he would ever be able to dream again. If it were twelve fifteen it would be June thirtieth and the group of people that were going to be in the Control Center would be saying their good byes to their family and friends later today. They would spend the last night with eleven others sealed in a room, protected from the temporal wake that would change life as they had known it.

He turned on his back and opened his eyes trying to bring into focus the ceiling of his bedroom. It was too dark to make out any details so he lay there continuing to think about all that was about to happen. He thought of those people that had given so much so that this could come into being. Some of those people were not going to exist after the change had been made.

There were sixty two people that had worked continuously on the project over the past five years and of those people twenty one would not be part of the new time thread. Norville had told each one of them personally and had offered them the protection of the Control Center module, it could easily handle that many people for the time that they would be confined to it. Only seven of the people that were not critical to the operation and had to be there elected to join them. Norville wondered if he had made the right decision, perhaps he did not belong in the new time thread.

His thoughts turned to Austin, his young friend who was planning on standing watch while they sat safely inside. He would be at risk of going back to prison or worse. Still it seemed as though Austin was destined to be seated outside of the room and he had seemed at peace lately, even though he had been put through a truly amazing ordeal, being falsely arrested and beaten. The man stood as a beacon showing the path to contentment.

Tomorrow morning, this morning, he would get up and travel to the business that Norville Forest had created for the sole purpose of providing the illusion of something other than a Control Center for the manipulation of the time thread, he thought. Adria would call it the modification life's processes, the shifting of the sequence of events in life causing us to move this vast machine at a different pace and for a different purpose. That woman could be so exasperating when it came to explanations, he mused.

Time was measured by us, it was nothing more than a recording of what was. Future time was taken on faith, that things would be as they had been, but if the earth's rotation slowed or the orbit was modified, our understanding of time would be altered as well. The only element of time that was truly meaningful was the one that you were experiencing at that moment, the point you were at on the cog of life. It was about what you were experiencing while you were inter-meshing with those around you.

Norville opened his eyes and could see that it was clearly morning. The light was streaming through the seam between the window shades and the sill, it painted a yellow stripe on the steel blue carpet. Norville couldn't believe that he had dropped off to sleep and once again had not a recollection of dreaming. He struggled out of bed, his feet hitting the floor with an awkward thump and the tingling sensation that was omnipresent caused him to wince with pain. The day was beginning and he had a great deal to accomplish. He wanted to call several friend and hear their voices once last time.

****

Kate had been sitting at her desk since six o'clock and now that it was getting close to eight there were more people present and her ability to concentrate on the planning was being challenged with the arrival of every voice.

"Mrs. Foster may I get you some coffee?" Smithson asked upon noticing that Kate was at her desk.

"No thank you. You can call the surveillance teams so that I can hear their report and their plan action for the day. Thank you." Kate said without looking up. She made the determination that she would detain Morton and that if Philip Lee did not show any further signs of movement, she believed that it would be a good idea to detain him as well.

Smithson came into her office and announced that the team that was shadowing Morton had called and they were on hold waiting to speak with her.

"Good, put the call through." she said abruptly. "What do you have to report?" she asked immediately.

"Mrs. Foster, the subject left his home approximately twenty minutes ago and we are following him. It appears that he is making his way to the train station and once there we will be able to ascertain his destination." the operative stated.

"Good. Keep a close watch on him and if it appears that he is attempting to avoid your surveillance you are instructed to detain him, using any reasonable force that may be required." Kate said firmly.

"Yes Mrs. Foster, that is understood." the operative replied and Kate disconnected the call.

"Katherine Foster you seem to be working too hard these days." Foon said to the Kate when she finally connected the call.

"Foon, it is good to hear the voice of a friend. Do you have anything interesting to share with me?" Kate said her voice betraying the smile she had on her face.

"I have one piece of information for you that might prove to be useful. I have heard that the Control Center for the group that you are pursuing is located in Baltimore Maryland. The source I have tells me that they will know the exact location by noon tomorrow." Foon said.

"That's a good start. Unfortunately this whole thing could be over before noon tomorrow. How have you been?" Kate asked.

"I have been surprisingly well. I have been having the most amazing dreams about my brother and I finally reconciling all our differences. It has given me such peace." Foon said candidly.

"I have been having some very unusual dreams as well. In them I find great joy. It's very hard to feel joy during the day with the stress of the job." Kate said and then laughed.

"Who would think that I would miss the days of undercover work, all that mystery and subterfuge." she continued.

"Katherine, when this is done, I would hope that we can find time to have lunch." Foon said.

"Yes, I would enjoy that very much. Have a good day and call me if you find anything more. Take care my friend." Kate said fondly.

"You too my friend." Foon replied. Neither party disconnected the call, they waited to see if the other had more to say, but the line disconnected due to inactivity after twenty seconds of no conversation.

****

Rush stood inside the abandoned manufacturing plant outside of York Pennsylvania. The last of the transports was overdue. All of the others had arrived on schedule and with no incidents. It is better that it happened at this time then tomorrow morning on the way to the drop, he thought. He heard the whirling sound of the engines and knew that the transport was close but he could not see it.

"What are you doing Harker?" Rush yelled in his PCU.

"Sir, the gyroscopic stabilizers are not functioning properly. It appears that we may have a serious problem developing here." Harker responded. The gun metal gray transport appeared suddenly above the line of houses to the south. It was clearly not functioning properly as it approached Rush's location flying sideways. This arrival was calling unwanted attention to the transport and to the abandoned plant as a number of residents appeared outside of their houses to see what the noise was. Most people had not seen the LTA series vehicles since it was determined that it made little sense for man to clutter the sky with vehicles. Harker brought the transport close the building and lowered it carefully to the ground. It settled awkwardly on its skids, which were extended at the last minute before the transport touched down.

Rush approached the vehicle and surveyed it looking at its exterior for any visible damage that may have cause it to malfunction. There was nothing obvious. He looked at the faded silhouette of the company logo of the vehicle's last owner which bled through the paint slightly, 'Robert's Moving and Storage', and thought this unit must have seen some extreme abuse during its time in service. They extended the wheels of the transport and pushed it into the building through one of the three large doors.

"I need to know quickly whether we can make this thing operational or if we will have to make other arrangements." Rush told the lead mechanic.

"We will know within a couple of minutes, once I get it hooked up to the diagnostic system." the man replied.

"How are you today Mr. Forest?" Rush asked as he took the call while he awaited the results of the diagnostic scan. He had hoped that he would have had an understanding of what they were going to do regarding the ninth LTA before he talked to Norville but he was not a man that avoided his responsibilities.

"Rush my boy, this is a glorious day. I am hopeful that everything will go according to plan. Have the transports arrived at their location?" Norville asked.

"Yes they are all here. We are experiencing a problem with one of them and I am awaiting the results of the diagnostic test to determine whether it will be serviceable." Rush said.

"How will that affect the deployment?" Norville asked with a slight display of concern.

"I won't know until I see the results of the diagnostics, I was just confronted with the problem ten minutes ago." Rush replied.

"Very well, please call me when you know the results so that we can determine our options." Norville said.

"Absolutely sir, I will be in touch with you as soon as I know." Rush said.

****

It was approaching noon and Kate was disturbed that she had not heard from the surveillance teams regarding Morton or Philip. She had received calls from the president and vice chairman but nothing from her teams. Internal Security was scheduled to call regarding the three potential areas where there may be a deployment of whatever devices they were going to use to perform this task. She still knew so little about what they were up against and how it was going to be done.

There had been some positive developments regarding Adria Constantina and Avery Silcox for they both appeared on manifests for trains bound for Harrisburg Pennsylvania. It was unclear how they would get to Baltimore from the train station but there would be teams in place to follow them when they arrived. Kate decided that there should be an even greater WBOI presence in Gettysburg and directed Smithson to mobilize the remaining agents from the region and have them report to Gettysburg. She then requested that a team of five agents be assembled and accompany her to Baltimore in an attempt to locate the Control Center that was believed to be located there. One of the people that they were tracking was bound to show up at the Baltimore train station and they would be there to follow them. She told Smithson that she would be leading the effort from that location. She then told Smithson to pack a bag and come with her. They were going to spend the next thirty six hours in Baltimore.

****

The tenth transport arrived on the back of a Norwind equipment mover. The flat bed vehicle could haul up to one thousand tons and the Olds transport was dwarfed by its size. The gyroscopic unit in the transport that arrived was functional whereas the one that had arrived earlier was determined that it needed to be replaced. It was also decided that it would most expeditious if the entire transport was moved and not just the gyro. The technicians insisted that they could replace the unit within three hours, though the specifications stated it was an eight hour job. Everyone moved quickly knowing that there was no margin for error.

****

Norville arrived at his office. The two double oak doors to the conference room mid-way down the hall were closed. As he walked passed them accompanied by Nelson Truax he turned to him and stated, "Tomorrow is the day that we have been working toward for these many years my friend. Nelson you have been a loyal aide and confidant, are you certain that I cannot persuade you into joining us in the Control Center?" Norville asked.

"Sir, it has been an honor to work for you these past seven years but I believe that if I am not part of the future then I know I have been part of a glorious past." Truax stated. Norville looked at the man and smiled.

"You know Mr. Barnaby will be part of the new time thread?" Norville added.

"Yes, he will have a new life. Even if I were to elect to join you everything that I know, except for you, will be different. None of my friends and family will be with me. The decision was an easy one to make." Truax replied.

"Please let me know when the others arrive. I am going to call some of my friends to hear their voices one last time." Norville said parting company with Truax.

During the next several hours Truax was joined by Barnaby and by seven of the group that would be entering the Control Center. He opened the doors to the large conference room to reveal a metallic room within the room. It was twenty five feet by fifteen feet and seven feet in height. Off to one side, next to an antique globe of the world, there was the power generation equipment. Once allowed inside of the Control Center the group began to go through the checklist in preparation for the early morning events. There would be no sleep this night and the anxiety was beginning to show on those that worked to complete their tasks.

****

Morton knew that he was being followed. He had placed a call to Norville and Norville in turn had dispatched Truax to assist him. Both Truax and Barnaby found him sitting in the main concourse of the Harrisburg train station. They also detected three people that were watching him. Barnaby suggested that one of them walk up to him and give him a news tube. This would appear to be a hand off of some information and should inspire those performing the surveillance to follow both parties. This would enable an observer to determine whether they had identified all of those that were involved in Morton's surveillance. Truax agreed and since Barnaby had superior skills in this type of operation, he would be the one to stay and observe the scene as it unfolded.

Truax approached Morton, catching his eye when he was within ten feet. Morton remained seated and Truax sat down next to him. Truax instructed him to pick up the tube and then proceed to the rest room. Truax explained that he would move in the opposite direction. Morton understood that Truax was a professional and he attempted to do what he was instructed to do. When the two men stood up and began to walk the surveillance team became animated and a fourth individual, an older woman seated across from where Morton had been seated revealed her role as coordinator. Barnaby waited and watched. Soon the surveillance team had moved off two following Morton and a third following Truax, the older woman remained stationary but was clearly giving instruction. Barnaby decided to move.

He simply walked up to the woman and told her, "If you value you your life you will call your team back to this location." The woman looked at him with a puzzled expression. "I will not say it again. Order them back now!" he said firmly as he sat next to the woman and poked her ribs with a pen he had concealed in his pocket.

The woman squirmed in her seat and then ordered the team back to her location. It took but a few minutes for the three agents to appear in the concourse. At that moment Barnaby got up and moved away from her in a deliberate fashion. Both Morton and Truax were able to make their way to the car that was waiting in the alley behind the station. Truax did not hesitate, he knew that Barnaby would be followed and most likely apprehended. It was the cost for getting Morton away safely which he did.

****

Both Adria and Avery left the train in Philadelphia and after an elaborate routine of doubling back and phantom exchanges boarded a car that was waiting for them in the historic district just down the street from the Liberty Bell. They would make one stop in south Philadelphia to pick up Willie Lawrence who insisted in stopping to get a cheesesteak sandwich since he wasn't sure that they would still be made after today.

The vehicle with the trio pulled into the parking lot of Norville's company shortly before six. They were the last group to arrive and they were welcomed warmly by everyone present. Norville upon seeing them was extremely emotional. He seemed to want to spend every moment treasuring each individual contact. The phone calls that he had made throughout the day had only made him realize how much he was going to miss. It was as at the peak of the welcoming of them that the call came in from Austin. "Hello my boy, it's great to hear your voice. I was hoping that you would call me. Have you come to your senses and decided to stay where you are?" Norville asked.

"Justin, I mean Norville. I am in transit to Baltimore now and I just need your address so that I can find the location." Austin replied.

"Son, you really don't have to do this." Norville said trying to encourage him to change his mind.

"Please there is no changing my mind." Austin replied. "I know what must be done and I know what will happen. My dream last night revealed it to me." Austin said. With that statement Norville gave him the address. He was glad to be able to see him one last time.

The next several hours the group enjoyed a diner and each other's company. Everyone seemed in great spirits especially after Norville received the call from Rush stating that after six hours and twenty minutes of very hard work they had replaced the gyro in the number nine transport, tested it and everything was okay.

****

591

When Kate arrived in Baltimore she was not in a great state of mind. Her surveillance team had been intimidated by a retired Philadelphia policeman that had ties to Justin Welsh through a man named Nelson Truax. Video images of the third man on the scene confirmed Truax's presence as well and that they had used him as a decoy to identify all the members of their surveillance team. The end result was that they lost Morton and that meant that Philip was the only individual on whom they continued to have surveillance. Avery and Adria had not arrived in Harrisburg and it seems that they had eluded surveillance as well.

The day that had started with such promise for success and now looked as though the likelihood of finding the location of the Control Center was becoming extremely remote. It was at that moment that she thought of Austin and her dreams that they were together, each night's dreams had become more vivid than the last. Perhaps the new time thread would offer her a chance for real happiness, but that wasn't her job and that time thread wouldn't include her boys.

****

Philip had decided that he would spend the night with his parents. He made the journey from his home in Pittsburgh to Harrisburg hoping to see Austin as well. He had concern about his well-being and had not been able to reach him for the past two days. When he walked into his parents' home, his childhood home, he sensed the tension in the atmosphere. His mother was busy moving about the house in a way that she did when Austin had first been arrested. It was if the constant movement would somehow keep her from dwelling on the unpleasant aspects of her life. She barely acknowledged his presence as she moved about. Gregory looked at him with such pain in his eyes that he instantly knew that there was something significantly wrong.

"Where is Austin?" he asked his father.

"I don't know for certain but I think that we may have seen him for the last time." he father said as he let the tears that he had been fighting back begin to flow.

"What are you talking about? What is he doing?" Philip asked sternly in hopes of getting through the wave of emotion that clouded his father's thoughts. Gregory realized that Philip might be able to talk his brother out of what he was doing.

"He went to be with Norville." he said finally.

"Why would he do that?" Philip asked quietly realizing the magnitude of the problem. He now knew who would be making the sacrifice for them, in some way he had always known.

"I think I know where he is. I will go get him and stop him from wasting his life on something that..." Philip said and then stopped in mid-sentence.

"You were going to say, has no meaning. Weren't you?" he asked his son.

"Yes, but it does have meaning. Probably more meaning than I could ever imagined before I became aware of this project. How could something so difficult have such a positive force?" Philip asked not expecting an answer.

During the next several hours Philip sat quietly with his mother and father. MacKenzie had finally exhausted herself and had collapsed on the sofa next to Gregory. The two of them numb from the ordeal.

"I have to call Jessica. Please excuse me." Philip said standing up and walking into the kitchen out of earshot of his parents.

"Hello Jessica. I needed to hear your voice. I apologize for the hour but there is a lot happening as you know and I wanted to talk to you about a situation." Philip said.

"What time is it?" Jessica asked sleepily.

"It's a little after midnight. It sounds like I woke you up. Please go back to sleep. I will call you tomorrow." he said.

"No, I want to talk to you I was hoping to hear from you and you need to know that you can call me anytime." she said emphatically. "What is wrong?" she then asked.

Philip went on to tell her about Austin and how his sacrifice corresponded with the dreams that he had been experiencing.

"I know. I was dreaming that you were calling me and wanted to ask me if you should go to Baltimore to stop him from making the sacrifice." she replied.

"I had a waking dream just minutes before I called you and in it we were having this very conversation and at the end you encouraged me to go, but not to stop him but to be there for him if he needed me." he said.

"Yes, that is exactly what I dreamt that I had said." she responded.

****

It was twenty minutes passed one o'clock and Austin was sitting in the Baltimore train station in the main concourse. It was surprisingly filled with people moving quickly from one train in hopes of catching another. It was clear to him that he had struck out on a journey were he did not actually know the final destination and how he was going to get there if he were fortunate enough to discover it. He did not know how he was going to complete the final leg of his quest.

Austin's presence did not alert the surveillance group since they did not have his profile loaded into the recognition program that was monitoring the people moving in and out of the train station. Kate was only a few dozen yards away from where he was sitting and had she seen him there she might have detained him. Austin knew that she was there and yet made no effort to hide his presence he knew that she would not detect him being there.

"Mr. Lee?" Truax asked even though he knew Austin from the image that was displayed on his PCU he felt that he should make every effort to make his arrival as stress free for him.

"Yes." Austin answered tentatively.

"Please come with me. I have been sent by Mr. Forrest to take you to him." Truax replied. Austin stood up and dutifully follow Truax out of the station and to the two passenger PTU that was waiting at the curb.

The trip took only a few minutes and they were soon at the door and were walking inside. For Austin, everything looked very familiar. He felt as if he had walked through those doors a hundred times. The feel of temperature in the lobby as they entered the antiseptic smell that greeted them, he had experienced them as well. He knew that the first person that they would encounter would be Willie Lawrence and that he would make a joke about the late hour of his visit. Then it would be Norville who would greet him and it would be a very emotional moment for both of them. He felt the strangeness of the precognition but there was total peace in knowing that what he was about to do was to fulfill his purpose.

It was as he had envisioned and the emotion that had been welling up within him burst forth as both he and Norville both quietly shed tears. When the two men had composed themselves Norville said, "My boy, you are a very brave man to be doing this. I am not even certain I understand but I do know that your dreams seem to be foretelling the events that are about to unfold."

Norville then escorted him into the Control Center where the team was beginning to start the initiation sequence. He introduced him to each person slowly and methodically. He was making certain that each of the people in the room knew Austin and that when the time came for them to shut the doors that they would realize what Austin was about to do, to protect them and ensure the missions success.

The time passed slowly as the team readied themselves for the final moments. Norville had received a call from Rush, who enthusiastically told him that his men, though there were three women pilots, were ready and would execute the plan flawlessly. Norville had smiled when he heard those words and then was asked by Willie what he found to be so humorous. "Willie, the man we selected to deliver those units to the each of the sites couldn't be more perfectly suited for the job if we had created him for it ourselves." he said with a laugh.

Austin stood back after he had been introduced and watched the people working. They were sitting in front of pyramid displays that rotated at varying speeds according to their needs. Willie saw him standing alone and approached him smiling.

"Austin, it has been a very long time since I have seen you. I think that I was still in school. Your hair is certainly a fashion statement." he said motioning and indicating its length.

"Willie, you have been working on this project for the last several months. Why are you here?" Austin asked pointedly. Willie looked at him smiling and then he slowly came to the realization that Austin wanted a response that was genuine and not the usual 'Willieism'.

"I joined the project for the same reason Roger did, for the challenge. Do you have any idea the level of the detail and creativity that went into visualizing the solution and then bringing to life?" Willie asked rhetorically. "It is the opportunity to solve the unsolvable!"

"I didn't ask you why you decided to participate, I asked you why you were here, that is to say present at this spot and at this time?" Austin asked.

Willie looked at him and saw that there was something odd about his demeanor. Austin seemed to have a quiet intensity about him. He was a man on a mission of some sort, a dangerous mission perhaps, but he was committed to fulfilling it. "I am not sure why you are asking this question." Willie responded hoping that Austin would allow him to avoid answering.

"You were given the opportunity to participate with Roger on what could be the most import mission that mankind has undertaken to date and yet you elected to stay here. You don't believe that the project will succeed and yet you are giving every effort to ensure that it does. Why are you here?" Austin asked again.

"It is where I am supposed to be." he said slowly and deliberately.

"Yes, exactly and I am here for the same reason. I have seen it. I know what you are going to say to me next and I also know that you are having a difficult time accepting the fact that this is all meant to occur in exactly the way that it is going to occur." Austin said passionately.

Norville observed Willie and Austin's interaction and he felt it necessary to intervene. Willie had more work to do and the time was rapidly nearing when everyone would simply sit back and watch the drama play out before them.

"Austin, I need to speak with you alone. Please excuse us Willie." he said as he joined the two men. Willie, felt the weight lift from him as he walked away to join the others as they prepared for the event that would take place within the next several hours. Norville motioned for Austin to join him and the two men left the Control Center through those two very familiar oak doors and went down the corridor to Norville's office.

Norville turned and looked at Austin. He remembered him as he was when they first met. There was no long hair, there was an intense fire in his eyes. He was keen on making a name for himself and establishing himself as a force to be respected within the financial community. When Norville convinced him to join his firm and later to become part of the conspiracy there was still that reckless passion that flared up, much like what Norville saw in Willie Lawrence and to a lesser extent Roger Lee.

Austin was not the same man. Perhaps it was prison that had changed him but Norville looked at him intently and saw a man that was at peace with himself and that was when he knew that Austin was functioning at another plain, a much higher one than Norville or those that were in the Control Center had experienced. He could not know for certain what he was witnessing but rarely had he seen this kind of contentment exhibited by anyone under the stress that he was under. Only one instance came to mind and that was a recording of the last interview given by Christopher Leesop. He was completely calm and was prepared to meet his end with a sense of destiny.

"Son, I am so very glad you came though I am saddened by the potential harm that will be done to you." Norville said.

"Justin, I mean Norville... you know I can't quite get used to the name change. Why did you do it?" Austin replied stopping in mid-sentence to ask a question that had troubled him.

"I didn't, Norville Forest is my real name. Though I don't have a daughter, that girl that was in your brother's class was hired to motivate him to take the assignment. Justin Welsh was the created persona, he never really existed though I tried to make him reality, to assist me in putting on the corporate mantel that I thought my father always wanted for me. It turned out that all he really wanted for me was peace and joy. I found that when I met you. You have been the catalyst for change in my life son. It has been a blessing to have shared life with you." Norville said stopping to collect himself, his voice noticeably quaking with the deep feelings that surged from the dark well where they had been carefully secured.

Austin looked at the old man that he saw in front of him. "Norville you said that you feared what would become of me. I know what will become of me and I know what must be done. I gladly do it for you all." Austin said with a smile.

"I know you do my son. It is still very painful to know that you have to do it." Norville responded. At this point Norville decided to share his true feelings, the thoughts that had been troubling him so much over the past week of dreamless nights.

"The thing that will be the most difficult to accept losing are the memories. The associated images linked permanently to a person that is precious to you. You know what I mean, like when you hear a piece of music and associate it with a friend and an experience. The memories rush upon you and you let them wash you clean, cleansing you from all of that bothersome stuff, of that baggage that we all collect as we go about living. As we are washed clean we can start anew. That, I am afraid will be gone, I am not sure what, if anything I will be able to remember. Will it be like not being able to dream again? I wonder?" Norville said as his voice trailed off to a soft whisper.

Austin understood intellectually and he grasped the concepts but could not feel Norville's profound sense of loss. Just like Norville would never fully know the contentment he felt as he awaited his fate. Every time he closed his eyes he saw the scene play out in greater detail. It was if that each vision was a rehearsal and that everyone was learning their parts while the others saw themselves in the alternate time thread.

It was almost two thirty and the schedule dictated that they were to seal the Control Center and activate its systems. Norville was about to tell Austin that they should rejoin the others when Austin said, "I know that you are going to tell me it is time to rejoin the others. I have seen this moment clearly, multiple times over the past week. I also know that you will once again tell me that I don't have to do this and that I can leave and there will be no harm done, but that is where you are wrong. There will be great harm done if I do not sit in that hallway and stand watch in front of those two oak doors."

Norville looked at him and nodded his head but still said the words, he had to say them even though he had been told that he what he was going to say. After saying it he asked Austin as they walked the corridor to the Control Center, "Did you envision this as well?"

"I did and the funny thing is that in these dreams or visions as you call them, I know your reactions to me telling you that this has all been foretold." As they entered the Control Center all heads briefly turned to see who had just arrived, but they quickly returned to their work, everyone working feverishly at their respective tasks.

****

Rush was alone in what he called his briefing room. The pilots would be joining him within the next half hour and they would be given their final instruction at that time. Each unit was to be deployed according the carefully calculated schedule of events. They all had to touch down at exactly the same time. They would at that point be live and if for some reason one were to be delayed even by a few moments it was possible that the LTA could be intercepted and destroyed. He leaned back in his chair putting his hands clasped behind his head.

After a few moments he began to daydream. He saw himself walking on a path. There were two children running ahead. The boy turned and called to him saying, "Come on Dad, don't be so slow." and he responded by picking up his pace. He knew that it was his son Eric and that the girl was his daughter Bernadette. Everything seemed so peaceful as he felt the warm breeze tug at this shirt and caress his face. They were on their way to the lake to fish and their mother, his wife had dutifully stayed behind to make certain that their home was comfortable and inviting. The dream state was so real and it was so enticing that he did not want to leave it, yet reality pulled at him as the sound of an incoming call notification caused him to wake from it.

"Rush here." he said sleepily.

"Rush its Norville are your people ready to go?" Norville asked prematurely.

"Norville, the team will be assembling within the half hour and we will be ready to go according to the schedule." Rush replied enthusiastically.

The call was just Norville's way of letting Rush know that he expected him to keep him apprised of the operation as it proceeded.

"That is good to know son. Now you will keep us updated on the goings on out there. Won't you?" he then added to punctuate the meaning of his call.

"Yes sir. It is very important for me to make certain you know what we are doing and when we do it." Rush replied firmly.

"Very good. I won't keep you any longer. I will speak to you soon. Good luck." Norville said.

"We don't need luck sir. We will make you proud and happy that you selected us for this important mission." Rush replied.

"Good bye then." Norville said and disconnected the call.

****

Philip was on his way to Baltimore and to Norville's company. He knew exactly where it was. The trains would not get him where he need to be so he had made arrangements to have a PTU waiting for him. He did not realize that the rental of the unit had been to signal that he was in motion to those that he were following him. He had somehow accidentally eluded the agents that had been assigned surveillance and had been waiting outside of his parent's home. Philip did not suspect that he was being followed.

When he arrived at the kiosk to pick up his transportation there was a team of agents ready to follow him. One of the members of the team was Kate. She was coordinating the surveillance since she lacked confidence in the team whose performance thus far had been substandard. She had never met Philip but Austin had spoken of him several times and when she saw him come into view she immediately saw the resemblance, he looked very much like his older brother. If she had not been given a description of him, she would been able to determine who he was because of her familiarity with Austin. She watched him walk with long strides to the kiosk and then fumble with the payment. She instructed her team to be patient, and that they knew where he was going and that the PTU had been programed to emit a signal allowing them to easily track it. There was no reason to be careless and let him detect the surveillance.

Philip was soon underway and was being followed discretely by two teams. The seven minutes that it took to arrive at Norville's company passed very quickly Philip. The PTU came to a stop in front of the doors and transmitted an arrival notification to the building whose doors opened to greet him. He entered the darkened reception area and looked about to see if he could determine where to go. There was no indication of where he should go and he weighed his options and decided the best course of action was to simply explore until he found where they were. It was a three story building with a central staircase that was a very large and graceful spiral. Philip decided that he would try the third floor and work his way down from there.

As he climbed the stairs he wondered what he was going to find. All of his dreams had been involved with his life with Jessica and their child. He had never seen any of this the way Austin described it. Austin had seen his alternate life and he had dismissed it. What did Austin know that he didn't? Why did Austin think he needed to be here and why did he not feel that he should try to talk Austin into not following through with whatever he felt he needed to do, Philip thought.

When he reached the third floor he looked down the corridor to the right and there was one light at the far end which appeared to indicate an exit. He turned and looked the opposite way and saw a light at the end of the dark corridor as well. It appeared to him that the floor was unoccupied but as he turned to descend the stairs he heard the sound of footfalls coming from the corridor to his left. He slowly turned and he saw the silhouette of two men outlined against the dim lighting at the end of the corridor. He knew that one of the men was Austin, seeing his tall lean frame and long hair. He assumed that the other was Norville.

"Philip is that you?" he heard Austin call out.

"Yes, but I suspect that you knew it was me before you even saw me standing here." Philip replied.

"What are you doing here my boy? You have a place in the new time thread, there is no reason for you to be here." Norville said.

"It was important for him to be here, without his presence I would not have been needed." Austin stated and then continued, "That does not mean that you were responsible for what is about to happen, it was preordained and must transpire."

At that moment Philip felt contentment, it flowed over him like a warm water from a refreshing shower. As his brother drew near and he could see his face, he noticed that Austin appeared to be at peace.

****

Outside of the office building Kate waited for her second team to arrive. One of her agents reported that the thermal scan indicated that there were at least three people located on the third floor. Another agent reported that there was a very high output magnetic signature that also emanated from the third floor. Kate knew that this was the location that they had been seeking. She ordered that additional agents be sent to the location and then placed a call to Wa.

"We have found the location, sir. At this time I am waiting for additional manpower because I am uncertain how many people are inside." Kate told Wa.

"Good work Mrs. Foster. How long before the others arrive?" he asked.

"About ten minutes." she replied.

"Move as quickly as you can. If they close the doors to the Control Center I am not certain you will be able to get through to stop them." he said encouraging her to move quickly.

"Very good sir, I will call you with an update soon." Kate said reassuringly.

"I want to know when you have Justin Welsh in custody." he said and then disconnected the call.

****

Rush walked to the warehouse section of the plant where the Olds LTAs were housed. He had wanted to own one of these when he was a child. He used to see them gliding along twenty feet above the snarled traffic that was below them. They had distinct whirling noise and they created a blast of hot air that push down from them which made them a bit of a nuisance to pedestrians and those that were in their path. The LTA's were things to behold, he thought. As he walked around them he marveled at their design. They were roughly eighteen feet long and wide with rounded wing like extensions that provided stability. The tapered rear section was the access point to the cargo area. The height of the vehicle was adjustable and could expand to accommodate a cargo that was more than twenty feet high, but without any cargo the unit was a little more than seven feet high.

The LTAs sat quietly arranged in two rows that faced the double doors where they had entered the warehouse and where they would exit. The lighting was subdued and would remain so in order to not attract a great deal of attention when the units exited the building. The noise would be enough of an attention grabber, he thought. As he walked past the first unit and he reached out and touched it. He felt its brushed aluminum skin and as he walked he allowed his hand to drag across the seamless metal. He reach the cabin door and when his hand contacted the actuator panel the door sprung open with a jerk. He glanced inside looking at the cockpit which more resembled an aircraft then a transportation vehicle. This was not an easy thing to fly, he mused. He then thought that the people that were about to make this trip were going to earn their pay today.

Helen walked into the warehouse and saw Rush standing next to the LTA that she would be piloting. She took this assignment because of Rush, as did the other eight members of the team. She had been a pilot for more than fifteen years and had flown the LTA before. It was a temperamental machine but it was very durable and she knew that she could have it perform at the top of its capabilities.

"What are you doing to her? You wouldn't be tampering with my seat position would you?" she asked jokingly.

Rush was slightly startled by the sound of her voice but responded, "I thought that I would make certain that the whoopee cushion I installed was properly placed."

"What is a whoopee cushion?" she asked shaking her head.

"It is a rubber bladder that is filled with air and during the mid-Twentieth Century people would place them under a seat cushion so that when someone sat on them it would make the sound of very loud flatulence." Rush responded very matter of fact tone. Helen looked at him quizzically and then the two of them laughed.

"Leave it to you to know some odd trivia relating to sophomoric behavior." she said smiling.

The rest of the team filed into the briefing room and waited for Rush to arrive. Rush poked his head into the room and saw that the eight remaining members were all present.

"Alright, it appears that we will have a mission after all." he said clapping his hands together one time. That was the last bit of levity that he would permit himself. He knew the precision that was required for this mission and he had to impress upon the team that they must adhere to the script precisely. He handed each one their specific assignment that was recorded on a wafer that would be installed in the LTA. The unit would then broadcast the details to the pilot's PCU and they would see the visual information in holographic form.

"Every one of you will be responsible for being on precisely on schedule. You are not to be late nor are you to be early. The margin for error is one minute on either side of the objectives. You will do this by flying the right course and by arriving and picking your cargo and then depositing it at the proper coordinates at the proper time. This units will begin to emit a magnetic pulse before they go completely active. If they are still in your cargo bay at that time the LTA will be destroyed. It will not be pretty. Every one of you has to come home safely, I promised your families." Rush said solemnly. The time had come to stop talking and to execute the plan. They were scheduled to commence the mission in less than ten minutes.

"That's it. Go out there and make me proud." he said and upon hearing that the pilots stood and purposefully left the room and each one hurried to their respective LTA. Helen would be the first to depart and Rush considered her to be his best pilot and she had the longest and most difficult mission. She was to place her Yom along a stream in York. She would have to negotiate a narrow flight path that would have her flying between rows of multi-story buildings.

The sound of nine units powering up within the confines of the warehouse was deafening. Rush walked to each unit and gave a thumbs up to every one of the members of the team. The time had come for Helen to depart. Rush signaled to the members of the ground crew to open the doors and as soon as they began to move Helen began to move her unit forward as though it were an anxious horse poised to leave the starting gate in an all too important race. The doors continued to open as the LTA approached. The unit passed through with only a few feet of clearance, Helen was airborne in a very few seconds and was making her way to her rendezvous with the Yom in seventeen minutes. Her airspeed was going to be rough three hundred knots and the unit detected the cross wind and adjusted the power level and heading to compensate for it.

Over the next seven minutes each LTA departed exactly as determined by the schedule and each pilot began to follow the flight instructions that had been provide as part of the mission parameters. When the last LTA left the warehouse Rush quickly assembled the ground crew and told them to commence the clean-up. They immediately began to sanitize the site so that there would be no evidence of their presence. He told them that they had one hour to accomplish this task and then they were to leave. He thanked them for their efforts and told them that they would be contacted in the future.

Rush went to the briefing room and sat down at a computer to watch the units as they progressed through the mission. The units all displayed in green indicating that they were performing according to the scenario. When the unit accomplished their first objective, the retrieval of the Yom, the unit number will display on the right side of the computer screen. The units were to arrive at the location to pick up the Yom units within the one minute time window. They all had almost the exact amount of flight time to their final destination, two minutes. After they deployed the Yom each LTA was to be piloted to a safe location more than an hour's flight time from where they were to make the drop.

****

Willie came to the doorway and Interrupted the conversation between Philip and Austin. "Norville they have begun the operation and we are tracking them now. It is time to close up the Control Center." he said.

Norville looked at the two men and said, "I was present when your Uncle Robert addressed the crowd at the food riot in 2090. He was remarkable and so charismatic. He spoke of how our need to extend ourselves and reach out to help each other at whatever the cost was the second most important thing of all. He told us that we would have the rare opportunity or gift to know someone that could put all things right. Unfortunately the government executed that man two years after your uncle was killed.

"Austin are you certain you want to do this? They could become very aggressive and use force, even deadly force."

"If I am killed in this time thread does that mean I will be dead in the other one as well?" Austin asked rhetorically. Austin did not expect an answer.

"Don't worry the answer will not make a difference in my decision. This is the right thing to do. We can't go on treating each other as if the only thing that matters is 'us'. We are here for only one purpose, failing to recognize it leads to loneliness and despair." Austin said these things and then gently pushed Norville in the chest so that he could close the door.

"Good bye son, I shall see you both on the other side." he said with a reassuring smile.

The door sealed and the low hum of the magnetic generators increased in volume. Austin stepped back several feet and watch the color of the control center exterior walls turn from bronze to a very pale yellow. The hairs on his arms stood straight up and leaned in the direction of the cabin. His PCU glasses presented a view of static snow and the ear piece whined and squealed. It was obvious that they would not function. At that point Austin looked at Philip who fainted because the implant in his temple had emitted a burst of energy which had caused those synapses to overload and as such he lost consciousness. Austin began to drag his brother out of the room and away from the magnetic field that was continuing to build in intensity.

When he finally reached the double doors he propped his brother against the corridor wall. He then turned his attention to closing the large double doors. He was amazed how easily they moved even though they were at least three inches of solid oak with a one inch steel plate that was hung on the interior of the doors. As he closed the doors he felt them vibrate in sympathy with the magnetic pulse that were coming from the Control Center cabin. They had opened outward into the hall and as they closed completely they made a whoosh sound. Austin tried to open the door and could not, in fact he felt a very sharp pain when his hand came in contact with the door handle. It was obvious to him that soon anyone that would come in contact with the door handle could suffer a serious injury.

He heard footfalls and turned to see Truax walking down the corridor toward him.

"Mr. Lee, is he alright?" he asked pointing at Philip.

"Yes, I believe so but if you could help me move him to an office that has a sofa where he would be more comfortable that would be helpful." Austin responded.

"We can take him to Norville's office. There is a very large and quite comfortable sofa there." Truax said as he grabbed Philips arm in an attempt to move him.

The two men managed to get Philip in a position where they could half carry and half drag him with legs and feet trailing behind them. After much effort they managed to get him into the office and onto the sofa.

"Would you be so kind as to stay with my brother until he regains consciousness? It will only be for a short time." Austin asked Truax even though he knew that he would stay. He would be alone for the next two hours and then he would be joined by Kate, his brother and several other people that he did not know. Shortly after that they would converge at the entry to the conference room where Norville was initiating the process. Then and only then will they all know what he knew.

After Truax agreed to stay with his brother and Austin turned and walked back to his place outside of the double oak doors. They continued to vibrate to the magnetic pulses that were being generated, and Austin ran his hand across them carefully avoiding the handles. He sat down in the chair that had been positioned outside of the room and waited.

He closed his eyes and let his mind drift where it wanted to go, he made no attempt to direct his thoughts, no meditation. It was just a quick look at the image from a movieola of conscious playgrounds, the scattered thoughts of past, present and unreality.

He found himself sitting at an octagonal shaped steel table with a deck of playing cards. He looked at his fingers, the nails were long and unevenly manicured. Jake joined him, sat down and began to laugh. At that moment Austin consciously interjected into the vision that was streaming before him; he wondered if Jake would be part of the new time thread or would he be one of the millions that would cease to be, their existence erased from eternity. What a loss, he thought.

****

Rush continued to watch the display as it showed the progress of each LTA. All of them were almost on time to the second, well within the minute margin for error. The crucial second phase was about to commence and he nervously watched as they all approached their objective, the picking up of the Yom units. He watched all them arrive at virtually the same moment. What precision, he thought. This was something to see and to brag about to his peers, though he knew he would never have the opportunity to do so, this mission was considered classified at best, illegal at worst.

The Yom units were to be retrieved within two minutes and once locked into place the LTA was to proceed to the final objective point where they would deploy the Yom. Rush watched anxiously and he imagined what his team must be feeling, the pressure that they were experiencing. They had been in place for almost two minutes and there was no indication that they were about to take off when suddenly he saw the images of eight of the nine jump into motion. The ninth unit just sat there, it was Helen's.

Helen was being challenged by a slow moving Yom. The units were designed to move at speeds up to ten miles per hour. This one was barely moving at two. The time for departure came and passed and the unit was at that point on the access ramp. It took another forty five seconds for it to position itself in the LTA and then another twenty seconds to lock itself in place. They were late and outside of the margin for error. Helen did not hesitate she accelerated quickly and exceeded maximum thrust for the LTA which shook violently as has it reached cruising speed. At that time Helen elected to exceed the speed limit set for the mission. She was attempting to make up for the lost time, and at the rate she was going she would be within the window of error when she reached the point of deployment.

She had an additional concern. The unit was moving too slowly to traverse the terrain and position itself properly before it activated the magnetic shielding and deploy itself for implant. It would be necessary to place the unit exactly where it needed to be. This coupled with the tight navigation would make the final two minutes of the mission extremely interesting, she thought.

Rush saw that Helen was outside of the mission's guidelines but he also saw that she was making up for the time differential. When the others had arrived at their point of deployment she was less than a minute behind them. He watched the image intently hoping that she would be able to have that thing out her ship before it activated. He imagined what would happen if the Yom powered up while inside the LTA, and the thought made him shudder.

Helen approached the landing zone weaving between buildings and trees. It was a difficult approach and she was exceeding the speed to accomplish it under normal conditions. The collision detection alarm had gone off so many times that she turned it off. Perspiration formed on her forehead and dripped into her eyes causing them to sting, but she could not take a hand off the controls to wipe it way.

She entered the touch down point into the console and watch the display show her relative position. The mission clock showed in the yellow as the LTA came to rest. The doors opened and the Yom unlocked itself from its position and began to slowly move down the ramp. The mission clock showed forty nine seconds and the Yom was not clear and in position. In the final seconds it would have to travel twelve feet to be at its proper location.

Rush watched the display. There was only one LTA that had not departed for their new location, and Helen's unit was dangerously close to being consumed by the Yom when it went active. He hoped that she would use sense and get out of the ship if there was any way that she could not take off in time. Then he saw the image move and a smile exploded on his face. His team had completed the mission.

"Rush, my boy you have done it. All of the Yom units are in place. We are just verifying the exact location on two of them to be certain they positioned themselves correctly. A great job." Norville said to him.

"Norville, it was touch and go there with one of my pilots. I am not certain what happened but I suspect the Yom must not have been working properly. Please let me know how it turned out. I am going to shut things down and get out of here." Rush replied his tone betraying the stress he had been under.

"Again you and your team have accomplished the mission and now it is up to us to make the rest of this morning as memorable as it can be. Good morning my friend and good luck." Norville said as he disconnected the call.

"Okay, people it is time for us to run the final diagnostic systems check before we initiate the Startling procedure. Willie will you please work with Avery to determine whether the telemetry data coming from the Yom units is according to program specifications. Adria you will sit with me here at the command console and you will keep me apprised of the integrity of the images that we are implanting into the time thread. You know that we have done simulations of this entire event and we have learned from our mistakes. If everything checks out properly we will initiate the Startling procedure in roughly thirty minutes." Norville said loudly and with great enthusiasm.

"There would be no reason why this will not work. All of the planning and the testing and the trials have lead them to this moment. We will succeed and there will be a new world order a new life for all of us. We will have no memory of the past and the terrible things that have been done will be forgotten. We shall start anew!" Norville said with enthusiasm that built to a high pitch. The mood within the Control Center was as electric as the magnetic energy was plentiful.

"Norville, I hope you are aware that when we step out of this Control Center we may cease to exist." Adria said to him quietly.

"Yes my dear I am very much aware of what may happen, but when you think about it there is no point in worrying. We are going through with this and the outcome will be as it is supposed to be." he replied with a smile.

Adria returned his smile and nodded her head approvingly, she felt that they would come out of the Control Center and would lose all memory of all past experiences and they would also have no understanding of the world in which they were entering. This was a fresh start, a completely clean slate.

****

Kate waited patiently for the backup that she had requested. Originally she had been told that it would arrive within ten minutes but ten minutes passed and she received a call stating that they would arrive within twenty additional minutes. Her people were very good at quoting times, though they did not think much of actually honoring their commitments, she thought. Her team continued to monitor the magnetic energy that was being produced within the building. It had reached a level that threatened to exceed the measuring capabilities of the equipment they were using.

The longer the delay the less likely that they would be able to stop the process and whatever would happen as a result of this initiative would occur. She was feeling the stress build within her and elected to close her eyes for a moment.

At that point she saw herself sitting in a room. There was a fire in the fireplace and she knew it to be her home. A man called to her from another room and she answered him, 'I am in her dear.' She then turned and looked at him as he walked through the doorway, her husband Austin smiled down at her. She then stood to embrace him.

"Mrs. Foster, President Wa is calling for you." her aide said. She opened her eyes and immediately felt a sense of loss.

"Yes, uh yes. Mr. Wa what can I do for you sir." she said stammering.

"Mrs. Foster, have you apprehended Justin Welsh?" he asked directly.

"No sir, our back up has been delayed. It will not arrive for another fifteen minutes." she replied.

"What is the problem with your people, why are they so unreliable. When this is over I want you to make changes or you will be replaced. Is this understood Mrs. Foster?" he said.

"I will..." Kate replied but then realized that she was speaking to no one.

****

The Yom that was located in York was positioned three centimeters from the optimum location. It had begun its insertion routine on schedule and had created the trenches in which the panels were inserted. Like all of the units its magnetic field was so strong that it could withstand any attack that could be made against it. The Yom glowed a pale blue as it began the synchronization protocol. It was sifting through the faint magnetic signatures of those people and things that once occupied the space and it would take almost thirty minutes for the Yom to find the exact set of signatures. At that time it would transmit a message to the control center and await the command to insert the fabricated image.

The unit systematically cycled through the sequences until it reached the desired point. It sent the signal to the Control Center that it at achieved the objective and went dormant awaiting the initiation command.

****

"Sir, that is the last message. All units have completed the synchronization and we are standing by and ready to proceed." Willie informed Norville.

"This is the moment we have all worked so very hard to reach. I ask you all to join me in a moment of silent reflection and when we have finished we will initiate the Startling sequence." Norville said then he closed his eyes and bowed his head. He could not find any thoughts to bring to mind, he did not remember anything, who he was, where he was and what he was about to do. There was nothing within him and it frightened him. He opened his eyes with a start and then gathered his thoughts. Did every one of them have the same experience he wondered? He looked at the others that were with him. All of them seemed to be bewildered, they must have experienced the same emptiness that they he had felt.

"Adria, when you closed your eyes what did you experience?" he asked quietly.

"Nothing, there was nothingness." she replied solemnly.

"What do you think that means?" Norville asked for the first time showing uncertainty in his voice.

"It means that we have no past in the time thread that we are about to initiate. Beyond that I do not know if we have a future, since those that have dreamed have seen visions of their past in the time thread, the only one that has seen the future is the man that is guarding our door. Are you having second thoughts?" Adria asked candidly.

"Of course I am having second thoughts, third ones too, but I cannot do anything other than what has been set in motion. The man guarding the door has seen his future and I think he knows that he will not survive. How can I do anything but follow his example?" Norville said with emotion distorting his words.

"Norville the time has come to initiate the Startling protocol. We are seeing evidence that Internal Security has mobilized and they are at two sites and converging on three more. We don't want to injure anyone and they most certainly will become injured if they attempt to interfere with the Yom units." Willie said interrupting the intimate moment that Adria and Norville were sharing.

"You are right my boy, let us get this underway." Norville replied.

"Initiate the first Yom's insertion." he ordered. The Yom acknowledged the command and began to weave the image of Lee's order to J. E. B. Stuart that caused him to move from his inopportune location to one where he could be used as part of the offensive on the first day of the battle. As the image became part of the magnetic signature there was a loud noise that echoed through the Control Center.

Norville requested that the cameras that were embedded on the outside of the Control Center to be turned on. It appeared that the walls of the building were no longer in place and that they were suspended in midair above an open field. The city of Baltimore was quite different in appearance, it was much smaller and there were signs of vehicles moving on roads in the distance. The sun was coming up and it revealed a much greener landscape, many more trees and open areas of grass with a smattering of flowers.

Everyone stopped and stared at the scene. It was as if there was no urgency, no pressing need to go back to the task at hand. Willie was the first to notice the effects that held them captive, it was mesmerizing.

"Norville, we have to keep the process going." he called out in a loud voice. This was enough to startle everyone and cause them to return to their tasks.

The second Yom was activated this was the unit that Helen had delivered and it created the intelligence that would be used by the third Yom which delivered that intelligence to General Lee along with a letter that was drafted from Stuart indicating the exact positions of the Union army on the first day.

As the Yom units came on line and initiated their piece of the program the scenery that was visible by the camera changed. The landscape was altered and the city changed about them. It was obvious that Baltimore was not a thriving contemporary metropolis but more like a second rate city in a less technologically advanced era. There was more evidence of people moving about out of doors, and dressed in such a way as to indicate that the weather might have been warm but the climate was not oppressive. The scene changes occurred before their eyes and the image would blur slightly and then some shapes would materialize and while others would disappear. It did not happen instantly it was if the viewers were looking through a telephoto lens at an image out of focus and someone was adjusting the lens in an attempt to bring about clarity.

Adria noticed as each piece was brought on-line that the effects on the personnel after it had been completed seemed be growing in intensity. There was a general loss of concentration and there were also periods where the people seemed to be in a trance of some kind.

"Norville I think that we should automate the final five Yom activations. I think if we are responsible for the activations we will most likely will be unable to finish them." she said to him quietly.

"I agree, it is very difficult to remain focused on what we are doing. I find myself staring at nothing and worse yet thinking of nothing." Norville replied.

"Willie please come here." he said gesturing for Willie to join them. "Son, I need to set the automatic sequencing program into motion. It appears that the effects of the time thread alteration is having a negative effect on our ability to concentrate. Can you make that happen, please?" Norville requested.

"Yes, I understand. I have been fighting to remain focused and there are times I don't know what we are doing here." Willie said. "I will do it immediately, before I forget what it is that you asked me to do." he continued.

****

Helen was piloting her LTA to a small warehouse located outside of Cincinnati Ohio. All of the units were to be taken to isolated areas for storage. As she traveled there she noticed that the terrain seemed to be changing and there were towns where there was to be open areas. She glanced at the environmental display and saw that the outside temperature was twenty degrees cooler than it normally would be at this time of the day, and then there were the unexplained loss of focus and she decided to place the unit on auto pilot but when she did the unit began to change course direction and it behaved as though it could not get a fix on the destination. Helen decided that the only thing she could do was to continue piloting the craft until she was unable to do so any more. At that time she would have to find a suitable landing zone.

****

When Rush arrived at his home he immediately began monitoring the team's progress. He found himself experiencing waking dreams that seemed so real that he was having difficulty remembering what was real and what was not. While he experienced these events the team ceased to exist. Those that were part of the new time thread were elsewhere living their lives under that scenario. Those, like Helen that were gone, it was as if they never existed. There was also a sort of nether region where the time threads overlapped. It was in those instances that Helen saw the topography change and the climate altered.   These episodes would become more frequent as the other time thread began to dominate reality and to replace the old existence.

****

"Out with the old and in with the new, well at least the different since it will feel to those participating that it has been that way always." Willie said. When he said it the automated sequencing of the next insertion occurred. This one was the order from Lee to Ewell encouraging him to press on to take the higher ground. The results of this action would put the both forces in exactly opposite positions than they were. This is the last insertion was based upon the historical accounts of the event. The final five insertions would be built upon the changes that had occurred as a result of the insertion of the first four magnetic images, the 'forgeries'.

Willie seemed to be able to concentrate better than most of the others. He watched as the view of the outside would change from moment to moment. At first they would see the new time thread's present and then moments later they would see nothing, the camera's view being obstructed by the walls that were still in place. After each phase was initiated there would be a period of time when the new time thread was extremely vivid and real, this was followed by a gradual fading back into the previous time thread what they had all know as reality.

Austin sat in his chair motionless waiting for the events to unfold. He was confident that the process would proceed exactly has he had seen it. Two days before he had visualized this moment when he would be thinking the very thoughts that raced through his brain. As the waves of the alternate time thread cascaded over him he found himself standing in the living room of what he knew to be his home. Kate was in the kitchen, he knew this even though he had not seen her or heard her stirring. He knew that she would be with him shortly and that she would walk up behind him and give him as forceful a hug as her small frame could manage. This was a hug that expressed her deep feelings for him, a love that he knew and reciprocated with all his being.

He also knew that after the next wave passed that he would see her. Not in the alternate time thread but in that corridor outside of the Control Center. She would be with several armed men and they would be there to gain access to the room, access that would prove to be fatal to her and her team should they attempt to enter. That was why he was there, not to stop them from terminating the program that was in place, but to prevent Kate from being killed. He knew that she would realize that it was done for her and that she would be sad, but she had to know that she, in another time thread, was happy with him, that they shared a life and had a child together and that memory would not fade.

As Kate waited for the other agents to arrive she found herself swept up and carried to a home that she knew was hers in a kitchen that was so familiar that she instinctively knew where everything was located. She was making diner for her husband Austin and their young son Christopher played happily at her feet as she move effortlessly across the room from task to task. Her husband was in the living room and she wanted to go to him to hug him and show him how happy she was. Her eyes then opened and she was crouched down outside an office building once again waiting for the agents to arrive. She found the smile lingering on her face and it disturbed her.

"Mrs. Foster the agents have arrived." Smithson informed her.

It was at that moment that the sixth Yom initiated the insertion process and she was once again back in her home. This time the strength of the image was even greater and the detail crisp and clear. She knew that this is where she wanted to be and that her happiness there was complete.

Then it passed and she felt extremely tired as she regained her concentration and focus on the assault on the building. Most of the team seemed visibly shaken by the fluctuations between the two time threads. Two of the team seemed as if they were in a trance. These two were not part of the new time thread and were being gradually pulled away from life into nothingness.

The team moved forward advancing so that they could cover the other members of the team as they moved toward the objective. They encountered no resistance and moved rapidly through the lobby to the staircase. They knew that the most likely location for them to come into contact with the perpetrators was on the third floor, the location of the magnetic energy.

They reached the corridor at the moment the seventh Yom began its insertion and Kate found herself back in her kitchen. This time she cooked the meal and when she was finished she walked into the living room and saw Austin with his back to her. She walked quietly up behind him and grabbed him tightly hugging him with all of her being. She loved him so much that the tears welled up in her eyes from the joy of being with him. He turned and smiled down upon her and she could see clearly into his very soul. There was no mystery, nothing hiding. Austin was transparent to her and she loved him for that too.

They sat down together and Christopher went between them making his presence known with hugs and kisses. He was just like his father she thought, a kind and gentle boy of four; precocious and curious, energetic and enthusiastic, a special boy for them both to dote over and love. They sat there for a time and then adjourned to eat the meal Kate had prepared. Time passed, they sat and talked it was sheer joy. Kate had no recollection of any other life other than the one she was experiencing at that moment.

When the time thread shifted back it was with a small jolt. Kate felt her body convulse and she staggered under the shift. She looked at her team and two stood mesmerized unable to move and the other five were in a similar state as Kate's, they all looked around as though they had lost something precious. Kate remembered the thread and she remembered her feelings and her confusion was amplified when she entered the corridor and saw Austin sitting in the chair. He turned at the moment she entered the hallway and looked her directly in the eyes. It was the same look she saw in his eyes in her dreams. Her breathing became difficult as she attempted to regain her composure.

Inside the Control Center the team struggled to regain their bearings. Some did not recognize the other members of the team others had trouble remembering who they were. Norville sat in a chair staring at the floor. Willie looked at him and thought how old he looked and then he wondered who he was. He wondered why he was standing in front of a screen that showed nothing. He turned to find the door and as he did his eyes came in contact with Adria's and then he remembered why he was there and what was about to happen.

"Adria, will we regain consciousness after the ninth Yom completes its insertion?" he asked.

"Willie, I don't know. With each insertion the alternate time thread appears to be strengthening and if you remember this program was constructed to not be fully implemented until the last insertion occurs.

That means that we will have these wild fluctuations as we are pulled between to the time threads. How we will ultimately respond in the final environment is unclear at this time." she answered.

Willie looked at the people that he was sharing this space. "I thought the magnetic field would protect us from the effects?" he asked.

"It is protecting us physically but I am not sure if there is any way to protect our minds." she responded.

"You mean we could be stuck here without any mind at all, no way to think?" he again asked with an air of panic in his voice.

"I am not sure Willie, we have to wait and see." she replied with a calm voice but the look in her eyes betrayed the fear that she felt, it was the same as his.

At that moment the eighth Yom began its insertion and the change of threads was much more intense and abrupt. The magnetic bubble that protected the control center and what ensured that the computers continued to complete the necessary programming began to buckle under the stress of the changes. It was as if the time thread's immune system was trying to expel the foreign object that infected it. No one in the Control Center noticed, they were all entranced, lost in a pool of nothingness, isolated from everyone and everything.

When Austin saw Kate at the end of the hall he had looked into her eyes and saw the same look he had seen repeatedly, it was a bleeding over of the two threads, he was the conduit between them. It was through him that all of the images flowed. He watched her succumb to the eighth insertions effects. Her eyes were open but she was not present, she was in another place with him. He could feel her near him yet he was now aware of both threads simultaneously and he knew that the moment was approaching when everything would change forever more. He waited for the effect of the shift to wear off but knew that this effect would wear off with less than a minute before the ninth and final Yom would begin its insertion. Once that time had arrived the final protocol would be initiated and the time thread was to become permanent. Only Austin knew the outcome, only Austin could watch the drama unfold.

Philip regained consciousness and saw Truax standing over him, a blank expression on his face. His eyes were open but it was obvious that he was not seeing anything. He was not there. Philip had been with Jessica and looked around to see where she was but then realized that she was not there, in fact he was not where he had been only seconds before, riding his horse with Jessica in the meadow near the stream where they had met Christopher Leesop. He was having difficulty understanding where he was and why he was there. He stood up shakily gaining his feet and staggered into the wall as he made the effort to reach the door and gain access to the corridor. As he reached the corridor he saw Kate and her team approaching Austin who was standing in front of the door. He was blocking it, preventing Kate from entering. He watched Austin turn to him and mouth the words, "I love you."

"Austin, please move out of the way. I must get in and stop this before…" Kate said and then realized that if they succeeded she would be happy, joyful and a new life would be hers to live. But this was her job, she had to follow through and complete the mission.

She attempted to grab the handle and Austin grabbed her wrist and said, "This is for you Kate, it's because I love you." he said and then he released her wrist and pushed her gently back.

"No, don't do it Austin" Philip found himself yelling. He now knew what was going to happen, why Austin was there, what he was going to do and why. Austin reached for the handle of the door and the charge lifted him from the ground and thrust him across the hall to the opposite wall where he impacted it with his head at the same time the ninth Yom initiated the insertion and everyone was violently transported to the alternate time thread.

****

As the Startling occurred Helen saw a brilliance that blinded her but she did not look away. She experienced a feeling of total well-being she felt as if she was a little child and that she was resting in the arms of her loving mother. Rush had watched the image her LTA and that all the members of his team's ships vanish from the screen as he experienced a momentarily lag before being transported to his home with his family. He was now only concerned about his family and their well-being, he like everyone else, had no recollection of any other existence.

Kate was in Austin's arms and he was staring down at her, he was smiling as he said to her, "It's time to go back, to go on. Don't worry I will always be with you."

She did not understand what he was saying to her she only wanted to be in his arms, safe. The room began to shake the roof of the house flew straight into the sky disappearing into a cloud. They watched as Christopher was lifted before their eyes and then he was suddenly gone. Kate had a look of terror on her face but as she looked into his eyes she began to feel calm and at peace. The world around them dissolved and then it was just them in a dimly lit corridor surrounded by armed agents and Philip Lee who was leaning against the wall in shock.

Austin was barely conscious and was looking into Kate's eyes. He was looking at her as he always looked at her. She felt the tears streaming down her face. They were just together in utter bliss and now this, he was hurt and she was back living the life that she had been living.

"Kate, you were there weren't you. We had a life together, didn't we?" Austin asked her.

"Yes Austin. We were there, it was so real." she replied her voice barely audible.

The door to the conference room opened and Norville came out bleary eyed and seemingly confused. He saw Austin on the floor being attended to by Kate. He smiled at him and Austin returned the smile. Kate turned to see who had drawn Austin's attention.

"Kate I would like you to meet Norville Forrest, a friend, a second father to me. Norville this is Kate Foster." Austin said weakly.

"Why are you telling me this?" Kate asked.

"It is time to start anew. You saw how it could be." Austin replied.

At that moment a call came in from President Wa.

"Mrs. Foster, you are to stop your operation and return to New York. Sherwood DeMasters has decided that we must move on and leave this witch hunt as he put it and come up with some positive way of improving the lives of everyone." Wa said.

"Mrs. Foster, you have been through a great deal I want to personally thank you for what you have done. I look forward to seeing you." he continued.

There was a pause and Kate responded, "I will leave for New York shortly. There is someone here I must help first." she said.

"Yes, of course. Please make certain you take the time that you need." Wa replied. "Be careful in your travels. Good bye Kate." he said in closing.

"Good by Mr. Wa." and when she had said that he disconnected the call.

Norville turned to Adria who had joined them. He asked her, "What has happened? We are back where we started."

She looked at him smiled and said, "Are we? Don't you see what has happened? It was the Epiphanal Startling not as Jenkins interpreted it but as Leesop had said it would be. The realization that life's meanings all come in our need to focus on our purpose and efforts to fulfill it, on each other and our service to that calling. The people that experienced it are those that were in both time threads. They have seen how it could be. We need to follow their vision. That vision will be our hope, our good hope."

Epilog

"Who are we going to see?" Billy Foster asked.

Kate looked at her son and smiled saying, "Billy I have told you already. We are going to see your Uncle Austin."

"Why?"

"Because he is sick and needs you to help cheer him up and make him feel better." Kate said.

They walked through the hallways of the hospital and toward the intensive care wing. This was the second time that Kate had visited Austin. The first time he was not conscious but when she received the call from Philip telling her that Austin had regained consciousness she told Michael that she wanted to see him and he suggested that the boys go with her.

When they arrived at the room she observed that there were several people standing in the hall outside. She recognized one of them as being Sherwood DeMaster's executive assistant and he was speaking with another man that seemed very familiar looking. The men looked at Kate and smiled. She then heard the sound of several men laughing and it came from inside Austin's room.

Kate approached his room and as she did Sherwood appeared at the doorway along with Norville and Gregory. Sherwood appeared to be taken aback by the sudden encounter but recovered quickly.

"Mrs. Foster what a pleasant surprise. We were just talking about you. Are these your boys? They are certainly very handsome young men. What are their names?" he asked smiling.

"This is my oldest Billy and this is Theo."

"Theodore." Theo said proudly, "Theodore Michael Foster."

"Boys this is Mr. DeMasters and he is a very important man where mommy works." Kate said kneeling so that she could encourage the boys to make a polite response.

Norville smiled at Kate who begrudgingly returned the smile for she was still not certain how she was to feel about the man she had sworn to apprehend. Still she introduced her sons to both Norville and Gregory.

Gregory told her that Austin was awake but had not spoken to anyone and then he added that he was certain that he would be glad to see her. After a few more cordial exchanges of pleasantries Kate pushed ahead and entered the room. She was uncertain of what she would find.

Inside she saw Austin, his head was turned facing the window. He had a very serene expression on his face. Kate felt her knees buckle slightly and she fought back tears. He was alive. She had been so certain that she would never see him again and yet there he was in front of her. She glanced down at her boys who were staring at him. Theo's mouth was open as though he was in awe.

She watched him breathing a slow rhythmic cadence, the only other movement was his eyes which blinked at regular intervals.

Theo was doing his best to be quiet but the effervescent energy of the five year old was about to explode and spill over into the lives of those with whom he came in contact imparting a contagious grin to everyone nearby. He ran to Austin's bed and came close to his face. He stared at him and said, "Are you my Uncle Austin?"

Austin lower his eyes and looked at Theo and turned his head and saw Kate. He instantly smiled and then said, "I am. You must be Theo and that is your brother William or Billy to his friends." Theo stepped back, he was surprised by Austin's voice. Kate returned his smile responding to the joy she felt to see him and in hearing his voice. They were apparently the first words he had spoken since the event that had occurred two weeks earlier. So much had changed in that short period of time, so much seemed right.

Kate wanted to ask him how he felt and to tell him that she was so glad that he was alive, but instead she started talking about the past two weeks and how there were so many people that had suddenly felt their lives had changed. They had lived through the 'Startling', experienced the alternate time thread and had a glimpse of how their lives could be. There seemed to be a resurgence of hope that was infectiously spreading.

Austin listened and smiled for he knew that it would be that way. He and experienced it and was confident. There was no need to be fearful, to worry about returning to prison for no matter where he was, he knew that that was where he was supposed to be.

"Austin it is so good to see you." Kate said her voice unsteady with emotion.

Behind her Gregory had returned to the room having heard his son's voice. He was followed by the other two men and they strained to see him.

"Hello Dad." he said.

The greeting startled Kate in that she had not noticed the men had returned, she was with Austin and him alone. It was a peaceful feeling that she could not bear to let go. The three men then realized that they might be intruding and withdrew to wait for their time with him.

"Kate, I am so glad to see you and to finally meet your two sons."

"How did you know their names?"

"I know so much about you. How is it that you don't know how connected we truly are?"

"I don't understand." she said after a significant pause.

"You will, it will just take time."

"Austin, I am confused as to what to do. We were so happy together. What should I do?" she ask finally coming to terms with the true reason she needed to see him.

"You must follow your path and remain true to your purpose. The journey starts anew each and every day."

"But what about you? How can I..."

"Kate, I want you to take this and read it." he said interrupting her. Austin then took a tube that he had concealed under his blanket.

"This will help you to see. You and I will always be together as you and Michael journey toward the destination that has been set for you."

The boys began to fidget and were clearly expecting an outing with much more entertainment involved. Kate took the tube and held it in her hands. And looked lovingly at Austin. She was comforted in knowing that he would remain as part of her life.

"I think that there are others that would like to see you and that you should get some more rest. Can I visit you again soon?" she asked.

"Absolutely, I will see you very soon and very often, it is our destiny. Please send my father, Norville and Sherwood in as I have to speak to them about what will next happen." he replied with a broad smile.

She bent down and kissed his forehead and turned to the boys and instructed them to say their good byes. Austin shook each of the boys' hands and wished them well. Kate then turned and ushered them from the room turning at the door to get one last look at him. He had turned his head again to the window and he had the look of contentment that she had seen on his face when she first saw him. She smiled and left to tell them to join him.

Kate left feeling content. As she saw the three men and told them that Austin was expecting them and she smiled at them all. There was no room for residual malice. She no longer sought to blame. She only knew that she was given a chance to hope and that hope was a guarantee that things would be right.

Bibliography and Citations

1. "The Killer Angels" by Michael Shaara - copyright © 1974 by Michael Shaara
2. The Gettysburg Campaign – A Study in Command" by Edwin B Coddington - copyright © 1968 Caroline Q. Coddington, Executor of Estate of Edwin B. Coddington

Educational Institutions Mentioned

Franklin and Marshall College – Lancaster, Pennsylvania
Temple University – Philadelphia, Pennsylvania
The University of Pennsylvania Wharton School of Business
    Philadelphia, Pennsylvania
Princeton University – Princeton, New Jersey
University of Southern California – Berkley, California

"...'The kingdom of God does not come from observation; nor will they say, 'See here!' or 'See there!' For indeed the kingdom of God is within you.'"

Luke 17:20, 21